CLASSICAL MYTH AND FILM IN THE NEW MILLENNIUM

CLASSICAL MYTH AND FILM IN THE NEW MILLENNIUM

By Patricia Salzman-Mitchell and Jean Alvares

NEW YORK   OXFORD
OXFORD UNIVERSITY PRESS
2018

Oxford University Press is a department of the University of Oxford. It furthers the University's objective of excellence in research, scholarship, and education by publishing worldwide. Oxford is a registered trade mark of Oxford University Press in the UK and certain other countries.

Published in the United States of America by Oxford University Press
198 Madison Avenue, New York, NY 10016, United States of America.

Library of Congress Cataloging-in-Publication Data

Names: Alvares, Jean author. | Salzman-Mitchell, Patricia B. author.
Title: Classical myth and film in the new millennium / by Jean Alvares and
    Patricia Salzman-Mitchell.
Description: New York : Oxford University Press, 2018. | Includes
    bibliographical references and index. | Includes bibliographical
    references and index.
Identifiers: LCCN 2016038130 | ISBN 9780190204167 (pbk. : alk. paper)
Subjects: LCSH: Myth in motion pictures. | Mythology in motion pictures.
Classification: LCC PN1995.9.M97 A48 2018 | DDC 791.43/615—dc23 LC record
available at https://lccn.loc.gov/2016038130

ISBN 9 8 7 6 5 4 3 2 1

Printed by Webcom Inc., Canada

To all our students, fellow teachers, and mentors—in this millennium and the past one.

ABOUT THE AUTHORS

Patricia Salzman-Mitchell is professor in the Department of Classics and Humanities at Montclair State University, New Jersey. Her interests lie in Latin poetry, Ovid, gender and sexuality in antiquity, and the reception of Classics in film and in Latin American literature and art. She is the author of *A Web of Fantasies: Gaze, Image, and Gender in Ovid's Metamorphoses* (Ohio State UP, 2005), and coeditor of *Latin Elegy and Narratology: Fragments of Story* (Ohio State UP, 2008), with Genevieve Liveley, and of *Mothering and Motherhood in Ancient Greece and Rome* (University of Texas Press, 2012), with Lauren Hackworth Petersen. She has published numerous articles on Latin literature and Ovid.

Jean Alvares is associate professor in the Department of Classics and Humanities at Montclair State University, New Jersey. His interests are in Greek and Roman Literature, and ancient narrative; the humanities tradition and current approaches to the humanities; utopian thought and literature; and technology and teaching. He has published numerous articles on the Greek and Roman novels, and coedited *Authors, Authority, and Interpreters in the Ancient Novel: Essays in Honor of Gareth L. Schmeling* (Barkhuis, 2006).

BRIEF CONTENTS

CONTENTS

ACKNOWLEDGMENTS

This book could not have been written without the support of many people, in particular our editor, Charles Cavaliere, who showed great interest and believed in the project from the beginning. We are grateful to the whole editorial team at Oxford University Press for their hard work in making this a much more polished book. We also want to thank Paula James, Gregory Daugherty, Emma Scioli, and the anonymous readers of Oxford University Press, who painstakingly and with great care read both the full manuscript and our early book proposal. Their input and many sagacious observations have made this a much better work, though of course, any errors or omissions are solely our responsibility.

We are also grateful to our colleagues at Montclair State University for their support and especially to Timothy Renner for help with proof-reading. In particular we thank the university for awarding Patricia a summer grant to work on this project a few years ago. Parts of this research were presented as conference papers and lectures in England, Argentina, the United States, and China. We are thankful for the many comments from these audiences. But more importantly, we want to give our appreciation to the students at Montclair State, including the members of the Montclair Myth Society, who through many years of discussions on myth and movies in courses such as Mythology; Troy and the Trojan War; Classics and Films; Ancient Religion; and Women, Gender and Sexuality in the Ancient World among many others, have offered their insights on the meaning of myth in the new millennium.

Many friends in the United States, Argentina, England, and China gave insightful comments and encouragement throughout this project. On a more personal note, Patricia would like to thank her husband, Ken Mitchell, and children, Alexander and Luciana Mitchell, for their inspiration and for many family movie nights watching Harry Potter or Percy Jackson, and especially to

Alexander for his constant feedback and fact checking on Young Adult books! She also thanks her parents, Irma and Roberto Salzman, in Argentina, for their unfailing support, for always being there. Jean would like to express his gratitude to Glen Gill, master of many mythological worlds, whose brain he has picked many times, and to Dr. Fan Ling, who opened perspectives gained from linguistics and Asian studies. Thank you all.

CLASSICAL MYTH AND FILM
IN THE NEW MILLENNIUM

It is the year 2016 CE, and if we ask people under forty where they had their first or most vivid encounters with Classical mythology, chances are many would mention a movie or television show, a comic book, or sci-fi film, or maybe a video game or some internet site.[1] Movies on Classical and mythological subjects appeared soon after movies themselves did, more than a century ago,[2] and experienced a revival after the 2000 blockbuster *Gladiator*. Part of this book's impulse was indeed the surprising number of mythically inspired films produced after the year 2000. We cannot know with any precision why this phenomenon occurred, and technological advances may well have played a role. Clearly this resurgence of Classical myth in popular culture is strong and pervasive, and indeed this reflects many concerns of the early twenty-first century. It is no coincidence that some of the most popular children's books series (*Harry Potter* and the various Rick Riordan collections, for example), TV shows, video games, and of course blockbuster movies have mythology at their core.

WHY WE ARE HERE AND WHAT WE ARE DOING

Our purpose here is not necessarily to "teach mythology through film." In fact, although we recount the main points of myths central to our discussions, we do not provide extended explanations of every myth we mention. For that, we refer readers to good mythological dictionaries, compendia, or the many useful introductory myth textbooks. Instead, we aim to offer thoughtful interpretations of the myths and myth patterns that appear in our movies. We hope that this book will be of interest both to college instructors and to students, as well as to scholars and a broad readership of myth and movie lovers. Thus, even though much

---

1 Indeed, two recent volumes explore the presence of the Classics in comics and science fiction. See Rogers and Stevens (2015) and Kovacs and Marshall (2011).
2 See Michelakis and Wyke (2013).

additional material is offered for further intellectual exploration in footnotes and appendixes, our goal is that the reader will enjoy our focused, accessible discussions in the chapters and feel enthused to explore the field further, for which we offer discussion questions at the end of each part.[3]

Most contemporary presentations of classical mythology don't closely follow the so-called canonical narratives. This is a necessary situation; after all, Hesiod, Sophocles, and Ovid were once "contemporary artists" who took liberties with prior texts and traditions, as was Shakespeare. A serious difficultly has always been that movies were from the beginning linked to mass-market consumer culture and entertainment, with only a few "art house" films deserving critical attention.[4] But think how pretty much the same thing can be said about most novels written or plays produced. In fact the high-low culture dichotomy has been more an ideological construct that privileges certain perspectives, classes, and beliefs and obscures the actual practiced realities of the culture. Despite the purists' complaints, it was recognized early how movies, thanks to their mass appeal and distribution, despite inaccuracies, some flagrant, would still raise public consciousness and interest about the past in a positive and significant way.[5] And we must recognize that today movies, television shows, and the like, in their vast variety of quality and content, are a central medium for narrative. Thus any teacher or scholar today must have an appreciation of this new reality and even learn to embrace it, as part of the dialectal understanding of past and present in the classical tradition.[6]

Again, as Winkler notes, important (but complex) is the contrast between a myth's past and present forms. For a truer understanding of Classical mythology, we should study the Classical versions of major myths (those of Homer, Sophocles, Ovid), in their literary and cultural contexts (e.g., Athens and Rome), how these myths compare to other major systems of mythology (such as those of the Egyptians, Mesopotamians, or Celts), and how later eras received, reinterpreted, and revamped those ancient myths—including works of our own era (Joyce's *Ulysses*) and the kind of movies we discuss. Standard Classical mythology introductory textbooks deal mostly with the first goal, but also increasingly connect with these other matters.

---

3   Unless otherwise indicated, translations of ancient and modern works and film texts are our own. We have transcribed texts directly from the movies, and compared them to the published scripts when available. Our translations from Spanish of the texts of *Pan's Labyrinth* and *Such Is Life* are slightly different from those in the English subtitles of the DVDs.
4   See the blistering critique of Adorno and Horkheimer (1994 [1944]). See also Corrigan (2014), 1–7; Winkler (2001), 3–4; Paul (2008), 305.
5   Winkler (2001), 5–6, cites Ullman (2015).
6   Winkler (2009), 20. As Rose (2001) observes, the familiar and comfortable world of movies can furnish a space where students can encounter what is truly unfamiliar—if the instructor can break the instinct to treat movies as items mostly designed to be consumed without thought.

Our book's central objectives are to produce a rich set of interpretations and readings of selected contemporary movies that (1) reflect the earlier expression of a particular myth (requiring some explication), (2) manifest the history of some major forms that myth took in later eras, and (3) delineate connections between cultural currents and those productions, with a special focus on the cultural currents experienced by those living in this new millennium, while also setting out the major theoretical models that allow this analysis. We hope that our volume will present wider perspectives on how classical myths and themes are employed in movies, their intended audience, and the realities of their reception, while never losing sight of the historical and cultural meaning those works originally had. Our volume is unique in its substantial use of myth theory. Therefore, we can show how many "modern" themes have quite ancient analogs, and understanding the difference between past and present versions tells much about the basic nature of the mythic theme and the shaping forces of our own culture. Such a comparison also questions prevailing notions of which cultural elements have to be "natural." We cannot understand the past "as it is," but only through the limitations of our own contemporary (biased and fragmented) perspectives. As noted, the reception of these myths as they have been retold through time is always an important issue. Within the limits of our abilities, we want to produce serious, close readings of these cinematic works, as one would do for any work of literature. But they are only one set of possible readings; we also invite our readers to employ their own imaginative and creative energies.

In our exploration of the Pygmalion myth, for example, found in movies like *Lars and the Real Girl* and *Ruby Sparks,* we lay out first the version of the myth created by the Roman poet Ovid, and consider briefly some later versions (including less direct ones), such as found in the *Romance of the Rose* or the plays of Gilbert and Shaw. All of our chapters provide examples of how mythic patterns, themes, and motifs have been handed down, received, and reinterpreted. And in this sense, our book sets itself within reception studies, which focus on the way a work of art represents how the creator (or audience) receives (that is processes and understands) some other work of art, tradition, or time period.[7] Issues such as adaptation, appropriation, and borrowing (discussed further below) arise. It has become clear that reception is a two-way street.[8] An adaptation of an earlier work can make us see the old work in a new way, as we show in our two chapters on *Lars* and *Ruby Sparks.*

 How this reworking is accomplished, and what elements shape and motivate the nature of this interpretation, reveal much about the original material

---

7   On reception studies and movies, see Paul (2008). For Classical reception, see Hardwick and
    Stray (2008), Martindale and Thomas (2006).
8   Paul (2008), 307.

and our own culture's preoccupations. It will be important to lay out the cultural elements that influenced Classical versions (such as a real belief in statues being inhabited by gods or being able to move), as well as modern versions (the rise of technological substitutions for real women). Displaced versions of the myth are noted (e.g., *My Fair Lady*), where Professor Higgins "shapes" a living woman. We consider issues that Ovid gave less attention to or even ignored, important in modern versions, including the role of trauma, or the nature of the couple's emotional relationship after the statue's animation, or the role of the community. Non-Classical myths (which also influenced Classical myth) will be looked at too, especially those coming from the Judeo-Christian tradition. To give one example, in Hesiod, after a great battle, the losing Titans are cast into Tartarus, where they remain for a while, if not permanently. But Titans are not devils; nor are they pictured as a permanent threat to the Olympians. However, influenced by the Judeo-Christian tradition of the Fall of Satan and his rebel angels (who become devils or demons), movies such as *Clash/Wrath of the Titans, Immortals,* or the *Percy Jackson* series view them as a constant threat, with Hades an enemy of Zeus, as Satan is an enemy of God.[9] And there are "modern myths" worth considering, such as the "myth of the defeated South," important for *O Brother, Where Art Thou?* as well as whole cycles of newly forged myth, such as found in the *Matrix* or *Star Wars* series.

Our third point in particular aligns with the goals of *Classical Myth and Film in the New Millennium*. Here we consider the varied ways Classical myths and themes are reused and reworked today and touch on specific matters that concern contemporary audiences. To illustrate, the Classical Perseus is a paradigmatic hero who successfully performs his Quest and helps fashion the political *status quo*. But today the *status quo* is widely seen as corrupt, and our heroes (such as Jack Bauer of the Fox TV show *24*, 2001–2010) are often quite problematic; today the heroic protagonist is more likely to be an outsider in some way.[10] Thus the Perseus of today's *Clash of the Titans* hates the gods (despite being half-god himself), and at the end becomes the leader of a human-centered world after the gods' downfall. Another example: today, becoming adult is far more problematic than it used to be, and *Troy*'s Paris has echoes of the "man-child" seen in many modern productions; the protagonist in *Lars and the Real Girl* wonders how one can really know when one becomes a man.

Irony is a major creative mood today, and parody widespread. Parody can, in its more lighthearted mode, arise from a choir of textual voices described as "Carnevalesque" because they partake of the freedom of the carnivals or

---

9   This influence works the other way: Milton in *Paradise Lost* makes the fall of the rebel angels recall that of the Titans.

10   Theodorakopoulos (2010), 19–20.

Saturnalias and their lords of misrule, which allow no perspective to domi-nate.[11] Further, as noted above, today the widely felt insufficiency and corrup-tion of dominant institutions promotes a mocking distrust of all those who take themselves seriously, and here parody can be quite savage. This is gener-ally not the case with our movies. Further, when dealing with unfamiliar or unusual Classical myths, it can seem difficult to suspend disbelief, and this gap also inspires parodic treatments. This element of lighthearted, sympathetic, not destructive parody is evident in the Percy Jackson movies, but also in *O Brother, Where Art Thou?* and to a lesser extent in *Clash of the Titans*.

RE-PRESENTING THE PAST

None of the movies discussed in this book claims to be an exact reproduction of *any* classical myth, where at most we are dealing with borrowed, shared, or reworked elements. This is quite obvious in *Pan's Labyrinth* and even more so in *Harry Potter and the Chamber of Secrets*. But even Homer's partial telling of the Trojan War was simply the most successful version, and Homer had other, sometimes radically different, competitors. The playwright Euripides was noto-rious for creating new versions of myths (for example, Medea as willing child-murderess) and Hellenistic and Roman-era authors took even more liberties. The Classical tradition, in respect to Medea, for example, is the sum of all the ways Medea and her story have been translated, adapted, appropriated, borrowed, or even parodied, from the earliest depictions in pottery to our own date.

Here we need to distinguish between adaptations, appropriations, inven-tion, and intentional borrowings/reworkings and unintentional use of simi-lar themes, plot devices, and other elements. To simplify what Sanders[12] and other scholars detail, when an artist transfers a work of literature into an alien genre or medium, even the most faithful craftsman still creates an adaptation, because the two genres cannot map onto each other exactly. A book, for ex-ample, will tell more, the movie will show more; the experience of reading is different from viewing, and so forth. An adaptation can be comparatively free or strict. Appropriation is when authors or artists take some work and adapt it for their own purposes, which may have nothing at all to do with the innate purposes of the original work. Appropriation is particularly apparent in com-mercial forms of cultural borrowings. In China, for example, during the month of December one sees all sorts of Christmas decorations, but they have been appropriated for a purely commercial practice, since religious aspects of the holiday are virtually nonexistent in China. One might remake the American novel by Nathaniel Hawthorne *The Scarlet Letter* (1850; see Roland Joffé's 1995

---

11 See Bakhtin (1981 [1941]), Genette (1997), Hutcheon (1985), and others that we discuss more fully in our *Percy Jackson* chapter.
12 Sanders (2005).

film version) to have overt feminist or sexual themes quite alien to the original. It can be argued that, to some extent, all modern movies, however faithful, are to some extent expropriations (the demands of the market must be met), but clearly some are more slanted that way than others. For example, *O Brother Where Art Thou?'*s reworking of the *Odyssey* has many elements that might be seen more as appropriation than mere adaptation, especially in those politically weighted scenes evoking the Ku Klux Klan. On the other hand, *Pan's Labyrinth* is an example of invention and intentional borrowing, as are, to a far lesser extent, the Percy Jackson movies. The myth of *Pan's Labyrinth* is mostly an original creation, although many elements, especially Pan himself, are quite intentionally adapted from Classical mythology. Our Pygmalion movies also fit into that model, while *Such Is Life* is more an adaptation veering into appropriation. Parody, which figures significantly in *O Brother Where Art Thou?* and especially in *Percy Jackson*, which we discuss more later, can certainly be seen as a form of appropriation.

We shall observe the quite unintentional borrowing or duplication of themes, elements, etc. Winkler in *Apollo's New Light* justifies making jarring comparisons, such as between the movie *Pleasantville* (1998) and the second-century AD Greek novel by Longus *Daphnis and Chloe*, where central motifs have been unconsciously shared.[13] As Winkler demonstrates, various forms of "genre cinema" (westerns, gangster movies, war movies, etc.) employ narrative patterns familiar from antiquity.[14] But how is this possible? There is a simple explanation, which connects with our later discussion of archetypal and reoccurring themes and elements. Just as in nature different organs can evolve in unconnected species because of similar pressures of natural selection, so similar plot elements can likewise arise due to similar cultural realities. In our discussion of *Clash/Wrath*, we note how those two movies present a plot where the human order supplants a corrupt divine order, a destruction in part willed by the chief god, here Zeus. A similar plot is found in the German composer Richard Wagner's *Ring of the Nibelung* cycle (completed in 1848), which starts off with crime and conflict and ends with the elimination of the Germanic gods, one willed by its chief god, Wotan, the prelude for a new Human age. We do not at all suggest that *Clash/Wrath* are consciously borrowing from Wagner. But both Wagner and the writers of *Clash/Wrath* lived in times of political turmoil, where old regimes were seen as oppressive and corrupt; the divine order has always existed as a metaphor for the political order, and artists have always exploited the potentials of that metaphor. These two instantiations of this metaphor, products of different eras, cultures, and artists' personalities, and received by different audiences, can profitably illuminate each other, permitting

---

13 Winkler (2009).
14 Winkler (2001), 3; see also Cawelti (1976), 12; Wollen (1998), 163–73; Holtsmark (2001), 24–25.

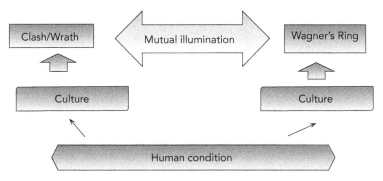

FIGURE I.1 The relationship of influence between an earlier work and a current movie

a richer understanding of past and present expressions.[15] Figure I.1.1 illuminates this dynamic.

Winkler, adopting the critical perspective of the Italian director Vittorio Cottafavi, notes how modern artists find ancient mythology and history and associated motifs, themes, and images continuously relevant and fascinating, but feel no need at all to follow their formats and templates, appropriating and reusing these items for their own purposes, which Winkler calls "neomythologizing,"[16] a practice occurring from antiquity until this very moment.

Clearly, the polyphonic mythic "mash-up" is not a solely modern creation. This variety of myth arises because every significant myth, all variants considered, presents a debate, a (sometimes Titanic) clash of perspectives, and many (often contrasting) traces of ideology, historical settings, and material conditions.[17] For example, Heracles can be seen as a "master of animals," an over-muscled comic buffoon, or a proto-Stoic saint. But ultimately, any movie must be considered in how it functions as a work in itself, and not just a reflection of some earlier narrative.[18] Subsequently, if the movie *Troy* fails as a myth, this failure is not due to unfaithfulness to Homer (who himself altered the Troy tradition), but because the myth it does craft out of various elements (as Homer formed his own Troy story) functions poorly. Thus when we consider synthetic

15 Cyrino and Safran's volume (2015) likewise makes unexpected but profitable comparisons, such as between Sophocles' *Philoctetes* and modern films such as *Cast Away* and *Papillon*.

16 Winkler (2009), 16, citing Leprohon (1972), 174–79; also Winkler (2007a). The often wildly noncanonical plots of Hercules/peplum movies likewise presents considerable. neomythologization: see Cornelius (2011), 4, citing Bondanella (2009), 159.

17 See Jameson (1981).

18 There is a longstanding critical debate over the director's duty to be historically accurate. Winkler (2009), 15–16, for example, argues for artistic freedom, while others insist on the need for historical accuracy. Theodorakopoulos (2010), 1–29, with discussion of Realism vs. Formalism in cinema. See also Wyke (1997), 8–9.

productions such as *Pan's Labyrinth*, we shall offer substantial readings of the movie's unique myth, and show how its borrowed Classical elements help form that whole.

Movies, as moving pictures joined with sound and music and special effects, have the ability to engage the audience powerfully and vividly, rather as dramas do, but taken to another level, through the ability of films to absorb us in the richness of their creators' vision.[19] This is a real critical challenge to those grounded in text-based philology, for Winkler is certainly correct in quoting Umberto Eco's opinion that individuals now increasingly think and remember in terms of images, not text.[20] Here we must narrow our focus to the film's mythic elements and their interplay, which our own areas of expertise allow us to analyze. The visual and aural components furnish a whole other level of meaning that we can no more than hint at. Theorists of cinema and painter-directors such as Jean Cocteau (as well as the director of *Immortals*, Tarsem Singh) compose cinematic images inspired by classical paintings, and thus the critical apparatus for interpreting painting is of relevance. Films can present a rich vision of a whole lost world, as we can admire in movies such as *Spartacus* or *Gladiator* or the television series *Rome*. We will hint at this richness, citing images of an apocalyptic battle in *Clash*, or the Christian tableaux in *Immortals*, or the polemical visions of the American South or post–Civil War Spain. It is this energy that allows films, chosen carefully and discussed even more carefully, to be powerful tools for educators.

But we cannot go into much depth regarding aspects of importance to more specialized scholars of film, for example, the setup of shots, matters of editing, details of lighting and filters, transitions, and so forth. As Fred Mench has done in respect to the *Aeneid*,[21] and Winkler has shown in respect to *Troy*,[22] and Theodorakopoulos in respect to some major films on Roman history,[23] the staging of scenes can echo motifs and metaphors found in Classical texts, and there is much work to be done in this area by future scholars.

Nor can we begin to survey all the films with mythical themes appearing since 2000; far from it. And there are movies that have come out since we started this project, notably *Air Doll* (Japanese title: Kūki Ningyō, 2009), *Ex Machina* (2015) and *Her* (2013) for the myth of Pygmalion. But we think thirteen films are quite representative of a recent resurgence of the Greek and Roman myths and mythic motifs in film. Some of them intended blockbusters, such as *Troy* (2004), the new version of *The Clash of the Titans* (2010), or *Hercules* (2014). Others are less-known independent movies such as *Lars and the Real*

---

19 Theodorakopoulos (2010), 12–14.
20 Winkler (2001), 6, quoting Eco (1986), 67, 213, 217.
21 Mench (1969), 232, declared that "the flexibility that we associate with the cinema is a hallmark of Virgil's epic."
22 Winkler (2007b), 54–56, mentioning *Iliad* 4.422–29, 446–56.
23 Theodorakopoulos (2010).

Girl (2004) and *Ruby Sparks* (2012). Two Spanish-language films explore how Classical myth has been recreated outside the United States: *Pan's Labyrinth* (2006) and *Such Is Life* (2000).

CLASSICS AND FILM

In the past two decades the study of Classical themes in modern movies has moved from the slighted margins to a notable, if not always appreciated, area of study, one parallel to the growing importance of reception studies, a significant influence on our book.[24] We will here address some watershed books in the discipline and some that have been particularly useful in researching our book. We highlight those texts written from the perspective of Classical scholars, though we indeed recognize the many contributions of critics outside the discipline. For a more complete list of books on Classics and film, see the Appendix at the end of the book. There are many useful articles as well, which we use in the chapters, too numerous to mention in this introduction.

A major first was Jon Solomon's *The Ancient World in the Cinema*,[25] a comprehensive account of classical themes in films. Since much of ancient myth is transmitted through tragedy, filmic recreations of these classics are useful to us and were early on discussed in groundbreaking volumes such as Marianne McDonald's *Euripides in Cinema: The Heart Made Visible* (1983), Kenneth MacKinnon's *Greek Tragedy into Film* (1986), and Pantelis Michelakis' *Greek Tragedy on Screen* (2013). There have been studies whose central aim is to (attempt) to sum up the appearances of a Classical character or theme in the movies; a notable example is Wenzel's 2005 survey of more than thirty films on Cleopatra.

Criticism of classical or mythological themes in movies tended earlier to focus on films that were clearly based on some Classical antecedent (e.g., *Helen of Troy*, 1956), and "faithfulness to the original" was a prime consideration. Direct borrowings of elements were also considered.[26] But as the interests of the field of classics and classical reception have (for most scholars) radically broadened and become increasingly multidisciplinary. Martin Winkler has emerged as a key innovator in the field, beginning with *Classics and Cinema* (1991), which was substantially revised and republished as *Classical Myth and Culture in the Cinema* (2001). This book of collected essays by scholars such as Hanna Roisman, Fred Mench, Janice F. Siegel, Marianne McDonald, Peter W. Rose, and Mary-Kay Gamel very broadly studied how Classical works, topics, and themes were adapted to film, often quite indirectly, for example exploring the Oedipal conflict implicit in *Chinatown*, Aristotle's models for tragedy in *The Searchers* by John Ford, the *katabasis* theme in nonclassical movies such as *100*

---

24 See in particular Wyke (1997, 2003); also Martindale (1996).
25 Solomon (1978 [2nd, rev. ed. 2001]).
26 See Paul (2008), 305–8.

Rifles and *The Wild Bunch*, or parallels between the comedy *9 to 5* and Greek Old Comedy. Winkler also demonstrates a sophisticated knowledge of formal film studies, unfamiliar to most Classicists. Four more volumes authored and edited by Winkler (see Appendix) followed, making him a true innovator and pioneer in this bourgeoning field. Earlier, Winkler had called for a philology of film,[27] but in *Cinema and Classical Texts: Apollo's New Light* (2009) he laid out the theoretics for "classical film philology."[28] First because films show rather than tell, details explicitly narrated in written texts must be set out in a less-obvious, even displaced fashion. Thus to appreciate less-apparent details requires the sort of close reading practiced in classical philology. As is clear in literary studies, few words, phrases, or even scenes mean much by themselves. Their full meaning depends on the three contexts: the text itself, the cultural and historical circumstances of the work's creation and reception, and the peculiar resources the reader brings when engaging the work. Likewise, images, cinematic words, and sounds have only contextual meaning, and only close readings will reveal the meanings arising from these contexts.

Winkler stresses the visual dimension of ancient texts, which allows a type of continuity in criticism from Aristotle to *auteur*. His work situates itself very much within modern reception studies, a field that considers the historically real audience for a movie, not some idealized professorial reviewer.[29] Contemporary audiences interpret such movies through a variety of filters and processes, with knowledge of and respect for the "classical antecedent" being fairly low on the list. And, even though the purist may cringe, it is these more popular interpretations that have the greatest cultural impact today. In 2006, Winkler edited a series of essays on *Troy* (2004), titled *Troy: From Homer's Iliad to Hollywood Epic*. In 2007, Wolfgang Petersen's director's cut of *Troy* appeared, and subsequently Winkler edited *Return to Troy: New Essays on the Hollywood Epic* (2015). This second volume not only gives more background on the theatrical versions but provides new perspectives on the meaning of a movie, for example, how obligated are we to assume the themes that receive more stress in the director's cut should be given greater weight when we (re)consider the theatrical version?

Recent treatments of myth in film are offered by thoughtful essays edited by Konstantinos Nikoloutsos (2013), *Ancient Greek Women in Film*, within the Oxford University Press series "Classical Presences." It is encouraging that major academic presses have lately launched series dedicated to the reception of the Classics (Oxford, Edinburgh, Palgrave, Brill). An important new volume of essays is *Classical Myth on Screen*, edited by Monica Cyrino and Meredith

---

27 Winkler (2001), 18.
28 Winkler (2009), 13.
29 On Classics and reception studies, see the edited volumes by Hardwick and Stray (1998) and Martindale and Thomas (2006).

Safran (2015). The various chapters explore how films and modern media texts engage with the classical past and myth, variously embracing them and rejecting them. The authors recognize how the "classical" elements in movies become mixed with other mythologies (e.g., biblical sources) and items of pop culture and modern mythologies (the *Die Hard*–type hero). Consider just two titles: Lisl Walsh's "'Italian Stallion' Meets 'Breaker of Horses', Achilles and Hector in *Rocky IV* (1985)"; and Hunter H. Gardner's "Plastic Surgery: Failed Pygmalions and Decomposing Women in *Les Yeux Sans Visage* (1960) and *Bride of Re-Animator* (1989)." The focus is not on whether X borrowed from or adapted Y, but rather on how shared themes mutually illuminate each other, an approach we employ.

One particularly important book for us is Paula James's *Ovid's Myth of Pygmalion on Screen: In Pursuit of the Perfect Woman* (2011), since it focuses on the development of one specific myth, with sagacious observations useful for our interpretations of *Lars and the Real Girl* and *Ruby Sparks*. One fairly recent work by Monica Cyrino is *Screening Love and Sex in the Ancient World* (2013). As Cyrino notes,[30] books and movies set in pre-Christian antiquity (one rendered with many liberties) were always a locus where archetypal stories of heroism adventure and love could be displaced, and alternative views of sexuality could be explored and exploited, and items such as the "orgy" were certainly expropriated. And, as we shall see in our discussion of the Hercules tradition, they could be recast in ways that reflect Christian anxieties about these earlier traditions. These and similar volumes explore how movies tend to speak more about our own time and preoccupations than attempt to understand the ancients.

Early on, large-scale movies on Classical subjects (e.g., *Ben Hur* or *Spartacus*) were billed as "epic," a category of the American Film Institute.[31] Clearly, epic is a "multi-discursive system,"[32] defined (albeit quite loosely) by a collection of common traits and by popular reception,[33] a large-scale sweep connected to a notable epoch with historical dimension. There is also a subgenre, the "sword and sandals" epic, and many of its examples can be classified as "peplum" movies, which are centered around some well-muscled hero such as Hercules who usually fights for the oppressed against some obvious form of evil, such as a tyrant. The visual and ideological conventions of these movies clearly influenced *Troy*, *Clash/Wrath*, *Immortals*, and *Hercules*. Joanna Paul's *Film and the Classical Epic Tradition* (2013) considers the elusive definition of epic, as she explores various features such as the nature of heroism, the allure of the spectacle, and epic parody, as well as other matters like the nature of adaptation.

30 Cyrino (2013), 1–5.
31 http://www.afi.com/10top10/category.aspx?cat=10. Accessed Oct. 11, 2016.
32 Altman (1999), 208.
33 See Paul (2013), 11–36, on the problematics of even defining epic.

Useful for thinking about epic (and epic movies) is the distinction between *primary* epic and *secondary* epic.[34] In primary epic, (e.g., the *Odyssey*), the hero triumphs by restoring a lost order, and by the epic's end, little has really changed; in a secondary epic, such as the *Aeneid*, the hero, his home often destroyed, must create a new home for his people or a new order of things. *Clash/Wrath of the Titans, Immortals*, even *O Brother Where Art Thou?* suggest secondary epics, as do the three series whose individual movies we consider: *Harry Potter, The Hunger Games*, and *Percy Jackson*. Accordingly, books that studied filmic versions of ancient epics help us think about this set of issues. *Hellas on Screen: Cinematic Receptions of Ancient History, Literature and Myth* (2008), edited by Irene Berti and Marta García Morcillo, provides an essential survey of the reception of ancient Greece from the silent film era to the new millennium. Cyrino's *Big Screen Rome* (2005) deals with famous "epic" movies, such as *Spartacus* and *Quo Vadis* and, among many other concerns, shows how these movies still shape (or distort) the way we think about the ancient world, Rome and the Roman empire being a powerful (if sometimes lurid) device for considering our own time, with the decline of a decadent, imperial United States visible to many observers.

Finally, we should briefly mention the existence of many books that detail how movies create new mythologies (e.g., the *Star Wars* and *Matrix* mythologies), or new mythological creatures (cyborgs), often out of prior elements, demonstrating the new possibilities posed by technology. We observe this sort of neomythologizing obviously in science-fiction movies (and thus films like *Ex Machina*), but themes and elements of these movies also appear in more "Classical" movies, such as the depiction of Hephaestus' laboratory/workshop in *Wrath of the Titans*.

MYTH THEORIES, STRUCTURES OF MEANING, AND ARCHETYPES

THE THREE CATEGORIES OF MYTHS; MYTH AND TRUTH

To study myth, one needs systems of interpretation.[35] One of our book's advantages is that we employ myth theories extensively to analyze these movies. Most introductory myth books contain chapters providing overviews of the major modern trends in criticism, including psychological approaches, anthropological and ritual criticism, "charter" theories, structuralist and poststructuralist approaches, and gender perspectives.[36]

Some suggest that myth must be sealed off from the reader's world.[37] We disagree. Indeed, "Mythical" does not mean either necessarily "fantastic" or

---

34   C. S. Lewis (2006), 33–51.
35   See Csapo (2004), Edmunds (1990), and Dundes (1984).
36   Popular textbooks are Morford, Lenardon, and Sham (2013); Harris and Platzner (2011); Powell (2015); and now the new Maurizio (2015).
37   Bakhtin (1981), 3–40.

"false," and myth commonly engages the complexity of the human condition, regardless of where or when the myth is set or how realistic it is. That is why myths continue to thrive. They are often slotted into three categories: (1) True or High Myth, (2) Legend or Saga, (3) Folktale.[38] High Myths are mainly serious myths about, for example, the gods, and include the major creation stories. Legend concerns itself with human beings, and reflects aspects of human culture and even history. The most notable examples are the cycle of legends surrounding the Trojan war, which reflect the realities of Late Geometric and Early Archaic Greek culture and even (however faintly) memories of Bronze Age history. Folklore can involve gods or humans, and what distinguishes it (often a hard distinction to make) is its less serious, sometimes comic or satirical tone. Tricksters and fools play important roles in folktale, as do odd prohibitions and tricks. For example, Odysseus fooling the Cyclops by telling him his name is "Nobody" is one of the *Odyssey*'s many folktale elements.

But what is a myth? Walter Burkert (1931–2015) provides a good definition, slightly revised here: "Myth is a traditional tale with secondary, partial reference to something of collective importance."[39] A problem lies in the word *traditional*, an issue taken up by *O Brother, Where Art Thou?* In that film, Ulysses Everett and his Soggy Bottom Boys spontaneously create a new hit song, "Man of Constant Sorrow," which has the feel of an "old timey" tune, but which the villain Homer Stokes declares is not "even old timey." What makes a song (or tale) traditional is not just passed time, but rather the work's set of elements embedding it within a culture's stream of mythic narratives, and a myth is thus often transmitted orally. So, instead of "traditional tale" we might instead write "a tale made out of traditional elements."

MYTH, STRUCTURE, AND ARCHETYPE

Myths present in artistic productions manifest both universal themes (e.g., the need to transition to adulthood) and cultural specifics (the need for a young man to pass a specific ordeal). Structuralist approaches, as well as that form of structural criticism often referred to as myth-thematic or archetypal criticism, can be usefully employed to interpret artistic representations of myth. Structuralist approaches to culture or to thought demonstrate how we live and act according to persistent patterns that give structure to our lives and ideas. The archetype is an important element of this conceptual framework. It is incorrect, as many do, to view "archetypes" as deriving solely from Carl Jung's psychological theories. The term is older.[40] The myth-thematic approach first appears with

---

38 See the organization of the mythology handbook by Rose (1959).
39 Burkert (1982), 23.
40 The notion of archetype goes back at least to Plato and his theory of ideal forms. The actual word ἀρχέτυπος is used by Plato-inspired philosophers such as Plotinus and Philo. "Archetype" comes into English in the works of Sir Thomas Browne and Francis Bacon.

comparative mythologists coming out of anthropology, such as Sir James Frazer (1854–1941)[41] of the Cambridge Ritualist School,[42] who charted mythic themes across many cultures. It was given more rigorous underpinning by formalists such as Vladimir Propp (1895–1970),[43] who in his analysis of Russian folktales found a certain empirical "grammar" of characters and actions.

Archetypes[44] are not mystic entities of some collective unconscious, as Jung would have it. Rather, our archetypes are persistent patterns of thought (as linguistic structures are) and creative expression that have arisen because they express in a compact or compelling form some matter of human interest. They emerge out of the lived experience (physical, mental, emotional, spiritual) of human beings. These archetypal patterns usually have metaphorical significance; we have all heard the phrase "life is a journey," which can expand into an archetypal narrative known as the "odyssey." The creators of our movies may be deliberately borrowing a pattern from a specific ancient work, but this is hard to prove; better to say that the modern movie and its Greco-Roman antecedent employ the same archetypal pattern.[45] And, as has been detailed, standard, nonexperimental cinema uses long-standing literary narrative traditions.[46]

Myths also reflect their culture, time, and place of composition. This is obvious in terms of material culture: Perseus wields a scimitar, while Luke Skywalker flashes a light-saber; Homer's *Iliad* strongly reflects social and political realities and ideologies of Late Geometric and Early Archaic Greece. There Thersites, the common soldier who dares speak his mind, is described as ugly and is thrashed by Odysseus to general acclamation (*Iliad* 2.211–77). This thrashing reflects the perspective of archaic Greek aristocrats appalled to hear "common people" speak out.[47] Marx, Malinowski, Lévi-Strauss, and subsequent scholars have shown how myths (especially those connected to religion or history) furnish part of the ideological superstructure that helps legitimate society.[48] Movies evoking Classical traditions can invoke their implicit ideologies (e.g., authoritarianism), or fight against them, offering a sort of counternarrative against the dominant ideology, or, as often happens, leave the contradictions unresolved or confused.

The myth-critical system of Northrop Frye (1912–1991), which offers a version of structuralist criticism, has considerably influenced us, especially as

---

41 See Frazer (1905–1915); Csapo (2004), 36–43, 44–67; Ackerman (1991).
42 See Segal (1998).
43 Propp (1968).
44 The notion of archetypes remains quite productive, and is used by major scholars. For example, see Winkler (2001), 1ff.
45 Useful is Sowa (1984), who uses the insights of Propp, Lord, and Levi-Strauss to identify nine persistent narrative patterns in the *Homeric Hymns*, and how different poems are structured by these recurring patterns, also referred to as archetypes.
46 See Winkler (2001), 9, citing Chatman (1978) and Bordwell (1985).
47 Postlethwaite (1988).
48 Malinowski (1926), Lefebvre (1982), Strenski (1992).

presented in the *Anatomy of Criticism* and *The Secular Scripture,* whose points about the hero's career are congruent with those of Campbell, Rank, and Raglan, as mentioned below.[49] Important also is Frye's formulation of the meta-genre of Comedy (Comedy in the sense of *Divine Comedy*), which often features a hero, basically good, but more lucky than able, who triumphs over obstacles that often involve breaking bad laws and concludes with the formation or restoration of a society. Although we think of the comic protagonist and the heroic protagonist as very different figures, ever since the rise of the ancient Greek and Roman ideal novel (what has been called "Epic for Everyman")[50] and its celebration of nonmartial values, the comic hero, as one who triumphs over cultural, amatory, or psychological forces, and whose basic decency, cleverness, or simple resilience is the reason for those victories, has become an important model of the hero. These heroes are not limited to just those latter-day Pygmalions, Calvin and Lars; we see their traits in such protagonists as Percy Jackson, Harry Potter, and Ulysses Everett.

Frye, considering the hero's full career, describes basic elements, showing up again and again in our movies, of the Hero's Descent: the initial crossing into a very different world that threatens one's identity and life, nighttime/ nightmare worlds, dark prisons, forests and winding labyrinths, confrontations with doppelgangers, and baleful judges and tempting Calypsos, often concluding in some demonic epiphany and death struggle.

A particular version of this descent is the *nekyia* (journey to the place of the Dead), or the *katabasis* (the decent to the underworld, the place of the Dead), which occurs in real, symbolic, or displaced form in many of the films we analyzed. Needless to say, it is the hero's supreme achievement to confront and defeat the powers of death. Gilgamesh does it in a fashion when he crosses the Waters of Death to visit Utnapishtim; Odysseus, Heracles, Theseus, Orpheus, and Aeneas also descend and return, as does Persephone every year, and other dying and rising gods such as Attis and Adonis. There the hero gains special knowledge of his own life, human destiny, and sometimes greater power and riches. The greater heroes (Heracles, almost Orpheus) actually rescue loved ones, as does Percy Jackson. This journey is also symbolic of death and rebirth, as Trojan Aeneas goes down and returns, and is central for dying and rising gods such as Persephone. This type of descent often concerns questions of identity and status. And, on a psychological plane, the *katabasis* is also a descent into the depths (and sometimes horrors) of one's own mind, a theme observed

---

49 Another common misconception is that Frye's critical system is outmoded. As the publications arising from Frye's centenary show, his thought remains very much alive and even foundational. See in particular Denham (1987), and Denham and Lee (1994), although much has been done since the publication of those two books. Note Julia Kristeva's tribute (reprinted in Lee and Denham, ed. 2002; original 1992).

50 Perry (1967), 48.

in *Wrath of the Titans,* where Perseus and his company enter an underworld labyrinth that plays with their minds.

Depictions of mazes and labyrinths can be forms of descent and reach back into the Paleolithic (indeed, some caves in which paintings are found are themselves mazelike), and always seem to contain some spiritual symbolism, such as being the route to the dead, the road to some form of salvation, or, particularly important for us, to some form of initiation and rebirth.[51] They also, as Frye notes, can be a feature of the confusing and dangerous Dark Woods and underworlds of epic and romance. These two views are aligned; one must travel through the underworld and its dangers before rebirth is possible. There is often some Lady/Goddess of the Labyrinth who leads the youth to a place of testing, where he faces some monstrous (and usually male) creature who represents some destructive aspect, real or psychological, such as a Minotaur (who also appears in three of our movies), which the hero must overcome. Having done so, he obtains tokens of success and social status, as when Theseus returns after killing the Minotaur in the Cretan Labyrinth and becomes King of Athens, despite other obstacles in his path. If the hero survives and returns to the surface, the enslaved are freed, evil laws are broken, the innocent are acquitted, one's true identity is found, and home is restored; and sometimes a new society is created.

MYTH, STRUCTURE, AND PSYCHOLOGY

Psychological approaches are central to many scholarly interpretations of myth. Although we will not always present them as specific "Lacanian" or "Freudian" readings per se, these approaches are quite important for our analyses. Certainly, many scholars find psychological theories diffuse or unverifiable and thus discount them. Yet it is undeniable that human psychology has powerful effects on all aspects of life; thus mythology, a central way for humans to think about and express their feelings and ideas of human nature, has to reflect life. To make psychological criticism more rigorous, we ought to recognize the underlying similarities between modern versions of psychoanalytic theory and those forms of structuralism influenced by the concrete insights of anthropology and historical study.[52] Both Freudian and post-Freudian approaches see the human psyche as providing structure for the way we think and act, such as drivers of emotion, action, and development, as well as fundamental conflicts that need to be resolved. The important difference is that more recent psychological theory suggests the basic structures of human personality are emotional, not rational,

---

51   On later Roman and Medieval labyrinths, see Tidworth (1970), 184–89.

52   A fine exposition on applying current revisions of Freudian theory to myth interpretations is found in Caldwell (1990). See also Caldwell (1974, 1976, 1981). Segal (1978) demonstrates the congruence of structuralist and psychoanalytic approaches. See too Slater (1968) and Arthur (1977). On myth and psychoanalysis, see also Zajko and O'Gorman (2013), Eisner (1987), and Schneiderman (1981).

and arise before the child can even speak, whereas structuralism tends to see the structures as embedded in language. But note that structuralists including Walter Burkert understand how these underlying structures of thinking and language are altered in various ways by culture and history. Thus in the course of early childhood there arise in us various preverbal and emotional structures that create patterns for thinking, structures later expressed through, and modified (in part) by language and culture.

Further, as the French psychologist Jacques Lacan (1901–1981) and others have argued, the roles that various individuals or objects play in these structures of thinking and communicating are relative to each other, not absolute. To give a simple example, one can see how the role of "mother" in the lives of some people is not played by their biological mother, but by one who does the tasks associated with motherhood. Psychologists, starting with Freud, have realized that the psychological language and symbolism of any particular individual is likewise contextual, depending on the individual's own life and the surrounding culture and language. In dreamwork sometimes a cigar is just a cigar, but sometimes it is much more. Important too in psychoanalysis and structuralism (as well as myth criticism) is the principle of *redundancy and repetition*, where the same pattern of behavior or language occurs again and again, as if it were a type of compulsion. That we can easily find one myth after another showing, in obvious or indirect form, various "mommy and daddy issues" is clearly one such repeating pattern that reflects real psychological tendencies.

Certainly the psychological dynamics of the growing child, its relations with its parents and itself, what the child desires, and what society allows (including forms of knowledge, sometimes forbidden) provide areas of conflict and trauma reflected in adult life and illustrated in various mythical patterns, among which we find those associated with the Oedipus complex.[53] Consider how, initially, the infant cannot recognize any real separation between itself and its mother. This is a fairly blissful situation, and some suggest that dreams of nirvanalike states, where the individual ego is dissolved, represent an attempt to regain that state which we still remember and desire at some level. But at some point the young child recognizes, fearfully, the mother is an independent entity who may never come back; that fear will develop into a desire for the mother/parent and a corresponding resentment/hatred of all obstacles to her possession. But along with this desire for the mother comes a fear of being unable to please the mother, and an anger at being so helpless, compared to adults. What the child first desires is what it does not have. Blocking (and potentially dangerous) "Father" figures have what the child desires, and they show up again and again in myth as dangerous and obstructing characters. This pattern of energized desire, resentment, and fear provides a structure for our development that in

---

53 On Freudian criticism, see also Mullahy (1955) and Downing (1975).

turn the myths reflect, as, for example, in the myth of Phaethon, a young man who is not sure his father is really Helios the sun god (and thus is unsure of his mother's virtue), and in going to see Helios he symbolically seeks sexual information about his father and mother. Phaethon tricks Helios into letting him drive his fiery sun chariot, which he fails to control, and before he burns up the entire earth (symbolic of the mother) he is blasted to death by the thunderbolt of Zeus, both a sky god and a father god. Thus, indirectly, Helios kills his son who has taken a parental power without the full consent of the father.[54] There are many repetitions of this pattern of father-son conflict.

The insights of Lacan likewise reveal how the child encounters its first major crisis when it realizes the independence of other individuals and its own dependence on others, who can also exert control.[55] Accordingly, a key Lacanian concept is the "Name of the Father," that entity (not necessarily male) who has the power to "lay down the law," which defines who you are as an individual and as a member of society, and how your desires must be regulated/repressed. Again, note how in *Lars and the Real Girl* Lars has to be the voice and personality of his doll-love Bianca, and thus (for a while) lays down the law of her existence. In *Such Is Life* Julia's husband Nico and the leader of the *vecindario*, the Sow, utter words that try to force Julia to change her identity and status. Lord Cotys tries again and again to define Hercules as merely a mercenary and a murderer. Relevant too is the concept of *displacement*, where new items are slotted into other places within a symbolic structure of meaning, like a type of metaphor. Thus the character "Mother" can stand for all objects of desire, and "Father" for what blocks that desire. Lacan suggests that projection (a form of displacement) is a central feature in many human relationships. Thus lovers, for example, never engage the object of their love as he or she exists *in themselves*, but rather their own projected construction—obvious in Lars's Bianca.

Another very useful idea is *decomposition*, where the contradictory aspects of one being are broken into two or more figures. For example, in several myths there is a figure who stands for the good aspects of a Mother (being loving and nurturing) and another for the bad aspects (being hard to please, angry, able to abandon or destroy the child). There can likewise be good Father figures and, more commonly, bad ones, which fill the Freudian role of the Father who is in competition for the Mother with the child and therefore seeks to harm it. Thus in the Perseus myth, one finds a female figure who presents positive aspects of the mother (Perseus' real mother, Danaë) threatened by a hostile father figure (King Polydectes, who is trying to seduce Danaë), and another female figure who incarnates the threatening aspects of the mother (Medusa, who tries to

---

54 But, in contrast, Pelops and Telemachus are successful examples of living up to the father.
55 For Lacanian interpretations and theory, we rely on Janan (1994), Bowie (1991), Homer (2005), Fink (1995), and Evans (1996). On the "Word of the Father," see also Homer (2005), 57–59; Evans (1996), 119; and Janan (1994), 23–24.

kill Perseus), who must be defeated, as is the bad father figure. All this allows Perseus to finally marry outside the family (Andromeda, whom he saves) and progress to becoming a hero, which culminates in his killing of another father figure, king Acrisius, Danaë's father (who had also tried to kill him), which leads to his kingship of Mycenae. In *Clash/Wrath*, Zeus and Hades incarnate two aspects of the biological father figure, as well as the "Father" in the Lacanian sense as one who keeps us from the object of desire, Hades or the Underworld as the ultimate blocker of Desire—with whom in the movie Perseus reconciles.

Since family dynamics are important for studying our myths, just consider how an absent parent seems the rule rather than the exception for our protagonists' family situation.

Perseus	Mother dead, real father absent, adopted parents both dead, motherlike first wife dies
Katniss	Father dead, mother debilitated, sister is (eventually) killed
Calvin	Father dead, mother in relationship with wacky guy
Lars	Mother died in childbirth, father depressed and then died, abandoned by brother
Heracles	Absent/unknown father, kills wife and children
Julia	Leaves/abandons hometown, including presumably her mother and father, kills children
Harry Potter	Both parents killed
Ulysses Everett	No mention of his parents, but he is dead to his children and wife for a while
Theseus	Absent father, mother dies, abandons own son Acamas
Achilles	Father apparently died early, mother a bit wacky
Bianca, Ruby	Have no parents except their creators, both thought to be orphans
Percy Jackson	Absent father, remarried mother (who symbolically dies), vile stepfather
Ofelia	Father dead, mother dies in the film

To rephrase what Luke says in *Percy Jackson: The Lightning Thief*: "Everybody in our chosen movies has parent issues."

While society forces individuals to repress, and even hide, certain desires and fears, these elements reappear in myth, sometimes explicitly, often in displaced and indirect form; thus the abundant occurrences of infanticide, incest, rape, murder, castration, even cannibalism. Likewise there are many episodes in which heroes see things or creatures forbidden and deadly, and then destroy them and wield their power (Perseus and Medusa). Figures such as the hybrid centaur, the biform Pan, or Titans hint at the nonhuman dimensions that nevertheless form us or in some way represent the power of our repressed (but not destroyed) past, for example the "Cerberus" of Hercules' nightmares.

And whereas we otherwise avoid Jungian perspectives, useful is his notion of the Shadow, that representation of those forbidden, frightening elements that remain essential parts of our psychological makeup, and that need to be confronted, encounters that myth presents in narratives of journeys across dangerous Dark Woods, Deadlands, or Labyrinths.

Myth does not so much represent humanity's "collective unconscious" as functions like a form of common, shared dreamwork—or nightmare. The myths of preliterate peoples often show a similar disregard for the "reality principle," because they follow structures of emotion and feeling, not rational and instrumental thought. Many of our movies, for example *Such Is Life*, but also *Clash/Wrath* and *Immortals*, present surreal, dream, or nightmarelike images (i.e. the Djinn of *Clash*, who have made their bodies increasingly inorganic), scenes, or even plot developments. The great Italian director Pier Paolo Pasolini felt that any reasonably sophisticated film presented, out of necessity, concrete images while at the same time possessing a level that was dreamlike, irrational, even uncivilized, and thus powerfully mythical and metaphoric.[56] As Walter Benjamin (1892–1940) and others have noted,[57] the current technology (especially in the age of advanced editing techniques and CGI) invites the radical refashioning, rejuxtapositioning, and "mashing up" of the elements of a visual narrative, making it difficult to find the threads of traditional meaning making and even storytelling. But they are (usually) there. Although for some critics these extreme elements make a movie incomprehensible, we propose that films sometimes need to be interpreted more as dreams, more as purely symbolic structures of signification, especially those connected to emotion and feeling, freed from the limitations of the real world.[58]

GENDER, OTHERNESS, AND MYTH INTERPRETATION

The problem with myth and most classical texts is that almost all of our evidence comes from men living in patriarchal societies. Think, for example, of the misogynist and oppressive myths that have come down to us: Gilgamesh slut-shamed Ishtar, Adam accused Eve, Pandora brought evil to the world, Helen caused war and destruction, and Medusa became a terrifying monster, perhaps due to her sexual excesses. There are "good" females as well, like Danaë or Alcmene, and the positive, generalized power of the Earth Mother is divided among various Greek goddesses – Athena, Aphrodite, Artemis, Hera, Demeter, and so forth. As we discuss in more detail in our sections on *Pan's Labyrinth* and *The Hunger Games*, and in our discussion of the Demeter-Persephone myth, the generational and intense mother-daughter bond, reflecting early memories of selfless unity with the

---

56 See Winkler (2009), 52–53, quoting Pasolini (1988), 171–78, 182, 184.
57 Benjamin (1936), 221, 224; quoted in Winkler (2001), 17.
58 See also Eberwein (2014).

mother, becomes a figure for the experience of bliss and a type of eternity. Also we should be aware of how myth can offer two models for creation, one coming from above and one from below; the one concerning life born from the earth is a more feminine and sexual one, where the earth nurtures and protects, a contrast to a male sky god, who intelligently fashions everything.[59] Movies such as *Pan's Labyrinth* and *The Hunger Games* series suggest the first model, while *Clash/Wrath* and *Immortals,* and, in a sense, *Ruby Sparks* suggest the second.

Since nearly all these tales have been transmitted in some form of male-authored testimony, as Lillian Doherty points out, we are probably "missing something important." Thus we lack stories, folklore, and even myth versions created for women and by women.[60] To some degree, issues regarding gender are implied in most other theoretical approaches.[61] One important insight of feminist scholars concerns how male-oriented views of myth, such as Campbell's, Freud's or Jung's, have a tendency to universalize experience in ways that create a sort of encasement of women that keeps them "in their place."[62]

The goal of feminist readings of myth is, at least in part, to fill some of those gaps. Telling the stories from the viewpoint of female mythical characters was one strategy some feminist readers and critics have used.[63] An important dimension of the feminist critique is "revision," a form of questioning and re-reading of male-oriented myths, texts, and stories.[64] The central question is what a feminist reader can do with myths. One strategy is to resist, and appropriate these patriarchal stories. And indeed, "many feminists have chosen to revivify ancient narratives to arm contemporary struggles [. . .yet] the transformation of normative stories into potent tales of resistance has sometimes been a controversial endeavour for feminists."[65] Some like Cixous in their work appropriate and align with the female figures of myth (seen in her own "Laugh of the Medusa") and "myth's inspirational potential for feminism."[66] A more deconstructive stance is adopted by readers like Lucy Irigaray (1930–), who "shows how myth fossilizes existing hierarchies."[67] As Zajko and Leonard write,

---

59 Frye (1976), 112.

60 Doherty (2003), 21.

61 Doherty (2003), 45.

62 Doherty (2003), 47. Some feminist scholars attack the universalizing approach of much archetypal theory, especially Jungian forms. Doherty notes: "Feminists who believe there is such a thing as 'essential' femininity or femaleness . . . may accept Jung's theory of the archetypes in principle. . . . Feminists who reject the notion of 'essential' femininity tend to reject Jung altogether. To them, the collective unconscious is a dangerous concept, one that can serve to keep women in their place in an era when they are trying on new roles and forging new identities." However, there are many feminist critics, such as Paglia (2006), who appreciate archetypal theory and even Jung.

63 See Cahill (1995), for example.

64 The articles in Zajko and Leonard (2006) offer some useful perspectives, which we draw on.

65 Zajko and Leonard (2006), 2.

66 Zajko and Leonard (2006), 3. See also Cixous (1976).

67 Zajko and Leonard (2006), 4.

"Feminists' simultaneous aim of exposing generalized structures of power, and their particular manifestations in personal politics, offer a distinctive contribution to reception theory."[68] This revisionist look at myth and the "effort to reclaim a distinctive 'women's classical tradition' appeals to many women and at least some men at the turn of the millennium."[69] As we discuss later regarding *Ruby Sparks*, the question remains of what to do with these male-biased texts, myths, and stories. As Amy Richlin wonders, should we "throw them out, take them apart, find female-based ones instead?"[70] Similarly, feminism posits questions for film criticism, especially with readers like Mary Devereaux,[71] who promotes rereading and re-vision, and the influential Laura Mulvey, who dismantles the presumed neutrality of film by positing, among other things, the existence of a controlling male gaze.[72]

Women are central in many of our myths and movies, and these feminist perspectives raise questions for us. Can Ruby Sparks react to her creator's power in a way that Pygmalion's statue could not? Can we see any agency in the life-size doll Bianca? Is Julia in *Such Is Life* simply an evil murderess or the product of male oppression? Does Ofelia in *Pan's Labyrinth* entirely comply with the beneficial fertility goddess figure, or are there also rebellious, anti-male-establishment aspects in her? How millennial and unconventional is Katniss's femininity, who is both warrior heroine and mother goddess at the same time?

Relevant too is the concept of Otherness or Alterity, taken from Continental philosophy, anthropology, and cultural studies, and especially useful for gender studies.[73] In its less philosophically complex version, it refers to our difficulties in relating to persons distinctly unfamiliar to us, whether people of other races and nations or, too often, women. Thus myths reflect how cultures make a woman or a foreigner an Other who must be despised or feared, but on occasion also admired. We can demonize and destroy the Other, or learn from him/her/it. And sometimes the Other is also part of Ourselves, as when Harry Potter, as we will discuss, realizes part of Voldemort resides in him. In particular, this concept is central to ancient Greek ideology as Greeks self-constructed their identity, in opposition to the Barbarian Other, a definition that once appeared linguistic (those whose speech sounded like "bar-bar," not speaking Greek). At the center of this world view is the free Greek male, women being different, Others perceived with dangerous potentials who must be suppressed. The feeling is found in Roman ideology with its sense of Rome's centrality versus the periphery of the rest of the known world.[74] The concept is pervasive in the conceptualization of women,

---

68 Zajko and Leonard (2006), 10.
69 Doherty (2003), 21.
70 Richlin (1992), 161.
71 Devereaux (1990).
72 Mulvey (1975, 1989, and 1996).
73 See Attridge (2004) with bibliography.
74 Augoustakis (2010), 2–3.

slaves, and those outside the male patriarchal elites.[75] And we ought to note that, as Julia Kristeva recognizes, women themselves may feel in a constant state of strangeness or otherness.[76] This notion surfaces clearly in tragedy in particular, as Edith Hall and others have shown,[77] and it is a useful concept for analyzing our movies. Picture Medea, for example, who is doubly a Barbarian and Other, a non-Greek female from the remote land of Colchis who has odd primitive customs and is exceptionally clever as well. We shall observe the complexities of this thinking in *Such Is Life*, but also in more displaced ways in constructions of threatening, uncontrollable females such as Medusa.

SOME OVERARCHING NARRATIVE AND SYMBOLIC STRUCTURES

In the introduction to each section of our book, we provide an overview of the myths and contexts that are particularly relevant. But there are two mythic meta-narratives that play some role in all our movies. The first pertains to the overall life of the cosmos, the second to the individual: the macrocosm and the microcosm, the origins and evolution of the universe, and the nature and career of the hero.

TITANS VS. OLYMPIANS: CREATION AND SUCCESSION MYTHS

Every narrative takes place in some sort of universe, and the nature of that universe, its origins, evolution, conditions and fate, provide context for the lives of the characters who live in it. The central Hellenic creation story is found in Hesiod's *Theogony*, with many elements borrowed from Middle Eastern creation narratives.[78] All these stories posit a succession myth, where a younger generation of gods deposes an older generation. This conflict is sometimes simplified into a battle between good and evil forces. The universe generally does not emerge through a god's will, but through Necessity or natural processes. Only later does the main god (e.g., Marduk) put his finishing touches on the universe. To simplify the complex Greek creation story, first there was Chaos, the "gap." Out of this came Earth (Gaia), Eros (Love), Nyx (night), Tartarus (the space beneath the earth), and Erebus (a primordial deity who personifies Darkness). From Gaia came a line of gods that leads to the human universe, and from Nyx came another baleful series of divinities. Gaia, being female, produced, among other beings, her

---

75 See Hallet (1989) and the very useful introductory chapter of Augoustakis (2010), who states that, at least for the texts he studies, "Roman identity ultimately rests upon the absorption of elements from outside, which bear the marks both of the radically different—the monstrous—and of Rome's truest self, that is, its idealised virtues and merits" (9). See also Konstan (2000) and Wells (1999). A good discussion of Kristeva's views of women as Other is found in Augoustakis (2010), 14–21.
76 See Kristeva (1991). See also Smith (1996).
77 Hall (1989).
78 On the Greek succession myth and its Middle Eastern sources, see Woodard (2008), 86–108ff; Burkert (2004).

husband Uranos (Sky), and together they produced the Titans. The Titans are usually thought of as crude, violent, and powerful gods, but some of the Titans were clever (Prometheus) and holy (Helios, the solar god). Very important for our movies is the fact that Kronos was the leader of these Titans, and father to various Olympians, the next generation of gods, led by Zeus, whose brothers were Poseidon and Hades. The Olympians and Titans had a war, the Titanomachy, which the Olympians won, and the Titans were confined to Tartarus, beneath the earth. Later an angered Earth produced the Giants (= Earth-Born), whom the Olympians defeated in the Gigantomachy. A theme more evident in our movies than in the myths is that the Titans represent an evil force that might reemerge, a theme influenced by Christianity, as noted above, where Satan and his angels, although defeated by God, are able to still find human allies and cause vast problems, but who will be finally defeated in an apocalyptic battle.

After the Titans were cast down into Tartarus, Zeus and the Olympians put their finishing touches on the universe by mating with each other, producing the younger Olympians (e.g., Athena, Apollo, Hephaestus, Ares, etc.), and with various mortal women, producing heroes such as Heracles and Perseus. In the *Percy Jackson* series the gods still "hook up" with mortal women. Greek mythology is vague on humanity's origins, and there is no central account that stresses humans were created by the gods.[79] Although Hesiod describes five ages of Humanity, and Ovid four, important for our movies is the notion that, right before our era, there was an Age of Heroes, which began with the repopulation of the world after the Flood and ended with the virtual apocalypse of the Trojan War. Many of the Greek legends are set in the Greek Bronze Age (1600–1100 BCE), which for Greeks was the Age of Heroes. This reflects a cultural memory of the glories of the Mycenaean world, which collapsed sometime around the canonical date of the Trojan War (according to Eratosthenes, 1194–1184 BCE). The Age of Heroes was characterized by larger-than-life individuals and deeds (as *Troy* underscores) and a more active relationship between humans and gods, all lost in our coarser Age of Iron.

Unlike most modern religious texts, Greek myth shows the gods as morally problematic; they lie, cheat, fornicate, murder, do battle, and play dirty tricks, etc., often with complete disregard for humane sensibilities. A theme, present but not stressed in Greek myth, is the possibility of Zeus' overthrow.[80] The realm of the gods serves as a metaphor for the overarching political order, and thus the generic evils of our world find their equivalent in the faults of current political systems. Thus, the dream of radical political change is reimagined as the downfall of the regime of corrupt gods.[81] Further, because the ancients saw

---

79 Although such accounts do exist, as with the myth that Prometheus made humanity: Paus.10.4.4, Hor. *Carm* 1.16.13ff.

80 For a decent summary of the evidence of resistance to Zeus, drawing on other scholars, see Yasumura (2013).

81 See Shelley's *Prometheus Bound* for example.

the gods as human enough to have husbands, wives, and children, the succession myth is also a conflict of generations, in particular of fathers against sons who are often allied with the mother, and thus these myths have rich psychological undertones. Myth tells truths through exaggeration. The domineering parent of real life becomes Kronos, who swallows his children, or Apsu, who wants to kill the young gods for making too much noise. For children to develop their own personalities, they have to separate themselves from their parents, and rebel; naturally mythic exaggeration of this rebellion is the killing of the parent. But in ancient societies a son is often defined by his father; myths, like those of Oedipus, Phaethon, and Ion, hinge on the question of who is the hero's parent and what that might imply. Today's books, television shows, and movies even more strongly present children forced to deal with problematic parents.

THE HERO AND THE COMPONENTS OF THE HERO'S CAREER

Turning to the microcosm, we consider narratives of the individual protagonist or hero. Here three myth paradigms interpenetrate: (1) the coming-of-age narrative, (2) the Hero's Quest or journey, and (3) the marvelous-child paradigm. As noted, the truly major narrative patterns/archetypes grow out of the experiences of human life. All children must transition into adulthood, a complex process rife with dangers. One basic pattern for this transformation can be elaborated this way: (1) a young person leaves the protection of the home and engages the potentially dangerous, but also rewarding, wider world; (2) to succeed, a young person must meet and gain the help of adults with some authority and power; (3) with this help and thanks to personal initiative, abilities, and luck, the young person achieves various goals (often on what can be termed a Quest); and (4) as a consequence, the young person can be seen as a fully functioning adult and gains status in the community. Now consider this sequence: (1) young adult leaves Satsuma, Florida, to attend Montclair State University in New Jersey; (2) student meets helpful professors and mentors and gains friends; (3) student obtains BA degree and meets future spouse; and (4) student returns to Florida to a successful career and marriage. Now think how this pattern applies to Perseus' life: (1) Perseus is sent away from Seriphos on an impossible quest; (2) Perseus gains the help of Athena and Hermes; (3) Perseus cuts off Medusa's head and rescues and weds Andromeda; and (4) Perseus returns to Greece, saves his mother, and becomes king of Mycenae. This simplified four-part version of the Quest motif is the one we employ. There is an obvious relationship between the Quest pattern and elements found in coming-of-age rituals and narratives, and this similarity will be noted in the movies we examine.

This simple, four-part structure can be extended and elaborated with subparts and embellishments. The most popular extended version of this simple pattern is the seventeen-part Hero's Journey paradigm, the "monomyth" made popular by Joseph Campbell (1904–1984). However, Campbell does not provide anywhere-near-sufficient evidence to prove his full seventeen-step paradigm is universal,[82] although elements of it are common enough. Furthermore, the scheme he presents is too androcentric, and reflects the preoccupations of Western culture.[83] However, Campbell was a considerable popularizer. A famous textbook for screenwriters, Christopher Vogler's *The Writer's Journey: Mythic Structure for Writers*, stems from a brief internal studio document, "A Practical Guide to *The Hero with a Thousand Faces*," and is grounded on Campbell's ideas of myth,[84] which Vogler wrote while working at Walt Disney. Rick Riordan (author of the Percy Jackson series and other young adult novels) uses this pattern fairly explicitly, which is why we present it below; In *Percy Jackson: The Lightning Thief* the satyr Grover notes that, although extensively trained, he has never been on a Quest. Campbell's pattern has three main parts: Departure, Initiation, and Return. Each part is further subdivided.

Departure	**Initiation**	**Return**
1. The Call to Adventure	6. The Road of Trials	12. Refusal of the Return
2. Refusal of the Call	7. Meeting the Goddess	13. The Magic Flight
3. Supernatural Aid	8. Woman as Temptress	14. Rescue from Without
4. Crossing the Threshold	9. Atonement with the Father	15. The Crossing of the Return Threshold
5. Belly of the Whale	10. Apotheosis	16. Master of Two Worlds
	11. The Ultimate Boon	17. Freedom to Live

Often the hero is a marvelous child, whose career usually reflects the Freudian family psychodrama mentioned above. Key elements of this pattern that we employ are that (1) the child is the son or daughter of a god or king; (2) the birth of the child is often accompanied by scandal involving the mother, and sometimes an attempt is made to kill the child; (3) the child is deprived of its birthright and exiled; (4) the child grows up not knowing its true nature, often among poor people in a pastoral surrounding; (5) the child discovers its true nature; (6) the child, after conflict (perhaps a Quest), regains its proper status and often brings benefit to its community. The best-known version of this was

---

82 For a very good critique of the problems with Campbell's theory of myth, see Gill (2006), 73–100, and Segal (1984).

83 The complex patterns described by Campbell, Rank, and Lord Raglan are elaborations and options of the more fundamental and simple patterns we have discussed.

84 This can be found online; see for example http://www.tlu.ee/~rajaleid/montaazh/ Christopher%20Vogler%20-%20Writers%20Journey.pdf. Accessed May 27, 2016. Print edition Vogler (2007).

produced by an associate of Freud's, Otto Rank, in 1909. Lord Raglan, in the steps of the Cambridge myth-ritualist school, in turn developed in 1936 an even more complicated twenty-two-part version in order to explain common Indo-European mythical patterns of the Hero. One notes, for example, how the life of Jesus corresponds to this mythic pattern.[85] But these complex patterns again are hardly universal, although individual elements occur in many myths and in our movies too.

On the anagogic level of interpretation, where deeper wisdom is found, the hero/marvelous-child myth suggests that we all are born with potentials that we do not know or recognize, and that must be discovered. It likewise recognizes we are often born in a station beneath what we should be, and in negative circumstances not of our making, with our parents, relatives, and fellow citizens oppressed in various ways. Thus it is the task of each of us, to the extent possible, to discover and recover what we are and our true station, and, as possible, help our families and fellow citizens do the same. In the movies we consider, Theseus, Percy Jackson, Ofelia, Harry Potter, Achilles, and even Katniss Everdeen are marvelous children.

WHAT IS MYTH GOOD FOR?

All works in the Humanities reflect some dimension of human culture, history, or psychology in varying degrees of realism or distortion. In our own millennial time, a period of rapid change and breakdown of the established order, members of the audience can seek a space where their hopes, fears, dreams, and so forth are displayed in the most engaging way. For some people the most appealing myths are partially (or wholly) divorced from the reality principle, a form of dreamwork. Classical myths, like science fiction and fantasy, are set in a universe of alternate possibility, where displaced versions of our fears and dreams can be enacted. In this regard, the formalist concept of *defamiliarization* is important. That is, fantasy can show us the familiar in a strange light, and thus make us appreciate our own reality more fully. As noted before, these myths are popular because they touch on widely experienced themes, and also illuminate them in a more attractive way. Thus myth offers a cognitive space that can entertain and even educate by allowing us to experience other realities and gain or experience new insights into our own reality. They also allow us to live a fantasy and to work through notions hard to deal with in conventional circumstances. We have already mentioned the anagogic element of movies; this aspect, when joined to a visual (and communal) spectacle wherein viewers can experience the full spectrum of joy and horror possible in life, can kindle the moral imagination and awaken our better selves. Movies can make powerful tools for propaganda,

---

85 Lord Raglan (2011: reprint of essay of 1909).

but also for progress. Thus learning and teaching how to closely read movies, as opposed to merely passively consuming them, is vital.

REFERENCES

Ackerman, R. *The Myth and Ritual School: J. G. Frazer and the Cambridge Ritualists.* Garland, 1991.

Adorno, T. W., and M. Horkheimer. "The Culture Industry: Enlightenment as Mass Deception." In *Dialectic of Enlightenment.* Continuum, 1994 (original from 1944).

Altman, R. *Film Genre.* British Film Institute, 1999.

Arthur, M. "Classics and Psychoanalysis." *Classical Journal,* vol. 73 no. 1, 1977, 56–68.

Attridge, D. *The Singularity of Literature.* Routledge, 2004.

Augoustakis, A. *Motherhood and the Other: Fashioning Female Power in Flavian Epic.* Oxford UP, 2010.

Bakhtin, M. "Epic and the Novel: Toward a Methodology for the Study of the Novel." In M. Holquist, ed., *The Dialogic Imagination* by M. M. Bakhtin. University of Texas Press, 1981 (original from 1941).

Benjamin, W. "The Work of Art in the Age of Mechanical Reproduction" (*Das Kunstwerk im Zeitalter seiner technischen Reproduzierbarkeit,* originally published in *Zeitschrift für Sozialforschung*). Houghton Mifflin Harcourt, 1936 (first published in English as *Illuminations,* 1968).

Berti, I., and I. García Morcillo. *Hellas on Screen: Cinematic Receptions of Ancient History, Literature and Myth.* Franz Steiner Verlag, 2008.

Bondanella, P. *A History of Italian Cinema.* Continuum, 2009.

Bordwell, D. *Narration in the Fiction Film.* University of Wisconsin Press, 1985.

Bowie, M. *Lacan.* Harvard UP, 1991.

Burkert, W. *The Orientalizing Revolution: Near Eastern Influence on Greek Culture in the Early Archaic Age.* Harvard UP, 2004 (original 1992).

———. *Structure and History in Greek Mythology and Ritual.* Sather Classical Lectures. University of California Press, 1982.

Cahill, J. *Her Kind: Stories of Women from Classical Mythology.* Broadview Press, 1995.

Caldwell, R. "Psychoanalysis, Structuralism and Greek Mythology." In H. R. Garvin and P. Brady, ed., *Phenomenology, Structuralism, Semiology.* Associated UP, 1976, pp. 209–30.

———. "The Psychoanalytic Interpretation of Greek Myth." In L. Edmunds, ed., *Approaches to Greek Myth.* Johns Hopkins UP, 1990, pp. 342–89.

———. "Psychocosmogony: The Representation of Symbiosis and Separation-Individuation in Archaic Greek Myth." In W. Muensterberger and L. Boyer, ed., *The Psychoanalytic Study of Society,* International UP vol. 9, 1981, 93–103.

———. "Selected Bibliography on Psychoanalysis and Classical Studies." *Arethusa,* vol. 7, 1974, 119–23.

Campbell, J. *The Hero with a Thousand Faces.* New World Library, 2008 (1st ed. 1949).

Cawelti, J. *Adventure, Mystery and Romance: Formula Stories as Art and Popular Culture.* University of Chicago Press, 1976.

Chatman, S. *Story and Discourse: Narrative Structure in Fiction and Film.* Cornell UP, 1978.

Cixous, H. "The Laugh of the Medusa." (trans. K. Cohen and P. Cohen). *Signs,* vol. 1 no. 4, 1976, 875–93.

Cornelius, M., ed. "Introduction: Of Muscles and Men: The Forms and Functions of the Sword and Sandal Film." In *Of Muscles and Men.* McFarland, 2011, pp. 1–14.

Corrigan, T. *A Short Guide to Writing about Film.* HarperCollins, 2014.

Csapo, E. *Theories of Mythology.* Wiley-Blackwell, 2004.

Cyrino, M., ed. *Big Screen Rome.* Wiley-Blackwell, 2005.

———. *Screening Love and Sex in the Ancient World.* Palgrave-Macmillan, 2013.

———, and M. Safran, ed. *Classical Myth on Screen.* Palgrave-Macmillan, 2015.

Denham, R. D. *Northrop Frye. An Annotated Bibliography of Primary and Secondary Sources.* University of Toronto Press, 1987.

———, and A. Lee. *The Legacy of Northrop Frye.* University of Toronto Press, 1994.

Devereaux, M. "Oppressive Texts, Resisting Readers and the Gendered Spectator: The New Aesthetics." *Journal of Aesthetics and Art Criticism,* vol. 48 no. 4, 1990, 337–47.

Doherty, L. E. *Gender and the Interpretation of Classical Myth.* Bloomsbury, 2003 (first publication 2001).

Downing, C. "Sigmund Freud and the Greek Mythological Tradition." *Journal of the American Academy of Religion,* vol. 43 no. 1, 1975, 3–14.

Dundes, A., ed. *Sacred Narrative: Readings in the Theory of Myth.* University of California Press, 1984.

Eberwein, R. T. *Film and the Dream Screen: A Sleep and a Forgetting.* Princeton UP, 2014.

Eco, U. *Travels in Hyperreality: Essays.* Trans. W. Weaver. Harcourt Brace, 1986, reprint 1990.

Edmunds, L., ed. *Approaches to Greek Myth.* Johns Hopkins UP, 1990.

Eisner, R. *The Road to Daulis: Psychoanalysis, Psychology and Classical Mythology.* Syracuse UP, 1987.

Evans, D. *An Introductory Dictionary of Lacanian Psychoanalysis.* Routledge, 1996.

Fink, B. *The Lacanian Subject: Between Language and Jouissance.* Princeton UP, 1995.

Frazer, G. B. *The Golden Bough: A Study in Magic and Religion.* Macmillan, 1911–1915.

Frye, N. *Anatomy of Criticism. Four Essays.* Princeton UP, 2000.

——— *Secular Scripture: A Study of the Structure of Romance.* Harvard UP, 1976.

Genette, G. *Palimpsests: Literature in the Second Degree.* University of Nebraska Press, 1997.

Gill, G. R. *Northrop Frye and the Phenomenology of Myth.* University of Toronto Press, 2006.

Hall, E. *Inventing the Barbarian: Greek Self-Definition Through Tragedy*. Clarendon Press, 1989.

Hallet, J. P. "Women as Same and Other in Classical Roman Elite." *Helios*, vol. 16 no. 1, 1989, 59–78.

Hardwick, L., and C. Stray, ed. "Introduction: Making Conceptions." In *A Companion to Classical Receptions*. Wiley-Blackwell, 2008, pp. 1–9.

Harris, S., and G. Platzner. *Classical Mythology: Images and Insights*, 6th ed. McGraw-Hill, 2011.

Holtsmark, E. B. "The *Katabasis* Theme in Modern Cinema." In M. Winkler, ed., *Classical Myth and Culture in the Cinema*. Oxford UP, 2001, pp. 23–49.

Homer, S. *Jacques Lacan*. Routledge, 2005.

Hutcheon, L. *A Theory of Parody: The Teachings of Twentieth-Century Art Forms*. University of Illinois Press, 1985.

James, P. *Ovid's Myth of Pygmalion on Screen: In Pursuit of the Perfect Woman*. Bloomsbury, 2011.

Jameson. F. *The Political Unconscious Narrative as a Socially Symbolic Act*. Cornell UP, 1981.

Janan, M. *When the Lamp Is Shattered: Desire and Narrative in Catullus*. Southern Illinois Press, 1994.

Konstan, D. "Women, Ethnicity and Power in the Roman Empire." Accepted for publication by Judith Hallett and Janet Martin, ed., *Proceedings of the Second Conference on Feminism and the Classics*. Published in *Diotima* with permission of the editors, February 2000 (http://www.uky.edu/AS/Classics/gender.html and http://www.stoa.org/diotima/essays/konstan1.pdf). Accessed Mar. 17, 2016.

Kovacs, G., and Marshall, C. W., ed. *Classics and Comics*. Oxford UP, 2011.

Kristeva, J. "The Importance of Frye." In A. A. Lee and R. Denham, ed., *The Legacy of Northrop Frye*. University of Toronto Press, 2002 (original 1992), pp. 335–37.
———. *Strangers to Ourselves*. Trans. L. S. Roudiez. Columbia UP, 1991 (original 1977).

Lee, A. A., and R. Denham, ed. *The Legacy of Northrop Frye*. University of Toronto Press, 2002.

Lefebvre, H. *The Sociology of Marx*. Columbia UP, 1982.

Leprohon, P. *The Italian Cinema*. Tr. Roger Greaves and Oliver Stallybrass. Secker and Warburg; Praeger, 1972.

Lewis, C. S. *A Preface to Paradise Lost*. Atlantic Publishers & Distributor, 2006.

MacKinnon, K. *Greek Tragedy into Film*. Routledge, 1986.

Malinowski, B. *Myth in Primitive Psychology*. Norton, 1926.

Martindale, C. "Introduction: Thinking Through Reception." In C. Martindale and R. Thomas, ed., *Classics and the Uses of Reception*. Blackwell, 2006, pp. 1–13.

Maurizio, L. *Classical Mythology in Context*. Oxford UP, 2015.

McDonald, M. *Euripides in Cinema: The Heart Made Visible*. Centrum, 1983.

Mench, F. "Film Sense in the *Aeneid*." *Arion* 8, 2001 (original 1969), 360–97.

Michelakis, P. *Greek Tragedy on Screen*. Oxford UP, 2013.

Michelakis, P., and M. Wyke, ed. *The Ancient World in Silent Cinema*. Cambridge UP, 2013.

Morford, M., R. J. Lenardon, and M. Sham. *Classical Mythology*, 10th ed. Oxford UP, 2013.

Mullahy, P. *Oedipus: Myth and Complex-A Review of Psychoanalytic Theory*. Grove Press, 1955.

Mulvey, L. *Fetishism and Curiosity*. Indiana UP, 1996.

———. *Visual and Other Pleasures*. Theories of Representation and Difference. Indiana UP, 1989.

———. "Visual Pleasure and Narrative Cinema." *Screen*, vol. 16 no. 3, 1975, 6–18.

Nikoloutsos, K., ed. *Ancient Greek Women in Film*. Oxford UP, 2013.

Paglia, C. "Erich Neumann: Theorist of the Great Mother." *Arion*, vol. 13 no. 3, 2014, 1–14.

Pasolini, P. P. "The Cinema of Poetry." In *Heretical Empiricism*, ed. Louise K. Barnett. Indiana UP, 1988.

Paul, J. *Film and the Classical Epic Tradition*. Oxford UP, 2013.

———. "Working with Film: Theories and Methodologies." In L. Hardwick and C. Stray, ed., *A Companion to Classical Receptions*. Wiley-Blackwell, 2008, pp. 303–26.

Perry, B. E. *The Ancient Romances: A Literary-historical Account of Their Origins*. University of California Press, 1967.

Postlethwaite, N. "Thersites in the *Iliad*." *Greece & Rome*, vol. 35 no. 2, 1988, 123–36.

Powell, B. *Classical Mythology*, 8th ed. Pearson, 2015.

Propp, V. *The Morphology of the Folktale*. University of Texas Press, 1968.

Raglan, Lord. *The Hero: A Study in Tradition, Myth and Drama*. Dover, 2011.

Rank, O. *The Myth of the Birth of the Hero: A Psychological Interpretation of Mythology*. Grove Press, 2015 (first published in German in 1909).

Richlin, A. "Reading Ovid's Rapes." In *Pornography and Representation in Greece and Rome*. Oxford UP, 1991, 158–79.

Rogers, B., and Stevens, B. *Classical Traditions in Science Fiction*. Oxford UP, 2015.

Rose, H. *A Handbook of Greek Mythology*. Dutton, 1959.

Rose, P. "Teaching Classical Myth and Confronting Contemporary Myths." In M. Winkler, ed., *Classical Myth and Culture in the Cinema*. Oxford UP, 2001, pp. 291–318.

Sanders, J. *Adaptation and Cultural Appropriation*. Routledge, 2005.

Schneiderman, L. *The Psychology of Myth, Folklore and Religion*. Rowan and Littlefield, 1981.

Segal, C. "Pentheus and Hippolytus on the Couch and on the Grid: Psychoanalytic and Structuralist Readings of Greek Tragedy." *Classical World*, vol. 72 no. 3, 1978, 129–48.

Segal, R. A. "Joseph Campbell's Theory of Myth." In A. Dundes, ed., *Sacred Narrative: Readings in the Theory of Myth*. University of California Press, 1984, pp. 256–69.

———. *The Myth and Ritual Theory: An Anthology*. Wiley-Blackwell, 1998.

Slater, P. E. *The Glory of Hera: Greek Mythology and the Greek Family.* Beacon Press, 1968.

Smith, A. *Julia Kristeva: Readings of Exile and Estrangement.* St. Martin's Press, 1996.

Solomon, J. *The Ancient World in the Cinema.* Yale UP, 1978 (rev. ed. 2001).

Sowa, C. *Traditional Themes and the Homeric Hymns.* Bolchazy-Carducci, 1984.

Strenski, I., ed. *Malinowski and the Work of Myth.* Princeton UP, 1992.

Theodorakopoulos E. *Ancient Rome at the Cinema. Story and Spectacle in Hollywood and Rome,* Bristol Phoenix Press, 2010.

Tidworth, S. "The Roman and Medieval Theseus." In A. G. Ward, ed., *The Quest for Theseus.* Praeger, 1970, pp. 175–194.

Ullman, B. "Editorial: The European War and the Classics." *The Classical Weekly,* vol. 8 no. 26, 1915 (May 8).

Vogler, C. *The Writer's Journey: Mythic Structure for Writers.* Michael Wiese Productions, 2007.

Wells, P. S. *The Barbarians Speak: How the Conquered Peoples Shaped Roman Europe.* Princeton UP, 1999.

Wenzel, D. *Kleopatra im Film: Eine Königin Ägyptens als Sinnbild für orientalische Kultur.* Gardez! Verlag, 2005.

Winkler, M. *Cinema and Classical Texts: Apollo's New Light.* Cambridge UP, 2009.

———. *Classical Myth and Culture in the Cinema.* Oxford UP, 2001.

———, ed. *Classics and Cinema.* Bucknell UP, 1991.

———. "Greek Myth on the Screen." In R. Woodard, ed., *The Cambridge Companion to Greek Mythology.* Cambridge UP, 2008, 453–79.

———. "The *Iliad* and the Cinema." In *Troy: From Homer's Iliad to Hollywood Epic.* Blackwell, 2007.

Wollen, R. *Signs and Meaning in the Cinema, 4th ed.* British Film Institute, 1998.

Woodard R. ed. *The Cambridge Companion to Greek Mythology.* Cambridge UP, 2008

Wyke, M. "Are You Not Entertained? Classicists and the Cinema." *International Journal of the Classical Tradition* vol. 9, 2003, pp. 430–45.

———. *Projecting the Past: Ancient Rome, Cinema and History.* Routledge, 1997.

Yasumura N. *Challenges to the Power of Zeus in Early Greek Poetry,* Bloomsbury Publishing, 2013.

Zajko, V., and M. Leonard. *Laughing with Medusa: Classical Myth and Feminist Thought.* Oxford UP, 2006.

Zajko, V., and E. O'Gorman, ed. *Classical Myth and Psychoanalysis: Ancient and Modern Stories of the Self.* Oxford UP, 2013.

HOMERIC ECHOES

TROY (2004)
O BROTHER, WHERE ART THOU? (2000)

"SING, OH MUSE!" HOMERIC ECHOES, MODERN ISSUES IN MILLENNIAL FILMS

To use a hackneyed phrase, the *Iliad* and the *Odyssey* are a "study in contrasts." But through such contrasts each illuminates the other and makes itself more comprehensive. This will be true of our examination of two very different movies, Wolfgang Petersen's somewhat old-fashioned Hollywood blockbuster *Troy* (whose interpretation is complicated by a later director's cut) and the Coen brothers' quirky, complex, sometimes confusing *O Brother, Where Art Thou?* These quite contrasting stories provide answers to two questions: First, what is the nature of the hero and his career? And second, what is the nature of the universe the hero must struggle through?

Achilles and Odysseus are contrasting heroes, the leading characters of two fundamentally different kinds of stories. Achilles, the greatest of warriors, belongs to Tragedy. He is bound by fate and ruled by passion and power in a tragic world where all mortals will be undone by Zeus, and the best a man can do is to live, fight, and die to protect his family and make a lasting name for himself. We tend to agree with Aristotle that the best tragedies are simple, with their hellish machinery clear, remorseless, and easily set in motion, let us say by an ill-thought insult of a stressed Agamemnon. The traits that define their often stubborn heroes and heroines are simple too, such as Achilles' wrath, which gives the *Iliad* its first word.

The character of Odysseus, however, belongs to Comedy as defined by Frye. The comic hero generally has far more possibilities and freedom than the tragic hero. He is less bound by fate than by chance. He has his passions, but can be cool and clever, even decidedly criminal. Real intelligence is even optional, and the comic hero always has a bit (sometimes a large bit) of the fool in him. The great distinction is that the comic hero survives and even wins, although sometimes having suffered terribly, and sometimes more by luck than by choice and personal action. And in his victory often others are saved. Where the tragic universe tends to the simple, the comic cosmos is complex, and the hero's travels are more like odysseys, giving the comic hero the opportunity to gain many and varied experiences and even knowledge. The genre of Comedy is much more fluid, accepting (and even glorying in) heterogeneous material and different voices—very much like the Coen brothers' movies.

The core stories of Achilles and Odysseus are easily stated. The demigod Achilles must come to terms with life's tragic confines. Dishonored by Agamemnon, he withdraws from his warrior society, which is devastated, but, waiting too long to reconcile, becomes responsible for his comrade Patroclus' death. This compels him to avenge his friend and set in motion his own death; but before he dies, he gains the needed tragic knowledge. Odysseus, blown off course with his problematic crew, struggles to save them and to get back to his beleaguered wife. Through cleverness, luck and some divine intervention, he learns to temper himself, and, although his mates are destroyed, he returns home, defeats his rivals, and restores his household, with the promise of a peaceful death.

Petersen's Achilles differs from Homer's mainly in how he seems always to have been a disillusioned and violent man, recalling the modern nihilist. The Coen Brother's Ulysses Everett falls very short of the Odysseus he imagines himself to be. But they have core similarities: both suffer an exile for which they are partly responsible, wander through a semifantastic world, and endure many threats to the body and soul (e.g. Circe, the Sirens, Polyphemus, encounters with the dead, Poseidon). Both play fast and loose with identity, becoming beggars, hobos, and various manifestations of the Other. Both are hunted by powerful, vengeful figures, and confront and even overmaster the powers of sex and death. And most importantly, they have wives threatened by suitors, and a broken family to be restored. The *Iliad* and *Troy* emphasize reputation and fame. but the *Odyssey* shows a greater consciousness of the role of the epic singer, and Odysseus borrows the bard's narrative power for his Phaeacian tales; Everett succeeds by becoming the 1930s equivalent, a radio folk singer. And, unlike Achilles, Everett survives with family restored. It should be noted that both Tragedy and Comedy can be tempered with romantic themes suggesting Love's redemptive power. Everett's struggles, like Odysseus', are motivated by desire for his Penny; but for Petersen's Achilles, unlike Homer's, it is the beauty of romantic love that reconciles the dying Achilles to the human condition, not his empathetic encounter with Priam or the full realization of the lesson of the two jars of Zeus.

Both Epic and Comedy make implicit demonstrations of the nature of the universe and life's meaning. Both our movies connect this issue with the question of religion's place. Petersen has eliminated the gods as actual characters. It is Priam's misplaced religious faith that destroys Troy, while Achilles declares that the gods envy human mortality. *O Brother* takes place within the Bible Belt, and much of its imagery, themes, and especially music draw with apparent sincerity from the Christian-Protestant tradition. Although Everett calls candidates for baptism "chumps," he succeeds by reinventing himself as "Jordan Rivers," whose "Soggy Bottom Boys" sing "songs of salvation" and his own salvation is foretold by a blind oracle who speaks in biblical cadences. In the end, it seems Everett will learn to temper his rationalism, while still hoping for a new Enlightenment, "like the one they had in France".

The tale of the Trojan War was a foundational historical myth for the Greeks, and the *Iliad* a powerful transmitter of political and cultural ideology, as well as a tool with which to think about war. Petersen's *Troy* presents scenes evoking American/Western imperialism and realpolitik, the power of religious extremism, and the deluged heroism of war. The Coen brothers, by setting their *Odyssey* in a definite but also mythologized historical period, the American South of the Great Depression, and giving their movie a purposely bygone flavor, create a more historically concrete version of the *Odyssey*'s ideal political ending, where the god-supported king and his house are restored, and the upstart, ignoble minor nobility are put in their place. Everett secures the endangered "Pappy" O'Daniel's rule, but also, aided by the force and beauty of music, creates a moment of social transcendence where the people of Mississippi accept a "miscegenated" band and ride out on a rail the Grand Dragon of the Ku Klux Klan. This ideal subplot contrasts with the current expansion of unapologetic racist ideology and violence in the United States.

Both these movies are a lot of fun, but they also reveal much about the transmission and reception of Classical myth, and how myths can be made to speak to us today.

CHAPTER 1

PETERSEN'S *TROY*

Reimagining Homeric Heroes

> Why should I blame her that she filled my days
> With misery, or that she would of late
> Have taught to ignorant men most violent ways,
> Or hurled the little streets upon the great,
> Had they but courage equal to desire?
> What could have made her peaceful with a mind
> That nobleness made simple as a fire,
> With beauty like a tightened bow, a kind
> That is not natural in an age like this,
> Being high and solitary and most stern?
> Why, what could she have done, being what she is?
> Was there another Troy for her to burn?
> —"No Second Troy," by William Butler Yeats[1]

Yeats's implied Helen is Maud Gonne, whom Yeats met in 1889 and deeply loved. Gonne was a feminist and militant in the cause of Irish independence and in 1900 she founded the revolutionary Daughters of Ireland. Yeats suggests Helen and Maud were both willing to destroy entire societies, although the contrast between Helen the adulteress and Maud the violent revolutionary could hardly be greater. Additions to what we call "the Matter of Troy" hardly ceased with Yeats; nor did it begin with Homer. "Homer" is not "Troy"; nor is "Troy" "Homer." "Troy" is much bigger than that. "Troy" is an evolving, multiform collection of themes, traditions, and works of the Humanities. "Troy" is mirror, projector, computer, something of a Muse, even a demiurge.

Troy (2004), with a script by David Benioff and directed by Wolfgang Petersen, is, along with *Hercules*, considered a Hollywood "blockbuster," starring top talent such as Brad Pitt, Eric Bana, and Orlando Bloom. *Troy*

---

1   Yeats (1916), 91.

PLOT SUMMARY

In 1250 BC King Agamemnon is conquering Greece, and Achilles is his greatest fighter. Menelaus' wife Helen runs off with Paris, helped by his very reluctant brother Hector. Agamemnon launches a huge expedition. Achilles' mother tells him if he chooses Troy and glory he will never return. Achilles goes and storms the Trojan beach, despoils Apollo's temple, and captures its priestess, Briseis. Agamemnon claims credit for the victory, and seizes Briseis to humble Achilles. When Achilles withdraws from the fight, Hector beats the Greeks. Paris duels Menelaus and is saved by Hector, who kills Menelaus. The Greeks lose again. The desperate Agamemnon returns Briseis to Achilles, who learns to love her and who is humanized by her. His cousin Patroclus fights disguised as Achilles and is killed by Hector, who realizes his time has come. Hector duels and is killed by Achilles. Priam comes for Hector's body, and we see Achilles change, as he gives both Hector and Briseis back to Priam. The Greeks take Troy through the trick of the Trojan Horse. Agamemnon is killed by Briseis, and Achilles is killed by the arrows of Paris, but dies reconciled by the love of Briseis. Helen escapes, as does young Aeneas, holding the sword of Troy. The director's cut makes it clear that Paris also survives.

was also nominated for numerous awards, and at the 2005 ASCAP Film and Television Music Awards it won Top Box Office Film, and Brad Pitt received the Choice Movie Actor—Drama/Action Adventure award. It was among the top two hundred most profitable movies and number eight in the year 2004. Reviews were decidedly mixed. It has a 54 percent Rotten Tomatoes rating; the generalized view is that *Troy* is "a brawny, entertaining spectacle, but lacking emotional resonance."[2] *Troy* is one of a number of films inspired by the success of *Gladiator* (2000), and like that movie, it gave impetus to more presentations of the ancient world in popular media.[3] As one can imagine, the criticism of Classical scholars was savage, as had been their criticism of *Gladiator*.[4] In 2007 Petersen produced a longer director's cut, which included some significant alterations of his original, especially the ending. And in 2015 Martin Winkler came out with a new volume, *Return to Troy: New Essays on the Hollywood Epic*. Our initial chapter was based on the "theatrical" version, although the director claims the newer version was more what he had in mind. In proceeding, we shall consider selected alterations found in the director's cut, which we suggest constitutes a type of argument Petersen's *Troy* myth is having with itself. Winkler thinks the changes are all for the better; we are not so sure.[5]

Director Petersen received a fine Classics education at Johanneum (Academic School of the Johanneum), an elite Gymnasium in Hamburg, and

---

2   https://www.rottentomatoes.com/m/troy/. Accessed Aug. 10, 2016.
3   Winkler (2015), 1.
4   Winkler (2015), 2–4; see also Solomon (2007), 482–534.
5   Winkler (2015), 6 and n. 13.

read Homer in Classical Greek. He sees *Troy* as illustrating eternal truths, such as how the supposed "glory of warfare" clouds men's minds to war's horrors, as well as reflecting on current events, such as American imperialism. He also wants to tell "grand stories that touch everybody . . . I want viewers to recognize their personal experiences in the film."[6] Petersen recognizes that *Troy* is not a true adaptation of the *Iliad*: "It is a retelling of the entire Trojan War story"[7] and even Homer is only part of the tradition, and not the whole, although there are many items in his movie that recall the *Iliad* directly.[8] Our analysis will consider how Petersen has achieved his main objective: to produce one more addition to the Trojan War tradition that reflects core ancient themes, segments of the grand tradition, and contemporary concerns and perspectives. And we will look at Petersen's *Troy* as a myth in its own right, with its own unique perspectives that must be separated from those of Homer.

 Troy is largely a story of heroes and presents the tragic tale of three heroes in particular: Achilles obviously, but also Hector and even Paris. The heroism of Briseis also looms large, especially in the director's cut. The importance of fame is clearly relevant, but there is a romantic dimension, for love redeems our Achilles, an attitude alien to the Classical tradition. Finally, Agamemnon's actions exemplify the use of brutal and amoral power to attempt to transform the world, practices evident in the past century. In our discussion of *Clash of the Titans* we consider how the myths of Perseus connect to various other myths (of Prometheus, Io, Heracles, Thetis, Peleus, and Achilles), a framework for much of the Heroic Age, especially its establishment. The major myth cycles that come together in the Trojan War myth provide an even more substantial framework for the Heroic Age, but one that stresses its flaws and problems, particularly in the sequence of horrors connected to the family of Tantalus. The story of Troy is an apocalyptic battle of East and West, which concludes the Heroic Age.

 Here we will outline some main themes and archetypal patterns and their connection with the Trojan/Homeric tradition. We will first focus on how current history is reflected in myth and continue by discussing several pertinent aspects of heroic myth, paying attention specifically to different facets of the hero displayed (and modified) in our film. Central will be Achilles, whose nihilistic heroism is defined by a thirst for glory and contrasts with Hector's more selfless devotion to nation and family. We must not forget the peplum movie traditions either; Achilles starts out as the opposite of the peplum hero, but, by his death, he has fulfilled several elements of the peplum hero's role. Hector

---

6 Winkler (2007), who quotes from Petersen with Greiwe (1997).
7 Winkler (2007), 8–9, n. 24.
8 In addition to what will be covered later, consider how Ajax is depicted as massive and a bit primitive (although he would never have used a war hammer); the scene in which, after a day of losses, bonfires burn throughout the camp; and the attack of Greeks and Trojans recalling the Homeric simile of the wave. See *Iliad* 4.422–29, 446–56, and Winkler (2007), 54–56.

TROY (2004) Warner Brothers	
Director: **Screenplay:** **Cast:**	Wolfgang Petersen David Benioff Brad Pitt (Achilles), Brian Cox (Agamemnon), Nathan Jones (Boagrius), John Shrapnel (Nestor), Brendan Gleeson (Menelaus), Diane Kruger (Helen), Eric Bana (Hector), Orlando Bloom (Paris), Garrett Hedlund (Patroclus), Sean Bean (Odysseus), Julie Christie (Thetis), Peter O'Toole (Priam), Saffron Burrows (Andromache), Rose Byrne (Briseis), Tyler Mane (Ajax), Frankie Fitzgerald (Aeneas)

as hero represents the family man, while Paris presents a more romantic hero who nevertheless evolves into a man conscious of his community and others. Briseis, much different from the Homeric character, shows the humanizing female perspective on war, even presents a narrative of female empowerment, and constitutes an important alternate center for the film.

THE MATTER OF TROY

As director Petersen knows, his *Troy* is simply one of a long line of retellings that began before Homer.[9] Like any major myth cycle, the saga has been endlessly re-shaped to reflect the cultural and social needs and interests of the author's time. The *Iliad* narrates only around fifty-one days in the last few months of the war, although there are flashbacks to earlier events, such as the omen the Greeks obtained at Aulis. Important backstories, such as Paris' abduction of Helen, are mentioned only vaguely; the story of the Trojan horse and the destruction of Troy is recalled, with little detail, in Homer's *Odyssey*. More details were provided by a series of "Cyclic" epics, among them the *Aethiopis*, *Cypria*, the *Little Iliad*, the *Illupersis*, *Telegony*, whose details often diverge from Homer's account; the Greek tragedies and Vergil's *Aeneid*, of course, provide even more. There are substantial arguments that Homer himself made radical changes to the prior tradition; for example, it was probably Memnon, not Hector, who was the great opponent of Achilles.[10] The reworking of Dares and Dictys of the Trojan War is far more radical, and Medieval writers created their own versions of the Matter of Troy. Further, the large majority of Classical artworks concerning Troy do not depict Homeric episodes.[11]

As the myth goes, Zeus, reconciled with Prometheus, learned that the goddess Thetis was destined to bear a child greater than its father. Zeus and the

---

9   See Burgess (2001b); Davies (2003); West (2003).
10   On the neoanalysts who have mapped out the pre-Homeric traditions, see Wilcox (1996), 174–92, Burgess (2006), 148–66.
11   On the great diversity of the Trojan War tradition, see Solomon (2007) with notes, Scherer (1963), Danek (2007).

other gods made sure she married a human being, Peleus, a notable hero and one of the Argonauts. All the gods came to their wedding, save one, Eris/Strife, who was not invited. She crashed the reception anyway, and tossed among the gods the famous golden Apple of Discord, which was dedicated "to the most beautiful woman." Aphrodite, Hera, and Athena all claimed it, and Zeus, unwilling to judge himself, let the Trojan Prince Paris Alexander judge this beauty contest. Needless to say, each goddess attempted bribery, Aphrodite offering Paris the world's most beautiful woman. Paris picked Aphrodite, making mortal enemies of Hera and Athena. Aphrodite kept her promise, and helped Paris gain Helen. Just one minor complication: she was married to Menelaus, king of Sparta.

In a diplomatic visit to Sparta, Helen elopes with Paris to Troy. The nature and motivation of Helen is a major issue in Greek myth and art. Is she the ultimate "bad woman" who betrays her husband and family for lust and the desire to live in the world's richest city? Is she a victim of an arranged marriage and Aphrodite's machinations? In the classical world, intense erotic passion was always thought to be dangerous; most elite marriages were arranged, and love had little to do with it. This issue will be important for our analysis of the Medea tradition in the film *Such Is Life*.

Menelaus sought help from his brother Agamemnon, king of Mycenae, the most powerful Greek kingdom. They raise a huge expedition and it sails to Troy. In one of the most famous accounts, Aeschylus' *Agamemnon*, Agamemnon— deeply desiring the fame of a great city sacker —is willing to sacrifice his daughter Iphigenia so that the Greek fleet can sail. Agamemnon and the Greeks commit various atrocities while conquering Troy, excesses evident in our movie. The angered gods punish them. Not only are countless Greeks killed, but once Troy is destroyed, the Greek leaders quarrel and go home separately, and some perish in a storm raised by gods. Clytemnestra, furious over the sacrifice of her daughter Iphigenia, together with her lover Aegisthus murders Agamemnon when he returns.

The Trojan saga involves various themes, such as how the evil of a rich and great family can begin and grow from generation to generation, success breeding excess, the public effects of sexual desire, transgression, and the lust for power, revenge, and justice. Patriarchal authority is questioned, as well as divine benevolence and control. In somewhat later accounts, after the rise of the Persian threat to Greece, the battle of East versus West becomes a more prominent motif, with the West representing civilization, and the East Barbarism. But this theme is hardly prominent in Homer; and Ahl makes a convincing case that *Troy* shows the *Greeks* as the Barbarians, and the Trojans as more civilized,[12] but also deluded and overconfident.

---

12 Ahl (2007), 180.

KEY TERMS

Bronze Age: Coming after the Stone Age, and before the Iron Age, the Bronze age begins in Greece around 3000 BCE and ends around 1200 BCE. This period saw the rise and fall of the great palace civilizations of Crete and Mycenaean Greece, and Asia Minor. Much of Greek legend and the Homeric epics are set in his period.

Trojan Saga: Narrative found in myths, literary texts, and artworks dealing with the events leading up to the Trojan war, the war itself, and returns of the surviving heroes and other consequences of the Trojan War.

Nihilism: Philosophy that questions the existence of any clear purpose or meaning in life, as well as the value of religion and sometimes even morality.

Age of Heroes: The fourth of Hesiod's Five Ages of Humanity. Mythologically speaking, it is the period between the time after the flood, and the end of the Trojan War.

Heroic code: An aristocratic code found in Homer, and implied in Troy, which stresses obtaining personal glory as a type of immortality, glory gained primarily through (often reckless) bravery in battle. The downside to such heroism is a high probability of an early death and the ruin of one's family.

HISTORY MYTHOLOGIZED

History often becomes myth, and myth becomes history, or furnishes a substitute for history, or even provides an alternate history. The Trojan War is a paradigmatic tool for thinking about war in general,[13] even in our time.[14] Further, Homer's audience and many subsequent Classical Greeks had concrete, often dreadful experiences of war, and these stories furnished a meditation on martial values.[15] Although the Greeks acknowledged the Trojan War's greatness, it was clearly a conflict with few victors, and it left both sides ruined. In the United States we wonder, after trillions of dollars spent on wars in Iraq and Afghanistan and untold dead, if there are any positive outcomes which offset the horrors endured. Petersen's Trojan War is likewise pointless, with only Odysseus and maybe Nestor surviving of the main Greek heroes; Troy is destroyed, but the promise of Rome (which will conquer Greece) remains. In fact, the Greek destruction of Troy *causes* Rome.

By and large the Classical Greeks (e.g., Thucydides) believed the Trojan War occurred in some form, although rationalizers (again like Thucydides) realized that much of Homer's narrative was fantastical and tried to tease out possible facts.[16] As noted, there were many other later and different versions of

---

13 Ahl (2007), 171, cites Erskine (2001), 258, on the changing meaning of the Trojan War. On the constant reinterpretation of Homer in the Classical world, see Zeitlin, (2001), 199–266.

14 Ahl (2007), 163, cites Achcar (2002) in particular.

15 Ahl (2007), 166–67.

16 See, for example, the first twenty chapters of Book 1 of Thucydides' *History of the Peloponnesian War*, which is often termed "The Archaeology."

the Trojan Saga, among them Flavius Philostratus' *Heroicus*, where the spirit of Protesilaos (the first Greek killed at Troy) claims that the Greeks never even took Troy![17] Although by the nineteenth century most Classical scholars dismissed the stories of the Trojan War as legends lacking any historical basis, starting with Heinrich Schliemann and extending to Manfred Korfmann today archaeologists have rediscovered the realities behind Homer's epics, finding that Troy (Wilusa) was a vast, rich city, probably a client kingdom of the Hittites.[18] The richest of the Troys, Troy VI, was probably wrecked by war, while the later, inferior Troy VII was destroyed by an earthquake, which may be connected to the story of the Trojan horse. There may well have been various conflicts between the Greeks, who were active in the region, and the Trojans, which gave rise to the legend of the Trojan War.[19]

As *Troy* was being crafted, statements appearing on its online "production journal" gave the sense that the movie was based on substantial historical reality, as shown by archaeological discoveries.[20] *Troy*'s first few minutes, with a voiceover complete with map giving background, evoke historical movies or documentaries. But archaeology can tell us nothing about any Agamemnon, Paris, or Achilles; thus the movie has a strong focus on the myth-making process.[21] *Troy* implies that Homer recorded historical realities, which had become overlaid with myth. This is particularly shown in the scene in which Paris shoots Achilles with several arrows; Achilles pulls out all of them except the one in his heel. The assumption is that the Greeks found him dead with one arrow in his heel, producing the legend of the Achilles' heel. *Troy* in some way recalls the film *King Arthur* (2004), directed by Antoine Fuqua. It supposedly gave a more "historically accurate" account of the story of Arthur based on archaeological evidence,[22] and Troy shows some similar perspectives. Early in *Troy* a young boy asks Achilles if he is invulnerable; the implication is that Achilles is being mythologized even while he is alive. In *Hercules* Iolaus is likewise mythologizing the living Hercules.

For Petersen the Trojan story reflects persistent truths about individuals and society. We observe in *Troy* what we see in *Immortals*, *Clash/Wrath of the Titans*, *Hercules*, *The Hunger Games*, and even (with much less brutality) in the *Percy Jackson* movies, that the ruling elite are vicious, incompetent, or

---

17 See essays in Aitken and Maclean (2004), also Solomon (2007), 504–8; also Maestre (2004) 127–41, Merkle (2004), 127–141.
18 Latacz (2004), 101–2.
19 On the evidence for some manner of "Trojan War" see Korfmann (2007), Dalby (2007), especially 50–55.
20 Shahabudin (2007), 109.
21 Shahabudin (2007), 116–17.
22 See Sumner (2004), http://www.geocities.ws/vortigernstudies/articles/guestgraham1.html. Accessed Aug. 20, 2016.

deeply corrupt. *Troy*'s Agamemnon is a dictator who sees himself, somewhat like Napoleon, as bringing modernity to a disunified Greece. He declares "Before me, Greece was nothing. I brought all the Greek kingdoms together. I created a nation out of fire worshipers and snake eaters! I build the future, Nestor. Me! Achilles is the past." But his actions also recall the aggressions of the United States and the West. He is something of a Nietzschean tyrant, asserting "Peace is for the women . . . and the weak. Empires are forged by war. . . . Old King Priam thinks he's untouchable behind his high walls. He thinks the Sun god will protect him. But the gods protect only . . . the strong! If Troy falls . . . I control the Aegean." Clearly getting back Helen is only a prete xt for the war against rival Troy.[23] Like many such tyrants, the cost in lives means nothing to him. After Hector's death, Agamemnon says "I will smash their walls to the ground . . . if it costs me forty thousand Greeks." The monstrous tyrant Hyperion in *Immortals* likewise aims to recreate the world, as does the Fascist Captain in *Pan's Labyrinth*. Popular culture likes a powerful villain, but Homer's portrayal of Agamemnon, who, although a man with deep flaws, also has some considerable virtues, is far more nuanced than Petersen's somewhat monotone despot. Further, in Homer's *Iliad* good and evil are balanced out between sides, with the Trojans in aggregate the more at fault, but with the doomed Hector often seen as the noblest of the heroes.

Some details in *Troy* evoke events in modern history. The landing at Troy recalls some D-Day movies,[24] where soldiers die coming out of the landing craft and others go up the beach under fire trying to reach the German emplacements.[25] The dawn attack at Troy, with exploding hay bales and fire arrows that look like tracer rounds, are reminiscent of modern battle scenes. Hector asks Priam, too confident in Apollo, "And how many battalions does the sun god command?" recalling Stalin's famous dismissal of the pope. But overall the movie's image of the society of Greek soldiers is thin; one of the strengths of the *Iliad* is the great attention paid to matters of social ritual, whether it is forms of address, feasting, giving out awards, reconciling, and so forth. The epic tradition does not really reflect the modern world of mass warfare, where anonymous uniformed men are part of a machinelike military organization and become statistics. Although Petersen would acknowledge the role of these common soldiers (as he did in *Das Boot*), we suspect the

---

23 As many suspect the United States has concocted pretenses for its wars for domination.

24 Ahl (2007), 167–70, makes some interesting parallels, with the Trojans being something like noble and habitually obedient Germans trapped because they must obey a deranged leader.

25 It is a bit amusing that the Greeks make a Roman testudo out of Bronze Age shields.

constraints of time, interest, and ability made him focus more closely on the lives of a few heroic individuals.

NO GODS, JUST HEROES

A major front in our ongoing culture wars is the validity (or foolishness) of religious belief, an issue current movies often reflect. In a millennial movie we do not consider in this volume, *300* (2006), Sparta's perverted ephor-priests try to stop Leonidas' mission before it begins; in *O Brother* Everett spitefully mocks religious belief, until he himself is touched by the miraculous; and in *Immortals* the president of the Hellenic Council takes pride in their secularism, right before we view a bloody rematch of real Olympians and Titans. No gods appear in *Hercules* either, but some divine forces are implied. Some scholars suggest that the undignified way in which Homer depicted the gods indicates that he had no real belief in them,[26] but that is almost certainly wrong. Instead, Homer's deathless gods (at least in the *Iliad*) have their own agendas, unbound by human notions of justice or fair play. Similarly, there are forces, often associated with the divine, that seem equally powerful and capricious, which in particular is thematized by erotic passion. We observe this in *Iliad* book 3.146–60, when the old men look at Helen's unearthly beauty, but confess that she should be returned to Greece. In the *Iliad* Helen is more victim of Aphrodite than villain. Homer there also reflects a tragic and fatalistic view of life, which will be softened in the *Odyssey*.

Troy disregards the gods and instead focuses on mythical heroes, though its characters, more historicized, are responsible for their own actions, not driven by ancient curses or treated as divine puppets. *Troy*'s Greeks (quite anachronistically) have little regard for religion, while Priam is ruinously religious.[27] Agamemnon links primitive religious beliefs and the lack of national social organization. Priam indulges Paris, too secure in his faith in Apollo and the supposedly divine walls of Troy, to Hector's dismay. Priam's religious beliefs cause the Trojan horse to be brought inside the walls, which leads to Troy's destruction. It is fitting that Priam is butchered in the temple of Apollo by Agamemnon, who here recalls Neoptolemus killing Priam at the altar. But *Troy*'s Achilles seems to hate the gods in a more singular way. In the initial assault Achilles and his men desecrate a temple of Apollo and butcher his unarmed priests, and after his captain Eudorus suggests he might restrain his men from plundering the shrine, he personally decapitates the statue of Apollo, his enemy (also his enemy in the traditional legend), and tells his

---

26 Grube (1951), 62.
27 Ahl (2007), 173.

men to take what treasure they want. This excess will foreshadow the atrocities committed during the sack of Troy, showing that Achilles is more like Agamemnon than he realizes.[28] He mocks Briseis' warning of Apollo's impending vengeance, suggests that the Gods may fear him, and later claims that he knows more about the Gods than she does. With the divine apparatus gone, the emphasis on human action and heroism becomes clearer, as does the fact that war is not only created by men but also a tragedy for humankind. Underscored too are perils of excessive religious credence, which can be connected to modern developments, noting how many recent millennial wars, originating for the most part in the Middle East, are tied up with religious struggle.

Further, Latacz suggests,[29] Homer's greatest innovation may have been to move the focus from external events of the war to a more human story about the choices, actions, and consequences of a few central characters, both Greek and Trojan. Homer's *Iliad* engaged the very personal concerns of his aristocratic (and embattled) audience, something the listeners could more closely identify with. Petersen likewise sees this ability to engage personal and human questions as central to his production, although with a much tighter (and limiting) focus. As Greece became richer and more populated, aristocrats of the late Geometric and early archaic era needed to be more than regional warlords with local concerns. But early Greece was still very clan- and tribe-oriented, and it was difficult for aristocrats to work together, even when circumstances demanded it. The *Iliad* explores the disastrous consequences of leaders who allow their emotions and desires to overrule their understanding of the common good. But the *Iliad's* humanistic dimension allows us to see Achilles' side of the story, and even to question the heroic code that held aristocratic society together.

ACHILLES: LIFE, DEATH, PASSION, AND GLORY

The *Iliad* is structured around pivotal moments, when Achilles comes to terms with his nature and life's constraints, before the fated death his actions have engineered. The "evolution/development of the hero" is a notable mythic motif and a metaphor for our own personal evolution, one often problematic, even tragic. Elements of this tragedy appear in the vastly older *Epic of Gilgamesh*. Both heroes are sons of minor goddesses; Gilgamesh and Achilles do marvelous deeds, lose close friends, withdraw from their communities, and finally accept the tragic limits of life. Like Gilgamesh, Achilles must learn how his nearly godlike nature can be accommodated within the strictures of human society. The

---

28   Blume (2015), 170.
29   Latacz (2007), 30–31.

heroic code, as spelled out by Sarpedon (*Iliad* 12.309–329), shows the connection between courage and fame, which is all the afterlife Greeks can hope for. Agamemnon's insult, coming after years of fighting, makes Achilles reconsider the worth of such fame. The heroism of Homer's Achilles is chiefly motivated by the desire for glory, when it is not fueled by rage. *Troy*'s Achilles, however, in part recalls a modern nihilist, scornful of most people and institutions, which sharpens his need for lasting glory, especially after his choice to go to Troy.

Petersen, a famous creator of "epic" movies like *Das Boot*[30] and *A Perfect Storm*, myths in themselves, in *Troy* shows an evident interest in how legends arise. There is an implication that people remember more what a person does, the great deeds accomplished, than what sort of person he or she was, and that sometimes people cook up fanciful narratives in connection with the remarkable, such as a force of nature like Achilles, a point made in other movies like *Hercules*. Odysseus' opening voice-over intones:

"Men are haunted by the vastness of eternity. And so we ask ourselves . . . will our actions echo across the centuries? Will strangers hear our names long after we're gone . . . and wonder who we were . . . how bravely we fought . . . how fiercely we loved?"

And ends with Odysseus' voice saying: "If they ever tell my story, let them say. . . I walked with giants. Men rise and fall like the winter wheat . . . but these names will never die. Let them say I lived in the time of Hector . . . tamer of horses. Let them say . . . I lived in the time of Achilles."

This initial voiceover, like an epic's proem, stresses three concerns: that Troy is an archetypal tale (and thus it will stand the test of time), and it will concern both fierce fighting and love. The film's coda, which invokes enduring Homeric language,[31] when considered in the context of the opening lines, implies that Hector and Achilles have become legendary giants. Further, Homer's prologue stresses the vast cost of the war, as well as the consequences of Achilles' wrath. This issue is particularly stressed in the opening sequence of the director's cut, as a dog searches and finds the body of his master, already feeding the birds. The following sequence, in which two armies face each other, with the issue settled by the duel between Achilles and Boagrius, is a metaphor for what is to come: two vast armies in conflict, but it will all boil down to the actions of an unnatural hero, Achilles.[32]

---

30 On similarity in themes between the two movies, see Winkler (2015), 10–14.

31 Especially the generation of leaves metaphor with its sense of time, *Iliad* 6.146–48: "As the generations of leaves, so the generations of human beings; through the wind the leaves pour upon the ground, but the oak flourishing bears others, when the hour of spring has arrived. Thus the race of men on the one hand rise up, and on the other hand pass away."

32 See Winkler (2015), 7–8.

The overall story of Achilles fits what we denote as "the tragedy of the exceptional hero" paradigm. Such a hero, like Gilgamesh, often part god, is even more unstable, the divine power ill-suited to human limitations. Can that exceptional hero ever come to terms with those limits? Our first sight of Achilles suggests a dissolute rock star of war, having enjoyed a drunken night with his groupies, arrogant in his power and fame, but finding little meaning in his success or status. There is some truth to Agamemnon's description of Achilles as "a man who fights for no flag. A man loyal to no country." Briseis asks why Achilles chose the warrior's life, and he replies without hesitation: "I chose nothing. I was born, and this is what I am." Achilles, a natural warrior, has yet to find a war, cause, or leader (certainly not Agamemnon!) to give his talents some greater purpose. He says to young Patroclus, whom he is training: "I taught you how to fight, but I never taught you why to fight. . . . Soldiers, they fight for kings they've never even met. They do what they're told, die when they're told to. . . . Don't waste your life following some fool's orders."

He offers to Briseis this revelation: "The gods envy us . . . because we're mortal. Because any moment might be our last. Everything's more beautiful because we're doomed." Unlike the Iliadic model, our Achilles seems half in love with death, perhaps because he has never seen the full beauty of life, killing being his only meaningful action. As does the *Iliad*, *Troy* explores the choice of Achilles of fame over life. Achilles was too young to have competed for Helen or to have taken the oath of Tyndareus.[33] Thus the "Classic" Achilles chose glory over a long life when barely an adult, and without much life experience. In the *Iliad* Thetis (as well as Zeus) often laments the basic distinction between short-lived mortals and the deathless gods. Recall too that the *Odyssey* reveals Achilles in the Deadlands implicitly regretting his choice, stating, "I would wish, being a sodbuster, to serve as serf another man, a poor one, to whom there is not much provision for living, than to rule over all the wasted dead" (*Od.* 11.487–90).

But in *Troy* Achilles has been responsible for many of Agamemnon's victories, as Odysseus notes, and has no illusions about Agamemnon or the justness of the Trojan War. Fame furnishes the major rationale for Achilles' fighting. Note how, when the young page says of Boagrius, "I wouldn't want to fight him," Achilles replies, "That's why no one will remember your name." Later Odysseus tells him, "Your business is war, my friend. . . . We're sending the largest fleet that ever sailed. . . . This war will never be forgotten."

In Homer, Achilles does not wholly trust wily Odysseus; but *Troy*'s Achilles is much more sophisticated, and thus the perceptive, pragmatic, and also somewhat cynical Odysseus is Achilles' closest friend among the Greek chiefs, and serves an essential role in helping sort out the chaos Agamemnon creates. In

33 Because so many Greek kings competed for his daughter Helen, Tyndareus made all the suitors swear to protect the marriage of Helen and whomever she married, to discourage later attempts to destroy it.

FIGURE 1.1 Achilles rouses his men. "We are lions!"

the director's cut Agamemnon's ambassadors encounter Odysseus disguised as a peasant, supposedly angry at the misbehavior of Odysseus, perhaps a reference to the madness Odysseus feigned to avoid going to Troy, accompanied by a dog meant to recall the *Odyssey*'s loyal Argus.[34]

After his encounter with Odysseus, Achilles then goes to speak with his mother, a slightly daffy prophetess of the sea, later reimagined as a goddess. Following the canonical story, she tells Achilles that if he does not go to Troy he will have a happy and fruitful family life, but eventually his name will vanish. If he goes to Troy, "They will write stories about your victories for thousands of years." We learn later that Peleus died young, his mother Thetis now being the parent Achilles will never see again. And as he and his troops are about to storm the Trojan beach, Achilles points at Troy (Fig. 1.1) and proclaims: "My brothers of the sword. I'd rather fight beside you than any army of thousands. Let no man forget how menacing we are. We are lions! Do you know what's there, waiting, beyond that beach? Immortality! Take it! It's yours!"

The "we are lions" evokes a common Homeric simile.[35] And in Apollo's temple, when Hector asks "Why did you come here?" Achilles answers, "They'll be talking about this war for a thousand years; our names will remain." The issue of fame also features in the Achilles-Agamemnon quarrel as well as power issues. As in the *Iliad* Agamemnon has resented Achilles for a long time, for although Agamemnon has the power, it is Achilles who is the better fighter by far and more admired.[36] And like many such tyrants, Agamemnon is also an egomaniacal fame seeker, as his exchange, which starts their quarrel, makes clear when

34 On Odysseus in *Troy,* see Loudon (2015), 180-189
35 See, for example, in *Iliad* 3.23–25, when Menelaus, seeing Paris in front of the battle line, is compared to a lion that sees a stag, or *Iliad* 10.296–98, when Odysseus and Diomedes, heading out at night, are compared to lions.
36 Agamemnon's statement "Of all the warlords loved by the gods, I hate him the most," reflects Agamemnon's declaration in *Iliad* 1.176, "You are most hated by me of the Zeus-nurtured kings."

he tells Achilles: "You came here because you want your name to last through the ages. A great victory was won today. But that victory is not yours. Kings did not kneel to Achilles. Kings did not pay homage to Achilles. . . . History remembers kings! Not soldiers. Tomorrow, we'll batter down the gates of Troy. I'll build monuments on every island of Greece. I'll carve 'Agamemnon' in the stone."

Because Achilles refused to see himself as a mere functionary, and feeling upstaged because his soldiers chanted "Achilles" after the victory, Agamemnon decides to put Achilles in his place by seizing Briseis, as in the *Iliad*. Achilles' withdrawal fits the "withdrawal-devastation-return pattern,"[37] whose basic elements are that the hero-protagonist is separated from his society, which is devastated, and then is brought back. But, as noted, Achilles, a quasi-god, has always been separated from his natural society, part of the plight of the extraordinary. As does the *Iliad*, *Troy* narrates the tragic events that prompt Achilles to rejoin society (at least after a fashion), but here he will not only be reconciled to life's limitations; he will learn to find real value in it.

Achilles' greatest loyalties are to his Myrmidons, like the Spartans of *300*, a war-focused, highly trained group of men bonded by love of slaughter and glory. There is one slight exception, his cousin, an orphan, whom Achilles has taken under his wing,[38] not the slightly older near equal whom Achilles calls the best of the Myrmidons (*Iliad* 18.10).[39] Patroclus is something of a humanizing force, and it is due to Achilles' stubborn and socially transgressive refusal to reconcile with Agamemnon and rejoin the Greek army that Patroclus dies. Note the near tenderness of Achilles when he tells Patroclus he must guard the ship because he is not ready to fight. The fact that Patroclus can so precisely assume the identity of the armored Achilles points out the closeness of their relationship, and perhaps the Achilles that might have been. But putting on Achilles' armor does not make any Patroclus an Achilles and, compared to the Iliadic Patroclus, this Patroclus accomplishes little, except that his death prevents Achilles from leaving Troy. Achilles must kill Hector to avenge Patroclus, which begins the countdown for his own death. Achilles' fury at Hector is as excessive as was his anger at Agamemnon.[40] The rage that Achilles feels after Patroclus' death is a combination of the remorse of the traditional Achilles, who blames his own actions for Patroclus' death, as well as that of Aeneas, who has been a surrogate

---

37 On this pattern in the *Iliad* and *Odyssey*, see Burgess (2001a), 26.
38 There was considerable criticism on not presenting Patroclus as Achilles' same-sex lover, but as his cousin; see Winkler (2015), 2. Krass (2012), 166–72, shows how *Troy* suggests that there was more than a homosocial relationship between the men, since Achilles removes the seashell necklace, a gift from his mother Thetis, which he must have given to Patroclus, and finally belongs to Briseis. On the tradition of Achilles' various loves, see Fantuzzi (2012).
39 Here "Myrmidon" seems to designate a member of a crack combat unit, not a tribe. See Blume (2015), 168.
40 On how the lament of one male for another close male friend is a common feature of the literary history of male friendship, see Krass (2013), 153.

father to Pallas, tasked with introducing him to the world of great deeds. But the inexperienced Pallas is killed by Turnus, and Patroclus likewise dies badly at Hector's hands. Greek tragedies such as the *Philoctetes* or the *Iphigenia at Aulis* often presented young people willing to sacrifice themselves to the war effort, blinded by ideology, desire for glory, and official lies. This is Patroclus' tragedy and a factor in his death.

But Achilles' death is preceded (and prepared for) by an acceptance of the human condition. In the *Iliad,* Achilles acts with more humanity during the funeral games for Patroclus, stopping quarrels and even awarding a prize to Agamemnon *honoris causa*) His mercies to Priam, and his parables concerning Niobe (*Iliad* 5.602–17), which tell how, although all her children had been killed, she finally consented to get on with life and eat, reveals a restored, deepened connection with the human community. His parable of the two jars beside Zeus' throne (*Iliad* 24.524–34) demonstrate his acceptance of our tragic condition; Zeus sends all human beings misfortune, the only question being how much. Thus all we can do is endure and let life go on with dignity that comes from our connection to the human community

Achilles dies during the sack of Troy after being shot by Paris, first in the heel and then several times in the chest. Here the dying Achilles is gentle, telling Briseis to depart with Paris, that she has made his life worth this death. As Ahl notes, Achilles' death occurs the first time he shows true, sacrificial concern for somebody outside his men.[41] Now recall what he told Patroclus earlier:

> At night, I see their faces, all the men I've killed. They're standing there on the far bank of the River Styx. They're waiting for me. They say, "Welcome, brother."

Note how Achilles calls the dead Hector "brother" as he prepares to return his corpse to Priam. Dillon, however, further correctly observes that *Troy* displays a modern, romantic undercurrent quite alien to the spirit of Classical Greek epic and its audience,[42] about the importance of romantic love to a fulfilled life. Here concludes Achilles' "death struggle," which is fought on two fronts, first, for those he cares about (Briseis, the Myrmidons, and to a lesser extent the other Greeks), and second, for those forces that would kill his own humanity. And Briseis is saved, and Achilles gains the afterlife of fame, his humanity also rescued.

BRISEIS: EROS AND THANATOS

As noted, *Troy* has a romantic dimension, and we can take stock of our various characters through their interactions with women, particularly Paris, of course, and Achilles too. Briseis in and of herself plays a small role in the *Iliad,* and she speaks only once, during the lament for the dead Patroclus (*Iliad* 19.282–302).

---

41 Ahl (2007), 174.
42 Dillon (2006), 128–29.

Troy's Briseis,[43] whose role has been intensified in the director's cut,[44] is a kinswoman of Hector's, and royalty (as Achilles notes), a committed virgin priestess of Apollo, unafraid to speak her mind. She recalls Cassandra, Priam's daughter, and in some traditions she is even Apollo's cursed lover. She also evokes Polyxena, a daughter of Priam with whom Achilles fell in love. In later accounts Achilles, going to meet her, is ambushed by Paris; in *Troy* Achilles, helping Briseis, is likewise trapped by Paris. Her seizure by Agamemnon when she is praying to Apollo inside Troy recalls the rape of Cassandra by Ajax the Lesser.

In Homer and probably in the pre-Homeric tradition, Achilles' initial loss of Briseis stings more as a matter of honor, not love, although later (*Iliad* 9.342–43) Achilles admits that he had come to love Briseis as deeply as any chieftain loves his wife. In *Troy* Briseis is even more central to Achilles' reformation, as are Patroclus, Eudorus, and all the other Myrmidons. From the time Briseis is captured alive in Apollo's temple, he treats her with decency and increasing concern, making the masculinist assumption she needs saving. The moment where he bathes naked before her, serves, of course, to attract her attention, but also symbolizes Achilles' potential vulnerability. Soon afterward she assumes Athena's role in keeping Achilles from killing Agamemnon, suggesting her humanizing potential.[45]

After the Greeks' second defeat, Odysseus quickly persuades Agamemnon to return her. Agamemnon's assertion "I haven't touched her" recalls the oath Agamemnon makes in *Iliad* 19.261–63, that he never had relations with Briseis. Achilles, having rescued her from impending rape, praises Briseis' active resistance, although she curtly dismisses his compliment. In their conversations Achilles is surprisingly verbal, picking at the contradictions and condescension in Briseis' perspectives. A man "born to take lives," aware of life's shortness, Achilles asserts that Briseis will never be more beautiful than she is now. Reluctantly impressed by this powerful humanistic statement, Briseis says, "I thought you were a dumb brute. I could have forgiven a dumb brute." But what sort of brute is Achilles? The brutality of *Troy*'s Achilles reflects his considered disconnection/disillusionment with human beings, relationships, and institutions, and a belief that violence is built into the universe's nature; he knows that Ares too is a god. *Troy*'s Achilles reflects a modern archetype, the intellectual antihero, capable of a level of disengagement from the mores of society impossible for a member of a traditional culture as is found in Homer.

The night after she is returned to Achilles, Briseis creeps up and puts a knife to Achilles' throat (Fig. 1.2). Achilles almost eagerly says "Do it," allowing her to experience his role as master of death, and the choice of Eros or Thanatos. Note how later she will kill Agamemnon with a ceremonial dagger. Women with

---

43   For what follows we are particularly indebted to Allen (2007).
44   Weinlich (2015), 191.
45   And in the director's cut her intervention at this moment is more powerful than in the theatrical version. Weinlich (2015), 197–98.

FIGURE 1.2 Briseis with her knife at Achilles' throat.

knives in Classical myth are seen to assume a somewhat masculine and active role (cf. Medea, Clytemnestra, and even Dido, for example). This marriage of freedom and danger breaks barriers for each of them, marking a turning point. They choose Eros. Odysseus' subsequent conversation with Achilles suggests that Achilles now imagines a radically happier life with Briseis away from the world of war. Achilles apparently was even able to sleep (?) through the Trojans' dawn raid. It is a dangerously irresponsible daydream, and it leads to the death of Patroclus. Likewise, earlier Paris fantasized that he could live with Helen happily ever after without fatal consequences. But, as we shall soon observe, *Troy* shows Paris, tutored especially by the example of his brother, shaking off that illusion, and how Achilles, stunned by Patroclus' death, further instructed by the examples of Hector and Priam, achieves a more empathetic outlook in the face of his own willed death.

The next morning Achilles sends Briseis back with Priam to Troy[46]; they will meet again only at the end of the film. In her most un-Homeric killing of Agamemnon, she necessarily recalls Clytemnestra. To some critics this seems a somewhat trite quasi-feminist female-victim-who-does-not-need-rescuing-and-gets-revenge-on-piggish-oppressor theme,[47] but there is another important dimension.[48] Amid their quarrel, Achilles says to Agamemnon, "Before my time is done, I will look down on your corpse and smile." When Briseis kills Agamemnon, she stabs him in the neck area, in roughly the same place that Achilles stabbed Boagrius and later Hector. Agamemnon's senseless war brought destruction to Achilles; through Briseis Achilles has his revenge on Agamemnon, and Achilles sees the dead Agamemnon as promised. Thus not only does Briseis give Achilles peace after a lifetime of war, but she more concretely avenges Achilles as well as the Trojans. In the director's cut the line about

46 Weinlich (2015), 197–98, notes that in the director's cut Briseis seems almost relieved to go, suggesting a less symmetric love between the two, which Achilles is aware of.

47 Morrissey (2004).

48 Allen (2007), 161–62.

how Helen didn't want a hero, but somebody to grow old with, is thought by Winkler to be the film's most ridiculous sentence and was excised[49]; but as we note in our survey of Hercules movies, so often what the striving hero most wants is exactly to settle down and have a family, and thus that dimension should not be totally discounted. Briseis also recalls Cassandra, who, in the *Trojan Women*, gains some consolation knowing she will be in some way partly involved with Agamemnon's murder. But the death of Achilles, like the canonical death of Paris (or like the death of Jack in *Titanic*, 1997), follows an "ancient theme that great love must be paid for in death."[50]

HECTOR: FOR FAMILY AND MOTHERLAND

The *Iliad* is also, secondarily, the tragedy of Hector, who exists in dialectical relationship to Achilles. Achilles exists at one pole of greatness, while Hector provides a contrast with both Achilles and Paris. We saw Achilles' speech to his troops, but compare Hector's address, which comes immediately before: "All my life, I've lived by a code. And the code is simple: Honor the gods, love your woman . . . and defend your country. Troy is mother to us all. Fight for her!" Hector is not fighting primarily for glory (although that is important), but for the survival of his wife, child, and family, in a war he knows the Trojans will lose. In the *Iliad* these realities make his own excesses and self-delusions, however fatal, more understandable, for he so wants to believe that Zeus has changed his mind, and that the terrible fate he imagines for his wife and child will not come to pass, that he can even beat Achilles. He is proved terribly wrong, and must sacrifice himself in a duel with Achilles to atone for the shame of this error.

In *Troy* Hector is even more so the experienced, responsible elder brother, who has absolute love and loyalty to his family, who upholds the *mos maiorum*, a man of heroic skill, but also of humane morality. He loves his brother but also knows in his heart his brother's abduction of Helen is wrong, a violation of the Zeus of hospitality and the sacredness of marriage; and he is horrified at how Paris has wrecked years of peace negotiations by running off with Menelaus' wife. Hector is trapped by his loyalty to family, which forces him into compromises with his integrity. He is a good counselor, suggesting practical advice that the religiously gullible Priam will ignore. But when faced with the choice of giving up Paris to Menelaus or taking him and Helen back to Troy, his love for his brother wins. Similarly, after Paris proposes a duel between Menelaus and himself, and is defeated, he embraces his brother's feet. Hector in effect violates the truce he swore to and ends up killing Menelaus, again to protect his brother.

For all the contrasts between Hector and Achilles, they are both equal in their worth as men of honor and as warriors. During the initial assault, the

---

49 Winkler (2015), 6.
50 Morrissey (2004).

odd interchange inside Apollo's temple between Hector and Achilles displays both mutual differences and their intertwined fates. Achilles stresses the immorality of fame, while Hector is shocked at the slaughter of unarmed priests, the needless bloodshed to come, and how Achilles treats warfare as a game. Surprisingly, Achilles allows Hector to go—but note the very pensive expression on Achilles' face right after he does so. We remember his shout after he has killed Boagrius: "Is there no one else? Is there no one else?" There Achilles could not find somebody whom he could measure himself against. He knows Hector is a great warrior, another man of the sword, a potential equal; thus Hector's words have the power to touch him.

Troy's Hector is increasingly haunted. After killing Menelaus he leads the Trojans to a rout of the Greeks, and, a couple of days later, in their dawn offensive, the Trojans again seem to have the military momentum. Then the Myrmidons led by Achilles come into battle. Hector slashes the throat of the supposed Achilles, only to find it is the young Patroclus, whom he must finish off for mercy's sake. Hector stops the battle instead of pressing a decided tactical advantage. And very soon afterward he shows Andromache the secret escape route out of Troy. When she keeps asking, "Why are you telling me this?" he tells her that he does not know how long Troy will last after he is dead. He then adds: "I killed a boy today. He was too young. Much too young," suggesting his guilt. This offers one explanation of why he accepts the one-on-one duel with Achilles; note how he declares this moment of confrontation has been in his dreams, perhaps a reference to the dream metaphor in *Iliad* 22.199–200.

As he leaves to fight Achilles, Hector bids friends and family farewell, and the last person he looks at is Helen. The Iliadic Hector's choice to fight Achilles is driven by shame at making a tactical mistake that cost countless Trojan lives, which makes his suicidal choice understandable; nevertheless, pathetically, his parents beg him to retreat inside Troy's walls. But *Troy's* Hector is under no such compulsion. While Achilles is outside panting in his rage, as Hector goes off to nearly sure death, there is almost a wistful peacefulness among the Trojans, save for Andromache. This odd peacefulness does not agree with the later intense grief of Priam, and this somewhat artificial scene serves to demonstrate that the Trojans are aware of how dutifully Hector has served his family and city, and that he is now reaching the *telos* of his burdened life. As Achilles bids Briseis farewell, as Paris sent away Helen, so here Hector says goodbye to an even wider community, to which he is tied in a way that Paris is not, and Achilles could never be. And here Andromache, like Hector, is an icon of duty, propriety, family, and suffering. Her loss of Hector is much more profound than the losses of Briseis or Helen, and, of course, much less deserved.

With Patroclus' death, Achilles has reverted to his prior brutal self, which views life as a cycle of unending violence. Three scenes suggest the heroes' interconnected fates, bound up in Troy's impending fall. Achilles lights Patroclus' pyre, which he tends all night, recalling the guilt-ridden obsession of the Homeric Achilles for revenge. Hector is seen looking pensively at the young Astyanax while Paris conducts late night archery practice. Their subsequent twin arming scenes likewise entwine their fates. The next day there is purposeful brutality in Achilles' refusal to make a pact with Hector, recalling a similar refusal in *Iliad* 22.262, in his mocking of him, and in how he drags Hector's body, looking back with a half-smile at the watching Trojans. These scenes again provide a stark, tragic contrast of hero types, one possessed by rage and desire for glory, the other more dutiful and in control of his emotions, whose main concern is his family.

That night, after Hector's death, as Achilles sharpens his sword, Briseis remarks that Hector killed his cousin, and Achilles has killed hers, and then asks, "When does it end?" "It never ends," says Achilles, and Briseis goes out to the seashore to contemplate and grieve. Priam then sneaks in, kisses Achilles' hands as in Homer's epic, and makes his anguished plea for Hector's body. Priam's bravery and indifference to death resonate with Achilles. The theme of fathers and sons occurs here as in the *Iliad*. Priam declares that he knew Achilles' father, who died early (which may explain much about Achilles), lucky not to have seen his son fall. When Achilles declares that "Hector killed my cousin," Priam points out all the cousins, brothers, and so forth whom Achilles has slain. When Achilles petulantly declares giving Hector back will change nothing, for they will remain enemies, Priam counters that even enemies can respect each other and perform the civilized religious actions that bind all humans together.

When Achilles goes outside to cover Hector's body (as he does in the *Iliad*), he breaks into uncharacteristic sobbing, and says "We'll meet again soon, my brother," with an immediate cut to the dead Hector's face. Achilles' transformation, which began with his relationship with Briseis, is now accelerating. Now, as in the *Iliad*, Achilles can weep with Priam, perhaps for Hector, perhaps for the horror that he has caused, perhaps for the human situation, and for the tragedy that binds all of them together. Achilles now realizes the necessity of his own death. He apologizes to Briseis for any hurt he may have caused, and gives her the necklace he received from his mother before he left for Troy, which Patroclus once wore. As in the *Iliad*, he grants Priam the twelve days needed for Hector's funeral games. His change in heart is evident as he praises Hector and later asks Eudorus' forgiveness, pointing out how he valued his loyalty, saying "Go, Eudorus. This is the last order I give you," kissing his head in a poignant farewell gesture. He knows he has one more battle to fight. Thus with his death, Hector indirectly bestows some of his heroic traits on Achilles, the capacity to think of others first, to empathize and care for them.

PARIS: WHEN LOVE IS NOT ENOUGH

Both *Troy* and the *Iliad* present a critical opposition between Achilles and Hector. But in the way *Troy*'s story of Paris departs from Homer, there arises an interesting contrast between Achilles and Paris, and in some respects (don't laugh) a better narrative of Paris' life. We must also take into account the difference between the director's cut and the earlier theatrical version. There is something cartoonish about the frivolous Paris of *Iliad* Book 3, who tosses out a challenge duel to all comers without thinking of the consequences, or who is shameless in his desire for Helen after his disgraceful duel with Menelaus. Homer gives no indication that Paris ever really faces the consequences of what he has done, although, to be fair, Homer's Paris is actually a decent warrior. Not so *Troy*'s, which in fact depicts the sorrow-tinged maturation of Paris. Paris and Helen can serve archetypal representations of ourselves as helpless victims of transgressive but irresistible desire. Our *Troy* presents a romantic (romantic in the sense that *Madame Bovary* and Goethe's *Faust* are romantic) perspective, but filtered through a modern (and self-indulgent) fantasy that becomes more tragic and realistic at its conclusion. The basic initial romantic and modern presupposition asserts an individual has the right to find and make a life with his or her "true love," no matter what the cost to others.[51] This perspective is further justified by the sense that those individuals and institutions that block the desired love are in some way oppressive and illegitimate. But it is one thing to cause chaos to a family and young children as a renegade modern spouse might today; it is another to willingly make choices that will destroy countless innocents.

A modern audience looking at Paris might identify him as part of that species of "man-child" so distressingly common in modern media.[52] The *Iliad*'s Helen is a haunted woman, endlessly blaming herself, and, we think, pictured as Aphrodite's pawn. In the *Odyssey*, while Menelaus has retrieved his goddess, they live in a sterile marriage; one suspects that this was not the first time Helen put drugs in their wine. *Troy* has no divine Aphrodite, but presents Helen as an almost suicidal victim of an arranged marriage (at the age of sixteen) to a boor, as half-unhinged by her first experience of great sex and what seems true love (of course at the hands of an expert seducer). She is even willing to return to Menelaus but is told by Hector that such a return would change nothing. Earlier, as Hector notes, Paris was an immature, reckless seducer of other men's wives, probably the tack he took initially with Helen. Paris runs away with her

51 The ancients knew also that the desire for love or sex can be so overpowering that it makes even the most responsible people do actions that injure themselves, their families, and even their countries. The modern fantasy is that it will all work out somehow. The Greeks and most romantics knew better.

52 Scott (2014).

without really thinking through the consequences for Troy and his family, including Hector. Even when he begins to understand the trouble he has caused, he still lives in immature fantasy of simply running away and living off the land, as even Helen notes, saying, "You're very young, my love." But the observation of the cost of war begins to change him, to make him perceive that being with Helen is not enough.

Paris is much the mirror image of Achilles. Achilles is a war machine who must learn that glory without love is not enough; Paris is a love machine who must learn that love without honor is also lacking. The pivotal moment comes when Paris chooses to duel Menelaus. He is given the sword of Troy to fight Menelaus with, which he drops, and Hector must retrieve it, which symbolizes the fact that Paris is not ready to lead Troy and that Hector must pick up after him. In the *Iliad*, the duel between Menelaus and Paris is a symbolic enactment of the fact that the Trojan War is really about their war over a woman. Here, the inability of Paris to fight his own battles is evident, Hector being his brother's enabler, as he was when he permitted Paris to sail with Helen back to Troy. And, as even Paris knows, it is he who should have died, not Menelaus. This episode finally wakes Paris up to his own humiliation and need to become more properly heroic, to find values beyond those of romantic love.

In the duel's aftermath, Paris heaps upon himself the opprobrium that Helen in the *Iliad* heaped on Paris.[53] When Helen reminds him he did what he did for the sake of love, it seems clear that mere love is no longer enough for Paris; he understands that love cannot justify his faults. He too wants to be a hero, not in the sense of having immortal fame, but somebody, to use an expression from *O Brother*, who is bona fide, a respected upholder of the community and its values, not just somebody whom Helen can "grow old with." With Hector's death, Paris, the surviving son, matures further. He advises the Greek horse be burned, but like Hector, he is ignored by Priam and condemns the festivities so soon after Hector's death.[54]

As Troy burns, Paris urges Helen to take the escape route out of Troy, while he will stay behind, to protect Priam and try to find Briseis. When Helen begs him to stay behind, Paris says, "How could you love me if I ran now? We will be together again, in this world *or the next*." Paris had just given the sword of Troy to young Aeneas and asked him to lead the Trojans to a new home. This is a reference to the *Aeneid*, in which Aeneas leads the remnant of the Trojans to Italy to establish the future Roman people. The suggestion is that, out of the ruin their love has caused, an even greater Troy will rise. In the theatrical version, we last see Paris leading Briseis to the escape route. According to the canonical legend, Paris cannot survive Troy, and Helen (whose character here

---

53 Cyrino (2007), 144–45.
54 The way the Trojan population wave palm fronds recalls Jesus' entry into Jerusalem, in which initial joy turns to disaster.

changes little) must. Right after his final moment with Helen, Paris comes to the massed group of Trojans preparing to make what they know is their final stand, as the general Glaucus says, "The boatman waits for us. I say we make him wait a little longer!"[55] and then clasps the arms of the returning Paris, who kills various Trojans with his bow before he sees Briseis. It is the death of his brother, which his actions have caused, that has shaken him from his infatuation. As we analyzed the initial release, we thought that we were to understand that Paris had offered his death and abandonment of Helen as a kind of atonement and maturation. But the director's cut unraveled this interpretation.

HEROES AT THE END

The final scene, where Odysseus lights the pyre of Achilles in Troy's burned-out center, is shot in bleak, ashen colors. We hear Odysseus' voice-over: "Let them say I lived in the time of Hector . . . tamer of horses. Let them say . . . I lived in the time of Achilles." Homer's *Odyssey* suggested that Odysseus, not Achilles, was the more successful hero, for he survived and restored his homeland; but here, Odysseus clearly sees himself subordinate in honor to Achilles. There is an end-of-the-age feeling; in Greek myth the Trojan War signals the end of the Age of Heroes, when more archetypal figures ruled. The sense of apocalypse, of the end of an era, will be common in our movies, suggesting, as we observed before, that the current situation cannot go on.

But, in the director's cut, between the segments showing Achilles' cremation, we observe a line of Trojan refugees in the bright sunlight, climbing up a narrow path to find sanctuary on presumably Mt. Ida, where, according to the *Aeneid*, they built ships that took them to Italy. This group includes Helen, Paris, Andromache, little Astyanax, and Briseis, who stops to look back at the smoke rising from Achilles' pyre. The implication is that Troy will live on; indeed, the future is with Troy. Weinlich[56] points out the strong contrasts of perspectives in these intercut scenes: Odysseus is focused on having had the honor of sharing the world with these examples of archetypal heroism, but Briseis is looking down on her smoldering city and its thousands dead. Her troubled glance says it all.

Concerning Paris's survival, we strongly preferred the earlier version, in which we were convinced that Paris had resolved to die fighting with the majority of Trojan soldiers, in atonement for the disaster he had caused, as well as to fit the traditional plot line. Retooling our interpretation, we consider how at one point Helen tells him, "You're very young, my love . . . you're younger than I ever was." The director's cut makes explicit a theme of rebirth from the ashes of disaster; in some way, Paris was right to abscond with Helen, which was a

---

55 Cf. Leonidas' memorable line from *300*, "Spartans! . . . tonight we dine in Hell!"
56 Weinlich (2015), 193–94.

type of rescue, and his willingness to duel Menelaus, to stay behind and kill Achilles and rescue Briseis, signals a virtue needed for the refounding of Troy, and justifies his living.

TROY AND THE MILLENNIUM

Troy presents a myth that engages politics and the personal in ways relevant to our era. On the political level, it portrays the ever-repeatable results of egomaniacal leaders motivated by the will to power, international aggression, and the effects of patriotism as well as religious delusion. But its more powerful and tragic stories concern how four lives demonstrate the relations between romantic and familial love, innate character, maturation, and the demands of society and circumstance. It accords with the myth of the *Iliad*, which suggests that a true grasp of life's lessons is achieved only in the face of death, and every man accepts and even wills his own death both as a function of duty and gaining that knowledge. There is a slightly old-fashioned feel to *Troy*.[57] It indeed reflects millennial themes, recalling the lawless international aggression that is currently happening. With the breakdown of so many cultural standards, moderns, like Lars, do dream of "becoming a man," which involves "doing the right thing." But we know in our time doing the right thing is very hard; accordingly, for our movies' heroes, doing the right thing is linked to their death. We sense that the tragic heroism of Achilles and Hector belongs to a vanished world echoing the common feeling that our society is no longer up to challenges that promote nobility and greatness.

REFERENCES

Achcar, G. *The Clash of Barbarisms: September 11 and the Making of the New World Disorder. Monthly Review Press.* 2002.

Ahl, F. "Troy and the Memorials of War." In M. Winkler, ed., *Troy: From Homer's Iliad to Hollywood Epic.* Blackwell, 2007, pp. 163–85.

Aitken, B. E., and Maclean, J. K. B., ed. *Philostratus's Heroikos, Religion, and Cultural Identity in the Third Century CE.* Society of Biblical Literature, 2004.

Allen, A. "Briseis in Homer, Ovid and *Troy*." In M. Winkler, ed., *Troy: From Homer's Iliad to Hollywood Epic.* Blackwell, 2007, pp. 148–62.

Blume, H.-D. "Achilles and Patroclus in Troy." In M. Winkler, ed., *Return to Troy: New Essays on the Hollywood Epic.* Brill, 2015, pp. 165–79.

Burgess, J. *Homer.* Tauris, 2001a.

———. *The Tradition of the Trojan War in Homer and the Epic Cycle.* Johns Hopkins UP, 2001b.

———. "Neoanalysis, Orality, and Intertextuality: An Examination of Homeric Motif Transference." *Journal of the Oral Tradition*, vol. 21 no. 1, 2006, 148–89.

---

57 Shahabudin (2007), 110.

Cyrino, M. "Helen of Troy." In M. Winkler, ed., *Troy: From Homer's Iliad to Hollywood Epic.* Blackwell, 2007, pp. 131–46.

Dalby, A. *Rediscovering Homer: Inside the Origins of the Epic.* Norton, 2007.

Danek, G. "The Story of Troy Through the Centuries." In M. Winkler, ed., *Troy: From Homer's Iliad to Hollywood Epic.* Blackwell, 2007, pp. 68–84.

Davies, M. *The Greek Epic Cycle.* Bristol Classical Press, 2003.

Dillon, J. "The Tears of Priam: Reflections on *Troy* and Teaching Ancient Texts." *Humanitas* vol. 19 nos. 1 and 2, 2006, pp. 126–32.

Erskine, A. *Troy Between Greece and Rome: Local Tradition and Imperial Power.* Oxford UP, 2001.

Fantuzzi, M. *Achilles in Love.* Intertextual Studies. Oxford UP, 2012

Grube, G. "The Gods in Homer." *Phoenix* vol. 5 no. 3/4, 1951, 62–78.

Korfmann, M. "Was There a Trojan War? Troy Between Fiction and Archaeological Evidence." In M. Winkler, ed., *Troy: From Homer's Iliad to Hollywood Epic.* Blackwell, 2007, pp. 20–26.

Krass, A. "Over His Dead Body: Male Friendship in Homer's Iliad and Wolfgang Petersen's Troy." In A-B Renger and J. Solomon, ed. *Ancient Worlds in Film and Television.* 2012, pp. 151–173

Latacz, J. *Troy and Homer: Towards a Solution of an Old Mystery.* Oxford UP, 2004.

———. "From Homer's Troy to Petersen's Troy." In M. Winkler, ed., *Troy: From Homer's Iliad to Hollywood Epic.* Blackwell, 2007, pp. 27–42.

Lang, M. "War Story into Wrath Story." In J. Carter and S. Morris, ed., *The Ages of Homer.* University of Texas Press, 1995, pp. 149–62.

Loudon, B. "Odysseus in Troy." In M. Winkler, ed., *Return to Troy: New Essays on the Hollywood Epic.* Brill, 2015, pp. 180–189.

Merkle S. "Dictys and Dares: The Trojan War." In H. Hofmann, ed., *Latin Fiction.* Routledge, 2004, pp. 155–66.

Mestre, F. "Refuting Homer in the Heroikos of Philostratus." In E. Aitken and J. Maclean, ed., *Philostratus's Heroikos: Religion and Cultural Identity in the Third Century.* Society of Biblical Literature, 2004, pp. 127–41.

Morrissey, C. "Pomo Homer": A Review of the *Troy* Movie." http://www.anthropoetics.ucla.edu/views/vw304.htm, 2004. Accessed Aug. 24, 2016.

Petersen, W., with U. Greiwe. *Ich liebe die grossen Geschichten: Vom "Tatort" bis nach Hollywood.* Köln. Kiepenheuer & Witsch, 1997.

Scherer, M. R. *The Legends of Troy: In Art and Literature.* Phaidon Press, 1963.

Scott, A. "The Death of Adulthood in American Culture." *New York Times Magazine,* Sep. 11, 2014.

Shahabudin, K. "From Greek Myth to Hollywood Story." In M. Winkler, ed., *Troy: From Homer's Iliad to Hollywood Epic.* Blackwell, 2007, pp. 105–18.

Solomon, J. "The Vacillations of the Trojan Myth: Popularization & Classicization, Variation & Codification." *International Journal of the Classical Tradition,* vol. 14, 2007, pp. 482–534.

Sumner, G. Review of *King Arthur,* the Movie (2004). http://www.geocities.ws/vortigernstudies/articles/guestgraham1.html, 2004. Accessed Dec. 11, 2016.

Weinlich, B. "A New Briseis in Troy." In M. Winkler, ed., *Return to Troy: New Essays on the Hollywood Epic.* Brill, 2015, pp. 191–202.

West, M. *Greek Epic Fragments*. Harvard UP, 2003.

Wilcox, M. "Neoanalysis." In I. Morris and B. Powell, ed., *A New Companion to Homer*. Brill, 1996, pp. 174–92.

Winkler, M., ed. "Editor's Introduction." In *Troy: From Homer's Iliad to Hollywood Epic*. Blackwell, 2007, pp. 1–19.

———. "Introduction: *Troy Revisited*." In *Return to Troy: New Essays on the Hollywood Epic*. Brill, 2015, pp. 1–15.

Yeats, W. B. *Responsibilities and Other Poems*. Macmillan, 1916.

Zeitlin, F. "Visions and Revisions of Homer." In S. Goldhill, ed., *Being Greek under Rome: Cultural Identity, the Second Sophistic and the Development of Empire*. Cambridge UP, 2001, pp. 199–266.

CHAPTER 2

RESINGING THE *ODYSSEY*

Myth and Myth Making in *O Brother, Where Art Thou?*

When 'Omer smote 'is bloomin' lyre,
He'd 'eard men sing by land an' sea;
An' what he thought 'e might require,
'E went an' took—the same as me!

(From Rudyard Kipling: *Introduction to the*
"Barrack-Room Ballads" in The Seven Seas)

Kipling knew there is no end to borrowing from Homer. And Homer himself took from here and there to make up his wondrous tales of heroes, gods, and monsters. Thus are epic songs spun, from Bronze Age ballads to millennial rap songs. So in the year 2000 the Coen brothers with *O Brother, Where Art Thou?* provocatively reinterpreted Odysseus' adventures in the Depression-era American South. This was, of course, neither the first nor the last movie reprising Homer's *Odyssey* and its themes. Notable examples include the NBC TV miniseries *The Odyssey* (1997), directed by Andrei Konchalovsky; *Ulysses* (1954), directed by Mario Camerini; and more displaced versions in Mike Leigh's *Naked* (1993) and Tim Burton's *Big Fish* (2003), though in some ways, every movie based on a journey has something of the *Odyssey* in it.[1]

A box office success, *O Brother* received nominations for two Academy Awards (adapted screenplay and cinematography), and George Clooney was awarded the honors of Best Actor at the Golden Globe. Though the aggregate of reviews was quite favorable, some critics saw it as an entertaining, but shallow, episodic pastiche. The Coen brothers are known for the subtle complexity and intertextuality of their movies, but some critics found no real center to

---

1   See also Pischel (2013) for other titles. Apparently, Hugh Jackman is in talks to star in a new version of Odysseus' tale by Francis Lawrence, who directed *The Hunger Games*. See http://www.theguardian.com/film/2015/aug/21/hugh-jackman-embarks-on-the-odyssey-homer. Accessed Apr. 7, 2016.

PLOT SUMMARY

The imprisoned Ulysses Everett McGill learns that his former wife, Penny, is about to re-marry. He convinces Pete and Delmar to escape with him, promising a share of hidden loot, soon to be submerged. A blind man prophesizes they will suffer much, but gain salvation. They are pursued by the devilish Sheriff Cooley. Among their adventures, they are betrayed by Pete's cousin and then encounter a congregation being baptized. They give a lift to Tommy, a young black man who has sold his soul to the Devil to be able to play the guitar really well. Posing as the Soggy Bottom Boys, they record "Man of Constant Sorrow," which becomes a huge hit. Afterward, they encounter Siren-like women who drug them, and seem to turn Pete into a toad. They are beaten up and robbed by the one-eyed Big Dan Teague. Returned to Ithaca, Mississippi, Everett finds Penny has told their daughters he was killed, and she is about to marry Waldrip, the campaign manager for Homer Stokes, who is running an insurgent campaign against Governor Pappy O'Daniel. Penny rejects him. In a movie theater they encounter Pete among a group of prisoners and rescue him. They then save Tommy from being hung in a Ku Klux Klan ceremony. They sneak into a rally for Homer Stokes as the Soggy Bottom Boys; they are joyfully received and Homer Stokes rejected. Penny accepts Everett back, but demands he get their original ring from their old home. Everett, Pete, and Delmar are nearly hanged by Sheriff Cooley, but Everett's inspired prayer is followed by the TVA flood, which saves them. Although still bickering, Penny seems to be willing to take Everett back, as the blind man slowly rides away on his cart.

O Brother. As Roger Ebert put it, "I had the sense of invention set adrift; of a series of bright ideas wondering why they had all been invited to the same film."[2] This pastiche quality reflects a current postmodernist aesthetic that purposely and playfully ironizes everything,[3] but it is also argued that the Coen brothers, by intermixing elements of high and low culture, "democratize" them, a process aligned with the film's evident themes of political, racial, and economic justice. The Coen brothers employ a varied mash-up of references, Classical, American, pop culture, and modern film, which, taken as a whole,[4] and held together by songs carefully chosen, provide a narrative, however fanciful, of a hero's journey as well as of American history and its reception.[5] And, as our reading of the *O Brother* mythos shows, it does present a substantial whole to those who know how to listen to its thought-music.

Epic was the ancient world's most "open" form, and the epic bard had the freedom to add material from other genres such as pastoral and folktale, to

---

2   http://www.rogerebert.com/reviews/o-brother-where-art-thou-2000. Accessed Apr. 22, 2016.
3   See Rowell (2007), 244, who refers to *O Brother* as a "cinematic mosaic that cherry-picks plots, methods and themes."
4   Siegel (2007), 214.
5   Rowell (2007), 244.

be both deeply serious, touching on the most fundamental issues of life and society, and rudely comic, as when Demodocus describes Aphrodite and Ares being caught during sexual intercourse. Accordingly, we begin this chapter by discussing how the Coen brothers reprise the epic genre in its inclusiveness, producing a visual and literary pastiche with a strong poetic voice, and how it presents moral, social, and historical questions relevant to our time, as well as recasting the mythical role of the bard and the centrality of song with a view to its historical setting. Second, we will focus on the Coen brothers' reworking of the hero's Quest/Journey, extended by wanderings, strange sights, and other adventures, experiences that help both the hero and audience understand the nature of life. The context for the Coen brothers' adaptation, as was the case with Homer's Bronze Age past and with the Spain of *Pan's Labyrinth*, is a past that has become mythologized and partially idealized so as to offer lessons and even hope for today's problematic times.

ODYSSEUS' JOURNEY AND *O BROTHER*

Odysseus, king of the small island of Ithaka, known for his clever, trickster ways, reluctantly joined Agamemnon's Trojan expedition and was responsible for its success through his ruse of the Trojan Horse. As Odysseus' men left Troy, their destructive unruliness during their raid on the Cicones foreshadowed the disobedience that would destroy them. Storm-blown into unknown territories, they encounter numerous threats to the soul and body. First there were the Lotus Eaters, whose fruit makes men forget their homecoming. Odysseus, overly confident and curious about the Cyclopes, is trapped by the savage Polyphemus, who eats several of his men before Odysseus gets him drunk with magic wine and then gouges his eye out. Odysseus, escaping, pridefully taunts the Cyclops, who prays to his father Poseidon, and Odysseus is cursed. He is entertained by the god of the winds, Aeolus, who provides a bag of winds so he can sail home smoothly. But his greedy men open the bag, and they are blown back to Aeolus, who drives Odysseus away. Soon after Odysseus, alienated from his men, escapes with one ship when his men encounter the cannibalistic Laestrygonians. But Odysseus subsequently rescues his men from the goddess/witch Circe. He stays (and loves) Circe for one year, but must go to the Deadlands to consult Tiresias. There he meets figures from his past, such as Agamemnon, Ajax, Achilles, his mother, and his crewman Elpenor. Afterwards he survives the alluring Sirens, who tempt ships to destruction with their song, and the combination of monster and whirlpool of Scylla and Charybdis. Finally, they are becalmed on the island of the Sun, and his disobedient men, driven by hunger, eat the Sun's cattle. Zeus blasts his ship and only Odysseus survives, washing up on the land of Calypso, who wants him to be her perpetual consort.

Meanwhile it has been nearly twenty years since Odysseus left Ithaka, and he is widely presumed dead. One hundred twenty suitors are trying to force Penelope to marry, eating up Odysseus' goods in the process. Athena persuades Zeus to order Calypso to release Odysseus, and she, in disguise, visits Telemachus at Ithaka and prompts him to search for his father. Odysseus, leaving Calypso, is nearly destroyed by Poseidon, but washes up on the land of the Phaeacians and is befriended by King Alcinoos and his daughter Nausicaa. At a banquet Odysseus relates his adventures. The Phaeacians take him home to Ithaka, where he, disguised as a beggar, gradually meets up and tests his loyal servants and Telemachus and is tested in turn. He also probes the suitors and even meets with Penelope, who may recognize him. Penelope sets up a contest where Odysseus gets possession of his old bow, and he and his allies kill all the suitors save two. He is reconciled with his wife and family, and Athena makes peace with the families of the suitors. Odysseus, as Tiresias in the Deadlands prophesizes, reconciled with Poseidon, will die in peace surrounded by his loved ones.

O Brother's dependence on the *Odyssey* is indicated by the title credit "Based upon 'The Odyssey' by Homer"[6] and the appearance of the epic's opening lines. Like the *Odyssey*, *O Brother* begins toward the end of Everett's adventures. Ulysses (the Roman Odysseus) Everett McGill is in jail, a type of exile, for which his own rashness is largely responsible. Both men have problems with refractory comrades, and endure fantastic travels and adventures that also reveal much about human life and culture as well as fate and the divine. Both are traveling back to their homeland, and have a spouse (Penny/Penelope) in danger of being compromised by suitors. Both meet a blind prophet (the railroad man and Tiresias) who offers structurally relevant prophecies; they encounter "Lotus Eaters" of sorts, in *O Brother* represented by a "blissed out" religious congregation; Everett and company meet Sirens (here merged with the Homeric Circe) who entice them with melodious singing and allegedly turn Pete into a toad. They deal with an aggressive Cyclops-man and have real or symbolic confrontations with the Deadlands. They both lose and reclaim identity in ways that rehearse their pasts, and they are even transformed. Persecuted by a powerful and vengeful figure (Poseidon/Sheriff Cooley), they both return home, restore the political order, and save their wives (who test them) and families from menacing suitors/antagonists and reestablish themselves as recognized and important members of society.[7]

---

6   The Coens claim that they never read the *Odyssey*, which is somewhat risible. See Siegel (2007), 213–14, and Flensted-Jensen (2002), 14.

7   Good overviews of the allusions to the *Odyssey* in the movie are found in Toscano (2009), 49–50; Siegel (2007); and Flensted-Jensen (2002).

KEY TERMS

Great Depression: period in America between 1929 and 1939, featuring a disastrous economic crisis, characterized by a stock market crash, low industrial output, poverty and very high unemployment.

Ku Klux Klan: extremist white supremacist organization in the United States, born after the Civil War to oppose the rights of newly freed slaves; particularly strong in Southern states.

Ancient oral poetry: oral stories narrated by traveling bards in ancient Greece and other nations. These are mostly narrative epic tales with common characteristics (such as epithets and re-peated phrases to aid memorization) that later gave origin to epic poems such as the *Odyssey*.

Nostos: story or myth of return home.

Nekyia: a journey to the land of the dead, often to consult its spirits, not necessarily a descent to the underworld, in contrast with *katabasis*.

REAL AND MYTHOLOGIZED HISTORY: AMERICAN MYTH AND CINEMA

As noted, *O Brother* furnishes a type of mythologized history. The way the Coen brothers have cast Clooney/McGill to look like Clark Gable, the use of 1930s-style broad acting, the sepia overtones, scenes borrowed from famous films (such as the *Wizard of Oz*), the use of "old-timey music," and other traits recalling manu-factured memories of the Old South all serve to give the sense (as Homer does) of participating in a reworked form of cultural memory, which grants the movie a deeper, and thus more authoritative, resonance. *O Brother*'s South is a mythical space, inhabited by typical denizens of Southern popular storytelling. Our movie includes many references to other American/Southern myths, including the figure of the manic depressive Babyface Nelson and even the talented guitarist Tommy Johnson.[8] Homeric poetry was always chanted with musical accompaniment, and the Coen brothers' extensive use of antiquated music[9] and formulaic scenes and language gives the movie a kind of bardic quality. Even Everett's insistence on using fanciful Greek and Latin rooted words (*paterfamilias*) points to this sense of regen-eration of a new work from fragments of the past, including the Classical past.

Thus an important context for *O Brother* is the Depression-era American South, the New Deal, and an active KKK, an era now remote enough to be a mythical world in its own right, amenable to artistic manipulation. The invoca-tion of the mythological South is at times as robust as the Homeric intertext.[10] Indeed, *O Brother* sometimes seems like a memory of a South that might have been, a historical fantasy,[11] which had suffered a defeat but whose culture lived

---

8 Goldhill (2007), 264, remarks that George Nelson's depression matches well with the general theme of the Great Depression.

9 Rowell (2007), 244.

10 Filene (2004), 59; Siegel (2007), 217; Cant (2007).

11 Toscano (2009), 50–51; and Ruppersburg (2003), 6 and 24.

on.[12] Despite parodic elements, there is often a noticeable "Gothic" aspect to these "tales of the South."[13]

As Franco's Spain in the 1940s was a dark period that still scars Spanish history and looms large in the collective memory of many Spaniards, so is the American South of the Depression. The Great Depression tested capitalism and the integrity of the American state. President Franklin Roosevelt struggled against entrenched conservative and corporate interests to enact the social welfare programs of the New Deal. The American South, very poor, had been hit hard. The American Civil War and the following period of the Reconstruction had ended only in 1877, and resistance to civil rights for blacks was still fierce. The racist domestic terror organization, the Ku Klux Klan, was powerful, with many important men its undisguised members. The myth of the Antebellum South and the noble Lost Cause of the War Between the States was strong. Southern governments were sturdily class-bound, as they had been in the plantation era. Conservative forms of Protestantism furnished ideological support for reactionary policies as well as demagogues like the Roman Catholic Father Charles Coughlin, who with his radio show argued for social justice yet at the same time had an anti-Semitic tone, veering toward Nazi support.

Connecting Homer and the American Depression is Preston Sturges's 1941 movie *Sullivan's Travels*. There, Sullivan,[14] known as a successful director of lightweight movies, desires to make a socially serious film about the Depression's ills. Sullivan has his own fretful odyssey through the regions of deprivation, often dressed like a hobo, losing his identity, and being jailed. The name of his putative film is *O Brother, Where Art Thou?* While viewing an animated cartoon in jail, Sullivan realizes that comedy can be as instructive as serious social commentary. The implication is that *O Brother* is the movie Sullivan could have made, and that the Coen brothers thought that through a light touch they could make serious points about U.S. history and forward a progressive vision.[15]

SING O MUSE! THE POWER OF SONG

Although the name Ulysses recalls Odysseus, the name Everett recalls "Everyman,"[16] suggesting that movies can be a type of "epic for Everyman."[17] As noted, Homeric epic was an assemblage of originally independent phrases, plots,

---

12 Ruppersburg (2003), 12.
13 Cant (2007), 66.
14 Toscano (2009), 53; Bergan (2000), 208–9; Weinlich (2005), 90.
15 McFarland (2009), 40–43; Ruppersburg (2003), 8.
16 Ruppersburg (2003), 21, notes the similarity of *O Brother* to "the medieval mystery play *Everyman*, in which the main character episodically encounters one person after the other. . . . The plot of *O Brother* is intensely episodic, almost picaresque. In some ways the film sets itself up as a spiritual quest."
17 See Perry (1967), 48.

songs, and other elements created through centuries of poetic practice and given its final shape through "Homer." *O Brother*'s noted mixture of high and low styles is seen in the *Odyssey*, with its many lower-brow elements of folktale and humor. Thus, beyond comparable episodes, there is something quite Homeric and mythical in the film's construction of its narrative through diverse pieces of stories and voices, in the same way that the *Odyssey* was forged. It is a treasury of traditions.

The movie begins with the *Odyssey* poet's initial invocation to his Muse;

> O Muse!
> Sing in me, and through me tell the story
> Of that man skilled in all the ways of contending,
> A wanderer, harried for years on end . . . [18]

Such a beginning underscores the centrality of music, song, and storytelling to the narrative format of *O Brother*, and also suggests a kind of divine inspiration.[19] The Muse of Homer, originally an oral poet, is Calliope, the inspiring spirit of epic poetry, whose verses were sung before a varied audience to the accompaniment of some stringed instrument, often the lyre or its ancestor the *phorminx*.[20] So even though the Greek reads *ennepe*, "sing" is a very appropriate translation and even more fitting for a film that conveys its meanings as much in song as in dialogue. Thus appropriating the Homeric proem to introduce their own film, the Coen brothers are placing themselves in the same role as Homer or the performing bard (*moi* in the Greek must certainly refer to the bard who both composes and performs his epic verses). The bards who appear as characters in ancient epic, such as Demodocus, reflect the traditional singers of antiquity and are seen as metapoetic reflections of the poet himself. [21]

The classical bard is often both a storyteller and a transmitter of cultural values through the ability to give *kleos*, "glory," or its reverse to individuals, cities, and events. One finds a mythical archetype in figures such as Orpheus, Demodocus, Phemius, and Homer himself. *O Brother*'s invocation of the Muse suggests a transpersonal power that makes the bards (and movie makers) produce their exceptional artwork. Its varied songs bind the segments and themes of *O Brother* together; and various critics have pointed at their diegetic character.[22] The power of music will help lighten the human spirit, connect individuals with the divine, bind communities, enable salvation, promote political

---

18   The Coen brothers mostly use Fitzgerald's Penguin translation (1998 [1962]).

19   "Song is *O Brother*'s ultimate connector"; Rowell (2007), 265, and also 244.

20   For more on the craft of the musician in the ancient world, see Kemp (1966).

21   Thus because Demodocus is blind, it was assumed Homer himself was blind. For the role of the bard in the composition of the Homeric poems, see Edwards (1987), 1–23; and Scodel (1998).

22   Chadwell (2004) and Harries (2001).

ideas and alliances, and even stimulate resistance. Music functions as a kind of chorus, providing comment and contrast to the action.[23]

The controlling fantasy of *O Brother* is that music, as an expression of a positive collective aspiration and long tradition, locates its prophetic channel in a problematic Everyman, Everett, who, in finding his bardic calling and abandoning false perspectives (which include his view of religion), restores himself, his family, his comrades, and even the State of Mississippi through song's power to rebuild community. *O Brother*'s Grammy-winning soundtrack has inspired a revival of interest in folk music. Such revivals occur periodically; some current musicians (e.g., the technopop star Moby) explore these older music forms, seen as an origin point for their own work. But many 1930s revivalists viewed folk compositions as more than living fossils; rather, folk music was a living and evolving tradition that could serve real cultural needs and would continue doing so. Further, the Depression led to a crisis of confidence in what American culture had become in the era of triumphant capitalism and mass society, its background music furnished by the radio and phonograph. Folk music was posited as the expression of a more authentic American counterculture, less a product of capitalist consumer culture, again epitomized by songs heard on the radio. But as Filene notes, the music of *O Brother* and similar folk music is prized today because it appears authentic, as opposed to modern commercial music, while at the same time being seen as remote, even alien, not a vital tradition for today. Note how the Coens wanted *O Brother* shot so it would look like a relic of a prior time, "brown and dirty and golden like a period picture book of the Depression,"[24] and the inserted notes in the CD to the soundtrack of *O Brother* suggest that the earlier, pure, delicate folk music was corrupted by later innovations.

Consider carefully how in *O Brother* this old time music is promoted by another recorder of songs. The radio station owner has been identified with Homer, undoubtedly because he is blind and has discerning taste for music, and here he helps transmit a form of oral poetry.[25] Homer has always symbolized a tradition and stream of "Classic" poetry. Everett and the Soggy Bottom Boys, who have never even practiced together, suddenly produce a rousing "hit" song; their lack of professional lineage would fit the model of the authentic folksinger as "coming out of nowhere" but also the divinely inspired bard, through whom the Muse sings. Delmar's ability to sing a solo later shows he too had imbibed folk music. The wondrously pleased blind station owner thus can represent both the then-current practice of exploiting musicians and also

---

23 The role of music in *O Brother* has been well analyzed by Chadwell (2004), Rowell (2007), and Cant (2007), 68ff., among others.
24 Bergan (2000), 213.
25 Toscano (2009), 58. See also Weinlich (2005), 92, for the radio owner as both Homer and a sort of Demodocus.

O Brother Where Art Thou? (2000)	
Touchstone Pictures, Universal Pictures	
Directors:	Joel and Ethan Coen
Screenplay:	Ethan Coen
Cast:	George Clooney (Ulysses Everett McGill), John Turturro (Pete Hogwallop), Tim Blake Nelson (Delmar O'Donnell), John Goodman (Big Dan Teague), Holy Hunter (Penny), Chris Thomas King (Tommy Johnson), Charles Durning (Pappy O'Daniel), Michael Badalucco (George Nelson), Wayne Duval (Homer Stokes), Ray McKinnon (Vernon Waldrip), Daniel Von Bargen (Sheriff Cooley).

that bardic tradition, which has tested and accepted the Soggy Bottom Boys, making them an instant success for whom the whole South is "going ape."

When the station owner asks for "old timey" tunes, Everett quickly asserts (probably truthfully) that they are "steeped in old-timey material"—which fuels their powers of composition.[26] Though this term refers to a specific genre popular in the 1930s,[27] we can metacritically think of "old poetry" as legitimated by a tradition. The radio station itself symbolizes a new, and problematic, form of mass communication; in Homer's day the bard's winged words (a phrase much used by Homer) were carried from city to city by their force and beauty. But in our day, anybody who has the money can mass-communicate. The scene in which the Soggy Bottom Boys and Pappy O'Daniel and his aides pass by each other implies what might be gained and what lost in this new world of mass communication. These episodes suggest an ideal synthesis: folk music that arises from prior and varied traditions and engagement with the present, which uses modern methods to transmit its important message without being compromised by it. Later a business associate talks to the blind station owner about "beating the competition," but the owner, more tied to the spirit of music, agrees with this statement only ironically. The production of music is not about beating the capitalist competition.

Why did the Coens choose to name a chief villain Homer? "Homer" can be a kind of shorthand for a "folksy" person, and we do not know Homer Stokes is a villain at first; indeed, since Pappy as governor presides over the brutal conditions of the chain gang, he could be a villain. But Pappy actually recalls W. Lee "Pappy" O'Daniel, owner of Hillbilly Flour, who funded radio programs playing country music in the 1920s and 1930s, along with two groups of country music. O'Daniel even pardoned Leadbelly, in jail for murder.[28] He was later the populist (but ineffectual) governor of Texas. The song "You Are My Sunshine" (1940) was actually a campaign song of Jimmie Davis, governor

---

26 But note Everett is willing to present himself and his fellows as Negroes; the fact that the Soggy Bottom Boys are integrated (in Homer Stokes's view, miscegenated) recalls how "old timey" music was in fact influenced by black music, and should transcend racial barriers.

27 Chadwell (2004), 5.

28 Ruppersburg (2003), 16.

of Louisiana. In *O Brother* the first time we hear of Pappy is on a commercial for Pappy O'Daniel's Flour Hour. The blind radio station owner drops a significant detail: "I'm lookin' for some ol'-timey material. Why, people just can't get enough of it since we started broadcastin' the 'Pappy O'Daniel Flour Hour'. . . ." This folk music tradition can be seen as living and evolving; the music of the Soggy Bottom Boys is an example of old-timey traditions used to produce a new, but still authentic, folk song.[29] In turn, the false Homer represents the tradition of frozen authenticity; thus at the rally he claims the music of the band is not even "old-timey." His view of history is as an ideological weapon, typical of the Southern demagogue who claims to speak for the "little man" and against the status quo but does so in the service of reactionary ideologies—something familiar today. And after the expulsion of Homer Stokes, Pappy pardons the felons (as the real Pappy did) and admits the Soggy Bottom Boys as his laureate band. So *O Brother*'s Pappy, recalling his historical model, is responsible for the promulgation of this important oral music that expresses the pure feeling of the people, true populism according to *O Brother*'s myth of authentic music.

ODYSSEUS REBOOTED

Both Odysseus and Everett during their heroic journeys must "reinvent themselves."[30] Odysseus is Everett's implied role model, but he often fails to measure up. The hero's process of gaining heroic status and *andreia* (manliness) usually involves the discovery and use of skills he never knew he possessed. To return to Ithaka, Odysseus must learn to control his words, even to remain silent, and not blindly indulge in heroic aggression. There is a buffoonish quality to the Everyman Everett, who uses his snowstorm of words as a defense mechanism. Everett thinks of himself as a silver-tongued and skilled-in-ways-of-contending Odysseus, but survives more by luck[31] than cleverness. Big Dan Teague, the Bible salesman who recalls Polyphemus, overpowers him both with words and with physical force. Everett/Everyman, seduced by his gift for gab, was jailed for practicing law without a license, thus illegally helping lay down the law—in other words, taking the rights of rulers. Odysseus assumes multiple identities, often in great contrast to his true identity, for example, claiming to be a Cretan, a beggar, or "Nobody." Everett also assumes disguises (for example, dressing as a member of the KKK color guard), and claims to be much more (and less) than he is.

---

29 On authenticity in the film, see Chadwell (2004).

30 Siegel (2007), 219.

31 Everett is often rescued by interruptions; for example, when Pete first questions Everett's leadership, the sound of pursuing dogs stops the confrontation; the argument about the stolen watch is stopped when they hear the music of the congregants; when Pete is about to catch Everett's lie, surprised he had no plan, again the pursuing police halt further argument; the fight that begins when Pete learns about Everett's lie about the treasure is cut off when they see Tommy is about to be hanged at the KKK rally.

The stories Odysseus tells to the Phaeacians belong to a species of "Tall Tales," "Phaeacian Tales" becoming later a byword for a fantastic story.[32] Everett too knows how to spin a tall tale.

Homer's Odysseus is morally problematic, willing to buy poison for arrows (Hom. *Od.*1.262), to cheat Ajax of Achilles' armor, and Athena remarks on Odysseus' compulsive deviousness (Hom. *Od.* 13.291–93). Similarly, Everett has no problem with lying, stealing, and potentially wreaking the lives of his comrades to achieve his goals, although his actions, functionally speaking, do challenge the oppressive status quo and make him a hero of the "little man."[33] Further, as part of Everett's attempt *not* to be a Southern "Everyman," he has adopted a secularist, mocking rationalism out of place in the 1930s American South.[34] Comedy accepts that even good individuals can acquire evil habits if they are displaced from their natural position.[35] Everett and his companions become heroes through moral action, which begins with Delmar and Everett rescuing Pete and ends with Everett's saving and seemingly heartfelt prayer before the flood. Odysseus' *andreia* lies in his martial strength, courage, and cleverness with words, qualities Everett lacks initially but gradually and partially acquires. Finally Everett gains his *nostos*; he escapes prison, defeats the evil master of his wife's suitor, and regains his wife and family, victories made possible because he discovered and accepted his gift as a singer/bard and took great (and unlike Odysseus', successful) risks to save his companions; but his *nostos* is not a return to the *status quo ante*. And whereas Odysseus conquers the suitors with physical strength and wit, Everett's most significant triumphs are connected to surprising song.

EVERETT'S ODYSSEY

ESCAPE AND DESCENT

The film's onset presents the voices of guards and the rhythmic crack of hammers, all blending with the prisoners' cries of "Po' Lazarus!" and their subsequent song of suffering and contending, encouraging communal support in adversity. Its hero is a sort of "Po' Lazarus," an outcast and criminal exile, just as Odysseus and Everett are, who need to somehow return to their major roles in the community (think here of Harry Potter in the cupboard), and be reborn.

---

32 Kim (2010), 152.
33 Rowell (2007), 249, 256.
34 See Toscano (2009), 56: "Everett's obsession with keeping his hair just so, with his hairnets and Dapper Dan pomade, embodies his commitment to reason and control."
35 Alvares (2002), 6. Note how the *Odyssey* lends itself to very different reinterpretations, ranging from comedy to almost unwatchable tragedy. See discussion in Goldhill (2007), 245. For other versions of Odysseus in film, see also Verreth (2008).

"Po' Lazarus"[36] is an African American "bad man" ballad, telling how the white sheriff orders his deputy to bring Po' Lazarus in. The allegedly dangerous Lazarus is however seen with his "head hanging down," and without even being allowed to surrender, he is shot. Implied too is the dead Lazarus whom Jesus raised, and the implied hope of renewal and rebirth. The line of chains linking the prisoners together symbolizes both oppression and community.[37] There will be a very different and satisfying linking at the movie's conclusion.

The title and credits of *O Brother, Where Art Thou?* are accompanied by the "The Big Rock Candy Mountain," a utopian fantasy answering the earlier images of oppression played during the escape attempt; the song's first mention of the word *hobo* coincides with the three escapees jumping up from the grass. The hobo-singer tells of his intention to travel to a dreamlike place, a golden age paradise where no work or effort is needed. This dream utopia recalls the country of Homer's Phaeacians, a land of abundance, where people are helpful, and where Odysseus is fed and clothed without much struggle.[38] Meanwhile, the escapees are depicted stealing and eating with some relish a farmer's chicken in a quasi-parody of a banquet scene; freedom from the chain gang, and their quest for seeming riches, has a utopian feel. The version of "The Big Rock Candy Mountain" that the Coen Brothers include is actually the original first recording by Harry McClintock, with some improvements, from 1928. McClintock himself was briefly a hobo, and the lyrics seem to be based on his life roaming the United States.[39] Just as Odysseus, who will become a storyteller in the court of Alcinous, appears as a sort of itinerant hobo (twice in the poem he is dressed as a beggar, and in book 6 he is referred to as "a wanderer . . ./, from an island of far off men", *Od.* 6.279–80),Homer himself, as wandering bard, was a sort of ancient hobo, like McClintock, who actually performed this very song as a street singer.

An argument between Everett and Pete about who is in charge is interrupted as we hear the sound of a creaking handcar with a blind driver (Fig. 2.1), whose statement that "I work for no man" can be a reference to Odysseus/Ulysses

---

36 This song is a field recording done by Alan Lomax of Jimmy Carter and some fellow prisoners in 1959, who were serving time at the notorious Mississippi State Penitentiary, widely known as Parchman Farm; see Filene (2004), 58. Parchman Farm, a terrible place, figures in the "Southern Gothic" of Faulkner, especially "the *Old Man* section of *Wild Palms*"; see Cant (2007), 66.

37 For the imprisoning and paralyzing effects of Ogygia and the penal farm, see Weinlich (2005), 91–92.

38 For utopian views of Scheria in its abundance of food, wine, and perfect weather, see *Od.* 7.113–132.

39 Just as Homer wrote down, "recorded" in a way, a canonized version of Odysseus' tale, McClintock seems to have done the same with a song that was already popular and traditional, of which various versions existed, and still do. Other previous "hobo" songs may have served as inspiration too.

FIGURE 2.1 Everett, Pete and Delmar meet the blind prophet on his railroad pushcart.

Everett[40] and to the workings of a mysterious force of fate. Everett's pompous reply is interrupted by the blind man's oracle.

> You seek a great fortune, you three who are now in chains. . . . And you will find a fortune—though it will not be the fortune you seek. But first, first you must travel—a long and difficult road—a road fraught with peril, uh-huh, and pregnant with adventure. You shall see things, wonderful to tell. You shall see a cow on the roof of a cottonhouse, uh-huh, and, oh, so many startlements. . . . I cannot say how long this road shall be. But fear not the obstacles in your path, for Fate has vouchsafed your reward. And though the road may wind, and yea, your hearts grow weary, still shall ye foller the way, even unto your salvation.

This oracle resembles that of the *Odyssey*'s Tiresias in two points[41]; the clearer one concerns their struggles, and the second concerns salvation, in the sense of "getting right with god," in Odysseus' case the angered Poseidon. We hear Christian overtones in references to "chains," "difficult roads," "weary hearts," and "salvation." A protagonist whose career is shaped by a prophecy is a staple of myth, seen for example, in the myths of Achilles, Oedipus, or Narcissus. This oracle structures *O Brother*; it gives an indication of its magical and mythic aspect, and how it will be a tale of upsettings and transformations. But our problematic heroes must first further travel more widely in this netherworld.

As in the *Odyssey*, the theme of hospitality is important, as well as kinship bonds.[42] Pete's cousin receives them and removes their shackles. The Great Depression's hardships are obvious; instead of the feast of Alcinous' palace, they eat nearly rancid meat from a horse that Wash Hogwallop had to butcher. We learn of suicides, foreclosed homes, a child dead of mumps, and his wife,

40 Rowell (2007), 253–63.
41 See Flensted-Jensen (2002), 17–18; Heckel (2005a), 58. References found in Siegel (2007), n. 21.
42 Toscano (2009), 50.

Cora, who "run off." As they sit in the darkened parlor, "Pappy O' Daniel Flour Hour" is on the radio, playing "You Are My Sunshine"; the governor's disembodied voice sounds godlike, oracular. Broken by poverty, Wash betrays them for the reward and they wake to the voice of the deputy demanding surrender. Everett wants to "negotiate," but he can do little except confess "we are in a tight spot"—four times. At this point, unlike his Greek counterpart, Everett seems at a loss for words. The truly demonic figure of Sheriff Cooley appears, a pursuing Devil figure whose mirrored glasses reflect Hellish fire. But here the demons are also buffoons, and cause their own ammo truck to explode.

They escape, thanks to Hogwallop's small son, not Everett's cleverness. When their getaway car breaks down in a town "two weeks from everywhere," Everett declares that, as a tactician, he is prepared, and, grinning, tosses to Pete an expensive watch stolen from Pete's own cousin. Pete is shocked and angered; how can such a man be trusted? Their argument is interrupted by the gentle voices of a white-clad congregation walking to the river to be baptized, singing "Down to the River to Pray," an old time hymn, in origin African American, with coded references to escape from slavery. They wear rapt expressions and move as if in a trance, recalling the Lotus Eaters in the *Odyssey*.[43] The Christian search for salvation, often connected to water and baptism, is likewise evoked, and saving water, along with hellish fire, are two major symbolic elements for this movie. The skeptical Everett says, "I guess hard times flush the chumps. Everybody's lookin' for answers," while the simple Delmar suddenly rushes forward. Delmar is a holy fool, a decent fellow once driven by desperation to commit crime, and yearns to be saved. His confession, and joyous proclamation of his forgiveness, even goads the otherwise nasty Pete, who also rushes to be baptized. The desire for forgiveness, purity, a fresh break with a sinful past, is a perennial utopian dream, a vision of paradise central to the mythos of Southern fundamentalism. Everett, here the scornful rationalist, will be saved by his own prayer and a much vaster baptism, the TVA deluge, as he and his friends are about to be hanged.[44]

THE RECOVERY OF MUSIC

At Delmar's urging, they give a ride to Tommy, a well-dressed black man with a guitar. Tommy claims he was at a crossroads the previous midnight, to sell his soul to the Devil to receive the gift of playing the guitar "real good." Tommy, unrelated to any character in the *Odyssey*, is modeled on the legendary Southern blues guitar player Robert Johnson, who died at twenty-eight, sometimes conflated with his contemporary Tommy Johnson. He had disappeared for a while

43 Flensted-Jensen (2002), 18.
44 Rowell (2007), 251. Note, for example, the saving flood at the end, and how Sheriff Cooley, when Pete is reprieved from hanging, says, as it begins to rain, "Sweet summer rain. Like God's own mercy." See Pollio (2007), 24–26.

and then came back a much better player, hence the legend that he sold his soul to the Devil.[45] This is an old archetype, traced at least to Jesus' famous saying, "For what will it profit a man if he gains the whole world and forfeits his soul?" (Mark 8:36, Matt. 16:26), and it connects to various later Christian legends and the Faust legend. There are ample versions of the Faust legend in American literature (especially "The Devil and Daniel Webster," by Stephen Vincent Benét, made, for example, into the 1941 movie *All That Money Can Buy*, and the television episode "The Devil and Homer Simpson"). Significantly, Tommy sold his soul because he wasn't using it. For an African American, whose ancestors could be bought and sold, and who were then living in apartheid conditions, the implication is that to prosper, and even to survive, required making a deal with the Devil, that is, the white power structure, who looks exactly like Sheriff Cooley, down to his big dog.[46] Sheriff Cooley's character has evident religious, historical, and metatheatrical dimensions. Southern fundamentalism thunders on about Satan's power; the Southern sheriff is a common symbol of corrupt Southern politics and culture.[47] If we consider instances of police brutality in Baltimore, Ferguson, and elsewhere, this image has current resonances. The name Cooley probably evokes the evil Warden in *Cool Hand Luke* (1967), a prison escape movie important for *O Brother*.[48]

But Tommy recalls another singer-musician who had dealings with the king of Death: Orpheus, who interestingly has been portrayed in modern cinema as a talented black young man, seen most prominently in Marcel Camus' Brazilian version of the myth, *Black Orpheus* (1959), but also in the 2000 Hallmark miniseries *Jason and the Argonauts*.[49] Tommy and Everett are both uncanny (and musical) men of destiny, whose fortunes are linked in supernatural ways to bring benefit to both themselves as individuals and to their larger communities, including transcending racial boundaries. Everett, of course, comically declares that he remains "unaffiliated," choosing neither God nor Devil. But when Tommy mentions the possibility of making money through song,

45 See Flensted-Jensen (2002), 15, and Ruppersburg (2003), 17; Clarke (1999), "Johnson, Robert."

46 One of the standard features of Hades is the dog Cerberus. But Cooley's dog, used to track the prisoners, is probably a bloodhound, which is how the Furies are characterized in Aeschylus' *Eumenides*, uncompromising spirits of retribution who scorn modern concepts of law—like Sheriff Cooley.

47 See Placide and LaFrance (2014).

48 Ruppersberg (2003), 12.

49 On this see Cyrino (2015), who discusses the idea of "back enchantment" in cinematic representations, applicable indeed to our Tommy Johnson and his enthralling guitar music. Cyrino refers to Gabbard's idea (2004, 6) of "Black Angels" as "a transformational figure, who appears, seemingly out of nowhere, in the plot of the film to help, heal, and ultimately validate the white protagonist" (Cyrino, 2015, 122). She notes how this trope appears profusely and strongly in the films of the new millennium. On Tommy Johnson as Orpheus and "Black Angel," see Cyrino (2015), 130. For other millennial examples, see Cyrino (2015), 131.

Everett's cunning instincts pay attention. They come to a radio station (with the humorous letters WEZY); and, Everett, saying "All right boys, just follow my lead," tells more than he knows.

Myth's divine poet is inspired, untaught by anybody, and the Hesiodic bard can utter divine secrets. Accordingly, Everett, despite his recent mockery, introduces himself and his band as "Jordan Rivers and the Soggy Bottom Boys" and declares they sing "Songs of Salvation to Salve the Soul." This is a critical episode in the Quest/Journey when the mythic hero faces a contest or situation that reveals previously undiscovered powers, like unschooled Telemachus giving a proper formal greeting to Nestor. It is also a moment when the hero asserts some aspect of his true identity. This moment has its parallel when Odysseus finally reveals his identity to the assembled Phaeacians and then plays his bardic role as he narrates his recent (and highly symbolic) life for the first time. Marvelously, Everett produces a wonderful and engaging song at first go; the Muses must be at work, and Everett is revealed as an authentic folksinger, as Odysseus is an exceptional storyteller.[50]

The very title "Man of Constant Sorrow" recalls the etymology of Odysseus' name[51] but also the phrase *mala d'eimi polustonos* "I am a much suffering man" (*Od.* 19.118), a phrase Odysseus uses to identify himself to Penelope.[52] Odysseus' pain and sorrow are foregrounded on the proem and help define him ("who suffered deep in his heart many pains upon the sea" *Od.* 1.4), a persona he maintains in his Phaeacian tales.[53] It also recalls the "man of sorrow" and acquainted with grief, described in Isaiah 53:3, later interpreted as referring to Jesus (e.g., Handel's *Messiah*).[54] Odysseus gave nearly as good as he got, but there is nothing triumphant in the "Man of Constant Sorrow," however bouncy the tune. The song becomes a huge hit precisely because the problematic Everett voices the sorrow of the Depression's suffering and hopeless population. The loss of helpful friends, of home, and of love are metonyms for the entire spectrum of human loss, as heaven is for human hope. "Man of Constant Sorrows" is juxtaposed to Pappy O'Daniel's "You Are My Sunshine," which can represent utopian hope, but also the Reaganesque "morning in America" sloganeering whose sugar-coated dreams mask the people's real agony.

---

50   For the epic poet as instructed by the gods, who sing through him, see Finkelberg (1990) and *Od.* 8.73–74, 22.347–48.

51   The name Odysseus is linked to the Greek verb *odussomai*, which suggests one who is angry but also incurs anger. See Stanford (1952) for further discussion.

52   Goldhill (2007), 265.

53   E.g., "Cares are to me in my soul even more than contests, / I who earlier suffered many things and toiled much." (*Od.* 8.154–55), "But now I am held by evil and pains; for I have suffered many things, experiencing the wars of men and painful waves" (*Od.*8.184–85). There is also the epithet "the long-suffering hero" (*Od.* 8.199 and famously in the proem.)

54   Ruppersburg (2003), 21.

"Man of Constant Sorrow" is also a traditional American folk song, which first appeared in a 1913 songbook and was first recorded by Dick Burnett,[55] himself a partially blind fiddler hailing from Kentucky, curiously, like George Clooney.[56] The lyrics seem to be autobiographical and refer to Burnett's blindness "for six long years" and thus have a literal meaning as well.[57]

The Coens' intercut shots of the Soggy Bottom Boys singing enthusiastically with the radio-owner listening, smiling, and clearly loving the music. This juxtaposition guides our interpretations, as does Everett's reaction as he finishes singing, one of genuine joy, a thrill beyond cold cash. He tells Tommy with happy irony, "I almost believe you *did* sell your soul to the devil!" They then briefly encounter the coarse Pappy and his counselors (he dismisses them as "crackers"), again a strong juxtaposition of the power of mass communicating and true communication. And the excesses of Pappy and his obese son provide a strong contrast with the sorrowful tune Tommy later sings at the campfire, "Hard Time Killing Floor Blues." No song of feel-good evasion, this ballad describes the rigors of the thirties' Depression; composed by Skip James in 1931, it speaks of the hardships of being black and poor and working at the slaughter houses (killing floors), its detail more truly capturing the horror of poverty and its accompanying degradation.

DESCENDING DEEPER

That evening, Everett asks Delmar and Pete what they are going to do with their share of the money from his supposed heist. In different ways, they both have dreams of being somebody with status, of being bona fide, of escaping the prison of poverty. Everett's Odysseus has manipulated his men's desire for a true homecoming, which is more than a physical return, also a return to respectability, an important theme of the *Odyssey* as well. Delmar says he will buy back the family farm, for a man without land is nobody. This loss of the family farm explains Delmar's fall into crime. Pete almost catches Everett out again—why has Everett no plans?—but Everett is saved by another interruption. The sheriff's men have comically assumed they are hiding in another barn and intend to burn it down with them in it, without giving them a chance to surrender. They flee, their car abandoned.

Their fortunes improve, paradoxically in meeting Baby Face Nelson, a mythic figure of America's native underworld mythology, a chaos monster, a

---

55 The song in the film is itself performed by Dan Timinski. As with other traditional songs, it has been rerecorded multiple times.

56 See also Wolfe (1973). See further the Daily Show interview with Ralph Stanley, on Oct. 9, 2009. http://thedianerehmshow.org/shows/2009-10-14/#27945. Accessed Nov. 20, 2014.

57 And the layering of roles here goes much deeper; see Chadwell (2004), 3–4. Weinlich (2005), 98, interprets the lyrics as autobiographical for the singer Everett, and containing a sort of covert message to Penny.

suitable figure for this *Odyssey*.[58] Outlaws were then a staple of popular myth (think Bonny and Clyde or Dillinger). Nelson, like Everett, is overcompensating for feelings of inferiority. His maniac proclaiming of his identity as he defies the police recalls Odysseus' foolish mocking of Polyphemus during which he tells him his name and brings the wrath of Poseidon down upon himself[59]; both are addicted to the rush of "being on top." Of course, "being on top" is part of the new American way, as is the violence he indulges as in a game, as he machine-guns the cattle. After Nelson's crime spree, they sit on broken Greek and Roman columns, probably the remains of a ruined plantation house, representing the broken mythos of Southern traditions, of a time when the Old South was more "on top." We recall how Greek myth itself looks wistfully back to the imagined glories of the Bronze Age. Meanwhile a music producer is seeking the Soggy Bottom Boys, since, unknown to them, the whole state has "gone ape" over their song.

Soon they discover three seductive, lightly clad, and wet women washing clothes by a river, singing a sensuous lullaby song "Go to Sleep You Little Baby." The scene, recalling the *Odyssey*'s Sirens, speaks to the irresistible and powerful danger of song and temptation; note the line "You and me and the Devil makes three." The *Odyssey*'s Circe is also alluded to, since the sorceress (who also can sing beautifully) turns Odysseus' men into swine, while here Pete is turned into a "horny toad," as Delmar believes.[60] But the scene also recalls Odysseus' meeting with Nausicaa when she is washing clothes (*Od.* 4.57–98), with ironic changes.[61] There Odysseus follows the "Shipwrecked Sailor meets the Princess Pattern" and immediately comments on Nausicaa's beauty and potential as a wife. Here again Everett fails his model; Odysseus is a master manipulator of women (except Penelope), but Everett's words and cunning prove useless and he cannot save his "transformed" comrade.

At a fine restaurant, where the governor eats with his team (with Homer's bust in the background), Everett and Delmar meet the one-eyed Big Dan Teague, equated to the Odyssean Cyclops. Like Polyphemus, Teague marks out these strangers and potential victims, and shows considerable appetite as he eats the food provided for him.[62] The Cyclopes were notable for their monstrous form and lawlessness, having no respect for the Gods (or God, since he claims to

---

58 As Ruppersberg (2003), 13, notes, almost nothing about Nelson in *O Brother* conforms to the historically real figure.

59 Siegel (2007), 238; also Flensted-Jensen (2002), 27.

60 Siegel (2007), 223; Danek (2002), 87.

61 Toscano (2009), 49. Also Weinlich (2005), 105.

62 Siegel (2007), 224. Note that Odysseus first helped himself to the Cyclops' cheese; but here it is the Cyclops who cages a meal from Everett and Delmar. Goldhill (2007), 266–67, cleverly observes that whereas Polyphemus in the *Odyssey* eats Odysseus' companions "marrow, bone and all," "Teague eats a chicken fricassee, sucks on the bone . . . and then squishes what the travelers think is their companion."

make money selling God's Word)[63] or the sacred rituals of hospitality.[64] Teague is able to prey on Everett's own greed, belief in religion as a scam (note how Teague states that "Folks're lookin' for answers"), a tendency to be impressed with ornate formal vocabulary, and his confidence in his powers, to set Everett up for robbery and assault with a branch, a very primitive weapon. The way Teague crushes the toad/Pete recalls the gruesome way Polyphemus handled Odysseus' men. And it is Delmar who fights back and gets beaten up, while the "hero" Everett doesn't even try to resist.

HITTING ROCK BOTTOM

The nadir of Everett's fortunes comes as they finally return as hitchhikers to Ithaca,[65] Mississippi, and to Penny, Everett's Penelope. Everett recognizes his daughters at a rally for Homer Stokes, singing the gospel tune "In the Highways." These musical girls recognize their father immediately. In *Odyssey* 16 Odysseus' reunion with Telemachus, who at first doubts the beggar is Odysseus, is problematic. Here the children were told by Penny that he had been hit by a train and was dead, unlike Homer's Penelope, who insists Odysseus is alive when she has good reason to think the opposite. As Telemachus tells Odysseus about the suitors, the girls inform him that Penny has a suitor who has given her a big ring. They agree with their mother; Everett is not bona fide. Thus to those who mean the most to him, Everett has become No-Man, symbolically dead. And her suitor Waldrip is the oily campaign manager for the evil Homer. Meeting Penny and Waldrip in the Woolworth's, Penny berates Everett as a shameful man with no prospects, and since her girls are looking to her for answers, she must do what it takes to survive. Penny's harsh realism is a perfect counterpoint to Everett's delusions. She seems hardly the loyal Penelope, but, as Pollio[66] notes, she wrote to Everett in prison to tell him she was getting married, and the wistful look on her face after she meets him indicates some love remains. Further, it should be noted that Odysseus' Penelope, by announcing the bow contest, could not foretell the outcome—which could have resulted (as far as she knew) in having to marry one of the suitors.

---

63 Pollio (2007), 25. Teague, like Polyphemus, is also a sort of "shepherd"; Siegel (2007), 224.

64 Polyphemus says to Odysseus: "You are childish-, O stranger, or you are come from far away, / you who order me to either fear or avoid the gods! / For the Cyclopes do not care for aegis-bearing Zeus, / Or the great gods, since we are braver by far. / Nor would I, fearing the hatred of Zeus, spare / either you or your comrades, unless my heart should command me" (*Od.*9. 272–78).

65 Everett's return as a hitchhiker can be tied to Odysseus' returning in another's ship, fulfilling the curse of Polyphemus.

66 Pollio (2007), 26.

Waldrip intends soon to marry Everett's former wife and uses his Dapper Dan as the suitors eat Odysseus' pigs and court Penelope.[67] At the palace Odysseus gains increasing command of the situation, while here, after exchanging insults, Waldrip beats him up in a fight Everett provoked, recalling the bout between the beggar Odysseus and Iros, whose brutal beating foretold Odysseus' future victory against the suitors.[68] After he is tossed out of Woolworth's, Penny says of him, "He's not my husband . . . just some no-account drifter."[69] This is the lowest point of his quest, for he has truly lost the identity and hope he struggled to come home for. But then the dramatic curve bends upward.

The scene in the cinema recalls Odysseus' *nekyia*, his journey to the verge of the underworld, where he confers with souls and receives the prophecy of Tiresias. Mythically speaking, this is an episode where the hero in some way dies to his old self and is reborn. After their trips to the Deadlands, both Odysseus and Aeneas gain new strength to accomplish their missions.[70] Indeed, Everett recalls Aeneas, as one who has repeatedly fallen short in his true path, especially in respect to Dido, and needs to be transformed to Roman Aeneas. The theater's darkness suggests an oracular and necromantic moment where the dead meet the living. There is indeed something ghostlike about the pale troop of prisoners in the flickering light. In *Sullivan's Travels*, Sullivan, still a prisoner, is brought into a black church to watch cartoons, and the pastor welcomes them as souls who need forgiveness, and Sullivan recognizes the power of popular comedy.[71] *O Brother*'s movie, where aristocrats watch an alluring woman in shorts dance and do gymnastics, is cartoonish, and provokes Everett's various misogynistic comments; He sounds more like the bitter Agamemnon in the Deadlands than Odysseus. An armed guard whistles in a troop of ghostlike prisoners, including Pete, who warns Everett and Delmar the Sheriff is prepared to ambush them, as Agamemnon warns about a possible ambush when Odysseus returns to Ithaka.

THE ASCENT UPWARD BEGINS

This moment of encounter with the symbolically dead Pete revives the heroism of Everett. A scene at Pappy's mansion has shown his campaign is on the ropes too. Having lost Penny, Everett has no real reason to rescue Pete, but faces real danger in doing so. This choice also reflects the choice of Odysseus to return to Penelope; he has not seen her in twenty years, and has no idea what he might find other than assured opposition and the prospect of old age and death. But

---

67   Everett, seeing the baby in Penny's arms, asks "What's this?" The baby looks under a year old, but not a newborn, and it is possible that Everett went to prison before Penny even knew she was pregnant. Or has she had out-of-wedlock relations with Waldrip?

68   Danek (2002), 86; Heckel (2005a), 60.

69   Just as Penelope first thought the beggar Odysseus was.

70   Siegel (2007), 230. See Holtsmark (2001) for further information on adaptation of the *katabasis* pattern in modern film.

71   Rowell (2007), 248.

his love for Penelope and his home make him choose a return to struggle. Amid darkness, thunder, and lightning, Everett and Delmar invade the jail barracks (adorned with the sign of the noose) and rescue Pete. Note how they put on blackface, which helps them travel unnoticed at night, as well as making them "black." Forgiveness is a major theme, and this rescue prompts Pete's remorseful confession that he betrayed them. This honesty goads Everett to admit his own lies about the hidden loot, a confession that is also part of regaining his identity and self-understanding. And there is risk involved.

In the ensuing fight Pete and Everett roll downhill, a metaphoric form of descent into a deeper region of Hell, here the edge of a KKK lynching ceremony. The ceremony is far more elaborate than any historically real ceremony, presenting what Roger Ebert called a cross between "Busby Berkeley and 'Triumph of the Will',"[72] while also recalling the "March of the Winkies" from the *Wizard of Oz*, another American myth.[73] The Coens make the Klansmen look both menacing and ridiculous at the same time.[74] The torches and the burning cross evoke the same hellfire that Sheriff Cooley is associated with.[75] Going to the rescue, the three evoke the scene in *The Wizard of Oz* where the Tin Man, the Cowardly Lion, and the Scarecrow (all on their own quests) steal uniforms to rescue Dorothy from the Wicked Witch of the West.

Here we see, mythically speaking, a nocturnal mystery ritual, a type of human sacrifice (also seen in *Pan's Labyrinth* and *Such Is Life*), a ritual centered around the symbol of the burning cross and handing over to the infernal powers an accursed victim.[76] The song "O Death" sung by the Grand Dragon (Stokes) in a red costume underscores this dimension, as do the white-robed Klansmen and the burning cross. Here embattled Southern culture will make a human sacrifice in an attempt to preserve itself. The opening of the speech by Stokes aka the Grand Dragon connects the ideological dots (Fig. 2.2).

> Brothers! We are foregathered here to preserve our hallowed culture'n heritage! From intrusions, inclusions and dilutions! Of culluh! Of creed! Of our ol'-time religion! We aim to pull evil up by the root! Before it chokes out the flower of our culture'n heritage! And our women! Let's not forget those ladies, y'all, lookin' to us for p'tection! From darkies! From Jews! From Papists! And from all those smart-ass folk say we come descended from monkeys! That's not *my* culture'n heritage! . . . (A ROAR FROM CROWD) Izzat *your* culture'n heritage? . . . (ANOTHER ROAR) . . . And so . . . we gonna hang us a neegra!

---

72 http://www.rogerebert.com/reviews/o-brother-where-art-thou-2000. Accessed Apr. 28, 2016.
73 Toscano (2009), 53.
74 Siegel (2007), 232.
75 Pollio (2007), 24.
76 In Classical myth and religion, black victims (like Tommy) were sacrificed to the underworld (chthonic) gods. Note how later Homer Stokes declares "And these boys here trampled all over our venerated observances an' rich'ls!" Siegel (2007), 232.

FIGURE 2.2 Homer Stokes, Grand Dragon of the KKK at rally.

Note the mention of the need to protect white women. In 2015, the young man steeped in white extremist thought who was shooting up a black church in Charleston, South Carolina, made explicit mention of how black men were raping white women. As mentioned, here the coming TVA flood symbolizes a wave of change that threatens the traditional South; a similar wave is now present.

The truly great Greco-Roman heroes rescue humans from the powers of death, as Heracles does. The guilt ridden Tommy thinks "the devil's come to collect his due!" But the central Christian hero, Jesus, is through grace able to save even those whose sins should send them to Hell. Everett, Pete, and Delmar, like Jesus, save the basically noble Tommy from what was more mistake than Satanic sin. Everett's role as true hero began with Pete's rescue. Now they will defy more formidable powers: Homer, Dan Teague, and the massed Klansmen. They take down the three-man color guard (presenting Homer's great fear, as he proclaims, "The color guard is colored!") and manage to smash the Cyclops (Teague) by breaking the infernal symbol of power, the flaming cross, which also recalls the burning olive pole that Odysseus thrusts into the Cyclops' eye.[77]

THE SUITOR DEFEATED, AN EVIL PURGED

The ensuing scene of recognition and restoration of our hero takes places in a great hall (here the town hall), a political rally for Grand Dragon Homer Stokes, as with the climactic battle in the *Odyssey* occurring in Odysseus' *megaron* or great hall. But first Pete again challenges Everett: "Who elected you leader of this outfit?" and lists the troubles he has gotten them into; even Delmar is unsupportive. Note how Everett says, regarding who has turned against him, "The whole world and God Almighty . . . and now you," reflecting how a god turned against Odysseus.[78] Earlier Everett confessed his deceit; here he drops his verbose bluster, admits mistakes, and pleads for one last chance. Odysseus disguised himself as

---

77   Heckel (2005a), 60.
78   Pollio (2007), 27.

a beggar to infiltrate the palace, and Everett and company disguise themselves as hillbillies[79]; just as Odysseus' victory began with a display of his unique skill (here archery), Everett uses his unique musical skill to save the day. In the *Odyssey* Odysseus revealed who he really was, while Everett does not so much show who he really is (escaped convict) as display the new identity he has assumed. Delmar plays a crucial role; while Everett tries to speak to Penny, Delmar sings his solo of "In the Jailhouse Now" (and suddenly his identity as simpleton slips away). It tells of "Ramblin' Bob / Who used to steal gamble and rob / He thought he was the smartest guy around . . . He's in the jailhouse now." This clearly relates to Everett, who overestimates his intellect, practices deceit, and ends up in jail. Everett indeed still does not grasp the need for honesty, since he tells Penny he plans to practice dentistry with a fake license.[80]

Penelope in the *Odyssey* does not know the beggar is Odysseus in disguise; Penny indeed knows it is Everett, but not that he leads the Soggy Bottom Boys. She rejects him and his usual lying ways. But as the first cords of "Man of Constant Sorrow" play, the audience erupts; there occurs an a-ha moment of recognition for Everett, when the hero finally acknowledges potentials he was not aware he had, is accepted by his family and community, and reenters society in a privileged position. Homer, enraged about the recently disrupted KKK rituals, declares to all how the Soggy Bottom Boys are not white, have interrupted the Klan's performance of a lawful lynching, and are escaped criminals who should be remanded back to prison. It is ideologically significant that Homer declares that their music is not even "old timey." Homer is unplugged, pelted with vegetables, and ridden out on a rail.[81] Although Pappy dismissed Everett and company earlier, now the portly Pappy climbs onstage, attempts down-home dancing, pardons them, and even promises to make the clearly integrated band members his "brain trust."

Odysseus was trying to regain his identity as king of Ithaka and husband of Penelope, but many forces conspired to make him No-man, either through threats to his life or through a loss of identity. The *Odyssey* plays with identities; not only does Odysseus don a beggar's disguise, but also the background (and noble behavior) of Eumaeus shakes the presumption of aristocratic virtue and servile vice evident in the *Iliad*. Hospitality and how one treats the stranger and poor man is also a mark of civilization in the *Odyssey*, where there is a Zeus of Friendship, and beggars come from Zeus. *O Brother* also upends traditional racial structures. The first chained prisoners we observe are black, and

---

79 Toscano (2009), 50; Siegel (2007), 235.

80 Interestingly, Weinlich (2005), 95, notes how "While many of Odysseus' falsehoods originate in his intention to save himself and his comrades from death, Everett is mainly self-centered when he is lying."

81 Siegel (2007), 236, makes an interesting comparison with the brutal punishment Melanthios suffers before his execution.

the prophet is black, as is the Faust-like figure Tommy. Not only does Everett claim to the radio station owner that he and the crew are black, but in several places they are assumed to be black to some extent or another.[82] The horrified Homer even suggests they are the product of black-white interrelations, probably a black man and a white woman.

But now instead we have a utopian moment when the powers of music and the feeling of oppression it expresses moves classes, races, and even leaders to change heart, to transcend traditional boundaries, to expel the forces of evil and reject the ideology of virulent racism. Soon the Soggy Bottom Boys, including a black member, are singing at Pappy's behest "You Are My Sunshine," which recalls "Happy Days Are Here Again," the campaign song for Roosevelt's 1932 run. Ulysses Everett has now realized his true potential as bard and speaks with a newfound sincerity, but he also preserves the cleverness and adaptability of Odysseus; when the governor asks them to sing his theme song, he says, "Governor, that's one of our favorites"; O'Daniel replies "Son, you gonna go far," pointing to the possibility of a continuation of this more ideal configuration.

THE TEST AND DEATH STRUGGLE

Everett's prior clueless cunning lingers; he figures they'll just get married with the ring that Waldrip gave Penny, to which she indignantly replies, "We ain't gettin' married with *his* ring. You said you'd changed!" The restoration of Odysseus involves a rehearsal and renewal of his past. The stories he tells to the Phaeacians, prefaced by the declaration of Odysseus of his identity ("I am Odysseus, child of Laertes" *Od.*9.19.20), help sum his life, especially the account of his visit to the Deadlands (where figures from his past provide important details and perspectives). In book 19 the discovery of Odysseus' scar leads to an account of how he acquired that mark of adult status, and, then moving further back, explains the origin of his very name, given to him by his grandfather, the master thief Autolycus, which symbolizes his cunning nature. The bow contest replays the contest through which Odysseus obtained Penelope. Even after he has killed the suitors and reunited with her, he must visit Laertes, a kind of *deus otiosus* (an idle god), who once planted a garden for Odysseus, as Yahweh did for Adam in the Bible.

Likewise, Everett must face new tests after Homer is cast out and Pappy is made secure in his rule. He must firmly confront the past to move on to the future. Accordingly, Penny demands Everett obtain the original wedding ring from their cabin, which is exactly in the region where Everett claimed the stolen money was. The true ring is located in the original place of their marriage.

82   Rowell (2007), 263–64.

In the *Odyssey* Penelope tricks the trickster into revealing a secret of their marriage, the immovable bed he fashioned, symbolic of their marriage's enduring quality. Everett must prove that, amid his transformations, he is able to find the true enduring symbol of their wedlock. That cabin was tied to their initially more idyllic wedded past, as well as to the delusions that seduced Everett, symbolized by the needless number of Dapper Dan cans. So the quest to find the true ring is a test of the identity of Everett as husband, a form of displaced punishment and atonement, a final confrontation with his past, and a heroic deed that brings benefit to his community.

The hero often faces a direct encounter with the forces of death and evil, here in the form of Sheriff Cooley, who like Poseidon is a lawless pursuer who has set an ambush. But he is a sort of Hades figure as well, fitting perfectly with Tommy's description of the Devil. As Frye points out, a central theme of comedy is the breaking of unjust laws.[83] The Sheriff is a demonic figure representing blind vengeance, bad justice, bad guilt, and so forth. Interestingly, when Everett tells Cooley that he cannot hang them because the governor has just pardoned them ("It went out on the radio!"), Cooley responds, "Well, we ain't got a radio," which mirrors Poseidon's defiance of Zeus' command that Odysseus be allowed to return and attempt to drown him,[84] which can be connected with his statement that the Law is a human institution.

While they face hanging, the three black gravediggers sing "Lonesome Valley"; in the context of Southern black lynchings, they suggest spirits of the dead giving advice to those about to die. The critical lyric is "Oh, you got to ask the Lord's forgiveness / Nobody else can ask Him for you." It is time for Everett to drop disguises and accept a truth he knows, and that Delmar and even Pete accepted before, that he, as a sinful man, has done wrong. His prayer also repeats movingly Odysseus' own desire to be back with his family,[85] which has been broken by his actions, and to save his friends, who face death because of him. Everett displays the true bardic power in his improvised prayer, which (mythologically speaking) moves even the gods. Prayer and singing are often linked. And God seems to answer with an apocalyptic deluge; note that the song continues to play in the background as items representing his life (e.g., a banjo, a phonograph, and the Sheriff's dog and sunglasses) float by. The numerous Dapper Dan cans represent Everett's pretension; they pop up from the water as he does.

---

83 Frye (1957), 163–70.

84 Toscano (2009), 50; Siegel (2007), 239. A further irony here is that it is Sheriff Cooley, the Poseidon figure, who is drowned.

85 Siegel (2007), 218. See *Od.* 7.223–25: "But you with dawn's appearing rouse yourselves to place me wretched and having suffered many things upon my fatherland. Let life leave me having seen my possessions, my slaves, and my great, high-roofed house." See also Pollio (2007), 25–26.

Emerging from the water after another baptism, the three cling to a coffin,[86] again symbolic of rebirth and escape from death; Odysseus, nearly drowned by Poseidon, comes up and sits in the fragments of his broken raft (*Od.* 5. 324–26).[87] Pete declares it a miracle, but Everett tries to walk back his confession and returns to his Age of Enlightenment shtick[88]; the deluge is the sign of a new era; note that the promise of the TVA's coming transformations were often couched in religious terms.[89] But when he sees the prophesized cow on the roof, Everett repeats the words "about time" sotto voce, suggesting that he realizes it is "about time" to temper his rationalism. At least, as Toscano notes,[90] Delmar and Pete were promised (falsely) great wealth, the canonical American treasure. But they have gotten a greater boon: social forgiveness and reintegration into society.

THE HAPPY ENDING AND LOOKING FORWARD

In the final scene in town, Everett declares to Penny, "I'm awful pleased my adventuring days is at an end." In the *Odyssey*, once Odysseus has demonstrated he is bona fide, they finally reunite: "And rejoicing they came to the bond of their bed of old" (*Od.* 23.295–96). But when Everett gives Penny the ring, she claims this is not the correct ring, and she seems prepared to walk away. A watershed (forgive the pun) moment, though, has passed. There is no returning to the status quo ante; for Everett, their relationship and even their society have evolved and remain dynamic. As Penny, Everett, and their strung-together children walk away, a sign appears: "Power and Light," alluding to the introduction of power through the TVA, and thus progress. The old world, and its ring, are gone and a new world has begun. Electrification is symbolic of the new era that will lighten the world, symbolizing the enlightenment Everett optimistically hopes for.

We observe ring composition, a "framing device,"[91] as the last shot shows the old blind railroad prophet, his prophecies now realized. Railroad tracks and trains are important reoccurring symbols in *O Brother*, signifying movement and guided direction, which is another word for both fate and the cleverness of the author's plotting. Although the couple are still bickering as they leave our sight, we hear the children's voices, and then the black prophet whose handcar is going away singing, "My latest sun is sinking fast, my race is nearly run, / My strongest trials now are past, my triumph has begun! / O come, angel band, come and around me stand / O bear me away on your snowy wings to my immortal home." These are good indicators that Everett's adventure days

---

86 Cant (2007), 67–68, notes a connection to the end of *Moby Dick* here.
87 Siegel (2007), 240.
88 Pollio (2007), 26.
89 Rowell (2007), 256.
90 Toscano (2009), 57.
91 Ruppersburg (2003), 10.

are done and he has arrived home, and has fulfilled his destiny. Everett could never go back to the same home again; he is more like Aeneas, whose *nostos* is a new beginning for himself and his people.[92]

IDEAL DIMENSIONS IN REGRESSIVE TIMES: PUBLIC BENEFIT, COMMUNITY, AND INDIVIDUAL REDEMPTION

More than seventy years later, some see Everett's South as containing many retrograde and racist aspects and backsliding into darkness. But to assert that the film suggests no rebirth, no social change, misses the main thrust of this historical fantasy, that the power of music, channeled through its problematic but basically noble hero, could, for a brief shining moment, make hard-core racists reject the Klan, and joyously support a governor who will make an interracial band part of his "brain trust." It is myth of an imaginary past that can give hope for now.

The truly happy ending should be public, benefiting the hero's society or even creating a new one.[93] The exile/incarceration of Everett, Pete, and Delmar engage issues of public justice, although the Coens declare no manifestos.[94] The *Odyssey* begins with a discussion of justice: Zeus had warned Aegisthus not to take Agamemnon's wife, and has gotten proper punishment from Agamemnon's son Orestes. Zeus acknowledges Odysseus' unjust exile, and finally helps him. *O Brother's* opening scene evokes the prison or prison escape movie (e.g., *I Am a Fugitive from a Chain Gang*,[95] *Cool Hand Luke, Down by Law*), in which issues of justice are often central, and the transformation/redemption of escapees not uncommon. *O Brother*, with its focus on the hardships of the underclasses during the Depression, and revelation of the corruption of the wealthy, fairly openly criticizes American and Southern style democracy and capitalism, although the works of the TVA suggest how government can be a force for public betterment.

The issue of community is likewise important. Chains furnish an important framing device, for the chains of the prisoners seen at the opening will, in the last frame, be transformed into the string that ties the children of Penny and Everett to their parents,[96] and thus become a symbol of an enduring bond. The larger issue concerns what binds people together, and what breaks them apart, issues important for the *Odyssey* too. The question "O Brother, Where art Thou?" refers to the brother we can call on. The Klan is a demonic brotherhood, as well as an alternate government.[97] In a world where various forms of

---

92 This fact makes some critics doubt how committed the Coens were to the *nostos* theme. See Flensted-Jensen (2002), 24–25.

93 See Alvares (2002), 3–4.

94 Rowell (2007), xi, sees *O Brother* as providing a considerable critique of issues of justice.

95 Toscano (2009), 53, and Ruppersburg (2003), 12.

96 Rowell (2007), 246.

97 Siegel (2007), 232, quotes from Dixon's (1905) "To the Reader," who notes how the KKK has leaders for state, congressional districts, counties, and townships.

economic and political violence have sundered the bonds of community, what force can restore them?

O Brother is a tale of redemption and restoration for the protagonist, his comrades, his family, and his state. Not only are Delmar and Pete formally pardoned, and gain employment as the Soggy Bottom Boys, and even become part of the Governor's "brain trust"; they also have personal moments of redemption, as when Delmar is baptized and admits to robbing the Piggly Wiggly, or Pete confesses that he betrayed them, which is answered by Everett's own confession about the nonexistent treasure. Tommy is saved from hanging. Everett's family is restored too. There is a battle for control of the kingdom (Mississippi), with Menelaus "Pappy" O'Daniel fighting for his political life with a villain, Homer Stokes, a Grand Dragon of the KKK, a baleful secret society. The dragon symbolism is obvious. "Pappy/Father" of course is a major ancient honorific; thus Augustus was particularly proud of being named Pater Patriae (Father of the Fatherland). The Homeric Odysseus is being threatened by upstarts, as is Pappy, whose columned house recalls memories of the Old South. Often in myth sons have to save (sometimes problematic) fathers, which can represent the canonical political system. Thus Everett plays the role of the scorned outcast who ends up saving the King and the Kingdom from the forces of darkness as well as his family and himself.

The *Odyssey* provides a utopian ending, of sorts, in which the old order based on the traditional *basileus* (but with liberalizing modifications) is restored. In *O Brother* a transcendent love for music induces bigoted Mississippians to reject the Grand Dragon and confirm the (now improved) old order, again with liberalizing dimensions: elite society and the lower orders combine, pointing to a democratizing ideal.[98] The cleansing flood is tied to the TVA's electrification project, which Everett suggests will bring a new Enlightenment, just as they had in France, where the old "mumbo-jumbo" is dispensed with, and we are all "hooked up to the grid." The TVA's flood is a symbolic event that divides the premodern South from the modern (and electrified) present.[99] It is this present that Homer Stokes then and radical conservatives today are warring against. Images drawn from Judeo-Christian apocalypse, of battles between fire and water,[100] God and the Dragon, are joined to enlightenment utopian images. Everett tends to dismiss religion, but his own hit song has religious references,[101] and later, he makes the heartfelt prayer that precedes the saving flood. It may well be that, in this conflict of reason and religion, Everett comes to accept some of the sensibilities (if not the formalities) of religion as mediated by song. We cannot be quite sure.

---

98 Rowell (2007), 249, believes that Everett "epitomizes a truly democratic hero" who thrives in a group, unlike Odysseus, who alone survives.
99 Ruppersburg (2003), 23.
100 See Pollio (2007).
101 Rowell (2007), 254.

What makes this a movie for the new millennium? It shares with our other movies an adaptation and reworking of abiding cultural icons, mainly from the *Odyssey* and elements of Southern culture, but ones fitted to more current tastes, hopes, and fears, and, as Weinlich suggests, the sense of unpredictability and lack of control in a twenty-first-century hero's life.[102] The pastichelike quality reflects the postmodern attitude, which avoids overriding interpretive structures, an array of materials, mostly ironically presented, that invite each viewer to create his or her own valid *O Brother*. In the grim depiction of the Depression-era United States and the life of the lower class, their songs of pain and dreams of hope, the bankrupt political structures, the film evokes our current financial and political desperation. But we live in a time when many of us cannot believe in big heroes, and we all seem more like stooges than saints. We like to feel superior to Everett, but in his haplessness we also identify with him, and with the hope that we can find in ourselves, despite ourselves, some power and ability to restore our world. It is a hope beyond reason and knowledge, which may seem as silly as "The Big Rock Candy Mountain," but nevertheless one we respond to, and sometimes find ourselves believing in.

REFERENCES

Alvares, J. "Utopian Themes in Three Greek Romances." *Ancient Narrative*, vol. 2, 2002, 1–30.

Bergan R. *The Coen Brothers*. Orion, 2000.

Cant, J. "Homer in Tishomingo: Eclecticism and Cultural Transformation in the Coen Brothers' *O Brother Where Art Thou?*" *Comparative American Studies*, vol. 5 no. 1, 2007, 63–79.

Chadwell, S. "Inventing that 'Old-Timey' Style: Southern Authenticity in *O Brother, Where Art Thou?*" *Journal of Popular Film and Television*, vol. 32 no. 1 2004, 3–9.

Clarke, D. *The Penguin Encyclopedia of Popular Music*. Penguin, 1999.

Cyrino, M. "Magic, Music, Race: Screening 'Black Enchantment' after *Black Orpheus* (1959)." In M. Cyrino and M. Safran, *Classical Myth on Screen*. Palgrave Macmillan, 2015, pp. 121–132.

Danek, G. "Die *Odyssee* der Coen-Brüder. Zitatebenen in *O Brother, Where Art Thou?*" In K. Töchterle and M. Korenjak, ed., *Pontes II. Antike im Film*. Studien Verlag, 2002, pp. 84–94.

Dixon, T. *The Clansman: A Historical Romance of the Ku Klux Klan*. Doubleday Page, 1905.

Edwards, M. W. *Homer: Poet of the Iliad*. Johns Hopkins UP, 1987.

Filene, B. "Oh Brother, What Next? Making Sense of the Folk Fad." *Southern Cultures*, vol. 10 no. 2, 2004, 50–69.

---

102 Weinlich (2005), 106.

Finkelberg, M. "A Creative Oral Poet and the Muse." *American Journal of Philology*, vol. 111 no. 3, 1990, 293–303.

Fitzgerald, R., trans. *Homer's Odyssey*. Penguin, 1998 (original 1962).

Flensted-Jensen, P. "Something Old, Something New, Something Borrowed: The *Odyssey* and *O Brother, Where Art Thou?*" *Classica & Mediaevalia*, vol. 53, 2002, 13–30.

Frye, N. *Anatomy of Criticism: Four Essays*. Princeton UP, 1957.

Gabbard, K. *Black Magic: White Hollywood and African American Culture*. Rutgers UP, 2004.

Goldhill, S. "*Naked* and *O Brother, Where Art Thou?* The Politics and Poetics of Epic Cinema." In B. Graziosi and E. Greenwood, ed., *Homer in the 20th Century: Between World Literature and Western Canon*. Oxford UP, 2007, pp. 245–67.

Harries, M. "In the Coen Brothers' New Film, the Dark, Utopian Music of the American South." *Chronicle of Higher Education*, Feb. 2, 2001. B14-15.

Heckel, H. "Odysseus am Mississippi." *Des altsprachliche Unterricht*, vol. 48, 2005a, 58–62.

———. "Zurück in die Zukunft via Ithaca, Mississippi. Technik und Funktion der Homer-Rezeption in *O Brother, Where Art Thou?*" *International Journal of the Classical Tradition* vol. 11 no. 4, 2005b, 571–89.

Holtsmark, E. "The *Katabasis* Theme in Modern Cinema.' In M. Winkler, ed., *Classical Myth and Culture in the Cinema*. Oxford UP, 2001, pp. 23–50.

Kemp, J. "Professional Musicians in Ancient Greece." *Greece & Rome*, Second Series, vol. 13 no. 2, 1966, 213–22.

Kim, L. *Homer Between History and Fiction in Imperial Greek Literature*. Cambridge UP, 2010.

McFarland, D. "Philosophies of Comedy in *O Brother, Where Art Thou?*" In M. T. Conrad, ed., *The Philosophy of the Coen Brothers*. UP of Kentucky, 2009, pp. 41–54.

Perry, B. E. *The Ancient Romances: A Literary-historical Account of Their Origins*. Sather Classical Lectures, vol. 37. University of California Press, 1967.

Pischel, C. "'Include me out'—Odysseus on the Margins of European Genre Cinema: *Le Mépris, Ulisse, L'Odissea*." In J. Solomon and A.-B. Renger, *The Ancient Worlds in Film and Television*. Brill, 2013, pp. 195–212.

Placide, M., and C. LaFrance. "The County Sheriff in Films: A Portrait of Law Enforcement as a Symbol of Rural America." *International Journal of Police Science & Management*, vol. 16 no. 2, 2014, 101–12.

Pollio, D. M. "Baptizing Odysseus: *O Brother, Where Art Thou?* and Homer's *Odyssey*." *Classical Outlook*, vol. 85 no. 1, 2007, 23–27.

Rowell, E. "*O Brother, Where Art Thou?*: A Song." In *The Brothers Grim: The Films of Ethan and Joel Coen*. Scarecrow Press, 2007, pp. 243–76.

Ruppersburg, H. "'Oh, so many startlements . . . ': History, Race, and Myth in *O Brother, Where Art Thou?*" *Southern Cultures*, vol. 9 no. 4, 2003, 5–26.

Scodel, R. "Bardic Performance and Oral Tradition in Homer." *American Journal of Philology*, vol. 119 no. 2, 1998, 171–94.

Siegel, J. "The Coens' *O Brother, Where Art Thou?* and Homer's *Odyssey*." *Mouseion*, Series III, vol. 7 no. 3, 2007, 213–45.

Stanford, W. B. "The Homeric Etymology of the Name Odysseus." *Classical Philology*, vol. 47 no. 4, 1952, 209–13.

Toscano, M. "Homer Meets the Coen Brothers: Memory as Artistic Pastiche in *O Brother, Where Art Thou?*" *Classical Era: Film and History*, vol. 39 no. 2, 2009, 49–53.

Verreth, H. "Odysseus' Journey Through Film." In I. Berti and M. Morcillo, ed., *Hellas on Screen: Cinematic Receptions of Ancient History*. David Brown, 2008, pp. 65–73.

Weinlich, B. "'*Odyssey*, Where art Thou?' Myth and Mythmaking in the Twenty-first Century." *Classical and Modern Literature*, vol. 25 no. 2, 2005, 89–108.

Wolfe, C. K. "Man of Constant Sorrow: Richard Burnett's Story." *Old Time Music*, vol. 10, 1973, 6–11.

DISCUSSION QUESTIONS FOR PART I

1. The character of Odysseus is important in *Troy*. What do you think his role is, and why does the director include him as a sort of narrator of the tale, almost as if the movie gave his perspective?

2. One of the functions of myth is to provide solutions to insolvable problems. One is that we want to live, but we know we are going to die. What are some possible solutions to this issue that our movies present?

3. *Troy* makes two very radical departures from the canonical tale of Troy: having Menelaus killed early on, and having Briseis kill Agamemnon. How well do you think these alterations work for the story as a whole?

4. Myths as they are transmitted from one era to the next acquire components and perspectives alien to their original forms. How successfully does *O Brother* blend Christian and Classical themes?

5. How are both films, in different ways, about a confrontation of the modern world, or its perspectives, with older, more traditional cultural practices?

6. *Troy* and *O Brother* each has a female character who is a significant departure from the classical model, Briseis and Penny. How successful and significant are those portrayals?

7. In the *Iliad*, Achilles carries into battle a shield containing pictures of the whole cosmos and scenes summing up human life, suggesting the universality of his story. How "universal" do you think the story of Achilles in *Troy* is?

8. *Troy* is also very much the story of Hector too; to what extent is his story universal, perhaps even more so than Achilles'?

9. How do the ways in which *Troy* considers the power of fame and *O Brother* the power of music complement each other?

10. How effectively do you think *O Brother* presents substitutes for the Sirens, Circe, Polyphemus, Tiresias, and the Lotus Eaters? And do the members of the KKK function well as mythical beings?

PART

II

THE RELUCTANT HERO

HERCULES (2014)
CLASH OF THE TITANS (2010)
WRATH OF THE TITANS (2012)
IMMORTALS (2011)

HERCULES, CLASH OF THE TITANS/WRATH OF THE TITANS, AND IMMORTALS

The Fate of the hero, the Fate of the Gods

Jesus (citing *Psalm* 82) asked, "Is it not written in your scriptures, 'I have said you are "gods"'?" (John 10:34) The Classical Heracles was a man-god. Later, Classical heroes were replaced by miracle-working Christian saints. Nietzsche in *The Joyous Science* (1882) proclaimed "God is Dead," and Wagner,[1] once Nietzsche's inspiration, produced a great cycle of music and myth ending in the *Twilight of the Gods*, in which Wotan and the rest of the compromised gods perish. In *The Wild One* (1953), when Mildred asks, "Hey Johnny, what are you rebelling against?" Johnny (Marlon Brando) responds, "Whadda you got?" It seems everybody is looking for an antihero. Further, Freudian psychology, inspired by Greek myth, reveals the sometimes barely hidden desire to kill our parents, who stand as allegorical symbols for the current social order. Sordid family history maps onto brutal and blood-soaked national traditions; it is no accident that many languages speak of "motherland" and "fatherland." Yet a more positive view is that humans should surpass (even redeem) the gods, as parents should be surpassed (and even redeemed) by their children, as we move toward perfection, perhaps even toward a technological Singularity, with, in H. G. Wells's words, "Men Like Gods."

Myth's varied traditions present not a lecture, but an argument. We begin this section with the hero of heroes, Hercules, who has been reimagined in countless ways, including many sword-and-sandals and peplum movies. As in *O Brother, Where Art Thou?* there is a desperate situation, where divine forces,

---

1   Reading Aeschylus' *Oresteia* profoundly influenced Wagner's production of "stage festival dramas." See Ewans (1983).

both within and without, seem to be at work. In different ways, *Hercules* and *Immortals* present an ideal hero (and marvelous child) who has suffered trauma and disgrace, and must learn to accept fully his nature and potentials, which will have world-shaking consequences. Hercules is trapped between the mythologizing of his cousin Iolaus ("You know nothing. His father was Zeus!") and his terrible and real guilt over having killed his beloved family, guilt which defines and burdens him. In *Immortals*, after he has killed his own son Ares for helping Theseus, Zeus screams, "I have faith in you, Theseus. Prove me right! Lead your people!" which is a critical turning point for Theseus, as is the moment when the prophet Amphiaraus declares to the chained Hercules, "We have faith in you. . . . Remember the man that you are. Remember the deeds you have performed, the Labors you have accomplished! Now, tell me! Who are you?" In these critical moments Hercules and Theseus will tap into a hidden potential within them, as Ulysses Everett (also a disgraced criminal estranged from his family) did when asked to sing something properly "old timey," which began a transformational chain of events. Although we cannot break chains or topple massive statues of Hera, we can nevertheless identify with the earthiness of this Hercules, and allow his example to inspire us to break free of what chains us, and become who we are meant to be.

Clash of the Titans (*Clash*) and its sequel *Wrath of the Titans* (*Wrath*) and *Immortals* start from the same two mythic foundational elements and their implied questions, but come to far different conclusions, reflecting modern differences of perspectives and dreams. The elements: (1) The battle of the Olympians and the Titans, who are cast down into Tartarus; (2) The relationships of Olympians, Titans, and Humans in the evolving universe; and (3) Two subquestions, (3a) In what direction is the universe and its inhabitants evolving? and (3b) What is the relationship between gods, humans, and human choice and fate in that evolving universe?

In *Clash*/*Wrath* the Olympians created humanity to preserve their own immortality. They are brutal toward humans and to each other, especially Zeus, although they sire mortal children. A revolt against the gods has begun. Zeus's son Perseus, an exiled marvelous child, a quest hero, hating the gods, wanting vengeance for his murdered family, will both fight and rescue them, and even partially redeem a few, as he destroys the last traces of Titanic rule. But as Wagner's Wotan knew, there is no place for these compromised gods. As *Wrath*'s Zeus himself declares, "There will be no more sacrifices. No more gods. Use your power wisely, Perseus." Zeus crumbles away; Hades shuffles off. Helius, Perseus' son, raises his father's sword, an image of the new human and heroic future.

In *Immortals* the victorious Olympians have caged the Titans for eons and rule unseen, protective of human free will. Titanic evil takes mortal form in King Hyperion, to be opposed by Theseus, a marvelous child trained (unbeknownst to him) by Zeus, whose exceptional virtues mirror Hyperion's exceptional evil. Theseus was "once a faithless man," but no antihero like the Perseus of *Clash/Wrath*; his mother was murdered, but he will, after a difficult hero's journey, destroy Hyperion, though not before the Titans are unleashed, and several Olympians killed. Theseus earns godhood, and is destined to fight, alongside his son, against the Titans. In *Immortals* the gods do not die out, but incorporate the best of humanity into their ranks for the struggle against Titanic chaos, and humans and gods will make a future together. Both Perseus and Theseus must reform themselves, but the spiritual elements are much more pronounced in *Immortals*. Perseus is both helped and hindered by women, and his Andromeda, transformed from quiet sacrifice to warrior Queen, will have his back in battle. In contrast, the prophetess Phaedra displays the sorrowful and sacred feminine that draws Theseus upward. Both movies too can show a surreal, dreamlike/nightmarish quality, but the imagery of *Immortals*, more than *Clash/Wrath*, seems more convincingly to hint at deeper truths. And even though Hercules does not become a god, he does become a tested and proven hero as well as a free man, one ready for further triumphs.

All four of these movies take considerable liberties with canonical stories, especially *Immortals*, although they richly employ themes and elements found in Classical myth and literature. However we might think of them as movies, on the level of myth, in displaced fashion, they touch on important questions both universal and personal. And now think: How will you watch, how will you respond? Which vision will you like best?

CHAPTER 3

WHAT'S OLD IS NEWISH AGAIN

Hercules

Heracles, Zeus' son, I will sing, he whom, very much best of those upon the earth, Alcmene birthed in Thebes of the lovely dances, having coupled with the Son of Kronos, gatherer of clouds; who, formerly, traversing unspeakable ranges of earth and sea at the commands of King Eurystheus, himself committed many wanton deeds, and endured many. But now in the beautiful home of snowgirt Olympus he abides, delighting himself, and holds Hebe of the lovely ankles.

Hail, O Lord, Zeus' son! And grant both excellence and wealth.
(*Homeric Hymn 15 to Heracles the Lion-Hearted*)

We begin this section of the book on heroes with possibly the most archetypal of heroes, whose prominence in art, literature, art, and cinema makes his figure iconic. But it's not so simple. Early in our movie, Iolaus, Hercules's cousin and spin master, says to the pirate king concerning Hercules: "You think you know the truth about him? You know nothing." Our research for this chapter truly underscores how the short poem from which we quote above merely points to one high peak among the vast mountain range of Heracles/Hercules tradition, which for thousands of years has offered riches (and labors) for everyone. Within our study of myth in films of the new millennium, we have chosen one recent version, *Hercules* (2014), with Dwayne Johnson, "The Rock," as protagonist and directed by Brett Ratner, among numerous others that came out, including two from the same year. But our movie had more popular, "blockbuster" status, which is why we have selected it for analysis.

This chapter will first present an overview of the complex Heracles/Hercules tradition in myth, society, and art including discussion of the Hercules tradition in cinema. Then we shall consider our own movie, which departs considerably from the Greco-Roman "canonical" version, but less than does, let us say, the TV-series *Hercules the Legendary Journeys*, much less *The Three Stooges*

Meet Hercules (1959).[2] The Hercules tradition is vaster and more complex than that of all our other heroes put together, and thus a more extensive presentation of background information is given to better appreciate our movie. In sum, *Hercules* (2014) tells, in a context of a quasi-realistic world where invisible powers are at work, how Hercules, a marvelous child, is displaced from his proper status, first by his illegitimate birth, and next by what he believes is his slaughter of his wife and children. Hercules must find his true nature, which involves, as is common with many of our heroes, recognizing and releasing powers within himself and fighting attempts to keep him in his false consciousness, which allows him to become truly Hercules.

Five other issues are central: (1) the power of comrades and community for the hero's development; (2) the ability of the hero to redeem himself and his comrades, and to save entire communities; (3) the need, in desperate times, for a hero people can believe in; (4) how myths arise and; (5) corruption in high places, deception, and imperialism. In terms of myth theory, we start from the archetypal pattern of the marvelous child and Quest hero, which is flexible enough to allow many "side trips" and inflections. As before, we must use cultural insights to discern the significance of various components of Heracles and his career.

HERACLES, THE HERO, AND HIS CANONICAL CAREER

Heracles, or Hercules for the Romans, a more widely known name, has the best "branding" of all the Greek heroes.[3] Although Hercules was a truly Panhellenic hero, he is also the most misunderstood of the major Greek heroes, quite unlike the others in significant ways.[4] Roughly, one can identify six types of Heracles: (1) Primitive "Master of Beasts"; (2) Leader, Helper, Cultural Hero, and Savior; (3) Tragic Hero; (4) Sexually Transgressive Hero; (5) Transcendent Heracles; and (6) Comic Heracles. The earliest stories of Heracles may well belong to folktale, with Heracles an archetypal strong man and pre-urban "Master of Beasts."[5] Note how eight of the twelve canonical labors simply involve hunting beasts, recalling a time when animals were major threats and sources of food, and how he fights with a club (though the bow is his favored weapon) and wears a lion skin.[6] No other hero experiences such extremes of tragedy and triumph. Greeks drew firm bounds between gods and humans, but Pindar calls

---

2 O'Brien (2011), 187–202.

3 Perhaps referred to in Disney's *Hercules* by a sequence showing products with his name on them, like "Herc Air" sandals.

4 For what follows, we are particularly indebted to Padilla (1998), 19–33, with bibliography. See also Galinsky (1972), Blanshard (2005).

5 Burkert (1985), 208–11.

6 Many elements of his myth are imported; for example, the image of a man fighting a lion has Middle Eastern connections, and particularly recalls the skin-wearing and club-wielding Ninurta, son of the storm god Enlil. Burkert (1985), 209 and n. 5, with more bibliography.

him a hero-god *(hêrôs theos: Nemean* 3.22). Shrines of Heracles are found all over Greece, Rome, and later beyond. Like the shaman, Hercules can cross the borders between our world and the world of divinity, especially during his last three labors, where the transcendent Heracles finally conquers death itself,[7] as he does when he saves Alcestis, and he is widely worshipped as both man and god. This status will make him a kind of rival to Jesus[8] in later antiquity. He battles cosmic and chthonic snake monsters and supports the Olympian order against the Giants (Pindar, *Nemean* 1.67–68), but he also fights against Hera, Ares, and Apollo, among other gods.

The Greek "hero" can be responsible for terrible evil, and is prone to violence, even madness. In our movie, Autolycus makes reference to Hercules' "Blood Rage." The question of what exactly *is* a hero will be a major consideration for our Hercules movies. Heracles stands apart from the more socially oriented Homeric heroes, and Homer provides a sense of Heracles' lawlessness and savagery[9] *(Iliad* 5.392–404 and *Odyssey* 11.600–615). The skin-wearing Heracles is the most beastlike of the major heroes,[10] yet he is also Odysseus-like in cleverness and tricks, and Athena is his patron too. Heracles can be counted as one of the most important helper/savior divinities, worshipped all over Greece as the Averter of manifold evils.[11] He is deadly to his enemies, but often a threat to his friends.[12] He is the lone hunter, but also a visitor to aristocratic courts.

Heracles is claimed (albeit indirectly) as ancestor of the Doric peoples and, because of legends which have him mating with many women, and his extensive travels, he is credited with founding many cities. Greek colonists used his myth to connect themselves with Greece.[13] There is also a tradition of Heracles as outstanding general,[14] one central to our movie, who sacked, among other places, Elea, Pylos, and Troy, some of which may connect to historical realities of the Bronze Age; as Tiryns was dependent on Mycenae, so Heracles must obey Eurystheus.[15] He serves as well as a culture hero in other ways,[16] founding the Olympic Games (Pindar's *Tenth Olympian Ode* 55ff.), being patron of ephebes, young men undergoing civic and military training,[17] and particularly when he takes the girdle of Hippolyta, an Amazon queen, which represents the triumph of the male order. He is an exemplum of hypermasculinity and

---

7   See Fontenrose (1959), 28–45.
8   See Aune (1990), 3–19.
9   Galinsky (1972), 9–15.
10 Segal (1975), 31; Padilla (1998), 20–22.
11 Galinsky (1972), 4.
12 See Pike (1977), 73–83; Slater (1992), 364–69.
13 Padilla (1998), 30, who cites Malkin (1987), 90; West (1985), 150.
14 On Hercules as general and conqueror, see Padilla (1998), 28.
15 Webster (1958).
16 For Heracles as cultural hero and villain, see Padilla (1998), 22–25.
17 Galinsky (1972), 4–5.

misogyny,[18] yet he is clearly bisexual and he (and his priests) engaged in considerable gender bending.[19] The Greek historian Megacleides underscores his many erotic relationships, as well as love of soft beds and overall voluptuousness.[20] Indeed, the portrayal of Hercules as a tragic figure is far overshadowed by the number of appearances in comedies, where Heracles/Hercules is often shown as an overmuscled, oversexed, underbrained creature of great appetites, more interested in fine food than great deeds.[21] Finally, the Sophist Prodicus (400 BCE) made him a philosophic hero, faced with a choice between females representing Duty or Pleasure, in the famous Choice of Heracles transmitted in Xenophon's *Memorabilia* 2.1.21–34. Cicero, Dio Chrysostom, and Epictetus also idealized Hercules.[22]

Hercules was very popular among the Romans,[23] who focused on his more serious dimensions. Vergil's *Aeneid* strives to make Aeneas the kind of hero among the Romans that Hercules was among the Greeks, with a better character.[24] Note how Vergil stresses his persecution by Juno, just as Hercules is pursued by Hera, and the constant references to Aeneas' labors, including a descent to the Underworld. Most famously, *Aeneid* book 8 describes Hercules' defeat of the fire-breathing volcano-monster Cacus. Aeneas during a festival dedicated to Hercules is invited into Evander's humble home (*Aen.*8.362–65), and the host tells him

> Hercules the Victor went beneath these lintels, this palace received him.
> Dare, O guest, to condemn luxury, and fashion also yourself worthy of a god,
> Come, without harsh attitude because of poor possessions.

Just as Hercules put down the fire of a monster and became a god, so Aeneas, by putting out the fires of war, can also become a god (as he does, along with Augustus).[25] Many Roman emperors (Caligula, Nero) made (or had made for them) a connection with Hercules.[26] The later Roman emperor Commodus especially honored him, as is memorialized in one of the most famous, if jarring, busts ever carved (Fig. 3.1).

---

18 See Austin (1990), 119–20. According to Plutarch (*On the Pythian Responses* 404a) there is in Phocis an oracle of Hercules the Misogynist.
19 Plutarch (*Greek Questions* 304c–e) declares the priest of Heracles at Antimachia wore a female headdress and bridegrooms welcome their brides wearing female garb.
20 Padilla (1998), 28–29, citing Megacleides *Fragments of Greek Historians* 4.443; see also Spina (2008), 60–61.
21 Padilla (1998), 293, Spina (2008), 59.
22 Although some Romans took to euhemerist interpretations, such as Lucretius and especially the polymath Varro, who discerned forty-seven men behind Hercules. See Galinsky (1972), 131.
23 Note how *Mehercule!* (By Hercules!) is a stock expression in Plautus.
24 Galinsky (1972), 131–49.
25 Propertius also tells the story in the beginning of Elegy 4.9, as an introduction to another story that connects Hercules with the shrine of Bona Dea.
26 See Galinsky (1972), 141; Anderson (1928) 7–58; Vermeule (1977), 289–94.

FIGURE 3.1 Commodus as a dainty Hercules.

This bust is found in the Capitoline Museum at Rome and shows the emperor Commodus as Hercules. He carries the apples of the Hesperides in his hand, suggesting the apotheosis of the Emperor.[27] But we think of Hercules as a rugged fellow—yet note the fine pincurls of Commodus' hair.[28]

Thus Heracles never goes out of fashion because there is always one or more versions of Heracles to fit a time period. Because of his tradition's vast complexity, he is a great "tool to think with" concerning the fluid nature of the mythical hero, seeing the contrasting elements of human life and potential that confront each other in his personality,[29] and the forces shaping elements of the classical and even modern traditions. Goethe in *Faust Part II* saw Heracles as the best symbol of the Urmensch, whose nature is beyond the poet's ability to express (7395–7396).[30] That is why too he has been depicted in every age in various ways, as well as in countless movies.

---

27 Another interesting painting where the labors of Heracles appear as an allegory for contemporary events is seen in a work of Toussaint Dubreuil (circa 1600, now in the Louvre Museum), which depicts Henry IV of France defeating the Lernaean Hydra, which represents the Catholic League.

28 Hannah (1986).

29 Padilla (1998) 19, notes how "the stories and attributes of Herakles embody a rich set of liminal tensions," citing Kirk (1974), 212; Burkert (1985), 210; Holt (1992), 38–59.

30 Grafton, Most, and Settis (2010), 428.

Here is a thumbnail (and composite) sketch of Heracles' career.[31] Zeus made love to Alcmene disguised as her husband, the hero Amphitryon, who also mated with her the same night and produced Iphicles; in his comedy *Amphitryon* Plautus gives a humorous account of this event. Hera, hating Hercules, arranged for Eurystheus to be born a day early, and Heracles a day late, which is why Eurystheus became King of Mycenae/Tiryns and why Hercules had to serve him. Hera constantly caused him trouble but was reconciled with Heracles when he entered Olympus (Diodorus Siculus 4.39.2), and allowed him to marry her daughter Hebe.[32] Heracles had notable tutors, such as Chiron the Centaur, Autolycus, Eurytus, Castor, and others, including Linus, whom he killed. While tending cattle for Amphitryon, a massive lion was ravaging the cattle of the King of Thespiae, who let Heracles sleep each night with one of his fifty daughters, until he slew the beast. For service to Thebes, its king gave him his daughter Megara to marry.

Later on Hera drives Heracles into a madness in which he kills his wife and children. He goes to Delphi for purification, and is ordered to perform twelve labors for King Eurystheus.[33] The canonical labors are (1) slaying the Nemean Lion; (2) killing the Lernaean Hydra; (3) retrieving the Golden Hind of Artemis; (4) seizing the Erymanthian Boar; (5) cleaning the stables of Augeas in one day; (6) destroying the Stymphalian Birds; (7) seizing the Cretan Bull; (8) stealing the Mares of Diomedes; (8) obtaining the girdle of Hippolyta, Queen of the Amazons; (9) stealing the cattle of Geryon, a monster who lives at the world's edge; (11) obtaining the golden apples of the Hesperides; and (12) catching and retrieving Cerberus, the three-headed hound of Hades.

There were various side labors, most famously, while he drove the cattle of Geryon back to Greece, he encountered the volcano-monster Cacus (*Aeneid* 8.184–275) and killed him. He kills a sea monster ravaging Troy, and, when cheated by King Laomedon, sacks Troy and kills him. Apollonius makes him take part in the voyage of the Argo, but when his boy companion Hylas was captured by water nymphs, the Argonauts left Mysia without him. He arrives in Pherae the day on which Alcestis, wife of King Admetus, agreed to die for him. Heracles was able to wrestle death and give her back to Admetus. He frees the chained Prometheus, bringing about Zeus' reconciliation with the Titan. He wrestles the

---

31 In the classical world, the best "biographies" are found in Apollodorus, *Library* 2.4.8–2.9.1 and in Diodorus Siculus 4.8–39. Padilla (1998) gives an abundantly footnoted survey of the various myths, rituals, and social connections of the Heracles myths in Greece from prehistoric to Hellenistic times.

32 This notion of glory gained due to the opposition of a god with whom the hero is reconciled is often seen in epic. See Padilla (1998), 26, citing Nagy (1981), 303.

33 One of the most interesting depictions of the Labors of Hercules is found in the eighteen ivory panels on the Throne of St. Peter, which was given to the Pope by Charles the Bald in 875, and was once believed to have been used by St. Peter himself. By the ninth century many Christian writers had, like the Stoics, spiritually allegorized the deeds of Hercules.

river god Achelous in a competition for Deianira as wife. Later, when Deianira was about to cross a river, the centaur Nessus pretended to help her but attempted to rape her instead. Enraged, Heracles shot the centaur and fatally wounded him. The dying Nessus convinced Deianira that his blood (infused with Hydra venom) could be used as a love potion. Later Heracles loves Iole, princess of Oechalia. Her father King Eurytus had promised her to the winner of an archery test. Heracles won, but, because he was already married, King Eurytus refused to give her to him. In one version, out of anger, he kills Iole's brother Iphitus. For this crime he served Queen Omphale of Lydia, wearing women's clothes and doing women's chores. He then sacked Oechalia and brought Iole back home. Deianira smeared Nessus' blood on a cloak, which she gave to Heracles, hoping to regain his love. But the poison ravaged Heracles' body, and he built a pyre to gain release in death. The father of Philoctetes, Poeas, lit his pyre, for which he received Heracles' bow. The mortal portion of Heracles was burned away. He became fully god and married Hebe, goddess of youth. His children, driven out of Greece, returned a century later to found the Dorian people.

HERCULES/HERACLES AND THE SWORD-AND-SANDALS OR PEPLUM MOVIE

Hercules (2014) is based (although toned down)[34] on the five-part graphic novel *Hercules: The Thracian Wars* (2008), by Steve Moore, who took legal steps to dis-associate himself from the film.[35] *Hercules* opened up at second ranking to the action adventure (and Scarlett Johansson vehicle) *Lucy*, a strong but somewhat disappointing showing. Reviews were mixed, with some critics seeing it as a grand misfire, and others as an impressive and even epic revision of the Heracles myth. Many gave Dwayne Johnson credit for making the movie better than it deserved to be. Rotten Tomatoes gave the film a basically positive score of 60 percent, and Metacritic gave it a 47, which indicates a more mixed set of reviews.

The director, Brett Ratner, is well known for his often comically inflected action movies, such as the *Rush Hour* film series (1998, 2001 2007, *The Family Man* [2001], *21* [2008], *Red Dragon* [2002], *X-Men: The Last Stand* [2006], and *Tower Heist* [2011]). He was also a producer for the Fox drama series *Prison Break* (2005–2009) and movies such as *True Crime* (2016), *Mirror Mirror* (2012), *The Revenant* (2015), and even the adapted Bollywood movie *Kites* (2010). He has directed more than thirty music videos featuring major singers such as Mariah Carey, Madonna, and Miley Cyrus, as well as Cannibal Corpse. He is seen not

---

34   Scott Foundas, http://variety.com/2014/film/reviews/film-review-hercules-1201267840/. Accessed May 31, 2016.

35   "Alan Moore Calls for Boycott of 'Wretched Film' Hercules on Behalf of Friend Steve Moore." http://www.bleedingcool.com/2014/07/17/alan-moore-calls-for-boycott-of-wretched-film-hercules-on-behalf-of-friend-steve-moore/BleedingCool.com. Accessed May 23, 2016.

PLOT SUMMARY

Hercules grew up an orphan on the streets of Athens with his friend Autolycus and then entered the army. The Athenian king Eurystheus sends him on increasingly dangerous missions, where he gains as his companions the prophet Amphiaraus, Atalanta, and the barely humanized Tydeus. He is accompanied by his nephew Iolaus, who has fabricated the story of the twelve labors and suggested he is the son of Zeus hated by Hera, who provoked madness in him, which led to his killing his wife and children and being driven out of Athens. Hercules is tormented by dreams of his dead family and Cerberus. Princess Ergenia, working for her father Lord Cotys in order to protect her son Arius, hires Hercules to train the Thracian armies to fight against the supposed wizard Rhesus. Lord Cotys insists the Thracians defend the Bessai, who, they find, have been (supposedly) bewitched by Rhesus. Hercules and his fellows make a formidable fighting force. They then attack and capture Rhesus. Heracles decides to halt Lord Cotys, and everyone joins him except for Autolycus. Captured, they learn that Eurystheus, now Lord Cotys' ally, drugged Hercules and used his hounds to kill his family. Goaded by Amphiaraus, Hercules embraces his true nature, rips away his chains, kills the three hounds (the Cerberus of his nightmares), and then kills Eurystheus. They then face Lord Cotys, who holds Arius as hostage, and his army. In the nick of time Autolycus shows up, and he and Tydeus free Arius. Tydeus sacrifices himself. Hercules topples the statue of Hera, killing Lord Cotys, and the Thracian soldiers submit. Ergenia and Arius are now Thebes' rulers.. Hercules and company will now head for other adventures, realizing also their greater purpose and destiny.

so much as a cinematic artist, such as Ang Lee, but an A-list go-to director who is very competent and controlled and will produce a quality (if not visionary) product.[36] The selection of the Rock as Hercules suggests its commercial bent.

Hercules, as well as *Troy, Clash of the Titans, Wrath of the Titans,* and *Immortals,* should be seen in the context of the sword-and-sandals movie, or the Italian peplum movie,[37] which arises from the famous silent film *Cabiria* (1914) and comprises a series of movies about a Hercules-like former slave called Maciste, although the peplum designation is mostly used for about 170 movies from the 1950s and 1960s. These movies are often historically fanciful[38] and show considerable neomythologization[39]; for example, in *Tiranni di Babilonia* (1964), Babylon has conquered Greece. Hercules battles not only traditional monsters like the Hydra, but also Moon Men and Vampires. Although they display hierarchical and patriarchal (and violence-prone) perspectives, the hero is often engaged in a fight against the ruling powers (such as tyrants or usurpers) or

---

36 See styleblazer.com/135911/cinematic-mercenaries-15-journeymen-filmmakers-on-hollywoods-a-list/. Accessed Apr. 22, 2016.

37 See Introduction (1–14) and essays in Cornelius (2011); also Blanshard and Shahabudin (2011), 58–76. Ennio De Concini, a pioneer of the genre, prefers to call them "sandaloni" = "big sandals"; see Spina (2008), 61, n. 18, citing Giordano (1998), 39.

38 See Spina (2008), 62 n. 19; and Nisbet (2006), 45–66.

39 Cornelius (2011), 4, citing Bondanella (2009), 159.

otherwise defending the oppressed. There is usually a seductress trying to distract the noble hero. The Hercules figure recalls a supernatural being in his power, but remains human and accessible, even inviting a certain level of identification with the audience, ready to fight for the people, even a whole nation, in the name of justice.[40] Our Amphiaraus notes in his concluding epilogue, "The world needs a hero they can believe in." Sometimes the muscle-hero has morally rigorous motives for his actions, but often he merely seeks revenge, as seen in, for example, the actions of Maximus in *Gladiator*. These movies tend to present straightforward contrasts of good and evil, with little psychological realism. The hero, although he overthrows the tyrant, does not want power for himself, but gives it to the proper ruler—as happens in our movie.[41] It has been argued that the movies' emphasis on the hero's massive musculature suggests his heroism arises because only he has the resources (in his brawny physique) to accomplish the mission, and his sheer strength is enough to defeat the often supernatural forces arrayed against him. This productive muscularity thus defuses (to some extent) the homoerotic dimensions of constant display of the hero's semi-unclothed body, which often can be connected with a campy, "gay" subtext or with problematics of the "straight" and "merely admiring" male-on-male gaze.[42] The excessive muscularity of Dwayne Johnson certainly aligns with this. But, as Wyke has pointed out, the rise of body building in the nineteenth century was inspired by classical attitudes and their love of ideal bodies. Classical figures, especially Hercules, have shaped modern attitudes toward the depiction of the male body—they do not call him "Mr. Olympia" for nothing[43]—and are powerful conveyors of current ideologies.[44]

---

40 Spinazzola (1974), 334.

41 D'Amelio (2011), 16ff., sees the peplum hero as presenting a strongman recalling the fascist dictator, who saves the people (as the dictator claimed to do) without seizing power for himself.

42 Pallant (2011); see also Wyke (1997), 59–63.

43 To give further context to the connection with body building: the Italian American Angelo Siciliano morphed into Charles Atlas, who co-wrote the bestselling *Health and Strength by Charles Atlas*. Charles Atlas Ltd. offers an exercise and fitness program for the "97-pound weakling." This focus on male body and physical fitness is well sent-up by the famous song in *The Rocky Horror Picture Show*, "I can make you a man" (easily found on YouTube). The Hercules/bodybuilder/self-improvement vibe hovers around many Hercules movies, including this one.

44 Wyke (1997); for example, the muscled hero whose virtue exceeds the flabby, indulgent, and perverse tyrants, such as Nero, or more "Asiatic" or "alien" types. The working-class hero who played Maciste tied in with rising Italian imperialist movements as a symbol of "patriotic recovery" (58). The Italian intellectual Giovanni Bertinetti, who promoted the genre, even wrote an article, "Il cinema, scuola di volontà e di energie" ("Cinema, the School of Will and Energy"; 1918), which argued that the cinema was particularly good at teaching Italian youth the patriotic lessons of strength and action.

Savior hero: a hero who can be appealed to by individuals, for help against all manner of evils.

Master of animals: a type of hero whose principal action is killing or capturing often fearful animals.

Culture hero: a hero whose deeds are seen to uphold social values, for example, freedom.

Apotheosis: when a human becomes a god, often through great deeds.

Hero as founder: a hero who is credited with being the founder or establisher of a people.

The Greek hero: not one who necessarily does great deeds, or even good deeds, but one whose life is so uncanny that it seems, somehow, to be touched by the gods.

HERACLES/HERCULES IN THE MOVIES

There have been uncounted movies made about Hercules or having him as a character,[45] which mirrors the endlessly reinvented classical tradition. The earliest American movie we can find is a spoof, taken from a stage play, *The Warrior's Husband*, where Hercules acts the coward. Our analysis needs to be conducted in the light of that vast tradition. Accordingly, we will survey three works each of which highlights some facet of the Hercules movie tradition. First we consider *Le fatiche di Ercole* (English title *Hercules*), a 1958 film from Italy quite popular in the United States, which started a series of sword-and-sandal movies, and even had tie-ins with consumer products.[46] Hercules is played by the famous body

---

45 Here is a short (!) list of films that are mentioned most often. Again: there are hundreds more. *Hercules and the Queen of Lydia / Hercules Unchained* (1959); *Hercules and the Masked Rider* (1960); *La vendetta di Ercole (Revenge of Hercules)*, aka *Goliath and the Dragon* (1960); *The Loves of Hercules / Hercules vs. the Hydras* (1960); *Hercules and the Treasure of the Incas* (1960), *Hercules and the Conquest of Atlantis* (1961), *Hercules at the Center of the Earth / Hercules and the Haunted World* (1961); *Hercules in the Vale of Woe / Maciste Against Hercules in the Vale of Woe* (1962); *Hercules vs. Ulysses* (1962); *The Fury of Hercules* (1962); *The Three Stooges Meet Hercules* (1962); *Hercules Against Moloch* (1963); *Hercules, Samson and Ulysses* (1963); *Hercules of the Desert* (1963); *Hercules, Prisoner of Evil* (1963); *Hercules Against Rome* (1964); *Hercules Against the Moon Men* (1964); *Hercules the Avenger* (1964); *Hercules Against the Sons of the Sun* (1964); *Hercules and the Ten Avengers / The Triumph of Hercules* (1964); *Hercules Against the Tyrants of Babylon* (1964); *Hercules the Invincible* (1964); *Hercules and the Princess of Troy* (1965); *Hercules Against the Barbarians/Mongols* (1965); *Hercules in New York* (1969); *Hercules* (1983); *The Adventures of Hercules* (1985, a sequel to the 1983 movie); *Hercules: Zero to Hero* (1999; Disney, straight-to-video animated movie); *Little Hercules in 3-D* (2009); *Hercules Reborn* (2014, a straight-to-video production); *The Legend of Hercules* (2014, or *Hercules: The Legend Begins*). There are also the TV shows *Hercules: The Legendary Journeys* (1995–1999); *The Mighty Hercules* (1963–1966); *Hercules and the Amazon Women* (1994); *Hercules and the Lost Kingdom* (1994); *Young Hercules* (1998–99); *Hercules and the Circle of Fire* (1994); *Hercules: The Animated Series* (1998–99); *Hercules in the Underworld* (1994); *Hercules in the Maze of the Minotaur* (1994); *Hercules and the Arabian Night* (1999); *Young Hercules* (1998). We might also mention the German movie musical *Amphitryon* (1935), which is based on plays by Molière, Plautus, and Heinrich von Kleist. For a good compilation of Hercules-related movies see: https://en.wikipedia.org/wiki/List_of_films_featuring_Hercules. Accessed October 22, 2016.

46 Blanshard and Shahabudin (2011), 63.

builder Steve Reeves.[47] It set the pattern for many subsequent movies, visually and thematically, including our own. Second is Disney's *Hercules* (1997), a film many of our readers have seen, one profoundly commercial, ideologically revised, and sanitized, with some notable parodic qualities. Finally, we'll look more briefly at the two-part TV miniseries *Hercules* (2005), directed by Roger Young and produced by Robert Halmi, Sr., both long associated with Christian-oriented programming. Its radical reworking of the canonical myths reflects, as Safran notes, Christian anxieties.[48] In 2014 there also came out *The Legend of Hercules*, a poorly made, poorly received movie that presents an Oedipal battle between Amphitryon, Hercules, and Alcmene. There was also *Hercules Reborn*, a production so barely noticed that Rotten Tomatoes hasn't even been able to muster one review for it, but simply gives a short descriptive blurb.[49] Almost certainly these movies were made to cash in on the anticipated popularity of our *Hercules*, just as, right after the initial *Star Wars* movie (1977), there was a spate of horrible science fiction knockoffs, such as *Battle Beyond the Stars* (1980).

The initial scrolling in the Italian *Hercules* (1958) links Heracles to the divine world. There are two versions of what follows: "Yet from lesser men he learned one eternal truth—that even the greatest strength carries with it a measure of mortal weakness . . . ," while another version declares, "But one day men crossed his path, they were willing to sacrifice their brief treasure, for knowledge, for Justice, for Love." We can observe here two ways to stress Hercules: Is he tragic, or inspirational? In this movie Hercules goes to Jolco to tutor Iphitus, the son of the evil King Pelias, and forms a relationship with Pelias' daughter Iole. The Nemean Lion mortally wounds Iphitus before Heracles can kill it. The wrathful Pelias commands Hercules to kill the Cretan Bull. Unexpectedly, Hercules first visits the Sibyl, and gives up his immortality so that he can love Iole and have a family. Now mortal, a sort of superhuman Everyman,[50] he kills the Cretan Bull. Hercules participates in the entire Argonautic journey, with Ulysses, not Hylas, as his pupil. There is no Medea, no Aeetes, and Jason must kill a dinosaur-like dragon to get the Fleece. Upon returning to Jolco they must still fight Pelias. In a trope appearing in several Hercules movies (such as our own), the imprisoned Hercules pulls his chains from their moorings. The evil Pelias, defeated, takes poison, and Jason is restored to the throne. Here, as fits the standard peplum hero, Hercules seeks not power, but only justice. As the couple sail off into a beautiful sunset, a voiceover declares, "Now there is

---

47 We mentioned the "gay subtext" of Hercules movies. Note one stanza to "Sweet Transvestite," where Dr. Frank N. Furter sings, "Let me show you around / Maybe play you a sound / You look like you're both pretty groovy / Or if you want something visual / That's not too abysmal / We could take in an old Steve Reeves movie."

48 Safran (2015), 133–46.

49 See http://www.rottentomatoes.com/m/hercules_reborn/. Accessed May 26, 2016.

50 Wyke (1997), 64.

justice. . . . Out of great sorrow and spilled blood, forces of good are sometimes born. Hercules and Iole are leaving now to find a new happiness. They will seek among the race of men where justice and peace will be with them again. Farewell Hercules . . . farewell Iole. . . . Life awaits you with all its glory and all its shadows. But even through the most difficult tasks the Gods may prepare for you, you'll have each other to the end of time."

In the canonical account Hercules must earn immortality, a theme also stressed in Disney's *Hercules*. Yet, we will see in *Clash of the Titans* how Perseus rejects Zeus' gifts and Olympus, wanting to succeed as a mortal. Achilles in *Troy* declares that the gods envy our mortality, because it makes life sweeter, which agrees with a theme of the *Odyssey*, where Odysseus could have remained immortal as the boy-toy of Calypso, but chose love, danger, and impermanence— and meaning. This Hercules, like Odysseus, embraces the problematical human condition, a life with struggles, finding comfort in the enduring love and companionship of a good woman.

Any Disney film must be considered in the context of a globalized media company that leverages a movie to sell other products. *Hercules* (1997) is a production of the Eisner era, the chief who revived the animation division with hits like the *Little Mermaid* (1989) and *Aladdin* (1992). *Hercules* (1997) follows this same formula, which demands great stories, great characters, and technological sophistication,[51] and whose elements fit many aspects of Joseph Campbell's notion of the heroic career.[52] Disney exists as a significant part of the ideological superstructure of American/Western consumer-based capitalism (which the movie indeed shows an ironic awareness of), and the conservatism of its movies is often noted and scorned. But it remains a very successful formula even in the new millennium.

The movie begins in a museum's Greek gallery, and focuses on a vase with a hero fighting a lion. Charlton Heston (of *The Ten Commandments* fame) intones: "But what is the measure of a true hero? Ah, that is what our story is." The Muse Thalia breaks in: "Will you listen to him? He makin' the story sound like some Greek tragedy," her interruption suggesting a contest between canonical "serious" perspectives, and a less serious, even parodic, take on Hercules fitting modern sensibilities.[53] But Heston's question still lingers; what is the nature of the hero? *Hercules* presents various classical facets of the hero, and redefines him largely in terms of a Christian-inflected ethic, with an irony that may be a reminder that we consumers should not take all this moralizing talk too seriously.

---

51 Blanshard and Shahabudin (2011), 196–97. See also Leitch (2007), 200.
52 Earlier we noted how Christopher Vogler wrote a brief studio memo, "A Practical Guide to *The Hero with a Thousand Faces*," based on Joseph Campbell's mythological ideas, while working at Walt Disney.
53 Burchfield (2013), 3.

The Muses then sing "The Gospel Truth," which tells of the early world being crushed by the Titans, until along comes the glowing, Nordic-patriarchal Zeus, who brings order to the world by imprisoning the Titans. Zeus, Hera, and baby Hercules reflect Disney's ideology of the ideal nuclear family, not the disturbing relationships found in Greek myths. Hades, as in *Clash*, hates Zeus and his child; his inept minions kidnap the infant Hercules and make him a mortal, to be adopted by the farmers Amphitryon and Alcmene. His great strength makes him clumsy and he becomes a social reject, rather like Percy Jackson. Zeus tells him he must regain his immortality by becoming a true hero. This is his call to adventure; but as in *Immortals*, Zeus will not help Hercules. He must achieve divinity by his own efforts.[54] Zeus sends him Pegasus[55] (see *Clash*), and together they find Philoctetes, a satyr and athletic trainer, his "magic helper." Heracles shows up in often rude satyr plays more than any character, and thus a satyr is a natural companion to a more comic Heracles[56] (we recall the rather comic Grover as Percy Jackson's companion here too) and hints at the problematical tradition that Disney sanitizes. Phil's training allows him to go from "Zero to Hero."[57]

In our movie Ergenia, daughter of Lord Cotys, to protect her son must trick Hercules into fighting for a villain; similarly, the wisecracking Megara has sold her soul to Hades (Christian motif!) for the sake of a disloyal lover, and is working with Nessus, while Hercules thinks he is saving Megara.[58] Hercules becomes a celebrity, and Disney plays on that status by revealing all the marketing tie-ins connected to him. The notion that being famous does not make Hercules a true hero in Zeus' eyes is a perspective alien to classical Greeks[59] but in alignment with Christian views. Megara distracts Hercules by proclaiming her love, and this makes him reject Philoctetes. Disaster follows. Hades forces Hercules to relinquish his power to save Megara. As in *Wrath*, Hades then unleashes the Titans to destroy Zeus. Summoned by Megara, Philoctetes assures the nearly beaten Hercules that he believes in him, and this empowers Hercules to defeat a Cyclops. As Io's death in *Clash* was the prelude for

---

54 See Burchfield (2013), 19.

55 In Carracci's painting *Hercules at the Cross Roads* (Ecole al bivio, 1596) Virtue points to a harsh mountain path near whose summit is Pegasus, symbolic of his transcendence of morality. See Burchfield (2013), 18.

56 Spina (2008), 60, n. 60, who cites Krumeich, Pechstein, and Seidensticker. (1999).

57 Again, the notion of "going the distance" echoes the notion of "Are you tough enough?" *Hercules* provides another training scene as a metaphor for those actions that toughen us up for life. "Phil" notes how a lot of "-euses" let him down, suggesting Hercules' exceptional status. There is a pointed contrast with Achilles, another candidate for top Greek hero, who fails because of "that furshlugginer heel of his!" Burchfield (2013), 16.

58 Here Nessus is described as a "river guardian," and this episode may (ironically) correspond to Campbell's "Crossing of the Threshold" at the start of the heroic career. Burchfield (2013), 13.

59 See Burchfield (2013), 19–21.

Perseus' conquest of the Kraken, when a pillar lethally crushes Megara, so too Hercules regains his strength, and, again like Perseus, he flies off on Pegasus, frees the Olympians, and destroys the Titans by tossing them into space, where they explode.[60] Hercules' willingness to plunge into the waters of Death and give his life for Megara earns him immortality. As Io is resurrected at the end of *Clash*, so Megara returns to life. This version of the transcendent, virtuous, and self-sacrificing Hercules likewise reflects Christian perspectives. Although offered a life on Olympus by Zeus, like Perseus in *Clash*, and like Hercules in the earlier Italian movie, he chooses to live a human life on Earth, with Megara.

For a third contrast, we consider the TV miniseries *Hercules* (2005).[61] This Hallmark production offers another mythical mash-up undercutting Greek religion and mythology and traditional positive views of Hercules, making its Hercules have a "conversion" to a more Christian-seeming conception of God and morality. Like the Disney *Hercules*, the maturing hero must deal with a dangerous and morally problematic world. Hercules' true father is a supernaturally strong and evil Cretan criminal called Antaeus (a worshipper of the Earth Goddess), who rapes his (Hercules') mother, Alcmene, who, when she realizes the rapist was not her husband, declares him to be Zeus, due to his thunderbolt scar. This young Hercules starts out as a fairly brutish fellow, for example, raping Megara, an assistant priestess of Hera, while she is drugged. The result is three sons Megara will use to try to kill him, whom he will slay instead. While we see centaurs, satyrs, and various monsters, the gods themselves never appear, and Hercules comes to realize that the excesses of Greek religion (especially human sacrifices practiced by Hera's priestess, his own mother, Alcmene) are human abominations, not divine commands. Eventually Tiresias (a blinded hermaphrodite) tells him he must abandon his role as hero and god, and be "reborn as a man." Hercules comes to reject the notion of Zeus as his father, what Safran sees as his "born again" moment, and prays to the gods as "one" (implying monotheism) rejecting all the immorality and injustice imputed to them. During their final combat, Hercules realizes that, although Antaeus is his father, not Zeus, what counts is what he has made of himself. At the end, Iole (Megara's daughter by Eurystheus) and Hyllus, his son by Deianira, a good wood nymph, are wed, which hints at a political reconciliation, as are Hercules and Deianira herself, to live happily ever after. As happens in several movies, this Hercules embraces the mortal condition, helps end long-standing conflicts, and embraces a newer, more moral view of divinity.

----

60 In the mostly scorned 1984 *The Adventures of Hercules* featuring the famous body builder Lou Ferrigno, Hercules has a tendency to toss monsters into space.

61 For what follows we rely on Safran (2015).

Hercules (2014) Paramount Pictures and Metro-Goldwyn-Mayer	
Director:	Brett Ratner
Screenplay:	Ryan Condal and Evan Spiliotopoulos
Cast:	Dwayne Johnson (Hercules), Ian McShane (Amphiaraus), John Hurt (Lord Cotys), Rufus Sewell (Autolycus), Aksel Hennie (Tydeus), Ingrid Bolsø Berdal (Atalanta), Reece Ritchie (Iolaus), Joseph Fiennes (King Eurystheus), Tobias Santelmann (Rhesus), Peter Mullan (Sitacles), Rebecca Ferguson (Ergenia)

OUR *HERCULES*: ARCHETYPAL PATTERNS, MYTH INTO TRUTH, TRUTH INTO MYTH, AND THE NEED FOR A HERO

As does *Troy, Hercules* claims to tell a more "realistic" story; no gods are present, nor mythological monsters. Our movie presents several archetypal patterns, various elements of the canonical Heracles tradition, plus items borrowed from other traditions and movies. The movie as a whole does not directly recall any particular classical Hercules tale, but several segments of the Heracles tradition inspire it. First, there is the notion of Hercules as a marvelous child whose abilities allow him to accomplish great deeds and inspire others, but these abilities contain fearful potential for violence. Hercules thus commits brutal murders for which he is cursed and which he needs to atone for. This atonement will also involve a certain amount of self-discovery. Second, Hercules is the savior of the oppressed. And third and finally, there is the tradition of Hercules as commander of armies.

The classical Heracles is a marvelous child with a life inflected by tragedy, triumphs, marvels, and even deification. Our Hercules is a marvelous child too, who never knew his father. Like Theseus in *Immortals*, a child of rape by unknown men, Hercules may be divine. At crucial moments he exhibits special talents, such as snapping heavy metal chains. He is clearly born beneath his natural station, and must overcome considerable obstacles to discover his true identity.

Our Hercules leads a band of skilled mercenaries, sort of a Bronze Age cross between *The Expendables* and *The A-Team*. This band is trying to make one last score to earn enough money to retire. Atalanta, a female heroine known particularly for her participation in the hunt for the Calydonian boar, becomes an Amazon princess whose family was avenged by Hercules—no girdle of Hippolyta here.[62] The spear-wielding Amphiaraus was the famous seer tricked into participating in the siege of the Seven Against Thebes, knowing he would die there. He did not exactly die, but was swallowed by the earth to produce a famous oracle. Autolycus is Heracles' close friend (and master knife thrower),

---

62 Roger Ebert says of the Amazon that she should have "Katniss Everdeen" tattooed across her beautiful forehead. http://www.rogerebert.com/reviews/hercules-2014. Accessed May 31, 2016.

who in classical Greek mythology is a son of Hermes, the world's greatest thief as well as Odysseus' grandfather. However, he appears as a friend and occasional helper to Hercules in the TV series *Hercules the Legendary Journeys* (1995–1999, NBC), and thus here one modern myth influences another. Another radically repurposed figure is Tydeus, also a major character in the *Seven Against Thebes*. Banished from Calydon for a murder, he ended up in the court of King Adrastus at Corinth, where he met Polynices, who had been exiled from Thebes and was seeking to regain the kingship of Thebes. At Thebes he was matched with Melanippus, whom he killed but in so doing was mortally wounded. The goddess Athena, who had planned to make him immortal, refused after seeing the dying Tydeus eating the brains of Melanippus. This might well explain the nature of this movie's Tydeus. In our account Heracles comes to Thebes, whose population is all dead except a young Tydeus. He has been extremely traumatized; he cannot speak, and has to be chained at night due to his horrid nightmares. Heracles rescues or redeems them all, and perhaps Tydeus most strikingly. The name "Lord Cotys" derives from the names of at least four actual kings of Thrace of the Odrysian and Astaean lineage, starting with Cotys I (383–358 BCE).[63] Eurystheus was the famous king of Mycenae whom Heracles had to serve, and who pursued the children and grandchildren of Heracles to Athens, where he was defeated and killed, which may explain why here he is made an Athenian.

Like *Troy*, our movie, in a more complicated, and ironic, manner, suggests how myths arise. The initial and concluding voiceovers bookend this project. The movie begins with the voiceover of Iolaus, accompanied by depictions of some of Hercules' canonical deeds:

> You think you know the truth about him? You know *nothing*. His father was Zeus. The Zeus. King of the gods. His mother, Alcmene, a mortal woman. Together, they had a boy. Half human, half god. [At this point we see them lift the newly born Hercules toward a mosaic of Zeus on the ceiling, and the little baby seems to clutch Zeus' thunderbolt.] But Zeus' queen, Hera, saw this bastard child as an insult, a living reminder of her husband's infidelity. Alcmene named the boy Hercules, which means "glory of Hera," but this failed to appease the goddess. She wanted him dead. [We see twin snakes coming out of the eyes of a statue of Hera, which the infant Zeus strangles.] Luckily, he took after his father. Once he reached manhood, the gods commanded him to perform Twelve Labors, twelve dangerous missions. If he completed them all and survived, Hera agreed to finally let him live in peace. He fought the Lernean Hydra! [Interestingly, the Hydra here looks like the Hydra in *Percy Jackson: The Lightning Thief*] . . . But his greatest Labor was the Nemean Lion. This was no ordinary beast. It had a hide so tough, no weapon could penetrate it. But even this monster was no match

---

63 Paunov (2015), 280, fig. 18.4.

for the son of Zeus. [We see Hercules killing the lion by spreading his jaws until its skull breaks. This method will be used later when he kills one of the three wolves, who have in his dreams become "Cerberus."]

At this point Gryza, the pirate king, says "What a load of crap." He has captured Hercules' nephew Iolaus, Hercules' promoter and propagandist. Bad move. Hercules and his comrades arrive and readily dispose of the pirates.

The prophet Amphiaraus, having missed his expected death, provides the concluding voiceover: "You want to know the truth about Hercules? There it is. To be honest, I prefer it to the legend. The world needs a hero they can believe in. Is he actually the son of Zeus? I don't think it really matters. You don't need to be a demigod to be a hero. You just need to believe you're a hero. It's what worked for him. What the hell do I know? I'm supposed to be dead by now." This epilogue distinguishes between Iolaus' mythological fabrications and the historical "truth." But it also sums a repeated theme, important for our own time, concerning the need for a hero, and how the heroism arises from proper self-trust, a perspective now evident in a "New Age" emphasis on self-esteem and a rather mystic sense of human potential. That transition takes time for Hercules. When Ergenia tells Hercules, "I feared nothing could ever be good again, till you arrived," Hercules merely responds, "I'm just a mercenary fighting for gold," still bound up in a negative view of himself. Ergenia's reply is telling: "How we view ourselves is of little consequence. How others perceive us is important. And your name, like it or not, is a rallying cry. I have seen too much reality to trust in legends, and I am not alone. Nobody has any faith anymore. The people need a hero. They need someone to look up to. My son believes in you. Bring us peace, and . . . I will believe in you, too." As we look upon today's social and political chaos, we see that people have lost faith in institutions and leaders. At the same time, many seem to crave a strong leader to believe in, to be led by, to be saved by. This seemed to be true for post–World War II peplum movies, and it seems true now.

To what extent our protagonist accepts his heroism is a major issue for our movies. Theseus of *Immortals* offers himself as a hero, while Perseus is more reluctant. Theseus knows he is a good man, but Percy Jackson thinks he is a screw-up; Perseus hates the gods and yet feels unable to be equal to them. Ulysses Everett, of course, is a convict, albeit quite self-confident. And *Troy*'s Achilles is deeply cynical about Agamemnon and the war, and sees himself, like Hercules, as not having much of a choice in what he has become. Further, our Hercules has his own dark fears.

Earlier, Princess Ergenia asked Iolaus, "a good storyteller," about rumors concerning Hercules' murder of his wife and three children. Again, the question is raised about narrative and truth. When Iolaus mentions Hera, she insists: "No myths. I want the truth." Autolycus says, "No one knows the truth.

Not for sure. We found Hercules alone. His wife, Megara and the children, dead. He remembers nothing." Autolycus further explains:

> We grew up together, both orphans, trying to survive in the streets of Athens. We found a home in the army. . . . Kings of Athens started to send him on all the most dangerous missions. ["The Twelve Labors," says Ergenia, suggesting how this element of the legend arose.] And he took me with him. To fight by his side. And with each mission, our numbers grew. Scythia, the Amazon kingdom where the royal family had been assassinated." At this point Atalanta says, "My family was gone. Everyone was gone. Hercules helped me avenge their murder. He became my brother-in-arms." Autolycus continues: "Thebes, the city of corpses, where we found a single child, still alive. Hercules took Tydeus in when everyone else saw nothing but a wild animal. You know how a rumor spreads. How a legend grows. Hercules' deeds were so incredible, they could not possibly have been performed by a mere mortal. So we played along. We encourage people to think Hercules was the son of Zeus. It's good. Scares the enemy. Iolaus helps. He talks nice.

We later observe how the Hydra myth arose from Hercules' killing of robbers wearing snake masks, and how men on horses (Rhesus and his army) were confused with centaurs, their destruction being a major part of the Hercules tradition. And as we shall see, Cerberus, the three-headed Hades hound that Heracles captured, is simply three savage dogs, just as in *Percy Jackson*.

In our movie, after Hercules has defeated his army, the captured Rhesus is paraded in chains and suffers abuse. Hercules realizes that Rhesus was actually resisting the incursions of Lord Cotys. In response to his objections, Cotys retorts, "A mercenary who has long since sold his conscience for gold can hardly presume to judge his employers." Cotys constantly tries to keep Hercules in the old frame, and further inflames Hercules by declaring that the Thracian troops he has so wonderfully trained will train others, creating a vast army that will be unstoppable—and this imperialism will be the true legacy of Hercules.

As they leave the palace, Hercules offers his gold to Autolycus, declaring, "There will be no more innocent blood on my hands. I can't leave without setting this right." This signals the moment when the true Hercules begins to emerge, when he is willing to risk impossible odds to correct an evil he is responsible for. When he tells Atalanta she can go, because she no longer owes him anything, she retorts, "Debt? You think we follow you because we owe you? Look around, Hercules. We're family. All we have is each other. We will fight for you. And if it's our time, we will die for you. Because you would die for us. . . ." This exchange illustrates a point we'll see again, that a community of friends who believes in you, is willing to live and die for you, is essential for your personal transformation, as Philoctetes restored Hercules' faith at a critical moment in the Disney movie. And when Hercules orders Iolaus to leave, he refuses, wanting to cease to narrate other people's stories and start living his own. Note how in *Troy* Achilles' cousin Patroclus, against orders, goes to fight the Trojans and is killed. In *Wrath*, Helius, Perseus' son, tries to defend his father against Ares, and distracts him enough for Perseus to kill him, and later accepts Perseus' sword. Iolaus will actually save Heracles' life when he is attacked by General Sitacles.

ARCHETYPAL PATTERNS AND THE MYTHICAL ARC

The traditional Heracles finds his labors rewarded by godhood. Like Ulysses Everett, a convicted felon, and *Immortals*' Theseus (who could not save his mother), our Hercules is cursed by the murder of his wife and children and fears, like *Troy*'s Achilles, who was "born to take lives," that he is a latent monster. Autolycus explains "Hercules is a warrior. And there is something that haunts warriors. It can cloud their minds. We call it the Blood Rage. This rage afflicted Hercules. He made me vow to keep the world away from him. To make sure that he would never harm innocents again. And that, my Lady, is the truth. Whatever the truth, the death of his loved ones haunts Hercules."

A common feature of Greek mythology, especially in the view of feminist critics, is those episodes in which the hero must in some way defeat or possess a woman or women, and our movies also hint at this ideological dimension.[64] Our film presents Iolaus' fabricated story of Hera wanting to kill the infant Hercules; yet, at the end, we see Hercules topple a massive statue of Hera, whose bouncing head seems to aim for Lord Cotys, who is demanding Hercules' death, probably a deconstructive nod to the traditional myth of Hera's opposition. But these traditional myths reflect male misogyny, attempts to assert masculine power, fear as well as a certain guilty conscience, which recognizes Hera has a right to be angry—she is supposedly the goddess of marriage, with one of the worst husbands on Olympus. Austin sees Heracles as symbolizing the negative outcomes when certain aggressive hypermasculinity disregards or opposes the female.[65] Our movie, like some current productions (e.g., Disney's *Hercules*), shows a quite different Hercules in this aspect. No excessive sexual athlete and predator, our Hercules is tormented by the death of his wife and children, and

---

64 For example, think how Percy Jackson, who is told that Annabeth can "squash him like a bug," defeats her at Camp Half-Blood, or how, after she tries to kill him, Achilles in *Troy* has sex with Briseis, or how Perseus in *Wrath* wordlessly grabs Andromeda and kisses her, or (with Phaedra admittedly prompting matters) Theseus has sex with and impregnates Phaedra; think how Ulysses Everett believes he can wed Penny with another man's wedding ring; needlessly the whole myth of Medea found in *Such Is Life* centers on themes of male domination, as, in a different way, the Pygmalion myths do as seen in *Lars and the Real Girl* and *Ruby Sparks*. Even Katniss must pretend to go along with Peeta as lover to get more sponsorships in *The Hunger Games*.
65 See Austin (1990), 118–23; also Slater (1992).

the romance that we half expect will develop with Ergenia never even flickers. Instead, a threatened mother and child needing protection will motivate him.

After Hercules fled Athens in disgrace, he became a mercenary, which mirrors his own negative self-conception. But, as in our other movies, the Powers, however hidden, are in play. Hercules is continually haunted by visions of his dead family, as well as of Cerberus, whose conquest Amphiaraus declares is the labor he must complete, a labor tied to the recovery of his true identity and vindication, which will require a trip to the underworld of his own psychology. In *Clash/Wrath*, Perseus must accept finally the duties his demigod powers demand, while in *Immortals* Theseus becomes a demigod who will help the surviving Olympians fight Titanic evil. Our Hercules transitions from disgraced mercenary to mortal superhero who will now serve humanity in his true role.

FATE, PROPHECY, AND THE FINAL CONFIRMATION OF IDENTITIES

Supported by his comrades in arms, Hercules now moves into the standard role of muscleman peplum hero, to defeat a tyrant and restore the rightful heir. After he is captured and chained up, he learns how Eurystheus, like *Troy*'s Agamemnon, resented and then feared Heracles' popularity among the Athenians, thinking that he might want the ruling power. But like the proper peplum hero, our Hercules had no such interest. Eurystheus determined to disgrace him, and drugging him sent in his three trained dogs to kill his family. As noted, the underworld journey can be a metaphor for uncovering secret truths buried in the subconscious. At some level, the drugged Heracles perceived the attack of the three hounds, which Hercules now realizes is the Cerberus of his nightmares. Lord Cotys prepares to execute his daughter Ergenia for assisting Hercules, while Hercules and his jailed comrades watch. One of these is Amphiaraus.

In *Immortals* Phaedra the prophetess seems glad to lose her gift of prophecy, a heavy burden to her. Amphiaraus seems quite obsessed by the foreshadowed death. He tells the upset Hercules when he announces his impending end, "Oh, cheer up, Hercules. I've lived, not always well, but long enough. I'm ready for what's next"—that is, ready for death. But just as Heracles must learn to live anew, unburdened of his curse, so must Amphiaraus. Nevertheless, the prophet now triggers Hercules' transformation. As they strap Ergenia, cursing her father, to the headsman's block and the executioner prepares his blade, Amphiaraus shouts to Hercules: "Who are you? Are you a murderer? Are you a mercenary who turns his back on the innocent? Are you only the legend? Or are you the truth behind the legend? We believe in you. We have faith in you. Have faith in yourself. Remember the man that you are. Remember the deeds you have performed, the Labors you have accomplished! Now, tell me! Who are you?"

Like many other heroes, Hercules is faced with a moment when he must recognize (Greek: *anagnorisis*), embrace, and fulfill his true nature, and reject his false, obstructing selves. Hercules, powerfully straining at his chains, screams

FIGURE 3.2 I . . . AM . . . HERCULES!

in an act of self-realization, "I am Hercules!"[66] and, having connected with his true potential, yanks the chains from their moorings and stops the execution. Recall how Hercules, right before the climactic battle with Rhesus, proclaimed to his troops: "In this moment, on this day, become the man you were born to be! You have it within yourselves to write your own legends! Let it be to death or victory!" They gain victory, as does Hercules now (Fig. 3.2).

Eurystheus releases his three dogs, Cerberus of Hercules' nightmares, which Hercules kills barehanded, slaying one of them just as in Iolaus' mythical account he killed the Nemean Lion, by forcing its jaws apart and breaking its skull. Amphiaraus tells Hercules, "The gods have revealed your innocence. The final Labor is complete," to which Hercules replies, "But I'm just getting started." Soon afterward Hercules liberates Amphiaraus from his supposedly foreshadowed death. In the melee a spear, flying through a flame, ignites, and Amphiaraus spreads his arms, ready to receive his death. Hercules intercepts it, to which Amphiaraus says "Excuse me. That was my moment, my fate." But recall that Hercules is one who can even break the powers of Death.

The next climax connects these themes, and brings a bittersweet redemption. While Hercules is hunting down and killing King Eurystheus, evoking his murdered family as he does so, Lord Cotys brings up his army against them. Lord Cotys shouts to them, "Hercules is mortal! Not a god!" His men bring out Arius, and offer Hercules the choice of either surrendering or watching the child die. But, just as Han Solo in *Star Wars* IV showed up in the nick of time to prevent Darth Vader's ship from blasting Luke's fighter, so Autolycus' knives suddenly take down the soldier threatening Arius, which allows the boy to run for it. Amid a hail of arrows, Tydeus rushes forth, shielding the boy

---

66 Which recalls a similar moment in the *Odyssey* (9.19–20) as Odysseus proclaims to King Alcinous, who is also demanding a statement concerning his identity, "I am Odysseus, son of Laertes, who for all kinds of tricks I am a concern to men, and my fame rises to heaven."

FIGURE 3.3 Tydeus' goodbye to Hercules.

with his body. Knowing himself fatally wounded, Tydeus rushes into a mass of Thracian soldiers, killing them all, and collapses. Heracles carries his pincush-ioned comrade to the temple steps, where Tydeus, looking genuinely happy, speaks his only word—"Hercules"—and dies (Fig. 3.3). Hercules closes his eyes, and says "Have peace, my brother," which recalls the words of Achilles in *Troy* to the dead Hector. In myth, often somebody must die so the hero can live. For example, consider all the people (including children) killed at the Battle of Hogwarts. Barnard,[67] in discussing the modern analogues to the myth of Philoctetes, notes how the power of speech is the defining characteristic of humanity for the Greeks, and even essential to sanity. In some sense, Tydeus represents a shadow self of Hercules, a type of brother, and following Hercules he has gained a noble death; by speaking a word of community, he has gained his humanity before leaving a world he could never have had peace in.

Tydeus' death sets the stage for the conclusion. The massed troops of Cotys, shields locked, tromp toward the steps of the temple. The confident Lord Cotys screams. "As you said, Hercules, there is no way to defeat a shield wall! . . . You're no hero! You're no god! You're nothing but a mercenary! Your wife and children deserved to die!" Cotys, as before, plays on Hercules' old identity and guilt. This goads Heracles to lift up the base of the massive statue of Hera, a miracle of muscle, which then topples over, shattering, its bouncing head taking out Lord Cotys. In peplum movies, it is almost never the hero who kills the tyrant, as here.[68] Interestingly, this statue is the large version of the same Hera statue out of which snakes emerge to try to kill the infant Hercules. The implication is that this miracle of strength (and perhaps Hera's support) further vindicates Hercules. With Cotys dead, the remaining Thracian soldiers kneel to Hercules. It seems clear that now Hercules the true hero has emerged.

---

67 Barnard (2015), 27–36.
68 D'Amelio (2011), 19–20.

THE CALL OF THE MILITARY, THE LOGIC OF EMPIRE

As noted, a less familiar mythological component presents Heracles as leader of armies, which our movie invokes. This episode falls into two segments. In the first, Heracles begins training the Thracian soldiers; this is interrupted by Rhesus' supposed invasion of the land of the Bessai, which leads Lord Cotys to force his unprepared army to fight a battle. Lord Cotys' willingness to sacrifice his men recalls that of *Troy's* Agamemnon. The battle scenes, according to some critics, have a significant level of detail and physicality.[69] The later scenes, which concentrate on the creation of the shield wall, an excellent defensive weapon, recall the 1969 epic *Alfred the Great*, where Alfred gets the idea for a successful defensive formation against the Danes by seeing a medieval manuscript with a picture of a "Spartan Phalanx."[70] The Bessai fight with an inhuman force, recalling the enemies fighting for Hyperion in *Immortals*, which tricks us into thinking Rhesus is a wizard who has bewitched these men. In the second part, the Pattonesque Hercules[71] finally trains them to use the shield wall and become an invincible army, which is proven in the climactic battle against Rhesus' forces. One can argue that scenes in which an army, treated as a collective entity, is rigorously trained figures as a social desire for a disciplined national unity, as well as reflecting dreams of rigorous rites of passage. The idea of hard training is a masculinist theme ("Can you take it, recruit? Are you tough enough, maggot?"). We see this in the theme of "going the distance" likewise in the Disney *Hercules*.

This movie also deconstructs aspects of American political dreamwork. Rhesus and his men, who supposedly use magic and fight as madmen, reflect aspects of our own time, where we think we fight against terrorists, and fanatical Others. We seem to be doing badly at first, and know it; however, we fantasize about a strong (but fair) leader who can mold us into shape to be an invincible fighting force. Note that once the Thracian army has succeeded against odds, Lord Cotys developed a lust for empire; the successful defenders become enslavers, and many think the United States is guilty in this regard. But the people of Thrace have been conned by their rulers, and they are in fact the imperialists in league with other evil powers; Hercules, like many of our own professional elites who enable our tyrants, at first functions as a clueless mercenary. So Hercules must defeat a monster he has created and expose the tyrants (our tyrants?) for what they are, as often happens in the peplum movie.

---

69 "We're a long way away here from the disorienting whiplash effect of most modern action movies, as sweeping overhead vistas give way to carefully framed medium shots and close-ups that hone in on specific bits of action. Bone and sinew smash against swords and chariot wheels. Arrows rain down from the skies (and, in the unusually good 3D conversion, right into the audience). Shields and armor clang resoundingly on the Dolby Atmos soundtrack . . ." Foundas (2014). Accessed May 4, 2016.

70 Aberth (2003), 54.

71 http://www.rogerebert.com/reviews/hercules-2014. Accessed May 30, 2016.

HERCULES THE MYTHICAL AND THE RESHAPED HERO: A MOVIE FOR THE MILLENNIUM

The canonical Heracles is the greatest of Greek heroes in the vast variety of his exploits, which include considerable criminal and sexual excess. Various traditions (the Disney *Hercules* most emphatically) make Hercules more acceptable. Although our Hercules racks up a sizable body count, he never kills needlessly or glories in bloodshed, and he even shows some mercy. The "out of control" dimension of his behavior is a frame-up, and he acts with remarkable self-control. The mythical Heracles was bisexual and was credited with dozens of illegitimate children; our Hercules has never gotten over his first wife. He provides the framework in which individuals find community, mature, and right wrongs. In the end, there is a nobility, but also a safeness, to our Hercules, and his virtue is within the possibilities of human imitation—save for the miracles of strength. But this elision of the more problematic aspects of Hercules, which we see also in *Immortals'* Theseus, as well as in the 1958 *Hercules,* represents a failure to deal with an inescapable flaw of human nature. And, a theme underscored by other movies, Hercules' true victory is the recovery of his full humanity, a triumph we can aspire to, not divinity.

As is noted, Hercules is a character who never goes out of fashion because he can be depicted in so many diverse ways. It is suggested that peplum-style movies are popular during periods of stress and breakdown, when we have collective fantasies of a hero who can save, individually and collectively. The army and battle scenes can be linked to hidden desires for discipline and order, military might, and domination of threatening Others, while the political machinations reflect the sordid world of actual power politics and our paranoid attitudes toward the political process and its compromised leaders. Hercules is a character we can identify with, and Hercules (as do other heroes) represents two powerful perspectives on ourselves. First, many of us feel in some ways traumatized, abused, cheated, even lost; at the same time we feel there are potentials by which, with the right breaks, we could be a contender instead of the bums we feel we are. We recognize the roles of both excellence and chance, and we yearn, as the Disney song goes, from "Zero to Hero." And finally, we know we cannot do it alone, and need a community to push us forward. We want our time under the heroic Sun.

REFERENCES

Aberth, J. *A Knight at the Movies: Medieval History on Film.* Routledge, 2003.

Anderson, A. "Hercules and His Successors." *Harvard Studies in Classical Philology,* vol. 39, 1928, 7–58.

Aune, D. "Heracles and Christ: Heracles Imagery in the Christology of Early Christianity Greeks, Romans and Christians." In D. L. Balch, E. Ferguson, and W. A. Meeks, ed., *Essays in Honor of Abraham J. Malherbe.* Fortress Press, 1990, pp. 3–19.

Austin, N. *Meaning and Being in Myth.* Penn State UP, 1990.

Barnard, S. "The Isolated Hero: *Papillon* (1973), *Cast Away* (2000), and the Myth of *Philoctetes.*" In M. S. Cyrino and M. Safran, ed., *Classical Myth on Screen.* Palgrave Macmillan, 2015, pp. 27–36.

Bertinetti, G. "Il cinema, scuola di volontà e di energie." *La vita cinematografica.* Special issue, December 1918, 145–50.

Blanshard, A. *Hercules: A Heroic Life.* Granta Books, 2005.

————, and K. Shahabudin. *Classics on Screen: Ancient Greece and Rome on Film.* Bloomsbury, 2011.

Bondanella, P. *A History of Italian Cinema.* Continuum, 2009.

Burchfield, A. "Going the Distance: Themes of the Hero in Disney's Hercules." Thesis, Brigham Young University. All Theses and Dissertations, paper 4291, 2013.

Burkert, W. *Greek Religion* (J. Raffan, tr.). Harvard UP, 1985.

Cornelius, M., ed. "Introduction: Of Muscles and Men: The Forms and Functions of the Sword and Sandal Film." In *Of Muscles and Men.* McFarland, 2011, pp. 1–14.

Cyrino, M., and M. Safran. *Classical Myth on Screen.* Palgrave Macmillan, 2015.

D'Amelio, M. "Hercules, Politics and Movies." In M. Cornelius, ed., *Of Muscles and Men.* McFarland, 2011, pp. 15–27.

Fontenrose, J. E. *Python: A Study of the Delphic Myth and Its Origins.* University of California Press, 1959.

Foundas, S. Review of *Hercules.* http://variety.com/2014/film/reviews/film-review-hercules-1201267840/, 2014. Accessed May 4, 2016.

Galinsky, G. K. *The Herakles Theme.* Rowman and Littlefield, 1972.

Giordano, M. *Giganti buoni. Da Ercole a Piedone (e oltre) il mito dell'uomo forte nel cinema italiano.* Gremese Editore, 1998.

Grafton, A., G. Most, and S. Settis. *The Classical Tradition.* Harvard UP, 2010.

Hannah, R. "The Emperor's Stars: The Conservatori Portrait of Commodus." *American Journal of Archaeology,* vol. 90 no. 3, 1986, 337–42.

Holt, P. "Herakles' Apotheosis in Lost Greek Literature and Art." *L' Antiquité Classique,* vol. 61, 1992, 38–59.

Kirk, G. S. *Myth: Its Meaning and Function in Ancient and Other Cultures.* University of California Press, 1974.

Krumeich, R., N. Pechstein, and B. Seidensticker. *Das griechische Satyrspiel.* Wissenschaftliche Buchgesellschaft, 1999.

Leitch, T. *Film Adaptation and Its Discontents: From* Gone with the Wind *to* The Passion of the Christ. Johns Hopkins UP, 2007.

Malkin, I. *Religion and Colonization in Ancient Greece.* Brill, 1987.

Nagy, G. *The Best of the Achaians: Concepts of the Hero in Archaic Greek Poetry.* Johns Hopkins UP, 1981.

Nisbet, G. *Ancient Greece in Film and Popular Culture* (rev. 2nd ed.). Bristol Phoenix Press, 2006.

O'Brien, D. "Hercules Diminished? Parody, Differentiation and Emulation in *the Three Stooges Meet Hercules*." In M. Cornelius, ed., *Of Muscles and Men*. McFarland, 2011, pp. 187–202.

Padilla, M. W. "Herakles and Animals in the Origins of Comedy and Satyr-Drama." In *Le bestiaire d'héraclès*. Presses universitaires de Liège, 2013, pp. 217–30.

———. *The Myths of Herakles in Ancient Greece: Survey and Profile*. UP of America, 1998.

Pallant, C. "Developments in Peplum Film Making: Disney's *Hercules*." In M. Cornelius, ed., *Of Muscles and Men*. McFarland, 2011, 175–86.

Paunov, E. I. "Introduction to the Numismatics of Thrace, ca. 530 BCE–46 CE." In J. Valeva, E. Nankov, and D. Graninger, ed., *A Companion to Ancient Thrace*. Wiley, 2015, pp. 265–92.

Piggott, S. "The Hercules Myth: Beginning and Ends." *Antiquity*, vol. 12, 1938, 323–31.

Pike D. "The Superman and Personal Relationships." *Acta Classica*, vol. 20, 1977, 73–83.

Safran, M. "Reconceiving Hercules: Divine Paternity and Christian Anxiety in *Hercules* (2005)." In M. Cyrino and M. Safran, ed., *Classical Myth on Screen*. Palgrave Macmillan, 2015, pp. 133–46.

Segal, C. "Mariage et sacrifice dans les *Trachiniennes* de Sophocle." *L' Antiquité Classique* , vol. 44, 1975, 30–53.

Slater, P. *The Glory of Hera: Greek Mythology and the Greek Family*. Princeton UP, 1992.

Spina, L. "By Heracles! From Satyr Play to Peplum." In I. Berti and M. Morcillo, ed., *Hellas on Screen: Cinematic Receptions of History, Literature and Myth*. Franz Steiner Verlag, 2008, pp. 57–64.

Spinazzola, V. *Cinema e pubblico: Lo spettacolo filmico in Italia 1945–1965*. Bompiani, 1974.

Vermeule, C. C. "Commodus, Caracalla and the Tetrarchs: Roman Emperors as Hercules." In U. Höckmann and A. Krug. ed., *Festschrift für Frank Brommer*. Von Zabern, 1977, pp. 289–94.

Webster, T. B. L. *From Mycenae to Homer*. Methuen, 1958.

West, M. *The Hesiodic Catalogue of Women: Its Nature, Structure and Origins*. Clarendon Press, 1985.

Wyke, M. "Herculean Muscle! The Classicizing Rhetoric of Bodybuilding." *Arion*, vol. 4 no. 3, 1997, 51–79.

CHAPTER 4

CLASH OF THE TITANS/ WRATH OF THE TITANS

Altered Prototypes and Aeschylean, Wagnerian Dimensions

Here is an interesting tidbit of Classical trivia to delight your friends. Although Richard Wagner is famous for operas on Medieval and Germanic themes, he had actually considered an opera on Achilles, who later provides a model for Siegfried. In Dresden 1849, Wagner wrote: "Man is the perfection of God. The immortal gods are the elements which only beget mankind. In Man creation accordingly achieves its end. Achilles is higher and more complete than the element-power Thetis"[1] (A.E. 8.367–68).

As we note earlier, Wagner's mythic tetralogy *The Ring of the Nibelung* concludes with *The Twilight of the Gods*; there Wotan wills the downfall of the compromised gods, so a new human race can emerge. We have seen how many current movies suggest the current regime is evil, corrupt, and incorrigible, the product of an evil past. Further, myth translates political conflict into family struggles; the son hates the domineering father as the citizen hates the tyrannical fatherland. *Clash/Wrath* tell of the fall of the gods, which is contained in their beginnings, as well as the rise of a new human order, and a conflict involving ancient Titanic evils, as well as the sad, but familiar, stories of shattered family relationships. It is also the tale of a great hero, but one who is angry, hesitant, defiant (the sort we moderns prefer), who suffers setbacks but also triumphs, who saves his comrades, redeems his parents, gets a proper love match, and secures his son's future. Not bad.

The creators of *Clash/Wrath* have radically repurposed the Perseus myth, transforming him from a foundational, unproblematic hero to a rebellious revolutionary who saves the world and sets up a new human-centered regime. Thus the

---

1   Ewans (2009), 77.

mythic arc in *Clash/Wrath* contains elements of the creation-to-consummation myth found in Aeschylus' *Prometheia*[2] and the Danaid Trilogy here transformed into a type of creation-to-apocalypse myth, marked out by a Zeus who, like Wagner's Wotan, as noted in the Introduction, understands the need for his own downfall and sets in motion events leading to the end of the gods. A central driver of this *Ring of the Titans* will be human personal bonds, especially those of father and son, and of course "daddy issues." Other myths (e.g., myths of Medusa, Andromache, and Kronos) will be substantially altered, and characters, images, and subplots added, often enhancing the movie's psychological "dreamscape." When the mythic elements of *Clash/Wrath* are thus read, a quite substantial and coherent mythic narrative emerges. This chapter will also serve to prepare us for a consideration of *Immortals*, which possesses many similar themes.

In our analysis, we will consider (1) the theme of the hero or marvelous child's journey/quest, which, as in many of our movies, is bound up in relationship between the exceptional hero and his society, and also presents the usual family tensions; (2) the theme of cosmic creation and evolution through a violent succession of gods, culminating (here) in their fall; and (3) the employment of other mythic elements, not only from the myths of Perseus and Medusa, but also elements such as the Labyrinth and the Journey to the Underworld.

Though with a very respectable cast of stars, *Clash of the Titans* and its sequel *Wrath of the Titans* are considered lesser-quality movies. *Clash of the Titans* (MGM 2010), directed by Lois Leterrier, is ostensibly a remake of the earlier 1981 *Clash of the Titans* (directed by Desmond Davis, with stop-action animation by the famous Ray Harryhausen). Rotten Tomatoes gave it a 29 percent score based on 225 reviews. A consensus opinion is that the film lacks enough visual thrills to offset the script's deficiencies. But Roger Ebert had more fun, saying, "I like the energy, the imagination, the silliness. I even like the one guy who doesn't have a beard" (Perseus).[3] *Wrath of the Titans* (2012), directed by Jonathan Liebesman, was given by Rotten Tomatoes a score of 25 percent, a consensus opinion being that "its 3D effects are an improvement over its predecessor's, but in nearly every other respect, *Wrath of the Titans* fails to improve upon the stilted acting, wooden dialogue, and chaos-driven plot of the franchise's first installment."[4] But, as we shall see, on the level of myth there is much the critics did not appreciate.

---

2 We assume that Aeschylus was the author of the trilogy. We are more than aware of the vast debate over authorship and the reconstruction of the trilogy. But authorship is not the critical issue here, and I follow the current consensus on the reconstruction of the trilogy, which seems reasonable. On the *Prometheus Bound*, see West (1990), 51–72; Conacher (1980); and Herington (1970).

3 http://www.rogerebert.com/reviews/clash-of-the-titans-2010. Accessed May 31, 2016.

4 https://www.rottentomatoes.com/m/clash_of_the_titans_2/. Accessed Aug. 12, 2016.

PLOT SUMMARIES

In *Clash*, Acrius' wife Danaë is seduced by Zeus. Acrius puts Perseus and Danaë in a chest and tosses it into the sea. Perseus is raised by the fisherman Spyros, but his family is destroyed when Hades punishes a revolt against the gods. Hades demands that Andromeda be sacrificed, or the Kraken will destroy Argos. Perseus joins Draco's expedition to find how to kill the Kraken, along with the demigoddess Io, his secret protector. They are hunted by Calibos. Information from the Stygian witches sends them to the underworld to get Medusa's head. Most of Perseus' men are killed, and Io is stabbed by Calibos, whom Perseus kills. Flying on Pegasus, he uses Medusa's head to petrify the Kraken. He rescues Andromeda, but rejects Zeus' offer to rule. Io is resurrected and marries Perseus. In *Wrath*, set ten or so years later, Io is dead, and Perseus has become a fisherman. Chaos is breaking out. Ares and Hades conspire to capture Zeus and drain his power to free Kronos. The dying Poseidon sends Perseus after his son Agenor, now imprisoned by the warrior queen Andromeda. Agenor, taking Poseidon's trident, leads them to the island of Kail, where they meet the crazed Hephaestus who later acrifices himself so they can enter the Labyrinth of Tartarus, where Perseus battles a Minotaur. They rescue the half-dead Zeus, whom Hades revives. To get the final part of the Spear of Trium, Perseus must fight his brother Ares, whom he defeats with help from his son. Hades and the revived Zeus fight Kronos, sacrificing their power so that Perseus can destroy him with the Spear of Trium. Perseus meets Zeus just before he dies, and Hades leaves, powerless. Perseus embraces Andromache, and gives his sword to his son, suggesting the future of a new human order.

THE PRELUDE: *CLASH OF THE TITANS I*

As an ostensible remake, *Clash of the Titans* (2010) contains many plot elements similar to the 1981 version (even at times parodying its model), but with a quite different tone.[5] Essentially *Clash I* narrates how a marvelous child grows up and pursues and saves the girl (Andromeda) from an evil suitor (Calibos) and his even more evil mother (Thetis). There are few of the major historical or cosmogonic issues seen in the millennial *Clash/Wrath*. Zeus and the other gods are generally supportive of Perseus and the main action arises due to Calibos, the son of Thetis and fiancé of Andromeda, princess of Joppa. As in *Clash/Wrath*, the Perseus-Medusa myth is subordinate to the Perseus-Andromeda myth. At the end Zeus gives the couple his blessing, and the constellations of Perseus, Andromeda, Pegasus, and Cassiopeia are created in their honor. Justice is done and evil punished, and the resulting world seems a better place for gods and humans, so unlike the conclusion of *Wrath/Clash*.

THE ARCHETYPES AND THEMES: CREATION TO APOCALYPSE

The classical Perseus, whose career will be also important for our interpretation of *Harry Potter and the Chamber of Secrets*, is the canonical marvelous child and Quest hero, whose life and career fills not only our simple four-part Quest pattern but

---

5   On the first *Clash of the Titans*, see Curley (2015), 207–17.

much of Rank's scheme.[6] Perseus is Zeus' son, as well as the product of the line of heroes sprung from the mating of Zeus and Io. Acrisius was a king of Argos, who, somewhat like Laius, father of Oedipus, was told by Apollo's oracle that the child of his daughter Danaë would kill him. Like various folktale ogre-fathers, Acrisius builds a brazen tower (or a cave), where he imprisons Danaë. Zeus visits her as a shower of gold and impregnates her. Acrisius puts Danaë and the infant Perseus in a chest, and tosses it into the sea. The chest washes up on Seriphos, where it is found by the fisherman Dictys. Perseus is raised in exile in humble circumstances, as marvelous children (e.g., Jesus) often are. Years later, Danaë is threatened by King Polydectes, and Perseus defends her. King Polydectes' ruse forces Perseus to go in Quest of the petrifying head of Medusa, the only mortal Gorgon. He gains Hermes and especially Athena as magic helpers. He is sent to the Graeae, spirits of old age, ancient hags who share one eye and one tooth, who help (under compulsion) Perseus, usually by telling him where to gain certain magic objects, such as flying sandals, a special bag called the *kibisis*, a mirrored shield, a cap of invisibility, and a curved sword. The flying Pegasus is a much later addition.[7] Perseus swoops down and decapitates Medusa. On his way back, he sees the beautiful princess Andromeda (from either Joppa or Ethiopia) about to be sacrificed to the sea monster Cetus because her mother Cassiopeia had insulted the sea gods. Perseus slays the monster, petrifies his erotic rivals, and marries Andromeda. Eventually he flies back to Seriphos, saves his mother, and petrifies his enemies. He accidently kills his grandfather Acrisius with a wild discus toss, and, because of the shedding of kindred blood, gives the rule of Argos to Megapenthes and becomes instead king of Tiryns. His descendent will be Heracles. Other Greek traditions also make him founder of Mycenae.[8]

As we noted before, the Perseus myth also has rich psychological undertones. There is the conflict between father figure and son over the mother, and the triangle of mother and son versus father. Danaë and Perseus in the chest together hint at the intense closeness of the mother-son bond, suggesting that the father figure rejects the mother because of her closeness to the son. The conflict between Polydectes and Perseus is likewise a father-son conflict over the mother. As noted, Medusa represents the threatening aspects of the female, as deadly Other, with Danaë representing the good points. The danger of even looking upon Medusa suggests the perils of forbidden knowledge. Conquering Medusa allows Perseus to move to the next stage of development and marry

---

6   On the canonical Perseus myth, see Gantz (1993), 299-311; Fowler (2013), 248-259.
7   In earlier Greek myth the flying horse Pegasus is actually born when Medusa is decapitated, and employed by Bellerophon to fight the Chimera. (See *Iliad* 6.180 ff., Apollodorus *Library* 2.3.2). Interestingly, the hubris of Bellerophon prompts him to try to fly Pegasus to Olympus, and he is struck down, perhaps after Zeus sends a gadfly, and becomes an example of human arrogance.
8   Fowler (2013), 259. See also Pausanias 2.16.3–6. Hekataios fragment 22, Stephanus of Byzantium s.v. Μυκῆναι).

somebody not his mother, Andromeda, but even there Perseus must defeat a sexually symbolic entity (for sometimes a snake is more than a snake). By getting the head of Medusa, he controls a deadly female power. And finally, he kills (albeit accidentally, although on the symbolic level there are no accidents) the first father figure before he is fully established as king of Mycenae. It is a fable of maturation, and both Hermes and Athena are traditional helpers of young heroes. The multiple steps Perseus must take even to get to Medusa are symbolic of the complex and uncertain path maturation must take. The threatening father figures serve to test Perseus, and reveal him worthy of his true father, Zeus. *Clash/Wrath* incorporate and complicate these psychological conflicts and resolutions.

But Perseus also has been made to fit into a wider Greek creation-to-consummation or creation-to-apocalypse myth, a form of secondary epic, such as Vergil's *Aeneid*, which presents a pivotal historical movement. In the Classical Greek drama *Prometheus Bound*, attributed to Aeschylus, the Perseus myth is (implicitly) a central link in a vaster creation/foundation story, a surprisingly good text to consider dialectally with *Clash/Wrath*. Foundation myths are important in several of our movies. There is a marvelous mythopoetic vision in Aeschylus, which presents, in a more allegorical manner, a form of process theology,[9] where the human and divine cosmos coevolve to the benefit of both.[10] We suggest that *Clash/Wrath* also present this story of coevolution of human and divine realms, and as with Wagner's *Ring* cycle, it ends with the downfall of the gods and a new human order.

In *Prometheus Bound* Zeus is the recent victor of the Titanomachy, and now appears as the tyrannical ruler of Olympus, intent on letting humanity die out.[11] The Titan Prometheus, who helped Zeus defeat the Titans, champions humanity, although in a willful, arrogant fashion, teaching them various technologies and survival skills. In *Clash/Wrath* the tyranny of the gods (including Zeus) is stressed and humans have finally been driven to revolt. Prometheus has a long history as the archetypal rebel against authority,[12] and in the *Prometheus Bound* he even hints that the tyrant Zeus will be overthrown (*PB* 908–31). In *Prometheus Bound* the lawless theft of fire was the last straw for Zeus, and Prometheus is chained to a crag in the Caucasus until he learns to obey.

---

9 Process theology grows out of process philosophy developed by Alfred North Whitehead (1861–1947), and makes God influenced by temporal processes, and thus able to evolve. For a decent survey, see Epperly (2011).

10 For example, in the *Oresteia*, on the human level, the chain of killing and counterkilling is stopped, and humans gain, through the institution of the trial by jury, a better way of justice; on the divine level the elder female gods (e.g., the Furies) are better incorporated into the Olympian system, becoming the Eumenides (the Kindly Ones).

11 In what follows I am indebted to the nuanced interpretation of White (2001), who demonstrates that the subtle Zeus would have been seen by the original audience as a lot less tyrannical than is generally thought by moderns.

12 Perhaps the modern tradition begins with Goethe's poem *Prometheus* (written 1772–1774).

Prometheus is then visited by the gadfly-stung, boviform Io, who also appears (albeit rather differently) in *Clash/Wrath*. *Prometheus Bound* tells of how Zeus forced Io's father to cast her out, and then turned her into a heifer to hide her from Hera; of the killing of Hera's watchman Argus; and of how she is now being driven across Eurasia by Hera's gadfly. Prometheus foretells how Io will travel to Egypt, where a kindlier Zeus with a gentle touch will restore her human form, and produce (perhaps by a form of virgin birth) Epaphus, who will engender a line of Egyptian kings.

As White and Zeitlin show, the world of Inachus is still primitive, filled with monsters—like the archaic world of *Clash/Wrath*. They will eventually be destroyed by various heroes, especially Heracles. *Prometheus Bound* suggests that the mating of Io with Zeus produces a new variety of human to make the world more civilized[13]; that this journey, which will be known to "all mortals," symbolizes her central role in the "shift of authority from the Titans to Zeus"; and that "her far reaching impact on the future of mankind is shown by the fact that her name is given to the Ionian sea" (841).[14] The marriage of Io's descendant Hypermnestra with her cousin Lynceus will produce a line of kings for Argos.[15] Out of her progeny shall come "a bold archer" who will free him: Heracles.[16] Io's "heroic career" is symbolic of the Greek (idealized) view of a woman's life; she is fearfully separated from her father's house by a strange and powerful man, and enters a new and strange word, but finally discovers the nobility and gentleness of her husband; through bearing his children she supports the family and *polis*, and gives honor to herself. Heracles, amid his labors, shoots the eagle that eats Prometheus' liver and frees him; in Aeschylus' *Prometheus the Fire Bringer* Prometheus tells Zeus the secret of Thetis' son, which leads to their reconciliation.[17] It appears too that Zeus, thanks to his fondness for Heracles, becomes more benevolent to human beings.

Although there are variants, the grandson of the Danaid Hypermnestra and Lynceus is generally thought to be Acrius, whose daughter is Danaë, who may give her name to the Danaans, a Homeric name for Greeks. Perseus, through his marriage to Andromeda, will produce Electryon, whose daughter Alcmene will bear Heracles to Zeus, who will free Prometheus and be (in Aeschylus' trilogy) instrumental in the reconciliation of Zeus with Prometheus and the Titans. Thus, Aeschylus' *Prometheia* encompasses a span of time from the era of Kronos, the battle of the Olympians and Titans, the harshness of the youthful Zeus's rule, until, centuries later, Zeus and Prometheus are reconciled, which brings about the marriage of Peleus and Thetis and the birth of Achilles.

---

13 White (2001); Zeitlin (1996), 229–32.
14 White (2001), 120.
15 On the Danaid Trilogy, see Winnington-Ingram (1983), 55–72; Garvie (2006). A stunning modern interpretation of this play is Charles L. Mee's *Big Love* (2000). See Mee (2015).
16 Conacher (1980), 56–65.
17 Conacher (1980), 98–119; Herington (1986), 172–74.

KEY TERMS

Creation-to-apocalypse narrative: a cycle of myths encompassing all mythical history.
Process theology: the notion that God and the universe are evolving together.
Succession myth: a form of creation myth in which younger generations of gods depose an
  older generation.
Decomposition: in myth, when contradictory potentials in one figure become two figures, such
  as good mother and bad mother.

The canonical Perseus is a founder of the status quo. He defends his mother
and obeys the gods, and the people he kills/petrifies deserve it; he is a famous
ruler and ancestor of great heroes. Perseus is no rebel, in contrast, for example, with Bellerophon or even the transgressive Heracles. And accordingly, the
"canonical" Perseus would make a proper link for an Aeschylean creation-to-
consummation myth where the consummation is Zeus becoming reconciled
with Prometheus and more just toward humans. But, as noted, a major undercurrent of artistic productions of the new millennium is that the status quo is
corrupt and decaying, often combined with a hope that some newer arrange-
ment is in the offing. The millennial hero tends more to be transgressive, an
outsider, even an outlaw or rebel. And even after the god's triumph, resistance
to Zeus is thinkable.[18] For example, in the *Iliad* Achilles, realizing how Apollo
has duped him, wishes he could really attack the gods (22.14–20). Even Greek
Old Comedy imagines rebellion against the gods,[19] a desire that is central to
Clash/Wrath, whose writers, by presenting Perseus as a rebel and making the
human rebellion against the gods a major theme from the start, created a space
where varied elements, alien to the canonical Perseus tradition, would naturally connect. This Perseus, instead of being an earlier link for the established
order, becomes the central player in the old order's demise and the beginning
of a new, and better, human one.

CLASH OF THE TITANS: PERSEUS' TRAGIC BEGINNING

The beginning of *Clash* narrates how the Olympians battled the Titans, who were
defeated only through the use of the Kraken (borrowed from Scandinavian mythology[20]), created by Hades out of his own body. The defeated Titans were sent
to Tartarus, where Kronos still dwells, trapped. In *Wrath* we shall see Kronos, a
massive, totally nonhuman fire monster who is destroyed by Perseus.

---

18 For a decent summary, drawing on other scholars, see Yasumura (2013).
19 In the *Birds* of Aristophanes, the birds, led by a human turned into a bird, create a blockade
    between Earth and Heaven and force the gods to bow to their power.
20 It was thought to be a giant octopus or squid, big as an island and living off the Norwegian
    coast; Eason (2007), 143. For information and historical background of the Kraken and its use
    in the original *Clash* as well as in video games and popular fiction, see Torjussen (2016). In
    Greek myth, Andromeda was to be sacrificed to a sea monster sent by Poseidon.

Clash/Wrath thus contain elements of the succession myth, of a cosmos that evolves through conflicts between generations of gods. And on a psychological level this myth reproduces those tensions within families between parents and children. Unlike Hesiod's creation myth, women play an even lesser role; in fact, save for the demigoddess Io, there are no divine women present—in contrast with the original *Clash*, where Thetis had a major part.

In *Wrath*, Hephaestus notes that Hades was once good, strong, and wise. After Kronos' defeat, Hades quarreled with Zeus, who, arrogant in his power, exiled him to rule the underworld; there is a similar exile of Hades in *Percy Jackson*. Hephaestus was exiled too. Hades has been twisted by his maltreatment; like Prometheus, he was responsible for Zeus' success, but very poorly treated, and now seeks revenge. Classical Greek mythology provides conflicting accounts regarding by whom and especially why human beings were created. *Clash*'s Zeus created mortals so their worship could add to their power and extend their immortality. Without human worship, the gods lose power and even become mortal. Interestingly, this explanation recalls one reason Marduk creates Humanity from the blood of a slain enemy in the *Enuma Elish*: to do the servitude in place of the defeated gods.

As *Clash* begins, humans have begun to revolt against the gods, refusing them reverence and even violating their temples. An early rebel leader was Acrius, king of Argos, whose wife (not daughter, as in the traditional story) was Danaë. Zeus, to punish Acrius, altered his form (as in the story of Zeus and Alcmene) and coupled with and impregnated Danaë. Acrius took the infant Perseus and Danaë and put them in a chest and tossed them into the sea. Zeus blasts him with lightning, transforming him into the monster Calibos.[21] As noted in the introduction, an evil parent-figure is often found in the hero's journey, and Perseus will deal with two such figures, first Acrius/Calibos, but also Zeus, at least initially.

The fisherman Spyros finds the chest containing the young Perseus, his mother Danaë already dead. Perseus is raised by Spyros, unknowing of his origins, as fitting the marvelous child, seemingly content to be a fisherman, clearly close to his adoptive father and family. While sailing, Spyros watches soldiers sent by King Cepheus (who is continuing the rebellion) topple into the sea a colossus of Zeus. Hades convinces Zeus to release the Furies to punish the Argives. The vessel of Perseus' family is capsized, and all are killed save Perseus. Perseus blames the gods, especially Hades. This loss of a beloved family, especially a father to whom he was close, starts Perseus' heroic career.

---

21   In the 1981 *Clash* Calibos is the son of Thetis and the jealous suitor of Andromeda, an aristocrat turned into a satyr by Zeus because he has ruined the Wells of the Moon and killed most of the flying horses, save Pegasus. Note how his name recalls the savage Caliban of Shakespeare's *Tempest*, whose name, in turn, evokes the word *cannibal*.

Clash of the Titans (2010)	
Warner Brothers	
Director:	Louis Leterrier
Screenplay:	Travis Beacham and Phil Hay
Cast:	Sam Worthington (Perseus), Liam Neeson (Zeus), Ralph Fiennes (Hades), Jason Flemyng (Calibos/Acrisius, Gemma Arterton (Io), Alexa Davalos (Andromeda), Tine Stapelfeldt (Danaë), Ian White (Sheikh Suleiman)

The rescued Perseus is brought to King Cepheus and his wife Cassiopeia, now foolishly glorying in their revolt. Recalling the canonical myth, the queen suggests humans are like gods and declares her daughter Andromeda more beautiful than Aphrodite. A rather subdued Andromeda (and *very* different in *Wrath*) is clearly upset with her parents' folly. Hades makes a fearsome epiphany, announcing that the Kraken will destroy Argos unless Cepheus sacrifices Andromeda by a set date. Hades also reveals Perseus is Zeus' son, which nearly gets him killed on the spot.

THE QUEST FOR MEDUSA

King Cepheus orders his commander Draco to find some means to kill the Kraken and save Andromeda. He is being pressured by Prokopion, a fanatic Hades-priest who implores people to return to their prior worship and urges Andromeda's sacrifice. Prokopion evokes the modern fundamentalist who doubles down on religion's often life-denying agenda. This depiction of religion is another millennial theme, and seen in the (completely nonhistorical) conflict in *300* between Leonidas and the ephors, depicted as pervert-priests, as well as in *Troy*. In prison Perseus is visited by Io, given immortality because she refused the advances of some deity, another form of rebellion.[22] But note she sees immortality as a curse (as Phaedra views her divine sight in *Immortals*), underscoring the mythical theme that humans are not made for immortality,[23] and that there are worse fates than death. The value of humanity versus the value of immortality is an important issue for *Clash/Wrath*, where Hades will go far to remain immortal, as well as in the *Harry Potter* series, whose Voldemort thinks death is the worst possible thing, and will more than sell his soul to obtain deathlessness. And this theme is also central in the Heracles tradition.

Io has been watching over Perseus since he was a baby, a substitute mother, who declares she has been waiting for the day "when you'll help bringing an end to the tyranny of the Gods." Io is a magic helper for Perseus, but *Clash/Wrath*

---

22 She recalls the *Aeneid*'s Juturna, sister of Turnus, who resisted Jupiter and was made a demigoddess (Verg. *Aeneid* 12.143–45).

23 This notion of the impossibility of immortality is illustrated by the failed attempts at immortality of characters such as Tithonus, Endymion, the Sibyl of Cumae, Demophoon, the children of Medea, etc.

will provide an interesting exchange of the roles of Io and Andromeda, which will make us reconsider in *Wrath* Io's role in *Clash*. Io convinces Perseus to join Draco's expedition.

Perseus' quest is initially indirect and hesitant; he is particularly conflicted since he bitterly hates the Gods, while being part god himself. This will, of course, be an element of the conflict within Percy Jackson and other characters from the series such as Hermes' son Luke. Thus an important dimension of Perseus achieving mature status will be to come to terms with what he actually is. Greek myths like those of Phaethon, Hippolytus, and Oedipus (as well as that of Luke Skywalker and Darth Vader) likewise stress the importance of knowing your family and yourself.

Draco serves a "tough sergeant, sacrificial father figure" role, a role Dumbledore will play for Harry Potter. This band of heroic comrades contrasts with the canonical Perseus, who quests alone, underscoring that achieving adult status must be done in the interactive context of society, a lesson vividly presented by the *Harry Potter, Percy Jackson,* and *The Hunger Games* sagas. A smaller such company will appear in *Wrath*. They seek out the Stygian witches (recalling the Graeae, spirits of old age who also appear in the second Percy Jackson movie) to learn how to kill the Kraken. Meanwhile Hades makes a deal with the monstrous Calibos, the transformed Acrisius, who welcomes the chance to kill Zeus' son. Hades infuses him with demonic power. Acrius was Danaë's husband, and thus, as Calibos, is a sort of demonic parent for Perseus, almost like the embodied curse of the circumstances of his birth. In *Harry Potter and the Chamber of Secrets* Tom Riddle's hatred for the established order and Harry's parents makes him persecute Harry and associates and turns him into a monster. Here Acrius' hatred for Zeus is transferred to Perseus, with Acrius likewise monstrously transformed.

Draco, teaching Perseus the finer points of sword fighting, attacks him aggressively, to rouse the god in him. Perseus responds automatically, and nearly kills Draco. During their journey heroes discover new potentials in themselves, and this corresponds to a scene in *Percy Jackson* where Percy is nearly defeated by Annabeth, Athena's daughter, until the voice of his father Poseidon tells him to "go to the water," which heals and turns him into a superlative fighter. Zeus, now aware of Perseus' mission, sends him a magic sword, which Perseus stubbornly refuses to use, much to Draco's disgust.[24] Perseus' attitude recalls Ajax, for he insists that, if he is to succeed, he wants to do so as a human, without the help of the hated gods, a problem prominent later in *Wrath*.[25]

---

24 On a psychological level of analysis, Zeus is handing Perseus a parental (and symbolically phallic) power, which he refuses, because, as we can see, at some level he does not think himself equal to the father.

25 At the end of *Deathly Hallows I,* Harry Potter insists that he wants to bury Dobby with his own hands, without magic. This rejection, if only momentary, of magical powers, speaks perhaps to the hero's deep connection to his own humanity and mortality.

FIGURE 4.1 Sheik Suleiman offers a coin to pay for passage to the Underworld.

Immortals, considered in our next chapter, provides a contrast, for there Zeus *forces* Theseus to succeed with human resources.

Calibos attacks and retreats only when his hand is lopped off. From his blood emerge huge scorpions, echoing legends of how the snakes of Libya were created by the drops of blood falling from the Gorgon's severed head (Ovid *Met.* 4. 617–20). Perseus and company kill (barely) these monsters; more scorpions arrive, but these are ridden by desert sorcerers (the Djinn, the name borrowed from Arabic myth[26]) led by Sheik Suleiman. There is an interesting contrast between Perseus, who insists on staying human, and the Djinn, who have replaced their human parts with inorganic materials (see Fig. 4.1 for Sheik Suleiman). But they too detest the gods, and are willing to help Perseus; indeed, Sheik Suleiman heals Perseus from the poisoned wound he received from Calibos.[27]

The theme of transformation looms large in mythology, especially as depicted in Ovid's *Metamorphoses,* which extends from the metamorphosis of mixed Chaos into the known universe, to Julius Caesar becoming a star. Physical form, like literary form, is unstable and uncertain in Ovid, and this mutability is evident in *Clash/Wrath.* Kronos is a vast, inhuman fire monster, but his children, Hades, Zeus, and Poseidon, look human and can mate with mortal women; yet Hades produces the monstrous Kraken out of his own body. Io has become a demigoddess, Acrius is changed into the monster Calibos, and the Djinn have made their bodies progressively inorganic. Medusa is part woman, part snake. These hybrid beings, as in *Prometheus Bound,* seem characteristic of

---

26 El-Zein (2005), 420–21.
27 Phaedra will tend Theseus' poisoned wounds from the "Beast" in *Immortals.* The "poisoned wound," which may suggest a spiritual taint, is another mythic pattern; for example, Telephus seeks healing from the wound that Achilles gave him; Tristan gets an incurable wound from Morold in Wagner's opera *Tristan and Isolde;* in *Lord of the Rings* Frodo's wounds from carrying the Ring cannot be healed in Middle Earth.

the early universe. This horrific potential for mutability fits the movie's dream-like dimension, and also expresses a current concern, where changes in society and technology are rendering problematic what it means to be human, and are revealing the inhuman and even monstrous roots and possibilities of human behavior. And this dreamlike (or nightmarish) mutability is likewise a major feature of the *Harry Potter* series, where the living, the organic, the dead, and the inorganic (like the Sorting Hat and the Ford Anglia) have been metamorphosed into characters in their own right. This also points at a feature of our deeper consciousness, where all manner of beings and symbols, impossible in the rational world, live and have their being and meaning. The Djinn will be essential for Perseus' success, suggesting that even those threatening and inhuman areas of human experience in fact can provide powerful resources. The radically Other can be useful indeed.

Perseus forces the Stygian witches to reveal that Medusa's head can kill the Kraken. They also prophesize that Perseus will die, causing some members to abandon him, as heroes such as Beowulf or Jesus were abandoned. Perseus, Sheik Suleiman, Io, and Draco and his remaining men proceed onward. Again Perseus angrily refuses Zeus' offer to live on Olympus.

They must cross the waters of the underworld in Charon's vessel. In the traditional myth Medusa lives at the world's edge, but here Perseus' company make a true death journey to confront a primal snakelike female.[28] As Medusa is generally depicted, she is *not* so snakelike, but rather a humanoid and sometimes very female (as in *Percy Jackson*) being with two arms and legs, although in archaic art she does look quite monsterlike.[29] Snakelike females are symbols of the primal earth/female power, such as a Tiamat or Typhoeus, spawned by Gaia (Earth). In many quest myths the hero must enter/descend into an underworld or dark wood and kill some entity or retrieve some valued object, as Gilgamesh and Enkidu enter the vast Cedar Forest and kill Humbaba and gain access to his cedar wood. Thus Perseus, descending to kill a dangerous demon-female (which is also symbolic of the child's fear of the mother), will bring back an item that allows him to employ her power.

But what is the nature of that power? As we discuss later, *Wrath* takes an increasingly masculinist direction (a factor also in Aeschylus), and Medusa's depiction is illustrative. *Clash* uses a variant of Ovid's Medusa myth (*Met*.4.794–803). Io, who herself resisted a god, recounts how Medusa, a beautiful girl, ran to Athena's temple for protection against Poseidon's lust. Poseidon raped her there, and Athena, instead of offering solace to the victim, turned her into this monster, who can never harm women, but instead turns men into stone. Note the twist here, not seen in *Percy Jackson: The Lightning Thief*, that she can

---

28 Also in 1981 *Clash*.
29 For important surveys on Medusa, see Wilk (2007) and the articles in Garber and Vickers (2003).

hurt only men. Now what might Athena's actions toward Medusa be caused by? There are various psychoanalytic theories concerning the significance of Medusa,[30] but for this suggestion we start from the fact that, in feminist scholarship, Medea is often a symbol of female rage.[31]

Athena seems one of the most repressed of Greek goddesses, being born from the male, from her father's head, in order to protect male power, becoming the son who cannot depose him. And we argue that the repressed returns, and *Clash* amplifies what was found in Ovid. Thus Athena creates Medusa as a kind of anti-self, a destroyer of young heroes, the primal serpent goddess. *Clash* puts her in a temple, which men alone can enter, which is a place of hidden riches, of female power linked to death and rebirth, and, in terms of psychology, the deeply repressed. Accordingly, this will be a site of real and symbolic death and rebirth. In *Harry Potter and the Chamber of Secrets* Harry will visit a kind of underworld located within the very foundations of Hogwarts, traveling through watery tubes, in order to defeat a Basilisk, who can likewise petrify. Now when Classical Athena has Medusa killed and has her head put on her shield, a circle is completed, a type of integration. Athena finally possesses a displaced version of her own female rage, which is directed at men, usually men in battle. Now in the hero's journey, as a result of his struggle the hero often obtains some boon, treasure, or weapon he can use. Medusa's head will allow Perseus to kill his enemies; in *Percy Jackson* the head petrifies the Hydra and later Gabe the evil stepfather; in *Harry Potter* the fang of the Basilisk is used to "kill" Tom Riddle's diary and the evil enchanted memory possessed by it.

While sailing on the river Styx, below deck Io prepares Perseus to fight a quick-moving creature he cannot directly observe. They tussle, and eventually Perseus ends up on top of the not-unhappy Io. Gaining erotic knowledge and often a mate is also part of the hero's maturation process, here signifying the power of life even amid the waters of death. When they arrive, Io waits outside the temple, which women cannot enter, while the warriors face Medusa. All but Perseus are killed, with Draco and Suleiman, Father and Other, sacrificing themselves so that Perseus can decapitate Medusa. Leaving the underworld, Perseus meets Io, who is immediately stabbed by Calibos. Perseus is forced to use the sword of Zeus, that parental power he had rejected before. Fatally wounded, Calibos reverts to human form and pleads, "Don't become like them"—as if Acrius, having gained a final moment of clarity, realizes what engagement with the gods can do, and warns Perseus. Again, the hero has helped a foe find some redemption. Likewise self-sacrificing, the dying Io tells Perseus to leave and rescue Andromeda. He obeys, flying off on Pegasus.[32]

---

30 On Freudian criticism and Medusa, see Freud (1993) and (1970); Mullahy (1955), 16–29; and Downing (1975).

31 Culpepper (1986).

32 As noted before, a common feature of hero myths is that people end up dying (sometimes willingly, sometimes not) for the hero.

PERSEUS, THE KRAKEN, AND ANDROMEDA:
THE APPARENT FIRST ENDING—PERSEUS GETS IO

The trip across the Underworld's waters, the battle with Medusa, and the death of all his company, including Calibos and Io, are the necessary preliminaries for the true demigod Perseus to emerge, signified by his use of Zeus' sword and his riding Pegasus. In *Harry Potter and the Chamber of Secrets* Harry gains the sword of Gryffindor and is towed through the air by Fawkes the Phoenix. Carrying Medusa's head, Perseus flies to Argos. The evil Hades-priest Prokopion has roused the Argives to ignore their king (whom Prokopion later kills) and tie Andromeda up to be sacrificed. Hades persuades Zeus to "release the Kraken." But once he does, Hades reveals that he has gained power through the people's fear, and subdues Zeus. In mythic-cultural terms, Perseus' conquest of Hades is a figure for the defeat of those cultural entities that bind and blind us through ignorant fear. The demand for the sacrifice of a young innocent woman is a touchstone of such institutions. Further, Zeus becomes the problematical father Perseus must save, whom he will also rescue in *Wrath*. In *Chamber of Secrets* Harry must save his virtual fathers Dumbledore and Hagrid and keep Hogwarts from being closed down. Percy Jackson not only takes his mother out of Hades, but he stops a potentially disastrous war between the Gods.

Perseus, riding Pegasus while being attacked by the Harpies, displays Medusa's head. The Kraken slowly petrifies and shatters, its massive pieces crushing the Hades priest and knocking the bound Io into the sea. Perseus, calling on Zeus, tosses his thunderbolt-infused sword at Hades, who is blasted back into the underworld. The image of Perseus, riding the winged horse, battling demonic Harpies, and defeating the vast, elemental Kraken and then Hades, resembles an apocalyptic battle of the heavenly armies with the forces of the underworld and Satan.

Perseus rescues Andromeda, but refuses her request to rule alongside her and returns home, an action we have noticed as characteristic of peplum heroes, who do not want power for themselves. Later, besides his fallen statue, Perseus meets Zeus, who offers immortality, again refused. Note what Zeus says: "You may not want to be a god, Perseus, but after feats like yours, men will worship you. Be good to them. Be better than we were." Zeus' admonition "Be better than we *were*" (note the past tense) points to the future world ruled by humans, not gods. Then Zeus, insisting that since Perseus is a son of Zeus he should not be alone, presents him with a resurrected Io. The son who rebelled against the power of the Gods is given by his God-father (who produced him through rape) a woman who spurned the sexual power of the Gods; the Freudian overtones are clear. The Quest hero-son has saved the father, has done great deeds (went to the underworld and back again, defeated a demonic female, defied Hades, saved the world), and has gained a wife. Zeus's comments seem to indicate that Perseus will now take up the status that his feats have earned him, lifting human aspirations as a man who can even defeat Hades, the lord of the Underworld and Profiteer of Fear, and hopefully rebuild a new human society as he will build his own family with the reborn Io.

WRATH OF THE TITANS: HEROISM REJECTED, THE DEATH OF THE GODS BEGINS

Maybe that was the end *Clash*'s creators had initially planned. But *Clash* ended with too many loose ends. Zeus admitted that Hades was merely biding his time, and there was still the question of the gods' eroding power. More importantly, what about Andromeda and Perseus? Where they not supposed to hook up? We suspect *Clash*'s incongruent dismissal of Andromeda indicated a planned sequel.

Wrath, whose plot repeats several elements in *Clash*, perhaps a bit too mechanically, opens around a dozen years later. The initial voice-over by Zeus gives essential information: "In ancient times, the world was ruled by gods and monsters. But it was the half-god Perseus, my son . . . who defeated the Kraken and saved humanity. For his courage, I offered him a place to rule at my side. But Perseus . . . was strong-willed and chose a different path. He vowed to live as a man. Even when fate took his wife . . . he would not pray for help, from me . . . or the other gods. And now the time of the gods is ending. But the son of Zeus cannot hide from his destiny forever."

This prologue functions like the epilogue of *Immortals*, and guides our interpretation. The world is becoming more human, as is the world of *Prometheus Bound*, and the era of "gods and monsters" is ending. At this point Perseus remains an abortive hero who has denied the destiny Zeus imagined for him. Perseus has returned to his fishing nets and buried his armor. Io and Perseus had a son, Helius, and Io died. Perseus has rejected any heroic career, in part out of a promise to Io, who had hated the gods and any involvement with them. He also fears greatly for his son; Perseus endured the traumatic loss of an adopted father, and he does not want his son to suffer the same fate. In addition Perseus did not think himself equal to the gods, echoing common Classical attitudes, as well as the son's fear of not being equal to his father. But a central point of the myth of *Clash*/*Wrath* is to overturn that notion. In *Clash* Zeus told Perseus "Be better than we [the gods] were," and in *Wrath* Zeus says to Perseus, "You will learn someday that being half-human makes you stronger than a god, not weaker." But this rise of humanity must go hand in hand with the death of the old father, here the destruction of the gods. *Clash*'s Zeus knows, and accepts, that "the time of the Gods is ending." He recalls the Wotan of Wagner's *Ring*, who, in act II of *Die Walküre*, recognizing the corruption of the gods, renounces his power and sets in motion their doom.[33]

---

33 Cicora (1999), 35.

Can humans be better than gods? Remember how Achilles in *Troy* declared to Briseis, "The gods envy us . . . because we're mortal." *Wrath* suggests family relationships are a central factor respecting this greater strength. Zeus in the prologue calls Perseus "my son," and in this sequel father, son, and family issues loom large. Zeus will emphasize the power that the love for a son gives, and we shall see three other sons: Ares (son of Zeus and Perseus' half-brother), Agenor (son of Poseidon, Perseus' cousin) and Helius (Perseus' son). Ares despises his father because Zeus has come to love Perseus more, and conspires with his uncle Hades to drain Zeus of his power in order to liberate Kronos, the once-hated father of Zeus, Poseidon, and Hades, to ensure that their problematic immortality will continue. Zeus will be forcibly made to grasp how badly he has treated his brother and Ares, and the divine brothers, at least, will reconcile. Although dying, Poseidon will prompt the renewal of his own son, Agenor. And sons will save fathers, as well as destroy them and nearly wreck the world. And as we will see, a second factor in mortal superiority will be humans' ability to hope against near-impossible odds, and then triumph. Perseus will be slow to gain such hope.

Alongside the question of the value of human versus divine life and the power of family relationships stands the question of the worth of female life versus male life. Consider again *Prometheus Bound*'s Io. After her ordeal, like any Classical Greek woman, she becomes a good wife and mother and produces glorious children. Her son Epaphus is the first in a line of kings and heroes who will civilize post-Titan humanity. Helius is the name for the sun god, symbolic of the dawn and thus of rebirth. At the end of *Wrath*, Helius holds Perseus' sword, and agrees they cannot go back to being fishermen, but must embrace their heroic destiny. Thus, as in *Prometheus Bound*, Io's son will produce a renewal of humanity. In *Percy Jackson: The Lightning Thief*, Zeus forbade the gods to associate with their mortal children because they were becoming "too human" and avoiding their divine responsibilities. Because of his domestic association with Io, Perseus has neglected his heroic responsibilities. He will fully embrace them once his father Zeus is dead, as he shares his life with the transformed Queen Andromeda. This contrast between Io and Andromeda evokes a question of feminist studies: Is it possible to be a mother and yet uphold feminist principles?[34] Does the ability to wear armor, command armies, and kill effectively make you a feminist heroine?[35] And does the way in which our couple are depicted as finally coming together represent a regression to patriarchal stereotypes?

Another famous myth resonates here: the narrative of Aeneas as reconfigured by Vergil who drew on the Jason of Apollonius Rhodius' *Argonautica*.[36]

---

34 See DiQuinzio (1999).
35 See essays in Jones, Bajac-Carter, Batchelor (2014).
36 See the lengthy presentation in Nelis (2001).

Aeneas, like Jason, does not willingly set out on his mission to refound the Trojan race, having rather died at Troy, and his father Anchises guides him. When Anchises unexpectedly dies, Aeneas is distracted by Dido, and would have remained with her (as Perseus remains with Io), with his destiny and that of his son Iulus thwarted, save that Jupiter sends Mercury to get Aeneas back on track (*Aeneid* 4. 221–278). But Aeneas must go to the Underworld, confront his father, and see the future of Rome, to be transformed into the Roman Aeneas who will complete the mission.[37] Our Perseus will likewise make a transformative trip to the Underworld to see his father Zeus. The Aeneas myth is Vergil's ideological creation, an allegory of the problematic path Octavian took from the time of Julius Caesar's murder to the political settlements of 27 and 23 BCE. Our Perseus is the world's reluctant refounder after the fall of the Gods, who makes mistakes and allows himself to be diverted from his destiny by a woman (here Io) in the process depriving his own son Helius of his destiny, as well as allowing needless suffering.

In *Wrath*, humanity's regard for the gods has sharply fallen, weakening the world's security. While Perseus teaches Helius fishing-net technique, Helius says, "I want to be a good god and do good things"; Perseus replies, "There are no good gods." Zeus appears, warning that the walls of Tartarus are crumbling and begging Perseus' help. Perseus rebuffs him, an action he will regret, a refusal of his destiny with terrible consequences. Accordingly, Perseus has anxious dreams, in which he repeats the line "I will never leave my son"; we recall how he was abandoned as a son, and lost a father, and knows, without admitting it, a crisis is coming.

The next day a vast Chimera attacks. Perseus digs up his armor and, using demigod derring-do, slays it. At a ruined temple Perseus tries to contact Zeus, but finds Poseidon, fatally wounded. He informs Perseus that he alone can save Zeus and the world from Kronos. When Perseus protests his lack of power, Poseidon tells him he must find another half-god, his son Agenor, to help him. Poseidon gives him his trident, dies, and crumbles into dust. This is the beginning of the death of the gods, and the triumph of the demigods, who will prove stronger than the gods by first saving them and then outliving them.

AGENOR AND THE SEARCH FOR THE FALLEN ONE

Perseus flies Pegasus to Argos; he is hailed as the Kraken's conqueror. But he is a latecomer, like Theseus in *Immortals*, having permitted others to bear his burdens. Andromeda, whose eyes light up seeing him, is no longer the passive, delicate princess of *Clash*, but has morphed into an armor-wielding warrior queen. The episode with the Kraken, her father's death, and her assumption of royal power have compelled her to embrace her radical potentials, to heed her

---

37   See Otis (1963), 290–307.

own "call to adventure"—unlike Perseus. Andromeda has commanded an army, fighting against monsters with unsustainable casualties. But Agenor, like Perseus, has left duty behind, and respectability too, becoming a thief. He is now in jail, having proposed to Andromeda (signaling suitability as a hero's wife); rejected, he attempted to steal her jewels. Like Perseus, Agenor has not lived up to his ancestry, or to the moniker "the Navigator"; later Hephaestus will consider Agenor a nobody. As noted, a hero awakens and redeems problematic others. The name Agenor suggests he is destined for an impressive future. According to the mythographer Apollodorus (*Library* 2.1.4), Agenor was a son of Poseidon and the nymph Libya, and became king of Phoenicia. Even more important, Agenor is usually named as the father of Europa (whom Zeus abducts and takes to Crete to father Minos), and of Cadmus, who, sent to find Europa, goes to Greece and founds the famous Greek city of Thebes.

Perseus starts by noting Agenor has his "father's eyes." Perseus needs Agenor to guide them (including Andromeda) to the hidden island of Kail, where the Fallen One, Hephaaestus, dwells. Agenor is reluctant to help, until Perseus further motivates him with the promise of a ship. Perseus even hands him Poseidon's trident, saying "Don't let our family down," stressing their kinship. When Agenor grasps the trident, it flames, connecting with his paternal power, and turns the ship toward Kail. A relieved Perseus says, "Never doubted you for a second, Agenor." This scene in part recalls the earlier moment when Perseus finally took up Zeus' sword. Agenor begins to accept his heroic lineage.

As in *Clash* the adventurers were attacked by scorpions, whose masters the Djinn later proved helpful; arriving at Kail, Perseus and company are set on by Cyclopes. Peace is made when Perseus reveals Poseidon's trident; in some accounts the Cyclopes are Poseidon's children,[38] although they also serve Hephaestus.[39] They lead the survivors to a Hephaestus gone schizophrenic, who nevertheless performs as a magic helper.[40] Hephaestus in Greek myth is the god of industrial arts, the divine craftsman. He is associated with the island of Lemnos, whose volcanic fires power his forge. The name "Fallen One" relates to a story found in *Iliad* 1.590–94: when Hephaestus tried to protect his mother Hera from Zeus' outrages, he was tossed so violently by Zeus that he fell for a whole day and finally crashed on Lemnos, which may explain his lameness. In *Wrath*, Hephaestus, after he had created the gods' three weapons (Zeus' thunderbolt, Hades' pitchfork, and

---

38 In the *Odyssey*, for example, which is why Polyphemus prays to Poseidon.

39 For example, in Callimachus' *Hymn to Artemis* 9, and they serve Vulcan in *Aeneid* 8.417ff.

40 It is an inside joke in *Wrath* that the alter ego whom Hephaestus keeps talking to is the mechanical owl from the earlier *Clash of the Titans*. In *Clash* Perseus picked up that same owl as he was choosing gear for his mission, and Draco told him to toss it away. But here there is the possible fitting allusion to the Classical Hephaestus, who made robotlike figures, such as the two mechanical dogs for Alcinous (*Odyssey* 7.91–93) as well as golden mechanical female helpers for himself (*Iliad* 18. 417–18).

Poseidon's trident),[41] supported Hades' quarrel with Zeus. He too was exiled, and, alone and hoping for a reconciliation, has gone mad. He mocks Perseus' plan to rescue Zeus, and foresees Kronos shattering the world. But Andromeda's resemblance to his lost (and loved) wife Aphrodite moves him[42], especially when, with deep softness, Andromeda says, "I'm sorry that you think being human is not enough; but we humans hope when there is no hope. And we believe when to believe is idiotic. But sometimes, in spite of everything, we prevail."

Here a remembered love awakens the good Hephaestus; Andromeda's speech reveals that special source of human power, the ability to hope.[43] Later, right before their descent into the Labyrinth, Perseus says, "I can't beat him [Ares]"; he is gently slapped by Agenor, who tells Perseus to "jump in" and commit himself to the hope his responsibilities demand.

Meanwhile, in Tartarus, Zeus, savaged by Ares, is nearly drained of divine power. Hades starts to question his actions. Justifying his willingness to do anything to stay immortal, Hades declares that human souls, when they die, go somewhere else, but for the gods death is "oblivion." We can infer that *Wrath's* gods are, in some sense, soulless; when they crumble, note how inorganic they appear inside. Nevertheless, remember how Zeus created humanity to augment the gods' immortality. Logically, somehow, positive human nature arises from Zeus our creator, and he puts some better part of himself into the creation of humans. Thus it is appropriate that, in *Wrath*, Zeus is able to finally recognize the true importance of family relationships, as does his brother, Hades. But like Wagner's Wotan, he also acknowledges the limitations of the gods. Amid his sufferings, Zeus can send a mental message to Perseus, who tells Zeus to "stay with him"; they retain a special connection.

THE LABYRINTH OF TARTARUS AND THE HERO'S ORDEAL

Hephaestus gave Tartarus a mazelike structure and a secret exit/entrance, which he now leads them to. Hephaestus lets Agenor (aka the Navigator) hold a special map of Tartarus, recalling how Poseidon taught him navigation.

---

41 A fitting role, since in the *Iliad* Hephaestus makes new armor and weapons for Achilles, and his Roman equivalent Vulcan makes armor and weapons for Aeneas in the *Aeneid*.

42 A question the movie leaves unasked and unexplained is where the goddesses who were there in the original *Clash* have gone. Apparently an appearance by Athena (who is referred to also) was edited out. The disappearance of the goddesses, and the existence of only one fully divine child (Ares) points to the sterility of the divine order.

43 The power of human hope is stressed, although problematically, in *Prometheus Bound*. After enumerating all the arts he has taught humanity, when Chorus asks him if he transgressed in other areas, he says (250–53): "PROMETHEUS: I stopped mortals from seeing their fate. CHORUS: Having found what sort of cure for this sickness? PROMETHEUS: I established in them blind hopes. CHORUS: Greatly useful this that you bestowed on them." And in our *Hercules* (2014) movie, the ability to truly believe in himself as a hero was essential to Hercules' transformation into superhero.

Hephaestus too is prodding Agenor to embrace his potentials. Suddenly, when one of Andromeda's naïve servants prays to the gods, Ares locates them and violently attacks—another instance of the movie's hostility to formal religion. Hephaestus sacrifices himself so the remainder can slip inside the Labyrinth. Another god is gone, but redeemed in his passing.

Wrath's trip through the Tartarus maze functions like the underworld journey to Medusa's temple in *Clash*. A labyrinth will also feature in *Immortals*. A labyrinth is a path, a symbolic (or real) route through an underworld, or through an initiation/rebirth process. The Tartarus maze also plays with their minds, and works on their fears, which they must overcome, for, as Hephaestus declares, "After all, the mind . . . is the biggest trap of all." The Quest hero often must journey to the underworld to battle monsters (e.g., Grendel's mother, from the old-English epic poem *Beowulf*) or to save a loved one (Eurydice). In the *Aeneid*, even after his father's death, dreams of Anchises keep summoning Aeneas, and his paternal piety makes him conquer death's realm (*Aeneid* 4.687–96), where he gains a revelation of Rome's future and truly becomes Roman Aeneas, ready for the *maior opus* (greater labor) awaiting him in Italy. The hero often confronts forces of chaos and illusion, as well as figures connected to his past and destiny. Thus in his journey to the underworld of Hogwarts Harry meets the phantom memory of Tom Riddle, who became Voldemort and killed his parents. Agenor leads them into the Labyrinth, and, as predicted, the maze plays with their minds and threatens them with its constant reconfiguring, rather like the tumblers of a lock, which will reveal the right route when Perseus completes his ordeal. There Andromache thinks she sees her slain servant, and Perseus and Agenor quarrel over the map, which Agenor declares is "useless," perhaps because the map (and the true struggle) lie in the mind.

The shifting maze dumps Perseus in a chamber where he imagines that he sees his son, who says "It's cold in here, isn't it?' and walks past him, as if a dead spirit. The distracted Perseus is immediately attacked by a Minotaur-man, who represents a demonic force the hero must conquer, and as well those hidden, bestial, and psychosexual forces and fears that stalk the mazes of our unconscious. In their fight, Perseus steers the monster into a wall, and a horn breaks off, with which Perseus stabs it. Percy Jackson kills his Minotaur with a similar trick. In *Immortals* King Hyperion's savage helper, "the Beast," wears a Minotaur helmet, and Theseus beats him to death with his own club. The phallic dimensions stand out; during Heracles' battle with Achelous, Heracles breaks off the river god's horn, which becomes the Cornucopia, the "horn of plenty" and an obvious fertility symbol.[44] But the fact that Perseus sees his son, and that, when the Minotaur-man is dying, he hears Helius' voice saying "Why are you doing this? Please, Dad, don't kill me," connects to Perseus' earlier worry

---

44 Roberts (1998), 19–20.

that the heroic life will destroy his child. This recalls when Odysseus visits the Underworld; he faces dead individuals, such as Elpenor, Anticlea, and Ajax, who represent what his career has cost others. Aeneas does the same in *Aeneid* 4. But, the final test passed, the maze reconfigures itself, reuniting him with Agenor and Andromeda and revealing the heart of Tartarus.

PERSEUS AND THE SECOND TITANOMACHY

Kronos, powered up, is nearly free. Zeus gains forgiveness from Hades by offering his own. As Perseus and Hades fight Ares, and Perseus struggles to free Zeus by using Poseidon's trident (Fig. 4.2), Zeus refers to him as "my son" and tells him to "use the power within you"—the supernatural power inherited from his divine father. They escape to Argos, where Andromeda's army has assembled. Perseus' actions (with assistance from Hades) will soon help Zeus redeem his failings in an act of self-sacrifice, and cement the future of Perseus and Helius.

They carry the nearly dead Zeus to a tent. Zeus explains that he recently tried to make the world safer for Perseus and his son Helius, but Perseus had rejected Zeus' plea for help. The results of this rupture now threaten the world as Kronos emerges, ready to destroy all. Note this exchange:

PERSEUS: I should have come with you.—I was just . . .

ZEUS: You pulled me . . . out of Tartarus. You saved me. How do you suppose you did that?

PERSEUS: I never stopped thinking about getting home to my son.

ZEUS: Then you use that. Fight for your son.

FIGURE 4.2 Perseus rescues Zeus.

Underscored again, before Perseus' great ordeal, is the power arising out of love for family, a significant theme also of *O Brother, Where Art Thou?*, where such powerful love motivates Everett's prayer. Aeneas emerged out of the Deadlands more willing to undertake new challenges, which he assumes in part for the sake of his son, Iulus/Ascanius. Now Perseus has been tested, has claimed his purpose, and is prepared for his last trials. Just as in *Clash* only Medusa's head could defeat the Kraken, here only the Spear of Trium, made from Hades' pitchfork, Poseidon's trident, and Zeus' thunderbolt, can destroy Kronos, and Ares has the thunderbolt. Perseus has held back, thinking himself unequal to the gods in general and unable to defeat Ares in particular. But now he prays to Ares, offering to meet him to prove to their common father Zeus that he is the better son. This confrontation will be his true death struggle.

As he leaves on Pegasus, there are grunt cheers borrowed from *300;* Andromeda plans defense. Agenor shows good military skills. Their mission resembles that of Aragorn's army in *Return of the King*: fight Sauron's overwhelming armies to give Frodo time to destroy the Ring. The gritty scenes of a worn army preparing for a near-hopeless battle provides a greater realism than kindred scenes in *Troy*. The massed Greek phalanx is likewise impressive. In *Hercules* there will be also a powerful scene of massed combat.

Whirling three-bodied monsters emerge and wreck havoc with the Greek army. Amid the chaos, Hades slips into the tent and clasps his brother's hand. "I forgive you," he says, and gives Zeus what power he can, his last offering. Reconciled, they now will, for a brief moment, relive their glory days when as young gods and true brothers they fought against chaos. They stride forth at ease in power and blast various monsters.

In contrast to these reconciled brothers, at the half-ruined temple Ares, who mockingly and repeatedly refers to Perseus as "brother," has abducted Perseus' son, declaring "I want you to know . . . what it feels like . . . when someone takes your father away from you." Ares prefers to keep beating Perseus instead of delivering a fatal blow. Helius steps forward with a sword, scared to death but prepared to defend his father. Inspired by Helius, Perseus is able to blindside Ares, and pierce him with Zeus' thunderbolt. Ares crumbles to dust. Perseus now soars off on Pegasus with the assembled Spear of Trium, which shudders with power.

Kronos, an elemental fire monster, rumbles toward the Argives. Zeus and Hades use their power to distract Kronos so Perseus can fly within range of Pegasus. The rain of lava and fire, the image of Perseus carrying the Spear of Trium, a living bolt of lightning, and the blasts of Zeus and Hades together suggest an apocalyptic battle, a rehearsal of the original Titanomachy, a closing of a temporal circle. Zeus uses his remaining energies to protect the Greeks and Hades, deflecting a fiery cascade. Perseus hurls the Spear of Trium down Kronos' gullet and Kronos explodes.

THE END OF THE GODS, A RECONCILIATION, A NEW BEGINNING

Perseus flies to where Hades waits with Zeus, who is about to die. Earlier we saw Perseus' guilt at not assisting Zeus; now Perseus' grief almost does not let him look his father in the eye. Consider their final exchange:

ZEUS: Your boy gave you strength.
PERSEUS: Yes.
ZEUS: As did mine.
PERSEUS: Perhaps Hades can heal you.
ZEUS: He already gave me my last chance.
PERSEUS: And you sacrificed it for him.
ZEUS: There will be no more sacrifices. No more gods. Use your power wisely,
    Perseus. Thank you, my son.

Again, nearly at curtain close, the power of the father-son bond is underscored. Zeus' next-to-last comment recalls his earlier statement in *Clash*: "Be good to them. Be better than we were." Like Wagner's Wotan, he understands why the gods must fall. Father and son finally make eye contact, partially reconciled, partially redeemed. As Perseus tries to embrace him, Zeus crumbles apart, with Perseus holding his hand to his heart in grief. This recalls the ending of Euripides' *Hippolytus*, where, as Hippolytus dies, father and son are reunited at a human level, understanding each other's sorrow and nobility, although much too late. It resembles Odysseus trying to give Anticlea the embrace he could not grant her in life. But it also strongly reminds us of another Hollywood blockbuster, the conclusion of *The Return of the Jedi*, where Darth Vader sacrifices himself for Luke, and dying, pleads to see his son with his own eyes before he dies. Note too how Hades, shuffling off, tells Perseus, "All my power is spent. Who knows? I might be stronger without it." In a sense, Hades has been freed too from the compromised burden of divinity, and being more human may indeed make him stronger.[45]

Back at camp, Agenor signals to Perseus that he should talk with Andromeda, calling Helius over to him. When Helius says, "I've read that you are a great disappointment," Agenor simply replies, "That's right, I am great," underscoring his readiness for the destiny his name implies. Andromeda, seeing Perseus, frantically begins to plan for further monster attacks. Wordlessly, Perseus pulls her to him and kisses her deeply. Again, no words, but her eyes do brighten. Her watery plunge after the Kraken's destruction spelled a kind of death and rebirth for a changed Andromeda. Now, in Hollywood fashion, a new life phase begins with a kiss from her Perseus Charming. Her past has awakened her potentials as queen and warrior, making her a suitable match for Perseus, as Io was not. We will speak more of the satisfaction of those potentials soon.

---

45   Of course, it is not improbable that Hades was left alive for a third movie (*Return of the Titans*, anyone?) which was contemplated, but not made.

In the final scene, father and son stand on a ridge, gazing over the blackened desolation. Helius declares, "I've decided being a boring fisherman isn't that bad," recalling Perseus' early refusal of his destiny. But now Perseus says, "You know we cannot go back." The son shakes his head in agreement, and then Perseus offers him the sword (and we recall Zeus once offered Perseus a sword): "Take it. You're Helius. You're son of Perseus . . . the grandson of Zeus. Take it." Helius reluctantly takes the sword, which seems too heavy at first, but then he raises it with more authority (Fig. 4.3). Note Perseus' invocation of Zeus; Perseus bids his son, as his son must, to accept his ancestry and destiny, and the glories and responsibilities it entails. Perseus says, "It's heavy," to which Helius answers, "Yeah, it is. Is it too much?" Helius replies, "No." The son has accepted what his father Perseus accepted only too late; recall how Agenor accepted Poseidon's trident.

And so *Clash/Wrath* conclude. With the primal order and its gods gone, the hope is that the battle-tested demigods and heroes/heroines will be rulers of a more human-centered universe, empowered by family bonds. The old father gods have done great harm, and been partially redeemed, but cannot share the world with the new generation. The fathers are acknowledged with a certain pride, but they remain safely dead. We have similar redemption in the *Oresteia*, where the problematic Agamemnon of the *Agamemnon* becomes a demigod prayed to in the *Choephoroi*, and in the *Eumenides* Athena is happy to accept the offerings that Agamemnon left her at Troy and protects his son Orestes. As noted, out of the deaths of problematic parents new dispensations can arise.

The *Oresteia* is thought to show the triumph of the masculinist order, with the male and female initially opposed on the divine and human levels. In the *Eumenides* resolution is achieved, but only with the acquittal of the matricide of Orestes through the tie-breaking vote of armor-wearing Athena, who favors the

FIGURE 4.3 Helius raises Perseus' sword.

male in all things, with the former Furies, now Eumenides, becoming protectors of the civic, patriarchal order of Athens. *Clash/Wrath*, despite the transformed Andromeda, are also noticeably masculinist. Only Io and Andromeda have significant speaking parts, and Io says much more than Andromeda. Of the Greek goddesses only Aphrodite and Athena are mentioned. In *Clash* the proud father Zeus gives his son the restored Io, who says nothing, a mute but smiling prize. *Wrath*'s "romantic moment" lasts only a few seconds, as the bloody Perseus seizes the armored Andromeda and kisses her wordlessly; she is apparently so taken with his manliness that verbal communication or consent is unneeded. It's all about his godlike attractiveness and big sword, we must assume. Accordingly in *Wrath*'s concluding scene Perseus hands Helius a sword, which he first holds horizontal, then shifts to the vertical, while Perseus looks on satisfied that his son can "handle it." The military, Freudian, and masculinist imagery is obvious. Father and son, proven descendants of Zeus, will rule by the sword—very different from the usual ending of a peplum movie, where Hercules or an equivalent hero moves on to right more wrongs. In times of obscurity and crisis like our own, there is always a retrograde desire for the return of the days of heroic masculine authority, for real heroes and the women who will armor up for them but look dewy-eyed at the appropriate moment and not say too much.

CLASH/WRATH: TWO MOVIES FOR THE MILLENNIUM

As do our other movies, *Clash/Wrath* imply that our own social and political order was built on violence and injustice, which the current political order must blindly and bloodily reproduce. But rebellions naturally arise, and these oppressive forces contain the seeds of self-destruction. There is a dream of a hero with innate special ability, who arises from our problematic circumstances, flawed, and thus human, who overcomes, as we can, still uncomfortable with his power, who will, at the end, take part in the apocalypse, even to willed self-immolation, which will be the preliminaries of a better, more human, order.

There is a theme, shared by most of our movies, that *Clash/Wrath* particularly emphasize: as teachers, we sometimes despair at how many students do well in high school and college, in their initial quest, so to speak; and then, instead of following the path their initial success displays, they settle for the safe, the mediocre, or worse. Sometimes it is because they never were convinced of their own ability, and sometimes because the abusive system itself disgusts them, and they cannot see the possibility of real change. Today there is widespread doubt that we can overcome the Titans who oppose us, and who are also part of us. This is Perseus' plight and ours. He is a compromised hero who must finally accept his heroism and leadership role, in the spirit of hope, not certainty. By not acting, perhaps we doom the world, and our children too. Sometimes, the only solution is to stand up and be counted, if only as a casualty. But that, alas, in our complex world may be too simple a solution.

REFERENCES

Cicora, M. *Wagner's Ring and German Drama*. Greenwood, 1999.

Conacher, D. J. *Aeschylus' Prometheus Bound: A Literary Commentary*. University of Toronto Press, 1980.

Culpepper, E. E. "Ancient Gorgons: A Face for Contemporary Women's Rage." *Woman of Power*, vol. 3, 1986, 22–24, 40.

Curley, D. "Divine Animation: *Clash of the Titans* (1981)." In M. Cyrino and M. Safran, *Classical Myth on Screen*. Palgrave Macmillan, 2015, pp. 207–17.

DiQuinzio, P. *The Impossibility of Motherhood: Feminism, Individualism and the Problem of Mothering*. Routledge, 1999.

Downing, C. "Sigmund Freud and the Greek Mythological Tradition." *Journal of the American Academy of Religion*, vol. 43 no. 1, 1975, 3–14.

Eason, C. *Fabulous Creatures, Mythical Monsters, and Animal Power Symbols: A Handbook*. Greenwood, 2007.

El-Zein, A. "Jinn." In J. W. Meri, *Medieval Islamic Civilization: An Encyclopedia. Vol. 1: A–K*. Routledge, 2005, pp. 420–21.

Epperly, B. G. *Process Theology: A Guide for the Perplexed*. Bloomsbury, 2011.

Ewans, M. *Wagner and Aeschylus: The Ring and the Oresteia*. Cambridge UP, 1983.

Fowler, R. *Early Greek Mythography. Vol. 2: Commentary*. Oxford UP, 2013.

Freud, S. "Medusa's Head." In P. Rieff, ed., *Sexuality and the Psychology of Love*. Collier Books (Macmillan), 1993, pp. 212–13.

———. "Das Unheimliche." *Studienausgabe. Psychologische Schriften*. Vol. IV. Fischer Verlag 1970.

Gantz, T. *Early Greek Myth: A Guide to Literary and Artistic Sources*. Johns Hopkins UP, 1993.

Garber, M., and N. J. Vickers, ed. *The Medusa Reader*. Routledge, 2003.

Garvie, A. F. *Aeschylus' Supplices: Play and Trilogy*, corrected ed. Bristol Phoenix Press, 2006.

Herington, C. *Aeschylus*. Yale UP, 1986.

———. *The Author of the Prometheus Bound*. University of Texas Press, 1970.

Jones, N., M. Bajac-Carter, and B. Batchelor, ed. *Heroines of Film and Television: Portrayals in Popular Culture*. Rowman & Littlefield, 2014.

Mee, E. B. "Charles Mee's (Re)Making of Greek Drama." In K. Bosher, F. Macintosh, J. McConnell, and P. Rankine, ed., *The Oxford Handbook of Greek Drama in the Americas*. Oxford UP, 2015, pp. 731–35.

Mullahy, P. *Oedipus: Myth and Complex*. Grove Press, 1955.

Nelis, D. *Vergil's Aeneid and the Argonautica of Apollonius Rhodius*. Francis Cairns, 2001.

Otis, B. *Virgil: A Study in Civilized Poetry*. Oxford UP, 1963.

Roberts, H. *Encyclopedia of Comparative Iconography: Themes Depicted in Works of Art. Vols. 1 & 2*, 3rd ed. Fitzroy Dearborn, 1998.

Torjussen, S. S. "'Release the Kraken.' - The Recontextualization of the Kraken in Popular Culture, from *Clash of the Titans* to *Magic: The Gathering*," *New Voices in Classical Reception Studies*. (2016), vol. 11, 1–13.

West, M. *Studies in Aeschylus*. Teubner, 1990.

White, S. "Io's World: Intimations of Theodicy in *Prometheus Bound*." *Journal of Hellenic Studies*, vol. 121, 2001, 107–40.

Wilk, S. R. *Solving the Mystery of the Gorgon*. Oxford UP, 2007.

Winnington-Ingram, R. *Studies in Aeschylus*. Cambridge UP, 1983.

Yasumura, N. *Challenges to the Power of Zeus in Early Greek Poetry*. Bloomsbury Academic, 2013.

Zeitlin, F. "The Politics of Eros in the Danaid Trilogy of Aeschylus." In R. Hexter and D. Selden, ed., *Innovations of Antiquity*. Routledge, 1992, pp. 203–52.

CHAPTER 5

THESEUS IN *IMMORTALS*

An Ideal Hero for a Rough Age

By the rivers of Babylon we sat and wept when we remembered Zion.
There on the poplars we hung our harps,
For there our captors asked us for songs,
Our tormentors demanded songs of joy;
They said, "Sing us one of the songs of Zion!"
How can we sing the songs of the Lord while in a foreign land?

(*Psalm* 137 1–4, New International Version)

Again and again, our essays consider the heroine, the hero, and the heroic career. Everybody is searching for a hero, right? Yet, how many times have we deployed adjectives like "problematic" or "flawed"? The modern world seems foreign, a Babylon for our hopes; can we sing the old song of heroism in this strange land? And how would it sound? Tarsem Singh's *Immortals* offers one solution. Its surreal cinematic style and narrative gives its protagonists and plot a very archetypal and mythic embodiment. It combines an old-fashioned dramatic arc about deep personal loss, faithless turn to faith, battles for the world's soul, sacrifice, salvation, and eternal reward within a mythic dreamscape. This is why the movie works as a substantial myth. In every one of our movies humans battle against looming, ingrained evil. Even in the "love stories" of *Lars and the Real Girl* and *Ruby Sparks*, psychological traumas inflict a heavy toll. We ourselves often feel at war against barely comprehensible, powerful obstacles, and yearn for a cosmos containing helpful powers equal to those obstacles. And now, when science, superstition, secularism, fundamentalism, fanaticism, individualism, and all the burdens of hatred and history weigh heavy on us, there are countless expressions of this hope, or its impossibility. Our movies demonstrate a wide swath of this spectrum, but *Immortals* offers an old- and new-fashioned view, as did *Hercules*.

PLOT SUMMARY

Before human history, the gods conquered and then caged the Titans inside Mt. Tartarus. King Hyperion aims to destroy Greek society and the gods. He is brutalizing Greece while seeking the Epirus Bow. Zeus in disguise has been training the peasant Theseus. Hyperion attacks Theseus' village, kills his mother, and condemns him to the salt mines. He is saved by the prophetess Phaedra, and they escape. Phaedra rebuilds Theseus' faith in his divine mission. While burying his mother, Theseus finds the Epirus Bow and kills the Minotaur-masked Beast. Theseus now believes in his destiny, and makes love to Phaedra. Ambushed, they lose the bow. Hyperion blasts open the gate to the fortress around Mt. Tartarus, where the Greeks are making a last stand. Hyperion frees the Titans, whom Zeus and the gods battle, while Theseus and Hyperion fight. Most of the gods are killed and Zeus pulls down Mt. Tartarus, while Theseus kills Hyperion. Zeus, the wounded Athena, and Theseus shoot upward like stars. Ten years later, Acamas, the son of Phaedra and Theseus, has a vision of a future battle of the gods. The disguised Zeus tells Acamas he will soon help his father in the cosmic battle against evil.

Immortals' creator Tarsem Singh earlier made music videos (he won a Video of the Year Award for his video of R.E.M.'s "Losing My Religion") and has directed dozens of television commercials. His breakout movie was the surreal, sadistic *The Cell* (2000), followed by *The Fall* (2006). Most recently he has radically repurposed the myth of Snow White (*Mirror, Mirror,* 2012). Singh is known for his visually stunning work.[1] In an interview he said, "I was wondering what it would look like if I took ideas from paintings instead. I thought if I looked at Renaissance paintings, I could use that as the inspiration."[2] A critic notes how "Tarsem's loves are diverse—among them, the writers Jorge Luis Borges and Gabriel García Márquez, Polish cinema, Coppola's *Dracula*, Tarkovsky, the painter Caravaggio, the photographer Joseph Koudelka, and erotic imagery as well as the imagery of different religious traditions; and viewers have seen in his work references to Derek Jarman, David Lynch, Alejandro Jodorowsky, visual artist Damien Hirst, *The Wizard of Oz*, and the stories of Grimm and Arabian Nights."[3] Two of the movie's producers, Mark Canton and Gianni Nunnari, worked on the highly stylized *300*.

---

1   For some his style is too stunning; Marc Olsen (review of *The Fall*, May 9, 2008, *LA Times*) wrote, "Tarsem underlines the film with truly obnoxious levels of pretentiousness that insist on the pretty pictures as having capital-M meaning, which only brings into sharp relief what a hollow exercise it all really is . . . his ideas of what constitutes 'artful'—mostly consisting of slo-mo, tableau framing, strange costumes and a romanticized exoticism—seem at best encased in amber and at worst completely regressive." http://articles.latimes.com/2008/may/09/entertainment/et-fall9. Accessed Aug. 14, 2016.
2   Quoted in Murphy (2011), MT 20.
3   Garrett (2008).

Immortals, filmed in 3D format, featured an international cast and notable actors such as Mickey Rourke, Henry Cavill, Freida Pinto, and John Hurt. Rotten Tomatoes rated it 35 percent, based on 114 reviews. The reviews tended negative; Roger Ebert wrote, "One image after another is gob-smacking but a lot of the time I had no idea what was going on."[A] However, in terms of myth work, this movie coheres, especially as a nonlinear dream-nightmare-fantasy. *Immortals* takes and alters various narratives and characters from Classical myth and inserts new material, often in ways that function through association. As with any complex "text," then, our movie's full meaning can be finally discerned when all its interlocked forms of signification are considered; every word, shot, special effect, and so on counts. This makes the movie seem more "art house" than "sword and sandals," but that impression would be incorrect; the focus on hero's well-defined (and well-shot) muscles, prodigious abilities, desire to defend and save the oppressed, and a wicked tyrant needing to be overthrown aligns with many aspects of the peplum movie.

Immortals treats, but quite differently, themes found in *Clash/Wrath* and *Troy*. *Clash/Wrath*, starting from the Titanomachy, Io, Perseus, and Medusa narratives, created an original myth about the Fall of the Gods. Its all-too-human Olympian gods oppress human beings, and a reluctant, angry, demigod Perseus is central to establishing a new human order. The Olympian gods of *Immortals*, especially Zeus, are fundamentally good, but also Other, and, hidden from human perception, have bound themselves to noninterference in human affairs. The Titans they battle are clearly more inhuman, more evil. But a king, Hyperion of Heraklion, has emerged. He embodies Titanic evil and ambitions, and ransacks Greece and releases the Titans, while another quasi-divine child, Theseus, trained in secret by Zeus, must grasp his call to adventure and lead the desperate human resistance. For his virtues, as great as Hyperion's evils, Theseus becomes an Immortal, a full partner in the battle between the gods and the Titans, as will be his son. We recall a similar focus on virtue in Disney's *Hercules. Troy* and *Immortals* both present a king who prefers power to morality and who wars to reset the world order. The Fascist captain Vidal in *Pan's Labyrinth* is cut from the same cloth. In *Troy* the problematic Achilles is saved by the love of a spiritual woman and priestess, Briseis; the salvation Phaedra provides Theseus is even more substantial. As does *O Brother* (but with different nuances), *Immortals* presents the fantasy-dream of a beneficent divine order worthy of our trust, which respects human choice, and mortal heroes and heroines who can transcend themselves and labor with the gods to shape the world's fate. Both *Pan's Labyrinth* and *O Brother* also present narratives of humans who work with divine forces under the sign of destiny.

To better illuminate *Immortals*, we will consider three archetypal structures and themes: (1) the marvelous child and development of the hero, including

---

4   Ebert, http://www.rogerebert.com/reviews/immortals-2011. Accessed Apr. 9, 2016.

the hero's quest; (2) the hero's quest as a central role in a conflict on which evolution of the divine and human cosmos turns; and (3) the full significance of that apocalyptic battle and its outcomes in respect to relationships between gods and humans, fate, free will, and the possibility of human heroism, immortality, and a new future. As before, we must judge *Immortals* not as if it were retelling the traditional Theseus myth, but rather on the quality of the unique mythical narrative Tarsem Singh has crafted.

TITANS AND OLYMPIANS

The movie begins with a quote: "All souls are immortal, but the souls of the good are divine." We then join Phaedra's nightmare: King Hyperion frees the Titans using the Epirus Bow. Then a voice-over ties these themes together:

> When this world was still young, long before man or beast roamed these lands, there was a war in the Heavens. Immortals, once thought incapable of death, discovered they had the power to kill one another. Lost in this war was a weapon of unimaginable power: the Epirus Bow. The victors declared themselves Gods, while the vanquished were renamed Titans and forever imprisoned within the bowels of Mt. Tartarus.[5] Eons passed, Mankind flourished. . . . And the great war receded from memory. But the evil that once was . . . has reemerged.

The accompanying pictures evoke the angular style of Greek Orthodox icons, implying a similarity between the Judeo-Christian account of the fall of Lucifer and his angels and the story of the Titans' confinement. The Titanomachy is a key element of the succession myth implied in our other movies. As in *Clash/Wrath*, the *Percy Jackson* series, and, in a displaced fashion, the Harry Potter universe, as well as our own political systems, the early cosmos featured an unresolved primal struggle. In *Harry Potter and the Chamber of Secrets* the story of the Basilisk and the Chamber of Secrets is so old as to be dismissed as myth; in the *Lord of the Rings* the One Ring has been forgotten. Here too memories of ancient evil have faded, and now will reemerge through its contemporary human incarnation. The gods have not directly interfered with human history, respecting the need for free will. Zeus, burdened with understanding the cosmic law, has secretly trained Theseus to oppose King Hyperion. Just as in *The Chamber of Secrets*, Tom Riddle / Voldemort, more than a thousand years later, revived the demonic plan to recreate the pure-blood world envisioned by Salazar Slytherin, and found human allies, so the Titan-like King Hyperion, leading a brutal army of soldiers drawn to his nightmare ideology, intends to release the Titans and recreate the world's broken remnants in his own image. As with *Clash/Wrath* (as well as the *Harry Potter* series), this movie deals with a major turning point in

---

5   In conventional Greek myth, Tartarus is a place underneath the earth where the Titans were confined, e.g., Hesiod, *Theogony* 119, 721–25; see West (1966), loc. cit.

FIGURE 5.1 The Gods on Olympus look down on Greece.

history, where exceptional humans will have to work to save the human universe, and the old order will be modified, although not destroyed.

Tarsem Singh's unique visual style renders uncanny his Titans and Gods. The Titans move in a crouched, quasi-animal, jerky style and never utter a human sound. The Olympians are generally gorgeous and golden, endowed with symbolic headgear. Their battle scenes physically convey their power; thus Ares moves so quickly that humans appear to stand still. When the gods hit a victim, their bodies explode in a gory shower. One of the movie's great shots gives a low-altitude aerial view of Theseus' village, which rises to show the whole Greek coast, to finally rest on Olympus looking down on the mainland from on high (Fig. 5.1).

In *Clash/Wrath* humans revolt against the Gods. In *Immortal*s the issue of the "silence of God" is raised. Theseus tells Phaedra: "My mother was a woman of faith. And her gods were absent when she needed them the most." The thief Stavros more ironically relates how he prayed as a child for a horse; unanswered, he stole one. King Hyperion, angered at his family's wretched deaths and the silence of the gods he prayed to, is determined to bring about their destruction by finding the Epirus Bow (a weapon forged by Heracles[6] in the Titanomachy) and uncaging the Titans. He is ransacking every Greek holy place in order to find it. He comes to the Monastery of the Sybillines, whose Oracle can give him vital information, but gains neither bow or information. His army then goes to Kolpos, Theseus' home, known for its famous Labyrinth, and slaughters most of the population, including Theseus' mother.

---

6   Heracles is sometimes said to have fought in the Gigantomachy; see Pindar, *Nemean* 1.67–69.

Titans: the earlier generation of gods

Olympians: the later generation of gods who overthrew the Titans

Sibyl: a female prophetess associated with Apollo

Hyperion: a solar god known for purity

God as hidden: the notion that god or the gods exist but, to preserve human freewill, must work in secret

Rationalist views of religion: a dismissive view that sees gods and miracles, at best, as metaphors for elements of the world and the human condition

THESEUS THE HERO IN CLASSICAL MYTH

The protagonist is named Theseus, but our movie's similarities to the traditional Athenian hero are subtle. The name Theseus is an understandable choice; "Theseus" is a by-word for "great Greek mythological hero," and other names, such as Perseus and Heracles, were used in prior movies. The leading Classical (if late) account of Theseus' myth is found in Plutarch's *Life of Theseus.*[7] Because Theseus was seen as a founder-hero for the Athenians, a hero crafted in part in response to Heracles as the Doric founder-hero, many legends about him (such as his six labors) were fabricated later to glorify Athenian accomplishment[8]; indeed, there is a saying reported in Plutarch that goes "Nothing without Theseus."[9] Accordingly, his character is endlessly employed by Athenian writers and myth makers. Thus, like Heracles, he becomes a hero whose life encompasses the highest highs and the lowest lows, filled with experiences both transcendent and brutal. Theseus, like Heracles, becomes a "hero to think with." He is a much more intriguing character than Perseus, but that very diversity makes it impossible to give any fixed character to him, a problem we saw regarding Hercules. In our analysis we detail how our Theseus reflects some of these canonical qualities, as well as the unique Theseus myth our movie presents.

Traditionally, Theseus's father was Aegeus, king of Athens. Aegeus, lacking children, visits the Delphic oracle, which gives the riddling command, "not to loosen the jutting foot of the wineskin…until I should again come to the paternal hearth" (Euripides, *Medea* 679-81). In Troezen he visits his friend, Pittheus the wise, who gets Theseus drunk and gives him his daughter Aethra to sleep with. The next morning, when Aegeus realizes what has happened, he puts his sword and shield under a large stone, and tells Aethra that, if she is pregnant and bears a boy, once the child is old enough to lift the stone and take the sword she should send him to Athens. In some accounts Aethra is also visited

---

7   On Theseus as a figure of the Athenian imagination, see Calame (1990). On "rationalizing" approaches to Theseus, see Hawes (2014), 149–74.

8   Walker (1995), 51ff.

9   Plutarch, *Life of Theseus* 29.

by Poseidon, which helps explain why both Poseidon and Aegeus are thought to be Theseus' father, although Aegeus is really probably a form of Poseidon.[10] Theseus thus grows up with an absent father in a type of exile, a detail our movie echoes. When Theseus matures and obtains the sword, he decides to travel by land to Athens to emulate Heracles' heroism and en route defeats various evil humans: Sinis, Sciron, Procrustes, Cercyon, and Periphetes. These labors became a popular topic for Athenian pottery. Medea, whom Aegeus befriended at Corinth, is now Aegeus' consort and tries to poison Theseus. Aegeus recognizes his sword and stops her. Medea flees to Persia, where her son Medus becomes the founder of the Medes.

Athens was being forced to send seven young men every year to Minos, king of Crete, to be sacrificed to the Minotaur. This story of youth sacrifice is also important for *The Hunger Games*. The legends of King Minos reflect the cultural and perhaps political dominance of Knossos over the Aegean; Thucydides (*History of the Peloponnesian War* 1.4) has Minos build the first fleet, and he subjugates Athens. In drama and poetry, Minos is often depicted as a harsh tyrant, although another tradition makes him wise, even an Underworld judge. The empire-building Hyperion comes from Heraklion, not far from Knossos. Ariadne, Minos' daughter, falls in love (or is made to fall in love) with Theseus, who, with her help, enters the Labyrinth and kills the Minotaur. This detail probably reflects the historical conquest of Knossos and the other Cretan palace centers by Mycenaean Greeks.[11] Theseus then escapes with Ariadne, only to abandon her on Naxos (an important site for her cult), where in some accounts she is rescued by Dionysus. Abducting women, especially women/goddesses connected with fertility,[12] is a part of Theseus' profile as hero. Ariadne curses him; Theseus subsequently forgets to lower the ship's dark sail. Aegeus believes Theseus is dead and jumps into the sea and drowns; it becomes known as the Aegean Sea. Afterward, Theseus is credited with taking the various towns of Attica and making them one unified political unit, Athens.

The "Phaedra" of *Immortals* in many details recalls her sister, the Cretan princess Ariadne. The sequence of Ariadne guiding Theseus through the Labyrinth and to the Minotaur ordeal, and their subsequent marriage, is symbolic of young-male's initiation. Indeed, Athenian ritual presents the young Theseus as an ephebe, a young man undergoing rites of initiation.[13] In some accounts

---

10 Rose (1959), 264, n. 32; Farnell (1921), 86, 337.
11 On the historical level, the myth recalls the mazelike nature of the palace of Knossos, "Hall of the Double Ax," in whose courtyard the dangerous ritual bull leaping took place. Knossos and the Minoan palaces were invaded and Knossos occupied by mainland Greeks. See Ward (1970), 113–31.
12 Walker (1995), 15–16. Note how Theseus also abducts Antiope, princess of the Amazons, and even young Helen of Sparta.
13 Versnel (1994), 57–61.

Theseus "marries" Ariadne, an event tied to the breaking of Minos' power.[14] Ariadne is clearly a Lady of the Labyrinth, and a vegetation goddess whose rites celebrate her death and return.[15] In Greek and Roman art Dionysus' rescue and wedding of Ariadne present themes of death and resurrection.[16] *Immortals'* Phaedra will likewise guide Theseus to his Labyrinth.

A few important points about Theseus' hometown, Kolpos. The anonymous reviewer on TVtrops.org[17] makes sniggering comments about how *kolpos* in Modern Greek means *vagina*, although it can also mean "gulf" as in Kyparissiakos Kolpos or "Gulf of Kyparissia." We suspect that this first meaning is quite intentional; Singh could have chosen other names. But *kolpos* as hinting at vagina is fitting, since Kolpos holds the shrine of the Labyrinth, which is also a vast cave/womb. In fact, in terms of imagery, *Immortals* presents a battle of cave wombs; the first is the vast hollow of Mt. Tartarus from which the Titans have their rebirth, and the second is the Labyrinth, from which a reborn Theseus emerges. Note how much of Kolpos is carved into a steep cliff side, as if its citizens must perpetually "live life on the edge." Its town square contains a vast sundial, suggesting the progress of time; indeed, we shall see one age die and another age being born.

As is the case with Heracles, some myths present Theseus as violent and lawless, others sacrificing and heroic. Theseus is often depicted as a protector of the weak, abused, or threatened.[18] Accordingly, the disguised Zeus of *Immortals* urges Theseus to think of the fragile and defenseless. In Sophocles' *Oedipus at Colonus*, Theseus gives aid and sanctuary to the old, blind Oedipus. In Euripides' *The Suppliant Women*, prompted by Aethra, Theseus forces Creon to bury warriors who died fighting against Thebes. He keeps Heracles from committing suicide after he is maddened by Hera and kills his children. We need to recall the notable tragedy of Theseus' life because in *Immortals* Phaedra is so different. In the canonical myth Theseus eventually marries Phaedra, Ariadne's sister, thus also from Crete, who is forced by Aphrodite to fall into obsessive love with Theseus' son Hippolytus, an extreme devotee of hunting, sexual purity, and Artemis. Framed by the maddened Phaedra for rape, Hippolytus is fatally cursed by Theseus, who learns too late of his son's innocence. The unpopular Theseus goes to the island of Skyros, whose king throws him off a cliff, a rather inglorious death. In 475 BCE Cimon, a major Athenian political figure,

---

14 As Sourvinou-Inwood (1978), 106ff., suggests, abducted goddesses such as Persephone become symbolic protectors of marriage.

15 Simone (1996), 17–22ff.

16 Thus Roman era sarcophagi are decorated with depictions of this myth. In Homer (*Odyssey* 11.321–25) Ariadne is the daughter of baleful Minos, and killed by Artemis at the behest of Dionysus. This alternate version may imply that Ariadne was loved by Dionysus before she was seduced by Theseus.

17 http://tvtropes.org/pmwiki/pmwiki.php/Film/Immortals. Accessed July 9, 2016.

18 For how Theseus is shaped to reflect Athens' ideal image of itself, see Mills (1997).

Immortals (2011) Universal Pictures and Relativity Media	
Director: **Screenplay:** **Cast:**	Tarsem Singh Vlas Parlapanides, Charley Parlapanides Henry Cavill (Theseus), Stephen Dorff (Stavros), John Hurt (Old Man/Zeus), Isabel Lucas (Athena), Kellan Lutz (Poseidon), Freida Pinto (Phaedra), Mickey Rourke (King Hyperion), Joseph Morgan (Lysander), Peter Stebbings (Helios), Daniel Sharman (Ares), Anne Day-Jones (Aethra), Greg Bryk (Nycomedes), Corey Sevier (Apollo), Robert Maillet (the Beast), Alan van Sprang (Dareios), Stephen McHattie (Cassander), Mark Margolis (the New Priest, a monk), Robert Naylor (Young Theseus), Gage Munroe (Acamas)

"found" the body of Theseus, and brought the bones back to Athens, perhaps putting them in the temple mistakenly identified as belonging to Hephaestus.[19] Theseus does not, unlike Heracles, become a god, although there was a considerable hero cult devoted to him,[20] as may be reflected (somewhat) at the end of our movie.

HYPERION

The name for our monster-king seems peculiar, because in Greek mythology Hyperion is a sun god (sometimes merged with his son, Helios) and, although a Titan, a deity who sees all and is associated with pure, life-giving light, so viewed as a deeply holy god.[21] "Hyperion" becomes a by-word for nobility and greatness.[22] Minos from Crete in Greek poetry and drama is presented as a cruel ruler and conqueror. Our Hyperion of Crete is even more murderous and sadistic; his brutal captain, called "the Beast," wears a Minotaur helmet and tends a bronze bull that cooks victims alive, recalling the infamous executions of Phalaris. According to Diodorus Siculus (*Biblioteca Historica* 9.18–19), Phalaris, tyrant of Acragas (now Agrigento) in Sicily, (ca. 570–554 BCE) had a hollow bronze bull constructed in which a victim was placed, with a fire then set underneath to roast the person.[23] Not only does Hyperion wear monstrous uniforms, which make him devil like, but his men scar themselves to look more threatening. Yet in his private quarters, he is usually shown barefoot, wearing animal skins, as if a survival from a primitive era (Fig. 5.2). Eagles and dogs also serve him.

---

19 Podlecki (1971), 141–43.
20 See Kearns (1989), 120–24; Walker (1994), 20–24.
21 *Oxford Classical Dictionary*, 4th ed., "Helios" and "Hyperion."
22 As we see in Shakespeare's *Hamlet* Act I Scene 2.143–44, where Prince Hamlet says of his father, "So excellent a king, that was, to this [his uncle Claudius], Hyperion to a satyr."
23 Some have postulated a connection with Eastern bull cults, perhaps linked to Carthaginian influence in Sicily. See Abbot (1901), 428–29.

FIGURE 5.2 Hyperion in his tent. Note the devil horned helmet, the skins he wears, and his bare feet.

Before the Greek traitor Lysander defects to Hyperion, he participates in a dialogue, which reveals what motivates Hyperion's army.

FIRST SOLDIER: They [Hyperion's soldiers] fight with a ferocity unlike anything I've seen.

SECOND SOLDIER: Almost as if they could see in the darkness. It's always suited them.

FIRST SOLDIER: You speak as if they are not human.

LYSANDER: They are human. The only difference is they fight for a belief which allows them to kill without restraint. That is why they will win.

Many today feel prior norms of religion and morality have lost their force, a sentiment particularly evident in *Troy* and *O Brother*. To some, the purity of nihilist violence and inhuman butchery is the only faith left, and faith is a major theme of *Immortals*. Lysander, despising conventional morality, butchers his comrades and flees to Hyperion. His hordes represent a contemporary nightmare, a fanaticism that inspires in its very rejection of conventional morality and mercy, as today ISIS/ISIL (Islamic State of Iraq and Syria/ Islamic State of Iraq and the Levant) appear to do, or fanatic death cults found in any number of movies. They are our deepest fears: fanatics who have no dread of death, and who are committed to a regime of utter barbarity without restraint. In *Troy* Agamemnon aspired to conquer all Greece and, with Troy's destruction, to control the Aegean, and to immortalize his name, but he was also inspired by a kind of progressive thought. Hyperion likewise desires a similar immortality, but his vision is utterly demonic.

As in our previous movies, fathers, mothers, sons, daughters, and paternity issues play an important role. When Hyperion hears that Lysander has no children, he says slowly: "A man's seed can be his most brutal weapon. For generations, your people will stare into the eyes of their sons and they will see my likeness. I will be remembered in every glance, every smile, every tear that is shed for eternity." He then has the Beast unman Lysander by crushing his genitals with a large mallet. Later, Athena notes that "their king (Hyperion) takes the greatest care with women that carry a child and personally sees to their slaughter. He ventures to eradicate the Hellenic future." Hyperion tells Theseus: "Long after this war is over, my mark will be left on this world forever. The sun will never set on my blood, Theseus. This is what I offer you: immortality." Hyperion means to overthrow the Olympian gods, usher in a reign of the Titans, and become a new creator of humanity apparently through mass rape. In contrast, early in the movie the disguised Zeus chides Theseus, as his mother does, about not marrying and having children. At the movie's end, the gods will reward Theseus by giving him a son, Acamas, who will follow in his footsteps and be a future leader, as Helius in *Wrath* will follow in the footsteps of Perseus his father. Note how the question, prominent in other movies, concerning the nature of proper immortality is stressed.

THESEUS' BEGINNINGS IN *IMMORTALS*

In *Immortals*, the dramatic thrust of Theseus' career is contained in the initial quote and summed up in a concluding voice-over. The first quote is falsely attributed[24] to Socrates: "All men's souls are immortal, but the souls of the righteous are immortal and divine." Then, near the movie's conclusion, as his son Acamas inspects a monument commemorating Theseus, Zeus' voice-over sums up the movie's lesson: "All men's souls are immortal, but the souls of the righteous are immortal and divine. Once a faithless man, Theseus gave his life to save mankind, and earned a place amongst the gods. They rewarded his bravery with a gift: a son, Acamas." Thus our story of Theseus is positive, describing the hero's evolution, from doubt to faith, from mortality to divine glory, all in the context of service to humanity, a benefit that will continue through his son. It tells how Theseus becomes one of the Immortals, which corresponds to the classical Hero.

Theseus is clearly another marvelous child. The mothers of such children are often involved in scandal or suffer abuse; his mother Aethra was supposedly raped by (unnamed) villagers, and has lived as a single mother, suffering frequent maltreatment. Theseus might be a demigod (which explains his outstanding abilities), reared in virtual exile. A mere peasant, he has yet to answer

---

24   The closest classical text is found in *Symposium* 212a: "Is it not possible for one who has begotten a true excellence and raised it, to become a friend of god and, if it is possible for another among human beings, [possible] also for that man?" This sentiment became installed in one of those often unattributed quotes seen in collections of quotes. Claude Pavur tells us early evidence of the quotation can be found in *A Choice collection of divine and pious sentences, selected out of the writings of some ancient heathen philosophers & etc*. Printed for Tho. Goddard, Bookseller in the Market-place, in Norwich, 1702. We thank Claude Pavur, Charles Young, and other members of the Classics-L list who assisted us.

a "call to adventure." For years Zeus, disguised as an old man, has mentored him, honing his skills as a warrior, both physical and moral, molding him for his destiny as an aid to the gods in a future Titanomachy.[25] Zeus as magic helper and pseudo-father remains hidden, remote, an issue prominent in *Clash/Wrath*. There Zeus and Perseus are reconciled, if too late; and at the end of the *Percy Jackson* series, the gods will acknowledge their human children. Here Zeus will rescue Theseus and take him to Olympus, made an Immortal, which did not happen in the myth of Theseus but may have been borrowed from the Hercules myth.

Moral training is as important as martial training. Consider what the disguised Zeus says as Theseus chops wood:

ZEUS: You know being a warrior is not just being able to strike your opponent down with a sword. It's finding good reason to draw your sword in the first place.
THESEUS: I draw my sword to protect those that I love.
ZEUS: What about the others?
THESEUS: They turned their backs on me.
ZEUS: The weak, the defenseless? Who is going to protect them?

Theseus must learn to be a protector (as is the Classical Theseus), but first he must make the decision to abandon his disengagement and disbelief (as Perseus must in *Clash/Wrath*) and to join the conflicts that threaten humanity.

"IT MUST BE HIS CHOICE"

General Helios announces that Hyperion is approaching, and the Kolpians must evacuate to the fortress of Mt. Tartarus, with its vast wall, the symbolic ultimate defense of civilization. Theseus and his mother are told by Lysander that they must wait and go later "with their kind." Theseus fights for their rights and safety, and gains a promise of assistance from General Helios, who expels Lysander immediately. Theseus refuses to join Helios' army when asked, still angry about their maltreatment, a refusal of the hero's "call to adventure," one that also echoes the insulted Achilles' unwillingness to rejoin the Greek army at a critical juncture. We learn that Hyperion himself was born a peasant, and later in disguise Hyperion will tell Theseus, "All are equal in Hyperion's midst." Hyperion will even offer him an alliance, for he "knows that you [Theseus] have no father, and like him, you were cast aside by your very own people. . . . They will never give you a say at their table. But you could sit at the head of mine." Young heroes are often tempted to join the side of evil, as happens to Harry Potter and even Percy

---

25 This molder of heroes is found in many hero stories, notably Yoda as trainer of Luke Skywalker, or Kesuke Miyagi as trainer for the Karate Kid, or the satyr Philoctetes training Hercules in the Disney movie.

Jackson. In our current world, the fires of fanaticism are arising where too many people, young males especially, cannot find decent employment or prospects for life, or any peaceful means to improve their social and political conditions. Thus they join violent organizations, where they are at least feared.

As Theseus defends the peasants and defies the aristocrats, Zeus again closely observes his moral development. Later we observe Theseus' daydream of his young self vigorously striking a tree, while the old man (Zeus) counsels: "Your anger moves you Theseus. You must learn to master your emotions." For the purposes of the movie, we must take seriously what Zeus tells Athena about Theseus' divine heroism: "He [Theseus] does not fear danger. No pain, defeat or ridicule. He fears only the failure to defend that which he holds so dear, his loved ones. If there is one human who can lead them against Hyperion, it would be Theseus. But it must be his choice." In contrast, we note in *Troy*, when Briseis asks why Achilles chose the warrior's life, Achilles replied immediately, "I chose nothing. I was born, and this is what I am." But our Theseus has a choice. Unlike the compromised and heavyhanded Zeus in *Clash/Wrath*, this Zeus, upholder of cosmic law, values the choice that makes human action meaningful. And Zeus can do so, trusting Theseus' exceptional and innate virtue.

But dangers remain for Theseus, and there is a price most great heroes must pay. During a tense meeting, Zeus comments on Hyperion's atrocities and then on the Greek response:

ZEUS: Effective! [Hyperion's actions] At least, thus far.

MALE GOD: Effective? Cowardly.

ZEUS: That may be. But the Hellenics have yet to adapt.

MALE GOD: And until they do . . .

ANOTHER MALE GOD: Isn't it time to intervene, Zeus? How can you stomach bearing witness to such atrocities while doing nothing?

ZEUS: I obey the law! No God shall interfere in the affairs of man unless the Titans are released. If we are to expect mankind to have faith in us . . . then we must have faith in them. We must allow them to use their own free will.

MALE GOD: And what if they unearth the bow?

ZEUS: If any of you come to the aid of man or otherwise influence the affairs of mankind as a God, the punishment will be death.

In *Immortals*, Theseus' desire to help those he loves must be expanded to include all Greeks, so that Zeus can command him to "Lead your people!" Theseus, like many heroes, will be motivated by tragedy. Early in the morning, he sees a soaring eagle, Hyperion's aerial spy; his townsfolk are being slaughtered. He fights to save his mother, killing many, until, tangled in nets, he must watch Hyperion slit his mother's throat, growling "Witness hell," a prophetic line to be repeated. Here Theseus has entered fully into his Dark Wood of testing.

BEARING THE CROSS, RESCUED BY THE MYSTIC
LADY OF SORROW, HOPE REGAINED

As Theseus marches with other prisoners to the salt mines, he carries a large wooden beam across his shoulders, a Jesus figure carrying his cross to Golgotha. Theseus will sacrifice himself for humanity, and, because of his merits, become a God, recalling Christ. Among the prisoners (also carrying wooden beams) are Stavros, a career thief; and Darius, both of whom join Theseus and Phaedra—an evocative quartet. Stavros is a common male name in Modern Greek, which means "cross." A major role of the hero is to redeem problematic others. The thief Stavros, who mocks religion, will become a kind of redeemed thief on the cross, and die defending Theseus. Darius will perish too, but not before calling the faithless and doubting Stavros a "heathen," as one of the thieves crucified with Jesus rebuked the disbelief of the other. As in other hero narratives, to accomplish his Quest and become the needed leader, the hero must possess a faith that is to be proven. And here that will require a heroine, a mortal woman, but also a magic helper, a sacred and wounded virgin. Although the faith of Theseus' mother is essential for the plot, even more important is the faith of Phaedra, the true prophetess of the Monastery of the Sibyllines, whose oracular dream opens the story.[26]

As do our other movies, *Immortals* reflects the contemporary, but uneven, dissolution of religious belief. Devout people, such as Theseus' mother, continue in their piety and lament its widespread loss. Unbelievers mock, often bitterly, as Everett does in *O Brother*. When his mother invites him to pray, Theseus says, "Mother, the gods are children's stories; my spear is not." Cassander, head of the Hellenic Council, a prototypical Greek rationalist, declares: "I understand that there are many Hellenics who put great faith in the myths and the gods, but we in the Hellenic Council do not. They are metaphors, son, nothing more. We are a society of laws based on negotiation and reason." And finally, there are those like Hyperion who have made darkness their light, embracing the evils traditional religion opposed.

After his trek across a desert, Theseus comes to an oasis, but, resigned to death, does not bother even to drink water. Hyperion has captured Phaedra, who is the true Oracle, and her three attendant women, who are also at the oasis. Phaedra receives another vision of Theseus and Hyperion in alliance, with Hyperion holding the Epirus Bow. Before them rests a corpse wrapped in red cloth. Theseus, she intuits, is God-touched, enfolded in the divine plan. In a richly evocative scene, Phaedra fills her mouth with clear water and dribbles

---

26 The Sibyls were largely legendary women who prophesized in an oracular frenzy. The Greek philosopher Heraclitus is the earliest writer attesting to a Sibyl: "And the Sibyl, according to Heraclitus, with prophetic mouth, sounding forth with her voice grave matters without adornment or scent, through the God, attains to a thousand years." For discussion of this passage, see Burkert (1985), 116–18, who cites Heraclitus, fragment 92.

this water of life into Theseus' mouth from above as he lies sprawled and list-
less, bidding him to live, evoking images of the Pietà. We note here the connections of water and birth and rebirth, and it is this water given by Phaedra
that brings the future savior back from near death. Theseus and Phaedra share
the spectrum of sorrow—he for the past, she for what is to come—as does the
Virgin Mary, who, like Phaedra, is submissive to the burden of the divine, a
woman of heartache and prayer.[27]

But also of action, Phaedra and her attendants kill several guards and escape,
though the other women are recaptured, and taken to martyrdom at Hyperion's
hands. They head north to confront Hyperion. Issues of faith, sorrow, and sacrifice are constant in *Immortals.* Stavros recalls Antenor in *Wrath*; he accepts
his role as a thief and makes suggestive sexual comments. Yet, although he
insults Phaedra, he chooses to stand with Theseus. While waiting for a vessel
to hijack, Theseus marvels at the risks Phaedra took for him. She replies, "Only
a faithless man would ask such a question." But Theseus remains the bitter
doubter. Theseus and his companions attempt to capture a ship, and find it
full of Hyperion's warriors. Phaedra, sensing Poseidon's coming intervention,
positions them to survive an oily tidal wave. Our faithful protagonists survive
this flood (compare the saving flood in *O Brother)*, while Hyperion's men are
swept away.

Later Phaedra's evident foreknowledge erodes his skepticism; the images of
the gleaming Phaedra and the besmeared Theseus, his eyes shining within his
blackened face, symbolize their spiritual states; the oil of the world does not
cling to her, and Theseus has eyes to see more. As is the obligation to produce
children, the obligation for family to bury the dead is a major theme in Greek
mythology, as the myths of Antigone and Hector, among others, vividly demonstrate. Thus Phaedra insists Theseus must return to Kolpos to bury Aethra.
When Theseus announces his disbelief in the gods, Phaedra counters: "But she
believed. *She believed*, Theseus. You must return to your village." Destiny and
Theseus' free choice, however motivated, however incomprehensible, will soon
change everything.

AT THE HEART OF THE LABYRINTH; BURIAL AND REBIRTH

The pace of the hero's journey for Theseus now quickens noticeably. At Kolpos,
shrouding his mother's body, he says, "I'm sorry I couldn't protect you, mother.
But I promise you our family name will not die with me." Death now leads to
his commitment to life, and also to the hero's statement of faith in the future. He
takes his mother's body into the Labyrinth, a vast stone crypt where the veiled
head of a goddess rests in a pool of water; think of the pool of water at the center

---

27   Mary is often called the *Mater dolorosa*, "the sorrowing mother," and Simeon, the prophet, says
to her, "And a sword will pierce your own soul too" (Luke 2.35).

of the Labyrinth in *Pan's Labyrinth*. This goddess is a mistress of the Labyrinth, mentioned above, whose waters promise life among the dead. Worshippers come and light candles there, as Aethra does during her prayers. The Labyrinth is both path to the dead and route of testing and initiation. Theseus is making the hero's journey into an underworld, which is a place nearly inescapable and filled with mystery. We see a similar labyrinth in *Wrath of the Titans,* and an even more significant one in *Pan's Labyrinth.* The ancestors rest here and powerful keys to the past are hidden, as well as a terrible test.

Theseus slides his mother's body into a stone niche, but a rock outcropping prevents him from sealing the grave. Carrying out the proper rites for his mother now brings Theseus to a weapon important for his destiny. Breaking the obstructing stone, Theseus reveals the Epirus Bow. This discovery corresponds to the episode in which Aethra points out the large rock that the young Theseus must lift to reveal his father's sword and shield, as well as the legend of how young Arthur pulled the sword of his royal father out of the stone. Indeed, there is evidence that Zeus himself hid this bow here.[28] Having gained one quest object, Theseus is ready for the ordeal that will confirm his heroic status. As with the underworld labyrinth in *Wrath,* guarded by a bull-like monster man whom Perseus must defeat to rescue his father Zeus, our Theseus must fight the Minotaur-helmed Beast; he wins only after a brutal struggle. Likewise, in *Percy Jackson: The Lightning Thief,* Percy must kill the Minotaur who has seized his mother before he can enter Camp Half Blood, and a new phase of life. Thus the labyrinth and a half-human beast symbolize a threshold, where the hero must confront his past, his own destiny, and an embodiment of real and suppressed evils. Meanwhile, outside, Stavros is certain that the Greeks will fall; Phaedra declares "You have no faith." Hyperion's scouts attack, and almost miraculously, Phaedra's faith repaid, Theseus appears in time to shoot Hyperion's men with the Epirus Bow. He then collapses.

Awakened in body and mind, and with Phaedra having tended his wounds, Theseus confesses the correctness of his mother's faith. Phaedra consoles: "Your mother's death was not in vain, Theseus. It was fate that brought you back . . . for the bow." But for human choice to matter, the future must not be so fully determined; Theseus will not use the Epirus Bow again and will have to use his own resources to succeed. The possession of the Epirus Bow and new knowledge mark another major inflection point. As noted, heroes often gain a mate during their heroic journey. Phaedra strips and gets into bed with him, and they make love. This is a turning point for Phaedra in another way too. Tradition shows both Cassandra and the Sibyl, God-possessed, being

---

28 Later, during the great battle, when the unleashed Titans seize the bow, Zeus tosses a war hammer and hits the bow with a magic force that seals it into the living rock again. This clue suggests that Zeus, who long ago grasped the future, hid the Epirus Bow away in the labyrinth in preparation for Theseus.

broken by their visions; likewise Phaedra's visions have become a curse; now she wants "to see the world through my own eyes, and feel with my own heart and to touch with my own flesh."[29] Again we observe the question of free will, faith, and humanity; to be human is to be able to act in faith without such clear forevision. She loses her prophetic vision with her virginity. As fits another mythic theme, human experiential knowledge is purchased at the price of truly divine knowledge. But their mating conceives the child Acamas, one so desperately desired by Theseus' mother, and promised to her by Theseus, who has also just properly buried her. Theseus has now become a true man and, as in some of our other stories of coming of age, has gone down to the bowels of the underworldlike labyrinth, confronted the Shadow-Beast, and obtained a magical element (recall how Percy brings back one of the Minotaur's horns from his encounter with him) and also a weapon that will allow him to "shoot far" and assert his masculinity. No wonder Phaedra sees his manly qualities and welcomes him into her fertile body. This far-reaching power of the Epirus Bow's magic arrows is symbolic of Theseus' own seed, which as Hyperion said earlier, may be a man's strongest weapon. And what is more far-reaching than conceiving a son?

PRELUDE TO AN ARMAGEDDON

The remaining Hellenics (too few) have retreated behind the great wall beside Mt. Tartarus. The tableaux is highly symbolic. The fortress walls themselves evoke a huge dam or levee, designed to keep out tsunamis of destruction. Hyperion's vast army stands assembled before it. Inside Mount Tartarus is a large hollow whose walls are held up by massive interlocked statues, which remind us of the Titan Atlas, who was condemned to hold up the sky, the home of the Olympian order, on his shoulders. At its center is the adamantine cage containing the Titans. Only a rock wall separates the Hellenic Council chamber, symbol of human control and rationality, from the interior of Tartarus and the caged Titans. The Hellenics, unaware, have been living forgetfully beside the most fundamental forces of chaos, just as the Basilisk and Salazar Slytherin's horrid Chamber of Secrets rest within the foundations of Hogwarts, both forces that will escape their prisons and unleash primal evil. This is a common, grand delusion; we build vast fortifications to keep out our enemies, ignorant of the greatest threats sharing our very walls.

At the monastery, Theseus and companions find Phaedra's three attendants being slow-roasted in the brazen bull, a fate later represented as martyrdom. They are ambushed by Hyperion's soldiers. In the melee Theseus drops the Epirus Bow, which is snatched by Hyperion's dog, who takes it back to his

---

29   And we saw in *Hercules* how Amphiaraus' ability to foresee his impending death was a quite
     problematic blessing.

master.[30] In *Clash/Wrath*, Perseus refuses the help of the Gods, demanding to succeed as a human; in *Immortals*, Zeus *forces* Theseus to succeed as a mortal. To save Theseus from his ambush, Ares and Athena intervene against Zeus' orders. Ares slaughters their enemies and Athena gives them divine horses to ride to Mt. Tartarus. The help that Ares and Athena provide against Zeus' will evokes episodes in the *Iliad*, where Zeus likewise forbids the angered Athena and Ares to help the Greeks (*Iliad* 8.5–40). Here Zeus, enraged, kills Ares but spares Athena. In the *Iliad* Zeus dislikes Ares but favors Athena, and this distinction is reflected here. But Zeus is not a tyrant homicidally enraged at disobedience; rather, more like Jupiter as implementer of Fate in the *Aeneid*,[31] he does what it takes to enforce the great law, no matter the cost. Thus Zeus, who has just killed his own son, bellows at Theseus: "No God will ever again come to your aid! You are on your own! Do you understand, mortal? I have faith in you, Theseus. Prove me right! Lead your people!" Zeus's faith, like Jupiter's faith in the struggling Aeneas of *Aeneid* Book I, is that humans must and can earn their own positive history.

They ride at full speed to Tartarus, and when they dismount, the divine horses immediately die. As they gasp their lives away, Stavros, wide-eyed, says, "The horse I prayed for when I was a boy . . . "; suddenly he perceives the subtle divine machinery, a preliminary to his heroic transformation. On Olympus the gods somberly place a war hammer on Ares' memorial, the slab of stone into which he was blasted by Zeus. Athena then says to an agonized Zeus, "In peace, sons bury their fathers. In war, fathers bury their sons. Are we at war, father?" This is King Croesus' famous response to Cyrus' inquiry about why he attacked the Persians, drawn from Herodotus book I. 87, where Croesus admits his foolishness and implies he was set up by the gods. In the *Iliad* there is a strong contrast between the Gods, who cannot die and who play at war, and the human beings, for whom death is very real. Zeus, disguised as the old man, earlier told Theseus he was "Just tired . . . It's not living as such that's important, Theseus. It's living rightly." The gods in *Immortals*, unlike the gods of *Clash/Wrath*, are more serious beings, and Zeus is wearied of maintaining justice for eons and perhaps shielding the other Olympians from this burden. Zeus has killed his son for violating his command, and he suffers greatly; this death has awakened Athena to dire realities, setting the stage for the Gods' own death struggle.

General Helios, seeing Theseus, says, "I hope you've come to join the fight." Perseus in *Wrath* will be similarly late to a fateful battle. The Greeks are terribly

---

30 This device seems silly, but it accords with Hyperion's reliance on a trained eagle to scout for him.

31 This passage recalls when Cybele pleads for help for her ships and Aeneas, and Jupiter tells her (Verg. *Aen*.9.94–97): "Oh mother, for what purpose do you invoke Fate? Or what do you seek for these? Shall ships made by mortal hands have immortal right? And shall Aeneas, secure, travel through uncertain dangers? To what God is such vast power permitted?" For Jupiter and Fate in the *Aeneid*, see Wilson (1979).

outnumbered, and civilization is facing its last stand. The coming conflict is given substantial philosophical and spiritual dimensions. The head of the Hellenic Council imagines that all can be solved with rational negotiation. Soon afterward, Hyperion, in disguise, going as his own messenger,[32] offers Theseus a share in his immortal fame and power, which Theseus refuses, asserting that "deeds are eternal, not the flesh." This is the preparation for the hero's final death struggle. But Theseus, like Perseus, is not beyond human doubt. "I don't know if I can do what Zeus asks me," he tells Phaedra, who replies philosophically, "By doubting, one comes to truth, Theseus. The gods chose well."

There follows, as in *Troy*, a preparation-for-battle scene, as Theseus and Stavros arm themselves, Helios ponders war maps, Phaedra prays, and the skin-clad Hyperion admires the bow, which he deploys the next morning to blast open the gate leading to a tunnel through the fortress wall,[33] allowing his hordes to flood inside, causing a Greek rout. This long tunnel evokes the narrow pass that permitted Leonidas and the Spartans to hold off vastly greater numbers of civilization-threatening Persians. Note also the somewhat postmodern look of this tunnel and other structures in the film, made of metal, which makes us think more of modern bunkers than of ancient architecture. Some structures in the dystopian *The Hunger Games* come to mind here, such as the metallic Cornucopia.

THE STRUGGLE FOR LIFE, DEATH, MEMORY, AND HISTORY BEGIN

Theseus' rousing speech halts the Greeks' terrified retreat. It is a fairly standard trope to have leaders address their warriors, especially when a situation looks bleak[34]:

> I am nobody to tell you what to do! I am Theseus, a good man. One of you, I share your blood and I share your fear! But to run now, we offer our souls and the souls of our children to a terrible darkness. Hold! We must stand and fight! Their numbers count for nothing in the tunnel! Stand your ground! Stand your ground! In formations![35] Just because they have scored their faces and scarred

---

32 In the myths surrounding Alexander the Great, he often goes disguised as his own messenger, as found in Pseudo Callisthenes, for example, to Darius (2.13–15), to Poros (3.3), and to Candace (3.21–23).

33 It is worth noting that the inside of the gate is marked with characters that resemble, some exactly (e.g., "wa" 𐀷), the Greek Bronze Age Linear B script, which fits the movie's supposed date of 1228 BCE. The true gate of civilization is connected to the production of the Word.

34 See for example the rousing speech Aragorn gives before his forces take on the hordes of Mordor toward the end of *Lord of the Rings*. Perhaps the best Western model of such speeches is found in Shakespeare's *Henry V*, the speech to the outnumbered English at Agincourt *(Henry V* Act IV Scene iii 18–67).

35 But even though fighting in formation behind a wall of interlocked shields is exactly the way to overcome the advantage of Hyperion's superior numbers, the Greeks in fact seem to fight in the tunnel a series of one-on-one duels, which, alas, makes better cinema.

their bodies, does not mean they are braver or stronger than we are. They are cowards! They hide behind their masks! They are human and they bleed like you and I [sic]. Listen to me! Stand your ground!

This speech sums up central themes, such as Theseus as a popular leader, bravery in the face of fear (*Troy*'s Achilles was incapable of that human emotion), and how they battle a dehumanizing horror. Stavros bangs his shield with his sword, affirming Theseus's proclamations, and soon all the Hellenics follow suit:

Fight for honor! (bang!) Fight for the man beside you (bang!) Fight for those who bore you! (bang!) Fight for your children! (bang!) Fight for your future! (bang!)

Fight for your name to survive! (bang!) Fight . . . for immortality! (bang!)

Let us write history with Heraklian blood! (bang!)

O Brother and *Troy* stressed the issue of the individual's ties to the community, a question even more important here, as is thought for their common future and lasting fame. This vision is much richer than Agamemnon's dream of raising monuments throughout Greece or Achilles, pointing to Troy, and telling his men, "There lies immortality. Take it." When we think of the problematic heroes (or antiheroes) of our other movies, we might find jarring Theseus' emphatic assertion, "I am a good man." But this points to a moral dream *Immortals* shares with movies of earlier generations, when one could present a hero who was not fatally compromised, and whose fundamental virtue was a divine force for inspiring others. Many of the traditional peplum movies of a generation ago presented such a moral figure. Again, we must take Zeus' positive opinion of Theseus seriously. With the spear-wielding, golden-armor-clad Theseus charging forward demigodlike, and Stavros behind him, the Hellenics rush into the tunnel, and furiously engage Hyperion's men.[36]

But this battle is mere diversion; Hyperion sneaks in and beheads the Council Leader, whose last words are "reason to," suggesting rationality's impotence facing primal evil. Hyperion uses the Epirus Bow to blow open a wall leading into Mt. Tartarus, and then to blast open the Titans' adamantine cage. Theseus and Stavros, chasing Hyperion, are knocked out and wake up dazed. Stavros valiantly gains possession of the Epirus Bow and briefly holds the Titans back, until he is butchered by them, a redemption of sorts. The Olympians arrive, golden and armed. Zeus dismisses Theseus to find Hyperion. Soon the Gods and Titans and Theseus and Hyperion are each engaged in their death struggle. Note that the room Theseus' battle takes place in is decorated with murals depicting scenes of Homeric-style warfare; the shields of the warriors

---

36 During the tunnel battle, Lysander fiercely advances, seemingly eager to be killed by Theseus, perhaps seeking redemption. When Theseus demands, "Where is your king?" Lysander, dying, asserts, "He is not a king."

have great eyes, as if the eyes of fame and history are on them. The grueling blows Hyperion gives to Theseus are paralleled by the violence the Titans do to the gods, who are killed one by one. When Athena is impaled and Zeus comes to her aid, she reminds him, "Do not forsake mankind." Zeus begins to pull to down the statues that support Mt. Tartarus, while Hyperion slowly takes up a knife, preparing to kill Theseus. As in *Troy*, the issue of memory and oblivion remains until the finale. Note this exchange:

HYPERION: What does it feel like knowing . . . that there will be no memory of you? I've won.
THESEUS: My death will make me a legend. And my deeds . . . will go down in history!
HYPERION: I'm writing your history.

VICTORY, APOTHEOSIS, AND THE FUTURE

Theseus, beaten half-senseless, asserts he will fulfill Zeus' trust in him. As the dying Poseidon screams "Do it," and Zeus pulls down Tartarus, finishing off the Titans and the prior order of creation, Theseus stabs the gloating Hyperion's feet, pins him, then slowly drives a knife into the throat of his wild-eyed antagonist, saying, "Look at me! I am the last thing . . . you will ever see. Witness hell!"—recalling Hyperion's words before slitting his mother's throat. The mutual faith of Zeus and Theseus is justified, and the true power of Zeus and Theseus against evil is revealed. Zeus lifts Athena's body, and both shoot like stars skyward. Mt. Tartarus implodes, its cascades of dust and rubble overwhelming Hyperion's army. Before Theseus is crushed, he glows too and his star shoots upward. He is deified, proving that, like Heracles, like Aeneas, like Jesus, it is possible for a man to gain divinity and immortality through heroic and moral deeds.

The movie leaps ahead some ten years, and back to Kolpos. We see Theseus' son, Acamas, as well as Phaedra, now working with the priests,[37] becoming a true mistress of the Labyrinth. In *Wrath*, at the end Andromeda becomes Theseus' warrior queen; here Phaedra becomes the priestess of Theseus' hero cult, a quite important contrast. Their son Acamas is shown inspecting a statue group showing his father killing the Minotaur, and the statue base's frieze, which displays major events of Theseus' career: Hyperion killing Aethra while Theseus watches, Theseus carrying the beam in his trek to the salt mines and meeting Phaedra, Poseidon's saving tidal wave, Theseus killing the Minotaur-man, the three Oracles (who have haloes, suggesting their status as

---

37 Acamas was a son of Theseus, who gives his name to the Athenian tribe Acamantis. According to Parthenius (*Amat. Narr.* 16), he accompanied Diomedes on an embassy to demand the return of Helen and supposedly loved Laodice, daughter of Priam, and with her had a son, Munitus. According to Vergil's *Aeneid* 2.262, he was one of the Greeks inside the Trojan horse.

Christian-like martyrs) roasting in the Bull, Theseus battling Hyperion.[38] The voice-over by Zeus declares the moral of our concluded hero, salvation and triumph: "All men's souls are immortal, but the souls of the righteous are immortal and divine. Once a faithless man, Theseus gave his life to save mankind, and earned a place amongst the gods. They rewarded his bravery with a gift: a son, Acamas."

The central statue group tells a rather different story about Theseus' conquest of the Minotaur than we saw earlier; this difference reminds us of *Troy*, which suggests it tells the "real" story of Troy before it was mythologized. Theseus' hero shrine has replaced the sundial, suggesting the emergence of a new sort of time, and the statue of Theseus and the Minotaur symbolizes Theseus' conquest of bestial forces. Acamas, when he touches Hyperion's relief figure, has a vision of a battle in heaven; he has inherited his mother's prophetic sight. The Old Man (Zeus) tells him not to fear his visions, that he knew his father, and soon his time will come, for "the fight against evil never ends, Acamas. War is coming to the Heavens. And your father will be there. Fighting for your future."[39] After Phaedra calls him back, Acamas closes his eyes, and has another revelation of a violent battle of Olympians and Titans, with his father fighting, the movie's final scene. In contrast to *Clash/Wrath*, at whose conclusion the era of gods and monsters is over, and a human- and hero-centered world is in place, with the future found in Perseus' son Helius and his sword, here a marvelous human has overcome personal disbelief, and, saved and inspired by a woman with a close connection to the gods, has fought the human incarnation of Titanic power, meriting Godhood for that. And in the union of the prophetess and hero, a new hero-son is promised to help continue the never-ending fight against evil, with human and god as partners. Echoes of Christianity and its hopeful message are hard to miss.

THE MILLENNIUM AND THE DREAM OF THE MORAL AND DIVINE

Immortals is more than a faux art-house sword-and-sandals flick, although it does draw on those traditions, and many of its elements resonate with the interests of the new millennium. As do many of our other films, it mirrors the widespread sense that the insufficiency or corruption of prior institutions has brought our rational civilization to the edge of apocalypse, with chaotic evil poised to triumph, aided by humans. But it acknowledges, in poetic and mythic

---

38 The statue group recalls nineteenth-century French and Italian neoclassicism, such as the statue group of Etienne-Jules Ramey Theseus Fighting the Minotaur (1826, Jardin des Tuileries, Paris) or Antonio Canova' Theseus Fighting the Centaur (1804–1819, Kunsthistorisches Museum, Wien).

39 This perhaps looks forward to a sequel of *Immortals*, which is apparently in the planning stages. See http://henrycavill.org/en/blog/henry-cavill-news/item/1158-immortals-sequel-in-the-works. Accessed July 21, 2016.

form, the intuition that these forces are in a sense spiritual (although not in the strictly theological sense) and not just material. The repeated depictions of apocalypses suggests that Titans (for example, widespread economic depression, endless local wars, new Cold Wars with Russia and China) and racist tendencies, once forgotten, are returning. The worse evil has a mystery of faith to it, and a mysterious attraction, which in *Immortals* can be met only by an equally mysterious virtue, which can be called divine and produce the sacred hero. *Pan's Labyrinth*, surreal in a very different way, nevertheless also posits that our hell-world intersects positively with magical and divine forces. *Such Is Life*'s adaptation of the Medea myth, also surreal, depicts powerful forces of evil, but without countervailing forces of good, ending with child murder and the escape of the murderess. In our chapter on *O Brother, Where Art Thou?* a type of hero and divinity were described, more parodic, subtler, but discernible nevertheless. But at the end, maybe *Immortals* best serves by recasting in a modern idiom an older ideal of an uncompromised and rewarded heroism.

REFERENCES

Abbot, E. *History of Greece: From the Ionian Revolt to the Thirty Years' Peace, 500–445 BC.* Longman, Green, 1901.

Burkert, W. *Greek Religion.* Harvard UP, 1985.

Calame, C. *Thésée et l'imaginaire athénien: Légende et culte en Grèce antique.* Sciences humaines, Editions Payot, 1990.

Ebert. R. "Immortals." http://www.rogerebert.com/reviews/immortals-2011, 2011. Accessed June 21, 2016.

Farnell, L. R. *Greek Hero Cults and Ideas of Immortality.* Oxford Clarendon Press, 1921.

Garrett, D. *Off Screen*, vol. 12 no. 9, September 2008. http://offscreen.com/view/fall_tarsem. Accessed June 21, 2016.

Hawes, G. *Rationalizing Myth in Antiquity.* Oxford UP, 2014.

Kearns, E. *Heroes of Attica.* University of London, Institute of Classical Studies, 1989.

Mills, S. *Theseus, Tragedy and the Athenian Empire.* Clarendon Press, 1997.

Murphy, M. "It's Gods vs. Mortals, and It Isn't Pretty." *New York Times*, Oct. 30, 2011, p. MT 20. See also http://mobile.nytimes.com/2011/10/30/movies/heads-are-exploding-in-tarsem-singhs-immortals.html. Accessed July 21, 2016.

Podlecki, A. "Cimon, Skyros and Theseus' Bones." *Journal of Hellenic Studies*, vol. 91, 1971, 141–43.

Rose, H. J. *A Handbook of Greek Mythology.* Dutton, 1959.

Simone, E. "Theseus and Athenian Festivals." In J. Neils, ed., *Worshipping Athena: Panathenaia and Parthenon.* University of Wisconsin Press, 1996, pp. 9–26.

Sourvinou-Inwood, C. "Persephone and Aphrodite at Locri: A Model for Personality Definitions in Greek Religion." *Journal of Hellenic Studies*, vol. 98, 1978, 101–21.

Versnel, H. S. *Inconsistencies in Greek and Roman Religion, Vol. 2: Transition and Reversal in Myth and Ritual.* Brill, 1994.

Walker, H. J. *Theseus and Athens.* Oxford UP, 1994.

Ward, A. *The Quest for Theseus.* Praeger, 1970.

West, M. L. *Theogony: Edited with Prolegomena and Commentary.* Oxford UP, 1966.

Wilson C. "Jupiter and the Fates in the *Aeneid*." *Classical Quarterly (New Series)*, vol. 29 no. 2, 1979, 361–71.

DISCUSSION QUESTIONS FOR PART II

1. What variety of models of women do these films present? Discuss Phaedra, Io, and Andromeda. Do they correspond to their traditional mythical predecessors? How do they correlate to models of the female in modern culture? Give examples.

2. *Immortals* provides a more spiritualized view of the world and humankind, while *Clash/Wrath* shows the death of the gods. How do these views of the divine correspond to millennial debates on faith and religion?

3. The labyrinth is a prominent theme in many of our movies. How is it displayed in *Clash/Wrath* and *Immortals*? What are its meanings and what does it symbolize in the hero's career? What sort of metaphoric "labyrinths" might a millennial youth encounter today?

4. What various interpretations of the figure of Medusa as she appears in *Clash* can we make? What can she represent? (Consider, for example, her relation to Athena.) Compare her re-creation with the ones that appear in other films.

5. *Clash/Wrath* seem to incorporate elements from various mythologies (not just Classical) and cultures. How might this speak to the modern idea of multiculturalism and diversity?

6. *Clash/Wrath* and *Immortals* deal with canonical Classical myths (Perseus and Theseus), yet the plots are very much changed from the traditional versions. Why do you think the creators felt the need to do so, and what are the results in the context of the new millennium?

7. One of the themes, especially stressed in *Hercules*, is that the more powerful the hero, the more unstable he is. How true do you think this notion is?

8. Our movies present confrontation between the rational and the irrational, the orderly and the chaotic. But where does Hyperion fit here? How might we see him as rational?

9. *Immortals* has somewhat of an unreal feel to it, presenting a rather dreamlike world. How does this work in terms of recreating a mythological world?

10. Both of our movies again reprise the mythical confrontation of Titans and Olympians and the threat of the evil forces reemerging. Why do you think this has become such a pervasive topic in millennial movies? What kinds of symbolic "Titans" might be threatening a resurgence in our modern world?

WOMEN IN THE MARGINS

PAN'S LABYRINTH (2006)
SUCH IS LIFE (2000)

MYTHICAL WOMEN IN THE MARGINS

We all know this: Medea was a terrible woman, for destroying life, the very fruits of her womb. The goddess Demeter, in contrast, is venerated, an all-powerful Mother who gives life to the world. But is it all that simple? In the next two movies we will explore the complexities of womanhood and motherhood and women's circumstances in patriarchal, often oppressive environments. What is a woman to do when she cannot conform to these patterns, or when these patterns fail to protect her?

For many of us, the most engaging stories present intense conflict, often with clear heroes and villains, let us say Harry Potter versus Lord Voldemort. This is certainly true also for news programs. In movies, some conflicts are embedded in a decidedly mythical world, but others are set in a specific place and time, and even within living memory. The best of these are not simple apocalyptic battles, but involve intricate depictions of oppression, resistance, hope in defeat, and sometimes victories. The very best always evoke the lived struggles of the viewer's society. *Such Is Life* (2000), directed by Arturo Ripstein, and *Pan's Labyrinth* (2006), directed by Guillermo Del Toro, are such stories of conflict that critically connect with our times. These movies, set in the margins, with liminal heroines in a non-English/American context, and calling for feminist and politically engaged readings, present two fine stories to explore.

Such Is Life may seem the more "mythological" since it adapts the "canonical" Greek myth of Medea as retold by the Roman Seneca. Briefly, this is the tale of an Eastern princess and witch, Medea, who was responsible for Jason's success and gave up her homeland for him. In Greece, after she has borne him two children, he abandons her for a new wife. In revenge Medea kills his new wife and the wife's father, and then her own children by Jason. Ripstein's movie, however, is set in a grittily realistic tenement in Mexico City and populated by contemporary characters not unfamiliar from Mexican *telenovelas*. Its echoes of the "supernatural" are products of the director's surrealistic approach, which reflects the probable mental breakdown of Julia, his Medea, and Ripstein's movies' more general take on life.

Pan's *Labyrinth* reproduces no set Greek myth, and yet its plot, characters, and themes are suffused with mythological elements, such as the god Pan, the descent into the Underworld, and the divine pair Demeter/Persephone. Each level has its own story. Its historically realistic narrative tells how the vile Falangist leader, Captain Vidal, takes his pregnant wife and stepdaughter to his military base in the mountains, where he attempts to destroy the last rebels against Franco; his wife dies in childbirth, and he kills his stepdaughter, only to be killed himself by the rebels, who will raise his child. But the mythic story is Ofelia's; she is an incarnation of Moana, princess of a magic underworld realm, whose actions awaken a kingdom of supernatural beings. It is ruled by a Faun, who assigns Moana three tests, which end in her own sacrificial death, and subsequent rebirth, and Vidal's execution.

Both films are anchored in a historically real world and complex social and political reality that remains significant. The persistent structures of oppression, both in Spain and Mexico City, are evident. These institutions are served by and profit men, these self-imagined heroes who dominate women as a natural right, all too easily degrading, brutalizing, and even killing women and children, among others. Both movies present life on earth as a kind of man-made Hell. Our oppressed and marginalized heroines appear powerless in the face of such evil, and it is a useful exercise to consider these two narratives in tandem, as providing two perspectives and sets of choices for women, both of which may seem appalling.

Julia has abandoned her hometown for Nico, and now is being kicked out of the tenement by the dominating father of Nico's new bride (known as "the Sow") with no place to go. Ofelia is a scorned stepchild with an ailing, burdened mother. What can they do? Or perhaps a better question: What do brutal circumstances force them to do? They compel the pair to make choices. Both films stress the programmatic roles and traditional obligations of daughter, mother, and wife in highly patriarchal societies, and the oppression of both Julia and Ofelia is bound to those roles. Extreme circumstances open portals to alternative ways of being and critical choices. Both women are healers with semimagical skills, and connect (or are thought to connect) with the hidden powers of nature. They are both exiles who lose through violence the most important person in their lives, one a husband, the other a mother. A major choice for both women involves the fate of a child dependent on them and threatened by an evil father, and both find their final identities by sacrificing that relationship. Ofelia's story echoes the ultimately positive fertility myth of the dying and rising and beneficent goddess Persephone and her powerful mother Demeter. Thus Ofelia self-sacrificially accepts the role of pseudo-mother and out of love gives her life for her little brother, to be reborn again in a fantasy world. Julia echoes Seneca's Medea, who embraces a hatred able to destabilize the universe, rejects the mores of motherhood, and kills her own children, but in our movie without even the hope of escape to Athens. Although both movies are innovatively crafted and rich in their depiction of political and cultural conditions, the obstacles, choices, and fates of Julia and Ofelia remain central, as they embody the realities of many, so many abused others.

CHAPTER 6

BLOOMING MAIDEN AND FERTILE GODDESS

The Myths of *Pan's Labyrinth*

But when the earth burgeons with every kind of spring's sweet smelling flowers,
at that time from the gloom of the darkness below
again you will rise up, a marvel to gods and humans liable to death.

(*Homeric Hymn to Demeter* 401–3)

She could be Snow White, full red lips and rosy cheeks on ivory skin, dark hair falling on her shoulders (Fig. 6.1). But she is not. She won't be saved by a prince or protected by friendly dwarfs, and an evil step parent will indeed kill her.[1] Yet this princess will gain her kingdom. The movie begins with the screen blank; we hear a girl's labored breathing. Titles inform us that it is 1944, and the Spanish Civil War is over, but in hidden areas bands are still fighting the Fascist regime, and armed camps have been set up to exterminate them. We see the form of a young girl dying, the dark ribbon of blood flowing back into her nose. This realistic scene leads immediately to fairy tale.[2]

The voice-over tells us that "a long time ago," in an underground (and dark) kingdom, a place without "pain or lies," a princess (who we learn later was called Moana) dreamed of the world of humans up above, a place with sunshine, light, and blue skies. She escaped from her father's realm, eager to go up to see the upper world. However, blinded by its sunlight, Moana becomes ill and dies. Her father, the king, believes that her spirit will return one day and vows to wait for her. Thus

---

1 For Ofelia's links to Snow White, see Zipes (2008), 237–38, and Kimura (2012), 83.
2 For the film's links to fairy tales, see Kotecki (2010) and Orme (2010).

187

FIGURE 6.1 The dying Ofelia, as her blood drips into the well.

PLOT SUMMARY

Traveling with her pregnant mother, eleven-year-old Ofelia journeys to a mill in the mountains to be with her stepfather, a captain of the Francoist army. She meets a faun and magical creatures and goes on a Quest to regain her status as princess of the underworld realm of Bezmorra. Her mother dies in childbirth, and as part of her third test, she refuses to spill the blood of her baby brother, which provides the ultimate proof of her worth to return to Bezmorra. In the real world, the evil captain is finally killed by resistance forces.

begins Guillermo Del Toro's 2006 *Pan's Labyrinth*,[3] a fantastic story of birth and rebirth, of myths of the earth, of women, fertility, and fecundity, all matters bound up with the historically real horrors of Franco's Fascist regime.[4]

A girl, dying, the moon in a pool, blood flowing, but backwards, perhaps to symbolize the rebirth that has been triggered. This first sequence symbolizes the film's complexities, part fairy tale, part historical horror story, part fertility myth. Acclaimed by both critics and scholars, the movie is in many ways a masterpiece.[5] Unlike some of our other movies, this film does not retell any

---

3   The English title may imply a link to Peter Pan. However, there is no mention of the name Pan at all in the Spanish version, just "a faun." Yet, for the English-speaking audience, probably the largest one for the movie, the connection between the god Pan and Peter Pan is not lost, a link observed by Merivale (1969), 152; and Lurie (1987), 193 and 198.

4   For earlier, seminal ideas for this chapter, regarding the transition to womanhood, the symbolism of blood in femininity, and the connections of the myth with the classical *katabasis* and the Demeter-Persephone myth see Salzman-Mitchell (2007) .

5   *NY Times* reviewer A. O. Scott (Dec. 29, 2006) refers to its "brilliance," the work of a "real magician," Del Toro's "finest achievement so far," and notes that the film "has the feel of something permanent" (http://www.nytimes.com/2006/12/29/movies/29laby.html. Accessed July 13, 2016). *Guardian* (Nov. 23, 2006) reviewer Peter Bradshaw calls it "so audacious and technically accomplished" (https://www.theguardian.com/film/2006/nov/24/sciencefictionandfantasy.worldcinema. Accessed July 13, 2016). Morgernstern's review in the *Wall Street Journal* (Dec. 29, 2006: http://www.wsj.com/articles/SB116735260876762064. Accessed July 13, 2016) is overwhelmingly enthusiastic and considers it one of the top ten movies in 2006. Roger Ebert (Aug. 25, 2007) calls it "one of the greatest of all fantasy films" (http://www.rogerebert.com/reviews/great-movie-pans-labyrinth-2006. Accessed July 13, 2016). There were many other laudatory reviews.

KEY TERMS

Spanish Civil War: civil war in the late 1930s in Spain in which the right-wing Fascists, supporters of Francisco Franco, fought against the elected Republicans

Falange (Española Tradicionalista): right-wing ruling nationalist party in Spain (1937–1977), led by Franco

Maquis: members of the rebels who opposed and fought Franco's regime

Fairy tale: a story, usually for children, with magical characters, places, and objects

---

specific mythological story but uses a vast range of sources and literary and filmic connections that speak at many levels.[6]

A young widow, Carmen, and her preadolescent daughter Ofelia travel to a liminal place, an old mill in the north of Spain, located up in the wooded mountains, to meet Carmen's new husband, Captain Vidal, a committed Falangist, who with his army is trying to suppress the last revolutionary forces of the Spanish Civil War. Carmen is in a stage of advanced pregnancy, and the film begins with a focus on her suffering during the long journey. The heroine's movement upward and into a more primitive region will begin her period of harsh testing in one world which will be a preparation for her ideal life in another.

There are many fairy-tale stories whose young heroines experience double worlds, as in *The Wizard of Oz* and Lewis Carroll's *Alice in Wonderland*.[7] This is a slightly displaced presentation of the persistent mythological notion that human beings are exiled from their original inheritance, whether heaven or the Garden of Eden, and can struggle to find their way back. Our film's setting is the backdrop for two parallel plots, one in the horrific and violent "above ground" world of post-civil war Spain and another in a peaceful and paradisiacal "underground world" to which Ofelia must earn her return. The majority of critics have seen the "unreal" side of the film as a dream, an escape fantasy of a young girl faced with the brutality of horrors that surrounded her.

The fantastic side of the tale, coupled with the comforting, rather haunting song Mercedes hums, can be seen as aiming to promote courage and ease our trauma at the violence and loss rising from such wars.[8] Our perspective accepts

---

6 Kotecki (2010), 243.

7 Though the master of modern film fairy tale, Disney, is unavoidably present in Del Toro's work, Del Toro's film "does not sanitize the past (like the Disney corporation does with its adaptation of classical narratives according to Zipes)"; Gómez-Castellano (2013), 4. Curiously, the next Disney movie, coming out in November 2016, features a Polynesian princess named Moana.

8 See Zipes (2008), 238; Hubner (2010), 45; Gómez-Castellano (2013), 11; and Orme (2010), 226. On Mercedes's lullaby as leitmotif in the movie, see Gómez-Castellano (2013). Maternal and uterine feminine strategies have often been employed to "voice political protest." Gómez-Castellano, 6. For fairy tales as a way for children to deal with trauma and *Pan's Labyrinth* as a "contribution to the revision of historical trauma," see Vivancos (2012), 882. Also Kimura (2012), 79: "without realizing it, she [Ofelia] is obliged to create the fantasy world as a means of withdrawal from the harshness of real life."

this fantasy as "real," and thus we shall treat it as we do other such content in our films. As noted, Del Toro's use of Classical myth is selective, eclectic, and indirect. For example, although the figure of the Faun and the lunar imagery is fairly straightforward, the themes of fertility and the descent to the underworld are more diffuse. Yet among the various other mythic traditions involved in the narrative, our focus will be on the themes and images of Classical mythology, and we shall discuss in particular myths of fertility, which involve four archetypal figures and motifs: the faun, the heroine's descent to the underworld, the figures of Demeter and Persephone, and the waning and waxing moon.

THE SPANISH CIVIL WAR AND FILMS OF RESISTANCE: REBIRTH AFTER WAR

Between 1936 and 1939 the bloody Spanish Civil War was fought between two factions: the left-leaning and pro-democracy Republicans and the Nationalists led by Falangist General Francisco Franco, whose authoritarian ideology had close connections with other extreme right-wing European leaders such as Hitler and Mussolini, though officially, Spain was never involved in World War II. The Nationalists won and Franco ruled unchallenged until his death in 1975. Yet after the war resistance factions, the Maquis, fought back for a while, often hidden in the hills and secluded areas. This is the setting of our film, where Captain Vidal is sent to hunt down these factions and exterminate, or "cleanse," Spain of them.

The remaining revolutionary forces were finally defeated and Spain endured a long period of totalitarian rule, with few liberties and a strong paternalistic, all-powerful figure in the person of Franco himself, who shaped the cultural makeup of Spain for thirty-six years. The Catholic Church remained a prevailing presence, and there was very conservative encouragement of the traditional family, ruled by a strong father obliged to provide for his numerous children and spouse; the latter's role was essentially that of being a mother and wife.[9] Franco himself was often seen as "father of the Spanish people."[10] He was not defeated by an election or a war, so at his death Spain had to reimagine herself, resulting in a tepid, problematic "pacto del olvido" or "pact of forgetfulness," a sort of collective amnesia that fits well with a Spanish tendency to silence the past.[11] The Spaniards basically decided to let the past be the past and not delve into the trauma of years and years of horror and violence.[12]

---

9 Vivancos (2012), 877–78 and passim.

10 Vivancos (2012), 877.

11 The virtual end of the "pacto del olvido" was set with the election of a Socialist Party president in 2004 and more precisely later in 2007 with "the passing of the Law of Historical Memory by the Spanish Prime Minister José Luis Rodríguez Zapatero." See Diestro-Dópido (2015), 26 and 25–39, for the meanings of war in *Pan's Labyrinth*. Many Spanish films since 2000 "refer heavily to this unearthing of the undead past which haunts the collective imaginary." Diestro-Dópido (2015), 26.

12 Gómez-Castellano (2013), 10. She sees (10) also that "Like the tale of Ofelia . . . Spain's recent past can be retold as the tale of a fallen princess that runs the risk of forgetting her true identity

Pan's Labyrinth (2006) Warner Bros.	
Language:	Spanish
Director:	Guillermo del Toro
Screenplay:	Guillermo del Toro
Cast:	Ivana Vaquero (Ofelia), Sergi López (Vidal), Maribel Verdú (Mercedes), Doug Jones (Fauno), Ariadna Gil (Carmen), Alex Angulo (Dr. Ferreiro)

Mexican-born Guillermo Del Toro has fully participated in the American mainstream blockbuster industry with movies in English, such as *Hell Boy* (2004), *Blade II* (2002), and *Pacific Rim* (2013), and was even involved as director initially in the *Lord of the Rings* movie series. His Spanish film production has also been acclaimed, and many of his films have been great creative as well as commercial successes and are true artistic statements in themselves.[13] He was not the first filmmaker to address the aftermath of the Civil War period; nor is this his first movie about it (cf. *El Espinazo del Diablo*, The Devil's Backbone, 2001).[14] Art can rarely be silenced, and we have not only artists of the resistance—painters, musicians, and so forth, often in exile in places like Mexico, where Del Toro comes from, which was the only Western nation that refused to accept the legitimacy of the Francoist regime[15]—but also a robust tradition of resistance cinema, which has significantly influenced Del Toro's work through films such as Victor Erice's *El Espíritu de la Comena* (*The Spirit of the Beehive*, 1973) and *El Sur* (*South*, 1983) and Carlos Saura's *Cría Cuervos* (*Raise Ravens*, 1976). In this Spanish resistance cinema, violence is a central feature, since "during the Francoist era, the depiction of violence was repressed, as was the depiction of sex, sacrilege and politics."[16] The film also follows a trend in modern cinema where a child appears as "a figure through which to explore the

if she keeps avoiding a traumatic encounter with her past." Ofelia's journey to recover what's hers is, in a way, like the Maquis' quests to regain Spain, yet both endeavors are doomed to end in "death and self-sacrifice" (Gómez-Castellano, 2013, 11). Thus "Ofelia stands for Spain, the orphan who lost her republican father in the war and who has to live in the house of her own enemy" (12). See also Hubner (2010), 46. Of course, "Fatherless and then orphaned, she conforms to the traditional fairytale hero" (53).

13 A very much awaited book written by Del Toro himself and Nick Nunziata to celebrate the ten-year anniversary of the release of *Pan's Labyrinth*, is expected to come out in October 2016, too late to be incorporated in this volume." We also direct the reader's attention to Olson (2016), which appeared too recently for us to properly address it in our book.

14 In the director's commentary to the DVD (2007), Del Toro thinks of *Pan's Labyrinth* as a "companion piece" to *Devil's Backbone*, set in 1939 Spain and released five years before *Pan*.

15 Vivancos (2012), 892. As Hanley (2007), 39, observes, Mexico is "a place of escape, the destination to which many Civil War exiles directed their hopes and futures." On the "Mexican connection" and the film, see also Diestro-Dópido (2015), 31–39. Interestingly, Del Toro himself is an exile, since he no longer lives in Mexico after his father was kidnapped. See Hanley (2007), 39.

16 Kinder (1993), 138.

legacy of war and genocide during the twentieth century."[17] Yet out of horror and violence there might come the mythical hope of rebirth. Our movie shares with *O Brother, Where Art Thou?* a setting in a historically real time that has become mythologized. Like *O Brother, Pan's Labyrinth* is a sort of history of what "might have been" but was not.[18] *O Brother* suggests a time when the power of music and a divinely connected (if problematical) hero could somehow defeat the KKK and help bring about a new, more enlightened age in deeply racist Mississippi. Here it is a magically connected young girl who helps forces that might defeat Franco's Falangists, saving a child from a demon father who can represent a possible future for Spain.

A QUEST FOR REBIRTH

Princess Moana's father, the king of Bezmorra, believes the spirit of his dead daughter will return one day. Now, after many years, she has been reincarnated in Ofelia, the story's protagonist, whose adventures in the upper world function as an inverted quest.[19] In order to rejoin her father's underworld kingdom, and later rule it, Ofelia must undergo three tests: retrieving a key from the insides of a frightful frog, then opening a lock in the house of a monster that kills children, and finally, spilling innocent blood." But as Del Toro mentions, what is important is not so much whether in fact she passes these tests or fails (in fact she fails the second one), but rather how one faces them, "how one goes about them."[20]

Although she is killed by Captain Vidal, we know that she has only died in the upper world, and instead has returned as princess Moana to the underworld kingdom to save it[21] and to meet her mother and father. Parallel to this plot, in the upper world, Captain Vidal fights the rebels and keeps on torturing and killing them, including the family physician, Dr. Ferreiro, who, together with the head housekeeper Mercedes, has been secretly aiding the resistance. Carmen's pregnancy worsens after momentarily improving thanks to Ofelia's actions, and she dies in childbirth. Toward the end of the film, Ofelia takes her baby brother away, but the Captain catches her; she dies when she lets her evil stepfather take the baby and, shot by the Captain, she sacrifices her own "innocent blood" in place of the infant's. But Mercedes the housekeeper and her brother Pedro appear, and the resistance fighters storm the Falangist camp, seize the newborn, and fatally shoot the captain. Moana is resurrected

17 Lebeau (2008), 141. See also the discussion in Clark and McDonald (2010), 56.
18 Toscano (2009), 50–51, and Ruppersburg (2003), 6 and 24. Also Spector (2009), 84.
19 Foley (1994), 80, notes how the *Homeric Hymn to Demeter*, which tells of the struggles of Demeter and her daughter Kore/Persephone, offers "a female version of the heroic Quest."
20 See DVD director's comments.
21 As the rebels fight to save Spain from Fascism. Lindsay (2012), 9.

in the underground kingdom, where she sees her father and her revived mother on lofty thrones, as well as the Faun, who we recognize has been managing Moana's Quest/trial. We learn that Moana ruled well for many centuries afterward.[22] Thus our movie presents a Quest or coming-of-age myth, with magic, magical helpers, and strange netherworlds playing a central role.[23]

Archetypes found in classical mythology help shape the narrative of her maturation, struggle, and triumph. As usual with Quest stories, the heroine is a marvelous child of quasi-divine origin (as is Perseus in *Clash of the Titans*, and Percy in *Percy Jackson and the Olympians*) whose coming of age is tied to a search to regain her own lost birthright, as well as to help a parent in distress. Note how the Faun tells Ofelia that she was engendered by the moon; and later she finds a sickle-shaped moon birthmark on her shoulder, which fits her, as the lightning-bolt scar fits Harry Potter. Her trip to the upper world implies a need to gain experience for her eventual return to Bezmorra and future queenship. Ofelia will need to discover her own fertility powers, not only in the transition to her own womanhood, but also as a sort of fertility deity who can give new life to the earth, as well as sacrifice herself for others. In her earlier life Moana is blinded and sickened by the sunlight, perhaps symbolic of masculine "solar" gods who often control women, or of knowledge she is not ready for. But it is images of the moon and moonlight that are most associated with Ofelia, not the garish sun.[24]

During her Quest, the young Ofelia must undergo a series of tests that will lead her from the innocence of childhood to becoming a woman with maturity, responsibility, and concern for others. Real or symbolic quests, of course, were once an important part of coming-of-age rituals. Lindsay suggests that menstruation, a major turning point in a woman's life, lies at the symbolic core of Ofelia's quest.[25] Indeed, allusions to Ofelia's growing up appear repeatedly

---

22 The *Homeric Hymn to Demeter* is a foundation myth for the formation of the ideal religious-political structure of Eleusis, which brings benefit to human beings, and *Pan's Labyrinth* is a foundation myth for the ideal rule of Ofelia. And just as Persephone can assist those in both worlds, so does Ofelia, as she sends signs for those who have eyes to see.

23 Lindsay (2012), 1–2, analyzes Ofelia's journey in the context of Campbell's scheme and its departures from it, acknowledging nevertheless that his views are rather male-centered and that postmodern criticism may be doubtful of overarching structures. Yet, as we mentioned in our introductory chapter, the influence of the hero's journey is paramount in modern movies.

24 Spector (2009), 82. On various mythical images of fatherhood and masculinity in the film, see Spector (2009).

25 Lindsay (2012), passim. "In appropriating the hero's journey as a metaphor for female menstruation, therefore, Del Toro transgresses the patriarchal cycle of womanless regeneration. In this way, although the film follows closely to and in some ways reaffirms the hero's journey as outlined by Campbell, it may also be read as feminist critique of this mythology" (7). On Pan's alternative refashioning of the monomyth, see also Perlich (2009), 103 and 123ff., and his discussion of the film in terms of the stages of the monomyth, 106ff.

in the film's dialogue,[26] and thus the plot presents a kind of rite of passage.[27] Fertility, so important in many myths, is obviously a central theme; Ofelia's coming of age, the fate of her pregnant mother, and her eventual delivery of a baby boy are tightly intertwined and linked to issues of procreation, mother-hood, femininity, nature, and agriculture, guided always by the Faun, a tradi-tional fertility deity.

THE WORLD BELOW, THE WORLD ABOVE

At the film's beginning the car in which Ofelia and Carmen travel moves up toward the mountains. This journey upward through the woods, the realm of the Faun and magical creatures, offers a setting symbolic of a coming-of-age journey with life-giving dimensions that Ofelia will undergo, as well as a transi-tion to another kind of world. Though great heroes like Heracles and Aeneas have journeys to the Underworld, we particularly focus on the initial, and then yearly, journey of Persephone to the Deadlands. This is a journey of life and death, as both Ofelia and her mother will die in the above-ground world, but will be reborn finally in the underworld. The Captain is far more concerned about his future child and heir than he is about the mother. Vidal embodies the rigid, hypermasculine patriarchal discourse of Franco's dictatorship, which Ofelia refuses to comply with,[28] and his focus on his unborn child, which he "has dictated" is a boy, aims at perpetuating this status quo. The perilous trip upward, to his camp in the mountains, is an expression of Vidal's desire to control all circumstances of his son's birth, as his father controlled the circum-stances of his own death. In *Immortals,* the monster King Hyperion makes sure pregnant women are killed, and apparently intends to control fertility when he is the world's master.

While the car is stopped because Carmen is nauseous, Ofelia wanders in the woods, which is, as we discuss in other films, often a real or symbolic Dark Wood. She discovers some insectlike "fairies" who lead her to ancient stones with the image of a faun.[29] These fairies are magic helpers such as Quest heroes often encounter. Heroes usually need guides, whether it is Hermes or the Sybil.

---

26 In the opening scene in the car, her mother insists that she is too old to be reading fairy-tale books. Later Carmen repeatedly tells her that she is now growing up and needs to understand that the world is a cruel place. Carmen does not give Ofelia a lot of "mothering" and seems to want her daughter to grow up quickly and be independent, perhaps so that she can focus on her new baby as well as have Ofelia's assistance. We see such a similarly harsh and negative view of life often expressed in the Mexican film *Such Is Life.*

27 Hubner (2010), 54.

28 Ofelia refuses to call Vidal father or to sacrifice her brother to the Faun. Kotecki (2010), 249, on the heroine's resistance to the "patriarchal order."

29 Longus in *Daphnis and Chloe* (1.4 and 3.12.2) mentions country effigies with the image of Pan on which little sacrifices are placed.

Ofelia comes across a piece of stone with an eye carved in it, which she places in an engraved effigy of a faun.[30] With this action she awakens the Faun and the supernatural world of the woods, thus setting events in motion. Del Toro has crafted a visual narrative where powerful images will dominate the screen and the viewer's imagination. It is, in a metafilmic way, the turning on of the camera.[31] Up to now, the fairy tale world has appeared only in the book Ofelia was reading in the car; now it has become visual. The car is moving upward toward the hills, but this opening of the "eye" will lead Ofelia/Moana on her quest downward.

During the first night in the Mill, Ofelia is awakened by fairies who lead her to "the labyrinth of the Faun" deep in the woods, which, as the Faun explains, is the last portal her father left open for her to return to his nether kingdom. The labyrinth is a richly symbolic structure that can be seen as a figure for the mysteries of the cosmos, of the human body, of the psyche, of destiny, and much more. It is a place of controlling spaces filled with dangers and revelations, which heroes must try to master. We are reminded of that very archetypal labyrinth the hero Theseus must confront, also with a half-human creature in it,[32] which reappears in *Immortals*. As Frye explains, in myths of subterranean descent "we find the night world, often a dark and labyrinthine world of caves and shadows where the forest has turned subterranean, and where we are surrounded by shapes of animals."[33] We will see this clearly in the "Forbidden Forest" in our Harry Potter film, for example.

In the specific historical context of the film, Lindsay observes that "Del Toro has proposed the monstrous possibilities of female dis-order and associations with nature as qualities to be embraced and preserved. In Del Toro's conception, the idea of Fascist Spain is a contrast to this, a representation of the worst of the masculine principle—cold, mechanical and unfeeling—that must be resisted."[34] These elements are clearly visible in Ofelia's Quest journey, for the girl's descent to the labyrinthine underground realm of the faun, set amid deep woods, occurs in the darkness of night, and earthly and female imagery of fertility and

---

30 Interestingly, Perlich (2009), 107, notices that "the open mouth of the statue mimics a pained expression and pleads with Ofelia for assistance."

31 Clark and McDonald (2010), 59, quote Del Toro himself saying that he often uses the camera as "if it were a curious child" (in Wood, 2006, 43). On the film "witnessing the world through, and adopting the gaze of, a young girl," see Perlich (2009), 106.

32 Kimura (2012), 82–83, discusses the mythical image of the labyrinth: "In its center, one can find one's new self. . . . Reaching the center of the labyrinth, one symbolically dies and is reborn as a new self, and going back to the entrance again is to accomplish one's rebirth. For Ofelia, the labyrinth is a place for enabling her growth as well as escape." Further, "In that labyrinth, there is a pool, which seems to represent the fluid of the womb—it is also the place of rebirth."

33 Frye (1976), 111.

34 Lindsay (2012), 10.

nourishing is pervasive. At the end of the initial journey upward, they find a dreadful world of killing and torture. Upward movement in the film generally implies death; note the horrific battles fought up in the hills. This makes sense in terms of the inverted mythical cosmos. Instead of the heaven-centered cosmos with its male sky-god, where good is "up," here, in this earth centered cosmos, controlled by a mother goddess, good instead is *downward*. In the end, the maiden Ofelia, whose name inevitably recalls Shakespeare's maddened heroine, must look to return to an underworld "without lies and sorrow" where life and happiness reign.

Frye further notes how in the journeys to a subterranean world "the normal road of descent is through dream or something strongly suggestive of a dream atmosphere."[35] This whole story could be seen as a wishful fantasy dream of a young girl to escape the horrors surrounding her, which leads her to her death.[36] Note how most of her adventures in this fantastic world of the forest occur in the middle of the night, and in all her encounters with the faun she wears a nightgown, though this may also reinforce the erotic nuances of her meetings with him, all suggestive of dream, an escape from reality.

The Faun's underground labyrinth is accessed first by a circular opening in the woods and then through a series of downward-spiraling stairs. The film's masculine world is denoted with straight lines, yet a world of the female with its spirals and turns appears in her first encounter with the world below.[37] Another circular opening in the ground also evokes a female aperture to Mother Earth, a large entrance to her body. These circles and spirals recall the female anatomy and in particular the entrance to the reproductive organs, of labyrinthlike shape themselves.[38] Thus, this return of Ofelia to the depths of Mother Earth can be seen as a return to the womb, and so from one perspective Ofelia's coming of age might have failed, her death returning her to the womb, rather than distancing herself from her mother. But in this inverted Quest world, as in Christian mythology, a sacrificial death does not mean failure. Jesus comes down from heaven, becomes human, gains knowledge, struggles and dies, and returns to heaven to rule, having benefited humankind. Ofelia comes up from the earth, becomes human, makes the earth fertile, gains knowledge, struggles, dies, and returns to her chthonic kingdom to rule, having benefited humankind.

---

35 Frye (1976), 99.
36 The Shakespearean imagery has further resonances here. Note how Sir John Everett Millais's famous portrait of the drowning Ophelia (1851–52) is also surrounded by flowers, linking her to maidenhood, to the girl at the verge of womanhood. See also how our dying Ofelia (Fig. 6.1) visually recalls Millais's painting.
37 See the "sharp phallic angularity of Vidal's world . . . the long columns of cars and men with guns . . ." Hubner (2010), 52.
38 See Lindsay (2012) in particular.

FAUNUS

In an interview with Del Toro, we read: "And the character of the faun is essentially the trickster. He is a character that is neither good nor bad. He's a character . . . that's why I chose a faun. Not 'Pan'. Pan is just the translation, which is not accurate. It's a faun, because the faun in classical mythology was at the same time a creature of destruction, and a creature of nurturing and life. So he can as easily destroy her as he can help her."[39]

Guillermo Del Toro's faun is a masterful creation, projecting a basic goodness while retaining an uncanny and even dangerous quality, a duality found already in this mythological figure.[40] The familiar imagery of coils and spirals in his forehead and horns (Fig. 6.2) suggests he represents the labyrinth's guiding intelligence and purpose. Just as is common with a young girl during the first brush with sexuality, Ofelia is both scared and intrigued by this male figure. Faunus is the Roman *numen* (ancient Italic deity, usually connected with some natural force) identified with the Greek Pan.[41] He is a male half-goat, half-man fertility god connected with the woods and the fecundity of the flocks,[42] and is considered particularly lustful. He symbolizes human beings as part animal, part human, and part god (and note that, unlike in Egypt, Greek and Roman mythology favors more anthropomorphic deities). Roman writers identified the figure of the Greek god Pan with Faunus or Silvanus, rustic deities who were often referred to in the plural as pans, fauns, or *silvani*.[43] In Del Toro's film, he is alluded to as one of many, "un fauno," "a faun." So even though Del Toro states that the translation of Pan for the *fauno* is not exact, he nevertheless accepts it as the English version for his film, which we understand as acknowledgment of how all these deities are closely related and blend into one another's imagery and identities, and in myth, they are much harder to distinguish.[44] There is no real reason the movie could not be titled "The Labyrinth of the Faun" in English, besides perhaps clarity and marketability. We understand that all aspects of Pan, Faunus, pans, *silvani* are related deities that serve as mythical background through which the figure of the Faun in the movie can be read, and thus the various traits here discussed add to our interpretation of this character.

---

39 Interviewed by Ian Spelling in *SCI FI Weekly*, Dec. 25, 2006. ftp://asavage.dyndns.org/Literature/scifi.com/www.scifi.com/sfw/interviews/sfw14471.html. Accessed July 13, 2016.

40 See Merivale (1969), passim.

41 *OCD*, 4th ed., "*faunus.*" For more on his name and related deities, see Borgeaud (1988) and Brown (1977).

42 As Frye (1976), 115, observes, animals are frequent companions of the hero in myths of descent to a subterranean realm. The Faun's partial animal nature fits into this pattern.

43 Clark and McDonald (2010), 58, who also note, though in passing, the presence of the mythological figures of Pandora and Persephone in the movie, recall echoes of C. S. Lewis's Mr. Tumnus from *The Chronicles of Narnia* in the figure of the faun.

44 Indeed, Del Toro (2007) asserts that only in America is the film called *Pan's Labyrinth*.

FIGURE 6.2 The Faun.

The name *faunus* seems connected with the Latin root of *favere* "to support"; thus *faunus* is "the kindly one," certainly a euphemism. In his connection with the enigmatic sounds of the woodlands, he is sometimes identified with Fatuus or Fatuclus, "the speaker."[45] As a god of the woodlands, Faunus lived in the mountains and caves of Arcadia, not in Mt. Olympus. It was said that if someone woke Pan up he gave a scream of terror, and from this comes our word "panic" to indicate the sudden terror that one may experience in the loneliness of the woods—just as in the countryside around the Mill.

This creature is celebrated also as a force of nature and country life against the destruction of city life, which aligns with the implied environmental messages of Del Toro's work. Hanley notes "Ofelia's movements between the interiors, ostensibly controlled by the villain/stepfather the Captain *el Capitán* and exterior or natural spaces, is echoed by the movements of Mercedes, the undercover Republican sympathiser."[46] There is much pastoral imagery here, of the kind seen in ancient texts by Theocritus, Vergil, and Longus. Plutarch even tells a story in which Pan is emblematic of the passing of the pagan world. Once, during the reign of Tiberius, Thamus, sailing by the island of Paxi, was commanded by a divine voice, "When you are at Palodes, announce that Pan the Great is dead." Thamus did so, and from that island came a terrible howling.[47] In this myth, Pan represents a god of an old, pagan world that is disappearing,

---

45 *OCD* 4th ed., "*faunus.*"
46 Hanley (2007), 38.
47 Plutarch, *Moralia* 5.17 (*De Defectu Oraculorum*). On Pan as an ambiguous figure, see Perlich (2009), 110, who also sees the faun as the "King of the Underground Realm" in the model of the monomyth.

which is also the case in *Pan's Labyrinth*, since the faun tells Ofelia that she is the only hope to keep the reign of Bezmorra and its inhabitants alive.[48]

The Faun functions as Ofelia's chief magic helper, and, accordingly, he guides all the actions of the protagonist and directs the plot. He is in a way a figure for the filmmaker and the narrator. Pan's image with his horns, pointy ears and hooves, and reputation for sexual activity gave birth to the image of the lustful devil.[49] This tradition of "the Devil as an Enlightening Pan"[50] helps explain his role as Ofelia's guide to the underworld and perhaps a figure alien to us, representing a form of knowledge and experience we fear and even hate, but must confront.

When Ofelia arrives at the Faun's labyrinth, she sees no one. She then begins to say "¡Eco!, ¡Eco! . . . ¿Hola?, ¿Hola?" ("Echo, Echo . . . Hello? Hello?") Interestingly, Greek myth tells that Pan loved the mountain nymph Echo, which gives some strangely erotic nuance to the relationship that Ofelia will have with this creature of the "mountains, the woods and the earth." The Faun is also extremely old (note the clouded eyes and moss all over his body)— though he does gradually become younger-looking and cleaner as the film progresses[51]—as is the pale man later, which contrasts with Ofelia's young age.[52] In fact, Ofelia is wearing only a nightgown in this scene and coyly makes an attempt at covering herself a bit with the woolen cardigan she is wearing. There is an implicit danger for Ofelia, for the Oread Echo was a famous singer and dancer; because she rejected the gods[53] she was killed, her body torn apart and spread over the earth. Her limbs were gathered by Gaia, the Earth Goddess, and only her sweet voice remained,[54] and at the end Ofelia will in fact die, but traces will remain of her in this world, as the echoes of Echo's voice.

---

48 The theme of the death of Pan as an indicator of the destruction of the natural world is also treated in the fourth book of the *Percy Jackson and the Olympians* series, *The Battle of the Labyrinth*, where we see the old god Pan withering away because, as he tells Percy and his friends, the world he represents is disappearing, and thus each of them is now responsible for caring for the forests and woodlands themselves. This, just as in *Pan's Labyrinth*, expresses the concern for the environmental destruction in the new millennium, in particular for millennial youth. An old god is here again revived to embody a serious preoccupation of our times.

49 For this connection see Merivale (1969), 14 ff. and chapter 5 for representations of "Sinister Pan."

50 This notion is seen in later occult practices. Cf. Levi (1896).

51 As Del Toro (2007) in the DVD commentary mentions, at the end of the film his eyes are clear, his teeth straight and no moss covers him. The director also remarks that if Ofelia had obeyed him in the third task simply because he looked good, then this would not have been a good choice deserving immortality. Del Toro (2007).

52 Hubner (2010), 56.

53 In *Daphnis and Chloe* 3.22, it is envious Pan who causes Echo's dismemberment.

54 Also on Pan and Echo, see the *Orphic Hymn 10 to Pan* and the *Homeric Hymn 19 to Pan*.

FORESTS AND MAGICAL WOODLANDS

City versus country provide a constant tension in many literary works, espe-cially pastoral ones, and Captain Vidal, in turn, embodies the foreign element of urban life that comes and irrupts into the peaceful setting of the woodlands and the mountains; he brings the modern cultural time (as we will see, he is ob-sessed with time and clocks[55]) of the city in contrast with the fuzzy/organic time of the realm of Pan, which he intends to replace. The forces of Spain's Fascist government try to destroy the rebels, many of them *campesinos* or "peasants" with a more primitive lifestyle, seen clearly in the two peasants who are hunting rabbits to eat and are senselessly killed by Vidal. Yet the fact that Vidal orders the squalid-looking rabbits to be cooked demonstrates how he depends on the Nature he needs to control.

Our story presents an underlying struggle between nature (the woods, the creatures of the forest) and the violent actions of men who wage war and destroy the woodland's serenity. Yet the woodlands, a prominent feature in Spanish "oppositional films," [56] also offer the promise of resistance and outlaw life, as we see Mercedes and the Maquis withdrawing into it at the movie's end.[57] But the woods also represent Vidal's own fears "of the un-known 'other', of all that is uncivilized and less easily controlled."[58] It is often an ambivalent space in fairy tales, which can work as both "oppressor and liberator."[59] The forest, "inhabited by the Resistance forces," symbolically represents "the organic and archaic."[60] Yet in fantasy genres the woodland is a "space in between, its liminality a pointer to something once seemingly understood as primeval, prior to discourse, providing an insight into an ar-chetypal understanding of human behavior."[61] Ofelia is connected to forces who defend this pastoral and archaic world. She is a healer who will bring light and flowers to the earth with her eventual death. And as she saves her brother from Vidal, she preserves the hope of a future no longer ravished by violence and two irreconcilable factions of the past that even Spaniards today have trouble with.

---

55 Note that clocks are central in *Peter Pan* as well and that Captain Hook, the villain of the story, has an interest in them. In the filmic version with Mary Martin (1960) and in the Universal Pictures 2003 version, Wendy's father and Captain Hook are in each film played by the same actor, drawing the connection to the evil father. We thank Paula James for this suggestion. Pocket watches, rabbits, and rabbit holes are found in *Alice in Wonderland* too.

56 Hubner (2010), 47.

57 Hubner (2010), 48.

58 Hubner (2010), 48.

59 Hubner (2010), 49.

60 See Clark and McDonald (2010), 54. They note, following Yocom (2008), 347, that "the mill's original function as a supplier of fundamental communal needs—the literal bread of life—has been perverted."

61 Hubner (2010), 51.

BLOOD, SLIME, SEXUALITY, AND LIFE

The three challenges that Ofelia must confront, which test whether she is still Princess Moana or has turned into a mere mortal, are described in the "Book of Crossroads" ("El libro de las encrucijadas") that the Faun has given to her.[62] The three tasks are tied to the fertile powers of this incipient goddess/heroine. The book, which recalls books of magic and destiny, details a turning point in Ofelia's life, a moment of passage and change from maidenhood to womanhood, but also from humanity to fertility deity, now seen as part of a grander design.[63] Similar magic books are important for the *Harry Potter* series. In the first test, the Faun instructs the girl to go to a tree that is being destroyed by a huge frog living inside of it who eats all the bugs. A long time ago, the book says, when the world was in harmony, men, animals, and magical creatures lived peacefully together and slept under this tree, which recalls the archetype of the "Tree of Life." If the frog is killed, the tree will "flourish" again. She must feed the creature three magic amber stones and then retrieve a golden key from its insides, a symbolic item that will serve as the key to open her own secrets of femininity and fertility.

This test has much to do with Ofelia's passage to womanhood, since it constitutes an emblematic first encounter with sexuality. First, the shape of the tree, although recalling the form of a faun's horns, also resembles the labyrinthine structure of the female reproductive organs, the uterus with the ovaries and Fallopian tubes. The very entrance to the tree is a crack that resembles a vagina[64] (Fig. 6.3).

---

62 We recall that crossroads are places where magic (especially that associated with witches and Hecate) is practiced. Del Toro emphasizes (Del Toro 2007) that all the movie's characters are at "crossroads" in their lives, and need to make choices. Carmen makes the wrong, but as she saw it, safer choice of not being a true mother to Ofelia and believing in magic, while the doctor makes the braver choice to defy the captain and kill the prisoner. Although these choices cost them their lives, the doctor's is a more meaningful and fulfilling death. Spain itself was at a crossroads at this time, reminds us.

63 Del Toro at first envisioned the character as younger, of eight or nine years of age, but during the casting he was so moved by eleven-year-old Ivana Baquero's performance that he decided to cast her, which forced him to adapt the plot to a central character of a maturing young woman. See Fischer (2006).

64 See Lindsay for this (2012), 3, who also notes the shape of Carmen's headboard and other architectural features. See also Clarke (2015), 43, who remarks that the bed frame "is carved with flowers and leaves, associated both of them with vegetation and fertility." The images of Ofelia's brother in the womb add to this too; Hubner (2010), 57. Del Toro himself acknowledges that he "deliberately designed the idea of the fantasy world to be extremely uterine . . . while everything in the real world is cold and straight." Also *The Guardian* interview with Del Toro: https://www.theguardian.com/film/2006/nov/21/guardianinterviewsatbfisouthbank. Accessed May 31, 2016. Del Toro (2007) also pays great attention to the color palettes of the film, with the real world painted in cold blue and green tones and the fantasy world in warmer red tones, though as the two worlds begin to intertwine this palette blends as well. On uterine images in the film, see also Clark and McDonald (2010), 60, who connect all the birthing imagery with the birth of the new nation of Spain. For Ofelia being reborn as she exits through the vagina-like crack in the tree, see also Perlich (2009), 113.

FIGURE 6.3 Ofelia approaches the tree with the evil toad inside.

Ofelia thus enters the world of her own sexuality during this test. Earlier, her mother gave her a beautiful new dress and shoes for the dinner party the captain was to host that night. The dress, however, reminiscent of the one Alice wears in Disney's version of *Alice in Wonderland*,[65] is rather puffy and childish, making her look like a doll. Yet when Ofelia approaches the tree and realizes that she will "get dirty" in this adventure, she removes this girlish attire and hangs it on a branch. She is now covered by only a light undergarment, which allows us to picture her developing womanly shape. Vivancos believes that the dress she wears points at "sanctioned femininity" and refers to her "desexualized underwear."[66] Accordingly, this undressing suggests Ofelia is removing, in preparation for her trial, an emblem of a false identity

Thus there are undertones of growing up, a scene not entirely asexual as the context insinuates. Having removed her "false" clothes, she will symbolically enter the world of her own femininity. The insides of the tree are muddy and dirty, recalling the world of fluids that the transition to womanhood implies; we do not see this getting dirty as childish, as others do, but rather as a reference to sexuality and its bodily fluids. She crawls in the mud toward the creature as the frog, with his long tongue, licks her cheeks—a scene with strangely erotic resonances.[67] Furthermore, the frog, "sapo" in Spanish, is

---

65 Kotecki (2010), 245. On the "Victorian-looking" dress, see Clark and McDonald (2010), 60.

66 Vivancos (2012), 886. Del Toro (2006) sees the dress as a quote to *Alice in Wonderland*, but it also exemplifies Ofelia's mother's focus on the mundane.

67 The encounter with mud hints at another kind of swamp, seen in a 1986 film called *Labyrinth*, with which our movie has many intertextual connections. In that film, a fifteen-year-old girl played by Jennifer Connolly embarks on a journey to save her toddler brother, who has been abducted by a Goblin King, played by David Bowie, who lives in a labyrinthlike palace. On her journey she has to go through "a stinky land of slimy mud called the Bog of Eternal Stench," which also symbolizes the contact with feminine fluids and sexuality, as at the end of the movie Sarah, the protagonist, decides to "grow up" and put away her childhood fantasy books. See IMDb summary of the film on http://www.imdb.com/title/tt0091369/synopsis. Accessed June 26, 2013.

a masculine word, and he of course brings to mind the common fairy-tale figure of the "Frog Prince," thus accentuating the scene's subtly amorous connotations.[68]

Ofelia defeats the frog, who literally "bursts through his mouth," and thus she gives new life to the dying tree. She retrieves the golden key. The following night, when a fairy visits, Ofelia tells her "I've got the key. Take me to the labyrinth." The key exists metaphorically to unlock her own sexuality and the desire to explore her own female nature, which includes life-giving power. Interestingly, when she next visits the Faun that night, he caresses her face with his hands, a scene that provokes both concern and an odd sense of erotic excitement. Perhaps these quasi-erotic encounters mirror the child's dream and fear of what will happen to all sexually active women, and what is happening to her mother, who after a recent marriage has clearly been sexually active and became pregnant, although we see no evidence of eroticism at the Mill.[69]

Ofelia manages to make the tree flourish again, her first act of life creation as fertility goddess. In a way she gives birth (or rebirth here) in the film, paralleling the birthing process her own mother is undergoing.[70] At the film's conclusion, once Ofelia has reached the underworld, a blooming flower is shown on earth as the sign of Princess Moana's abiding influence over the world: "y que dejó detrás de sí pequeñas huellas de su paso por el mundo, visibles sólo para aquél que sepa dónde mirar" ("and that she left behind small traces of her passage through the world, visible only to those who know where to look").

Next comes a horrific scene when Ofelia, alone in the bathroom, reads in the "Book of Crossroads" a prediction that her mother will soon start to bleed.[71] This event distracts her from beginning her next task. That night the Faun comes in person to her, showing a progression in the intimacy of both characters. In the first encounter they only talked; in the second he caresses her cheeks, and in the third he appears in her own bedroom. This male fertility deity will encourage Ofelia to discover her powers over fertility and healing. The Faun provides a mandrake root ("a plant that dreamt of being human"),

---

68 Lindsay (2012), 14: "The frog represents Ofelia's stepfather, feasting in luxury while the country scrapes by on ration coupons. The task is also representative of Ofelia's childlike desire to re-enter the womb of her mother." She emerges as in a sort of birth, covered in muck. Clarke (2015), 43, goes so far as calling the scene a "symbolic rape" by the frog.

69 Orme (2010), 228–29. This does not conform to the traditional male-desire expectations of fairy-tale narratives. Del Toro (2007) stresses how the movie is about choice and disobedience.

70 Del Toro states that "the film is about a girl giving birth to herself." See Spector (2009), 84, and Del Toro (2007).

71 In the bathroom, the attic and elsewhere, as Del Toro (2007) comments, we see circular windows for example, again connecting with the feminine and uterine world of fantasy.

which is thought to be a cure for barrenness in some cultures.[72] He tells her
that the root should be fed with blood and milk to help heal her mother. Ofelia
here is the nurturer of her own mother, and, generally, the more innocent child
who is forced to try to remedy and suffers for the world the adults produced.
Harry Potter, Katniss Everdeen, Percy Jackson, Perseus, and Theseus all, to one
extent or another, work to repair or redeem the horror world their parents have
created—another millennial theme.

Pan also mentions that "the full moon is approaching." This reference is
a time marker and indicates (an important mythological theme) that Ofelia's
actions are part of a fated and cosmically managed destiny. But of course, the
moon is a particularly feminine time marker, in contrast to Vidal's father's
watch, a patriarchal sign.[73] And matters of female reproduction are closely tied
to the moon. Such time imagery will be important in other movies we discuss.[74]

DEMETER-PERSEPHONE

The narrative of *Pan's Labyrinth* strongly engages the mother-daughter archetypes
seen in the fertility myths of Demeter-Persephone, best known from the *Homeric
Hymn to Demeter* and Ovid's *Metamorphoses* 5. There are some striking correspon-
dences between the myth and our film. In the myth, one day Persephone, who is
clearly on the cusp of womanhood, was picking flowers when her uncle Hades
took her away to live with him in the Deadlands, having gained permission from
her father Zeus. Her distraught mother, Demeter, goddess of agriculture and the
fertility of the earth, withdrew from Olympus, stopping the growth of vegetation. Zeus is forced to tell Hades to send her back. But because Persephone had
been tempted (or perhaps forced) and eaten seven pomegranate seeds, symbols
of sexual maturity, the Deadlands were now a part of her, and she was required
to return to them. Yet she would be able to spend a portion of the year with her
mother above ground, and this is when spring comes, when the flowers grow,
or, according to other versions, perhaps the fall when the crops are harvested, as
Demeter then smiles, rejoicing at her daughter's company. Demeter also teaches
the Eleusinians the Mysteries, and her daughter, Kore, who functions as a bridge
between the worlds of life and death, will be able to assist human beings.

As Foley notes, "the structure of the [Homeric] *Hymn* suggests strongly
that the rites originate above all from the divine relation between mother and

72 On the mandrake and fertility, see Josephus, *Bellum Judaicum* 7.6.3; the Bible, *Genesis* 30.14–17;
and John Donne, *Song 2* (*Goe and catche a falling starre/ Get with child a mandrake roote*, lines
1–2). J. K. Rowlings reintroduces the curative powers of the mandrake in *Harry Potter and the
Chamber of Secrets*. See also Harrison (1956) and Van den Berg and Dircksen (2008) for the
mandrake in antiquity.
73 Lindsay (2012), 11; and Vivancos (2012), 891.
74 In *Clash of the Titans*, Andromeda is to be sacrificed before a solar eclipse; in *Percy Jackson*, the
thunderbolt must be recovered by the Summer Solstice; and in *O Brother* the robbers' (supposed) haul must be recovered in a few days before the valley is flooded.

daughter,"[75] a focus that, compared with similar and older Near Eastern myths, such as that of Telephus, is unique.[76] Adrienne Rich and other scholars consider the power of the mother-daughter bond and the importance of the myths like that of Demeter and Kore for Classical literature.[77] Figurines of the mother-daughter dyad appear in the Neolithic period,[78] and the mother-daughter-child triad is represented in Bronze Age art; although they are in theory distinct individuals, they form an entangled unity. Thus Carl Jung recognizes a duality in the archetypal mother-daughter pair, and that the roles they play are somewhat fluid[79]: "The figure corresponding to the Kore in a woman is generally a double one, appearing now as a mother and now as a maiden."[80]

In respect to Kore the "primordial maiden," which we suggest Ofelia embodies, Kerényi notes that the image of "daughter with mother appears as life," while the relationship "young virgin with husband" appears as death.[81] Neumann's analysis suggests that, in this pattern, the entrance of the male is always disruptive, breaking the bond of mother and daughter, although the male is needed for the daughter to exist, and thus the entrance of the male can be equated with death.[82] Thus the Kore myth presents "an allegory of women's fate: the borders of Hades an allegory of the borderline between maidenhood and the 'other' life."[83] Indeed, Persephone was worshipped as the Queen of the Dead, and the rape of the bride was an allegory of death."[84] Persephone "is a creature standing unsubdued on a pinnacle of life and there meeting her fate—a fate that means death in fulfillment and dominion in death."[85] Del Toro's presentation of the Kore/Demeter archetype through Ofelia's interactions with her mother shows the needed fluidity. In the Classical versions Persephone is taken away from her mother by Death Himself; it is Ofelia's mother Carmen who is "taken" by death, both literally and figuratively.

---

75 Foley (1994), 118.

76 Burkert (1982), 138, calling the Demeter-Kore, mother-daughter myth a "crystallization of Greek Mythology."

77 Foley (1994), 82.

78 Burkert (1985), 140 and n. 12.

79 See also Jung and Kerényi (1993), 162; and Foley (1994), 119ff., with references.

80 Jung and Kerényi (1993), 158. Kerényi even suggests a certain identification of Demeter and her daughter, wondering if she was "really different from her mother," thus representing in a single figure "the motifs that recur in *all* mothers and daughters," and "the feminine attributes of the earth with the inconstancy of the wandering moon." Kerényi (1991), 32. On this see also Clarke (2015), 45.

81 Kerényi (1959), 107.

82 Foley (1994), 120, citing Neumann (1956), 63.

83 Kerényi and Jung (1993), 108.

84 Kerényi and Jung (1993), 108–9. Similarly, Robert May suggests that the Demeter-Persephone myth "with its pain and suffering, creative endurance and ecstatic return to fullness and growth—is the archetypal female fantasy." Foley (1994), 120, quoting May (1980), 8–13.

85 Kerényi (1993), 109.

In her renewal of the tree Ofelia recalls the fertility goddess Persephone, whose association with flowers is apparent in the *Homeric Hymn* and in Ovid. She was gathering roses, crocuses, violets, hyacinths, irises, and narcissi with the Oceanids when Hades came (*Homeric Hymn to Demeter [HHD]* 6–7).[86] In Ovid she gathers violets and white lilies (*Met.*5.392).[87] In the *Homeric Hymn* the flowers grow (*HHD* 11) to entice the girl, who tries to pick them and is swallowed down as the earth splits apart. Our Ofelia makes the tree flourish again, and flower imagery is pervasive in the film, both in the rose of immortality story and in the traces she leaves on earth after her descent.

THE CHILD-KILLING KING OF DEATH

Ofelia's second challenge is more complicated. With a piece of chalk, she must open a door in her bedroom and go to the abode of a strange white figure, who is sitting at a table loaded with deliciously tempting food, surrounded by images of himself killing children on the walls. As Frye indicates, "at the bottom of the night world we find the cannibal feast, the serving up of a child or lover as food . . . such a theme merges with the theme of human sacrifice in its most undisplaced form, which is the swallowing of a youth or maiden by a subterranean or submarine monster."[88] This Pale Monster thus fits well with the elements of myths of descent. The themes of food and child sacrifice are very evident in *The Hunger Games*. The Faun warns Ofelia not to try the food under any circumstances. "Your life depends on it," he says. This is a typical prohibition to those traveling to the underworld; as Persephone learned, if you eat of the underworld, you risk being claimed by it. Although one of the fairies points at the middle lock, Ofelia acts independently and figures that she must open the lock on the right with the key retrieved from the frog's stomach. She obtains a dagger, but strangely, and for no apparent reason, she gives into temptation and tries two grapes. In the *Homeric Hymn to Demeter* it is said about Hades "Nevertheless he himself with trickery gave [her] to eat the honey sweet seed of the pomegranate" (*HHD* 371–72), but Persephone tells Demeter that Hades forced her to eat the seed. Ovid writes that she actually ate seven seeds of the fruit by her own will, and was not tricked by Pluto (*Met.* 533–38).[89] Ofelia mimics the ambivalent actions of Persephone, which perhaps indicates a dangerous curiosity, as with Eve eating the forbidden fruit in the Garden of Eden. She was right in thinking for herself and acting against the fairy's directions before, but in disobeying the Faun she makes a tragic

---

86 Homer calls Persephone the one "with face like a budding flower" (*HHD* 9).
87 In Ovid the loss of virginity is clearly symbolized by the flowers falling out of Persephone's tunic (*Met.*5.399).
88 Frye (1976), 118. On the connection between the Hymn and immersion child sacrifices practiced in Sicily, see Burkert (1982), 139 and n. 8.
89 Hubner (2010), 56. Kimura (2012), 84, recalls Snow White's apple here (citing Bruno Bettelheim), by means of which the child in her dies.

mistake. The grapes that Ofelia consumes were placed on a tray next to what appear to be pomegranates, which has definite underworld associations.[90]

The "monster" doubles for Captain Vidal (the master of death) and Franco himself, since all three deadly male figures restrict the consumption of food, and tempt with their possession of it. It is interesting, as Del Toro himself notes in the DVD commentary, that this scene mirrors very closely the previous dinner party. Both Vidal and the Pale Man are sitting at the head of a large rectangular table loaded with food, with a fireplace in the background.[91] With the girl's transgression the monster is awakened, puts a pair of eyes in his hands that allow him to see (just as in the myth of the Graeae, also antagonistic creatures in the Quest myth of Perseus) and begins to chase her (Fig. 6.4). She barely escapes, but her irresponsibility costs the life of two of her fairy friends. On the one hand, it is clear that her temptation to eat recalls the temptation of Persephone to eat while in the underworld, a temptation that symbolizes the loss of maidenhood and her first encounter with sexuality. In an inversion of the story of Persephone, who after eating cannot remain in the upper world forever, Ofelia will not be able to return to the underworld. On a more human level, this episode illustrates the struggle between the girl and the woman, the reckless child versus the mature woman concerned for the well-being of others. And here, as in many stories of descent, the hero's return must be paid for by the death of others, often innocent.

This Pale Monster presents an image of death and old age that literally kills children, and will symbolically kill Ofelia's own childhood.[92] The figure looks like a grotesque and very old person, thin and almost emaciated, with folds of pale skin hanging from his arms and legs. He is also completely bald and lacks teeth, and his vision is limited (Fig. 6.4).

FIGURE 6.4 The Pale monster having regained his eyes.

---

90   For more on the pomegranate in the Persephone myth, see Kerényi (1991), 134.

91   Del Toro (2007).

92   Interestingly, the Pale Man and the Faun are played by the same actor, stressing the connection between them. Note that as Del Toro (2007) comments, he does hot really eat the fairies, who appear alive later.

He thus represents how old age ends up taking away youth and childhood, a very appropriate enemy for this developing girl. (Note also patent allusions to Nazism's destruction of children in the piles of shoes evoking images of concentration camps.[93] Ofelia indeed has been compared to a young Anne Frank.[94]) He also recalls a shriveled-up baby akin to the mandrake root,[95] which reminds us a bit as well of Voldemort's shrunken soul-part in the fourth and final *Harry Potter* movies and of the adult Voldemort himself.[96] Like the Greek god Kronos, he destroys children, and Ofelia is literally "on the clock" in this adventure. Let us here recall the phonetic similarity of the god's name with the Greek word for "time," a link that Greek intellectuals had remarked on.[97] In Spanish both words are spelled the same (*crono*, the god, and *crono-* as in *cronología*, for example).[98] Here, one cannot help but think about Goya's representation of the Roman equivalent of Kronos eating his offspring (*Saturn Devouring His Children*).[99] Perhaps, just as in the myth, this is an allegory implying that, in the end, time consumes all its children; we are all subject to the destruction of time.[100] And remember, Kronos is the father of Hades, as the *Homeric Hymn* reminds us, and that he is also referred to as a swallower of people ("The broad wayed Earth gaped throughout Nysa's plain, and with immortal horses the Lord who holds many, of many names, child of Kronos rushed upon her" (*HHD* 16–18). And further: "He at the suggestion of Zeus led her away unwilling, her father's brother, He who rules many, who holds many, the many-named son of Kronos" (*HHD* 30–32).[101]

Captain Vidal himself is obsessed by time, and repeatedly makes comments about people's punctuality. He carries around the watch that his father,

93 See Lindsay (2012), 17–18.

94 The year in which the movie takes place, 1944, is "the year that the Nazis captured Anne and her family." See Clark and McDonald (2010), 57 and 59: "This identity formation strengthens the link to Anne Frank, whose diary represented an alternative existence over which she had some control . . . the film offers a meta-textual dimension which attests to the transformative potency of fiction itself. In this way, the whole film can be seen as a celebration of storytelling as liberatory." See Orme (2010) as well for *Pan's Labyrinth* and storytelling as disobedient desire. Echoes of Holocaust films such as *Schindler's List* (1993) and Roberto Benigni's *Life Is Beautiful* (1997), as well as Del Toro's own recognition of the links with the "war on terror," are patent. See Kotecki (2010), 245.

95 Lindsay (2012), 17.

96 Del Toro tells us that for him the Pale Monster represents the church as well, and "represents fascism and the Church eating the children when they have a perversely abundant banquet in front on them." See Guillén, (2006).

97 Plutarch (*On Isis and Osiris*, 32) claims that some Greeks believed that Kronos was an allegorical name for Chronos (= time).

98 Del Toro even produced an earlier film—its theme is unrelated to this one—called *Cronus*.

99 Del Toro himself admits that he was greatly influenced by the works of Francisco Goya for this film. See Kermode (2006). See also Spector (2009), passim, and Gómez-Castellano (2013), 8.

100 See Lindsay (2012), 18.

101 Ovid calls Pluto Saturnius, "the son of Saturn" (*Met.*5.420).

a notable commander in the war in Morocco, threw to the ground and smashed at the moment of his death so that his son could know the time of his honorable death, an act that Vidal tries to mimic at the moment of his own death.[102] Vidal's office, where he is seen fussing with his watch, is in a former grain mill. Behind him are the mill's gears, symbolic of the deadly machine of Fascism and the workings of his mind. Vidal is also constantly obsessed with his son, emblematic of his attempt to control and create a future. Yet for all the love he supposedly has for his son, we never even learn the boy's name.[103]

Captain Vidal is presented as a devil incarnate, a king of death.[104] Sheriff Cooley in *O Brother* is another human devil, as is Hyperion in *Immortals*. He embodies, of course, what Franco himself was for many Spanish people. He is utterly inhuman, with few redeeming qualities, and evokes the ogres of fairy tales who personify evil, almost "a comic book figure of evil destined to provoke terror."[105] But he is also the male counterpart of the evil stepmother from fairy tales, as in *Cinderella* and *Snow White*, something perhaps a bit more "sanitized" and tolerable.[106] Again, time and death and the conquest of death figure prominently. The captain is responsible for many deaths, including Ofelia's and indirectly his own wife's, by forcing her to make a hard journey in such an advanced state of pregnancy. He even tells the attending doctor that if he needs to make a choice, he should choose the life of the child over that of the mother.[107]

Like King Hyperion, he seems to relish death and killing. The profuse images of blood and torture that some viewers have found disturbing add to his presentation as a devil, a king of death, Hades perhaps, who takes the lives of humans. He tells one of the prisoners whom he is about to torture, "Por encima de mí no hay nadie" ("Above me, there is nobody"), thus presenting himself almost as an all-powerful god. At a dinner party he hosts, one of the guests says, "Sabemos que no está aquí por gusto" ("We know that you are not here for pleasure, captain"), to which the captain responds "En eso se equivoca" ("In that you are wrong") and explains how he is there because he wants a new and clean Spain for his unborn son. This is an important clue. Vidal adds, "Pero hay una gran diferencia: que la guerra terminó, y ganamos nosotros, y si para que nos enteremos todos, hay que matar a esos hijos de puta, pues los matamos, y ya

---

102 Gómez-Castellano (2013), 13, comments about Vidal's father's watch: "a telling image that communicates the Fascist obsession with stopping history and smashing it like the *golpistas* did in 1936."

103 Spector (2009).

104 Paradoxically, his name has to do with the Spanish word for life, *vida*. He impregnates Carmen and creates life, yet he also has the power to destroy life. See Diestro-Dópido (2015), 40–41.

105 Hubner (2010), 52.

106 Hubner (2010), 54.

107 As Vivancos (2012), 883, mentions, the role of women in the film seems to be reduced to being reproductive bodies. And Carmen is "progressively deprived of any agency and autonomy"; even "her gradual disappearance culminates in her death in childbirth." See also Hanley (2007), 37.

está. ¡Todos estamos aquí por gusto!" ("But there is a big difference: that the war is over, and we won and if to make this known we need to kill those sons of bitches, then we kill them all and that's that. We are all here for pleasure!") and makes a toast. The demonic Vidal wishes to gain control over time and death by creating a new world that will live after him, as did some future-oriented Fascists like Hitler and the brutal Hyperion of *Immortals*. This desire to remake the world, at whatever cost in human life, is a trademark of totalitarian regimes of the twentieth century and very much part of Franco's plan to reshape Spain. Against him, a blossoming fertility goddess must rise. A feminine force of life and fertility will be its hopeful antidote, if only in the movie.

The captain designs a system to ration the peasants' food and medicines, so that they will not send any to the rebels, recalling a theme of *The Hunger Games* (and perhaps mirroring a greater millennial concern with food scarcity and excess, which we engage more fully in our chapter on *The Hunger Games*). Interestingly, the whole discussion about this rationing of food takes place at the dinner party where the privileged ones in power are present (a priest, the mayor, Captain Vidal, and Dr. Ferreiro). He is here directly responsible for the people's shortage of food, while in the myth Hades indirectly causes Demeter to grieve, and, in revolt, stop producing the products of the earth. In a sense, then—and again like the god Kronus—he wants to control fertility, the realm of Demeter, while Kronus wishes to restrain the products of his wife Rhea's womb by consuming them. But control over food is also a metonymy for control over desire, which in a patriarchal world is control over reproduction, sexuality, and women.

Food and eating are indeed important themes for the chthonic myths of Demeter.[108] There are several scenes in the mill's kitchen where the servants are preparing food, and a kitchen knife, a very feminine object, is the weapon with which Mercedes will defend herself and attack the Captain later on. The kitchen and caves in the hills are also feminine spaces of resistance.[109] Although the peasants' provisions are rationed and the two peasants who were hunting rabbits to eat are ruthlessly killed, the captain is always served well; he gives a lavish dinner party and Mercedes is constantly bringing him a tray with something. When Ofelia returns from her adventure with the frog, she is punished by being sent to bed without dinner. In this control over food, there is a remarkable contrast; in the *Homeric Hymn* Demeter restrains the ability of the land to produce food as a way of reasserting female rights over marriage and family, causing even Zeus, who tried to violate Demeter's rights, to relent and give her the honors she seeks. Here Vidal represents the tyrannical male power

---

108 At Eleusis Demeter refuses to eat, but consumes the *kykeon* beverage which, "Deo, the great Lady, took for the sake of sacred rite" (HHD 212). Persephone may or may not be *forced* to eat the pomegranate seeds. Finally, it is Demeter's refusal to let the crops grow that brings humankind to near starvation and causes Zeus to relent.
109 Gómez-Castellano (2013), 9.

that has usurped the capacity to control the products of fertility (not only food, but even a child) as a way of extending and maintaining power.

BLOOD, SACRIFICE, BIRTH, AND REBIRTH

On the fourth night, the faun appears anew in Ofelia's bedroom and asks what happened. He also mentions that "la luna estará llena en tres días" ("the moon will be full in three days"). When Ofelia tells him that there has been an "accident" and only one fairy has returned from the adventure with the child killer, the Faun, enraged, states that she has now lost the right to the throne and will have to stay on earth as a mere mortal. We suspect that the deaths of the fairies caused by her irresponsibility will have to be repaid with more death in the upper world. Accordingly, the following day brings a prisoner's execution, Dr. Ferreiro's murder by the captain, and Carmen's death in childbirth. After her mother's burial we see Ofelia packing, though it is unclear where she could possibly go; she is symbolically preparing for the coming journey of death and rebirth.

Ofelia's most important transformation, from innocent child to fertility deity and savior, soon occurs. After her mother's funeral the Faun returns to her room; he has decided to give her a second chance. Or perhaps her mother was a co-conspirator in Ofelia's testing, tempting her to "face reality" and stop reading those fairy tales that in fact point to the magic world Ofelia belongs to. Perhaps the Faun now can change his mind because the death of the fairies has been compensated by the death of Ofelia's mother, and one might even imagine that the newly arrived queen of the underworld, Carmen, can now plead for her daughter in her father's kingdom.[110] The Faun commands her to get her baby brother and come to his labyrinth. After she accomplished her first test successfully, the Faun showed her a stone with an image of a mother figure and a baby.[111] After Ofelia inquired, he answered while pointing at the mother figure, "y la niña sois vos" ("and the girl is you"). To Ofelia's follow-up question "¿Y el bebé?" ("And the baby?") the Faun gives no reply. Her fate of becoming a mother figure,[112] a life giver, a sort of goddess of fertility, mythologically speaking, it appears, is already written in stone, as her story was also written in the *Book of Crossroads.*

---

110 "Princess Moana's return to the Underground Realm of her father can be troubling to a feminist reading that commends the resistance to patriarchal dominance through the film . . . but he and the queen/Carmen are sitting upon tall, elegant and, dominating thrones that are hard not to see as phallic—in fact they look like giant erect penises—no nuance at all. . . ." But the fact that Ofelia does not quite "choose one world over the other" might be read as being resistant of patriarchy; Orme (2010), 231.

111 Del Toro remarks (2007) that this is a Celtic looking monolith, reminding us of the strong Celtic influences in the north of Spain, where the story is set. We recall how fantasy and fairy tale are indeed prevalent in Celtic culture.

112 See Spector (2009), 84.

As we noted, Ofelia's first two confrontations are symbolic (and progressively more violent) battles against Vidal. Now Ofelia must confront Vidal directly, and take from him what he values most, his son. Ofelia manages to slip a sleep-inducing drug previously given to her mother into the captain's drink, which slows Vidal down enough so she can take the baby away, becoming a symbolic mother herself. This transition was anticipated earlier when she put the mandrake root under her ailing and bleeding mother's bed and fed it daily with blood and milk, which helped her mother's condition improve.[113] She would prick her own finger for the blood to drip, and dip the root into milk. Thus she becomes a surrogate mother to the root, mirroring Carmen, who feeds her child with her own blood in pregnancy and presumably will feed him milk after the birth.[114] This too is a prefiguration of the blood she will give for her little brother.

When Ofelia runs with the baby to the Faun's labyrinth, the captain chases her. The Faun has told her that her last test is to sacrifice innocent blood, and asks for her brother. The Faun has been basically a helpful figure for Ofelia thus far, so how can we interpret this demand? "El portal sólo se abrirá si derramamos en él sangre inocente" ("The portal will open only if we shed innocent blood in it"), he says, a phrase that accentuates the symbolic connotations of deflowering and birth to come. First, one can say the "portal" to a woman's body must be opened with the blood of the virgin, and then in childbirth the passage is newly opened with blood. More simply, we can think of the common archetype of the virgin sacrifice, which sometimes is also a self-sacrifice. But note that Ofelia, like Abraham, is being asked, by a commanding Father figure, to make a child sacrifice. Here for the first time, Ofelia acts as a true mother and thinks of the baby before herself. She refuses to give up her brother, even knowing that this means she will not return to the underworld, and possibly will even face death. Persephone is turning into her Demeter side.

Unlike Abraham in the Bible, she rejects the commands of the Father-God. She has now grown from a child absorbed by fairy tales to a motherly figure who can love and care for this new life. Though she must hand over her brother at the end, she knows she is giving up her life for him. Again, a feminist reader may question if there is another image of "essential motherhood" presented here, where the role of a female heroine is defined by her sacrifice for the child, rather than on other heroic qualities. It is significant that Vidal shoots Ofelia somewhere in the lower abdomen, possibly in her womb, which Lindsay sees as an image of bloodletting, as the symbolic death of girlhood in the advent of adolescence.[115] The blood dripping from this place then flows into the circular

---

113 Clarke (2015), 47, makes the point that both Ofelia and Demeter are nurses who are "interrupted" in their task of caring for and saving a child.

114 On this, see Lindsay (2012), 16.

115 Lindsay (2012), 21.

entrance to the underground realm of the Faun, where the full moon is reflected, a scene that clearly evokes birthing imagery, as well as providing an indicator of time. Ofelia indeed bleeds and dies from a place close to where her mother bled and finally died. Yet this birthing imagery does not give birth to Ofelia's child, but rather to Ofelia's true identity, as she is reborn as princess Moana, a true fertility figure who can by her death make the earth bloom and also subsequently reign peacefully in the underworld kingdom of Bezmorra.[116]

Another figure aids the heroine and also undergoes a maturing transformation. Throughout the film, Mercedes the housekeeper is compassionate and understanding toward Ofelia, and is even sympathetic to her belief in fairy tales. As perhaps a third fertility figure, she is constantly handling food. She can play the helper role Hecate plays in the *Homeric Hymn*, someone who is sometimes thought to be more dangerous than Demeter or Kore. Nonetheless, she secretly aids the Maquis by bringing them provisions (like cheese and chorizo) and other supplies. Although she sadly admits to her brother that she is a coward, spending her days serving a monster, she gradually becomes a resisting woman in her own right. When Vidal discovers her treason and is about to torture her, she is the first person we see defending herself against Vidal, whose cheek she slices open. She is soon transformed into the movie's final mother figure. While Ofelia bleeds on the ground and Carmen appears, possibly holding an infant in the underworld, Mercedes holds the baby boy in the upper world and will thus become an independent woman and a mother herself.[117] Thus Mercedes, a former servant of a kind of Dark Lord, inspired by Ofelia, rebels and brings about his death and even supplants him, for it is she, not he, who keeps the child and will presumably give him her name; as part of her revenge, she makes Vidal know his child will never know his name.[118]

A secondary plot in the *Homeric Hymn* involves how the disguised Demeter becomes nurse to the late-born Demophoon, and tries to make him immortal. The interference of his mother, Metanira, prevents Demeter from achieving her goal; yet clearly Demophoon, having had a goddess for a foster mother, will become a great leader of Eleusis. Thus the *Homeric Hymn to Demeter* serves as a charter myth for the royal family of Eleusis, and points toward the future. We suggested Mercedes and her baby, who have been improved through contact with the divine, represent the possibility of a superior tomorrow. And yet Mercedes's declaration to Vidal that the baby will never know his name has

---

116 Note how, as Del Toro (2007) mentions the archway that acts as entrance to the labyrinth has a Latin text inscribed, which is hard to read in the movie: "In consiliis nostris, fatum nostrum est." "In our decisions lies our destiny."

117 See discussion of mothers in the film in Perlich (2009), 125.

118 Diestro-Dópido (2015), 53, notes that Vidal's desire for immortality "is every bit as strong as Ofelia's," given his wish that "memory will live on in the son who will bear his name."

complicated aspects.[119] Some critics posit, because Vidal will not be able to perpetuate the memory of male-dominated violence in his son, that a better future can unfold.[120] But in contrast, wouldn't Mercedes be repeating the cycle of erasing someone's memory, just as the Spanish people were compelled to do with the "pact of forgetfulness," or as the children of the disappeared in Argentina, for example, who were literally robbed of their memory and name when adopted by new families friendly to the dictatorship?[121]

But as noted, the Spanish Civil War is distant enough in time to be mythologized, yet still within the living memory of a few. Such a purposely forgotten and mythologized space is a perfect area for mythic projection, as is the "Old South" in *O Brother*. Ofelia's self-sacrifice, the victory over the Captain by the Maquis, and the survival of the child point to a future that might have been. Spain, having suffered decades of political unrest and oppression, needs to reimagine its future. Notice that Moana, even though she now rules in the underworld (as does the sacrificed Persephone), sends up indicators of her presence for those with eyes to see. And these indicators point to the possibility that what once was might exist again. For the risen Persephone is not just an allegory of the return of grain, but an allegory of spiritual rebirth, which can have a political vector.

Del Toro's narrative takes place in May and June 1944, evil times when Franco was cleaning up the last pockets of resistance, killing tens of thousands. But nevertheless it is springtime too; thus flower imagery has a relevant place. The circular opening or "portal" to the underground realm recalls the circular Well of Eleusis, where the goddess sat (*HHD* 98–99). This was known as the Virgin's Well "because it was connected with the destiny of a virgin, and Anthion, 'well of flowers,' presumably because a flowering from the depths was thought to take place here."[122] Indeed, the Eleusinians identified at least three entrances to the Underworld, one of them through the well of Eleusis.[123]

UNDER THE MOON

Thus the virgin's blood is spilled, a maiden's sacrifice to Mother Earth, blood that recalls menstruation, deflowering and loss of maidenhood, just as in Persephone's case, a sacrifice that in turn renews the world. Carl Jung, explaining the various manifestations of the Kore archetype, mentions that sometimes we witness "a true nekyia, a descent into Hades and a quest of the 'treasure hard

---

119 Del Toro (2007), as referred to in Clarke (2015), 48, hints that the knowledge that he will not be remembered by his son is what actually kills him, more than the gun shot.

120 Gómez-Castellano (2013), 13–14.

121 We thank Roberto Salzman for this suggestion.

122 Kerényi (1991), 36. "Vase paintings originating in the South Italian cult of Persephone show that a flowering was expected from the depths. They represent the event in the form of sprouting flowers, plants, or ears of grain" (Kerényi, 1991, 37).

123 Kerényi (1991), 39.

to attain', occasionally connected with orgiastic sexual rites or offerings of menstrual blood to the moon."[124] The moon plays a particularly important role. In Ofelia's first night at the mill, when she encounters the Faun, there is a sickle-shaped moon, which we must understand as a waxing moon since the Faun tells her that to successfully return to her father's realm she must complete the three tasks before the next full moon. Thus, the events of the film seem to take place within the span of about two weeks.

The moon does not appear again until the very end of the film, a thematic circularity. In the last scene, of Ofelia's ultimate sacrifice, the full moon is crossing the sky. Various cultural traditions relate the menstrual cycle to the moon. First, the very word *menstruation* or *menses* derives from the Latin *mensis*, "month." It is believed that menstruation occurs with the new moon and ovulation with the full moon, followed by a period of waning moon. Thus the cycle of the female body is the period between two new moons, which spans the twenty-eight days that it takes the moon to orbit around the Earth.[125] This period comprises a cyclical repetition of birth, maturation, death, and rebirth.[126] Accordingly, in Del Toro's presentation we witness the first half of the moon's and the menstrual cycles: from actual menses (new moon) to the full moon (ovulation). The full moon thus signifies the most fertile moment of the month, and it is on this specific night that Ofelia shows herself as a mother. The moon's fullness also symbolizes the girl's womanly maturity and even hints at the roundness of pregnancy.

Again, Jung makes evocative connections between the archetypal mother and the moon: "The Earth Mother is always chthonic and is occasionally related to the moon, either through the blood-sacrifice already mentioned, or through a child-sacrifice, or else because she is adorned with a sickle moon."[127] All of these aspects are observed in the film. Through a blood sacrifice Ofelia will soon return to the entrails of Mother Earth, where her own mother, Carmen, is now. Further, the Faun tells Ofelia that she was engendered by the moon and that she can find a moon mark on her shoulder. Indeed, later in the film, when Ofelia is about to take a bath—a moment of particular female intimacy—she looks in the mirror and finds a sickle-shaped birthmark on her shoulder. The moon is central in witchcraft, and the moon goddess in Classical myth is part of a female triad: Artemis on earth, Hecate in the underworld as goddess of magic in particular, and Selene as the moon in the sky. A similar split can perhaps be seen in the figures of Carmen, Ofelia, Mercedes, and the moon. While Mercedes stays in the woodlands, just as Artemis did, Ofelia and Carmen go to the underworld, while the moon still shines above. In our discussion of

---

124 Jung (1993), 158.

125 Apparently, in women living in urban settings, for example, artificial light affects the connections between the moon and menstrual cycles. See Lacey (1977).

126 See Kimura (2012), 85–86.

127 Jung (1993), 159.

The Hunger Games, we detail aspects of Katniss Everdeen that connect her to mothering (she mothers her little sister and then Rue), to Artemis (as huntress and goddess associated with woods), and even to a death-dealing goddess, especially in the Games.

The film's conclusion reprises the very first image—again, a ring narrative structure that points at the cyclical nature of women's lives—by showing Ofelia lying on the ground and dripping blood onto the circular opening (in the *Homeric Hymn to Demeter* it is said that the earth "gapes" to allow Hades to snatch the girl away; *HHD* 16). This visually arresting closure evokes the circle of life and death, of birth from the earth and return to the earth, as Persephone makes her trip upward and downward every year in the cycle of the seasons.

PAN'S LABYRINTH AND THE MILLENNIUM

So how does *Pan's Labyrinth* evoke the concerns of the twenty-first century? Admittedly, many of its problematics may not be specific to the new millennium, but they certainly reflect the concerns of our time. As in the worlds of the other films we consider, *Pan's* world is presented as being terribly flawed, controlled by savage powers, whether Fascists, demonic kings, or arbitrary gods, while the natural world is being destroyed and lost. The film does engage with millennial wars and is redolent of the battle against terror and the second Iraq war.[128] But it speaks more universally about the trauma of all wars and their aftermath. The hope of help (indeed, the very Greek etymology of Ofelia's name is "help") and salvation does exist, but, because of the sheer volume of horror, it seems to require something beyond this world, divine or superhuman, to achieve it. The older order is corrupt, and the savior-child thematizes the sought-for purity. But, as in *Harry Potter* and *The Hunger Games*, there must be much blood shed and sacrifice. The environmental message is strong as well, and the mythical fairy tale longs for a time when men and nature lived in harmony, a time that is dangerously coming to an end in the new millennium.

Where are we to find the solutions? As noted, one answer is the gods, in divine powers, or in humans who in some way incarnate divine powers; Ofelia and the child she protects are figures for that sort of power. Our world must pay increasing attention to the female dimensions of life and fertility, which, of course threaten male control, whose demonic embodiment is Captain Vidal. *Pan's Labyrinth* has correlates with some of the almost dreamlike/nightmarelike qualities of movies such as *Clash/Wrath* and *Immortals*, as well as the surreal aspects of *Such Is Life*. Movies of this kind, suggest that the true "reality" of our incomprehensible world cannot be captured by a linear narrative. This too is why most of our films play with forms of mystery and mysticism, reproducing

---

128 Kotecki (2010), 235–36. And Del Toro even mentions 9/11 as looming large early on in the director's commentary to the DVD.

our ancient (if often denied) feeling that there are secret powers and worlds above us and within us, which we need to confront, and perhaps profit by. And Ofelia, in our dark hour, serves as a messenger from that world.

REFERENCES

Bettelheim, B. (1976). *The Uses of Enchantment. The Meaning and Importance of Fairy Tales.* New York. Knopf/Random House, 1976.

Borgeaud, P. *The Cult of Pan in Ancient Greece.* University of Chicago Press, 1988.

Brown, E. "The Divine Name 'Pan'." *Transactions of the American Philological Association*, vol. 107, 1977, 57–61.

Burkert, W. *Structure and History in Greek Mythology and Ritual.* University of California Press, 1982.

Burkert, W. *Greek Religion.* Harvard UP, 1985.

Clark, R., and K. McDonald. "'A Constant Transit of Finding': Fantasy as Realisation in *Pan's Labyrinth*." *Children's Literature in Education*, vol. 41, 2010, 52–63.

Clarke, J. "Gender Roles, Time and Initiation in *Pan's Labyrinth* and the *Homeric Hymn to Demeter*." *New Voices in Classical Reception Studies*, vol. 10, 2015, 42–55. http://www2.open.ac.uk/ClassicalStudies/GreekPlays/newvoices/Issue10/clarke.pdf.

Del Toro, G. Director's Commentary and DVD Extras on *Pan's Labyrinth* DVD, 2007.

Del Toro, G., and N. Nunziata. *Guillermo Del Toro's Pan's Labyrinth: Inside the Creation of the Modern Fairy Tale.* Harper Design. 2016.

Diestro-Dópido 2015. Diestro-Dópido, M. *Pan's Labyrinth.* BFI Film Classics series. Palgrave. 2015.

Fischer, Paul "Guillermo Del Toro for "Pan's Labyrinth" *Dark Horizons* September 26 2006. http://www.darkhorizons.com/features/290/guillermo-del-toro-for-pans-labyrinth Accessed October 27, 2016.

Foley, H., ed. *The Homeric Hymn to Demeter: Translation, Commentary, and Interpretive Essays.* Princeton UP, 1994.

Frye, N. *The Secular Scripture. A Study of the Structure of Romance.* Harvard UP, 1976.

Gómez-Castellano, I. "Lullabies and Postmemory: Hearing the Ghosts of Spanish History in Guillermo Del Toro's *Pan's Labyrinth* (*El Laberinto del Fauno*, 2006)." *Journal of Spanish Cultural Studies*, vol. 14 no. 1, 2013, 1–18.

Guillen, M. "PAN'S LABYRINTH—Interview With Guillermo Del Toro" *ScreenAnarchy*. December 17, 2006. http://screenanarchy.com/2006/12/pans-labyrinthinterview-with-guillermo-del-toro.html. Accessed October 31, 2016.

Hanley, J. "The Walls Fall Down: Fantasy and Power in *El laberinto del fauno*." *Studies in Hispanic Cinemas*, vol. 4 no. 1, 2007, 35–45.

Harrison, R. "The Mandrake and the Ancient World." *Evangelical Quarterly*, vol. 28 no. 2, 1956, 87–92.

Hubner, L. *"Pan's Labyrinth*, Fear and the Fairy-Tale." In K. Hessel and M. Huppert, *Fear Itself. Reasoning the Unreasonable. (At the Interface/Probing the Boundaries*, vol. 61). Brill, 2010, 45–65.

Jung, C. G. "The Psychological Aspects of the Kore." In K. Kerényi and C. Jung, *Essays on a Science of Mythology. The Myth of the Divine Child and the Mysteries of Eleusis.* Princeton UP, 1993 (Mythos Reprint), pp. 156–77.

Jung, C. G. and Kerényi, K. *Essays on a Science of Mythology, Essays on a Science of Mythology.* The Myth of the Divine Child and the Mysteries of Eleusis Princeton UP Reprint, Mythos series 1993.

Kerényi, K. *Eleusis: Archetypal Image of Mother and Daughter.* Princeton UP, reprint, Mythos series, 1991.

———. *The Gods of the Greeks.* Thames and Hudson, 1951.

Kermode, M. "Interview with Guillermo Del Toro." November 2006 https://www .youtube.com/watch?v=iqdEKahV-gs. Accessed July 13, 2016.

Kimura, K. "The Fantasy World of a Girl: Guillermo Del Toro's *Pan's Labyrinth*." *International Journal of the Image*, vol. 2 no. 2, 2012, 79–88.

Kinder, M. *Blood Cinema: The Reconstruction of National Identity in Spain.* University of California Press, 1993.

Kotecki, K. "Approximating the Hypertextual, Replicating the Metafictional: Textual and Sociopolitical Authority in Guillermo Del Toro's *Pan's Labyrinth*." *Marvels & Tales: Journal of Fairy-Tale Studies*, vol. 24 no. 2, 2010, 235–54.

Lacey, L. *Lunaception: A Feminine Odyssey into Fertility and Contraception.* Coward, McCann & Geoghegan, 1975.

Lebeau, V. *Childhood and Cinema.* Reaktion, 2008.

Levi, E. *Transcendental Magic: Its Doctrine and Ritual*, tr. A. E. Waite. George Redway, 1896, pp. 288–92.

Lindsay, R. "Menstruation as Heroine's Journey in Pan's Labyrinth." *Journal of Religion and Film*, vol. 16 no. 1, 2012, 1–27.

Lurie, A. "Afterword." In J. M. Barrie, *Peter Pan.* Signet Classics. Penguin, 1987, pp. 193–200.

May, R. *Sex and Fantasy.* Norton, 1980.

Merivale, P. *Pan, the Goat-god: His Myth in Modern Times.* Harvard UP, 1969.

Neumann, E. *The Great Mother: An Analysis of the Archetype.* Princeton UP, 1970.

Olson, D., ed. *The Devil's Backbone and Pan's Labyrinth: Studies in the Horror Film.* Centipede Press, 2016.

Orme, J. "Narrative Desire and Disobedience in *Pan's Labyrinth*." *Marvels & Tales: Journal of Fairy-Tale Studies*, vol. 24 no. 2, 2010, 219–34.

Perlich, J. "Rethinking the Monomyth: *Pan's Labyrinth* and the Face of a New Hero(ine)." In J. Perlich and D. Whitt, ed., *Millennial Mythmaking: Essays on the Power of Science Fiction and Fantasy Literature, Films and Games.* McFarland, 2009, pp. 100–128.

Ruppersburg, H. "'Oh, so many startlements . . .': History, Race, and Myth in *O Brother, Where Art Thou?*" *Southern Cultures*, vol. 9 no. 4, 2003, 5–26.

Salzman-Mitchell, P. "Myth and Maidenhood in *Pan's Labyrinth* by Guillermo del Toro." Paper at CAAS Centennial meeting, Oct. 7, 2007.

Spector, B. "Sacrifice of the Children in *Pan's Labyrinth*." *Jung Journal: Culture & Psyche*, vol. 3 no. 3, 2009, 81–86.

Toscano, M. "Homer Meets the Coen Brothers: Memory as Artistic Pastiche in *O Brother, Where Art Thou*?" *The Classical Era: Film and History*, vol. 39 no. 2, 2009, 49–53.

Van den Berg, M., and M. Dircksen. "Mandrake from Antiquity to Harry Potter." *Akroterion*, vol. 53, 2008, 67–79.

Vivancos, A. "Malevolent Fathers and Rebellious Daughters: National Oedipal Narratives and Political Erasures in *El laberinto del fauno*." *Bulletin of Spanish Studies*, vol. 89 no. 6, 2012, 877–93.

Wood, J. *Talking Movies: Contemporary World Filmmakers in Interview*. Wallflower Press, 2006.

Yocom, M. "Pan's Labyrinth/El Laberinto del Fauno: Review." *Marvels and Tales*, vol. 22 no. 2, 2008, 345–38.

Zipes, J. "Video Review *Pan's Labyrinth* (*El Laberinto del Fauno*)." *Journal of American Folklore*, vol. 121 no. 480, 2008, 236–40.

CHAPTER 7

THE PERILS OF OPPRESSION

The Myth of Medea in Arturo Ripstein's *Such is Life*

> Thus thrice I would stand by my shield rather than give birth once.
> (Euripides, *Medea* 250–51)

Will the baby be healthy? Will labor be long or difficult? Will there be a lot of pain? These are common questions modern women ask themselves as the time of delivery approaches. What they do not normally ask, at least in the developed West, is, "Will I live or die" in childbirth? For ancient women, the odds of dying in childbirth, especially with multiple pregnancies, were very great. Thus, as Medea tells us, being a woman in the ancient world was a risky business. In Euripides' play, Medea voices the condition of Greek women, confined to the house, supposedly safe. Contrasted with men's freedoms, women suffer oppression and entrapment and thus the tragedy begins with the heroine stepping outside the palace, forcefully declaring she will not endure what she is expected to. The Classical Medea is an exotic Eastern princess and witch whose drama is set in a mythological world; but we must remember how these myths draw their power from life experiences. In 2001, the headlines told of Andrea Yates of Houston, Texas, who, suffering from serious postpartum depression, drowned her five young children in the bathtub. The ancients wondered, as we do now if something, besides mental illness, was needed to drive a mother to such an extreme act. The burdens of motherhood might have been too much for this woman to bear and might have overthrown her unbalanced mental state. We come up with many answers for filicide as we consider the oppressive structures of our own society, and the dark potentials found in intense human emotions.

In the previous chapter, on *Pan's Labyrinth*, we discussed a mythical, fairy-tale-like film that engaged vital women's issues, especially regarding fertility and reproduction. In some sense, most female mythical figures, as we discuss in

PLOT SUMMARY

Set in a shabby tenement of Mexico City, Nico, an unsuccessful boxer, decides to abandon Julia to marry Raquel, daughter of the landlord, La Marrana (the Sow). Unable to stand the abandonment, pain, and insults, as well as Nico's wish to take their children, Julia, an alternative healer, seems to go mad with love and rage; she kills her own children and flees in a taxi.

the chapter on *The Hunger Games*, reproduce some aspect of the Great Goddess or Great Mother, a life-giving and nurturing force of nature. *Pan's Labyrinth* offered the figure of a young heroine whose journey to womanhood and fertility led her to oppose the tyrannical control of her Fascist stepfather. This chapter's movie, just like the Classical versions of Medea, also has as its protagonist a life-giving helper for the (somewhat problematic) hero; she saves his life and gives him children. In myth, Medea also solves Aegeus' infertility and some of the rituals she performed in Colchis indeed may have had to do with the fertility of the land, (as clearly shown in Pasolini's film *Medea*) giving her character a certain aura of a fertility deity. Yet the Medea myth, albeit in extreme fashion, demonstrates what can happen when women do not conform to this mythical ideal and react to their silencing encasement in motherhood and wifehood, rejecting male domination and becoming figures for an alternative view of femininity. These issues of freedom, control, and selfhood are painfully relevant for our time, and thus Medea's story is also another powerful "tool to think with."

This chapter explores and unpacks Ripstein's film *Such Is Life* (2000), which has been somewhat ignored by the Anglo-Saxon Classical scholarly community so far.[1] Its reviews were varied. One critic, while recognizing Ripstein as an "outstanding Mexican director," felt the film "failed to sparkle" and showed little novelty, although the use of new technologies was praiseworthy. Some thought that the film lacked the necessary "poetry" to make tolerable the horrors of Medea's actions, and that it did not encourage any empathy with the protagonist.[2] Aguilera Vita (2011) sees the film as "artificial and cold, despite its rawness."[3] Other critics lauded the risks taken and the film's experimental nature,[4] so different from conventional Hollywood productions. For us, this is a carefully crafted film, worth our effort to produce a quasi-experimental analysis of our own, an important artistic creation that reimagines an ancient

---

1   In part this neglect reflects the denial of a space for alternative, countercultural interpretations in the "First World," but it is also based on linguistic differences, since the many recreations of Classical myth in Latin America are written in Spanish or Portuguese. See Nikoloutsos (2015), 333–34.

2   See Schwartz (2001).

3   Aguilera Vita (2011), 2.

4   See Colmena (2016).

myth—one of horrific revenge and transgression, but also of female resistance to male power and structures of oppression.

Medea, though she tried (somewhat) to conform to the ideals of fertile femininity and silent/passive motherhood, refused to accept Jason's abandonment and committed an unthinkable violation of her (supposed) essential femininity and, with premeditation, killed her own children. Feminist critics see Medea as offering a voice and actions that counter mythical ideas of the fertile and nurturing female and present an alternative, but one that embodies deep dangers, threats tied to women's lack of control and their possible disruption of the male order. Here we shall chart how Medea's metamorphosis from mother to murderer takes place: what causes it, what it involves, what justifies it, and how to find meaning in Medea's actions, and in actions like hers occurring today. We will first look at how the myth presents the value of marriage, the traumatic loss in its dissolution, her consequent and unbridled fury and rejection of conventional femininity, and her demand for revenge. Second, we will highlight some specific mythical aspects of the heroine, such as the figure of the Barbarian, the exile, and the witch and wise woman, all of which play a role in Medea's rebellion against her male-imposed roles as woman, wife, and mother.

MYTHS OF MEDEA

Medea herself is first mentioned in the eighth century BCE (Hesiod's *Theogony* 961), but the most widely known version of her story is the tragedy *Medea*, composed by the innovative Athenian playwright Euripides in 431 BCE. The tragedy takes place in Corinth, where Jason and Medea have settled and have two children. Medea, who did so much for Jason, even giving up her homeland, cannot endure being abandoned for the young Glauce, daughter of King Creon. After much internal struggle, plotting, and deceit, Medea kills both the new bride and her father and then murders her own children, all to revenge herself on Jason, who claimed he was marrying Glauce to offer greater opportunities to their children through his marriage into royalty. At the play's conclusion, Medea flies away unpunished, with the children's bodies on a chariot provided by her grandfather Helios, the sun god, leaving the ruined Jason bereft of everything important.[5] Critics posit that Euripides made up the story of Medea killing Jason's children for revenge; there is an older account that tells how Medea attempted to make them immortal and accidentally killed them (Eumelus, a seventh- and sixth-century Greek poet and scholion to Pindar; *Olympian* 13.13.74),[6] or that they were

---

5   The bibliography on Medea is vast. Good general studies are Clauss and Iles Johnston (1997) and Bartel and Simon (2010). Especially for discussions of Seneca's Medea, see Martin (1997).
6   See Eusching (2007), 102. On Medea trying to make her children immortal, see also Pausanias 2.3.11. See as well Graf (1997), 34–35.

KEY TERMS

Patriarchy: the system, political and social, in which male authority is dominant

Feminist resistance: a form of female refusal to conform to male power

Telenovela: a sort of typical Latin American popular soap opera

Casa de vecindario: a block of tenements with various small dwellings surrounding a patio; common in Mexico

Surrealism: cultural and artistic movement begun in the 1920s, allowing the unconscious to express itself in art without following the rules of reality

Otherness: the state of being or feeling different from the culture that surrounds us, or being an outsider

---

killed by the women of Corinth or Creon's family.[7] Medea reaches an agreement with Aegeus, king of Athens, who was struggling with infertility and to whom Medea promises help. She thus flies to Athens and with him produces a son, Medus, ancestor of the Medes, Persians who will be a nemesis to the Greeks and then to the Romans for more than a thousand years.

The earlier events of Medea's life are best known from Apollonius Rhodius' *Argonautica*, a third-century BCE Hellenistic epic, which differs substantially from the narrative found in Pindar's *Fourth Pythian Ode* (sixth century BC), which presents a more heroic Jason. The *Argonautica* tells how the tyrant Pelias, who had deposed Jason's father as king of Iolchus, sent Jason and the Argonauts to the edge of the known world to obtain the Golden Fleece, guarded by Medea's father Aeetes, the king of Colchis. Medea, both world-class witch and teenage girl, is compelled by Eros to fall in love with Jason. With Medea's help Jason harnesses fire-breathing bulls, scatters dragon's teeth, kills the warriors that then spring up, and puts to sleep the giant snake that guarded the Fleece. The Fleece obtained, Medea flees with Jason and the Argonauts. To escape pursuit, Medea prompts Jason to deceive and kill her own brother, Apsyrtus, for which they are cursed and suffer extensive wanderings. Other authors (e.g., Ovid, *Met.* 8.162ff.) tell how, when Pelias refused to surrender the throne, Medea tricked the daughters of Pelias into boiling their father alive. Because of this, Jason is exiled and ends up at Corinth. Jason's adventures with the Argonauts have been a popular theme of films, most notably the 1963 *Jason and the Argonauts* directed by Don Chaffey and more recently in a 2000 homonymous TV series with Jason London, directed by Nick Willing.

Among the Romans, in addition to numerous retellings (for example, Pacuvius' *Medus*), Medea's story is elaborately restaged by Ovid in his *Metamorphoses* 7, in his *Heroides* 12, and in his lost tragedy *Medea*. Lucius Annaeus Seneca, the orator, Stoic philosopher, and tutor to the Emperor Nero (who ordered him to commit suicide), wrote a *Medea* with a distinctive Roman

---

7   Tola (2014), 24, with reference to Martin (1997), 34–35, in n. 25.

and Stoic flavor. Ripstein chose Seneca, not Euripides, as the chief inspiration for his film. Seneca had written a philosophical treatise, *De ira* (*Concerning Wrath*), and his *Medea* offers striking examples of the tragic consequences of *ira* coupled with a loss of self-control.[8] Romans were (at least officially) very concerned with what we might today call family values, and accordingly Seneca's *Medea* emphasizes the marriage pact and the obligations it involves. Jason's major crime, an outrage to Medea, is that he has willfully broken that marriage pact, or *foedus*, a most Roman institution.[9] And, looked at more broadly, the Medea myth examines the possible and dire consequences of the neglect, oppression, and betrayal of another human being, one who is trapped and made vulnerable by circumstances and structures beyond her control.

MEDEA IN THE MOVIES

The myth of Medea has had a rich post-Classical existence, from famous works such as Geoffrey Chaucer's *The Legend of Good Women*, John Gardner's *Jason and Medeia*, and Jean Anouilh's *Medea*, and a Broadway production starring Diana Rigg (of *Avengers* fame), as well as numerous appearances in music (Cavalli's opera *Iasone*, Handel's *Teseo*, among many others) and art (the famous paintings by Frederick Sandys, 1868, or John William Waterhouse's 1907 *Jason and Medea*, for example, or Paul Cezanne's *Medea*, 1879–1882). In cinema, noteworthy versions focusing on the heroine are Italian director Pierre Paolo Pasolini's *Medea* (1969), Jules Dassin's *A Dream of Passion* (1978), and a made-for-television film by Lars Von Trier, *Medea* (1988). These works appeared in the span of twenty years, after the myth was practically avoided by directors for seventy years.[10]

In his usual and daring personal style, Pasolini's *Medea*, with Maria Callas as protagonist in a version not entirely based on Euripides,[11] recaptures the myths of Jason and Medea in a rather estranged setting, as is usual with this director. Yet Pasolini does not recreate Euripides' play but reworks various aspects of the entire saga. The film begins when Jason was a youth, being educated by the centaur Chiron; it then shows Colchis and a human sacrifice within a fertility ritual directed by the princess Medea as high priestess. The movie relates Jason's conflict with his uncle Pelias, and then his encounter with Medea at

---

8   Tola (2014), 25.

9   On marriage imagery in Seneca's *Medea*, see Henry and Walker (1967), 173–74. On the more specific connections with Roman marriage law, see Abrahamsen (1999).

10 See Christie (2000), 144. On representation of Medea in post-Classical times, see Hall, Macintosh, and Taplin (2000) and especially Christie's article in that volume, discussing the filmic versions of Medea. Two Spanish-language articles, Del Barrio Mendoza (2011) and Camino Carrasco (2013), are noteworthy. Nikoloutsos's book (2013) has a whole section on Medea in film, with articles on *Jason and the Argonauts* by Kirk Ormand, on Pasolini's *Medea* by Susan Shapiro, and on Von Trier's film by Baertschi. Dassin's version is mentioned, but Ripstein's does not appear.

11 See MacKinnon (1986), 147.

Colchis, the recovery of the Golden Fleece, and the murder of Apsyrtus. It even shows them returning to Iolchus and confronting Pelias once again. After a new and rather puzzling appearance of a centaur, the story gradually turns to tragic conflict, with a curious, possibly dreamlike and imagined double narrative.

After Jason's betrayal, Medea murders Glauce and Creon with the poisoned robe, though it is left somewhat open whether this last event was real or imagined, a fact echoed perhaps in Ripstein's version. Yet the narrative is repeated when Glauce and Creon appear alive again, only to die one more time by throwing themselves off the palace walls. Medea does, in the end, kill her children and attempt to burn down the city. Pasoloni's film also has a political dimension, as he shows Medea's world of Colchis, filmed in Cappadocia, Turkey, as the more natural and harmonic space, Medea's secret world,[12] and thus explains her difficulties in fitting into Corinth, which Pasolini sees as the more desecrated and modern world, which evokes his own despair at consumerism having "depoliticized the working class."[13] Critics have also seen an anti-Western colonialist message in the film.[14] As we will see, Ripstein and Garciadiego's version also highlights their interest on the conflict of Julia as a woman and the consequences of her oppression.

Another political take on the myth is made by Jules Dassin, a director ostracized in Hollywood's McCarthy era; the director's Greek wife and main actress Melina Mercouri was herself in exile. The movie is filmed three years after the fall of the Greek junta, a dictatorial government that ruled Greece from 1967 to 1974. In some ways, the movie engages with the question of the relevance of a Greek classic with the modern world, presenting the motif of the "play within a play."[15] In *A Dream of Passion* a somewhat faded Greek actress, now exiled in the United States, returns to Athens to perform the main role in Euripides' tragedy in an outdoor production set in the theater of Dionysus at the foot of the Acropolis, a performance that in fact took place.[16] The question thus remains: How can a late-twentieth-century actress relate to the feelings and motifs of the ancient heroine? In the process of the artistic creation of her character, she meets an American woman, who is now in prison for having killed her children after knowing her husband was planning to leave her for another woman, all alone and away from her land. This difficult yet intriguing relationship leads Maya

---

12 See Shapiro (2013), 97. Also, "There we see the Colchians, portrayed as an isolated and primitive culture, steeped in religious ritual (with Medea as high priestess) living a simple but peaceful existence before Jason and the Argonauts arrive to alter their civilization irrevocably." Shapiro (2013), 95. See also Shapiro (2013), 103–7, on Colchis in Pasolini. On Pasolini's *Medea* in the context of his filmography and the reception of the film, see MacKinnon (1986), 146–47.

13 Christie (2000), 153.

14 Shapiro (2013), 96 and 111–12 with refs.

15 Christie (2000), 160.

16 Christie (2000), 147.

(Mercouri) to comprehend much about the Greek heroine. Of the three Medea films that came before *Such Is Life*, this one is probably the most "modern" and "reflexive" of the three,[17] and probably the easiest to follow in some ways.

Lars Von Trier's *Medea* is a Danish adaptation of Euripides' play produced for television, based on a script by Carl Theodore Dreyer, the most renowned Danish filmmaker, and with influences of his style. With a dark, bleak, and watery setting, connecting Medea to nature, and with an underworldly feel to it, Von Trier seems to sympathize with the female figure, identified here strongly with water.[18] Baertschi refers to her as at the same time "protofeminist" and "Christian martyr,"[19] and as "a lonely and deeply wounded, yet strong woman, who faces an existential conflict in a patriarchal society and refuses to accept the role of victim that is expected from her. At the same time, Von Trier combines his feminist approach with a Christian re-interpretation of the story, presenting Medea as the incarnation of the oppressed female, who takes on the misery and suffering of all women."[20] The setting is a pagan and medieval-looking Denmark,[21] and Medea is very much presented as a "witch," a "wise woman."[22] Matters of Medea's control over fertility are also implied both in her relationship with Aegeus and in dialogues with Jason.[23] The narrative starts at the end, with an image of Aegeus' ship approaching the shores; from him Medea will beg assistance to leave Corinth after the murders (the children are hanged from a tree in this case). There is a sense of isolation surrounding the characters, who rarely communicate directly.[24] While Glauce and Creon die poisoned in the underground tunnels, Medea pushing a sled in the bogs arrives at a tree where the children will be hanged, the elder one even helping his mother first in the murder of the younger one.

Despite a certain sense of estrangement, Pasolini's, Dassin's, and Von Trier's versions are marked by a "politics of feminism" and resistance to patriarchy, possibly a product of the cultural changes of the 1960s, and of course all three of them are in constant dialogue with Euripides.[25] Ripstein's version is doubtless influenced by his predecessors, and we shall make references to them in our analysis. Yet Ripstein's distinctive innovation is to choose Seneca's text as his source instead of Euripides' and to place the drama actually in the Third World, in a non-European center, which gives the story its own original flavor and meaning. Ripstein's tale is set in a rundown tenement of Mexico City, and

---

17   Christie (2000), 147.
18   Sham (2014), 118.
19   Baertschi (2013), 119.
20   Baertschi (2013), 124.
21   See also Christie (2000), 146.
22   Christie (2000), 155.
23   Christie (2000), 156.
24   Sham (2014), 118.
25   Christie (2000), 147.

thus the director and screen writer adapt the myth to the environment they know best. Of all these versions, as well, Ripstein's is the only one written by a woman.

RIPSTEIN AND HIS CINEMA

In the year 2000, Arturo Ripstein, possibly the most established, respected, and prolific (his work on film spans at least fifty years) of Mexican film directors, and his wife and screenplay writer Paz Garciadiego, presented the strange yet thought-provoking *Such Is Life* (*Así es la Vida*, 2000), based on, as the final credits note, Seneca's *Medea*. His earlier black-and-white films such as *Tiempo de morir* (*Time to Die*, 1965), with original script by Gabriel García Márquez, and with dialogues by Carlos Fuentes, gave Ripstein recognition. His most recent cinema inserts itself in the "Nuevo Cine Mexicano," with its high-quality productions and filmmakers such as Alfonso Cuarón, María Novaro, Alfonso Arau, and Guillermo Del Toro. Our film was Ripstein's, and his partner Paz Garciadiego's, first film based directly on a Classical source and also the first one filmed digitally. Ripstein's previous noteworthy films also included *Deep Crimson* (1996), *Woman of the Port* (1991), *No One Writes to the Colonel* (1999), and many others. In addition to his collaborations with famous Latin American writers such as García Márquez and Fuentes, he has adapted a novel by the Chilean author José Donoso in *El Lugar sin Límites* (*The Place Without Limits*, 1978). Like *Such Is Life*, Ripstein's films tend to be dark, displaying a tragic and doomed perspective on life, and the impossibility of the usually dispossessed characters to conform to it. His works are set in dodgy, obscure, and bleak spaces and circumstances that often reflect a certain Latin American reality.[26] One can easily see that the subject and tone of this ancient tragedy fits Ripstein's interests well.

Another characteristic of Ripstein's cinematography, manifest in *Such Is Life*, is an unrealistic, almost dreamlike quality in the scenes, where things are reflected in other spaces—mirrors are ubiquitous in his work—as when characters appear on the TV screen, and then appear and sing in the living room, functioning as a chorus, commenting (obliquely) on events of the seemingly linear, "real" narrative. Ripstein's style of filmic storytelling presents a somewhat jarring alterative to the more straightforward narratives produced in Hollywood blockbusters. In his movies dreams and fantasies are often inserted in the narratives in a way that makes them indistinguishable from real events. As with the films of the Coen brothers, but even more so, Ripstein's characteristic style

---

26 Gorostiza (2002), 21, cited in Fresneda (2014), 63, thus describes Ripstein's and Garciadiego's cinema: "They decide to dive openly into the sewers of the world, in the muck of the forgotten, in the great dump of the Western world, to show us how the inhabitants of that underworld are born, live poorly and die."

presents an intentional aesthetic and artistic statement. *Such Is Life* is a challenging film that requires the viewer's active involvement and makes him or her think and rethink about what may have occurred onscreen. Our presence is even acknowledged when the characters seem to talk directly to us, to the camera, and toward the end when we even see the camera and crew reflected in a mirror, thus heightening the awareness that there exists an outside audience and that what we see is a constructed artistic product, hence breaking the illusion that the narrative is actually real.[27] Both Seneca's work and Ripstein's require a moral judgment from the audience.[28]

As a young man, Ripstein worked with the groundbreaking Spanish director Luis Buñuel, who was exiled in Mexico, like many other Iberian artists avoiding the Francoist regime. A surrealist filmmaker, Buñuel had directed films such as *The Golden Age* (*L'Âge d'Or*) and *An Andalusian Dog* (*Un Chien Andalou*) with the master surrealist artist Salvador Dalí. Not surprisingly, a surrealistic dimension is found in Ripstein's depiction of the entrapment of his characters, the exchanges between the masculine and feminine figures, and the transfiguration of sexual roles.[29] Surrealist cinema plays fast and loose with rationality, being dominated by dreams and imagination, taking a strange and provocative tone.[30] Note that the myths of preliterate peoples often possess this dreamlike quality, and thus myths (and Ripstein's movies) can be seen as a representation of the dream world.

Further, note in Ripstein's films that violence frequently emerges from characters' uncontrollable and unconscious passions.[31] Ripstein's films offer

---

27 Fresneda (2014), 65, notes that Ripstein reinvents the melodrama's hyperreality by using distinctive cinematographic techniques such as the long take, monologue, voyeuristic camera work (as when the characters are having sex and we or the camera seem to intrude in the scene), interpellation, and other theatrical techniques that provoke a sense of distance from the spectator. Rodríguez and Sinardet (2006), 141, point out the character of "filmed theatre"; see for example the technique of *"fondu au noir"* (fade out), which as in staged theater serves to separate scenes (142). On further theatrical aspects of the movie, see Aguilera Vita (2011). On the general traits of Ripstein's cinema, see Garrido Bigorra (2013), 162, who refers to Paranaguá (1997). On the interactions of the characters with the camera, see also Garrido Bigorra (2013), 172.

28 See Garrido Bigorra (2013), 171.

29 See Flores, Carlini, and Elizalde Robles (2008), 1, and passim for surrealism in Ripstein's filmography. In general terms, surrealism is a cultural movement born in Paris around the 1920s. Some crucial figures were André Breton, who wrote *The Surrealist Manifestos*, and the Catalan painter Salvador Dalí in the visual arts. Surrealism focuses on releasing the unconscious and thus often merges dream and reality in the superposition of incongruent, nonrealistic images.

30 Flores et al. (2008), 1.

31 Flores et al. (2008): "Arturo Ripstein, who briefly changes the focus of surrealism, characterizing it with passional desires hidden in the unconscious of the characters, making them affect their 'rational' form, pressuring them to act in an instinctive way, to the point of having a personal clash when they want to recognize what is right and what is wrong, what 'ought to be done' and what is 'allowed' in society. He presents aggressive personalities which emerge as a

considerable social criticism of a society unable to recognize these passions that thus inhabit (rather surrealistic) dreams.[32]

And yet, coupled with the fragmentation and distortion of reality, the films of Ripstein/Garciadiego also possess elements of the hyperrealism found in that most Mexican of genres, the *culebrón* or *telenovela* (soap opera),[33] where love and deep passions, almost tragic at times, unfold before our eyes in daily installments. Ripstein even directed one (*Dulce Desafío*, 1988), which shows a characteristically Mexican and Latin American focus on the family and children and their conflicts, as well as a sense of the protagonists' entrapment in psychological and social circumstances. And in our movie Ripstein establishes a dialogue with the TV set and the *telenovela*; indeed television programs provide both visual background and even characters for the film.

OF LOVE, MARRIAGE, AND *IRA*

So how does a Classical figure notorious for committing infanticide evolve into a lower-class, struggling character in a rundown tenement, or *vecindario*, in the Distrito Federal, Mexico's capital? Euripides's original tragedy contains a monologue by Medea that feminists often cite as an almost foundational cry for women's rights and exposition of women's oppressed condition. This tragedy ends as Medea escapes completely from the ties of husband, children, and family, leaving the scene in a flying carriage, unharmed and unavenged, ironically, to gain a new partner and family in Athens from which she will one day flee. Love is an important aspect of Euripides and of the later cinematic versions of Medea, but Seneca makes its sufferings even more evident. And, as Martha Nussbaum states in her analysis of Seneca's play, "Seneca's claim is that this story of murder and violation is our story—the story of every person who loves. Or rather, that no person who loves can safely guarantee that she, or he, will stop short of this story. . . . Medea's problem is not a problem of love per se, it is a problem of inappropriate, immoderate love."[34] For Seneca there doesn't seem to be a right form of love; rather, "There is no erotic passion that reliably stops short of its own excesses."[35]

---

consequence of the hostilities towards social norms such as transvestism and prostitution, the desire of what's forbidden . . . it is a manifestation of repressed instincts in the world, linked to hatred, pain, vengeance, and even fear. . . . We find that Ripstein presents characters trapped first in the image that they have of 'themselves', who tired of a certain claustrophobia, agoraphobia and personal exasperation, break the frontiers that exist between their rational part and their unconscious."

32 Flores et al. (2008).

33 See Fresneda (2014), 62ff. On hyperrealism in Ripstein, see Tovar Paz (2002), 179; and Fresneda (2014), 64–65. On melodrama, see also Garrido Bigorra (2013), 168.

34 Nussbaum (1997), 220–21.

35 Nussbaum (1997), 221.

Two aspects are central in Ripstein's reimagination as in Seneca: the importance of marriage and the breakage of the marital bond, and the nature of Medea's wrath and madness, *ira* and *furor*.[36] The play's first line invokes the gods of matrimony (Sen., *Med.* 1–2): "You, gods of marriage and you, Lucina, guardian of the marriage bed." Medea also cites various other deities in whose name Jason had sworn the pact that he now is breaking (Sen., *Med.* 7–8). Her monologue is filled with vocabulary related to her own union with Jason, the marriage bed, and also his upcoming new nuptials with Creusa (Sen., *Med.* 16, 22–23, 37, 53). Her Senecan speech focuses far less on women's difficult plight, as did Euripides' Medea, but insists on the breakage of *matrimonium*, a most fundamental Roman institution seen also, for example, in the *foedus* or "pact" Dido believed she had made with Aeneas in the *Aeneid*.[37] Dido is also a female character, an Eastern woman possessed by a *furor* provoked both by love and by Aeneas' abandonment, which leads to suicide. The emotion of *furor* was thought by the Stoics to be particularly dangerous, able to wreak havoc on the whole cosmos as it almost destroyed Rome. Guastella notes how Medea's "revenge will arise from a fusion of *ira* and *amor*."[38] Again, Seneca's focus is not legal issues per se, but the rupture of a solemn pact and subsequent abandonment that leads the heroine to a passion she cannot, or refuses to, control, one fueled by shame and anger and her intense love for Jason.[39]

The Chorus' subsequent allusion to nuptial songs (Sen., *Med.* 93), typical of Roman weddings drives Medea even deeper into despair and wrath: "I am dying. The wedding song has struck my ears" (Sen., *Med.* 116). She blames Creon for the dissolution of her marriage bond (Sen., *Med.* 143–46); the nurse mentions again Jason's lack of faithfulness (Sen., *Med.* 164). The Chorus clearly sees how the loss of her marriage brings about Medea's *dolor* and *ira*: "as when a wife deprived of her wedding torches burns with fire and hates" (Sen., *Med.* 581–82). When Medea reflects on her crimes, she insists: "No crime did I commit in anger: Unhappy love is raging mad" (Sen., *Med.* 135–36). Jason later refers to her fury and anger: "As she sees me, she is beside herself, is in a fury, she carries her hatred in front of her: all the pain shows in her face" (Sen., *Med.* 445–46). The fury is again seen in Medea's later, self-reflective speech, when she says "still you love him, mad one, [*furiose*]" (Sen., *Med.* 897). Conscious of the wrath absorbing her, Medea struggles with the choice of child murder; in a moment

---

36 Guastella (2001) links Medea's wrath in Seneca with his Atreus in *Thyestes*.

37 Vergil's depiction of Dido owes much to depictions of Medea; see Henry (1930).

38 Guastella (2001), 205. See Nussbaum (1997), 225ff., with references on Stoic aspects of Seneca's *Medea*.

39 Perhaps less obviously than in *Such Is Life*, given its great influence of the *telenovela*, Eros and its manifestation in love are important in Pasolini (see how Medea is transformed by one look and smile from Jason in Colchis); and the fact that the film ends in conflagration, a metaphor for passion, is significant. See MacKinnon (1986), 153. Fire imagery is also prominent in Ripstein.

of sanity, she wishes that motherly love were stronger than her wrath (Sen., *Med.* 943–44). But no. Such *dolor* and *ira* are precisely what Seneca's Stoicism teaches us to avoid,[40] because of such fatal outcomes. But it was not fate; Medea made a choice.

As we know, unmeasurable anger occurs frequently in all mythologies, giving this all-too-human and ruinous emotion an almost divine status. The *Iliad* itself begins with Achilles' wrath, an uncontrollable feeling that leads to multiple tragedies. The myth of Medea, at least as related by Seneca and Ripstein, is about the power of a great love and the great *dolor* arising from its loss, which often leads to *furor* and irrational actions.[41] Although ancient tragedy obviously highlights an extreme situation, we observe acts of passion-driven violence committed every day—just look at tabloid headlines—with graver or milder consequences.

These Senecan features also appear in *Such Is Life*. Julia, the film's Medea, seems half-crazy with feelings of betrayal and abandonment by Nico, with no place to go. And the pressures of her madness increase, building up to the movie's horrific climax and conclusion. Her plight seems to arise from her marriage's breakup; Nico is referred to by both Julia and Medea as *marido*, "husband," and the godmother at some point tries to console Julia by telling her, "Nadie muere de divorcio" ("No one dies of divorce"). Yet there is space to wonder what the actual nature of this marriage was. Julia does not seem to wear a wedding band, and Nico's decision to leave her appears to have been recent and sudden: "Porque . . . fácil, ¿no? Así nomás de buenas a primeras me dice: ya vete, ¿no?" ("Because . . . easy, right? Just like that, from one day to another he tells me: go away, right?") Is it so easy for a man to leave a woman, divorce quickly, and marry another in Mexico 2000?.

The marital status of Seneca's Medea may also be questionable; according to Ulpian, *Tituli Ulpiani* 5.4, *conubium* (marriage) with a foreigner is valid only if the right "has been granted (*si concessum sit*)." Medea certainly considers herself wedded to Jason (she refers to him as *coniunx* and to their union as *conubium*), but Jason calls her so only once, and Creon never does so.[42] In Roman law, for a marriage to exist there must be *affectio maritalis*, "the intent to regard one another as spouse." Thus the "subsequent marriage of one of the former partners confirmed that the original marriage had ended."[43] Clearly this is not the case in

---

40 Tola (2014), 27.

41 See Camino Carrasco (2013), 72: Medea is a "subject driven by her own passion, a passion without limits and without control . . . something so contrary to the Greek way of thinking." See also Casanova (2006), 201.

42 Abrahamsen (1999), 109. According to Abrahamsen (1999), 110, other details show that Jason's union with Creusa is "*iustum matrimonium*, unlike Jason's marriage to Medea." Guastella (2001), 198, believes that "the central issue of Seneca's play is the problem of ending a marriage, and he addresses this problem in particularly Roman terms."

43 Abrahamsen (1999), 111, with Treggiari (1991), 450 in footnote.

modern Mexico, and it strikes one as improbable that Nico could so simply and legally marry a new wife. Would Julia have actually agreed to a divorce? Might this new marriage actually be Nico's first legal one? Or is the movie simply over-looking legal practice for a more mythical approach? Nico's marriage to Raquel is an attempt to gain more proper status, which is why Jason marries the King of Corinth's daughter, as in the Greco-Roman world the choice of marriage partner was often governed by economic, social, and even political considerations.

In any case Julia keeps returning to the profound bond, the "pact" estab-lished between her and Nico, and on the *telenovela*-like passion and heartbreak of love lost.[44] Yet, unlike in the mythical heroine, Julia is unbalanced and self-destructive; she cuts herself, hits her head against a wall, and even repeatedly slaps her face till it bleeds. This love is stronger for her than anything, even the love of her children. After a suggestive scene where we see a vehicle (perhaps an ambulance) from behind cruising the streets of the city as if waiting for the inevitable outcome,[45] the film moves to a monologue in which Julia, like Medea, focuses on her suffering self: "¿Y yo qué? El se va con otra" ("What of me? He leaves me for another"). She has done everything for Nico, has given him children, left her hometown and family: "¿Y los hijos que te dí? ¿Y los años que te dí? . . . Tuve tus hijos por tí, para tí. Hice todo por tí. ¿Y ahora?" ("And the children I gave you? And the years I gave you? I . . . had your children because of you, for you").

As Shapiro explains for Pasolini's *Medea*, the problem is that she has re-placed her whole previous world, a world of primitive rituals and beliefs with her love for Jason, and now he is all she has, she "now lives her life for Jason alone."[46] Our Mexican tragedy, like Seneca's, explores her unbounded and dan-gerous love for Nico, and its horrific consequences, but in a more contemporary context. Yet some things do not change; as Camino Carrasco observes, "the obsessive person tends to destroy the object of his obsession and himself."[47] As with Seneca's Medea, or Vergil's Dido, Julia is convinced a profound pact has been unilaterally broken by her man; the subsequent semi-kitschy and grotesque imagery of the new bride Raquel with the tacky cake, dress, and so forth add insult to Julia's injury. Even when Adela, the *madrina*, who plays the role of nurse, tells her that all men are the same, that she should move on, start

44 As Garrido Bigorra (2013), 167, tells us, Ripstein had already showed us "the abyss of an ex-cessive love for which everything was sacrificed" in *Profundo Carmesí*. Garrido Bigorra refers to Aguilera Vita (2011), who even sees a sort of Medea in Coral, the central character in *Profundo Carmesí* – a nurse who abandons her children.

45 Rodríguez and Sinardet (2006), 142, note how the almost random appearances of the am-bulance help to fragment the story line, as presumably the trip of the ambulance only occurs in the last few minutes of the film, after the murders. Garrido Bigorra (2013), 165, does not necessarily see this vehicle as an ambulance but rather as a van which symbolizes the "process of existence, destiny."

46 Shapiro (2013), 111.

47 Camino Carrasco (2013), 73.

over, find another man and have new kids, Julia cannot forget or stop loving and asserts that there is nothing worse than having Nico leave her: "Si él me deja, ¿qué cosa peor me puede pasar?" ("If he leaves me, what worse can happen to me?")

On top of the lost love, what hurts Julia, perhaps not as much the mythical Medeas, is losing her identity as wife.[48] One of the central issues of Seneca's Medea is "who retains the legitimate identity as Jason's wife," and "Medea's actions now become a way of reconstructing her own identity."[49] Seneca manages to put Euripides' tragedy into a Roman context "in order to make her legendary criminality more troubling to a specifically Roman imperial audience/reader."[50] Julia, as she admits, has forged a role for herself as the devoted servant of Nico, and has lived for him and nothing else. Nico went to and from the house; she had to stay home and work. Like Jason, Nico is a deficient hero who needs a woman to do his dirty work for him. Julia makes a good case that Nico was nothing before her: "Antes de mí eras puro borracho de pueblo en pueblo, ni a las peleas llegabas" ("Before me you were just a drunk from town to town, you wouldn't even get to the fights"). Jason likewise owed his survival and success to Medea. Now Julia, who for Nico's sake is separated from her hometown, is left bereft of this identity and self-construction.

In Apollonius' *Voyage of the Argo* Medea transitions from a teenage girl to a wife who provokes her brother's murder. One explanation for this intense hatred is that Medea has really come to understand that the Jason she saved and abandoned her homeland for was duplicitous (he was willing to give her back to her father Aeetes, and a terrible death, to save his skin) and unworthy of the sacrifice she made, but now she is trapped, like a character in a *telenovela*, in the consequences of her actions. Nico is a boxer—a glamorous occupation (rather like a heroic warrior), particularly popular in Mexico—and we can imagine the naïve and infatuated Julia once being swept off her feet by him, only later to see he mostly loses his fights, and she realizes at some level Nico is more a parasite than a hero. And yet now he is leaving her?

The tradition tends to present Medeas as driven to (or past) the point of madness, and this is certainly the case with Ripstein's Julia; we assume some of the movie's more surreal scenes reflect her maddened perspective. Yet not all filmic Medeas stress the heroine's madness, though we do see this feature clearly in Brenda Collins of *A Dream of Passion*, a woman deeply in love and driven to crime and insanity by abandonment. Julia explicitly tells Nico that her world is shattered without him.

---

48 The question of identity in Ripstein is also explored by Garrido Bigorra (2013), 168. A different discussion of Medea's identity is given by Henry and Walker (1967), who do not see "a character with continuous identity" in Seneca's play (177).
49 Guastella (2001), 198.
50 Abrahamsen (1999), 107.

NICO: "Que sin mí no se acaba el mundo." ("The world is not over without me.")

JULIA: "El mío sí. Tú eres lo único que tengo . . . Estoy loca por tí . . . y yo me quedo con mi locura sin ti." ("Mine is. You are the only thing I have . . . I am crazy for you . . . and I stay alone with my craziness without you.")

Julia continues, hopelessly, obsessively, to beg Nico to love her again. Later, when the *madrina* tells her that she still has the kids, Julia responds: "Eso es todo lo que me queda. Odio y nada más . . . los hijos son de él" ("That's all that is left to me. Hatred and nothing else . . . the children are his"). And when she is about to kill her daughter, our Mexican Medea reflects: "Se me acabó el mundo [cf. *Nihilque superest opibus et tantis tibi* "Nothing remains of so many riches" in Sen., *Med.* 165] . . . Me ha agarrado la rabia" ("My world is over . . . wrath has gotten hold of me"). The viewer will tie Julia's unhinged state to those abuses connected to her use and abandonment by Nico, as well as to wider social conditions that give such power to repellent figures like La Marrana. But we also wonder about other causes.

The force of *dolor* finds a natural home in the movie's seedy, dark setting, full of lonely, unhappy characters that simply struggle to survive amid ruinous circumstances. As Rodríguez and Sinardet[51] see it, Ripstein provides a "degraded" version of the characters and the myth in general. The crowded, decrepit tenement is run by a fat old man who walks around most of the time in a bathrobe; his nickname is "La Marrana" (the Sow). Economic, social, and patriarchal oppression are undisguised. The movie stresses through image, word, and action the general toughness of life, while giving Medea's plight a more Mexican and Latin American flavor, like what can be found in the *telenovela*. This sense of fate, unavoidable and gloomy, is often mentioned, in particular by the *madrina*, concerned about Julia's welfare, an aged, embittered advisor, ranting about the general evil of men.

When Julia advises a patient on having an abortion, "Esta vida duele mucho, entonces si no lo dejas que nazca, la vida jamás le va a doler. Eso es amor de madre" ("This life hurts a lot, then if you don't let him live, life will never hurt him. That is mother's love"), the patient adds, "¡qué perra es nuestra suerte!" ("our luck is such a bitch!"). Even La Marrana (the Creon figure), although he has some sympathy for Julia as he kicks her out of the tenement, later says: "La vida es así. La vida es una gran cabrona" ("Such is life. Life is a bloody bitch"). Life's events seem beyond our control; when Nico explains why he has ceased to love Julia, he can only say "cosas que pasan pasan" ("things that happen happen"). Two surreal scenes underscore this repetitive, automatic dimension to events. In the first, Nico and his fiancée Raquel (who her father thinks is a virgin!) are naked in bed and engaging in sex. The camera eventually moves to

---

51 Rodríguez and Sinardet (2001), 141.

FIGURE 7.1 Nico and Julia undressing with a TV in the background.

the black-and-white TV set, which shows a naked couple in a bathtub, which in fact, turn out to be Julia and Nico. The second scene, a flashback, shows Nico and Julia earlier, undressing mechanically in preparation for sex with the TV visible, showing scenes from a boxing match (Fig. 7.1).

The TV may in fact reveal how Nico seduced each woman, Julia with the thrill of his boxing career, and Raquel with the promise of sex. And there is a general sense that destiny, as well as the male order, cannot be fought or changed but must be accepted. Though everyone asks Julia to surrender, to accept her fate and associated circumstances, the prospect revolts her. Instead she must strike out against male rule and forge an alternative identity of herself, different from the role of mother and wife.

The sense of loneliness and bereavement is persistent; Adela insists on her solitude and the characters all end alone. The *madrina* is packing her bags to leave for some unknown destination. Julia, having murdered her children, takes off alone in a taxi, and Nico finds himself holding his dead children. One imagines that marriage with Raquel is now impossible. For the lower classes of the Latin American poor, life can be tragic, and one must accept the inescapable doom and pain of living: such is life.[52]

THE EXILE, THE WITCH, THE LOST WIFE

In a broad sense, the myth of Jason and Medea presents the "heroic career" of the weak and resourceless hero, Jason, and provides an example of the Quest/ Maturation of the hero done badly. The motif of a hero abducting some exotic other, a female, sometimes a sort of goddess (think Theseus, Heracles, even

52 Medea seems to be a figure useful in thinking about the Third World. Pasolini already indicates so in interviews and by setting Colchis in the barren landscape of Turkey. He refers specifically to the plight of Africa. See MacKinnon (1986), 148: "For him, this story could be that of a Third World, specifically African, nation, which has experienced the catastrophe of contact with materialist, Western civilisation."

Paris), is a common one in myth. In these narratives the men and women are often from radically different backgrounds, which can have positive or negative impact. Certainly many heroes, like our Nico, have been helped by the women they took away. But these more exotic women can respond very differently to circumstances than Greek women might. Jason recalls Perseus, except that for Jason everything goes wrong. Instead of getting Andromeda, he gets Medea.

As noted, a central issue of Medea's own story concerns her betrayal and the resistance and chaos this violation engenders. What might happen when a woman, superior to her partner and to whom he owes his very life, is scorned and unjustly abandoned by him, and these offenses are supported by the dominant power structure? Revolt, however unimaginable, is an option. A secondary and related issue concerns how individual and social realities actually manufacture that oppression. These themes are developed in other Greek tragedies such as *Ajax*, which concerns the tragic aftermath of the cheated hero's need of revenge; and *Hippolytus* and *Ion*, who seek justice; and of course, to a great extent, the *Oresteia*'s character of Clytemnestra, who has significant similarities to Medea herself. All these myths reflect on the nature of justice in the face of oppression, and just as does Euripides, Ripstein offers considerable social criticism. More specifically, in the case of Medea and other heroines, the abuse they suffer is connected to their entrapment through patriarchal social structures that would relegate them to reproductive wombs first and human subjectivities second, conditions that often lead to excess and chaos as the heroine decides (or is given no other alternative but self-destruction) to reject the imposed roles in often extreme ways: Medea kills her own children, and Clytemnestra murders her husband. It seems shocking that the Medeas of myth seem to flee unpunished, but the implication may be that such oppression merits justice gained by "any means necessary," which can include the murder of innocents.

But Medea's myth also concerns the actions of the foreigner, the Barbarian, the Other, whose character and mores are different and threatening. Greek thought posited a deep ideological divide between Greeks and Barbarians, and Greeks defined themselves in opposition to them, which is sometimes depicted as a struggle between Civilization and Barbarism. Such a story begins with the difficulties Greek communities have with embracing and accepting the Other. Medea comes from Colchis, located at the eastern edge of the Black Sea. The exotic East is also often conceived as the home of secret and powerful knowledge, and Medea is also a wise woman, indeed, a witch. But Medea's struggle epitomizes the plight of any Greek or Roman wife, who must give up her own family and become part of, or a stranger in, her husband's household. One thinks of wives even today who take their father's name in place of their husband's and who are abandoned for a younger wife once the husband has become successful. In Seneca's tragedy Medea complains concerning her abandonment: "Was Jason able to do this? After he robbed me of my father, my

Such Is Life	
Facets Multimedia	
Director:	Arturo Ripstein
Screenplay:	Paz Garciadiego
Language:	Spanish
Cast:	Arcelia Ramírez (Julia), Luis Felipe Tovar (Nicolás), Patricia Reyes Spíndola (Adela, the Godmother-*madrina*), Ernesto Yáñez (La Marrana), Francesca Guillén (Raquel)

fatherland and my kingdom, in a foreign land, cruel one, to leave me alone?" (Sen., *Med.* 118–20) But when Medea and every ancient wife abandons her home, she also must, to some degree, forge a new identity in the service of her husband and his family. The new wife must self-construct her own persona as a new figure, whom the man can accept or discard as he pleases.

Exile and identity loss provide central themes. Julia has come to the DF from another town together with the *madrina*. Early on she says, "Me vine para acá" ("I came over here"), and she implies it was for Nico. Her new environment revolts her: "Esta ciudad que huele a mierda" ("This city that smells like shit").[53] This recalls the common plight of many Latin American internal migrants, who move to unfriendly large cities in search of work and better conditions, escaping the poverty of provincial towns. The *madrina* says that Julia was happy and well cared for in her home town: "Ella no tiene costumbre de la vida dura. . . . Allá en su casa teníamos todo, que si su frutita en la mañana, peladita y en la boca . . ."[54] ("She has no custom of hard life. There in her house we had everything, her little fruit in the morning, peeled and in the mouth . . ."). Julia here recalls Medea, who lived comfortably at her home in Colchis. As noted, Medea gave up her prosperity and identity in the service and love of a man later revealed as a failed hero.[55] Yet the resourceful Julia has found a way to make a living here, and the way she dresses in the film recalls a sort of service-oriented attire. A parallel with Apollonius' Medea may be relevant; Medea, to help Jason and herself, especially after their exile from Colchis, becomes a more "professional" witch, so to speak. Thus the compulsion of necessity caused potential skills in Julia to be manifested. But these skills are powerful and destabilizing.

Medea is in a type of exile, having left Colchis, and now she is condemned to a second exile by Creon when he expels her and her children from Corinth. Later Medea describes herself as "expelled, suppliant, alone, abandoned, on

53 On exile in the Medea movies of Pasolini, Von Trier, and Ripstein, see Camino Carrasco (2013), 71–72.
54 See Camino Carrasco (2013), 69, who sees this as a hint to Medea's noble past (she was a princess), and that she has given up all comfort to follow Jason/Nico.
55 One thinks of Medea's words in Seneca, when she calls Jason a mere passive spectator: "*spectator iste*" (Sen., *Med.* 993).

all sides distraught once I shone on account of my noble father" (Sen., *Med.* 208–9) and notes how fortune propelled her into exile (Sen., *Med.* 219–20) and that she carried with her nothing into exile, save the body parts of her brother (Sen., *Med.* 486–87). She is bereft and has lost her family identity, and there is no hope of return. And this is what exile provokes: the loss of who one was, of a personal identity and community belonging; in the case of Julia, potentially utter impoverishment.

When La Marrana tells Julia she must leave, and that he cannot tolerate her to be around the tenement where his daughter and new husband will live, Julia begs, "¿Y yo a dónde me voy? . . . Déjeme mi casa" ("Where do I go? . . . Leave me my home"), and even kisses his feet, as if he were a king; in fact, the other dwellers of the *vecindario* seem to treat La Marrana as a king earlier in the film. She adds, "Dejé mi familia, mi casa, mi pueblo" ("I left my family, my home, my town") and later will complain, "La Marrana me dejó sin casa, a la intemperie" ("The Sow left me without a home, out in the open"). La Marrana concedes one day for Julia to delay her departure, just as Creon does in Seneca and Euripides. Although she has probably been contemplating vengeance, this threat of impoverished exile pours kerosene on her emotional fires. In both Euripides and Seneca, Medea is an almost divine being, the Sun's granddaughter and perfectly capable of finding alternatives, as we see in the later myth, when she flies to Athens, becomes the consort of Aegeus, and even has a new son, Medus. Yet for Julia and many Latin American dispossessed women, life appears bleak. With the loss of her home and her husband, and her work, as she will also lose the *dispensario* in her new exile, she has lost even this new identity she forged for herself as wife and provider to Nico. We see a glimpse of Medea's difficult future when she says to the Marrana that a woman is accepted alone, but not with children hanging from her skirts.[56] This also speaks to the still-backward and hard situation that women find themselves in even at the turn of the twenty-first century, often suffering economic inequality, raising families on their own, with little governmental of societal support and the stigma of being poor or single.

In Euripides' *Medea* (550–75), Jason keeps insisting he was divorcing her and marrying Glauce for their children's sake; his emphasis on how valuable the children are to him gives Medea a motive for child murder and is a way to destroy what Jason claims is most valuable. Note that while punching the bag Nico tells himself how the children belong to him, and soon afterward he will tell Julia he plans to take away her children ("No los dejo a ellos. . . . Ellos son míos, tienen mi sangre. . . . ¿Por qué . . . se van con ella? . . . Mañana voy por ellos" ["I am not leaving them. . . . They are mine, they have my blood.

---

56 Camino Carrasco (2013), 70.

Why . . . are they leaving with her? Tomorrow I'll go get them"]).[57] Thus he will even deprive her of a mother's identity. But then this allusion to the shared blood becomes Julia's argument for the murder: "Ellos tienen la sangre nuestra, la tuya y la mía. Y hay que desunir nuestras sangres" ("They have our blood, yours and mine. We must separate our bloods").[58] In a way, this is tantamount to Medea's allusion to her newfound virginity in Seneca ("My stolen virginity has returned" Sen., *Med.* 984).

This new freedom from the ties of motherhood and marriage is visually expressed in Von Trier's version when Medea, for the first time in the film, once safely in Aegeus' ship, removes her black skullcap and lets loose her long red hair.[59] The allusion to the "disunion" of the bloods through the death of the children can be viewed as the dissolution of Julia's persona, which conforms to traditional ideas of womanhood. Not only will she not be a wife, she will stop being a mother and thus deprive Nico himself of fatherhood, an essential macho element of patriarchal societies both in ancient Rome and modern Mexico. And, as Christie mentions, there might be a castrating dimension in the figure of Medea, who controls and disrupts male fertility and the possibility of reproduction, since both the children and the new wife are dead.[60] Ripstein's films tend to break with the traditional view of mothers and motherhood of previous "Golden Age" Mexican cinema, which usually showed devoted, asexual, self-sacrificed mothers who lived only for their children and would give everything for them.[61]

The problem of exile and alienation can be examined in the broader context of contemporary Latin American art, culture, and literature. This exile is twofold. First, there is a community of writers and artists whose origins are in Europe and who feel, in some ways, that they are perpetual exiles in their own Latin American milieu. At various times in the twentieth century, many of them were forced to flee (often to Europe) the political persecutions and

---

57 Abrahamsen (1999), 116, observes that in Roman law, in the case of "*matrimonium iniustum* . . . the children followed the status of the non-citizen parent; and one can further infer from a passage of Cicero (*Topica* 20) that children of a Roman citizen father and non-citizen mother stayed with their mother following divorce." But "in a legal marriage, children generally stayed within the father's household."

58 Cf. Baertschi's remarks (2013), 132, on the encounter of Medea and Jason at the loom in Von Trier's version: "The only thing that they still have in common are their sons. But when Jason in the course of their quarrel 'pushes his hand through the warp, angrily undoing the symbolic fabric of the family' [quoted from Joseph and Johnson (2008), 122] it becomes evident that their lives that have been woven together must be separated once and for all, and that the children as representatives of this joint life must be killed." (Baertschi, 2013, 134).

59 On this, see Baertschi (2013), 134, and Joseph and Johnson (2008), 123. Also see the loose hair as an allusion to a recovered maidenhood: "once again a nymph . . . Medea has regained her virginity."

60 Christie (2000), 163.

61 See Esterrich (2010), passim.

oppressions in their own countries.[62] Julia thus embodies the struggles of the
Latin American exile at the crossroads of a new millennium, when television
is only a mirage and a distraction from the drudgery of the sordid life in the
urban periphery of society.[63] More specifically, Julia's struggles can mirror the
vicissitudes of someone like Ripstein himself, a Jewish director, of European
background, influenced by Luis Buñuel, also an exile, and living in a traditionally Catholic society in the new continent.[64] This struggle speaks of the
quandary of a whole community of Latin American men and women artists
and intellectuals, to find their place while feeling like outsiders, often seen as
transgressive, like Medea, like Julia, in their own countries.

As noted before, Medea possesses a special and powerful status as a wise
woman, a witch, who knows more than is proper for a woman, who delves into
dark, forbidden arts, and from whom people nevertheless seek needed help, as
Julia asserts: "Dicen que soy bruja . . . pero los muy cabrones bien que me usan"
("They say I am a witch . . . but those assholes certainly use me"). Has Julia
made a virtual pact with forbidden forces? Like Medea, Julia is a kind of witch
doctor, a practitioner of homeopathy and traditional remedies, and employs
various unsanctioned curative arts, including prescribing abortifacients. And
yet, though Jason was saved by Medea's witchcraft, Creon finds her practices
polluting and alludes to this when he banishes her (Sen., *Med.* 270). But in this
unsophisticated Mexican tenement, where scientific modern medicine is hard
to come by, there is a more general acceptance of unorthodox cures. Even La
Marrana feels comfortable sitting and chatting with Julia in her *dispensario*, a
quite feminine space in which his huge, larger-than-life figure seems domineering and intrusive. Notice that access to the *dispensario* is through a tiny,
almost hidden door; one descends to a sort of cellar or basement, thus recalling
the chthonic, underworld connotations of magic, and the secrecy of women's
activities, and in a desperate moment Julia even seems to hope to harm Raquel
with a sort of voodoo doll. Beyond this we do not see Julia performing magic
per se, yet her office is full of saints and other objects that allude to magical
or divine elements assisting her cures. More than the settings of Euripides and
Seneca, Julia's *dispensario* symbolizes an alternate culture where women (all the
patients we see are women) go for help. Even at the turn of the twenty-first century, there are few places lower-class women feel comfortable going to, where
they would receive assistance without being judged, like the young girl who
seeks an abortion and yet, when Julia says that she must rush to a hospital if
she is in a bad way, answers that she prefers to come to her.

Our movie's surreal narrative and images makes the viewer question what
is really occurring on screen. Are we viewing the psychotic projections of a

---

62 See Tovar Paz (2002), 177.
63 On the use of TV in the movie, see Garrido Bigorra (2013), 171.
64 See Tovar Paz (2002), 178.

FIGURE 7.2 A fatal fire in her tenement which Julia imagines/hallucinates.

shattered mind? The *furor* Seneca alludes to might indeed translate into delusions of unreal or surreal images in Julia's mind. The materialization of the bolero band in her living room perhaps manifests the demonic chorus within Julia's head. In Euripides' *Medea*, Glauce and Creon are killed when Medea sends the poisoned gifts that burn them alive. In the movie Julia, after tossing down a lighted cigarette, apparently imagines such a fatal fire (Fig. 7.2) in the tenement, a product possibly of a raging fever.

Stoics saw *furor* as a force that could disrupt the cosmic order; Julia's *furor*, arising from abandonment and desperation, has clearly unhinged her mind. The classical Medea and Julia both have dangerous powers over life and death, which, under conditions of humiliation and threat, can turn toward evil, as seen for example when Medea tricks Pelias' daughters into boiling him alive.

Medea is never shown using magic to purposefully commit child murder. The knife, the tool of sacrifice, is Medea's weapon, as well as Julia's, and this is the case in Pasolini and Dassin's versions; as we mentioned, Von Trier has her hang her children. In Euripides, in accordance with the traditions of Greek tragedy, the killings occur off-stage; both Seneca's Medea and her twentieth-century cinematic representations, as well as the millennial Julia, murder their children before our eyes. Seneca's and Euripides' theater has been referred to as "revolting," provoking nausea due to the horrors they expose openly.[65] There is probably a similar reaction to Ripstein's films, which at times force us to avert our eyes. The killing of the second child, done while Nico watches in his wedding suit, fulfills her desire for vengeance (for she can see his reaction) but also presents a public statement and even has elements of a ritual.

Now consider the unsettling sequence of the last killing. Julia murders her young son inside the house (we do not see that act), and she comes out carrying the boy's body, with the daughter walking beside her. The daughter seems calm, and

---

65 Henry and Walker (1967), 169–70. And Seneca is considered "as first parent of the Tragedy of Blood and Theater of Cruelty" (169).

appears to know what is to come, just as Medea's older son in Von Trier's account affirms: "I know what is to come." Why does Julia's daughter not try to escape, or even manifest fear at the prospect of being slashed with the knife? Von Trier's version also shows a sense of acceptance of this death on the part of the children.

A feature of ancient religion and ritual may offer a hint. In Greek animal sacrifice, the animal is made to seem to want to be sacrificed, and an animal struggling is not a good sign. Here Julia's own daughter, having observed and suffered with her mother's struggles, seems to accept what her mother must do, and in doing so the daughter can be said to justify her mother, and even her own murder, thus perhaps implicitly participating in her liberation. Note too Julia and her daughter climb up steps to where the killing takes place, as if they were stepping up to an altar raised on a platform.[66] Julia says right before stabbing her daughter, "Ellos tienen la sangre nuestra, la tuya y la mía. Hay que desunir nuestras sangres, Nicolás. Ya no va a haber una gota de esa sangre que llamamos nuestra. . . . Me vuelvo inolvidable" ("They have our blood, yours and mine. We must separate [*desunir*] our bloods, Nicolás. There won't be a drop of that blood we call ours. . . . I have become unforgettable"). In some sense, then, the children are not just killed; they are sacrificed in a ritual of separation, purgation, and domination. After this rite, Julia will haunt Nico forever. After she kills the children, she walks straight out of the tenement, and gets into the taxi, as if these sacrificed children opened the door for her escape.

Though indeed a tale of unleashed passions, where the protagonist cannot control her wrath and cannot submissively accept her fate, as Seneca and the *madrina* would prefer, the Medea myth displays the condition of female oppression and one woman's rebellion and liberation. Medea left her home and committed crimes for Jason. No doors are open to her anymore: "All the paths I opened to you, I closed for me" (Sen., *Med.* 458). She has borne children for him; she served as his wife and helpmate. In Pasolini's version Jason's lack of heroism can be perceived, because he doesn't even have to fight the fire-breathing bull or the men sprung from the dragon teeth. Medea just gives him the fleece. Similarly, Julia did everything for Nico, even traveling all over the country to accompany him to his boxing matches, which he mostly lost. It is ironic too that the name Nicolás etymologically is related to *nike*, "victory," and thus the name is parodically unsuitable for an unsuccessful boxer.

Nico, like Jason, seems to have only one real talent, his charisma and ability to seduce women; we recall the alternate scenes of sex with Julia and Raquel.

---

66 On the image of the staircase in cinema and Medea's liberation, see Aguilera Vita (2011), 6. In the movie *Iphigenia* (1977) by Michael Cacoyannis, we see at the end the young maiden ascending the steps of a sacrificial altar leading to her death. In the Von Trier *Medea*, the tree where the children will be sacrificed is on a sort of mount. See Baertschi (2013), 133. The idea of tragic children walking up to their own deaths, also here at the hands of a parent, directly as in Medea or indirectly as with Agamemnon allowing his daughter's sacrifice, seems a poignant visual intertext for Ripstein's film.

Jason's charming smile is at play in Pasolini's version as well.[67] Clearly both Nico and Jason are self-absorbed and narcissistic. Although perhaps in the grip of a partial psychosis, Ripstein's Medea wakes up, rebels, and stops being the serviceable mate. Through the extreme act of child slaughter, Julia is liberated from the essentialist construction of motherhood,[68] and even the idea of young women choosing to end pregnancy may also be read as women taking control and in a way ending the burden of womanhood. "¡Qué perra es nuestra suerte!" ("What a bitch our luck is!") is no more, and her rebellion declares "Life is not such." Julia has come to reject the way things are, the status quo Nico, La Marrana, and the nurse insist on. She has found, as terrifying and immoral as it is, a different path, through a kind of death struggle. In romance the hero tends to triumph and survive, but in tragedy the hero's triumph can come in death, even in the form of willed self-destruction, as when Oedipus gouges his eyes out. A suggested moral of the Medea story is that the structures of patriarchal regulation are so oppressive, especially for an exceptional woman, that it often forces her to choose between forms of self-destruction: be a submissive outcast and be destroyed while your oppressors benefit, or strike out, which will also destroy you but will punish your oppressors and prevent them from profiting from their evil.

NEW MILLENNIUM, NEW BEGINNINGS

Julia, after the murders, leaves alone in a yellow taxi, without luggage, suggesting either she has no future or the possibility of new beginnings. Satisfactory new beginnings seem rare in this movie's universe, which, as in Ripstein's other films, appears ruled by a destiny largely outside human control. We don't know much, but the idea of starting over and its difficulties is felt throughout the film.

The story's setting is only vaguely contemporary. The actors' generally drab clothing could have been worn at various times in the late twentieth century. The buildings are run down, yet the street traffic shows a sense of impatient urban modernity. This indeed is a puzzling feature of most Latin American cities, where fashionable new American-style malls coexist with decaying, broken neighborhoods. Perhaps the most telling symbol of the struggle between the old and the new is seen in the television, nearly always on, an old black-and-white set. The *madrina* even points out that if Nico had been a true man, he would have given her a color TV long ago. But his refusal to do so is symbolic of his desire to keep Julia's life monochrome, and suppress her polychrome potentials. This old TV performs a considerable symbolic narrative role in the movie's surreal, and sometimes absurd, psychotic cosmos, showing a

67 See discussion in Shapiro (2013), 108–9.
68 See Fresneda (2014), 63, who sees Medea's acts as symbolically resisting the oppression of the heteropatriarchal system. Garrido Bigorra (2013), 168–69, also notes how the typical patriarchal model of the melodrama is subverted and broken within Ripstein's melodrama-inspired cinema. On the concept of "essential motherhood," see DiQuinzio (1999).

weather woman always announcing storms, presenting scenes of boxing and bathtub sex, or the odd bolero band that acts as chorus, a clever translation of the Greek chorus to the Mexican reality.[69] This male chorus (Ancelmo Fuentes and his brothers) is less sympathetic to Julia than the Chorus of ancient tragedies.[70] The camera angles and shots likewise illustrate the confining nature of life in the tenement, where there are few ways out. And note that the TV turns into color only after Julia's departure.

The film presents a struggle between the past and the future, one allied with the struggles of the Third World to reach modernity. At times we observe La Marrana playing with what appears to be some electronic device, but beyond that, conditions seem backward. These elements point to a conflict becoming increasingly sharp in the maturing millennium, the co-existence of contrasting social formations, some representing archaic institutions (the Queen of England), some current society (London's Financial District) and some future formations (the "Silicon Fen" near Cambridge, UK). This conflict was an important issue for Greek mythology as seen in the *Oresteia* trilogy, which presents a struggle between the older female powers of the cosmos and the more modern male deities. Aeschylus' utopian answer is that all formations must have their place in the new order. But plays such as Sophocles' *Antigone* and Euripides' *Bacchae* suggest archaic forces must be given their due, no matter what rationalizing male politicians might think. Our movie suggests how the ancient oppressions and conflicts between men and women can take on particularly toxic and degrading forms in a modern world whose tools for repression outstrip those for liberation and allow for many tenements, structural and actual, where such men-sows wield life-crushing authority. This was Ripstein's first digital film, and in it he explored a modern medium that allowed him to improve cinematic features such as his widely used extended shot. He used a handheld camera, which, thanks to its portability, seems more able to capture life on the fly; and indeed the camera's presence is acknowledged by the characters and even challenged when it intrudes on intimate moments. Understandable, since the images expose the backwardness of the characters and conflicts.[71]

In concluding, we note the importance of transitions and passages for this film. A vivid, if mysterious, symbol of passage is the moving ambulance or van, seen at various times, where the vehicle often goes under bridges, into tunnels, or through other passages. These images first of all evoke the passage between life and death, which the children will suffer. But there are other passages, life changes more or less successful. Julia leaves the constraints of the males who have commanded her life (and the physical constraints of the tenement) in a taxi, and

---

69   Rodríguez and Sinardet (2006), 143.

70   Garrido Bigorra (2013), 166, sees that the bolero is a typical Mexican genre from the Golden Age, which often tells sappy stories of revenge, jealousy, hatred, and treason in women.

71   On the characteristics of the digital format and its benefits for Ripstein, see Garrido Bigorra (2013), 162–63.

perhaps will start a new life, not in the sense that *madrina* suggested, of another husband, more children, same old story. But who knows? Maybe the taxi will be like Euripides' flying chariot, with another Aegeus to betray and flee. Cinema is a male-dominated industry,[72] yet here the woman has the last image (almost), and as in *Ruby Sparks*, the script of this movie is written by a woman; it is, at least in part, "a female retelling" of the mythical, suffering, and tragic heroine.

REFERENCES

Abrahamsen, L. "Roman Marriage Law and the Conflict of Seneca's Medea." *Quaderni Urbinati di Cultura Classica*, vol. 62 no. 2, 1999, 107–21.

Aguilera Vita, A. "Medea. Las dos Medeas de Arturo Ripstein." *Metakinema. Revista de Cine e Historia* 9. http://www.metakinema.es/metakineman9s3a1_Antonio_Aguilera_Vita_Medea_Ripstein.html, 2011. Accessed July 13, 2016.

Baertschi, A. "Rebel and Martyr: The Medea of Lars von Trier." In K. Nikoloutsos, ed., *Ancient Greek Women in Film*. Oxford UP, 2013, pp. 117–36.

Bartel, H., and A. Simon, ed. *Unbinding Medea: Interdisciplinary Approaches to a Classical Myth from Antiquity to the 21st Century*. Legenda, 2010.

Camino Carrasco, M. "La pervivencia del mito de Medea en el cine contemporáneo. Pasolini, Lars von Trier y Ripstein." *Ubi sunt? Revista de Historia*, vol. 28, 2013, 66–77.

Casanova, C. "Medea o la radicalidad del deseo." *Desde el Jardin de Freud: Revista de psicoanálisis* 6. Universidad Nacional de Colombia, Bogota, 2006, 200–204.

Christie, I. "Between Magic and Realism: Medea on Film." In E. Hall, F. Macintosh, and O. Taplin, ed., *Medea in Performance 1500–2000*. Legenda, 2000, pp. 144–165.

Clauss, J., and S. Iles Johnston, ed. *Medea: Essays on Medea in Myth, Literature, Philosophy and Art*. Princeton UP, 1997.

Colmena E. "Así es la vida ¡Pinche Medea!". Criticalia.com. (2016), http://www.criticalia.com/pelicula/asi-es-la-vida. Accessed May 31, 2016.

Del Barrio Mendoza, M. del C. "Versiones y Revisiones cinematográficas de un mito clásico: las *Medeas* de Pasolini, Dassin, von Trier y Ripstein (1969–2000)." *Espacio, Tiempo y Forma, Serie II, Historia Antigua*, vol. 24, 2011, 651–70.

DiQuinzio, P. *The Impossibility of Motherhood*. Routledge, 1999.

Esterrich, C. "Para desbaratar a mamá: el último cine de Arturo Ripstein y Paz Alicia Garciadiego." http://www.hamalweb.com.ar/hamal/pdf/mexico/para-desbaratar-a-mama.pdf, 2010. Accessed October 31, 2016.

Eusching, C. *Granddaughter of the Sun: A Study of Euripides' Medea*. Brill, 2007.

Flores, D., S. Carlini, and R. Elizalde Robles, "Arturo Ripstein y su cine surrealista." https://palabrasdispersas.wordpress.com/2008/09/08/arturo-ripstein-y-su-cine-surrealista, 2008. Accessed May 21, 2015.

Fresneda, I. "Así es la Vida: la Medea de Arturo Ripstein. Violencia Simbólica y Estereotipos de Género en el Cine." *Comunicación y Medios*, vol. 30, 2014, 54–71.

---

72 Fresneda (2014), 59–60.

Garrido Bigorra, M. T. "Las trazas de otros lenguajes. Una aproximación a *Así es la Vida . . .*, de Arturo Ripstein." *Archivos de la Filmoteca*, vol. 72, 2013, 161–75.

Gorostiza, J. *Arturo Ripstein*. Las Palmas de Gran Canaria. *Cuadernos de Filmoteca Canaria*, 2002.

Graf, F. "Medea, the Enchantress from Afar: Remarks on a Well-known Myth." In J. Clauss and S. Iles Johnston, ed., *Medea*. Princeton UP, 1997, pp. 21–43.

Guastella, G. "*Virgo, Coniunx, Mater.* The Wrath of Seneca's *Medea.*" *Classical Antiquity*, vol. 20 no. 2, 2001, 197–220.

Hall, E., F. Macintosh, and O. Taplin. *Medea in Performance 1500–2000.* Legenda, 2000.

Henry, D., and B. Walker. "Loss of Identity: Medea superest? A Study of Seneca's *Medea.*" *Classical Philology*, vol. 62 no. 3, 1967, 169–81.

Henry, R. "Medea and Dido." *Classical Review*, vol. 44, 1930, 97–108.

Joseph, S., and M. Johnson. "'An Orchid in the Land of Technology': Narrative and Representation in Lars Von Trier's *Medea.*" *Arethusa*, vol. 41 no. 1, 2008, 113–32.

MacKinnon, K. *Greek Tragedy into Film*. Fairleigh Dickinson UP, 1986.

Martin, R. "Medée, d'Euripide à Sénèque." In *Analyses & Réflexions sur Sénèque Médée: l'humain et l'inhumain*. Ellipses, 1997, pp. 34–38.

Nikoloutsos, K., ed. *Ancient Greek Women in Film*. Oxford UP, 2013.

———. "Cubanizing Greek Drama. *José Triana's* Medea in the Mirror *(1960).*" In K. Bosher, F. Macintosh, J. McConnell, and P. Rankine, ed., *The Oxford Handbook of Greek Drama in the Americas*. Oxford UP, 2015, pp. 333–58.

Nussbaum, M. "Serpents in the Soul: A Reading of Seneca's *Medea.*" In J. J. Claus and S. Iles Johnston, ed., *Medea: Essays on Medea in Myth, Literature, Philosophy, and Art*. Princeton UP, 1997, pp. 219–249.

Ormand, K. "Medea's Exotic Text in *Jason and the Argonauts* (1963)." In K. Nikoloutsos, ed., *Ancient Greek Women in Film*. Oxford UP, 2013, pp. 75–94.

Paranaguá, P. A. *Arturo Ripstein. La Espiral de la Identidad*. Madrid. Cátedra, 1997.

Rodríguez, M.S. and Sinardet, E. "Du choeur antique aux Mariachis: *Así es la vida* (2000) d' Arturo Ripstein." Les modèles et leur circulation en Amérique Latine: 9° Colloque international du CRICCAL, Paris, 4-5-6 novembre 2004, Université de la Sorbonne no. 2006.

Sham, M. *Now Playing. Studying Classical Mythology through Film*. Oxford UP. 2014

Schwartz, D. Review of *Such is Life*. 2001, http://www.imdb.com/reviews/295 /29568.html. Accessed May 31, 2016

Shapiro, S. "Pasolini's *Medea*: A Twentieth Century Tragedy." In K. Nikoloutsos, ed., *Ancient Greek Women in Film*. Oxford UP, 2013, pp. 95–116.

Tola, E. *Lucio Anneo Seneca, Medea*. Editorial Las Cuarenta, 2014.

Tovar Paz, F. "*Medea* de Séneca en *Así es la vida* (2000), filme de Arturo Ripstein." *Revista de Estudios Latinos (RELat)*, vol. 2, 2002, 169–95.

Treggiari, S. *Roman Marriage: Iusti Coniuges from the Time of Cicero to the Time of Ulpian*. Oxford UP, 1991.

DISCUSSION QUESTIONS FOR PART III

1. Does *Pan's Labyrinth* have a satisfactory outcome? Would Ofelia's life have been better if she had conformed to the Captain's orders and wishes for her?

2. Do you think a subplot of the sort seen concerning the kingdom of Bezmorra adds something important to the myth of *Pan's Labyrinth*? Why?

3. Classical myth provides other female characters who act independently and refuse male power, such as Clytemnestra. How can we connect Medea and Julia with her?

4. Iphigenia, a young Greek tragic heroine, is unfairly sacrificed for a cause many consider unjust. Can we draw links between her and Ofelia?

5. *Pan's Labyrinth* came out in 2006. Can you draw connections between the film and other current wars and struggles (even local) against oppression?

6. What do we imagine Julia's life might be like after she kills her children? Would this correspond with Medea's life after Corinth? Are we even supposed to think about a life afterward for her?

7. How are *Such Is Life* and *Pan's Labyrinth* like dreams, and what is the connection between dreams and myth?

8. How are the forest in *Pan's Labyrinth* and the tenement in *Such Is Life* like characters in themselves?

9. Motherhood is an important theme in both these movies. How is fatherhood also an important theme?

10. We can see Ofelia as a heroine in *Pan's Labyrinth*. Can we think of Julia in any way as a heroine? Why or why not?

IV

COMING OF AGE IN THE NEW MILLENNIUM

HARRY POTTER AND THE CHAMBER OF SECRETS (2002)
THE HUNGER GAMES (2011)
PERCY JACKSON AND THE OLYMPIANS: THE LIGHTNING THIEF (2010)

fact influence our interpretations of the films. However, our concern is with the cinematic elaboration of the various myths these movies showcase and not necessarily with whether they are good or bad adaptations of the novels.

In a way, every heroic adventure, from Odysseus' to Jason's is a coming-of-age journey, even when the characters are not adolescents. Figuratively, confronting mythical monsters and vanquishing enemies is what we all must do in life to define ourselves as adults. Some myths, however, seem particularly adept to showing this process. Perseus fighting Medusa and her defeat are both present in Harry and Percy, boys who must vanquish the threatening divine female with paralyzing gaze. The legacy of Theseus fighting the Minotaur appears in *The Hunger Games* and in *Percy Jackson*, as emblems of a young person's struggle to suppress one's animal side. Harry slays a Basilisk as well as a vampiric projection of past and future evils. The *katabasis* motif (descent to the underworld) is prominent in all three of our movies, where the hero/heroine must metaphorically go down into a dangerous sort of netherworld, either to rescue a loved one (Percy and Harry) or to confront the nightmare dangers the higher powers impose on them (Katniss). This is a dangerous trip, and the myth of Orpheus describes a failed attempt, as he is not able to rescue his Eurydice. And, as in most coming-of-age adventures, there is an implicit quest for knowledge after an initial desire not to see. Thus Harry is a bit like Oedipus, who is ignorant at the beginning but must learn the truth. Percy's quest for knowledge is embodied in the search for the thunderbolt. Sadly, Katniss knows too well from the start the cruelty she will find at the Games.

These magical children, who grow up orphans or with an absent parent, gradually discover their histories and considerable potentials, labor for others, and, so to speak, save their world. But to do this they must bestride two realities and exist in a double universe. Harry lives partly in modern England, in suburban Surrey, with the Dursleys; Percy is a New York boy who must enter the world of Olympian gods and demigods and yet simultaneously deal with millennial American realities; Katniss lives in a future America, renamed Panem, in the poor District 12 she calls home, but she is transported to the rather surreal Capitol, where everything is fantastically made up. After undergoing difficult perils and finding a sort of consort, our three heroes will achieve both maturity and heroism, as well as benefit their communities.

CHAPTER 8

GAZE, KNOWLEDGE, SNAKES, AND RIDDLES

Harry Potter and The Chamber of Secrets as Foundation Myth

Avert your eyes or you will get petrified—or die. Those terrifying yellow eyes are lurking around every corner. If you are a Hogwarts student this year, this is what you have to contend with. Uncanny events are taking place at the school; a cat, a ghost, and various students are found immobilized, as if turned to stone. Harry is hearing strange voices, and creepy notes are written in blood on the walls. It is the Basilisk serpent, we'll learn, which threatens to harm and destroy.

This beginning may not seem too Classical, but the borrowings from Greek mythology in J. K. Rowling's Harry Potter series are countless.[2] Beginning with Latin or Latinized spells (petrificus totalus!) to names such as Albus, Severus, Lucius, and Hermione, classical echoes are patent. There are mythological allusions in names like Minerva McGonagall, the clever transfiguration professor; Pomona Sprout, the eccentric herbology teacher; and Argus Filch, the school's grumpy caretaker. Actual mythological characters such as the centaurs and Fluffy, the three-headed watch dog (alluding to Cerberus), abound in the Wizarding World. But beyond these scattered and obvious references, the plot reveals numerous classical themes.

The second movie of the series, *Harry Potter and the Chamber of Secrets* (hereafter, *Chamber of Secrets*) was an instant hit and a great commercial success, breaking various box office records. Reviews were overall very positive, and the film was nominated for international awards (BAFTA and Saturn Awards), especially in the technical departments. It is also the only film in the series whose narrative drive is Harry's confrontation with an actual mythological monster—which doubles here, of course, for his archenemy Lord Voldemort—with the

---

2   See Mills (2009), Hirsch (2008), Colbert (2008), and Dickerson and O'Hara (2006).

HARRY POTTER AND THE CHAMBER OF SECRETS (2002)

Terrible events are happening at Hogwarts this year: students are petrified and strange notes are written in blood on the walls. We learn that a thousand years ago, Slytherin, one of the founders of the school, created a deadly monster with a petrifying and murdering gaze, the Basilisk. Now the memory of Tom Riddle (young Voldemort) is controlling the beast, has possessed Ginny Weasley, and finally has her, half-dead, trapped in the Chamber of Secrets. Harry and his friends must find its entrance, go down to this subterranean space, rescue Ginny, and destroy both the serpent and Tom Riddle's diary—of course, with a bit of help from Fawkes, Dumbledore's Phoenix.

aid of another creature from Classical myth, the Phoenix.[3] This film's events are central to the entire epic and for the ultimate triumph of good versus evil. Our chapter deals with three specific mythological themes: an underlying struggle that recalls the confrontation between Titans and Olympians; the *katabasis* motif, or descent to the underworld; and how Harry's heroic journey and overall career echoes elements of the myths of Perseus especially, but also Oedipus and Cadmus, heroes who are central players in major foundation/restoration myths, each of them having his own quest, engagement with history (past, present, and future), and problematic destiny.

GODS, TITANS, AND GIANTS

Is religion absent in the *Harry Potter* series? Are even the mentions of Christmas and Easter perfunctory and devoid of any sacred content? Is this an anti-Christian work, Satanic, encouraging witchcraft? Or is it actually a Christian allegory, Narnia-style? Critics have been divided.[4]

These debates also arose regarding *The Lord of the Rings*, a substantial influence on the Harry Potter series. Although our focus is on mythological elements, the Judeo-Christian war between Satan and God has many similarities to the battle between Olympians and Titans. As discussed in our introductory chapter, such primordial struggles are found in Greco-Roman accounts of the early beginnings and initial ordering of the cosmos, a confrontation of unruly primal forces against the more orderly and humane power of the Olympian gods, seen in the Titanomachy and Gigantomachy. This confrontation is restaged in many of our films (*Clash/Wrath*, *Immortals*, *Percy Jackson*, *The Hunger Games*) and in many productions of the new millennium. We will see these creation and conflict themes in *Chamber of Secrets*.

Chamber of Secrets is critical for the *Harry Potter* series, for it reveals the mythic and flawed origins of Hogwarts, faults connected to wizardry's dark

---

3   See Gibbons (2005).
4   Blake (2002), 94ff.

KEY TERMS

Katabasis: a mythical descent to the Underworld
Mudblood "dirty blood," a form of pejorative and quasi-racist way of referring to wizards with no magical parents in the Harry Potter series
Oedipus complex: the psychological terms describing the love of a young man/boy for his mother
Foundation myth: a myth that explains the origins of a city, era, or new world.

---

aspects, embodied by the dormant serpent about to be unleashed. The film's imagery builds on myths that underscore the problematic struggles between the Divine and the Titanic side of human beings[5] and the complexities of foundational myths, for which the foundations of Tiryns and Thebes and their heroes, Perseus, Cadmus, and Oedipus, furnish models. Although in the Titanomachy and Gigantomachy the primal, chaotic forces were suppressed by the Olympians, it is imagined that the threat of their insurrection (literally from their prison under the earth) remains. Commonly, creation narratives introduce some flaw to explain current problems, such as the Temptation of Eve, Cain slaying Abel, Romulus killing Remus, the Battle between the Judeo-Christian God and Satan, and so forth. Thus the murder of Laius, for example, leads to the plague at Thebes. Further, many foundation myths involve the killing of a snake (symbol of ancient, material powers), as occurs in Babylonian Marduk's killing of Tiamat, and the snakes slain in Thebes and Delphi; there is a less drastic version at Athens regarding the snake baby Erichthonius.

We learn that a serpentlike monster, the Basilisk, created by a founder of Hogwarts, Salazar Slytherin, a thousand years ago, has been roaming through the school's pipes and paralyzing and killing various individuals. The underground chamber where it dwelled has been opened and thus Harry, aided by his comrades, must descend to this dreadful place, kill it, and rescue Ginny Weasley, whom the Basilisk and Tom Riddle have taken away. For a thousand years, then, the threatening forces present at the school's foundation have been waiting, only to reemerge fifty years ago, and now again at the turn of the millennium, the giant snake is arising out of its underground chamber, as the mythical Titans or Giants might do. Another primordial throwback, a faction of the Wizarding World, now strives to impose Slytherin's bigoted vision of "the true wizard"; and *Chamber of Secrets* foregrounds important battles against the hatred and discrimination these forces entail.

---

5   These themes are more openly addressed in Riordan's series *Percy Jackson* and subsequently *Heroes of Olympus.*

SERPENTS, BEGINNINGS, AND DEADLY GAZES

Salazar Slytherin's intentions were, through magic, to create and hide the enormous serpent in a secret chamber under the school so that one day it would be liberated and purge the school of "Mudbloods," what Tom Riddle calls "Slytherin's noble work." Though the other three founders adhered to an orderly, tolerant, and inclusive set of communal laws, Slytherin extolled a form of hatred and segregation, a more chaotic and primitive type of racist thinking, views that forced him to leave the school.[6] From the perspective of an American reader, all this sadly resonates, as in *O Brother*, with the myth of "real Americans," exclusively WASP and dangerously retrograde, who always want to revive "old traditional" ways. It is a sort of thinking still vivid in 2016, as this book is written. But the movie presents the contradictions often inherent in this belief. Tom Riddle, aka Voldemort, is proven to be the true heir of Salazar Slytherin, because he successfully opens the chamber; but Tom's father was nonmagical, which makes the son a half-blood, exactly the sort of wizard Slytherin despised. Further, as Hagrid says as he comforts Hermione, now, more than a thousand years after Slytherin, everybody has some Muggle in their lineage. Hence this notion of a "pureblood wizard" is a myth in the negative sense of the term.[7]

The legacy of Slytherin resembles those mythical Titanic forces, buried but not dead, that infect the school and the magical world in the form of his (problematic) true heirs: Voldemort; the memory of his young self, Tom Riddle; and the wizards and creatures that adhere to or are instruments of his cause, such as the Malfoys, Bellatrix, the rest of the Death Eaters, and of course creatures like the Basilisk and Nagini. There is a whole parallel world of dark magic found at the film's beginning, when Harry, by mistake, lands in Knockturn Alley, where he curiously finds Hagrid, a somewhat liminal character himself. But, Harry Potter is also a hero who rights old wrongs, discovering the innocence of Hagrid and who really killed Moaning Myrtle, as well as rescuing his future wife.

Snake imagery is pervasive and central in the Harry Potter series.[8] Think for instance of the anaphoric onomatopoeia found in the founder's very name (also names like Severus Snape and Draco Malfoy) and in traits of Voldemort. Indeed, Voldemort is a Parseltongue, able to talk to snakes, and so is Harry, a gift observed in the first movie, when he communicates with a Python at the London Zoo and helps her escape. Yet this skill does not entirely manifest itself

---

6   Morgenstern (Nov. 15, 2002) in his *Wall Street Journal* review talks about an evil that "is redolent, at least for adults, of Nazi-era eugenics."

7   Compare Pope Francis's recent words to a divided U.S. Congress in a message of tolerance and inclusion: "We, the people of this continent, are not fearful of foreigners, because most of us were once foreigners." Sep. 24, 2015. See full speech transcript at https://www.washingtonpost.com/local/social-issues/transcript-pope-franciss-speech-to-congress/2015/09/24/6d7d7ac8-62bf-11e5-8e9e-dce8a2a2a679_story.html. Accessed June 1, 2016.

8   Berman (2008). A valuable study of the snake in Classical myth is still Fontenrose (1959).

Harry Potter and the Chamber of Secrets (2002) Based on the novel by J. K. Rowling Warner Bros. Pictures	
Director: **Screenplay:** **Cast:**	Chris Columbus Steve Kloves Daniel Radcliffe (Harry Potter), Rupert Grint (Ron Weasley), Emma Watson (Hermione Granger), Bonnie Wright (Ginny Weasley), Kenneth Branagh (Lockhardt), Robbie Coltrane (Hagrid), Alan Rickman (Snape), Maggie Smith (McGonagall), Richard Harris (Dumbledore), Tom Riddle (Christian Coulson)

clearly until the second film, when he talks to a snake, produced, poignantly, by "Draco" Malfoy's wand (the spell he uses is "Serpensortia!") in a practice duel at the school. Harry persuades it to retreat and cease her attack.

The symbol of the house of Slytherin is a serpent, and Voldemort belonged to this house. His close companion is a gigantic snake named Nagini (Indian for snake), which later becomes one of his horcruxes, where Voldemort has hidden part of his soul. This quest for immortality is another important mythical theme, especially important for the last two movies, where possessing the Deathly Hallows is equivalent with being "master of death."[9] Finally, his very symbol, which also marks out his followers the Death Eaters (a name that may also indicate the desire to surpass death—or is it that they feed, vampirelike, on other people's death, as Tom Riddle does with Ginny?), has a viper intertwined with a skull.

The word *Basilisk* is of Greek origin, from *basileus* "king," especially a foreign one, and *Basiliskos*, "little king or tyrant," and was seen by various ancient authors as the king of snakes, perhaps also because of a crown-shaped crest on its head, an association with royalty confirmed in Egypt by Horapollo, *Hieroglyphica* (ca. 450 CE): "This the Egyptians call *Ouraion*, but the Greeks a *Basilisk*. They make this [snake] of gold and put it on the [heads of the] gods" (1.1).[10] Another influence is the Egyptian boa, which also advances raising its front and head and which can apparently kill without biting by spitting venom. From this fact probably arose the notion that the Basilisk can kill from a distance through his powerful gaze. In antiquity it is seen as a marvel of nature, but in the Middle Ages and beyond it becomes a fantastic monster.[11] Our earliest evidence for this name and creature comes indeed from ancient Rome. In his *Natural History*, Pliny the Elder tells us:

---

9 Note that by deciding to destroy the Elder Wand at the very end of the series, Harry chooses mortality (unlike Voldemort, who had basically wished to be a god), a choice faced by Classical heroes like Odysseus.

10 Boas (1993), 43. For the Basilisk as king, see also Lucan, *Pharsalia* 9.724–26.

11 For a good overview of the Basilisk, see Huey (2005), who gets her evidence mostly from Cirlot (1962) and Jobes (1962).

The Basilisk serpent also has the same power. It is a native of the province of Cyrenaica, not more than 12 inches long, and adorned with a bright white marking on the head like a sort of diadem. It routs all snakes with its hiss, and does not move its body forward in manifold coils like other snakes but advancing with its middle raised high. It kills bushes not only by its touch but also by its breath, scorches up grass and bursts rocks. . . . Yet to a creature so marvelous as this—indeed kings have often wished to see a specimen when safely dead—the venom of weasels is fatal: so fixed is the decree of nature that nothing shall be without its match" (8.33).[12]

Pliny does not mention the Basilisk's deadly gaze, but implies that it kills from a distance with its breath. Heliodorus (*Aethiopica* 3.8) alludes to the Basilisk's gaze who "with its breath alone and its glance completely withers and injures the one encountering it."[13] The Basilisk has a prolific afterlife in authors like Isidore of Seville, the Venerable Bede, Albertus Magnus, Geoffrey Chaucer and Leonardo Da Vinci. And so we come to J. K. Rowling, in a small book called *Fantastic Beasts and Where to Find Them*,[14] meant as a companion to *Harry Potter* that students of Hogwarts are supposed to read (it even has handwritten notes by Ron, Harry, and Hermione on the sides), under the pseudonym Newt Scamander explains: "The Basilisk is a brilliant green serpent that may reach up to fifty feet in length. The male has a scarlet plume upon its head. It has exceptionally venomous fangs but its most dangerous means of attack is the gaze of its large yellow eyes. Anyone looking directly into these will suffer instant death."[15] "Scamander" mentions that the Basilisk is not natural; the first one was created by a Greek dark wizard named Herpo. It is on this description that the celluloid Basilisk is fashioned.

Now, the serpent is a complex symbol, taken in some ways for the powerful and female earth, as it slithers on the ground, and it invokes as well dangerous female sexuality. But snakes also serve as phallic symbols, as the tempting male who seduces the feeble female and thus unchains disaster for the world, as in the Hebrew Bible. Serpents are symbols of both life and fertility in their capacity to regenerate and shed their skin, and Harry and Ron see a massive skin the Basilisk has left behind as they enter the chamber. At the same time their poison and deadly bite imply death, though their circularity may allude to the cycle of life and death that human beings are subject to.[16] All these aspects of

---

12 Rackham's 1940 translation.

13 See Ammianus Marcelinus (Yonge trans.), *History* 28.1.41, "He was indeed harmful from a distance, like Basilisk serpents"; and mentions of the snake in the Greek version of the *Old Testament* (Isa. 59:5 and Jer. 8:17) and Claudius Aelian's *On the Nature of Animals* 3.31 (2nd century CE). For an interesting modern account, see Borges (1970).

14 A highly awaited forthcoming movie released in November 2016, directed by David Yates and written by J. K. Rowling, shares the name of this book.

15 Rowling (Scamander, 2001), 3–4.

16 Berman (2008), 45–46. The shedded skin symbolizes the "process of death and rebirth"; Grynbaum (2001), 30.

the vipers, and also dragons, since the distinction between snakes and dragons is late and in myth they are kindred creatures, will be present in *Harry Potter*.

Our Basilisk also exists as a fulfillment of an ancient curse, like the plague of Thebes that arises from the curse of Laius' murder. Tom Riddle resembles Clytemnestra's ghost in Aeschylus' *Eumenides*, a malevolent force arising from a past deed that strives to destroy the living. Both Perseus and Cadmus will become kings, and in both foundation stories serpent monsters are killed: Perseus must defeat Medusa, and Cadmus kills the dragon. Here killing a king-serpent and transferring its powers to himself (in the form of the fangs and the sword) will be crucial to Harry's development as hero. Further, the Basilisk is also an alter ego for Voldemort, who, as Grimes recognizes, "represents the evil king in the archetypal heroic tale."[17] In this sense, the whole Harry Potter series will be the struggle for a new beginning after freeing Hogwarts, and himself, of dark forces. Human beings have divine and Titanic aspects, and Harry has been infected when part of Voldemort lodged itself in him as he tried to murder him. The struggle through eight films will then be for Harry to expunge his Titan side, so to speak, which can only be achieved in receiving the final killing curse from Voldemort. The final battle will show the triumph of the divine powers and of Harry, who will become a sort of refounder of the school, after it is literally destroyed. Hogwarts will have to be rebuilt from the rubble after two snakes are dead and Voldemort, who actually has some snaky features, is shattered as well.

PERSEUS, HARRY, MYCENAE, AND MEDUSA'S GAZE

THE HERO AND HIS ATTRIBUTES

Harry Potter's heroic career accords with Classical models, with the Greek Perseus especially, Zeus' son, whose career we described in our chapter on *Clash of the Titans*.[18] Perseus becomes the founder of Mycenae, a center of early Greek civilization. But before founding the city, he must also, like Harry, defeat a snake-headed primeval monster that represents dangerous forces. Medusa herself is directly linked to the Basilisk in ancient sources. Lucan, (*Pharsalia* 9.619ff.) recounts that Perseus flew over Libya with the severed head of Medusa, and the blood that dripped from it onto the earth produced the Basilisk.[19] The Medusa connection possibly explains its powerful gaze and the fact that it can be overcome by mirrors.[20] Interestingly, both in the novel and the movie, the monster is referred to only as "it," since a red crest is never mentioned and never appears; still, the consensus is that the Basilisk in *Chamber of Secrets* is a female serpent, complicating the idea that the Basilisk is a "king." In a later version, Medusa was originally

---

17 Grimes (2002), 113.
18 For a good study of folktale elements in Harry Potter, see Lacoss (2002).
19 Cf. also Apollonius Rhodius, *Argonautica* 4.1513–1517, and Ovid, *Met.* 4.
20 See *Gesta Romanorum*, 139, p. 244; translation by Swan (1894).

a woman, arrogantly beautiful, whom Poseidon raped in Athena's temple; as a punishment the goddess turned her into a monster whose head was covered in snakes and whose glance, when looked on directly, caused petrifaction. We have here a punishment for hubris about one's beauty and sexual excesses by a chaste goddess (oddly, as often in Ovid's rapes, it is the victim who suffers the punishment); the snakes symbolize threatening, unrestrained female sexuality.

Here, J. K. Rowling merges the mythical Basilisk, whose eye contact with victims is deadly, with the Medusa, whose lethal gaze petrifies.[21] In the myth Perseus decapitates her by looking at her image in his mirrored shield; in Rowling's version the petrifying power of Medusa's gaze is combined with the lethal vision of the Basilisk, not known specifically for petrifaction. First Mrs. Norris, Filch's cat, sees it in a puddle, Colin Creevey through the lens of a camera, Justin Finch-Fletchley through Nearly Headless Nick. Penelope Clearwater and Hermione Granger see it in Penelope's mirror.[22] All are paralyzed. Nearly Headless Nick looks at it directly, but since he was already dead, he can only be petrified. Just as Perseus must deprive the monstrous Gorgon of her agency and independence (although her eyes retain their petrifying power) and appropriate that power for himself, Harry must also destroy the monster, although it is Fawkes the Phoenix who blinds it, saving Harry. And just as Perseus uses Medusa's head to eliminate various enemies, Harry uses the Basilisk's fang to destroy Tom Riddle as Harry stabs Tom's diary with it.

Harry Potter recalls Perseus as a hero who must confront the dire forces that threaten or are even trying to reemerge, as with Perseus' Gorgons.[23] The tales of Harry and Perseus both present a young man gifted in flight and having a powerful sword, an object that makes one invisible. In both stories one finds the defeat of an ugly, snaky chthonic monster and the recreation of civilization, once these forces have been crushed. He also rescues his Andromeda, for by killing the Basilisk he mimics Perseus defeating the snaky Cetus, sent to eat Andromeda. Like Perseus, Harry is a good, fast flyer, as evident during

---

21 The connections with Medusa and the mirror that petrified Hermione were already noted by Yeo (2004), 6; and Grynbaum (2001), 29. Another Medusa-like figure in the Harry Potter film is the dark witch Bellatrix Lestrange, brilliantly performed by Helena Bonham Carter, with her flowing black tresses, bulging eyes, and horrifying laughter. Up to the fifth film she also has been living in the dark prison of Azkaban, but is released. The mere people also have Gorgon-like features, with large eyes and hairlike tentacles in their heads. They live in a liminal place, at the bottom of the Black Lake, but their alliances are rather unclear.

22 Yeo (2004), 6, also notes how Hermione, usually a powerful female, is paralyzed for about a third of the book here. She is unable to move, speak, act, or see, and the petrifaction with a mirror in her hand, in which she probably reflects herself, stereotypes women and shows them in a passive stance; thus Yeo sees an antifeminist, rather traditional, nuance to the story. For discussions of gender in *Harry Potter*, see Yeo (2004), Kellner (2010), Dressang (2002), Pugh and Wallace (2006), Bell (2012), Berndt (2011), and Berberich (2011).

23 Two important studies of the hero in Harry Potter, including Campbell's models, are Pharr (2002) and Grimes (2002).

Quidditch matches.[24] Later in the fourth movie, when he must face the challenge of dragons and is asked to find his strengths, he says, "I can fly. I mean, I'm a fair flyer." Harry flies with the aid of a magical object, his broomstick, given to him by Professor Minerva McGonagall, another magical helper. Perseus, although a demigod, was lent a pair of winged sandals or *talaria*, made of pure and indestructible gold by Hephaestus, the ones Hermes himself wears, allowing him to fly over Africa and Asia. These are divine gifts to near-divine heroes, which will help them reach liminal places to fight Titanic forces. Harry Potter's killing of the Basilisk recalls also Apollo killing Python to secure a place for his Delphic shrine, defeating a primal earth power.

But Harry has other forms of flight as well; the first time he leaves the Muggle world he flies with Hagrid on his motorcycle toward the Leaky Cauldron, a hidden London pub, hangout of wizards and magicals, emphasizing even more his sky connection. In *The Prisoner of Azkaban*, he flies the Hippogriff Buckbeak, and later in *The Order of Phoenix* he and his friends fly on the backs of Threstrals (horses with wings that look rather skeletal and have reptilelike faces) all the way to London. Perseus in later traditions flies a magical beast, Pegasus, as does Perseus in *Clash of the Titans*. *Harry Potter and the Chamber of Secrets* begins and ends with flight. Harry is first rescued from the Dursleys' house by the Weasley brothers on his birthday in a flying car, which by the way, also has an "invisibility booster," an ordinary Muggle car that has been magically altered by Mr. Weasley. After missing the train at King's Cross, Ron and Harry fly this car to the school, and interestingly, it is this car that rescues them from being eaten by the spiders in the Forbidden Forest. At the end of Harry's adventure in the Chamber of Secrets, Dumbledore's Phoenix Fawkes, another significant magical helper, comes to Harry's aid, first blinding the Basilisk and then bringing the Sorting Hat with the sword of Gryffindor hidden in it, with which he kills the monster. Finally Harry, Ron, Ginny, and the memory-wiped Lockhart escape the Chamber of Secrets by holding on to Fawkes's tail, as it flies back up to Hogwarts. Perseus and Harry are beings of the world above, celestial youths in a way. Perseus is a son of the sky god Zeus, and Harry, significantly, wears a mark of a thunderbolt in his forehead. In their heroic journey, however, they must both confront the forces of the world below, of Tartarus of sorts, and journey to the dark underworld and come back triumphant and thus attain true heroism.[25]

---

24 Harry is a "seeker" in this game, and as Pharr (2002), 56, observes, this is a symbolic title since "the Potter heritage calls Harry to become a seeker whose episodic quests for knowledge are unified by the grand themes of self-discovery and selfless valor."

25 Pharr (2002), 58, compares "going away to school" to the initiation journey of the archetypal hero (like Odysseus and Achilles going to Troy, or Frodo leaving the Shire): "Hogwarts is the nexus between the agony of their past and the uncertainty of their future—and not even its headmaster knows all its secrets."

In the myth of Perseus, Hades lends a helm or cap of invisibility so that he can approach Medusa unseen. The "cap of Hades" was originally given to him as a gift by the Cyclopes after the defeat of the Titans (see Apollodorus *Library* 1.2.1, first century BCE), again connecting this magical object with the destruction of the primal, chaotic forces. Its conflation with the cap of invisibility may be a later tradition. Perseus uses it to escape Medusa's Gorgon sisters Sthenno and Euryale.[26] This perhaps becomes the inspiration for Harry's "invisibility cloak," given to him by Dumbledore on his first Christmas at Hogwarts and said to have belonged to Harry's father, James. But Harry's invisibility cloak is a family heirloom; the Potters are descended from the younger Peverell brother, Ignotus, who once asked Death to give him something by means of which he could hide from Death itself, and Death took his own cloak and gave it to him, as we learn in *Deathly Hallows I*, and indeed, the cloak, together with the Elder Wand and the Resurrection Stone, will be part of the Deathly Hallows. The cloak thus points to an unusual heritage in our millennial hero, another element of the archetype.[27] In *Chamber of Secrets* Harry and Ron use it to escape the school and hide at Hagrid's hut, where they learn that both Hagrid and Dumbledore are being removed from Hogwarts, Hagrid being sent to Azkaban prison. From there they follow the spiders all the way to the Forbidden Forest, a realm of death of sorts, which, yet again, they manage to survive.

Finally, both our heroes have magical swords. In one version of the myth, when Perseus visits the Hesperides, they give him an adamantine sword from Zeus that can cut through any material. Harry is given the sword of Gryffindor, which will kill two monstrous snakes, first the Basilisk, and later on in the eighth film Neville will kill Nagini, the last horcrux (the sword also destroys the locket and the ring and comes to Harry, via Snape's *patronus* in the woods in *Deathly Hallows I*). This is then the sword of a primal founder, who through it still battles evil. After killing Medusa, Perseus later uses the Gorgon's head against his enemies, which is eventually given in thanks to Athena, as Harry uses the Basilisk's fang. And let us not forget, from a gender perspective, the phallic connotations of swords. Thus his killing of the Basilisk and Nagini with this weapon implies the triumph of masculine power over threatening, male or female, forces.

THE HERO'S DESCENT

Both Perseus and Harry must travel to a liminal place to destroy a monster. Medusa lives in an obscure lair at the world's edge, near the river Ocean, past Atlas. Perseus in some versions is helped by the Titan Atlas, exiled to the world's rim, as Harry is helped by the massive Hagrid, who has been unjustly exiled from

---

26 In the *Percy Jackson* series, Annabeth wears a baseball cap that doubles as a cap of invisibility, given to her by her mother, Athena, and Luke Castellan steals winged sandals from Hermes.
27 See Pharr (2002), 55–56.

Hogwarts proper. Many representations of Medusa (*Clash of the Titans,* for example) place her in an underworld, and sometimes the hero must cross the Styx to get to her. Hogwarts's deep foundations represent this subterranean world, the destination of the descent that heroes like Orpheus, Heracles, and Aeneas must undergo. And there they will find the Basilisk, who seems an infernal creature, the three-pronged crest of which may appear an inversion of the trinity.[28] The activity of ghosts, such as Moaning Myrtle and Nearly Headless Nick, also give Harry's adventures an underworldly aspect. In the novel, Ron, Hermione, and Harry attend a ghost party in which Nearly Headless Nick celebrates his "death day," and thus they miss the school's Halloween party, a holiday that helps humans negotiate their fear of death.

Even the Forbidden Forest, which Ron and Harry visit to talk to the giant spider, an "achromantula," Aragog, can be seen as a liminal space where the hero is tested and gains a boon, but must also escape. During Harry's mental voyage to the past through interaction with Tom Riddle's diary, we see that Aragog is kept in a box, and then escapes and finds refuge in the Forbidden Forest, where he appears to reproduce and form a huge colony (he calls the other spiders his "sons and daughters"). Again, the forces of chaos must be kept imprisoned, or at least relegated to a Tartarus-like space in a Dark Wood. Hagrid straddles two worlds, rather like a mythical wild man, and is at ease with the powers of civilization and the unruly (and sometimes hostile) aspects of the natural world.[29] Thus Aragog tells Harry and Ron that even though he does not allow the other spiders to attack Hagrid, he "cannot deny them fresh meat when it wanders so willingly into [their] midst." Aragog is king of this displaced Tartarus. Like other underworld characters (the ghosts Odysseus encounters, Aeneas' father), Aragog gives Harry important information.

Chamber of Secrets resembles a detective story where clues must be followed and criminals uncovered. Harry and Ron, after prolonged investigations, finally find the entrance to the Chamber of Secrets, in the girls' bathroom under a sink marked with a snake. Water flows there and Moaning Myrtle often floods it; Harry literally walks in the water. All of these provide symbols of feminine power and rebirth, but they also furnish a sort of crossing of the Styx. In creation stories male gods must ally with female powers to control or destroy them. Putting the entrance of the chamber in the nearly waterlogged girls' bathroom suggests symbolically his control of female power, a power over the waters of life and death. Water is connected with birthing in myth (note Moses and Romulus and Remus left in river streams as infants). First-year students alone are transported to Hogwarts in boats across the lake when they first enter the school, and Harry descends to the Black Lake (another form of

---

28 See Huey (2005), 67, with references to Cirlot (1962), 21–22; and Diel (1952).

29 For archetypes in the novels and Hagrid as the archetype of the wild man specifically, see Evans (2003), 12. For the archetypal journal in Harry Potter, see Boll (2011).

FIGURE 8.1 The face of Slytherin, from which the Basilisk will emerge.

underworld) to rescue a loved one in *Goblet of Fire*.[30] The fact that they cross a body of water to get to Hogwarts gives the school itself an underworld and initiatory dimension.

To open the first gateway to the Chamber, Harry must speak in Parseltongue before the snake-marked sink. Then Harry, Ron, and Lockhart must thrust themselves through an enormous downward pipe and descend toward Hogwarts's "underworld."[31] They immediately find there an enormous serpent skin; the viper imagery continues as they approach a door decorated with eight carved snakes, and Harry must again use Parseltongue to open it. They continue through a corridor lined by statues of serpents, at the end of which stands a massive sculpture with the face of, presumably, Slytherin (indeed he looks like a Titan, a great natural force, with long, flowing, almost snakelike hair), out of which the Basilisk will eventually emerge (Fig. 8.1).

This underworld is notably marked in the movie by the presence of large pipes and plumbing, being wet and flooded all over, though the novel insists more on its slimy, muddy quality (Lockhart says in the film: "It's really quite filthy down here") pointing more directly to the fluids of sexuality and the transitions to adulthood, as seen in Ofelia's muddy adventure with the frog and the tree in *Pan's Labyrinth*. As we discussed in the introduction, real or displaced *katabases* tend to begin with some cave or opening in the crust of the earth,[32] seen clearly in *Pan* and here in the hole left by the opening of the sink in the girls' bathroom. We also have a sort of king of the underworld at the underworld's bottom, embodied by Tom Riddle/Slytherin and a woman who needs to be rescued, another common element of the *katabasis* motif. And recall here Persephone being taken away by the king of Death, but also the myth of Orpheus and Eurydice, where Orpheus must descend to Tartarus to rescue his wife, who coincidentally has been killed by the bite of a snake, taken

30 Grimes (2002), 119–20.
31 Yeo (2004), 4, already noted the underworld connotations of the Chamber of Secrets.
32 Holtsmark (2001), 25.

to Death by a snake, so to speak.[33] Orpheus must also confront the king of the Underworld and persuade him with his own personal skill of music, though his rescue of Eurydice is unsuccessful.

But the bedrock Harry walks on suggests also a foundational dimension. Yeo, in her Jungian interpretation of the film as collective dream, sees biblical and patriarchal overtones of the dangerous snake tempting the weak girl and describes the sexual connotations of the chamber and the Chamber of Secrets as the dangerous female.[34]

> We have an innocent young girl, at the age of puberty, writing on the walls in blood. We have Harry and Ron, two adolescent boys trespassing in the bathroom. Harry finally deduces the location of the opening. Once this is seen as a wet opening into the female body, Harry's gesture in the film seems all the more telling: he literally caresses the faucet of the fountain, where he notices an emblem of a serpent. He must whisper in the secret language of serpents, and then falls into the cavern that opens before him. Inside the chamber, it is dark, wet, and ominous. It is dangerous; it is also the home of deep and evil magic that has been held at bay for many years because the chamber had been "sealed." This is the home of the Basilisk, who like Medusa, or the Old Testament cockatrice, can kill with a single malevolent glance.[35]

Of course mythical women who cannot resist temptation appear. Think of Pandora ignoring the prohibition and opening the lid of the jar, thus bringing all evil into the world. Psyche is another example of a girl who ruins everything in her desire to see the face of her husband Eros. Or the Athenian girl Pandrosos, who opens the basket to find the baby Erichthonius who was part snake, thus defying Athena's commands. And this episode of unbarred female curiosity bringing doom is, as in Harry Potter, at the core of a foundation myth, that of Athens.

A DANGEROUS "BOOK OF THE DEAD"

As in *Pan's Labyrinth*, an enchanted book also plays a central role, and books inside books always have metatextual meanings. Ginny Weasley, in her first year at Hogwarts, has been gradually possessed by Tom Riddle through his diary, a magical object from the past (never quite dead) that will bring its sinister creator to the present. There is a whole tradition of women being possessed by

---

33 Holtsmark (2001), passim and 25–26.
34 Mills (2006) proposes another curious interpretation of the snake, as a sort of "solid lump of feces that, Freud claims, is experienced by the child as sexually pleasurable and an indicator of potency in the course of excretion . . . sliding along inside the damp, slimy pipes and emerging in an attempt to destroy its victims" (9). This, Mills argues, is also true for Moaning Myrtle and for Harry, Ron, and Lockhart, when they slide down through the pipes (10–11). And thus the Basilisk may represent a part of ourselves that we reject and want to "expel." See Mills (2006), 10 and 4. On a Lacanian approach to this and the Oedipal struggle, see Seelinger Trites (2001), 476.
35 Yeo (2004), 7.

demonlike males in modern film, and as Kristen Day observes, it has a clear "parallel in the ancient world in the usurpation of women's bodies by deities for the purposes of prophecy."[36] This possession has been seen as symbolically tantamount to rape.[37] There are resemblances between Harry and Tom Riddle, as Harry tells Dumbledore, which, since Ginny has a crush on Harry, makes her seduction even easier. This diary was slipped into Ginny's cauldron at the shop Flourish and Blots in Diagon Alley early by Draco Malfoy's father, Voldemort's agent. From a psychosexual perspective, this is a book that preserves the memory of an evil and seductive man, and it is tellingly placed in a feminine-shaped object, a cauldron.[38]

Yeo sees "a darkly sexual undertone to this relationship," even with overtones of rape and violence.[39] Day further observes how in films where women are possessed by these male demons, "their characterization as more rational and self-possessed serves as a contrast to the vulnerability of women."[40] This controlling poise and stance is seen in Tom Riddle, who does not appear to lose his composure till the very end. Tom's diary is also a horcrux safeguarding part of Voldemort's soul. The diary's destruction by Harry with the Basilisk's poisonous fang is the first step to annihilating the powers of "The Dark Lord." During Odysseus' visit to the Deadlands, the dead must gain life force by drinking the blood of sacrificial victims. Ginny recalls such a victim, for her life force is being drained so that Voldemort can fully manifest himself.

And yet, it is a book that requires interaction from the reader since its pages are blank and only come to life if one actually writes on it. Ginny writes, and the diary writes back; consider how girls today can get into trouble with predatory men through a similar internet mediated interaction. This is also thought-provoking from a reader-response perspective, which sees that the meaning of a text is realized only through the active process of interpretation, indeed, creation of the text.[41] Needless to say, the use of this book and of the "Half-blood Prince's" (aka Snape's) potion book in the sixth film are notably metatextual, pointing at the power and even dangerous influence of texts over potential readers. The diary is also a portal to the past, since Harry literally learns

---

36 Day (2013), 85.
37 For this see Day (2013), passim. In cinema this male possession of the female body by a sort of demon is common in horror movies. Day (2013), 90ff.
38 Recall critical approaches such as those found in Peter Brooks's *Reading for the Plot* (1992), 3–36, which compare the act of reading to making love to the text, thus implying a quasi-sexual relationship between the reader and the writing.
39 Yeo (2004), 5. Note that Riddle feeds on Ginny's soul, as he says, "I grew stronger and stronger on a diet of her deepest fears, her darkest secrets." See the vampire connotations of this as well. For American vampire stories such as found in the *Buffy* TV series as context for Harry Potter, see Blake (2002), 22–23. For Tom Riddle and the vampire archetype in Jungian terms, see Grynbaum (2001), 26–33.
40 Day (2013), 92.
41 See in particular Tompkins (1980).

about the past in a sort of vision quest prompted by reading and writing in the diary, where he gains knowledge about Moaning Myrtle and the fate of the young Hagrid. But passed time prompts forgetfulness. In the movie Professor McGonagall tells the story of the Chamber of Secrets and how the Basilisk was born, but dismisses it as "pure legend." However, the film and books imply that many items adults and authority figures dismiss as "myths" of long ago are very real, and dangerous.

THE DAMSEL IN DISTRESS

Harry is twelve and Ginny eleven, and their future love is only hinted at. Ginny is clearly interested in Harry; she blushes and her eyes widen as Harry arrives at the Borrows home early in the film. Ron immediately comments: "She's been talking about you all summer. A bit annoying really." Controlled by Tom Riddle, Ginny opens the Chamber and releases the Basilisk after writing a message in blood on the walls of the school[42] ("It was me! But I swear, I didn't mean to . . . Riddle made me."[43]), but toward the film's conclusion she is taken away by Riddle and is lying immobile ("cold as ice") in the Chamber. She is alive, but "just barely," when Harry finds her. As noted, many myths require the death of one innocent female. Ginny, like Eve, is a victim of her own curiosity and the deceiving serpent.[44] But, as seen earlier, there are allusions to "archetypal representations of the female body . . . characterized as dangerous and terrifying."[45]

Ginny also evokes Andromeda, chained to a rock, unable to move (Ovid, *Met.* 4.672–75), a sacrificial victim to the sea monster Cetus (note all the water surrounding our Basilisk), which in its turn is by a simile assimilated to a serpent in Ovid (*Met.* 4.715, *draconem*) and which in some versions is indeed a sea serpent and is represented in ancient art with snake features. Harry in *Chamber of Secrets* will have to free all those paralyzed (and worse) by the past and its evils, even his problematic magic helper Dobby (who is made to look a bit like a Roman slave). Perseus sees the endangered Andromeda, kills the monster, and rescues and marries her. Ginny is infatuated with Harry; they become a couple and eventually get married. The novel tells us that the day that Ginny was taken away was "the worst day of Harry's entire life."[46] Harry risks his life,

---

42 On the symbolism of women, blood, and magic, see Yeo (2004), 4: "In a complex web of symbols, the blood becomes a feminine symbol of dangerous power, female puberty initiation . . ." And of course, Ginny is at an age when girls transition into womanhood, precisely through bloodletting.

43 With Yeo (2004), 4, one recalls the Biblical words of Eve: "The Serpent beguiled me, and I ate."

44 Yeo (2004), 1. Yeo sees a patriarchal and "oppressive view of the feminine" (1) in the movie: "I became disturbed by the underlying symbol system, which betrays a deep reliance on old representations of women as connected to evil, dark magic, and traditional roles of passivity and naiveté" (1).

45 Yeo (2004), 4.

46 Rowling (1999), 295. Further, see Adney (2011), 179.

kills a monster, and almost dies himself to save her. It is curious and unfeminist perhaps that Harry chooses this rather weak girl (though she develops into a brave young woman later, albeit a somewhat secondary actor in the plot) to be his wife, perhaps perpetuating patriarchal structures; the relationship between Ron and Hermione seems somewhat inversed, with Hermione the smarter, savvier, and even perhaps braver partner.

We have here a young man who must descend and penetrate into a hidden chamber, symbolic of femininity, its very entrance haunted by the female ghost of Moaning Myrtle, where a female serpent lies. Its defeat, as in the Perseus myth, is a story of sexual awakening and affirmation of heroism and masculinity, the snake as both threatening femininity and a phallic symbol. In Freudian terms, Medusa may represent the female genitals, especially those of the mother as well as the fear of castration.[47] Her conquest reminds the boy of his own successful manhood in the process of coming of age, and thus *Chamber of Secrets*, just like the myth of Perseus, is figuratively a tale of first love, sexual awakening, and coming of age. One could add in contrast that Orpheus's trip to the Underworld to rescue his beloved is unsuccessful since not only does he lose his bride a second time due to curiosity and disobedience by looking back when he was told not to, but also, figuratively, he does not defeat the snake/ Death which had taken her away. Unlike Perseus and Harry, in whose figures we can read a successful transition to manhood, Orpheus may be read as an example of failed masculinity.

THEBES AND THE SINS OF THE PAST

VISION AND DARKNESS

As we mentioned, the killing of the chthonic monster, the serpent, is also central in foundation stories. Perseus destroys Medusa, and snake figures appear as well in the foundation myths of Athens, with its first king Cecrops who was even half-snake. They must kill two serpents, the Basilisk and Nagini, before Hogwarts can be refounded at the end of the saga, though these two monsters are simple phases of one major Titanic force, Lord Voldemort, who has creepy serpentine traits himself.

The legends of Greek Thebes provide an example of a city whose flawed beginnings infect the lives of its later rulers, as is also the case with Hogwarts. Europa, daughter of Tyre's King Agenor, was loved and abducted by Zeus. Her three brothers are sent to find her. One brother, Cadmus, following Apollo's oracle, comes to Thebes. Some of his men, sent out as scouts, are killed by a dragon sacred to Ares, god of war. Cadmus then slaughters the dragon, but as it dies the beast curses him and declares Cadmus himself will become a snake. Nevertheless, Cadmus sows the dragon's teeth in the soil, and from them arise

---

47   See Freud (1955 [1922]).

the primordial Thebans. And indeed, both Cadmus and his wife Harmonia are turned into snakes at the end of their lives. In most versions Harmonia is a daughter of Ares, to whom the serpent belongs. Cadmus killed a sacred being, and this is instrumental for the cursed future of Thebes, which will see such abominable tragedies as the mother Agave killing her son Pentheus, whom Dionysius destroys by exposing his desire to see what is forbidden, that is, his mother's supposed sexuality; and later the parricide and incest committed by Oedipus; or Ino jumping into the sea with her child. But the killing of a serpent is central to this foundation story, as it will be in the refounding of Hogwarts. Later in Thebes, Oedipus too must confront a monster and solve the Sphinx's riddle to save Thebes and, in a way, give it a new beginning, yet again a flawed one, being built on father murder and unspeakable love.

It is not the physical gaze of the Sphinx at play in the Oedipus myth, but rather her intellectual sharpness. Harry and Oedipus, or rather Harry and the Oedipus complex, have connections.[48] In Sophocles' *Oedipus Tyrannus*, Oedipus is also haunted by the all-too-human, and heroic, desire to know and to change the baleful destiny ordained by Apollo's oracle. Oedipus can maintain his physical vision as long as he stays in the "dark" regarding past events, yet once he knows, the knowledge is blinding, and he gouges out the eyes that presented to him a deceiving reality. In *Chamber of Secrets*, Harry has been in the dark for years, without knowing the truth about who his parents really were or how they died. Enlightenment will gradually come as he grows as man and hero. But Harry's desire to know is weak at the beginning of our movie, perhaps implied by his broken glasses and the fact that Hermione repairs them in Diagon Alley with the Latin spell *"Oculos reparo"* ("I repair your eyes"). Later in the series Hermione with her intellectual acuteness will certainly teach Harry to "see more." Oddly enough, Moaning Myrtle wears the same round glasses as Harry and reveals that the last thing she saw before dying was "a pair of great big yellow eyes" by one of the sinks. Unlike Harry, she could not overcome the power of the Basilisk's gaze.

Just as in the myth, we find here another type of vision, the mind's sight, the prophetic vision of the future. The most renowned seer in Classical mythology is the Theban Tiresias, who predicts that one day Oedipus will murder his father and marry his mother. In the Perseus myth, an oracle given to Acrisius predicts he will be killed by the son of his daughter. We shall later discover that a prophecy about Harry has been stored in the Ministry of Magic, but we do not obtain details until the fifth movie; it predicts that Harry must kill Voldemort or die himself.[49] In *Chamber of Secrets* the house-elf Dobby assumes a prophetic role. Dobby knows things, in this case because he is a slave to the Malfoys,

---

48 Noel-Smith (2001) in particular.

49 Grimes (2002), 92, discusses the various father and grandfather figures in the book and sees both Dumbledore and Voldemort as contrasting grandfather figures.

but also because he is clever, and later in the book it is said that "Dobby has known it for months"[50] about the Basilisk and the Chamber of Secrets. Dobby unexpectedly jumps out of Harry's closet, with his "bulging green eyes the size of tennis balls"[51] (in the book the first thing of Dobby that Harry sees are a pair of big eyes bulging in the hedge[52]), to give him a prophesy of sorts, warning him not to return to Hogwarts.

And as oracles often do, Dobby does not speak plainly. His words must be interpreted: "Dobby had to come. . . . There is a plot, a plot to make most terrible things happen . . . Ooo . . . er . . . can't say . . . argh. . . ." But he never quite says what will happen clearly. Although he doesn't tell Harry why, this warning is based on certain knowledge that the Basilisk is there and that Voldemort is trying to rise again. Later in the film the elf appears in the middle of the night while Harry is in the hospital, perhaps hinting at an oracular dream. He speaks cryptically then as well: "Terrible things are about to happen at Hogwarts . . . now that history is to repeat itself." Dobby's vision is underscored by the prominence of his eyes; the Oedipus myth presents seeing as a metaphor for knowledge, knowledge that heroes do not always want to see and hear. The themes of sight and blindness are important for Oedipus, and for *Chamber of Secrets* too. As we mentioned, the snake is a symbol of sexual knowledge, but also of mystic knowledge, and both forms can petrify. Like Oedipus, who wants to find his real parents and "return home" in a way, Harry tells Dobby that he must return to Hogwarts because that is his home, and indeed that is where his parents met; it is the place that links him to them, just as Thebes is for Oedipus. It is curious and somewhat oracular that Dobby speaks only in the third person, and thus his speech is tinted with the mysterious formality of prophecies. In the Oedipus story there are questions as to who is loyal to Thebes, and whether Tiresias is a false prophet; Harry Potter must sort these questions out too, and he finds a "false prophet" in Lockhart and true prophets in Hagrid and Dobby, who even dies for him at the end of *Deathly Hallows I*.

Oedipus solves the riddle of the monstrous Sphinx, and thus saves Thebes.[53] The name Tom Riddle thematizes how Harry Potter is constantly asked to solve riddles dealing with past, present, and future; and visualization of the reordering of letters in the film to transform "Tom Marvolo Riddle" into "I am Lord Voldemort" certainly point in this direction. Significantly Tom Riddle says, "Voldemort is my past, present, and future." The plague of Thebes is the result of the untended evils of the past now infecting the present; the Basilisk and Tom Riddle are both holdovers from the past, a past of intolerance and even racist tendencies, which are polluting the present, as we see when Malfoy uses

---

50 Rowling (1999), 16.
51 Rowling (1999), 12.
52 Rowling (1999), 8.
53 A true Sphinx appears in *Harry Potter and the Goblet of Fire* (but not in the movie), is rather crucial for the plot, and poses a riddle to Harry in the labyrinth.

the term Mudblood to offend Hermione. Harry Potter must gather knowledge and solve riddles, but the question (still open in this movie) is whether he can survive the truths he finds. Voldemort is called "he who must not be named"—again, representing a past that cannot be confronted—and Harry must, somewhat like Tiresias and Oedipus, uncover and speak the uncomfortable truths of the past.

THE HERO AS EXILE AND SURVIVOR

Oedipus, Perseus, and Harry are exiles. Perseus is first cast out of his homeland by his grandfather and then is sent by King Polydectes far away to get Medusa's head. He flies around and finds adventures in various geographical locations but returns to Argos only briefly, the place he cannot inherit after accidentally (at least in most versions) killing his grandfather. Then he moves on to become king of Mycenae or Tiryns. Oedipus, who, like Harry, should have died, survives as an exile, living with adoptive parents, the king and queen of Corinth, and then, attempting to escape fate, unknowingly returns home, with terrible consequences. Harry is also an exile, living in a foreign world, removed from his true home where he lived as a baby with James and Lily, and placed in this unfriendly and narrow-minded suburban Muggle home, relegated to "the cupboard under the stairs," the epitome of exile. His uncle Dudley literally puts bars in Harry's windows to imprison him. But he eventually returns to his true home, the Wizarding World of Hogwarts (note the insistence throughout the books that "Hogwarts is my home"). Indeed, at the beginning of the movie Harry is shown looking at a picture of his mother and father and then at a photo of him with his new friends, who indeed have become his new family.

Oedipus and Harry are thus, as the oracle reveals, each embedded in a foreordained plan. They must deal with the consequences of ancient (and often evil actions) that involve issues of identity surrounding themselves and their community. Harry, Perseus, and Oedipus, all magical children of special parents, have been nearly killed but survive, and must learn about their past and regain their proper identity, in the process bringing various benefits to their people. Harry is called "the boy who lived," recalling Perseus, who was tossed into the ocean in a chest to die, and Oedipus, who also should have died but did not. Oedipus, like Harry Potter, must learn really what happened in the past, who his parents were, what their fates were, and his own identity. As Holtsmark reveals, both for the mythical motif of katabasis and for its symbolic recreations in modern film, "katabasis seems inevitably to entail at some level a search for identity. The journey is in some central, irreducible way a journey of self-discovery, a quest for a lost self."[54] The Chamber of Secrets contains not only a monster, but secrets from that past that influence the present. The foundations

---

54 Holtsmark (2001), 26.

and future of Thebes and Hogwarts are likewise problematic, and the story of Perseus connects to foundation myths of Mycenae. Harry must learn how he belongs at Hogwarts, as Oedipus learns painfully how he "belongs" at Thebes.

OEDIPAL COMPLEXITIES

Oedipus in fact goes on to murder his father, Laius, and marry his mother, Jocasta, in whom he will engender, incestuously, four children. Perseus has an absent father, Zeus, and a close relationship with his mother, Danaë. Not only do we have the physical proximity of mother and child huddled inside the box, but Perseus professes a very strong love for her, to the point of facing sure death in the Medusa Quest to protect her honor, and, remarkably, to protect her from a man who desires her. We see elements of the Oedipus complex in our Harry Potter myth as well. Harry does not kill his father, but just before their murders James tells Lily to go ahead and protect Harry, indicating a deeper connection between mother and son. The profound love of his mother is what finally saves him from Voldemort's curse.[55] And, considering the special importance of the gaze and eyes in the story, the fact, repeated over and over, that Harry has "his mother' eyes" signals this special bond. Plus, his memory of Lily remains idealized while Harry's memory of his father James degrades a bit in the last few movies.[56] And we can note the physical resemblance in the movies between Ginny Weasley, his future wife, and Lily Potter. After Harry has killed the Basilisk and is dying from its venom (Ginny is dying too, since Riddle says that "she is still alive, but only just"), the memory of Tom Riddle tells him, "You'll be with your dear Mudblood mother soon." Then Harry's gaze moves to Ginny, and so does the camera's. This develops the connection between Lily and Ginny further. One wonders if saving Ginny implies the fantasy of bringing the mother back from the dead as well.

Harry will learn that, during Voldemort's failed attempt to murder him, some of his powers, such as speaking with snakes, transferred over to Harry. And in subsequent books he will discover other disturbing truths about his parents. Heroes also often redeem those parents who have been disgraced or deposed, and Harry Potter helps both Hagrid and Dumbledore, who are at the same time father figures, one heavenly, one earthly. In different ways, both Voldemort and Snape become symbolic fathers to Harry, and he has part of all of them in him. Indeed, themes of resurrection are found in the scenes with the mandrakes, which the students learn to plant and grow, and with the Phoenix, a classical animal that provides crucial help to Harry because Harry

---

55 Noel-Smith (2001), 202. Noel-Smith even compares Harry's scar with Oedipus' swollen feet, 203. For a discussion of mother figures to Harry, see Grimes (2002), 114–15. She even sees Lily as a sort of Demeter figure, for whom motherhood is the most important thing.
56 Mills (2006), 8.

FIGURE 8.2 Harry and companions ascend to the upper world.

demonstrates great loyalty to Dumbledore in the Chamber.[57] But also a resurrection occurs for Harry himself, who was fatally wounded with the Basilisk venom, and can be revived solely by the tears of the Phoenix. Note how the Phoenix is the opposite of the Basilisk: the eyes of the Basilisk kill, but the eyes of the Phoenix heal.

Returned from virtual death, Harry will become a savior, or a "Child Redeemer."[58] Note that just like the baby Jesus in swaddling clothes, Harry is also delivered in a bundle by Hagrid to the Dursleys' house at the beginning of the first movie. The baby imagery is intriguing, since Lord Voldemort also appears as a sort of grotesque baby before his "rebirth" at the Riddle House in *Goblet of Fire*. Yet unlike baby Oedipus hung from his feet, Perseus in a box, and Harry bundled up (we recall his image in the barred crib repeated in the films), Voldemort's shriveled-up body is a mixture of life and death, small and unable to walk, like a baby in wait of birth, yet recalling the withered bodies of the old and the dead. And in the end the redeemer will ascend, taking the saved with him out of the bowels of Hell, a concept partially evoked by the image of Fawkes hauling through the air Lockhart, Ron, and Harry, who is holding Ginny, out of the lower world toward the upper world, brightened by a full moon (Fig. 8.2).

HARRY POTTER AND THE NEW MILLENNIUM

At the end Harry learns that to truly destroy Voldemort, he has to sacrifice himself and die, a scene that takes place in the Dark Forest, which is a sort of underworld in the last movie. It is Hagrid again who carries him in his arms, allegedly dead, back to Hogwarts, but in fact he has been reborn after his encounter with death. He will survive even Voldemort's deadly spell, thanks perhaps to the resurrection stone. From this apparent death—he even visits with the ghost of Dumbledore in the afterlife train station—Harry will return, save Hogwarts, and initiate a new era for it, a sort of refounding after apocalypse.

---

57 For a full discussion of the Phoenix, see Huey (2005), 75–78.
58 Yeo (2004), 3. On other Christian aspects of the novels, see Ciaccio (2009), Johnston (2011).

So how does this movie, as part of a series, which foregrounds a foundation myth, form part of the concerns of the new millennium? A new millennium is certainly a new beginning, a sort of rebirth from something that existed before. And yet, unlike the optimistic feelings surrounding the year 1900, with a hope of new technologies that would make life better for humanity, the advent of Y2K was fraught with fearful, quasi-apocalyptic views, a dread of certain chaos to come, symbolized on the surface as a fear that technology would crash and produce pandemonium.[59] But at the same time the 1990s were good years of economic prosperity in America and the West. Yet there is a certain hopelessness coloring the new millennium, with serious environmental concerns and out-of-control population growth that seems to presage the doom of humanity, and a widening income gap, which creates feelings of insecurity and demoralization and fuels all manner of violent bigotry. With the hopeful election of President Obama in particular, racist ideologies have emerged, like Titans thought to be forever chained, and yet seemingly rampantly unhinged again in 2016 as the writing of this book comes to its conclusion. But as with the myths of Oedipus and Perseus, the *Harry Potter* saga brings new hope that the forces of chaos can be contained and crushed, and that a new beginning, a rebirth, is possible. *Harry Potter*, a seminal work of literature and film, spanning the last years of the twentieth century and the first few of the twenty-first, can be read as a foundation myth with the hope of a new world, born out of chaos, where Titans and Giants and other dark forces are defeated and the word can be newly founded.

REFERENCES

Adney, K. "The Influence of Gender in Harry Potter's Heroic (Trans)Formation." In K. Berndt and L. Steveker, ed., *Heroism in the Harry Potter Series*. Ashgate, 2011, pp. 177–92.

Bell, C. *Hermione Granger Saves the World: Essays on the Feminist Heroine of Hogwarts*. McFarland, 2012.

Berberich, C. "Harry Potter and the Idea of the Gentleman as Hero." In K. Berndt and L. Steveker, ed., *Heroism in the Harry Potter Series*. Ashgate, 2011, pp. 141–58.

Berman, L. "Dragons and Serpents in J. K. Rowling's *Harry Potter* Series: Are They Evil?" *Mythlore*, vol. 27 no. 1, 2008, 45–65.

---

59 Blake (2002), 23ff., actually sets the novels in a more positive reshaping of England that he calls "retrolution" and that goes along with the advent of New Labor in the late nineties.

Berndt, K. "Hermione Granger, or, the Vindication of the Rights of Girl." In K. Berndt and L. Steveker, ed., *Heroism in the Harry Potter Series*. Ashgate, 2011, pp. 159–76.

Blake, A. *The Irresistible Rise of Harry Potter*. Verso, 2002.

Boas, G. *The Hieroglyphics of Horapollo*. Princeton UP Reprint edition. 1993.

Boll, J. "Harry Potter's Archetypal Journey." In K. Berndt and L. Steveker, ed., *Heroism in the Harry Potter Series*. Ashgate, 2011, pp. 85–104.

Borges, J. L. *The Book of Imaginary Beings*. Discus Books/Avon, 1970.

Brooks, P. *Reading for the Plot*. Harvard UP, 1992.

Ciaccio, P. "Harry Potter and Christian Theology." In E. Heilman, ed., *Critical Perspectives on Harry Potter*. Routledge, 2009, pp. 33–46.

Cirlot, J. *A Dictionary of Symbols*, tr. J. Sage. Philosophical Library, 1962.

Colbert, D. *The Magical Worlds of Harry Potter*. Berkley, 2008.

Craig, H. *The Critical Merits of Young Adult Literature: Coming of Age*. New York. Routledge, 2014.

Day, K. "Soul Fuck." In M. Cyrino, ed., *Screening Love and Sex in the Ancient World*. Palgrave Macmillan, 2013, pp. 85–98.

Dickerson, M., and D. O'Hara, *From Homer to Harry Potter: A Handbook on Myth and Fantasy*. Brazos Press, 2006.

Diel, P. *Le symbolisme dans la mythologie grecque*. Payot, 1952.

Dressang, E. "Hermione Granger and the Heritage of Gender." In L. A. Whited, ed., *The Ivory Tower and Harry Potter*. University of Missouri Press, 2002, 211–42.

Evans, A. D. "Discovering the Archetypes of *Harry Potter*." Paper presented at the seventeenth West Regional Conference of the International Reading Association (Portland, OR, Mar. 9–11, 2003), http://eric.ed.gov/?id=ED479487, 2003. Accessed May 14, 2016.

Fontenrose, J. *Python: A Study of the Delphic Myth and Its Origins*. Biblio-Moser, 1959.

Freud, S. "Medusa's Head." In vol. XXIV (Indexes and Bibliographies) of the *Standard Edition of the Complete Psychological Works of Sigmund Freud*, tr. J. Strachey, ms. from 1922, published posthumously 1940. Hogarth Press, 1955, pp. 273–74.

Gesta Romanorum; or, Entertaining Moral Stories, tr. C. Swan, W. Hooper, ed. Charles Bell and Sons, 1894.

Gibbons, S. "Death and Rebirth: Harry Potter and the Mythology of the Phoenix." In C. Whitney Halle, ed., *Scholarly Studies in Harry Potter: Applying Academic Methods to a Popular Text*. Edwin Mellen Press, 2005, pp. 85–105.

Grimes, K. "Harry Potter: Fairy Tale Prince, Real Boy, and Archetypal Hero." In L. Whited, ed., *The Ivory Tower and Harry Potter: Perspectives on a Literary Phenomenon*. University of Missouri Press, 2002, pp. 89–122.

Grynbaum, G. "The Secrets of Harry Potter." *San Francisco Jung Institute Library Journal*, vol. 19 no. 4, 2001, 17–48.

Hirsch, A.-C. *Names and Their Underlying Mythology in J. K. Rowling's Harry Potter Novels*. GRIN Verlag, 2008.

Holtsmark, E. "The *Katabasis* Theme in Modern Cinema." In M. Winkler, ed., *Classical Myth and Culture in the Cinema*. Oxford UP, 2001, pp. 23–50.

Huey, P. "A Basilisk, a Phoenix and a Philosopher's Stone: Harry Potter's Myths and Legends." In C. Whitney Halle, ed., *Scholarly Studies in Harry Potter: Applying Academic Methods to a Popular Text*. Edwin Mellen Press, 2005, pp. 65–83.

Jobes, G. *Dictionary of Mythology, Folklore and Symbols*. Scarecrow Press, 1962.

———. "Harry Potter, Eucatastrophe, and Christian Hope." *Logos: A Journal of Catholic Thought & Culture*, vol. 14 no. 1, 2011, 66–90.

Kellner, R. "J. K. Rowling's Ambivalence Towards Feminism: House Elves—Women in Disguise—in the 'Harry Potter' Books." *Midwest Quarterly*, vol. 51 no. 4, 2010, 267–385.

Lacoss, J. "Of Magicals and Muggles: Reversals and Revulsions at Hogwarts." In L. Whited, ed., *The Ivory Tower and Harry Potter: Perspectives on a Literary Phenomenon*. University of Missouri Press, 2002, pp. 67–88.

Mills, A. "Archetypes and the Unconscious in *Harry Potter* and Diana Wynne Jones's *Fire and Hemlock* and *Dogsbody*." In G. L. Anatol, ed., *Reading Harry Potter: Critical Essays*. Praeger, 2003, pp. 3–14.

———. "Harry Potter and the Horrors of the *Oresteia*." In E. Heilman, ed., *Critical Perspectives on Harry Potter*. Routledge, 2009, pp. 243–55.

———. "Harry Potter and the Terrors of the Toilet." *Children's Literature in Education*, vol. 37 no. 1, 2006, 1–13.

Morgenstern, J. "'Chamber of Secrets' Is More Sure of Its Magic." Review. *Wall Street Journal*. http://www.wsj.com/articles/SB1037313235288318468.html, Nov. 15, 2002. Accessed Aug. 5, 2013.

Noel-Smith, K.. "Harry Potter's Oedipal Issues." *Psychoanalytic Studies*, vol. 3 no. 2, 2001, 199–207.

Pharr, M. "In Medias Res: Harry Potter as Hero-in-Progress." In L. Whited, ed., *The Ivory Tower and Harry Potter: Perspectives on a Literary Phenomenon*. University of Missouri Press, 2002, pp. 53–66.

Pugh, T., and D. Wallace. "Heteronormative Heroism and Queering the School Story in J. K. Rowling's Harry Potter Series." *Children's Literature Association Quarterly*, vol. 31 no. 3, 2006, 260–81.

Rackham, H., trans. *Pliny: Natural History*. Volume III, Books 8-11. Harvard UP, 1940

Rowling, J. K. *Harry Potter and the Chamber of Secrets*. Scholastic Press, 1999.

——— (Newt Scamander). *Fantastic Beasts and Where to Find Them*. Scholastic Press, 2001.

Seelinger Trites, R. "The Harry Potter Novels as a Test Case for Adolescent Literature." *Style*, vol. 35 no. 3, 2001, 472–85.

Tompkins, J. P. *Reader-Response Criticism: From Formalism to Post-Structuralism.* Johns Hopkins UP, 1980.

Yeo, M. *"Harry Potter and the Chamber of Secrets*: Feminist Interpretations/Jungian Dreams." *Studies in Media & Information Literacy Education*, vol. 4 no. 1, 2004, 1–10.

Yonge, C. *Ammianus Marcellinus: The Complete Works*, tr. from 1962. Delphi Classics, 2016.

CHAPTER 9

ARROWS, ROOTS, BREAD, AND SONG

Mythical Aspects of *The Hunger Games*

May the odds be *ever* in your favor!

(Suzanne Collins, *The Hunger Games*, 2008, 19)

The Selective Service System of the United States conducted a lottery (on Dec. 1, 1969) to decide which young men would have to serve in the Vietnam War, with, as we know, a good chance that they might perish there. Your luck indeed depended on a random number. To those boys, we could have easily said the night before, "Good luck" and "May the odds be *ever* in your favor." A fictional ceremony in the future dystopian country of Panem decides which boys and girls from the Districts will participate in a spectacular survival contest, the Hunger Games, a fight to the death, where only one contestant remains alive and is crowned. Serving one's country in a war with possibly lofty ideals is, of course, not the same as being picked to participate in a live, televised, deadly fight. Yet the agony for young people to have their lives ruled by a government lottery is similar; and dystopian fiction is often a distorted, extreme version of things that happen or could happen in reality.

Classical themes abound in *The Hunger Games*.[1] For example, the sacrifice of youths for the common good and atonement of a past fault in the myth of Theseus and the Athenian youth condemned to fight the Minotaur in Crete as penance for the Athenians' killing the son of King Minos are essential plot elements.[2]

---

1 As shown by various conference presentations and articles: Mills (2015), Buggy (2013), Schofield (2013), OKell (2013), Graf (2015), and Makins (2015). Profuse discussions on the web debate Classical references from Shakespeare's *Julius Caesar* to the meanings of the name Panem.

2 Peksoy (2014), 84, even sees a connection with the episode of Polyphemus in *Odyssey* 9.

279

PLOT SUMMARY

In the future and dystopian country of Panem, a ruined version of the United States, every year, to atone for a previous rebellion, one girl and one boy from each impoverished district are picked to participate in the Hunger Games, a survival contest to the death, where only one tribute comes out alive. Taking the place of her younger sister Prim, Katniss Everdeen volunteers and, together with her old schoolmate Peeta Mellark, travels to the Capitol. The games are brutal, with much killing, violence, and sacrifice. Yet with a clever ruse, Peeta and Katniss manage to defy the Gamemakers and both win and survive, thus unleashing a gradual revolt against the Capitol's oppressive authority.

The gladiatorial spectacles in the historic Roman arena are revived in the Roman names of powerful characters in Panem's Capitol.[3] Youth sacrifice is turned into a reality show, a world created for television such as *The Truman Show* (1998) and the ever-more-lurid examples of reality TV.[4] In myth, many quests seem virtual suicide missions, for example, Jason sent against the fire-breathing bulls and the sown men to obtain the Golden Fleece, connecting to the idea of violence and combat to the death as spectacle. Perseus' pursuit of Medusa's head is likewise extraordinarily dangerous. Reviews of *The Hunger Games* were mostly positive (average of 67 in Metacritic and 85 for Rotten Tomatoes), though there was some comment on th director's unsuitability for this film and the lack of a sense of hunger and urgency compared to the novel.

Our chapter deals with the first movie of the four in the franchise. We begin with the film's reworking of the mythical primordial battle after which the world is precariously set in order, until the crushed population rebels and overthrows President Snow. A young heroine emerges, and thus we explore the construction of Katniss Everdeen as embodying aspects of the divine female, in particular those expounded by the figure of the Virgin Huntress and the Great Goddess. Katniss becomes a divine hero figure, and her character and journey serve to foreground issues of coming of age and femininity, and the themes of nature and culture.

---

3   Gladiatorial images are seen in the short introductory film at the Reaping and in Cato's parade costume. See also Mills (2015), 57 and 60.

4   Bartlett (2012). Suzanne Collins (2012) states that the idea for the books came to her as she was channel-flipping between reality TV and actual images of the Iraq War. Scholastic interview: http://www.scholastic.com/thehungergames/media/qanda.pdf. Accessed May 17, 2016. For the links of *The Hunger Games* with reality TV and the idea of surveillance, see Dubrovsky and Ryalls (2014), 395–99. Other recognized connections are William Golding's *Lord of the Flies* (1954) and the science fiction novel *Enders Game* (1985), as well as the Japanese cult movie *Battle Royale* (2000) and popular dystopian movies like *Death Race 2000* (1975, with remakes in 2008, 2010, and 2013), *Rollerball* (1975, 2002), and *Running Man* (1987). More recently, consider also the dystopian *Divergent* saga by Veronica Roth with its four movies (2014, 2015, 2016, and forthcoming).

PRIMEVAL BATTLES AND THEIR AFTERMATH

As we discussed regarding Harry Potter, most creation myths begin with conflict, usually a confrontation between two forces, commonly between generations for succession of power after which a precarious order is established, one usually more lawless and demonic than the other. Classical mythology presents this primordial confrontation in the Titanomachy and Gigantomachy, where the upper forces of light and enlightenment defeat the primitive powers and trap them in gloomy Tartarus (bright Zeus against his savage father Kronos). *The Hunger Games* reworks this myth in a fairly displaced fashion.

Unlike the book, the 2012 movie (a very close adaptation; Collins herself was deeply involved in script writing) begins with a televised interview between an almost clownish Caesar Flickerman, the "master of ceremonies," and Seneca Crane (note the reference to the Stoic philosopher and enabler of Nero, a great lover of the games), the head Gamemaker, emphasizing the film's self-reflectiveness concerning the damage and atrocities that provocative use of cameras can cause. We soon view a ceremony called "the Reaping," which includes a short introductory video explaining how, many years ago, there was an uprising of the thirteen districts of a country called Panem against the Capitol. They were defeated, but as penance and a memorial every year, each district must send one girl and one boy between twelve and eighteen as "tribute" to take part in the Hunger Games. In the movie (as opposed to the book), there is greater emphasis on the "media coverage of the Games that is prominent only in latter parts of the novel."[5] The Hunger Games is a show that also supports a "government's fabricated narrative of Panem's past"[6] (what exactly happened in the war of seventy-five years ago is unclear), and the film provides only a mediated and mediatized government version of those past events. Thus spectacle promotes a form of political amnesia and a substitute for the actual past.[7] It is clear, however, that a primeval battle took place a long time ago, involving a previous generation, and it divided the country in two. Yet, unlike what happens in other creation narratives, here the Titans are the victors.

KEY TERMS

Dystopian fiction: fiction that shows a negative, quasi-apocalyptic, and degraded view of a society's future; the glum pictures are the opposite of utopias and contrary to the author's ideology

Kourotrophos: quality of ancient gods of protecting the young

Great Goddess: all-encompassing Mother/Earth deity concerned centrally with fertility, in various ancient mythologies

---

5   Fitzgerald and Hayward (2015), 77.

6   Koenig (2012), 43.

7   Koenig (2012), 42 and 46.

Another primeval battle is also at play in *The Hunger Games*, similar to one contained in the myth of Theseus. As we discussed previously in our *Immortals* chapter, King Minos, a child of Zeus, sent his own son to Athens; evil Athenians, jealous because he beat them at their games, murdered him, committing the original sin, so to speak, of killing a quasi-divine guest. So Minos conquers Athens and forces the city to regularly atone for its sins by sending seven youths and seven maidens every nine years to be eaten by the Minotaur. Thus Athenian youth must pay for the crimes of a previous generation, just as in the Hunger Games the tributes are payment for an earlier generation's uprising.[8] But the son (Theseus) of another god, Poseidon, is willing to sacrifice himself to overcome the power of an oppressive king who also wishes to control fertility. The Labyrinth and the inhuman power of the Minotaur inside it are symbolic of the mysterious power Minos has, which of course relates to the realities of Minoan civilization, a seafaring people who used bulls in their worship, which almost certainly was concerned with fertility.

Theseus embodies the mythic archetype of "the young man gets the goddess" and is able to destroy that power and capture the powers of fertility. The way Ariadne, also a vegetation deity in origin associated with the Cretan Britomartis, is contained at Knossos, a mistress of the Labyrinth, recalls to some extent how Kronos and older male gods try to control the Earth's powers of fertility. In *The Hunger Games*, a goddesslike heroine connected to the fertility of the land raises up from the underworld of her poor and dark district, is thrown into a highly technologically built labyrinthlike arena—let's recall that the master inventor and builder Daedalus designed the Cretan maze— where she must fight hybrid beasts, among other things, and she dethrones the powers of the evil upper world of light. One notes a somewhat similar inversion in *Pan's Labyrinth*, where the ideal kingdom of Bezmorra is located in a dim netherworld, while the upper world is controlled by the demonic Fascist Captain Vidal, whom the heroine opposes.

The Hunger Games (2012) Based on Suzanne Collins's 2008 novel Lionsgate	
Director: **Script:** **Cast:**	Gary Ross Suzanne Collins and Billy Ray Jennifer Lawrence (Katniss), Josh Hutcherson (Peeta), Liam Hemsworth (Gale), Elizabeth Banks (Effie), Stanley Tucci (Caesar), Wes Bentley (Seneca), Woody Harrelson (Haymitch), Toby Jones (Claudius), Lenny Kravitz (Cinna), Donald Sutherland (President Snow), Amandla Stenberg (Rue)

8 Koenig (2012), 41, sees the shadow of the Vietnam War in this. Young men were drafted to fight a war rooted in a previous generation's fears, and they had no clear sense of what and why they were fighting.

A WORLD OF CONTRASTS

As with *Pan's Labyrinth*, we have an inverted world, where the Capitol is presented with bright colors and the dazzling lights of TV spectacle,[9] yet its characters and actors, including President Snow, symbolize the forces of inhumanity and cruelty, with no regard for life.[10] There is a sort of perverted Olympus, with its high buildings accessed by speedy elevators, into which the tributes oddly arrive by high-speed train,[11] in some ways recalling the upper world of Fritz Lang's classic *Metropolis* (1927), a vision of the triumph of the forces of capitalist oppression, with the workers relegated to the underworld; *Metropolis* now possess mythic status, and thus its myth of conflict furnishes a subtext for our movie and indeed for the third film of *The Hunger Games* series, where the oppressed and thought-to-be-annihilated District 13 hides in a subterranean complex.

Yet, as in *Pan's Labyrinth*, this upper world is controlled by violent and totalitarian forces. The districts, and in particular District 12, are impoverished and often desolate areas; consider the dull sepia palette and gloomy images of District 12 before the Reaping, which contrasts with the Capitol's colorful extravagance and artificiality, for example Effie's bright pink in opposition to the drabness of District 12's children, or the bright clothes of the crowds that Katniss and Peeta see from the train. The people of the Capitol recall the denizens of Petronius' *Satyricon* and Fellini's 1969 filmic version of that story. This luxury is tied to a civic religion of conspicuous and mindless consumption, found for instance in the excessive preening and styling of the tributes in preparation for the camera and to make them a "product" their mentors can sell.[12] This is of course an allusion to capitalism[13] and commodification (and a Marxist reading of the film is indeed very possible), as seen earlier in the movie *Rollerball* (1975 and 2002), where corporations rule the world. We note an unnatural embellishment of the body, especially in those involved in the visual spectacle, such as the Gamemakers and TV presenters Cesar and Claudius—only just a notch above what we see in some celebrities today.[14]

Amid this spectacle, as in Ridley Scott's *Gladiator* (2000), the games, both ancient and modern, appear as a social drug that keeps the masses distracted

---

9   On the Capitol's focus on the visual, see Koenig (2012), 42.

10 Discussions of hyperreality and the centrality of TV are, as with *Such Is Life*, also part of critical debates on *The Hunger Games*. See Shau Ming Tan (2013), 66–67.

11 Note the elevators that lead to "Olympus" in the six-hundredth floor of the Empire State Building in the *Percy Jackson* series.

12 Bartlett (2012), 10. On the queer gender implications, see Mitchell (2012), 135. On Katniss's gender neutrality, see DeaVault (2012), 192–93, and in contrast see Dubrofsky and Ryalls (2014) on Katniss as performing conventional white femininity. For the commodification of children's bodies in the tributes, see Shau Ming Tan (2013), 60. On body alterations and their political meaning in *The Hunger Games*, see Koenig (2012), 42–43, and as adornment, especially in Effie, see Dubrofsky and Ryalls (2004), 405.

13 See Fisher (2012), 28.

14 And dystopia is only a "distorting mirror of our own [world]." Fisher (2012), 27.

and unwilling to stand up for their freedom, a frequent criticism of today's mass media.[15] In *O Brother, Where Art Thou?* technology is partially associated with progress; but there are also problems with "mass communicating." President Snow is a master of media to a degree that Governor Pappy in *O Brother* could never dream of. Interestingly, though, the master image fabricator and enhancer, Katniss's stylist Cinna (recalling perhaps Lucius Cornelius Cinna, a four-time Roman consul), is the most genuine and sensitive man around and is dressed in simple dark colors, possibly in solidarity with the "underworld" of the districts, without any artificial hairdo or clothing. The first thing he says to her, instead of "congratulations," is "I'm sorry that this happened to you." He returns a bit of humanity to the horror show these cruel "gods" have created.

District 12 has underworldly features, underscored also by the importance of mining and the activities that occur beneath the earth. It is notably backward in culture and civilization; people barter for food in the Hob in an informal, rather rudimentary economy based on extracting raw materials from the earth, instead of having more developed industrialized labor. Since Katniss's father dies in a mine explosion, mining can denote violence to Mother Earth, giving the narrative an environmental undertone, as discussed later. The underworldly nature of the rebellious districts is highlighted in the trilogy's last book, where, as we mentioned, District 13 (which the Capitol thought to be annihilated) is revealed as surviving and prospering underground and preparing a revolution (somewhat like the human underworld in the *Matrix* series (1999, 2003, and 2003). In contrast to the carnivalesque horrors of the Capitol, this "underworld" presents the values of family, love, hard work, and community, as opposed to the Capitol, where we see little of family life, friendship, or affection.

This horrific upper world is governed by President Coriolanus Snow, whose white, flowing hair makes him fatherly-looking, maybe a bit Zeus-like, but instead a conniving and evil monarch, more like C. S. Lewis's White Witch in *The Lion, the Witch, and the Wardrobe* or the statue of Slytherin in *Harry Potter and the Chamber of Secrets*. The name Coriolanus is highly ironic, since it evokes, probably via Shakespeare, a rather controversial general of Roman legend who, like President Snow, tried to keep the state together in the face of rebellion. In Greek myth, Zeus is often fearful of revolt and threats to his power, as in the case of Prometheus, a Titan himself, who challenges his authority and aids mankind, using Zeus' fears of mating with a goddess who is destined to have a son who might surpass his father! The conflict of generations and their consequences is always hovering in the background. So Zeus is a complex figure himself in ancient myth, with bright and dark aspects, a partial inversion found in President Snow, fitting the manner in which the whole architecture and technologization of the Capitol and its people presents a perverted Olympus. Note the way the film shows how the Gamemakers control the arena's actions almost like gods,

---

15 Cf. the Canadian documentary *Manufacturing Consent: Noam Chomsky and the Media* (1992), and Postman (1985).

often arbitrarily orchestrating the movements of the tributes as the Olympians in Homeric epic steer events on the battlefields of Troy, or very much like a modern reality show, sending, for example, almost miraculous cures to their favorites in an arbitrary fashion.

MAIDENHOOD AND THE HUNT

Katniss Everdeen reprises various aspects of the Divine female, from the Maiden Huntress Mistress of the Wild (Artemis in Greco-Roman myth) to the Protective Great Mother and the Nourishing Earth (Demeter, Gaia, Cybele, and others) as well as the daughter/girl and her transition to womanhood (the Persephone type). The Great Goddess presides over life, transformation, and death. Katniss gives life, heals life, and helps transform life—and she takes it away. The archetype of the maiden huntress, so pervasive in Greek and Roman myth, is epitomized in Artemis, but extended also to her nymph companions and other heroic maidens such as the Amazons, Camilla, and Atalanta.[16] She is a hunter, a quality that defines her and gives her identity. But she is also a reluctant maiden who rejects marriage and motherhood (at this point), and a marvelous child who must learn her powers and help others.[17]

Homer defines Artemis as *potnia theron* ("mistress of animals"; *Iliad* 21.470), whose attributes are a bow and arrow and who takes pleasure in the woods and the hunt above all things.[18] Accordingly, our Katniss seems to be happy only when in the woods: "Gale says I never smile except in the woods" (Collins, 2008, 6), and she feels a strong longing to run into the woods and escape (25).[19] The Classical Artemis is a desirable virgin, yet one who will never be impregnated, while in the imagination always ripe and potentially fertile. Katniss reassumes the bow and arrow as hunting weapons, as means of sustenance, and the mythical figure of the huntress is well displayed visually in the film.

In Greek classical art the archetypal huntress Artemis is usually portrayed as a maiden, young, tall, slim, and fit, dressed in a girl's short skirt with hunting boots, a quiver, and a bow.[20] Perhaps one of the most famous and representative artworks that define our view of Artemis/Diana is one known as the Diana of Versailles, a Roman copy of a Greek original now found at the Louvre (Fig. 9.1).

---

16 On the Amazon in film, see Graf (2015), and further the TV image of *Xena the Warrior Princess*, with its many feminist critical responses. See also Pomeroy (2008), 113–14. For a well-received study on Amazons, see Mayor (2014). Mention of the connection between Artemis and Katniss is made as well by Mills (2015), 60.
17 See Pharr (2012).
18 See also the *Homeric Hymn to Artemis* 1–2 and Callimachus' *Hymn* 3, *To Artemis*. For aspects of Artemis see also Fischer-Hansen and Poulsen (2009).
19 See also Mitchell (2012), 130–31.
20 Sometimes Artemis appears with a hunting spear, as in her worship in Aetolia. See also Ovid, *Metamorphosis* 3.166.

FIGURE 9.1 Classical Diana the Huntress.

FIGURE 9.2 Katniss hunting.

Mythical hunters need companions. Like Artemis and her cohort of hunting nymphs, or like the mythical Amazons, Katniss lives only with women (her mother and sister). At the film's beginning we see our heroine putting on a leather jacket, wearing boots, her long hair in a braid, and running to the woods, then taking the bow and arrows out of a log and tree. This bow is wooden, handmade, forged by Katniss's father, but the bow and arrows she finds in the Games are metal, implying the inhuman and artificial meaning of the spectacle.[21] Note also, as Despain observes, that her retrieval of the father's weapons is meant to recall the scene in which Theseus lifts the stone and finds his father's sword, which he uses to defeat the Minotaur.[22] As Graf notes, Katniss and her contemporary screen peers Arya Stark (from the *Game of Thrones* TV series, 2011–present), and Princess Merida (in the 2012 Disney movie *Brave*), "actively contravene their society's norms by pursuing their masculine heroic ethos and independence over romance, marriage, needlework, appearance and other traditional feminine pursuits . . . these three girls share the sort of bond with their fathers that is usually reserved for sons, triggering associated social transgressions."[23]

But the maiden with the bow and arrows echoes other Classical heroines; the Roman Camilla comes to mind, as mentioned. Like Katniss, she had a special relationship with her father, who while trying to cross the river, as he was escaping from the Volci, tied her up to a spear and threw it to the other bank, pledging to Diana that Camilla would remain a virgin at her service. She was breastfed by a mare, "And when the infant had set down the first footprints with the soles of her feet, he [her father] armed her palms with a sharp javelin, and hung a bow and quiver from the little one's shoulder" (Vergil, *Aeneid* 11. 573–75). Camilla again incarnates the connections between the maiden huntress and nature, a figure who is one with the woods and hills. Unlike Camilla's

---

21 On gaze, gender, and spectacle in *The Hunger Games*, see Montz (2012).
22 Despain (2012), 70.
23 Graf (2015), 75.

father, the father of Atalanta, another mythical female huntress, abandoned her because he wanted a boy. Rescued and raised by hunters, she remained a virgin devoted to Artemis' service, and even participated in the Calydonian boar hunt.[24] But eventually she leaves the Diana stage, returns to her father, is slowed down through a ruse in a footrace (with Venus' intervention), and ends up marrying Hippomenes.

Yet, the identification of Katniss with Artemis (note the similar sounding names) gains another dimension when she is presented as part of a hunting pair with her friend Gale. It is Gale himself who reminds her that she is a great hunter and that she can win in the Games: "You are stronger than they are. You are. Get to a bow . . . you know how to hunt." Katniss replies, "They are not animals," and Gale retorts, "It's no different, Katniss." Her skills in archery give her the highest score, 11, from the Gamemakers, but also help her in hunting, which is central to the Games, where she slays other competitors, such as the male tribute who throws his spear at Rue, and the brutal Cato, a Career whom, while being eaten alive, she kills for mercy's sake. As Graf accurately asserts, compared to swords or rifles, which are expensive and heavier to wield, the bow and arrow are equalizing weapons for girls: "The bow is the weapon of the commoner. In a contemporary context of democratic uprisings, archery has reappeared predominantly in popular cinematic and television culture as the symbolic equalizer of the one and the 99 percent."[25]

Artemis is a complicated figure in gender terms, and Collins's Katniss challenges gender expectations. Although a maiden, she exhibits obvious masculine traits. And like the goddess Artemis, Katniss evades the traditional gender division of children's books by presenting "a female character who balances traditional masculine qualities such as athleticism, independence, self-sufficiency, and a penchant for violence with traditionally feminine qualities such as idealized physical female beauty and vulnerability."[26] Some think of hunting as a masculine trait,[27] but mythologically speaking, the Huntress Goddess, though problematically so, is notably female; not antifeminine like Athena, but one who presents the seductiveness and potentials of women at a stage when they are on the sexual cusp of readiness for marriage.

Katniss recalls early myths connected with hunting that still have a political and ideological relevance in the United States.[28] Hunting today is undertaken

---

24 Indeed, she is said to have wounded the boar first, although Meleager, who finished it off, then offered the prize to Atalanta, leading to considerable fighting among the male hunters. See Kerényi (1959), 116ff. Note how Atalanta in *Hercules* (2014) is also made an Amazon and archer.

25 Graf (2015), 78.

26 Lem and Hassel (2012), 118. For this see also Henthorne (2012), chap. 2.

27 Lem and Hassel (2012), 122; and DeaVault (2012), 195.

28 The centrality of hunting in the United States as part of the discussion on weapons and the Second Amendment has some resonance here.

with rifles, and seldom to procure food,[29] and archery is generally relegated to being a sport, sometimes viewed as a quaint remainder of arcane times. But Collins's reinvention of the huntress maiden and Gary Ross's cinematic recreation in fact resonate profoundly with modern audiences, especially young ones, and there has been a resurgence of archery both as a sport and in other TV and movie productions following *The Hunger Games*. Paleolithic hunter-gatherers, who hunted animals for survival[30] and used bows and spears, created rituals to appease a divinity, usually thought to be female, responsible for the life cycle of the animals they hunted. This goddess brought life and death to creatures. And thus in later times she is invoked as huntress, supportive of the hunter, as shown so clearly in Euripides' *Hippolytus*.

Members of less-advanced societies today (e.g., the bushmen of the Kalahari) may still use bows and arrows and hunting spears, but Panem, Katniss's country, is a future totalitarian, ruined version of the United States, a "distillation of all our darkest civic nightmares,"[31] where firearms are forbidden and hard to make; thus the use of bow and arrow fits well in a backward (but discontented) locale like District 12.[32] In Greek, Roman, Persian, and many other civilizations, hunting became more a matter of sport (especially for the elite) than survival, and even a substitute for war. Paleolithic hunting bands became in Greek myth (for example) Diana hunting with her nymph cohort. Men also hunted and fought in packs, and just as today, hunting is a pastime that fosters male bonding and (sometimes toxic) masculinity. Yet hunting remains a more nomadic and primitive form of obtaining sustenance than agriculture.[33] In *The Hunger Games*, the practice recalls its archaic role, a means of attaining food for survival, though of course, the special bonding between hunters is not lost, as is the case with Gale and Katniss.

Artemis is a twin sister of Apollo and sometimes he is her hunting partner. She is often fashioned as a kind of female Apollo (originally they were unrelated gods), as she represents the same mythical idea of the hunt that Apollo as her male counterpart does. What is more, sometimes they are seen as so close that their relationship is imagined as that of husband and wife, and one tradition actually states so (Eustathius, *Commentary to Homer's Iliad*. 20.70). Gale, Katniss's young hunting companion, who is also from the Seam, the poorest part of District 12, recalls Apollo in his character as the hunting double of an individual

29 Although Collins in the Scholastic interview mentions that for her own father, who grew up in the Depression, hunting was in fact a serious way to obtain meat. http://www.scholastic.com/thehungergames/media/qanda.pdf. Accessed May 18, 2016.
30 On hunting see Cartmill (1996).
31 Burton (2012). Dargis (2012): "Katniss . . . is a teenage survivalist in a postapocalyptic take on a familiar American myth . . . there's something of the American frontiersman in her." On recent female archers on screen, see Graf (2015), 73, with refs.
32 The thirteen districts recall America's original thirteen colonies, which suggests *The Hunger Games* saga implies a myth about the rebirth of a country.
33 See more on this in Despain (2012), 71.

of the opposite sex. Together, they embody this more primal yet hopeful world of nature. Gale represents what is similar and familiar, and Katniss hints at this fantasy of being brother and sister in the novel ("He could be my brother. Straight black hair, olive skin, we even have the same gray eyes"; Collins, 8) and the film certainly portrays them with the same phenotype, dark hair, light eyes.[34]

Yet their relationship is at the same time loaded with possible erotic under-tones, as in the fantasy of Apollo and Artemis being husband and wife. Gale proposes: "We could do it, you know? Take off. Live in the woods. What we do anyway." This desirous fantasy to live in the woods may echo anticapitalist, anti-modernist trends in modern America, of people who idealize the country side in search of "the organic and the local."[35] In mythical terms, this may be a fantasy of the refusal of the call to adventure. In the movie *Troy*, the irresponsible Paris also thought he and Helen could run away again and "live off the land." But the relationship becomes even more complicated with a certain assimilation of Gale to Katniss's father, also a hunter, which is, however, not so obvious in the film, their bond thus involving some Oedipal nuances.[36] Indeed, the hunt often gives place to sexuality, and in myth frequently nymphs get raped in the woods as they hunt. Even the first sexual encounter between Dido and Aeneas takes place when, during a hunt, they find refuge from a rainstorm in a cave, a natural element that will also be significant in the evolution of Katniss and Peeta's relationship.

Hunting in myth also involves a strong element of liminality. The woods are the world beyond what is allowed within civilization's borders, and thus the fact that Katniss has to illegally trespass the electrified (but often inac-tive) fence that marks the boundaries of her district is symbolic. The camera specifically focuses on a sign reading "District Boundary. No Access beyond this Point." Bad things can happen in the woods and during the hunt, as when Actaeon, while hunting, chances upon Diana bathing naked, or when Callisto (having been changed into a bear) is attacked by her own son Arcas. Hunting is an activity that takes place in wild nature and away from society, where cul-ture's rules do not fully apply; thus it brings humans into a world closer to animal life.[37] But the woods outside District 12 are easily violated, as an ultra-modern aircraft, a symbol of the Capitol's hypertechnological domination but also like an epiphany of the tyrannical gods, breaks through the sky above the woods where Katniss and Gale hunt. And as in the stories of Moses, Hesiod,

---

34 Dubrofsky and Ryalls (2014), 400–401, note that whereas this description of Katniss could have fit other ethnicities such as Latino or Middle Eastern, the movie version presents her as a white woman, with virtually no skin blemishes or signs of malnutrition, and that the images of the sun shining on her in several scenes shows her as "glowing," "a privilege of a certain kind of whiteness" that implies "cultural assumptions of whiteness as associated with virtue and innocence" (401).

35 Fisher (2012), 30.

36 Collins (2008), 111–12.

37 On Arya Stark, Merida, and Katniss in the wild, see Graf (2015), 76ff.

and Anchises, the wild areas are also where the gods manifest themselves; note how the following shot presents the highly artificial image of Effie Trinket, another significant last name pointing at the excesses of a materialistic, self-centered, and superfluous world of these gods.

Dystopian literature by nature presents a pessimistic view of the future,[38] although there are fantasies built on a romanticized idea of a better past.[39] Collins's reproduction of the maiden huntress motif recalls a better, more elemental world, a space where utopias are still possible.[40] The figure of the Maiden Huntress with a bow and arrow evokes a certain simpler, more authentic past where hope resides and humans have a more communal relationship with nature and each other despite the evident ruin of District 12. The sense of liminality while hunting makes it a good topic for a coming-of-age story—and teenagers are certainly at a liminal stage in life, and, for that matter, humanity seems to be at the crossroads of a new millennium. In a girl from a primitive district and her bow and arrow lies hope for a better future.

KATNISS *KOUROTROPHOS*

Most Greek goddesses reflect facets of an original Great Goddess, whose diverse qualities are divided among deities such as Juno, Demeter, Cybele, and Artemis. In Artemis the Virgin Huntress is given more protective and nurturing qualities. She safeguards young beings, both humans and animals, and also assists parturient women, often being invoked together with Ilithyia, goddess of childbirth, Artemis is a protectress of infants more specifically; she was even said to have assisted in the birth of her own brother. In this aspect of protector of the young she receives epithets like *kourotrophos* (Diodorus Siculus 5.73.5).[41] In Aeschylus, *Agamemnon* 142, she is referred to as protectress of young nursing animals that roam through the fields. As noted below, many of her rituals refer to her as protector of young girls, usually in their prepuberty years, a transitional stage in their lives.

Artemis as *kourotrophos* ties in with her image as a mother goddess figure, quite possibly her original nature before post–Bronze Age Greeks reimagined her solely as a virgin goddess. In this sense all the nymphs who had children could have been versions of the goddess, especially Callisto, whose name

---

38 On *The Hunger Games* and Lois Lowry's *The Giver* series as dystopian fiction, see Hubler (2014). On dystopia in young adult fiction and in *The Hunger Games*, Bartlett (2012), 12, explains, "It isn't difficult to imagine why broken worlds might appeal to adolescents. After all, they are confronting the collapse of childhood verities, and [are] faced with all the perilous uncertainty of adult life."

39 See DeaVault (2012), 190.

40 On the creation of America as a utopian nation in reference to *The Hunger Games*, see Shau Ming Tan (2013), 65–66.

41 See abundant references to the child-nurturing role of Artemis and other deities in Hadzisteliou Price (1978), for example 138ff.

FIGURE 9.3 Artemis of Ephesus.

recalls one of the epithets of Artemis, *kalliste* ("most beautiful").[42] The idea that Artemis is linked to the earlier Indo-European figure of the Great Mother is well attested in her identification with the cult statue of the Artemis of Ephesus in Turkey, once considered one of the Seven Wonders of the Ancient World (Fig. 9.3).[43] This Eastern deity was considerably different from the Greek Artemis. Although similar to the Phrygian Cybele (her priests appeared to have been eunuchs), she was worshipped by Ionian Greeks and identified with the Hellenic Artemis. This unusual figure presents numerous protuberances, which have been interpreted as breasts stacked upon each other or perhaps eggs, acorns, grapes, or testicles. As the illustration makes clear, in addition to the "breasts," the lower part of the statue was covered with figures of animals, probably connected to her role as "mistress of beasts." Evident indeed are its images of nurturing and fertility, whether we see rows of engorged breasts (see Fig. 9.3),

42 See for example, the temple of Artemis Kalliste in Elis; Pausanias, *Description of Greece* 8. 35.8. At http://philipharland.com/greco-roman-associations/membership-list-of-the-society-members-of-artemis-and-kalliste-236235-bce/ (accessed July 30, 2016), finds an inscription with the names of fifty-eight Athenians who were part of an association that honored Artemis Kalliste, who had a shrine in Athens.

43 A cult of a precursor of Artemis is apparently found in Minoan Crete as a great mother goddess associated with hunting and the mountains, Britomartis.

fruits, testicles, or a kind of pectoral, as is worn by similar goddesses.[44] Thus she embodies the earth's fructifying powers.

These maternal and *kourotrophic* aspects are also developed in the protagonist of *The Hunger Games* early on. The first time Katniss appears, she is hugging and consoling her frightened sister, who has woken up having had nightmares about the Games. Later, during the Reaping, Katniss volunteers to take her place as tribute. And here we recall Ofelia from *Pan's Labyrinth*, who is also willing to die—and in fact does so—for a younger sibling (Prim is the one who ends up dying in *The Hunger Games* saga). Prim is only twelve years old, and Katniss presents herself as a sort of surrogate mother to her, or an older sister who protects her, since their mother has not fully assumed a parent's responsibilities owing to her depression and isolation after their father's death.[45]

As with Harry and Percy, Katniss is a marvelous child, partly orphan with one impaired parent. Katniss occupies the place of the dead father when caring for her family,[46] but being a *kourotrophos* has a very feminine quality, part of her fundamental Artemis/Diana nature. The film shows this clearly when, as Prim dresses up for the Reaping, she calls to her mother, "Mom?" yet the mother remains silent and instead Katniss intervenes and quickly compliments her and fixes her clothes, as a mother would do. This Reaping is a time of major transition, and the children / potential sacrifices are dressed in their best clothes for a ceremony that will almost certainly send two to their deaths. In Greco-Roman sacrificial ritual, the animal to be slain was usually garlanded and decorated, and made to seem to agree to participate in the ritual. But the "Sunday best" clothes worn by the children also echo the mythical idea of "marriage to death," as these children presumably, if chosen, will never reach adulthood or get married themselves. Katniss affectionately calls her sister "little duck" in the book, for her untucked shirt in her back.[47] The appellative suggests the way mother ducks protect their chicks and it points anew at Katniss's connection with nature and as a guardian of the young. In fact, just as with Ofelia in *Pan's Labyrinth*, Katniss assumes the role of mother and keeper of her own incapacitated mother.[48]

---

44 The academic consensus suggests that these "breasts" were like knobs on a pectoral, which may have changed (including their interpretation) over time. See Burkert (1979), 130, nn. 7–11, and especially Fleischer (1973).

45 For a good study of mothering in *The Hunger Games*, especially on the relation of Katniss with her mother, see Arosteguy (2014).

46 Lem and Hassel (2012), 123.

47 Collins (2008), 15.

48 For maternal (and paternal) aspects in Katniss, see Mitchell (2012), 128 and 131; and Dubrofsky and Ryalls (2014), 406, who note that the only two emotional outbursts in the film for Katniss are when her sister is selected for the Games and when Rue dies. For Dubrofsky and Ryalls (2014), 407, then, these maternal traits make Katniss's filmic construction not feminist at all, unlike what some critics, in a rather superficial reading, believe, since it implies that "good women are always already mothers, and their value, strength and heroism stem from their maternal instincts and conventional heterosexual femininity."

There is a curious variation told by the Acadians, where instead of Leto, Demeter is Artemis' mother (Pausanias 8.37.6). This possibility emphasizes the connections of Artemis with the Great Mother, which Demeter embodies, and her associations with the Earth. The Arcadian Artemis is a deity primordially linked to the nymphs without any relation with Apollo. Names to refer to her in Arcadia are mostly linked with lakes, rivers, mountains, or other natural aspects. In Arcadia, together with her nymphs, Artemis held dances and sang in the mountains and forests. She was often referred to as *limnêtis* or *limnaia*[49] as her temples were often close to rivers and lakes.

At the training center in the Capitol, Katniss meets Rue, a female tribute from District 11, who is also only twelve, the youngest possible age to be entered in the "Reaping" and with whom Katniss establishes another sisterly/motherly relationship. Prim and Rue are not only the same age but they share other traits, such as being named after flowers (Prim is short for primrose and Rue, as Katniss explains in the novel, "is a small yellow flower that grows in the Meadow"[50]). The delicate image of small flowers stresses Katniss's character as defender of the young and weak, but also alludes to Persephone, who, returned to earth, brings spring flowers. Both Katniss's sister Primrose and Rue die at a young age, Rue in the arena and Prim in the third book of the trilogy, *Mockingjay*. Rue recalls a sort of nature spirit and thus is a natural love for Katniss, but she is also a sort of Patroclus to an Achilles-like Katniss.[51]

Both Prim and Rue are, archetypically speaking, nature spirits whose role is to attend the main goddess and protect her, as the fairies do with Ofelia in *Pan's Labyrinth* and are even willing to die for her. Katniss tries to protect the innocent, but in the end Rue, Prim, and Ofelia's fairies die. Both girls are also natural healers, a skill that Prim learned from her mother, who practiced that profession in District 12, though this is unmentioned in the film. Rue applies curative leaves to Katniss's tracker-jacker sting wounds while she is unconscious and nurses her back to health. Earlier, Katniss received a burn unguent from a sponsor, but later Katniss has to fight to death to obtain medicine for Peeta's leg. Here we find one further connection between Katniss and the archetype of the *kourotrophic* female deity: both have siblings who are experts in the healing arts and are themselves to some degree healers. Artemis can also demonstrate healing powers, like her brother. Homer in *Iliad* 5.447 tells us that the goddess, together with her mother Leto, healed Aeneas' wounds at Troy, and Strabo, *Geography* 14.1.6, recalls that her very name is connected with her ability to make people *artemeas* ("safe and sound").[52] Katniss takes care of Peeta's

---

49 Pausanias 2.7.6, 4.4.2, and 4.31.3.
50 Collins (2008), 99.
51 Mitchell (2012), 131, says that Prim is Katniss's "Achilles heel."
52 See also Pausanias, *Description of Greece* 10.35.7; and Aelian, *On the Nature of Animals* 14. 20. For Artemis in general, see Callimachus, *Hymn 3 to Artemis* and *Orphic Hymn 35 to Artemis*.

wounded leg and his agonizing fever at the cave, and in return, Peeta applies the curative unguent to the cut in her forehead.

Rue must be killed by others so that Katniss does not have to do so herself, and so that the romantic angle with Peeta may be pursued further. But Katniss is *kourotrophos* to the end, as she kills Rue's murderer, showing the vengefulness of Artemis; she holds Rue in her arms until she dies, and then covers her body with flowers, in an act that not only recalls her motherly and protective feelings for her, and perhaps the role of women as mourners, but also constitutes a visual challenge to the Gamemakers and an uncharacteristic break with the "fourth wall" illusion of the spectacle as the camera closes up on her enraged face. Katniss even places a bouquet in Rue's hands, making her look like "a bride to death," like the archetypal Persephone, but at the same time prepares her for a new birth, an image that indeed reminds us again of Hamlet's drowned Ophelia among the flowers immortalized in the painting by Millais (1852), which we mention in our *Pan's Labyrinth* chapter. And it is Rue's death that will save Katniss as Thresh will later spare her life for her kindness to Rue. Katniss sobs inconsolably after losing Rue, while in her toughness she has never cried before. But this is a heartbroken and desolate crying, fitting for a mother mourning her child, an older sister grieving for her ward, a pain that inspires a rage close to Achilles' at the death of Patroclus. In opposition, note the images of President Snow, who is shown gardening, pruning flowers (which symbolizes a desire for control over nature and fertility, in contrast with the wild flowers that Katniss arranges for Rue's funeral). His last name evokes the idea of cold and freeze, the absence of life, which destroys the fertility alluded to in the name Everdeen.

KATNISS AND THE EARTH

Artemis' "proper sphere is the earth, and specifically the uncultivated parts, forests and hills, where wild beasts are plentiful."[53] This earth connection, as noted, is rather part of a larger feminine mythical force. Artemis and the Earth Goddess are connected to rivers, pools, mountains, caves and groves, away from the cities.[54]

Katniss's choice of wall design for her room in the Games' training center is relevant; after gazing at the picture of woods, she abruptly switches to a more urban landscape, recognizing that her beloved woods are only a dream, part of the past. This image of the forest notably contrasts with the excessive artificiality of the furnishings. As Fish points out, the book starts out creating an Arcadian-Urban dichotomy. We remember that the pastoral genre was a creation of Hellenistic Greeks living in a vast, imperial, and alienating Alexandria.

---

53 OCD 4th ed., "Artemis."
54 See Callimachus, *Hymn to Artemis* 18–24. In Arcadia in particular, her surnames and epithets are connected with the names of rivers, lakes, and mountains.

The pastoral world of nature and love projected the dream of living a "natural" life, as opposed to the "society of the spectacle" of Alexandria, Rome, today's United States, and of course Panem. The woods represent the possibility of an authentic and naturally connected world. Further, the love affair of Peeta and Katniss, on an archetypal level, represents a more idealized form of love—and can such love survive the society of the spectacle, where to even eat you must compromise your identity? Again, like the lovers in ideal romance, they are an ideal couple who must set an example and free their people. And like the heroines of romance, she raises her young man to a higher level.

The name Katniss itself belongs to an edible root, which, significantly, her father taught her to recognize at the bottom of pools.[55] We are first made aware of this in the novel, when, once in the arena, Katniss decides to bathe in a pool and at the bottom sees the root for which she was named (Collins, 52). Interestingly, Pharr suggests that Katniss volunteers for her sister because she "quickly realizes that she belongs to her root society."[56] The name is actually the Sagittaria plant, which grows in various parts of the world and is what the Japanese call katniss. It is also known as "arrowhead" from the Latin *sagitta*, thus implying that at the heart of our heroine there are arrows.[57] Even her last name, Everdeen, sounds to us like "evergreen," evoking vegetation and hinting perhaps at the perpetual "greenness" and maidenhood of the Huntress Goddess.[58] Her father once told her, "'As long as you can find yourself, you'll never starve,'"[59] employing a pun on the name of the root and the name of the girl that makes us think of the Delphic maxim "know yourself."[60] As long as she finds a way to be herself, to hunt and to have knowledge of what the earth can provide, if she is one with the earth, she will survive.[61]

We notice that close to the cave she will share with Peeta during the Games there is also a waterfall, recalling again the *loci amoeni* where we often find Diana, as in Ovid's presentation in *Metamorphoses* 3, before Actaeon intrudes on her bathing. The movie is about the birth of two heroes, one who finds her

55   For a Lacanian interpretation of the mirror and definition of the self in this, see Shau Ming Tan (2013), 57.
56   Pharr (2012), 223.
57   Mitchell (2012), 128, mentions that this plant is unisexual, thus fitting a heroine who "blurs, erases, transcends, and challenges traditional representations of gender." Note also, with Graf (2015), 79, the heterosexual uniforms of the contestants and the lack of women's sexualization in the film. Both Peeta and Katniss are sexualized and exposed in the parade, but they are equally attired for the Games.
58   Susan Collins in an interview in *Entertainment Weekly* (http://www.ew.com/article/2010/08/12/suzanne-collins-on-the-books-she-loves; accessed June 1, 2016) mentions that her inspiration for Katniss's last name came from Thomas Hardy's protagonist Bathsheba Everdene in *Far from the Madding Crowd*.
59   Collins (2008), 52.
60   On the pun in the names, see Despain (2012), 73.
61   Stanley Fish (2012) sees that the central question of the book is how to be genuine amid a world of fabrication and falsehood.

inner goddess / Artemis / Mother Earth. Not only that, but as with other arche-typal heroes, she helps another proto-hero redeem himself. Though Peeta at first believes he doesn't have a chance at the Games, in fact Katniss needs him, for his ruse, telling viewers they are a romantic couple, actually helps them get ratings and thus more aid, which allows their survival. And at the end of the Games, as they prepare to eat the poisonous berries they look like a couple exchanging rings. Long ago Peeta gave her food when she was starving; now he gives her the emotional food she is hungry for too.

Peeta himself, a baker, embodies the fertility of the land, grains, and agricul-ture.[62] Katniss and Peeta thus complement each other, one symbolizing a form of sustenance seen more in nomadism, hunting, and gathering, and the other in civilization and a more settled life. The wildness of the woods of Diana meets the agricultural gifts of Demeter. Artemis is a goddess of the earth in its wildest state, the forest, the rivers, the animals who roam it freely; Demeter is also a chthonic deity, but one who works in harmony with it through cultivation. It is not the wild state of the earth she seeks but the rather tamed and cultured field, which necessitates stability of settlement in humans rather than the constant movement hunting animals requires. In this sense, agriculture has much to do with the divine female, but also with agricultural activity in contrast to hunting and gathering practiced by nomadic peoples. This dichotomy is central to *The Hunger Games* and to the protagonist's coming of age.[63] It is thus relevant that at the end of the series District 12 has become an agrarian society, perhaps a symbol of Katniss's own change, and no longer is practicing mining.[64]

This contrast is linked to Katniss's hesitation as to which mate to choose, the stable Peeta, who is very strong and yet somewhat of an artist as well, or her child-hood hunting companion Gale, who is restless, always moving, and in search of something[65]; of course the latter's name, evoking a strong wind, is fitting, con-trasting the stability of Peeta's name (Latin *petra* "stone"). He too is associated with nature rather than culture. As the Games are about to start, and the whole country is watching the live TV transmission, Gale sits alone in the woods, in a pensive attitude. As noted, Gale is in many ways very similar to her. Katniss strug-gles between the sameness of childhood and the small circle of what is known (perhaps showing a somewhat narcissistic and fearful desire for the same) and her transition to adulthood (which implies embracing what is different).

---

62 Mitchell (2012), 132, sees how Peeta being a baker also complicates gender roles in the story. On this, see also Graf (2015), 78. This blurring of gender differences and the box office suc-cess of the film "reflects a degree of blurring of traditional gender roles in society at large, as women continue to work outside of the home and men assume domestic responsibilities." Graf (2015), 79.

63 For the opposition of Katniss and Peeta in regard to food, see Despain (2012), 71. Peeta and the bread show some sort of community. On coming of age and sacrificed childhood in *The Hunger Games*, see Shau Ming Tan (2013), 56.

64 Frankel (2012), 57–58.

65 In the last book of the trilogy, Gale is one of the restless leaders of the rebellion.

Thus the process of leaving Gale and marrying Peeta at the end of the trilogy implies this movement away from hunting along with the instability of youth to a more settled life, epitomized in the coda to the last book, many years later (a scene influenced perhaps by the coda to the *Harry Potter* series, released in 2007).[66] The concluding chapter of *Mockingjay*, the last volume of the series, which acts as epilogue, presents Katniss as mother of two children sitting in a meadow with her husband, Peeta. Despite the destruction of District 12, the Goddess of the Earth, symbolized by Katniss, is not destroyed, and is ready to manifest herself and bring renewal to the community. And she must take a consort. In the cave, it is she who reaches down and kisses Peeta. Many myth systems present co-creators, such as Amphion and Zethus, Moses and Joshua, Romulus and Numa. Katniss and Peeta represent the twin poles of restored fertility: she the primal power of the woods, and he the power of the fields, inferior in strength to the woods. The primal goddess must not only save herself, but also help the depressed Peeta discover his own potential—which he does.

THE BREAD OF LIFE

Although themes of hunger and the need for food are pervasive in the book, in the movie such themes are largely absent. The characters look well fed (Jennifer Lawrence is not particularly thin and looks rather healthy[67]); we might imagine her hunting allows her more nourishment than is available to others in her district. But perhaps robustness allows Katniss/Lawrence to better evoke the maiden huntress, and the more formed and feminine shape of the actress's body makes hints at her connections to the Great Goddess. And yet, as Fish wonders, hunger here is also metaphorical and asks the question, "Just what is it that the characters, and by extension the readers, hunger for?"[68] It is more than food, for, as Jesus declares, "Man does not live by bread alone"—even in Panem.

The process by which the tributes (note the religious but also tax-related implications of this word[69]) are selected is a public lottery, which reminds us of the

---

66 Katniss's wildness has been then domesticated by the end of the series, and Graf (2015), 80, raises a good point in this regard. Have Katniss, Merida, and Arya been allowed this freedom because of their young age but possibly are expected to settle into more traditional femininity later in life?

67 Dargis (2012): "A few years ago Ms. Lawrence might have looked hungry enough to play Katniss, but now, at 21, her seductive, womanly figure makes a bad fit for a dystopian fantasy about a people starved into submission." Likewise, Dargis criticizes the movie for depriving the story of the sense of constant edge, toughness, and danger in the heroine, though the very few smiles may compensate somewhat for this. She also calls Lawrence's performance "bland."

68 Fish (2012) proposes that "food, however, is a metaphor in the trilogy for another kind of sustenance, the sustenance provided by an inner conviction of one's own worth and integrity." Pharr (2012), 223: "Collin's trilogy investigates and interrogates the way the human need for food and entertainment diminishes the human ability to make clear judgements about right and wrong. This diminution of judgment is itself a kind of ethical starvation, gradually destroying whatever is most humane among humans." For an excellent analysis of food and hunger in *The Hunger Games*, see Despain (2012).

69 Fisher (2012), 28–29.

drafts that various countries have adopted to select their military manpower.[70] The ceremony in *The Hunger Games* is symbolically called "the Reaping." In many ancient rituals, people sacrificed the "first fruits" of the harvest to the gods, and these youths are the first fruits of the harvest. In many societies mock battles are staged as part of end-of-the-year rituals. The idea is that these rituals enact the fears of society, here social division, which leads to civil war. As Burkert[71] has shown, in the ancient world young people, like the Athenian ephebes (young men undergoing civic training), were thought liminal, and in some societies they are still sent off to the borders to work out their uncivilized tendencies so that they can finally come back to the community as fully civilized beings. This is a myth behind the Classical "werewolves" of Arcadia. The idea of children as potential savages is well developed in William Golding's *Lord of the Flies*, another influence on Collins's trilogy.

Nayar believes that the word "Reaping" points at "what they have collaboratively reaped from their rebellion"[72] (note also the New Testament's "whatever a man sows, this he will also reap," Gal. 6:7) given that the Hunger Games are a form of atonement for the districts' past uprising, just as the sacrifice of Athenian youths to be devoured by the Minotaur is also a form of political atonement and control. And yet the word *reaping* has clear harvesting connotations. The tributes are like the grain or crops that must be reaped after the annual harvest; they are seen as products of the earth, and Katniss and Peeta are also products of this land. Bread is what moves the people of Panem and beyond. The specific use of the accusative form of *panis*, the Latin word for bread, alludes to the phrase *"panem et circenses"* (Juvenal, *Satire* 4.10.81).[73] We first see bread when Gale brings out a fresh roll in the woods. Later Katniss recalls how, years before, Peeta saved her life one past winter by tossing her some burnt bread and thus preventing her death from starvation. And soon afterward, spring begins (Collins, 32). All these connect with the myths of Demeter and Persephone and restoration of the bread-producing grain crops, a key to human survival, when Persephone is in the upper world with her mother.

Rue comes from District 11, where the main economic activity is agriculture; she has spent most of her life picking fruit destined for consumption in the Capitol, which controls all food sources, even forbidding the people of District 11 to eat the fruits of their alienated labor (Collins, 202). At Rue's death Katniss establishes a very personal connection with District 11, when, as an act of defiance to the Capitol, she decorates Rue's dead body with flowers and with a triumphant gesture to the camera dedicates this homage to her friend and to

70 Koenig (2012), 41. Despain (2012), 74, cleverly draws a connection on Katniss's enjoyment of the Capitol's lamb stew and the fact that she is like lamb prepared for slaughter.

71 Burkert (1986), 170–90.

72 Nayar (2012), 1.

73 On food as control and resistance in *The Hunger Games*, see Peksoy (2014), who even sees Panem as a living organism that must be fed (80).

her poor agricultural district. This sparks a revolt in District 11, as people burn the crops and thus prevent the Capitol from reaping the products of their land.

Food also serves to embody the Capitol's excessive lifestyle, in contrast to the food-deprived districts. In classical satire, food was a frequent symbol for decadence, most notably in Petronius' over-the-top depiction of Trimalchio's banquet, and there are many opulent displays of food in the film, first on the train, and then in the Capitol. And these images remind us of America as one of the "fattest" nations in the world—certainly a major concern of our times—a place where people eat, consume, and waste too much, thus harming both themselves and their planet, in contrast to the hunger that afflicts other parts of the world, as with the districts of Panem.[74] But more than hunger itself, *The Hunger Games* recalls the rising inequality in the United States, where the lower strata of society's economic circumstances have plummeted in the last few decades as the upper classes gain more and more economic comfort (the poor districts vs. the wealthy Capitol), the 1 percent versus the 99 percent.[75] In the scene when each tribute must demonstrate his or her own personal skills to the Gamemakers, after trying to shoot the target with her bow and arrow and having no success in being noticed, Katniss in anger shoots an arrow straight through the apple placed in the mouth of a roasted pig on the judges' table. This is a symbolic attack on what they control, a rebellion against the restrictions the Capitol inflicts on the people's survival.[76] But perhaps this might even be taken as entertainment by the Gamemakers, almost like the surprises Trimalchio puts on for his guests in Petronius' *Satyricon* and Fellini's movie. There is a perverted meaning in the film's depiction of the Cornucopia, which in antiquity is associated with Ceres, Demeter, the goddess of grain and plenty. At the beginning of the Games, once the competitors have been released into the arena, the Cornucopia, changed in the film from the traditional warm-looking wicker basket to a cold, metallic structure, is a distorted reference to the quintessentially American (and even utopian) Thanksgiving feast.[77] The Cornucopia is full of supplies that the competitors must fight to the death for, and indeed thirteen of them die in this very first battle.[78] Then toward the middle of the film, Katniss, with Rue's help, shoots an arrow at a sack of apples, which then breaks, and the falling fruits detonate several mines that were protecting the goods (mostly belonging to the Careers). The Careers now cannot

74 Despain (2012), 70: "Collins can count on her readers to find the Everdeen family's hand-to-mouth existence as unfamiliar as the hovercraft in her narrative."
75 Hubler (2014), 26; and Fisher (2012), 27. See also Henthorne (2012), 2, for the 2008 economic crisis as cultural context for *The Hunger Games*.
76 This scene also recalls the mythology of William Tell, who was forced by the evil Gessler, Vogt of Altdorf, put in power by the Habsburgs of Austria, to shoot an apple off the head of his young son with a crossbow; Tell leads a revolt that results in the formation of the Swiss Confederacy.
77 See Shau Ming Tan (2013), 67.
78 See also Pharr (2012), 221.

feed themselves, showing their weakness in comparison with Katniss the resourceful hunter. Finally, toward the film's end, the Cornucopia is the site of a deadly battle when Katniss and Peeta must confront a series of hybrid crossover creatures between humans and animals, very much recalling hellhounds. Katniss gains control over the Cornucopia and thus is mistress over food. Even the Gamemakers' very last attempt to change the rules yet again and force Peeta and Katniss to fight each other is confronted with an act of defiance when they plan to make a fatal meal of the delicious but deadly nightlock berries and thus deprive the Gamemakers of their needed single victor.

KATNISS AND THE COMING OF AGE

Katniss embarks on a type of hero's quest, as Harry and Percy do. As noted, the hero, more often than not, is in a form of exile and a marvelous child. Katniss is not exiled per se, but her people, robbed of their rights and heritage, suffer collective exile. And she indeed, for most of the movie, exists in the foreign space of the Capitol and must travel a long distance to it, as Odysseus did, and must endure the arena's strange and threatening space. Like Moses or Aeneas, her quest will involve the restoration of her people. The Quest hero, such as Perseus and Jason, has parents or parent substitutes who are in trouble or even dead; this is the case with Katniss, and note how the memory of her dead father motivates her. Many marvelous children, such as Romulus and Remus, are raised in rustic surroundings, and Katniss's liking for the woods recalls this. When her sister Prim is chosen for the reaping, this represents her "call to adventure"; it is similar to Theseus volunteering to be among the sacrificial youths sent to Minos. The train is the magical device that transports her into the Dark Wood or Belly of the Beast, where her adventures will occur. She finds there various magic helpers, for example Haymitch Abernathy and Cinna; the latter gives her magical objects (the flaming gown and chariot). The training center, a bit like Camp Half-Blood, is where she discovers skills she did not know she had. In many quests, the hero assembles a crew for a dangerous mission; here we have an inversion of the normal assembled company, a crew created to do battle with each other, though for some of them short-term, tactical alliances are forged. Like Perseus and other heroes, during this Quest-journey Katniss obtains Peeta, defies death, and emerges with a much higher, and even heroic, status.

And as with most hero journeys, Katniss has to confront a lowest point, a demonic epiphany, so to speak, a sort of Hell. The manufactured woods of the Games function as enchanted underworld, with booby traps and tempting items they must not eat.[79] Katniss nearly dies in the incident with the tracker-jacker poisonous stings; under the venom's influence she hallucinates and has visions

---

79 For all this, see again Holtsmark (2001). Holtsmark (2001), 42–48, sees displaced *katabases* in Vietnam-era movies as protagonists insert themselves in enemy terrain, a theme we can connect to *The Hunger Games*.

of her father in this sort of "deadlands," reminding us of Aeneas, a reluctant hero himself like Katniss, who encounters his father Anchises in the Elysian Fields. This experience puts our heroine at the nadir of her journey, from which she must return alive in a sort of rebirth and save her life and the future of her community, as Aeneas must do. And again, similarly to *Pan's Labyrinth*, the spatial inversion is clear: one must ascend through tubes to arrive in the arena. The fires Katniss encounters are also hellish, as are the way the rules keep changing. Katniss and Peeta are living sacrifices, fighting and conquering the powers of the underworld, and rising again to fight another day.[80]

The Hunger Games is, among other things, a *Bildungsroman* (character-building novel). Part of the mythical divine female's role is to assist girls through their "character-building" phase, especially concerning the transition to womanhood, marriage, and motherhood. Various Greek goddesses play crucial roles; Hera is goddess of marriage and the family, Aphrodite reigns over the sexuality needed for pregnancy and motherhood. Ancient "schools" for young girls, evoked in Sappho's poetry, worship that goddess in particular. Demeter embodies motherhood and the pain of losing one's daughter to marriage, thus helping Greek women negotiate this difficult reality. Artemis is also very much involved in women's transitions. Her assistance to birthing women is paramount, but also many of her rituals, in which she protects young girls, usually in their prepuberty years, involve a transitional stage in their lives. We think in particular of the cult of Artemis at Brauron, in Attica, where prepubescent girls, in preparation for future childbirth, played the roles of she-bears (*arktoi*) and danced for the goddess in a sanctuary, which, according to legend, was founded by another girl in dangerous transition, a sacrificial victim to the goddess herself, Iphigenia.[81]

At the beginning of *The Hunger Games*, Katniss is bent on remaining permanently in her "Diana stage." She swears that she will never get married or procreate ("I'm never having kids"). Like Diana, she is fine with protecting the young, in her role of *kourotrophos*, but does not want marriage or direct motherhood. Yet gradually, she will change and become a wife and mother, but only after her world has changed and the tyranny of the Capitol has been defeated. However, in the first film she is still in this phase, though we do have hints of her transition in her gradual closeness with Peeta and the fact that in the second movie domesticity is more prevalent.

---

80   On child sacrifice in *The Hunger Games* and its connections with Christ, see Shau Ming Tan (2013), 62–63.

81   Purposely or not, the film seems to pay homage to another film where Artemis and hunting are paramount. At the onset of Cacoyannis's *Iphigenia*, we see men pursuing a frightened deer. The first thing that Katniss does in the woods is try to shoot a deer, which Gale ends up scaring away. In both films the camera focuses on the frightened eyes of the prey. See also McDonald (2001), 90–91.

One aspect of the mythical transition of girls into women involves dancing and singing. Of the divine twins, Apollo is the god of music and poetry, usually portrayed with a lyre in art; Artemis also leads choruses of young girls who sing and dance.[82] Singing is in ancient myth an intricate part of the maiden's life in preparation for marriage later on. Think for example of Sappho and her choruses of girls. In the film, early we see Katniss singing with Prim, holding her in her arms. Peeta explains to Katniss in the novel that her mother, though she belonged to a merchant and wealthier class, rejected Peeta's father and fell in love with Katniss's own father because he was a wonderful singer (Collins, 300).[83] Significantly, in the novel, as Peeta tells her, he fell in love with her on the first day of school when they were both young children, as Katniss sang a song (301). Finally, Katniss sings to Rue's death as a dirge, after Rue asks her to do so[84]:

Deep in the meadow, under the willow
A bed of grass, a soft green pillow
Lay down your head, and close your eyes
And when they open, the sun will rise.

Fitzgerald and Hayward see the song as "redolent of pre-modernity" and point out that "traditional Appalachian ballad singing was usually unaccompanied," sung at home for friends.[85] These verses recall a mythic *locus amoenus*, a peaceful place in nature, often in the woods, where hunters and others stop to rest, as Ovid shows us in his epic, but it also reminds us of some of the hopeful gospel songs in *O Brother, Where Art Thou?* The desire to be somewhere else, in a place of peace and not in the horrors of death found in the arena, fills these verses, with their optimistic message of rebirth. And so Rue's death, as symbol of all the innocent youths lost in the Games, was not in vain.

Rue, through singing, communicates to her people back in the orchards of District 11 that it is time to go home after an arduous day of work. She whistles to the Mockingjays, who in turn will repeat the chant and transmit it to others. Nature gods use music, especially Pan with his reed pipe, and so this fits a nature spirit like Rue, whose voice is still alive, in a way, even after death. And song, of course, metacritically, hints at the power of the bard, the writer, the narrator, the director and script writer, a major theme of *O Brother*. Rue even teaches Katniss how to sing and use it as a means of communication and survival. This same bird, which is the symbol of District 12, represented in the movie by a pin a woman from the Hob gave to Katniss, emphasizes that the Mockingjay is an emblem of the people, which will accompany her

---

82 For example in *Homeric Hymn to Artemis* 14–20 and *Homeric Hymn to Pythian Apollo* 197–99.
83 Gant (2012), 89, suggests that song fills the place of the absent religion in *The Hunger Games*.
84 Fitzgerald and Hayward (2015), 77, refer to the region of Appalachia, where District 12 is supposed to be, as a rich "repository of Anglo-Celtic songs."
85 Fitzgerald and Hayward (2015), 79, with reference to Langrall (1986), 38.

through all the movies, and will become her own name and an emblem of re-bellion and fight against the power of the Capitol. The Mockingjay reflects the songs of the people, just as the songs of the Soggy Bottom Boys in *O Brother* reflect the hopes and fears and sorrows of the common folk, who may be ripe for change.

ECHOES OF WAR AT THE NEW MILLENNIUM

The Hunger Games not only reprises the theme of the primeval mythical battle but also alludes to war more generally. It is a "war story,"[86] with Vietnam and Iraq as major subtexts.[87] One can add that Afghanistan, Syria, and other more recent conflicts also inform our readings. Suzanne Collins admits that she was influenced in part by her own father's military service in Vietnam.[88] All wars demand the sacrifice of our youth in one way or another, and in the founda-tional war of the Greeks against the Trojans Agamemnon's daughter Iphigenia was sacrificed to Artemis to atone for the excesses of her father, and perhaps for those the Greek army would commit. But, as Marianne McDonald has lucidly shown in her analysis of Cacoyannis's 1977 film *Iphigenia*,[89] this story evokes all the children a nation must sacrifice to war, and the spectacle of Iphigenia walking up to the altar, with the crowds of Greek men watching, turns her death for Artemis into civic spectacle. When McDonald wrote her article, she was thinking of the first Iraq war; Collins in turn, found inspiration for Katniss's trials in reality TV taken together with footage of the second Iraq war. Not only does this war of the early millennium confront us yet again with the death of our youth for a not-entirely-clear or justified conflict, as Euripides does, but the very images of war have become commercialized, turned into spectacles in the nightly news.

Katniss's weapons against this are a bow and arrow, elements echoing the goddess of the wild, of hunting, of the simplicity of a mythical past and the land, where machine guns and drone warfare do not yet exist. So, to modern industrialization and technologization of the horrors of war and oppressive totalitarian governments, the response appears to be to go back to the earth, to nature, to feeding from Mother Earth, and to respect, harmoniously, what she has to offer. At the crossroads of a new millennium, *The Hunger Games* in its reappraisal of mythical themes rehearses the dangers of unrestrained tech-nology, artificiality, and war, where we all in one way or another sacrifice our children.

---

86 Lem and Hassel (2012), 125. Henthorne (2012), chap. 3.
87 Koenig (2012), 40.
88 See Scholastic interview: http://www.scholastic.com/teachers/article/qa-hunger-games-author-suzanne-collins. Accessed May 24, 2016.
89 McDonald (2001).

REFERENCES

Arosteguy, K. "'I have a kind of power I never knew I possessed': Transformative Motherhood and Maternal Influence." In D. Garriot and E. Whitney, ed., *Space and Place in* The Hunger Games. McFarland, 2014, pp. 146–59.

Bartlett, M. "Appetite for Spectacle: Violence and Entertainment in *The Hunger Games.*" *Screen Education*, vol. 66, Winter 2012, 8–17.

Buggy, S. "'If we burn, you burn with us': Spartan Influences in Suzanne Collins' *The Hunger Games* Trilogy." Paper presented at Swords, Sorcery, Sandals, and Space: A Science Fiction Foundation Conference, Liverpool, June 30–July 1, 2013.

Burkert, W. *Homo Necans: The Anthropology of Ancient Greek Sacrificial Ritual and Myth.* University of California Press, 1986.

———. Structure *and History in Greek Mythology and Ritual.* University of California Press, 1979.

Burton, E. "Reckoning Reality in *The Hunger Games.*" *Sightings*, https://divinity .uchicago.edu/sightings/reckoning-reality-hunger-games-emanuelle-burton. Accessed Oct. 13, 2016.

Cartmill, M. *A View to a Death in the Morning: Hunting and Nature Through History.* Harvard UP, 1996.

Collins, S. *The Hunger Games.* Scholastic Press, 2008.

Dargis, M. "Tested by a Picturesque Dystopia: *The Hunger Games*, Based on the Suzanne Collins Novel." *New York Times*, Mar. 22, 2012, C1. http://www .nytimes.com/2012/03/23/movies/the-hunger-games-movie-adapts-the-suzanne-collins-novel.html?_r=0. Accessed May 18, 2016.

DeaVault, R. "The Masks of Femininity: Perceptions of the Feminine in *The Hunger Games* and *Podkayne of Mars.*" In M. Pharr and L. Clark, ed., *Of Bread, Blood and Hunger Games: Critical Essays on the Suzanne Collins Trilogy.* McFarland, 2012, pp. 190–98.

Despain, M. "The 'Fine Reality of Hunger Satisfied': Food as Cultural Metaphor in Panem." In M. Pharr and L. Clark, ed., *Of Bread, Blood and The Hunger Games: Critical Essays on the Suzanne Collins Trilogy.* McFarland, 2012, pp. 69–78.

Dubrofsky, R. E., and E. D. Ryalls. "*The Hunger Games*: Performing Not-performing to Authenticate Femininity and Whiteness." *Critical Studies in Media Communication*, vol. 31 no. 5, 2014, 395–409.

Fischer-Hansen, T., and B. Poulsen. *From Artemis to Diana: The Goddess of Man and Beast (Acta Hyperborea).* Museum Tusculanum Press, 2009.

Fish, S. "Staging the Self: 'The Hunger Games'." *NY Times Review*, http://opinion-ator.blogs.nytimes.com/2012/05/07/staging-the-self-the-hunger-games /?_r=0, May 7, 2012. Accessed May 20, 2016.

Fisher, M. "Precarious Dystopias: *The Hunger Games, In Time* and *Never Let me Go.*" *Film Quarterly*, vol. 65 no. 4, 2012, 27–33.

Fitzgerald, J., and P. Hayward. "Mountain Airs, Mockingjays and Modernity: Songs and Their Significance in *The Hunger Games.*" *Science Fiction Film and Television*, vol. 8 no. 1, 2015, 75–89.

Fleischer, R. *Artemis von Ephesos und verwandte Kultstatuen in Kleinasien.* Brill, 1973.

Frankel, V. "Reflection in a Plastic Mirror." In M. Pharr and L. Clark, ed., *Of Bread, Blood and The Hunger Games: Critical Essays on the Suzanne Collins Trilogy.* McFarland, 2012, pp. 49–58.

Gant, T. "Hungering for Righteousness: Music, Spirituality and Katniss Everdeen." In M. Pharr and L. Clark, ed., *Of Bread, Blood and The Hunger Games: Critical Essays on the Suzanne Collins Trilogy.* McFarland, 2012, pp. 89–97.

Graf, B. "Arya, Katnis, and Merida: Empowering Girls Through the Amazonian Archetype." In M. Cyrino and M. Safran, ed., *Classical Myth on Screen.* Palgrave, 2015, pp. 73–82.

Hadzisteliou Price, T. *Kourotrophos: Cults and Representations of the Greek Nursing Deities.* Brill, 1978.

Henthorne, T. *Approaching the Hunger Games Trilogy: A Literary and Cultural Analysis.* McFarland, 2012.

Holtsmark, E. "The *Katabasis* Theme in Modern Cinema." In M. Winkler, ed., *Classical Myth and Culture in the Cinema.* Oxford UP, 2001, pp. 23–50.

Hubler, A. "Lois Lowry's and Suzanne Collins' Dystopian Fiction: Utopia and anti-Utopia." *Against the Current*, vol. 29 no. 3, 2014, 23–27.

Kerényi, K. *The Heroes of the Greeks.* Camelot Press, 1978 (original from 1959).

Koenig, G. "Communal Spectacle: Reshaping History and Memory Through Violence." In M. Pharr and L. Clark, ed., *Of Bread, Blood and Hunger Games: Critical Essays on the Suzanne Collins Trilogy.* McFarland, 2012, pp. 39–48.

Langrall, P. "Appalachian Folk Music: From Foothills to Footlights." *Music Educators Journal*, vol. 72 no. 7, 1986, 37–38.

Lem, E., and H. Hassel. "'Killer' Katniss and 'Lover Boy' Peeta: Suzanne Collins' Defiance of Gender-Genred Reading." In M. Pharr and L. Clark, ed., *Of Bread, Blood and the Hunger Games*: Critical Essays on the Suzanne Collins Trilogy. McFarland, 2012, pp. 118–27.

Makins, M. "Refiguring the Roman Empire in *The Hunger Games* Trilogy." In B. Rogers and B. Eldon Stevens, ed., *Classical Traditions in Science Fiction.* Oxford UP, 2015, pp. 280–306.

Mayor, A. *The Amazons: Lives and Legends of Warrior Women Across the Ancient World.* Princeton UP, 2014.

McDonald, M. "Eye of the Camera, Eye of the Victim: Iphigenia by Euripides and Cacoyannis." In M. Winkler, ed., *Classical Myth & Culture in the Cinema.* Oxford UP, 2001, pp. 90–101.

Mills, S. "Classical Elements and Mythological Archetypes in *The Hunger Games.*" *New Voices in Classical Reception Studies*, vol. 10, 2015, 56–64. http://www2.open.ac.uk/ClassicalStudies/GreekPlays/newvoices/Issue10/mills.pdf. Accessed Oct. 13, 2016.

Mitchell, J. "Of Queer Necessity: Panem's Hunger Games as Gender Games." In M. Pharr and L. Clark, ed., *Of Bread, Blood and Hunger Games: Critical Essays on the Suzanne Collins Trilogy.* McFarland, 2012, pp. 128–37.

Montz, A. "Costuming the Resistance: The Female Spectacle of Rebellion." In M. Pharr and L. Clark, ed., *Of Bread, Blood and The Hunger Games: Critical Essays on the Suzanne Collins Trilogy.* McFarland, 2012, pp. 139–47.

Nayar, P. "Growing up Different(ly): Space, Community and the Dissensual Bildungsroman in Suzanne Collins' *The Hunger Games*." *Journal of Postcolonial Networks* 2, http://postcolonialnetworks.com/tag/the-hunger-games/, May 2012. Accessed June 1, 2016.

OKell, E. "Beyond *'Panem et circenses'*: Roman Culture and Names in Suzanne Collins' *Hunger Games* Trilogy." Paper presented at Swords, Sorcery, Sandals, and Space: A Science Fiction Foundation Conference, Liverpool, June 30–July 1, 2013.

Peksoy, E. "Food as Control in the *Hunger Games* Trilogy." *Procedia: Social and Behavioral Sciences*. Fourteenth International Language, Literature, and Stylistics Symposium, vol. 158, 2014, 79–84. http://www.sciencedirect.com /science/journal/18770428/158/supp/C. Accessed Dec. 7, 2016.

Pharr, M. "From the Boy Who Lived to the Girl Who Learned: *Harry Potter and Katniss Everdeen*." In M. Pharr and L. Clark, ed., *Of Bread, Blood and The Hunger Games: Critical Essays on the Suzanne Collins Trilogy*. McFarland, 2012, pp. 219–28.

Pomeroy, A. "It's a Man's, Man's, Man's World—Except for Xena and Buffy." In *Then It Was Destroyed by the Volcano: The Ancient World in Film and on Television*. Duckworth, 2008, pp. 13-14.

Postman, N. *Amusing Ourselves to Death: Public Discourse in the Age of Show Business*. Heinemann, 1985.

Schofield, A. "A Game of Two Halves: The Past and the Future in Suzanne Collins' *The Hunger Games*." Paper presented at Swords, Sorcery, Sandals, and Space: A Science Fiction Foundation Conference, Liverpool, June 30–July 1, 2013.

Shau Ming Tan, S. "Burn with Us: Sacrificing Childhood in *The Hunger Games*." *The Lion and the Unicorn*, vol. 37 no. 1, 2013, 54–73.

CHAPTER 10

PERCY JACKSON AND THE OLYMPIANS

The Lightning Thief, an American Parody of The Hero's Journey

And she came to the borders of deep-flowing Ocean;
And there is a district and city of the Cimmerian men,
Wrapped in vapor and cloud; not ever
Does the shining Sun look down upon them with his beams. . . .
(Homer, *Odyssey* 11.13–16)

In the journey of our lives we all at some point have to travel to some deep, faraway dark place, real or symbolic, from which we can't be sure of returning. But what doesn't kill us makes us stronger, and so mythological heroes go to the edge of the world and meet the dark forces of the Dead. In the previous passage, Odysseus travels to the margins of the river Ocean, which surrounds the known living world, a dark place full of shadows where the sun never shines, to speak to the souls of the dead. Aeneas actually goes deep into the Underworld to return strengthened and prepared to accomplish his Jupiter-sanctioned mission. Heroes like Perseus, Theseus, and Hercules must journey to the edge of civilization to obtain a boon, but most importantly, to become truly men. In this chapter's movie, Percy Jackson embarks on a similar voyage, pushed to the limits of the familiar, to dark worlds of perils, monsters, the Dead, and to the West, to finally return home changed, enriched, and having grown up.

The film *Percy Jackson and the Olympians: The Lightning Thief*, based on the 2005 first volume of the widely popular collection by Rick Riordan and directed by Chris Columbus (*Harry Potter* I and II movies), centers around young Percy,

PLOT SUMMARY

Percy Jackson, a teenager from New York City, suddenly finds out that he is the son of Poseidon, Greek god of the Seas, and that he is being blamed for the theft of Zeus' thunderbolt, which, if not recovered, will lead to a war between the gods. For protection he escapes to Camp Half-Blood, a haven for the children of the gods in Long Island. After meeting various friends and helpers he embarks on a heroic Quest to free Percy's mother from Hades, which will lead him, Annabeth, and Grover through a series of adventures that include fighting Medusa in New Jersey and the Hydra in Nashville, and visiting the Lotus Casino in Las Vegas. They finally reach the Underworld in Los Angeles and recover the stolen thunderbolt and free Percy's mother. After returning to New York and fighting one last battle with the true thief, Luke, the order between gods and demigods is newly restored.

who learns that, instead of being a boy saddled with dyslexia and ADHD, he is actually a demigod, and belongs in a whole new community of divine and half-divine beings, recalling Harry's discovery of his own past and the alternate world of Hogwarts.[1] Although Riordan's series has received enormous praise as a book for a middle school audience, movie reviews have been mixed (49 in Rotten Tomatoes, and a 47 in Metacritic). Reviewers cite too many unnecessary, capricious changes to the book's plot line and the loss of Riordan's cleverness and humor, as well as a rather miscast group of actors and somewhat cheap special effects. Yet the film engages directly, more directly than our other movies, with both Greek myth and the problematics of the millennial generation, especially in the United States.

While discussing *Harry Potter* and *The Hunger Games*, we outlined their often displaced use of elements of Classical mythology. In *Percy Jackson* these elements are at the forefront. Indeed, characters often explain who this or that god or monster is, such as a minotaur or a centaur, or even some of the Olympian gods. In fact, negative criticisms aside, many reviewers recognize that the film encourages interest in Classical myth. There are more nuanced references, such as the reimagined Lotus Hotel and Casino. These "mashed-up" mythological elements do not recreate some prior myth, but—a purpose with even more entertainment potential—are creating "new" myths of the gods and demigods, and coming-of-age adventures suited for the American millennial child. As Riordan knows well, for many moderns the classical gods are hard to take seriously.

---

1   Some critics have condemned the series as copying J. K. Rowling, but then again, Harry Potter is also based on previous stories in the construction of the hero and the hero's journey. The *Wall Street Journal Review* (Feb. 12, 2010), http://blogs.wsj.com/speakeasy/2010/02/12/percy-jackson-and-the-olympians-the-lightning-thief-review-revue/ (accessed June 1, 2016), even begins by saying, "Percy Jackson, you're no Harry Potter" and ironically later discusses the puns on "lightning" to make fun of the movie.

The writing of a Rowling or a Tolkien has the imaginative power to make such an impossible world live; Riordan does not attempt that. Instead he creates an ironized and semicomic universe that does not need to be taken too seriously to make its points—and to entertain. In contrast with the *Harry Potter* series—more timeless in many ways, although it has a certain British nineteenth- and twentieth-century boarding-school vibe, Percy Jackson is more grounded in America, circa early 2000. Perhaps it is not so much a knockoff of the *Harry Potter* series as some want to see, but rather, an American response to it, as is *The Hunger Games.*[2]

This chapter considers our film as a partial parody both of ancient myth and also of myth theories, especially those related to the hero's journey (Campbell in particular) in the context of millennial American life. We will first discuss the mythical/folkloric theme of the magical child, and his birth and circumstances, and will then move to a close reading of the movie's parodic recreation of the hero's journey, fitting in a long tradition of a most American myth, the road trip through the country.

PARODY AND THE PARODIC JOURNEY

The Greek term *parōidía*, means "a song sung alongside another"; in literature, "it is a form of satirical criticism or comic mockery that imitates the style and manner of a particular writer or school of writers so as to emphasize the weakness of the writer or the overused conventions of the school."[3] The idea of parody, although problematic, is ancient, appearing in Aristotle *Poetics* ii.5. Its modern theorization owes much to the Russian formalist Mikhail Bakhtin, particularly his *The Dialogic Imagination.*[4] His complex views on parody focus on the notion of the carnivalesque, the polyphonic, and the dialogic aspects of a text that imitates another with sometimes wild freedom. What particularly distinguishes it is its desire to challenge in some way or to ridicule some target text. For Gerard Genette, as seen in his famous *Palimpsestes*, the notion of hypertextuality is critical, the referential relationship of one text to another; Genette believes it is the playful mood of such hypertextuality that characterizes parody.[5] Linda Hutcheon further notes: "What is remarkable in modern parody is its range of intent—from the ironic and playful to the scornful and ridiculing . . . Parody, therefore, is a form of imitation, but imitation characterized by ironic inversion, not always at the expense of the parodied text . . . Parody is, in another formulation, repetition with critical distance, which marks difference rather than similarity."[6]

---

2   See Shau Ming Tan (2013), 70.
3   Kuiper (2012), 177.
4   Bakhtin (1981).
5   Genette (1997), 5ff. and 28.
6   Hutcheon (1989), 87 ff. For further critical discussion of parody, see also Hutcheon (1985), Dentith (2000), Chambers (2010), Rose (1993), Danes (1988), Reza Sadrian (2010).

KEY TERMS

Quest/monomyth: the hero's journey, which results in personal transformation and attainment of a higher status

Parody: an imitation, often playful, of another work of art or literature

Pastiche: the combination of different elements and sources to create a new story or character

Economic crisis of 2007–08: a global financial crisis, suffered deeply in America, possibly second only to the Great Depression

Diversity and integration: general acceptance of various cultures, races, ethnicities, disabilities, and gender identities, and the effort to have all groups coexist harmoniously and in an integrated manner

Council of the gods: a common scene in ancient epic where the gods discuss their views on how to proceed concerning momentous human problems

---

Whereas most of the films we discuss possess some parodic elements, this dimension is much more pronounced in *Percy Jackson*. Rick Riordan's pentalogy and the two movies (so far) based on his novels provide constant references to various Classical texts, which tell versions of ancient myths, but these texts are playfully treated, both in content and tone.[7] *Percy Jackson* falls best into the category of the "ironic and playful" imitation. It does not parody one particular text, but creates a vibrant pastiche of Classical myth with some texts, such as Homer's *Odyssey*, receiving special focus. But this ludic imitation and often inversion (sadly less vividly shown in the films than in the books) extends not just to Homer or Ovid (e.g., use of epithets such as "daughter of Athena," "goat boy," "son of Poseidon," and the more humorous "seaweed brain") but also to the meta-mythology proposed by myth theorists, observed in the repeated use of terms like "Quest" (as in Campbell's monomyth) and other quasi-technical words, as when Chiron explains that monsters never die because they are "archetypes," a wink to theories of archetypes as in Frye, Jung, and Frazer.

The film parodies the typical American teenage movie, with its stereotypical characters and their interactions with their teachers and mentors, and also other film genres such as the "buddy movie," "road trip," "archetypal quest," and the "coming-of-age tale about misfits making their way despite, or because of, absent parents."[8] Grover the satyr even declares about Camp Half-Blood: "It's like high school without the musical."

As Campbell's Quest-myth paradigm details, only after a hero/heroine embarks on a journey where he or she must face dangers and temptations does the transformed and true heroic figure emerge. As expected, this coming-of-age journey is central to Percy Jackson's story, both in individual books and

---

7   This probably applies as well to his other series based on Classical mythology, *The Heroes of Olympus* and the recent *The Trials of Apollo*, as well as to his overall style in ancillary books such as *The Demi-god Files* and *Percy Jackson's Greek Gods*.

8   Biancolli (2010).

as an overarching theme for the whole pentalogy. Julia Boll notes, "The hero's journey is, in essence, a rite of passage . . . the movement of the monomyth corresponds exactly to the master plot of children's fiction (home-away-homecoming) . . . a cycle of separation, initiation and return."[9] And we see precisely this in the first movie of the series. Percy leaves his familiar home of New York City for Camp Half-Blood on Long Island, and then, to rescue his mother and save the world, goes on his true journey to the West (and back), like Aeneas, and returns first to New York to fight his final battle and ultimately back to Camp, his true new home.

THE MAGICAL CHILD AND THE PROBLEMATIC PARENT

Paul Collins, an author of children's stories himself, explains how *The Lightning Thief* fits well with Christopher Booker's classification of a basic plot, "rags to riches" (out of the seven he models for his book)[10]: "They are all essentially stories of growing up, about coming into the power and responsibility of adulthood, and about the dark forces that try to stop them. They begin, usually, with a child or youthful hero/heroine who is often an orphan or part orphan (like Aladdin, Percy has 'lost' a father) and who had been marginalized, forced to live in the shadows like Cinderella: neglected, scorned, undervalued, overlooked, and mistreated."[11]

As mentioned in our introduction, the birth of a marvelous child/hero is surrounded by mysterious circumstances.[12] Percy Jackson has lived with his mother, Sally Jackson, maltreated and disdained by his stepfather "Smelly Gabe Ugliano" (he is ugly and smells so bad he masks Percy's smell so that monsters can't find him) for as long as he can remember and has little understanding of who his real father was. Like Harry, Percy is figuratively blind and has the self-centeredness typical of teenagers at the series' beginning.[13] His quest will be for knowledge and self-awareness, which makes his search for the "lightning bolt" ("someone has stolen the light") highly significant.[14] At the end of the school term, through a series of bizarre events, such as an attack by a Fury at the Metropolitan Museum of Art, he discovers he is a half-blood, a demigod. The ancient gods are still alive, and every now and then they "hook up" (a term that ironizes and modernizes the ancient rape of mortal women by gods and whitewashes sexual violence) with mortals and create semidivine children.

---

9   Boll (2011), 87.
10 Booker (2006).
11 Collins (2008), 24.
12 On the birth of the magical hero, see Rank (2015).
13 Collins (2008), 27.
14 Collins (2008), 28.

The film begins at the school year's end, a moment of transition in which children "move up" to a new grade, symbolic of a new stage in life.[15] Percy will find his father, while being engaged in the figurative quest for masculinity embodied in the phallic shape of a magical object, the thunderbolt. The five books of the *Percy Jackson* series use the structure of mythic and natural time, except for book 3, all taking place during the summer months, always a transitional time. And let's not forget that, like Harry, Percy also has a summer birthday. Book 3 takes place over the Christmas break, a time of passage into a new year. The two films that have so far appeared leave this cyclical time rather vague, an outcome of the changing of the protagonists' ages.[16]

The earliest creators of myth did not know about the Big Bang or the quark-gluon plasma. What they did understand was human life, and their creation stories reproduce patterns of natural and human nature, in particular interactions between generations and within families. As Collins observes, "The gods of Olympus . . . are stand ins not only for the establishment (school, society, church) but also for those other godlike beings: parents." Further: "And this . . . is one of the secrets to the success of the series: it mimics the experience of everyone growing up—and of every person's troublesome need to become him- or herself."[17] Mythological heroes usually have problematic relationships with their parents, in particular with a dead one or often a divine one. But also they are very close (even dangerously so) to one of them: in an extreme, Oedipus marries Jocasta, but Perseus faces sure death when he defends his mother and tries to get Medusa's head. The Oedipal complex is at play here, as Percy risks everything to rescue his beloved mother from Hades, and their very special bond is evident. As noted, Sally is married to Smelly Gabe, so awful a man that he represents no competition for Percy, and he, we may say, can indulge in the Oedipal stage. Yet in subsequent books, we will see that Sally finds a much nicer guy, an English teacher who completely understands Percy. At the same time, Percy is developing his own love interest for Annabeth and for Rachel Elizabeth Dare, and thus outgrows the initial Oedipal stage.

---

15 Riordan (2008), ix: "Mythology especially appeals to middle grade readers because they can relate to the idea of demigods. . . . He [Percy] is constantly struggling to understand his identity, because he straddles two worlds but belongs to neither. Middle schoolers understand being in between." Riordan was a middle school teacher before becoming a full-time writer.

16 As Turan (2010) explains, the directors probably felt the need to expand the audience to "an older male demographic" and thus "they've deliberately restructured the plot to prioritize the action moments and emphasize the grotesqueness of mythological beings."

17 Collins (2008), 25.

Percy Jackson and the Olympians: The Lightning Thief (2010) Based on Rick Riordan's 2005 novel	
Director: **Screenwriter:** **Cast:**	Chris Columbus Craig Titley Logan Lerman (Percy), Brandon T. Jackson (Grover), Alexandra Daddario (Annabeth), Jake Abel (Luke), Pierce Brosnan (Mr. Brunner/Chiron), Sean Bean (Zeus), Steve Coogan (Hades), Kevin McKidd (Poseidon), Catherine Keener (Sally Jackson), Uma Thurman (Medusa), Rosario Dawson (Persephone)

Percy Jackson also tells the story of a boy who grows up with an absent father. In many patriarchal societies, a son was defined by his father (thus Achilles is called "Son of Peleus," and Medusa calls Percy "Son of Poseidon"). A son felt compelled to live up to his father's example, and a son was likewise shamed if he was disgraced. And, of course, paternity was an issue, as we mentioned regarding the myth of Phaethon. Even in the United States there is the persistent myth that a boy must "discover the father," often providing a subtext in discussions of the poor and their supposed absent fathers. Accordingly, in current blockbuster movies absent fathers/parents are crucial, as with Luke Skywalker and Harry Potter. In *Pan's Labyrinth* Ofelia's father is dead; in *Clash* Perseus' divine father is mostly absent, and in *Wrath* Ares is angry because Zeus comes to love Perseus more. In *Troy* Achilles' father died young. Hercules (in the 2014 film) never knew his father. Poseidon, despite being a god, is also flawed, especially as a parent and Percy insists that he would have liked to have seen him "just once." As a young man growing up, Percy must come to accept who his real father is, although that absence is not totally his fault. The motif of the orphan and the absent parent is timeless, but it is also particularly relevant today, especially to those growing up among the urban settings of the American new millennium, where traditional families are less than ever the norm. Further, a main concern of the entire series is the need for children to be recognized and loved by their parents. When at the end of the fifth book Percy is offered immortality as a gift for having saved the world, he declines and instead asks that all demigods be acknowledged by their divine parents.

So what is Percy's relationship with Poseidon like? The god of the oceans is the first character seen in the film, as he emerges, a giant, out of the water in Coney Island. He will not appear much in the film, but the fact that he appears first and larger than life is significant, implying how the father can be a towering presence for a growing boy. Although Percy does not see him until the end of the movie, his voice communicates with him at critical times, and he sometimes seems to be shadowing Percy. Sally talks about his absent father later on the ride to Long Island, without yet fully explaining who he is. But Percy will learn this from Chiron at camp, as he is directed to his sea-themed cabin.[18] When he picks up the trident he says, "This thing's got some weight to it," implying that he has a heavy destiny. At the end of *Wrath* Helius, son of Perseus, is given his father's sword, and when he asks to hold it, Perseus says yes.

Later, when Percy is seriously wounded by Annabeth, Poseidon's voice tells him, "Go to the water." At the Lotus Casino, Poseidon will "wake him up" again and warn him of the surrounding dangers. Their final encounter at Olympus is moving. Percy is angry at first and says of his Quest: "I didn't do it for you. I did it to save Mom." But gradually he warms up to Poseidon and seems to understand the complexities of the situation, as free will apparently is not always a choice for gods: "When I was with you and your mother, . . . I was becoming human. . . . That is why he [Zeus] passed the law [that gods could not contact their human offspring]. . . . If you ever need me . . . I will be there for you, in your thoughts." And indeed, Poseidon will always be with Percy in difficult times. The end of the movie shows Percy finding at last an ideal, even if mostly absent, father who will replace the horrible "bad father" figure of Smelly Gabe, who, ironically and humorously, as the coda (after the titles) shows, is petrified by Medusa's gaze as he breaks open the fridge to get a beer. And one can make the connection here with Theseus who at his return from Crete, involuntarily also kills his "foster" father (in a version where his true father is Poseidon) in order to become king.

In contrast, we have Luke, who though not a fundamentally bad individual is so angry and resentful of his father Hermes' abandonment that he intends to overthrow the gods. Fittingly, in the second Percy Jackson movie Hermes is running something that looks like a cross between Kinko's and UPS. As the *Homeric Hymn to Hermes* demonstrates, the god was a master thief and often helps Zeus in his problematic adventures. Luke is in many ways the epitome of the effects of abandonment and the lack of good masculine models in boys' lives. Percy turned out basically well, because he was raised by his good mother Sally Jackson, while Luke was left with an unbalanced May Castellan. Plus, we don't really see Hermes much involved in Luke's life either. As Percy is about to embark on his Quest, he tells them: "My dad's a jerk; I never met him. You too? Guess we all got Daddy issues . . . that's because all gods are the same, selfish. They only care about themselves." Indeed Luke spends the whole series hating his father and trying to find another father figure, fatefully, in his great grandfather Kronos, as we will see in the second movie. And thus Luke decides to steal Zeus' lightning bolt, which he admits right before the final fight with Percy over the New York skyline: "I'm the lightning thief." He goes on: "To bring Olympus crumbling down. . . . They've been in power for too long. I say it's time for our generation to take over." And thus, unlike Percy, who is willing

---

18 See Durst (2008) for a nice essay on parents in the series.

to work with the previous generation, despite its faults, Luke incarnates the succession myth of the battle for power between children and their parents.

Annabeth seems to have grown up with an absent mother and father, and become tough and resourceful. But she is also a rather sad character who longs for her mother's contact, which occurs only briefly in Olympus at the movie's end. The books provide more explanation, for Annabeth, like all of Athena's children, is a product of a rather intellectual relation instead of a physical one. Her loneliness recalls that of the Classical Athena, who is born from the head of Zeus after he has impregnated and swallowed Metis. Like Luke, for whom she feels a profound affection—not developed much in the film yet—she had lived alone but does not have the same hatred and resentment that Luke experiences; she accepts her situation, and tempers her potential rage—as the real Athena might be expected to do.

In *Clash/Wrath* and *Immortals* an important theme is the primordial battle between Titans and Olympians, which also foregrounds the generational struggles between parents and children. In the first film of the *Percy Jackson* series, this is only briefly hinted at when Mr. Brunner explains the Titanomachy at the Metropolitan Museum of Art, and there is a slight mention of Tartarus in the Underworld (in the book, the trio fall into this pit and are almost swallowed). Yet Luke's statement at the end of the film that the Olympians have been in power too long will lead to the major theme of the following movie, *Sea of Monsters*, even if this is not necessarily the theme of the second book, as the resurrection of Kronos happens later.

THE HERO

A common motif found in our movies (*Clash/Wrath*, *Immortals*, *Pan's Labyrinth*, *Harry Potter*, *The Hunger Games*) is a younger generation bound to fix problems caused or suffered by the older generation. Perseus must save his mother, and Theseus must mend what King Aegeus could not; in myth Romulus and Remus must save Numitor (their grandfather, rightful king of Alba Longa, who was however displaced by his brother Amulius), and Jason is trying to regain the kingdom for his father. *Clash/Wrath* and *Immortals* present a corrupt divine order, which has displaced variants in *The Hunger Games* and *Harry Potter*. In our film, tensions between the gods have simmered for years. It seems Zeus really wants this confrontation with Poseidon; note how hasty he is to blame Poseidon for the loss of the thunderbolt and to threaten war. Clearly there are problems, and Percy must avert apocalypse, however young he is.

This is the driving problem of the plot; the stolen thunderbolt must be found "in fourteen days," before the summer solstice, June 21, or there will be war between the Olympians. The lightning bolt as a central element is a symbol for Zeus' hypermasculinity, the power that allowed Zeus to conquer the Titans. It is this magical object that Percy must find, which will turn his entire exploit, we can interpret, into a young man's search for his own phallus, for his own masculinity; but as Collins observes, it is also a search for light, for knowledge and self-consciousness.[19] Still, as in Campbell's hero's journey, Percy initially refuses this call (note his isolation at the museum, when he listens to his iPod music, his ears plugged with earphones as Mr. Brunner lectures), thinking he is a loser. At Camp Half-Blood he begins to gradually understand his new destiny, as he verbalizes, "This is a lot to process."

As with many marvelous children, the hero-to-be (e.g., Perseus, Moses) is in a kind of exile in a station beneath him and does not know who his parents are or who he really is. Harry Potter lives in the cupboard with the Dursleys, not knowing about his magical heritage. Perseus again, after being cast in the ocean in a chest, arrives in a foreign land. Hercules, the greatest example of a demigod, lives with an adoptive father (and mother in the Disney movie) in a place where he does not entirely belong (again the Disney version makes this even more explicit; see the theme song). This initial exile is somewhat obscured in the film, where Yancy Academy is actually in New York City, while it is somewhere in Upstate New York in the book. All these heroes face a journey in which they will find who they truly are.

Percy Jackson's character is modeled on a collage of various Classical heroes, starting with Perseus, with whom he shares a name, but also Theseus as son of Poseidon, Odysseus, and Hercules in the adventures. Percy, although having special powers coming from his father Poseidon, mimics the exploits of many heroes. His role as Perseus is particularly significant. Perseus is a central status quo hero in canonical mythology, but here and even more in *Clash/Wrath* he is a more problematic figure, and in both cases exists in contrast to the Olympian gods.

But as with other heroes there is something defective about him. In Classical myth the defect is usually social, e.g., belonging to a poor or socially alienated family, a point emphasized in the case of Theseus in *Immortals*. Riordan has updated this motif through the theme of disability as exile, which his young readers can relate to. Here Percy has dyslexia and ADHD, both of which are getting worse. Thus he does poorly at school, but is able to read Ancient Greek inscriptions at the Met. One of the concerns surrounding the millennial child is integration. Schools strive to place children with various abilities in the same classroom, as well as working on the integration of those who are not traditionally considered mainstream from an ethnic, gender, or disability perspective. And just as with Oedipus and his defective feet, Harry Potter and his scar, Hercules with his abnormal size (in the Disney movie his strength makes him dangerously clumsy, and this makes him an outcast, a social "zero"), Percy is marked by a trait that makes him unable to adjust to the normal environment

---

19 The second movie actually focuses more on the feminine force of fertility in the Golden Fleece and its power to revive a tree that holds the life of a girl.

of the school.[20] And he also suffers from the common problem of a "broken family" and a vile stepfather. But Percy will discover that his brain is "wired for ancient Greek" and not for English,[21] and that his ADHD comes from his innate battle reflexes.

THE QUEST

CALL TO ADVENTURE

The setting of Percy's first brush with living myth, also the beginning of his journey of self-discovery, and his first "call to adventure," which begins his Quest, occurs appropriately in the Met, among Greek and Roman statues and artifacts. As he climbs the steps, his father's voice tells him, "Be prepared . . . everything is about to change." Poseidon is shown fleetingly in disguise standing across the street. The camera first directs the viewer's gaze to a sign that reads "The New Greek and Roman Galleries." This refers to the actual renovations that took place in this area of the museum for three years; it reopened to the public in the first few years of the millennium. In Percy's new world this is symbolic. It coincides with a revival of the ancient gods and creatures, and in a very American context at that, at the heart of New York. The reopening of the galleries matches the film's new millennial reincarnation of the ancient past. Just like the freshly arranged exhibits, Percy Jackson will be a renewed version of Greek myth, recontextualized in the United States at the onset of the 2000s.

Percy is accompanied by two teachers, both disguised mythological figures, one representing the forces of enlightenment in the figure of Mr. Brunner, the centaur disguised as a Latin teacher. His lecture in the museum provides needed mythical background, telling how the Olympians overthrew the Titans, how they are often at odds with each other, and how they go among humans to hook up. Mr. Brunner goads the tuned-out Percy to answer a question about demigods, and, looking at him intently, tells him many demigods became great heroes; he then asks Percy if he can name another demigod/hero, and gives him a clue. They have something in common. Percy then untangles the name Perseus, which allows him to provide an answer. This statement is obviously programmatic for the movie. But the sullen substitute English teacher, Miss Dodds, turns out to be the fury Alecto, a monster sent from the Underworld, who in *Aeneid* book 12 inflames Amata and Turnus to revolt and war. The three

---

20 Rick Riordan (2008), vii, reports that this explanation of dyslexia and ADHD came to him as a way of comforting his own child after he was diagnosed with these conditions. "In the story, Percy discovers that being different can be a source of strength—and a mark of greatness . . . Percy was my way of honoring all the children I've taught who have ADHD and dyslexia, but more importantly he was a myth for my son to make sense of who he is" (vii–viii).

21 As Wein (2008), 152, remarks, Percy's dyslexia and ADHD are not always consistent since at times he seems to have no trouble reading signs or seems actually quite focused and in control.

furies are servants of Hades, and Alecto in particular is the head torturer. In parodic and humorous imitation again, the film conceives her as an English teacher (a pre-algebra teacher in the book), a subject sure to be torture for the dyslexic ADHD Percy, as the confusing words on the board early in the film show.

The Furies or Erinyes are chthonic forces of revenge and famously pursue Orestes in Aeschylus' *Oresteia* for the murder of his mother Clytemnestra. They were born from the blood of Uranus' castrated genitals (after Kronos, his son, severs them). Thus their origin is a violent one. Another version has them born from the primordial dark power of Nix ("Night"). In the film Alecto appears as the first "eye opener" for Percy pointing to a whole other parallel world, which however is merged with the ordinary world of America and New York. She is a force of chaos and darkness that comes with a message from Hades: "You stole the lightning bolt. . . . Give it to me!" Hades is a milder version of the Titanic forces that will become increasingly central to the saga. Percy in his heroic career faces a series of evils and opposing forces and in the process he recovers the symbol of light and manhood (which oddly, has been with him since he left camp): Medusa, the Hydra, Hades, the land of the Lotus eaters, and more.

Percy's Quest is on. His cover exposed, with his mother Sally and Grover, Percy leaves the civilized world of New York City on a late night ride to Long Island. This marks the moment when the hero and crew "Cross the First Threshold." When, close to the Camp, they collide with "raining cows" and their car flips, Grover is revealed as a satyr and they must face a minotaur, again a hybrid form, as discussed in our chapter on *The Hunger Games*. Although in Greek myth the Minotaur is simply this half-man, half-bull offspring of Pasiphae and Poseidon's bull, here Hades has sent it to take Sally to the Underworld. The Minotaur again embodies the struggle between human and animal forces that battle inside us; at the end of the day we are all simply animals with higher intellect who constantly live trying to control our instincts, and this is what culture and civilization are about. Percy is at a liminal age for both the body and the mind, in which teenagers struggle with their most visceral, bodily instincts, yet at the same time begin to take pleasure in them. Adulthood requires us to learn to suppress them more, and the successful destruction of this hybrid beast is the first step in this direction.

The Minotaur pursues them to the barrier protecting Camp Half-Blood, a barrier his mother cannot cross; this is symbolic of those trials that must be done without the help of parents. The Minotaur makes his mother disappear in a cloud of flame. As Perseus in *Clash* had a sword of Zeus he needed to use, so Percy here has a pen that turns into a sword, Riptide, which does not help him much. But Percy defeats the Minotaur by tricking it into breaking off one of its horns, another masculine icon, and stabbing him with it. Perseus in *Wrath of the Titans* kills a Minotaur-man in similar fashion. There is something almost cartoonish in the way the monster dooms itself by crashing against a tree and losing a horn, suggesting an image of sexual castration but also parodically poking fun at the mythical monster. And here we recall Hercules as well, whose masculine prowesses are emblematized when he tears a horn off the river god Achelous (who was trying to abduct Deianira, whom Hercules himself marries after this:)

> "Nor was this enough; while he was holding [my horn] he broke it off, and ripped it from my mangled forehead. This, filled with fragrant fruits and flowers, the Naiads hallowed; [the goddess] Fair Abundance with my horn is enriched."
> (Ovid, *Met.* 9.85–88)

Thus the myth offers one explanation for the origin of a symbol of fertility, appropriate after an act of masculine prowess. And as we mentioned, Percy's fictional construction as a character is indeed a pastiche of various heroes, including Hercules, as we see later in his battle with the Hydra. The killing of the Minotaur sets up Theseus to be king of Athens, and this event thus sets up Percy for future greatness.

A NEW WORLD

From the trauma of the fight Percy faints and must sleep a number of days, metaphorically a kind of death and transition to a new world, here Camp Half-Blood. He assumes his mother is dead. Camp Half-Blood is a liminal place at the edge of Long Island bordering the sea, his father's domain, and there he recognizes a newfound community. This is the only place where neither monsters nor humans can penetrate—most of the time. The Camp is surrounded by a magical barrier and has a magical tree where the spirit of Thalia, a (now) dead daughter of Zeus, resides. It is symbolic of children's desire for protection from what they perceive as a violent and dangerous adult world.[22] This is clearly seen in the last film of the *Harry Potter* series, when Hogwarts is engulfed in a magical protective dome, and in the many protective spells Hermione casts when the trio are on the run in the woods ("protego, salvia hexia," etc.) and that are visualized in the movie as an invisible and concealing barrier.

Camp Half-Blood is both a safe haven and training ground for children of the gods where they are taught to fight and reach their heroic potential.[23]

---

22 But adults can also be humorously parodied, as Shulman (2005) observes: "Many readers will find parallels between the quarrels of the gods and those of the adults around them. What child hasn't felt at the mercy of mighty, unpredictable beings?"

23 Note how in the Disney *Hercules* (aimed at a similar audience) Hercules undergoes rigorous training to make him go from "Zero" to "Hero." Likewise in the evolving *Star Wars* saga, Luke Skywalker was put through rigorous and successful training, which had not worked well for his father, Anakin, who turned to the dark side. In the new series, we find that the mature Luke tried to rebuild the Jedi order, and to train Kylo Ren, son of his sister Leia and Hans Solo, but that training failed too.

This corresponds to that segment where the hero gains training and allies to prepare him for the "road of trials," here his road trip to Hades. He now is in the "Belly of the Beast," for he learns soul-shaking secrets, which is a mythological expression of how wrenching the move out of childhood can be; he gains allies, skills, and indeed enemies. The youths at the camp form a diverse and colorful group, which corresponds to our multicultural world, with a fantastic overlay. Myth in itself is a diverse world, with gods, monsters, demigods, and other fantastic creatures, and this "motley crew" of mythological beings speaks of the diverse millennial American world in which modern children are growing up.[24]

The first of these helpers is Percy's Latin teacher, Mr. Brunner, who was supposedly disabled too, confined to a wheelchair that somewhat magically hides the hind part of a horse, since he is actually Chiron the Centaur; he assumes the role of mentor in Campbell's model, who in myth trained Heracles and Achilles and many others, and is nicely played in this first movie by Pierce Brosnan.[25] Also interesting in terms of social inclusion and its myths is the presence of Percy's best friend, Grover. In the human world he is a boy with crutches, unable to walk properly, implying disability. But he is a satyr, part-human and part-goat, a creature that blends nature and culture. This duality allows him to operate successfully in two worlds, as is the case with Chiron.[26] The film goes one step further and casts the African American actor Brandon T. Jackson, foregrounding racial difference as well, which some may see as having racist overtones (the stereotype of the sex-driven black man who grows horns after supposedly sleeping with Persephone?). He is a protector-in-training, his care sincere, but his impulses somewhat immature. He will also develop on this journey. Similarly, in the second movie Percy will have built a close relationship with his half-brother, a Cyclops, whose single eye causes him problems and also makes him an outcast.

Camp Half-Blood will be central to Percy's coming of age and the revelation of Percy's own masculine instincts, for Quest-heroes often gain a consort. Percy encounters Annabeth, who afterward tells Percy that she has had very little experience with the outside world. We learn later in the series that she has an aloof yet loving father who lives in San Francisco. And like Percy, in the third book she will also have to travel West to find him. Annabeth is the necessary female/feminist model partner of the modern hero, recalling Hermione as well as Andromeda in *Wrath of the Titans*. Annabeth, a daughter of Athena, goddess of war and wisdom, is naturally smart, like Rowling's heroine, yet her most salient quality is physical strength and ability with a sword. Annabeth is also a good designer and architect, yet the films hardly explore this dimension.

24 See Rees (2008), 75.

25 Wein (2008), 154, on physical disability in the series.

26 Wein (2008). Interestingly, in the Disney *Hercules* Philoctetes the satyr is the trainer and mentor of the young Hercules.

Hermione does participate in battles, but she does so with a wand and rarely calls on actual physical force (she is not very good at flying, for example), and her interventions are mainly defensive. Annabeth is physically strong, a better warrior than Percy even, very good with weapons, and has had hundreds of victories, which makes her useful for his Quest. When Percy first sees her at camp, Grover laughs and tells him, "She will squash you like a bug."

A series of events follow where he begins to understand his powers (especially over water), which become truly godlike during the movie's conclusion. The film begins with Percy being able to stay under water in a pool far longer than normal human beings can; this makes us think of a sort of birth (it is interesting that the directors decided to begin the story with this scene right after the initial discussion of Zeus and Poseidon; the book does not start like this), and especially the healing powers of water, which all point at his divine nature. Again, the pool implies a new beginning, his new birth as demigod. And once more here, as we mentioned in our discussion of *Harry Potter*, there are birthing and initiation connections of water.

A critical moment comes when Percy participates in an intense game of "capture the flag." He is exhausted by running, and goes to wash his face in the water, when he sees the flag. He is ready to grab it, but is stopped by Annabeth, who challenges him, saying, "Let's see what you are made of." They get into an intense fight, and Percy seems beaten, until he hears a spectral voice intone "Go to the water, Percy . . . the water." He barely touches the water, which then climbs up his arm and heals his wounds, and turns him into an unconquerable swordsman, who twice overcomes Annabeth and gains the flag. Here Percy really begins to understand his true powers, although it makes him feel "like a mutant."

The central trial of Percy's heroic journey happens the evening after his victory. Annabeth lets him know that his father Poseidon and her mother Athena hate each other, and she has strong feelings for him—but she is not sure whether they are positive or negative. But then, just as Hades in *Clash* makes a horrific epiphany, demanding that Andromeda be sacrificed by the time of the eclipse or the Kraken will be released, here Hades appears, showing that Percy's mother is in fact alive but trapped with Hades, and that Percy must return the bolt to Hades to regain his mother. Percy disobeys Chiron's order not to get involved (for which he is later praised by the Centaur) and takes on a "Quest," which is also a death journey, to recover his mother from Hades, who is not quite dead (like Ginny in *Harry Potter and the Chamber of Secrets*?).

Many mythic heroes have to take impressive journeys, as do Odysseus, Perseus, Heracles, Jason, and Aeneas, sometimes with companions, sometimes alone. Although Percy initially intends to go by himself, Grover and then Annabeth join him. With a tip of the hat to myth theory, Grover declares he has never been on an "actual quest." As noted, this journey (in parodic form, of course) evokes the greatest of all journeys: to rescue one of the dead from the

Lord of the Dead, a task only a Heracles or a Jesus can succeed in. It will require all their resources. At the same time, their adventure revives a common plot in modern movies and books, the road trip, going back to Mark Twain's *Huckleberry Finn* or John Steinbeck's *Travels with Charley*. In the canonical Perseus myth, one of Perseus' magic helpers was Hermes, and it is fitting that Luke, the resentful and problematic son of Hermes, who already is Percy's nemesis, bestows a pair of (stolen) flying Converse high-tops on them (like the winged sandals Perseus obtains). Note how Luke's cabin is fitted with modern high-tech computer screens and machinery, and that Luke greets them by saying "Welcome to the Modern World." This will echo his proclamation later that it is time for the new and younger gods to rule; Luke's character also alludes to a modern type, the sometimes malevolent tech geek. But this thematizes as well an important current cultural issue, the conflict between ancient (here Greek) and modern values.

Luke tells Percy he must find the three pearls of Persephone to enter the Underworld. Pearls have rich mythology; we think of "pearls of wisdom" or "a pearl of great price," although here they are used by Persephone's amatory "visitors" to escape from the Underworld. Luke is able to help because his father Hermes (as *psychopomp* or "soul guide") can enter Hades. He also gets a magical shield, which recalls Perseus' special shield in which Luke has hidden the bolt. A magical map (like the Marauder's map in Harry Potter perhaps, an element absent in the novel) will lead them first to Medusa, who holds one of the pearls.

THE JERSEY GORGON

Medusa's lair is located "at the edge of the world," actually in New Jersey (!), in a tacky and unkempt garden statue shop they must reach by bus. This humorous parody will amuse the alert reader aware of the background of Medusa and of the local idiosyncrasies of New York and the tri-state area. Medusa in myth lives at the end of the world, almost at the river Ocean, which can be situated in the Underworld. Here Annabeth, Grover, and Percy take a bus headed to "Atlantic City," a place at the continent's edge, but also where people may be lost, a place that may represent darkness, tackiness, seediness, lack of refinement, at least from a New York perspective. It is also in Frye's demonic world where chance rules and form is unstable. And so the AC/DC song "Highway to Hell" plays on.

The trio gets off before reaching Atlantic City, where Auntie Em's (perhaps a parodic reference to the *Wizard of Oz* here as well? but also, because it is pronounced Auntie 'M', as in Medusa) Garden Gnome Emporium is located. It is a wasteland, a desolate and abandoned place lacking all culture, stereotypical of New Jersey as dirty, polluted, and industrial (let's think here of the beginning of the HBO series *The Sopranos*, 1999–2007). This "garden shop" is a degraded pastoral setting fitting for a degraded "Garden State." The film once again parodically recreates—and laughs at—the myth of New York as the best that civilization has to offer, in contrast to the bleak New Jerseyan landscape.[27] In Auntie Em's store stand many half-broken statues, prior victims of Medusa. And here again, as we discussed in relation to Harry Potter, Percy becomes Perseus, decapitating the Gorgon, depriving her of any agency over her deadly gaze (they do keep the head in a bag for later use, as Perseus does), this proving again his masculinity.

But Percy and Annabeth get a glimpse of the possibly negative actions of their parents. Note what Medusa says to Annabeth: "Daughter of Athena . . . You have such beautiful hair. I once had hair like that. I was courted, desired by many suitors. But that all changed because of your mother, the woman who cursed me." Then she displays herself in her deadly snaky glory and later tells Percy, "I used to date your daddy."[28] She never actually calls him Percy, but constantly makes reference to him as "Son of Poseidon." In Ovid's account, Medusa was raped by Poseidon in a temple of Athena. The goddess, angered because the purity of her temple was violated and she could not punish Poseidon, instead turned the beautiful girl Medusa into a Gorgon so she would no longer be sexually attractive (Ovid, *Met.* 4.801–3). With these mythological references, the film, in its parodic tone, expects clever readers to enjoy the process of teasing out the mythological sources and the nature of the modern imitation. And Percy must kill his Gorgon. Here the film plays again with the merging of times and technologies, since Percy doesn't see Medusa's reflection in a shield but rather on the back of his iPod, which, if you think about it, is a pretty magical technology too (Fig. 10.1).

FIGURE 10.1 Percy sees Auntie Em/Medusa.

---

27 Rees (2008), 73–74, discusses the importance of New York in the series and suggests that the gods have chosen it because of its frantic fast pace and energy, and its wealth: "They also can't stomach anything less than living the good life in ultimate luxury. I can't picture Aphrodite in a third-world country, can you? Now Saks Fifth Avenue is another thing."

28 The myth of Medusa can symbolize the confrontation with forbidden knowledge, things that must not be seen or known, as is parental sexuality from a child's point of view. Thus it is telling how Medusa reveals information about his father's sexuality outside of his relationship with Percy's mother.

AMERICAN ATHENA

That evening, beside the motel pool, Annabeth comes upon Percy, who is submerged; he looks up at her, the woman who will draw him upward. She congratulates him on his prowess; he notices her forearm is badly bruised and, using his water powers, heals her, a metonymy for the further healing he will help her find. Annabeth tells Percy that Poseidon and Athena dislike each other because of the quarrel over Athens; Percy learns she has never seen her mother, and why no god can associate with his or her children. Athena, just like Poseidon, speaks to her in times of crisis. And this brings us to the utopian theme, the idea of reconciliation of opposites (Poseidon and Athena). They will eventually become a couple, and thus the children here do better than their parents.

Our gods-crossed lovers seem on the verge of a more intimate moment at the pool, but they are interrupted by Grover, who announces new trouble. To their dismay, they see on TV that Percy is suspected of the abduction and murder of his mother, thanks to the lies of his stepfather, who depicts him as a sort of drug-using juvenile delinquent of modern mythology. The innocent man on the run is of course another staple of modern-media myth. After they accidentally scare a maid who sees Medusa's head, Annabeth says they had better flee before the arrival of "Homeland Security," a somewhat chilling current reference. On the run again, their next destination is Nashville (the Athens of the South) and the Parthenon, where the second pearl is disguised as part of Athena's diadem. This scene is not in the original novel; perhaps the filmmakers could not resist using such a special American monument, which indeed merges past and present, the Greek world and modern America, a second creation of Greek civilization.

Seeing her mother is significant for Annabeth, although only a lifeless, irresponsive statue, an emblem of the distant and uninvolved mother she has (Fig. 10.2). This is tantamount to teens and preteens saying "You never listen, you don't understand!" "I wonder if she really looks like that," Annabeth muses, and Percy assures her she will see her mother (as she will). They sneak in at night, and Annabeth uses her crossbow to shoot the janitors with sleeping darts. Grover objects to this treatment of "working-class Americans"; he thinks she has killed them, acting like an aristocrat who has no regard for the life of commoners. Percy uses the winged sneakers (with difficulty) to fly up and snatch the pearl. They are then attacked by the Hydra, which is like the Hydra of Lerna killed by Heracles, representing the savage forces of nature, here a fire-breathing monster. Percy becomes a sort of Hercules, who must destroy a monster hard to kill, and Perseus learns the hard way about the traditional reproducing heads. As he flies around slicing off the Hydra heads, he looks like Perseus killing the monster threatening Andromeda. We have a kind of cosmic battle as Perseus fights the fire of the Hydra with waves of water. It is actually Grover who petrifies the Hydra with the head of Medusa. It takes two to kill it, just as Heracles needed the help of Iolaus to defeat the monster.

FIGURE 10.2 Statue of Athena in the Parthenon, Nashville, Tennessee, by Alan LeQuire.

MILLENNIAL LOTUS EATERS

On the way to Las Vegas, their next destination, there is a special message on the news reports: an unusual storm cloud is threatening the world. The pictures echo various recent movies with weather apocalypses. Las Vegas is itself a major player in American mythology, as particularly seen in Hunter S. Thompson's *Fear and Loathing in Las Vegas: A Savage Journey to the Heart of the American Dream* (1971). Let us say there is much illegal drug use in it. The episode of the Lotus Hotel and Casino is a masterfully ironic and humorous reconceptualization of the Homeric Land of the Lotus Eaters,[29] another test and symbol of the many temptations the hero must surpass to return home, enlightened and profoundly changed. The Lotus reflects the mythical status of Las Vegas, a place of illusion, of dreams of happiness, of false allurements, and of time, money, and lives squandered. The movie captures a bit of Vegas's false wonder. Note its profound stress on material satisfaction, from the all-you-can-eat buffets to the glistening new cars. The later, sadder career of Elvis Presley is associated with Las Vegas. As they enter the casino, we hear Elvis singing "A Little Less Conversation," by Billy Strange and Mac Davis.[30] Its Sirens appear in the dancers and singers that enthrall Grover in particular, rather like the miniskirted female attendants who give you free drinks

29 Holden (2010) agrees: "It's the movie's most fully realized sequence."
30 Note one of the song's key lines goes "Close your mouth and open up your heart and baby satisfy me—Satisfy me baby."

while you gamble your savings away. The book depicts addiction much more in the presentation of video games that blur children's minds and do not allow them to grow healthily. The Peter Pan syndrome is evident, that desire never to grow up.

This is a particularly noteworthy moment, when the creators can capture the spirit of the ancient myth in a modern context.[31] Homer's lotus becomes an edible marzipan flower that makes you forget the outside world, but we can read in it the dangerous allure of drugs, video games, and the general American childishness and vanity (see Grover comically having a pedicure for example, or a "hooficure" rather!) for teenagers. The moment they eat the lotus flower and suddenly start to laugh, giggle, look silly, and want to stay awhile is an obvious reference to drug use seen in various cinematic "stoner" scenes. It is chilling to see that Percy indeed is about to forget his homecoming, as he forgets the "time-sensitive mission" he is on, and accepts Annabeth's stoned statement that their purpose in coming was "to have fun," to which Percy exclaims, "OK, let's never leave," at which Annabeth squeals in joy. The film changes the tone of the book here, since the older age of the characters allows them to flirt with sexuality—especially in the character of the lusty satyr.

To evoke another bit of American mythology, we see Grover dancing skillfully with a hat on and making dance moves that echo another pop culture mythic figure, Michael Jackson, whose estate was called, we remember, the Neverland Ranch, and who seemed tragically trapped in a drug-enhanced Peter Pan lifestyle. And this is a meta-moment too, since Grover is black, as was Jackson. At this critical moment, it is his father's voice that comes to his aid ("No. Percy. Don't eat the flower. It dulls the senses."—reminding us of Luke Skywalker hearing Obi Wan Kenobi declare, "Use the Force") and incites him to rouse his fellows, fight the guards, recover the pearl, steal a car, and escape. Like Odysseus, they have heard the song of the Sirens and lived to tell about it.

ABANDON ALL HOPE, YE WHO ENTER THE HOLLYWOOD HILLS

They have lost six days at the Lotus Casino instead of only a few hours, so they must hurry. They cross the Mojave Desert to Los Angeles, under an apocalyptic sky, while the radio proclaims increasingly extreme weather, sign of the impending god-war. The entrance to the Underworld is located beside the H (for Hades? Or Hell?) of the famous Hollywood sign. Percy's ability to read Greek allows him to interpret what seems Modern Greek graffiti, which proclaims "Woe to all depraved souls," which harks back to the inscription to the entrance of Dis in Dante, Canto III.9 *Lasciate ogne speranza, voi ch'entrate* ("Abandon all hope, you who enter"). We find here another level of parody and irony, just as New York is

---

31   Other brilliant moments later in the series are the personifications of the rivers Hudson and East and the recreation of the Achilles/Patroclus pair in Clarisse and Selena in the final battle of book 5. Riordan doesn't explain the myth here, but rather enacts it.

high and Olympian LA is low, subterranean, and hellish (though the entrance to Hell is actually in the Hollywood Hills), a dichotomy that actualizes the differences between the East and West Coasts of the United States, from a New Yorker's perspective. Here they make their death journey, the episode Campbell calls "the Ordeal," the lowest point in the mythological circle (the "Demonic Epiphany" in Frye's words), from which the hero either dies or emerges changed and triumphant. Appropriately, Percy must descend to the Underworld, rescue his mother (myth often has a parent or relation in the Underworld, his father Anchises for Aeneas and his mother Anticlea for Odysseus, or Eurydice for Orpheus), and obtain Zeus' stolen lightning bolt.

Gatekeepers and barriers must be faced, beginning with the customary Charon, ferryman of the Styx. Charon tells them to "die and come back" because the Underworld does not accept the living, which recalls the frosty reception Aeneas got when he tried to board Charon's skiff. They offer him dollars (a recollection of the coins put in the dead's eyes), which his touch burns, and Grover makes the pointed social comment, "You are burning money. We are in a recession." These words again convey the duality of the two texts, *Percy Jackson and the Olympians: The Lightning Thief* and the life of millennial American children, in parodic dialogue with ancient myth and its incarnation in the *Aeneid*, for example. Luckily, they have some gold drachmas taken from Auntie Em to pay the fare.

Charon transports them through a rather striking filmic construction of the Underworld, where we see broken objects and debris passing by, as they fly over flame-filled landscapes from which emerge the wails of the damned. Charon declares that this is the "scrapheap of human misery. Lost hopes and dreams. Wishes that never came true. . . . All lives end in suffering and tragedy." The death journeys of Odysseus and Aeneas served to firm their hero's resolve to live meaningfully; Odysseus learns from Achilles it is better to be alive at almost any cost, and the problematic Trojan Aeneas is transformed into the more mission-ready Roman Aeneas. But here we encounter themes we also saw in the episode of the Lotus Casino that reflect modern nihilistic perspectives. One can think of the sense of doom that engulfed the country at the height of the economic crisis of 2008 (the film appeared in 2010). But also this gloomy saying reflects the tragic lesson Achilles pronounces in the parable of the two urns of Zeus: that all humans get evil, and it is just a question of how much. (*Iliad* 24.525–33) This view might seem more common now as our religious, cultural, economic, and political systems have been tested and found wanting. Modern consumer culture is built in part on provoking desire, which leads to disappointment. Advertising and ideology promote dreams of success; hell is where those dreams come to die. As Bruce Springsteen says: "Now those memories come back to haunt me, they haunt me like a curse / Is a dream a lie if it don't come true / Or is it something worse. . . ." Hell is where dreams come to die— important for a young person, who still has dreams.

The traditional Cerberus is comically split into three hellhounds here, but ironically they are partially domesticated pets that respond to Persephone (absent in this scene in the book), who is cast as something of Hades' trapped and abused "trophy wife," the sex-thirsty queen of Hell, clearly unsatisfied with Hades' favors, seeking and receiving secret visitors for erotic encounters. This is indeed a major shift from the book; perhaps the directors felt more sexual innuendo was needed to entice an older audience. Indeed, the presumed sexual encounter of Grover the satyr with the queen ("I haven't had a satyr visit before")—and notice that he grows horns after that—hints at the process of sexual maturation, which is absent in the first volume of the series, where Grover gets his horns for being a good protector. The fact that satyrs, Pan, and fauns have some connection with the devil might explain this symbolism. But this accords with the traditional myth in which Persephone is forced to be the bride of Hades by his abduction and the pomegranate seeds she may be forced to eat. The *Homeric Hymn to Demeter* registers this resistance; *Percy Jackson* updates it by making Persephone trapped in a "Hellish" marriage to Hades, and eager for payback. Persephone, as a dying and rising goddess, was worshipped because she is a bridge between the realm of the living and the world of the dead, and can presumably, with the help of her mother Demeter, aid the worshipper in both realms, as she will do here.

At his palace they meet Hades, who has humorously assumed the shape of an aging, rather pathetic rock and roll legend (complete with red guitar), a good performance by Steve Coogan. "Stick to the Mick Jagger thing," says Grover after Hades shows himself in all his demonic might at the urging of the teenagers, as he had done earlier at the Camp. Again, the "aging rock star" is a sort of archetype for our time of faded glory, corresponding to the hopeless nihilism of Charon. The youthful Perseus must overcome the ancient Graeae, youth overpowering age. Here, allegorically speaking, youthful hope must overcome jaded and hopeless adulthood and keep the life and dreams of the young alive. Hades says Percy looks like his father[32] and tells Perseus how he was exiled to Hades by Poseidon and Zeus. He wants the lightning bolt so he can defeat his opponents and become "king of the gods" (as Hades tries to become in *Clash*, as well as in Disney's *Hercules*), and he accuses Percy of having stolen it. Hades presents Percy's mother to trade for the bolt, which is then discovered by accident inside the shield, put there by Luke. This is the "reward" or "seizing the sword" (a thunderbolt here) stage in Percy's journey. Percy evokes Aeneas, who has on his shield the images of the future greatness of Rome and hence is carrying a power he doesn't even know he has. Seeing the bolt and believing Percy has lied to him, Hades opens the gates of Hell. All seems lost for our trio, who are trapped between the burning damned and the threatening hellhounds. But

---

32 This is important for identity construction; when Telemachus is on his travels, note how Helen, for example, tells him he looks just like this father (*Od.* 4.138–46).

they are saved by Persephone, who, if Hades became ruler of the gods, would be trapped with him forever. So she feigns to kiss her husband passionately, steals the bolt, blasts him into unconsciousness, and sends them, all but Grover, back to the world of the living. She is the magic goddess who, in Campbell's system, often helps the hero escape. They (especially his mother) have had a symbolic death and rebirth, and Percy and company have managed the greatest of heroic deeds, to rescue a living person from Hades.

GODS AND DEMIGODS: THE RETURN HOME

To arrive before the summer solstice, the trio is magically transported back to New York, to the Empire State Building, where, on the six hundredth floor is the modern site of Olympus. But before returning the bolt, Percy must violently confront Luke. As in the *Harry Potter* series, after resurrection there is one final battle to win. The battle with Luke, as they fly like gods, fight with lightning bolts, and unleash cascades of waters, is indeed a battle of gods, not humans. Percy's assumption of Poseidon's power is underscored when he makes a water trident appear, with which he seems to finish off Luke—yet as we know from the second movie, he is not dead.

What follows is a slight parody of the "council of the gods" scenes we see in Homer and Vergil, as well as movies like the earlier *Clash of the Titans*, led by perhaps a bit-too-human Zeus nicely portrayed by Sean Bean. The gods (at least those who speak) in Olympus have British accents, embodying the modern myth of the Brits as being loftier and more refined from an American perspective. What is interesting in this scene is that demigods are allowed to access Olympus (using elevators, of course), though Percy's mother as mere mortal cannot; significantly, Percy won't be accepted back there until the final book, after he saves the world from Kronos and the Titans. The gods are depicted as giants, and Zeus seems particularly arrogant. Percy relates how Luke was the true lightning thief and tells the gods some home truths: that Luke was angry (at Hermes) and that he wanted the gods to destroy themselves, suggesting their own murderous folly. Athena has a brief communication with Annabeth, telling her how proud she was of her. Zeus, with some irritation, agrees to release Grover from the Underworld.

In *Clash/Wrath* there is a strong conflict between Zeus and Perseus, which is never quite healed until Zeus is on the point of death, and barely then. Here the gigantic Poseidon tries to reach out to Percy, but succeeds only when he reduces himself to human scale, which has symbolic meaning. His explanation of his absence (I was becoming human and cared less for my divine responsibilities) is an exaggerated description of the plight of many parents, who seem larger than life in the eyes of their child, but who cannot grasp the external responsibilities a parent may have, which keeps parent and child apart. But they are partially reconciled, for Percy does realize that his father is always with him at some level. Percy has accomplished a major step of the hero's initiation. Not only has he done great deeds, but he has reconciled with the father, an important step as seen in the lives of Odysseus and Aeneas, for example, and a motivator in many other myths.

Perseus also was able to defend his mother from an unwanted suitor, King Polydectes; our Percy enables his mother to kick out Gabe and be free of him. And just as Perseus petrifies Polydectes with the Gorgon's head, so Gabe is set up to self-petrify. Both have defended their mother. Full closure is finally achieved when Percy returns to Camp Half-Blood, his true home now, as his mother tells him, "This is where you belong." Even more than in the books, where Percy returns to New York to live with his mother every year, the film implies instead that Percy will live at camp now, or at least it leaves the matter open. This return shows the conclusion of the journey back, with a sense of recognition from the community of a hero who has been transformed by his Quest and helped humanity along the way. But Percy is not the only one who has been transformed; Grover has received his horns (with all the sexual innuendo) and is now a "Senior Protector," while Annabeth has met her mother for the first time and also seems to have a better understanding of who she is. And the scene, with a near kiss, suggests the future of Annabeth and Percy.

MYTH MAKES THE MILLENNIUM

In his introductory essay to *Demigods and Monsters*, Rick Riordan tells us: "Mythology is the symbolism of civilization. It contains our most deeply imbedded archetypes. Once you know mythology, you see it everywhere. . . . Mythology is a way of understanding the human condition."[33] This is precisely what we find in the thirteen movies we discuss in this book. We see in all of them a form of mythical structure, in some cases more direct and in others more displaced. Mythology does live on, with other characters and settings perhaps, but the mythical themes and archetypes remain. Thus we see in the two films based on Riordan's series how the Greek gods and heroes, even if parodied and ironically recreated, can live on in the new millennium at the center of American life; and how the archetypal struggle between parents and children is still relevant to the human condition, though they can, of course, be parodied and humorized.

REFERENCES

Bakhtin, M. *The Dialogic Imagination: Four Essays.* University of Texas Press, 1981.
Biancolli, A. "Movie Review 'Percy Jackson & the Olympians'," http://www.sfgate
.com/movies/article/Review-Percy-Jackson-the-Olympians-3273189.php,
2010. Accessed July 7, 2015.

---

33 Riordan (2008), viii–ix.

Boll, J. "Harry Potter's Archetypal Journey." In K. Berndt and L. Steveker, ed., *Heroism in the Harry Potter Series*. Ashgate, 2011, pp. 85–104.

Booker, C. *The Seven Basic Plots: Why We Tell Stories*. Bloomsbury Academic, 2006.

Campbell, J. *The Hero with a Thousand Faces*. New World Library, 2008 (original from 1949).

Chambers, R. *Parody: The Art That Plays with Art*. Peter Lang, 2010.

Collins, P. "Stealing Fire from the Gods: The Appeal of Percy Jackson." In R. Riordan, ed., with L. Wilson, *Demigods and Monsters: Your Favorite Authors on Rick Riordan's Percy Jackson and the Olympians Series*. Benbella, 2008, pp. 23–32.

Danes, J. A. *Parody: Critical Concepts versus Literary Practices—Aristophanes to Sterne*. University of Oklahoma Press, 1988.

Dentith, S. *Parody (The New Critical Idiom)*. Routledge, 2000.

Durst, S. "Percy, I Am Your Father." In R. Riordan, ed., with L. Wilson, *Demigods and Monsters: Your Favorite Authors on Rick Riordan's Percy Jackson and the Olympians Series*. Benbella, 2008.pp. 93–106.

Genette, G. *Palimpsests: Literature in the Second Degree*. University of Nebraska Press, 1997.

Holden, S. "Another Teenage Woe: The House of Hades." *New York Times Film Review*, http://www.nytimes.com/2010/02/12/movies/12percy.html?_r=0, Feb. 11, 2010. Accessed July 6, 2015.

Hutcheon, L. "Modern Parody in Bakhtin." In G. Morson and C. Emerson, *Rethinking Bakhtin. Extension and Challenges*. Northwestern UP, 1989, pp. 87–103.

———. *A Theory of Parody: Teachings from the Twentieth Century Art Forms*. University of Illinois Press, 1985.

"Percy Jackson and the Olympians: The Lightning Thief. Review Revue." *Wall Street Journal*, http://blogs.wsj.com/speakeasy/2010/02/12/percy-jackson-and-the-olympians-the-lightning-thief-review-revue/, Feb. 12, 2010. Accessed Apr. 2, 2016.

Kuiper, K. *The Britannica Guide to Literary Terms: Prose, Literary Terms and Concepts*. Britannica Educational, 2012.

Rank, O. *The Myth of the Birth of the Hero: A Psychological Interpretation of Mythology*. Johns Hopkins UP, 2015.

Rees, E. "The Gods Among Us." In R. Riordan, ed., with L. Wilson, *Demigods and Monsters: Your Favorite Authors on Rick Riordan's Percy Jackson and the Olympians Series*. Benbella, 2008. pp. 63–80.

Reza Sadrian, M. "Parody: Another Revision." *Journal of Language and Translation*, vol. 1 no. 1, 2010, 85–91.

Riordan, R. "Introduction." In R. Riordan, ed., with L. Wilson, *Demigods and Monsters: Your Favorite Authors on Rick Riordan's Percy Jackson and the Olympians Series*. Benbella, 2008, pp. v–x.

Rose, M. *Parody: Ancient, Modern and Post-modern*. Cambridge UP, 1993.

Shau Ming Tan, S. "Burn with Us: Sacrificing Childhood in *The Hunger Games*." *The Lion and the Unicorn*, vol. 37 no. 1, 2013, 54–73.

Shulman, P. "Harry Who?" *New York Times Sunday Book Review,* http://www
.nytimes.com/2005/11/13/books/review/harry-who.html, Nov. 13, 2005.
Accessed June 1, 2016.

Turan, K. "Review: Percy Jackson and the Olympians: The Lightning Thief."
Los Angeles Times, Feb 12, 2010, http://articles.latimes.com/2010/feb/12
/entertainment/la-et-percy12-2010feb12. Accessed July 6, 2015.

Wein, E. "Not Even the Gods Are Perfect: Disability as the Mark of the Hero."
In R. Riordan, ed., with L. Wilson, *Demigods and Monsters: Your Favorite
Authors on Rick Riordan's Percy Jackson and the Olympians Series.* Benbella, 2008.
pp. 107–118.

DISCUSSION QUESTIONS FOR PART IV

1. The myth of Medusa and its reincarnations in the classical tradition have been incredibly popular in coming-of-age and hero-maturation stories. Why do you think this is so? Can you think of other examples in modern film?

2. Another motif that is found in many coming-of-age stories is the *katabasis* or descent to the underworld. What do you think it symbolizes? What other *katabases* in art or modern film, literal or symbolic, can you think of?

3. Would you say that *The Hunger Games* presents a feminist story? If so, how does Katniss compare to the female characters in Percy Jackson and Harry Potter?

4. The three films we discuss deal with the question of diversity in one way or another. Why would this be an important mythical theme? If so, what sort of stories in Classical mythology would speak to it?

5. The theme of oppression is present in many of our films (think of *The Hunger Games'* President Snow, and the slave elves in Harry Potter, for example). Young Adult films and literature deal quite openly with it. How does this theme connect with current events? Give details.

6. How is a dystopian future portrayed in *The Hunger Games* likely? Mythically speaking, how does it speak to our time, for example, in respect to the struggle between the haves and have-nots, or the popularity of reality television?

7. Discuss the various mythical creatures adapted in our films (e.g., the Minotaur, Medusa, the Phoenix, the Hydra, etc.). Why do these monsters still fascinate us, and what does each of them represent? How do our heroes symbolically interact with them?

8. How do myths portray family and generational tensions? Why is this important for our movies too?

9. Another major motif of our films is the young person's discovery of his or her own hidden potentials, as well as the family's hidden history. Why is this such an important mythical motif? How effectively do our movies present it?

10. *Percy Jackson* stands out from our other movies in that it has more pronounced elements of parody. Do you think the parodic aspect lessens the effectiveness of the messages it conveys? Or does it make the film work better?

V

NEW VERSIONS OF PYGMALION

LARS AND THE REAL GIRL (2007)
RUBY SPARKS (2012)

NEW AND OLD PYGMALIONS

Part V discusses two movies that in different ways rework the myth of Pygmalion, the sculptor from Cyprus, its most canonical version given in Ovid's *Metamorphoses* 10.243–97. Disgusted by the apparent licentious conduct of the Propoetides, who were turned into stone by Venus for not respecting her divinity, Pygmalion lives a celibate life rejecting the company of women, until he fashions out of pieces of ivory a woman more beautiful than any real woman can be. The artist cares for her, offers gifts, and gradually falls in love with her. Finally, during festival to Cythera, he asks the goddess to give him a wife "like his ivory maiden." When Pygmalion returns, at his touch, the statue begins to come to life. Pygmalion and his maiden marry and have a child named Paphos, who gives her name to the island sacred to Aphrodite. Their grandson Cinyras bears a daughter Myrrha, who tricks her father into having sex with her, and who bears Adonis after being turned into a tree.

Yet before Ovid, others had told versions of the myth. Christian writers Clement of Alexandria and Arnobius, drawing upon the Hellenistic writer Philostephanus of Cyrene, describes a king (as found in Arnobius) with the name Pygmalion who managed to fall in love with a statue of Aphrodite and even had sex with it.[1] The story seems to be set in the context of fertility myths related to a Cyprian goddess identified with the Classical Aphrodite/Venus. The prostitution of the Propoetides probably reflects the Cypriot practice of temple prostitution, whereby women would offer sexual favors in the service of the goddess. Stories of agalmatophilia, or statue love, are found in ancient sources, a remarkable example being Pseudo-Lucian's narrative (*Amores* 13–16) of a man who, having fallen in love with a statue of Knidian Aphrodite, locked himself in her temple at night and had sex with her, even leaving a mark in her thigh. Euripides' tragedy *Alcestis* might also be one of Ovid's sources, since

---

1   Rosati (1983).

Admetus asks to have a statue of his dead wife Alcestis made by a sculptor and wishes to lie with her.[2]

After Ovid, Pygmalion has been one of the most prolific myths in the Classical tradition since ancient times to the twenty-first century. Highlights of its presence are found in Jean de Meun's continuation of the *Romance of the Rose*, the opera *Pigmalion* by Rameau and de Sovot (1748), *Pygmalion* by W. S. Gilbert, a play by G. B. Shaw (Pygmalion also appears in his *Back to Methuselah*), its adaptation *My Fair Lady* of course, and the series of Pygmalion-themed paintings by Jean Léon Gérôme, among countless others.[3] The myth finds prolific recreations in movies such as Hitchcock's *Vertigo* (1958), *My Fair Lady* (1964), *Pretty Woman* (1990), *She's All That* (1999), *Weird Science* (1985), *Educating Rita* (1983), *Cherry* (2000), and recently more displaced versions such as *Simone* (2002), *Her* (1913), and *Ex Machina* (2015).[4] Our next two chapters discuss a pair of millennial films that rework the original myth fairly explicitly. A young man creates his ideal girlfriend and falls in love with her: *Lars and the Real Girl* (2007) and *Ruby Sparks* (2012). The first problematizes the psychological complexities of falling in love with one's own creation and the connection with trauma; the second foregrounds issues of gender dynamics and male-female power struggles and domination.

The myth's implicit multiple themes have certainly contributed to its numerous adaptations in art and literature. Some concentrate on the artist's capacity to create life, or the problematic boundary between the living and the artificial. Others probe how Ovid's tale speaks metacritically of every artist's relationship with his or her work, which sometimes the artist loves excessively. The ivory statue stands as metaphor for other forms of literary and artistic production. And this leads to considerations of narcissism, since falling in love with one's work, which reflects aspects of one's personality, is certainly loving a part of oneself. Because our creations are in many ways "our children," the myth often involves overtones of incest. Pygmalion can be seen as delusional, and thus the myth prompts the exploration of underlying psychological issues. The story can be seen as male-oriented, dealing with questions of the "fetish object" and "womanufacture,"[5] and thus feminists have reread and resisted traditional interpretations, denouncing the male's oppressive control and offering alternate readings. All in all, the tale continues to fascinate us and every year more and more versions of Pygmalion are born out of artists' imaginations.

---

2   See also Salzman-Mitchell (2008). For more on 'statue love' see Scobie, A., and J. Taylor. (1975)

3   For example, Blühm (1988) shows 142 Pygmalion images from 1500 to 1900.

4   The best overview of the Pygmalion myth in film is James (2011).

5   Sharrock (1991).

CHAPTER 11

LARS AND THE REAL GIRL AND THE PYGMALION MYTH

Trauma, Community, and Desire

. . . Mi perfección no es mía	. . . my perfection isn't mine
la inventaste	you invented it
soy el espejo apenas	I am only the mirror
en el que tú te pules	in which you preen yourself
y por eso mismo	And for that very reason
te desprecio	I despise you[6]
—Galatea ante el espejo.	—Galatea Before the Mirror
(18–23)	(Claribel Alegría, 1993)

To find that perfect other is one of the great communal fantasies, particular in the West since the blossoming of individualism and romanticism. But the desire and fantasy for power and control are equally ancient, especially in a universe perversely indifferent to our needs, in which every major thought, word, and action is bound, in some way, with relations of power. At the same time, our selves are fluid and unknowable; if granted a wish to fulfill our desires, would our choices actually ruin us? And that desire known as "love" is particularly problematic in matters of knowing.[7] As we have claimed repeatedly, the great archetypal narratives present major human concerns compactly and compellingly. The narrative pattern associated with Pygmalion and Galatea certainly engages these issues. As expressed through two millennia of retellings, reinterpretations, and references, this archetype speaks in many voices, from the perspectives of many cultures.

---

6 Alegría (1993), 84–85
7 As we were completing final revisions, the famous French contemporary writer Alain de Botton wrote an editorial for the *New York Times*, "Why You Will Marry the Wrong Person." See De Botton (2016).

Here we shall look at the 2007 independent movie *Lars and the Real Girl*. The movie was nominated for an Academy Award for Best Writing in the Original Screenplay category, and Ryan Gosling was nominated for a Golden Globe Award for Best Actor in the Motion Picture Musical or Comedy category, among many other nominations. It opened to generally positive reviews, which tend to align with the comments of Roger Ebert: "The film wisely never goes for even one moment that could be interpreted as smutty or mocking. There are so many ways [it] could have gone wrong that one of the film's fascinations is how adroitly it sidesteps them. Its weapon is absolute sincerity. It has a kind of purity to it."[8] This supposed sincerity and sweetness repelled some critics, for example Manohla Dargis, commentator from the *New York Times*, who wrote: "American self-nostalgia is a dependable racket, and if the filmmakers had pushed into the realm of nervous truth, had given Lars and the town folk sustained shadows, not just cute tics and teary moments, it might have worked. Instead the film is palatable audience bait of average accomplishment that superficially recalls the plain style of Alexander Payne, but without any of the lacerating edges or moral ambiguity."[9] As we shall observe, the divergence of critical views of *Lars and the Real Girl* will in some way mirror those found for *O Brother, Where Art Thou?* Both movies mix highly mythic elements with items, sometimes quite problematic, taken from a historically real world. They also are founded on attitudes toward the world (e.g., sentimental vs. realistic, religious vs. skeptical), that are accepted or not as a matter of individual taste.

In this chapter we shall further discuss some aspects of the Pygmalion narrative found in Ovid useful for understanding our movie. Our introduction to this part has presented some later adaptations. Using this discussion as a framework, we will analyze in some depth and produce a reading of *Lars and the Real Girl*. This analysis will prompt us to think anew about the foundational Pygmalion myth, especially regarding certain psychological and social dimensions, and to understand these two works better, as well as subsequent adaptations of the Ovidian original and works employing (sometimes in displaced fashion) the Pygmalion pattern. And the question of how to read, and possibly employ, resisting readings, particularly by feminist critics, must be considered, an important issue for our subsequent analysis of *Ruby Sparks*. As before, we must not think of *Lars* or *Ruby* as simply a "retelling" of the Pygmalion myth, but also as a unique reading, a unique myth in itself.

---

8   Ebert (2007).
9   Dargis (2007).

PLOT SUMMARY

Lars Lindstrom, a decent young man traumatized since his mother's death, lives as recluse in his brother's garage. He buys online a very realistic life-sized doll and falls into a delusion that it is alive, naming it Bianca and providing it a history. He takes it over to live with his brother Gus and sister-in-law Karin. Thanks to Dr. Dagmar's intervention, his brother and the whole town participate in Lars's fantasy of a living Bianca. Because of this, new sides of his personality develop, including an interest in his coworker Margo. Lars and his brother also heal past hurts. Finally Lars's fantasy allows Bianca's death, after which Lars is ready for a relationship with Margo, a "real girl."

OVID'S PYGMALION MYTH: THREE THEMES

This section's introduction has briefly outlined Ovid's Pygmalion myth and some related issues, a myth whose basic theme (one person creating or shaping another according to his or her will or desire) is actually quite familiar. Here we are concerned in particular with three central themes.

The first is the fantasy of creating (and often dominating) a perfect mate or other individual. This motif extends from the dream of creating life, as in the case of Pygmalion's statue, to displaced versions where somebody is "made over," as with Eliza Doolittle. The power, usefulness, and danger of dolls, toys, and other transitional objects can be a factor here, as can be the notion of the fetish.

Second are motifs of coming of age and achieving proper status, of connecting with or finding love and a place in society, of doing the right thing, which, in displaced form, is a concern of the hero's journey, pertaining to both statue and creator, and evoking various issues of education, class, sexuality, commodification, and so forth.

A third persistent theme in myths, and in this myth in particular, is the stability and even reality of personalities and selves. This is why Ovid includes the Pygmalion narrative in the *Metamorphoses*, which explores in many ways the instability of permanent being. All these myths to some extent problematize the very notion of a "real girl" or "real boy."

As noted, each "version" of the Pygmalion myth explores the complexities and implications of these three strands to a greater or lesser extent (with other mythic and contemporary items included). Various elements can be emphasized, omitted, or skewed in one direction or another. Modern productions can question the very possibility of fashioning a perfect mate, difficulties linked to problems in the creator's own psychology, with issues of sexuality, transgression, and obsession looming large. This is the case in *Lars*.

KEY TERMS

Fetish: here, a material and manipulatable object created to allow another person to enjoy the illusion of power and control over what that object symbolizes

Phantasia: a mental image, not necessarily real

Projection: when our minds make us see qualities in other persons or things that they do not have, but that we have projected onto them

Resisting reading: a way of reading a text to circumvent or resist the sexist, racist, classist, etc. implications within that text

Trauma studies: a branch of critical theory that considers how personal traumas are expressed in various creative productions

Word of the Father: The authority of some father figure (not necessarily a male) to define by words aspects of the existence and conduct of another person; a Lacanian concept

---

PYGMALION AND TRAUMA

We suspect Ovid's audience would have assumed Pygmalion was a younger man. As we have seen, Greek myth commonly presents stories of young men (Hippolytus, Pentheus, etc.) unable to properly transition into a sexually mature male. Because Orpheus, whom Ovid makes sing the song of Pygmalion, is repelled by women after Eurydice's loss, Pygmalion, perhaps the king of Cyprus and revolted (traumatized?) by the sight of the Propoetides' prostitution, rejects all women and lives as a lonely, obsessed artist.

If Pygmalion were our contemporary, we might suspect his revulsion for women was connected to some personal trauma. This factor, although marginal in Ovid's account, is central to our analysis, since Lars, our protagonist, is deeply traumatized. The evolving field of trauma studies explores how literature bears the scars (or betrays evidence of hidden scars) of authors and their characters.[10] Literature can help us deal with trauma. The *Metamorphoses* is hardly lacking real or implied trauma, its victims both men and women. The brief verses "Since Pygmalion had seen these leading lives in crime, offended by the faults, many of which nature has given to the female mind, without a partner he was living as a celibate, and for a long while he was lacking a consort of the bed" (Ovid, *Met.* 10.243-246) suggests that the sight of these women engaging in prostitution (and perhaps their subsequent punishment[11]) so shocked or traumatized Pygmalion that he became convinced that all women were evil

---

10   Epstein (2014) argues that trauma "is the bedrock of our psychology." For more on Trauma Studies, see Tal (1996).

11   Interestingly, as the paintings of Burne-Jones illustrate, the Propoetides, turned to stone, can be seen as a sculpture group. Such a sculpture group would be symbolic and allegorical, the iconic (and fixed) portrayal of Pygmalion's negative view of women, the static nature of the Propoetides statues depicting his fixed and dismissive views. James (2011), 14.

by nature, and decided to live as a bachelor. But note this view is his personal perspective, not truly authorial.[12]

Where does Pygmalion's trauma come from? As noted in our Introduction, psychoanalytic theory posits that fundamental trauma arises from childhood anxiety about separation and vulnerability; the child, unable to fully comprehend a world independent from it,[13] needs the mother to meet physical and psychological needs, especially for recognition. The child's shock at maternal sexuality can be tied to the recognition that she may desire another person far more than the child—and might go away forever. The fear of loss can lead (as it also does in the case of *Lars)* to withdrawal and disengagement, and even forms of delusion. If we consider Pygmalion's reaction to the Propoetides excessive, and his non-Platonic treatment of the statue veering toward the abnormal,[14] then we might think more deeply (1) about how the statue is a manifestation of Pygmalion's mental state and (2) to what extent Pygmalion ever recovers from such problematic perspectives. In the Pygmalion myth, the Galatea[15] statue needs to soften and become human; in displaced versions of the myth, such as *My Fair Lady* or *Pretty Woman*, the "creator" needs humanizing as much as the created does, and the created helps this process. Likewise, Pygmalion, Lars, and Calvin (the protagonist of *Ruby Sparks*) also need to be humanized, and their statues/creations assist that purpose. But from a modern psychological perspective, they need to be *healed*.

As an alternative to rejected womanhood, Pygmalion creates from ivory his own ideal woman, his mind's sheer creation, like Ruby in *Ruby Sparks*. Note how Ovid in his *Fasti* (3.832) compares himself to a sculptor who can soften stones, using art to conceal art by making the artistic product seem natural. Before starting to carve his ivory, Pygmalion would have constructed a *phantasia* of his woman to be, that is, become a viewer of the statue before its creation.[16] Since the statue is made from ivory pieces,[17] we might expect, as the artists Zeuxis[18] and Albrecht Dürer advised, that Galatea would be an amalgam of female shapes Pygmalion found pleasing. The composition of Galatea would be a form of "womanufacture," being a male's construction of a male's ideal of a woman. Indeed, our Pygmalion stands in a line of males who (re)fashion women to suit male pleasures and purposes, going back to Hephaestus and Pandora, perhaps

---

12 Salzman-Mitchell (2005), 70.

13 Winnicott (1971).

14 A common theme found in reviews is how the reviewer expected *Lars* to present a sort of running pornographic joke, but in fact it did not.

15 The statue in Ovid has no name, but acquires "Galatea" later in the tradition, and this is the name we use in this chapter, while we prefer Sharrock's (1991) Eburna for our Ruby chapter For further discussion, see Law (1932) and Reinhold (1971).

16 See discussion in Salzman-Mitchell (2005), 69–70.

17 Salzman-Mitchell (2008), 294.

18 Kris and Kurz (1979), 61.

the first such fetish object in Western literature.[19] This successful act of creation suggests Pygmalion did have some considerable knowledge of women, at least in terms of form. What he understood about their personalities is another question. Lars too will "build" his woman out of pieces, since the Bianca doll is highly customizable, so he too, to some extent, is her physical creator; but Lars will be found to be an even more impressive, often real-time, creator of Bianca's personality.

Ovid makes no mention of any model for this statue[20]; it is rather Pygmalion's representation of the woman who would be ideal *for him*, yet not necessarily erotically compelling, as are many statues of Aphrodite. Lars too, in his own way, will create a woman who is safe (at least at first) for him. But Galatea remains a narcissistic projection/reflection of Pygmalion's own desires and perhaps fears.[21] To fall in love with your own creation, with a partial reflection of your desires, is to fall in love to some extent with yourself. Here a reading of Ovid's myth of Narcissus (*Met.* 3.339–510) is useful, which will be expanded on in the next chapter, since questions of narcissism figure even more prominently in *Ruby Sparks*. Pygmalion also is both the "father" and the "mother" to his statue, and thus there is an incestuous dimension here, and in the third generation there occurs the tragic incest of Cinyras and Myrrha, the grandson and great-granddaughter of Pygmalion. The early episodes of *Lars* do not assure us that the movie will have a happy ending, and the critic must not forget the potential for a tragic outcome in the evident narcissistic elements of Lars's behavior.

Modern readers, even taking cultural differences into account,[22] are made uneasy by quasi-psychotic behavior on the part of Pygmalion as he fondles the statue, kisses it, and gives her gifts, unsure whether it is alive. The Pygmalion narrative is fundamentally a discourse of desire, with only a few lines describing the statue's creation and his reaction to it. As Ovid relates: "In the meantime he auspiciously sculpted the snowy ivory with wondrous art, and gave it a form

---

19 On "womanufacture" and connections with Pandora, see Sharrock (1991), 36–49.
20 James (2011), 19–20.
21 Janan (1988), 124–26.
22 Most ancient Mediterranean civilizations maintained a lively tradition of treating statues as if they were alive. They did not make our clear distinctions between living and nonliving substances. There were often elaborate rites of feeding, clothing, and washing statues and so forth; they were even said to be capable of various forms of movement and action, especially in times of crisis. On the evidence for various forms of statue love, see Hersey (2009). Note Ovid in the *Amores* 3.2.55–58, looking at the procession of the statues of the gods before the chariot races, sees a statue of Venus and says in his mistress's hearing, "To you, sweet goddess, and to your boys [Cupids] powerful with the bow, we give applause. O divine one, nod in favor of my undertakings, and give the right attitude to my new mistress. May she allow herself to be loved. She [the goddess] nodded and by movement gave a favorable sign. What the goddess promised, may you promise yourself, we beg."

with which no woman can be born, and conceived a love for his own work. There was a face of a true virgin, which you would believe was living, and, if modesty did not forbid it, you would think she would want to be moved; so did art hide through its own art" (Ovid. *Met.* 10.247–252)

Here the artist's desires are so powerful they lead to projection and delusion.[23] Galatea becomes an object on which Pygmalion projects his fantasies (the face of a true virgin!) and desires, an artwork that also functions as a transitional object.[24] We must understand that Pygmalion, as he kisses her, touches her ("He believes his fingers push upon the touched members, and he fears lest a bruise come into the pressed limbs"; Ovid, *Met.* 10.255–58) and gives her pleasing presents, pretends or fantasizes, as Lars will, Galatea as being a personality responding to those kisses ("he gives kisses and thinks them returned" Ovid, *Met.*10.256), touches, presents, and words. Galatea is more than a sex toy for use; note he gives her gifts "pleasing to girls" (Ovid, *Met.* 10.259), suggesting that Pygmalion is treating her as a subject with feelings to be respected, a subjectivity that Pygmalion is trying to please. In giving these presents, in his admiration of her physical form, and even in a respect for his lover as subject, Pygmalion appears the stand-in for Ovid the elegiac, urbane poet and manipulative lover and Galatea for the *puella* of Roman elegy, as we will discuss more specifically in our chapter on *Ruby Sparks*, likewise more a creation of the author's fantasy and self-absorption than a living entity.

PYGMALION AND THE WORD OF THE FATHER

Note that Pygmalion, interacting with his statue, plays two parts; he is the lover trying to imagine and perform acts that will please his lover, and he is also the beloved responding positively to his mate's actions. Lars performs this dual role in a much more challenging and complex way. As we noted in the Introduction, Lacan posits the "Name of the Father," who has the power to "lay down the law."[25] When Pygmalion "speaks" to the ivory Galatea, and imagines being answered in turn, to the extent he does so in language he defines her, but because he uses language, which always has a regulatory function, his conceptions of Galatea's roles must (to some degree) acknowledge a world beyond the narcissistic Pygmalion-Galatea monad. However, what is a singular development in this movie is how Lars, willingly, allows many people to converse with and even speak for his Bianca, new notions that Lars's own proclamations of the "Word of the Father" will have to conform to, and thus educate Lars in wider social norms

---

23 Pygmalion's engagement with the statue recalls what Admetus promises to do with the dead body of Alcestis! See James (2011), 25.

24 Barolsky and D'Ambra (2009), 20, stress how Pygmalion is like a young girl playing with a doll, surrendered to make-believe.

25 Homer (2005), 54–57; Ragland-Sullivan (2016), 79–80.

and perspectives, all factors in Lars's subsequent healing and development. As we shall see, both Lars and Calvin in *Ruby Sparks* give up total control of their creation or fetish object, but Lars does it much more completely, and involves the community in doing so.

PYGMALION AS (TRAGIC) HERO-PROTAGONIST

Superficially, Pygmalion's story fills out the paradigm of heroic achievement; a young man of noble birth lives in a land that has suffered a scandal, and he himself as a result is displaced from his proper role (here being a married man with a family); through a marvelous act and aided by a magic helper (Venus), he resolves his problem, and, as heroes often do, obtains a wife.[26] Further, Pygmalion and Galatea appear the ideal couple, who, aided by Venus, produce a superior form of love for Cyprus, the island of love. They even rear a child so famous that she (or he) will give her name to an island.[27] Lars will reproduce much of this pattern in lower, more comic key. As our introduction notes, we might see here a postclassical and individualistic view of heroism, seen often in romances, where the protagonist's chief battles are not against monsters or armies, but against social and psychological forces.

Yet O'Sullivan notes how frequently in Pygmalion narratives (especially later ones) retribution seems required for unnatural and narcissistic acts, and disaster occurs in the third generation with the tragedy of Cinyras, and his daughter Myrrha, acting out the potentials in Pygmalion's own history. The mating of Pygmalion and Galatea remains uncanny, as are the matings of characters who mirror this narrative pattern. But we shall observe how the role of the community and communication makes possible a very different, happier ending for *Lars*, whose hero seems to win true psychological battles as he unmakes his Galatea, and allows this potential incest-tragedy to be circumvented.

WHAT ABOUT GALATEA?

Now, a modern reader might also ask, "What personality could the animated Galatea possibly have?" Galatea has no past, no memories, no experiences.[28] We see little evidence of Galatea's full agency, especially of the resisting kind that

---

26 Indeed, in some versions the statue is of Venus, so Pygmalion fits Sowa's paradigm of "the young hero who gets the goddess." See Sowa (1984), 39–43.

27 There is debate as to the sex of Paphos, since some manuscripts have *de quo* (from whom, male) but more *de qua* (from whom, female). Scholars tend to favor *de qua*, perhaps because islands in Latin tend to have feminine names.

28 Much of the plot of a 2009 Japanese movie *Air Doll* (*Kūki Ningyō*) turns on the misunderstandings and attempts at self-education and finding love experienced by an inflatable doll that comes to life.

figures in later versions of the myth, very much including *Lars* and even more so *Ruby Sparks*.[29] Galatea never speaks, but then, why should she, since all her thoughts are Pygmalion's in origin?[30] As happens often in Roman elegy, the central focus is on male desire and fantasy, whose full history is hard to visualize.[31] Is Galatea a Stepford wife *avant la lettre*, an unchallenging fabricated ideal fit for an artist unable to handle a real woman's truth?

As a short Google search reveals, the selling of life-size dolls is a thriving business today. Critics argue that such a statue/doll presents an image of a woman that is unstable, empty, and superficial, more performance than person; owing to the inventiveness of Lars and then the whole community, Bianca will put on quite a performance. But then, how different is the man-made Galatea from the man-regulated *puella*? Ovid advises women to refashion themselves, as with Myron making statues out of lumps of stone (Ovid, *Art of Love* 3.219–20), and adapt herself to the man,[32] like a self-fashioned Galatea. Modern self-help books often likewise recommend that women remake themselves.

THE ROLE OF THE COMMUNITY

One of the vital additions to Ovid's Pygmalion fable found in *Lars* is the narrative of his community's involvement. We have long lost many of our communal connections; we increasingly "bowl alone" and have four hundred Facebook friends but few ones known face-to-face. TV series like *Mayberry* or *Northern Exposure* present an American fantasy of a small, fairly close-knit community whose often quirky members help each other out through good times and bad. Americans are aware that it "takes a village" not only to raise a child, but to provide a proper environment for the development and happiness of all, and that it can take a village to heal an individual. As noted above, the collective "voice" of the community can produce the "Word of the Father," which, although it may unnecessarily curb the expression of desire, can perform useful educational functions as well as educate.

---

29 Liveley suggests as a "resisting reading" that we imagine Galatea, when awakening, retaining something of a *dura puella* ("harsh girl") of her time as a statue, and thus her response to Pygmalion is feigned, not natural. There is some possibility to this reading, if we remember that the living Galatea is also in part the creation of Venus, who has inspired various *durae puellae*. See Liveley (1999), 208.
30 Galatea is not the first woman whose voice is lost or appropriated in the *Metamorphoses*. Think of the story of Apollo and Daphne, who not only loses her form, but becomes a symbol of Apollo's glory.
31 As noted above, a common criticism of the movie was how unrealistic it was, especially in its lack of conflict, which, as Remington (2011), 1, notes, seems to be conceived as the only way major problems can be solved.
32 Liveley (1999), 210.

Lars and The Real Girl (2007) Metro-Goldwyn-Mayer	
Director: **Screenplay:** **Cast:**	Michael Gillespie Nancy Oliver Ryan Gosling (Lars Lindstrom), Paul Schneider (Gus Lindstrom), Emily Mortimer (Karin Lindstrom), Patricia Clarkson (Dr. Dagmar), Kelli Garner (Margo), Maxwell McCabe-Lokos (Kurt), R. D. Reid (Rev. Bock), Nancy Beatty (Mrs. Gruner)

LARS AND THE REAL GIRL: LARS CREATES HIS BIANCA

In Northrop Frye's taxonomy, *Lars and the Real Girl* counts as a comedy, where a protagonist, being more lucky than competent, overcomes obstacles despite himself, often benefiting his community and gaining social status and a wife. *Lars* is a kind of comedy of innocence, without true villains, just people variously broken by one set of circumstances or another, able to be healed or redeemed. Violent conflict to solve problems, evident in other movies, presupposes a polarization of good and evil, but in our movie-myth such polarization is avoided, for the townspeople intuit Lars only wants the love they all seek, and Bianca is a way for Lars to communicate with a world he has been unable to engage.

Lars Lindstrom, in his late twenties or early thirties, lives isolated in the garage apartment of the house where Lars and his brother Gus grew up and that they then inherited after their father's death. It is also a type of self-exile. Lars's mother died giving birth to him, his deeply bereaved father shut down, and Gus, unable to cope, left home early. Lars has become a recluse and avoids engaging with people, even family, being unable to tolerate human touch and showing little emotion. He carries around a baby blanket his pregnant mother wove, which is also a transitional object.[33] Karin, Gus's wife, is now pregnant, recalling to Lars the trauma of his own mother's death, as well as the possibility of her dying in childbirth and of further loss. At work Lars's "friend" Kurt habitually browses internet porn. A young, perky coworker, Margo, likes Lars, but he studiously avoids her. The movie's very first scene, shot from the outside, shows Lars peering out the garage window, and then transitions to show Lars standing in his dark room looking out that window. Lars clearly needs to escape from this dark trauma world, which is also a prison and even a sort of womb.

At church, which Lars regularly attends, the pastor announces the primacy of Jesus' command that we love one another; we see some community members who will later help Lars. This film is not religious per se, and the church symbolizes the dream of social institutions that can mold human nature into a loving community. They will assist through communal action, aiding their

---

33 See Jordan (2013), who cites Winnicott (1971), 1–25.

Venus (Dr. Dagmar). In a proleptic scene, Lars joins in as he sees children playing with small toy figures. In the parking lot, Mrs. Gruner (whose leadership will play a central role) tells Lars he should not wait long to get married and hands him a flower to give to somebody pretty, which he tosses away.

It is winter's beginning, and Lars's transformation is finished around Easter, the time of warming and rebirth. One day Lars's cubicle mate displays a website where one can buy sex dolls, very lifelike, flexible, anatomically correct, and customizable. Just as Pygmalion sculpted his Galatea to his fancy, Lars can choose options on hair color, eye color, and so on. Although Lars himself is an atypical client, this site epitomizes for the audience a nexus of sexuality, fantasy, objectification, and commodification of the world we all live in, dimensions important for other versions of the Pygmalion myth. Both his office mate Kurt and Margo own, play with, and even fight with small figures as surrogates. This movie explores how the lonely might use such productions of technology when real life fails them, but it also suggests how necessary a living community is for true healing.

The movie jumps ahead some weeks; a coffinlike crate is delivered to the garage (stressing the new arrival's deadness, or thing-like-ness); Lars brushes his teeth, admiring himself in a new sweater and carefully combing his hair, excited in his preparations. The next day Lars tells Gus and Karin that he has met somebody named Bianca over the internet, who must live with them, because she is quite religious and conservative. Significantly, Bianca will stay in the room where his mother once slept (colored a rather erotic pink); on the last night of Bianca's "life," Lars will sleep with her in that very room. Brother and wife, needless to say, are utterly stunned at the Bianca doll. Lars declares Bianca is from Brazil, a missionary, does not speak English, and cannot walk. "Everything is new to her," he says, as it would be to a new creation. The movie requires some suspension of disbelief, that there could exist an otherwise fully functioning human being who yet actually believes that a plastic Bianca is alive, although this remains in the realm of the possible, which is more than we can say about *Ruby Sparks*.[34]

LARS'S TRAUMA AND BIANCA

So, what might be wrong with Lars? As noted above, the child can be traumatized by the fear that one's mother, so essential to the child's needs and recognition, might go away and never come back. Death made Lars's mother leave forever,

---

34 Wheeler (1999), 156, suggests that the reader who believes in the reality of Pygmalion's living statue actually "loses his wits." "The narratorial audience, by contrast, is faced with the choice of identifying with Pygmalion's delusion or believing in the 'fact' of the artificiality of the statue. For these reasons one should be cautious about asserting that Pygmalion's desire is a myth about the reader; rather, it is a myth about one sort of reader, "one who loses his wits and believes too much in what he reads."

followed by the emotional withdrawal of his depressed father and the escape of his older brother, a traumatizing introduction to the world's otherness and independence. Sex and pregnancy bring deep fears of the possibility of death, loss, and vulnerability, making Lars relive those abandonments. To love a beautiful statue or doll you have created is to both possess your ideal object of projected desire and, (at least as long as it remains artificial) to have an entity who will never age, die, or be unfaithful.

As noted, it is unsure to what degree Pygmalion imagined his ivory Galatea as a full living personality. Lars's creation is certainly sexually attractive, but can adopt only a limited number of positions, with an unchanging facial expression. Some critics have stressed the doll's obvious "deadness" and its evident sexuality, a contrast to the aliveness and purity Lars (and later the whole community) must project on her. Earlier, as Pygmalion imagined a possibly sentient Galatea statue, his imagination had to play the part of the wooer and the wooed. Modern couples are encouraged to imagine the needs, desires, and fears of their partners; to make his delusion work, Lars in a sense must *be* both Bianca and himself. Think of the knowledge, even engagement, with the Other that this fact implies, and the complexity of Lars's ongoing act of imaginative creation as he fabricates Bianca's history and personality, which he must adjust in real time to exterior, chance circumstances, for example, answering questions posed by the brother and sister-in-law, or later, responding to actions performed by the locals who become cocreators of Lars's Bianca fantasy.

By making Bianca (whose name means white, which implies "purity" as Galatea is "milky white") Brazilian (although half–Dutch), he gives her an exoticism that excuses unusual behavior. Pygmalion keeps his Galatea statue in his private quarters, but Lars pointedly does not want Bianca to live with him. Bianca is an Other too, but her imagined profound conservatism (which mirrors Lars's own) makes her less dangerous; no demands that Lars cannot deal with—at least at first. Tellingly, Bianca in her inability to easily communicate with others mirrors Lars's own limitations. In his ongoing act of Bianca creation, Lars, unlike Pygmalion, must deal with many aspects of his own personality and its potentials and desires in the context of an expanding and deepening set of community relations. We shall observe something similar, but with darker dimensions, in *Ruby Sparks*. Lars will have to work beyond his desire for safety and control, and come to accept, and then need, a truly living woman as a self-determining subjectivity. Bianca is not merely a projection of Lars's fantasy of wholeness and perfection as Galatea is, but the projection of a somewhat broken human being who is fit for his own brokenness.

As detailed above, it is Lars who must initially pronounce the Lacanian "Word of the Father" that defines what Bianca is and what she can do, in a most literal (as in "letter") way. But because Lars (unlike Pygmalion) has the courage to include his community in the Bianca conversation, the community will pronounce its own "Word of the Father" (as Mrs. Gruner will do forcibly), pronouncements that will steer Lars into new behaviors and perspectives. We see none of that in Ovid's Pygmalion myth. Another insight: often lonely people are advised to get a dog, because, in the act of walking the dog, one will meet other dog walkers, and automatically have something to talk about. And because having a dog requires tending to the needs of another vulnerable being, having a dog often indicates a certain amount of empathy and even humaneness, attractive to potential partners. Notice how in *Ruby* Calvin's dog Scotty will play a part in Calvin's interactions with others. As his community intervenes, Lars's narcissistic mastery of the controlling discourse unravels, and in the end Lars will renounce his controlling Word and speak a conclusion to his Bianca fantasy, as Calvin in *Ruby* must do.

DR. DAGMAR, THE COMMUNITY, AND THE HEALING OF LARS

By putting Bianca out in public and involving the community, Lars prompts the communication needed to confront and heal the trauma that drove him to "create" Bianca. The artist's defining trauma, implied in Ovid's Pygmalion narrative, is explicit here. His sister-in-law Karin initiates the healing process. Since Bianca has been under much stress, they should make an appointment with Dr. Dagmar Bergman, medical doctor and psychologist. In Greek myth oracles and prophets play important roles, able to interpret the will of the gods and solve unsolvable mysteries. Such prophets can be tied to an older community figure, the shaman, who also actively mediates between the human and divine, between the known and the secret. Medical doctors and psychologists are professionals who have been, since Freud and Jung, often pictured as shamans, able to navigate the mysteries of the body and the unconscious. Although a shaman and avatar for Venus, Dagmar herself is a wounded woman, a very lonely widow[35] who had wanted children but could not bear them. Her surprising oracle is that Lars is neither psychotic nor the victim of faulty neural wiring. Instead, he is simply delusional.[36] Instead she suggests (as Socrates does in the *Phaedrus* 244a–245b) that some madness can be beneficial, a form of communication, a way to work through problems.

Indeed, Bianca, in a way, *is* real, and has been sent for a reason: Lars's way of working through the trauma he has been decompensating for. Galatea, Bianca, and to some extent Ruby are all psychosexual fabrications to deal with trauma that, because of the unknowableness of the process, function as divine manifestations. "Bianca is in town for a reason," declares Dr. Dagmar, and thus Bianca too functions as a magic helper. Through Dagmar's actions, Bianca (and

---

35 Indeed, Dr. Dagmar at one point says, "Sometimes I get so lonely I forget what day it is, and how to spell my name"—indicating a potential loss of self, which is what Lars's loneliness has also produced.

36 One suspects that most psychiatrists would put Lars on antipsychotic medications. See Scheff (2009).

therefore Lars) is able to more fully live and communicate. Central is Lars's need for somebody to listen closely, to accept the Bianca message as somehow real too, and to enter constructively into the Bianca-Lars-community conversation.

Dagmar immediately begins the listening-talking treatment; she (a quick improviser of fictions too) informs Lars that Bianca has a chronic condition demanding weekly extended visits, during which Dagmar will talk to (and thus treat) Lars, the real patient. During Bianca's "treatment," Dagmar explores Lars's anxiety about being touched, delves deeply if gently into his past, and connects issues. Lars eventually reveals that Bianca lost her family when she was young (as Lars did), and that her mother perished in childbirth (as did Lars's mother), and although Bianca is crippled, she does not feel sorry for herself and just wants to be treated normally (as Lars does too). And Lars's intense fear of potential loss is starkly presented when he panics while thinking about the remote possibility of Karin dying in childbirth.

Further, Dagmar, by suggesting Bianca is sick, opens an imaginative path for Lars to let Bianca decline and die, working through death and loss, as preparation for new love. Aphrodite fills Pygmalion's wish that his statue be alive and gives him a wife, but nothing beyond that. Our Dagmar is also something of a Great Mother figure controlling the entire process of life, love, transition, birth, and death, a Demeter/Kore, who, because they know the humanlike pain of loss, and have even lived among mortals, can help humans more than other gods. So, to be healed, to be able to love—and let die—a "real girl," Lars must circuit, guided by others, through the cycle of love, life, and loss, and even more importantly, he must will that loss, that removal of childish things and delusion, that experience of death. This Venus/Demeter/Great Mother, who knows both love and death, loneliness and loss, enables Lars to bring his statue to a full kind of life within a community (which Galatea may never have), to love, and die successfully, a prelude to having a proper life and wife.

Lars moves within a cosmos whose practical and salvic powers rest largely in women, starting with Karin, Gus's pregnant wife. This desire to help Lars arises first from them, and then is transferred to the men, even transforming some retrograde types. In Ovid's myth, only Venus as love goddess appeared, but in this miracle play, a wider range of female powers are on display. Although there is some male banter about sex and how Bianca is hot and flexible, there is notable lack of obviously aggressive masculinity in the protagonists, as we will see in *Ruby*; Gus is something of a stereotype of the inarticulate male, but even he is capable of deep gentleness.

Following Dr. Dagmar's advice, brother, wife, and then the entire town, although aghast initially, participate in the Lars-Bianca fantasy with growing enthusiasm and elaboration.[37] Eventually, they work on Bianca's hair style, get

---

37 Karlinsky (2008) notes how Dagmar's recommended course of treatment is traditionally unconventional, but how increasingly patients with delusions are being asked to discuss their delusions, which can be treated psychodynamically, and not just by medication.

her a job, involve her in charity work, even get her elected to the local school board. *Lars* presents a myth of a community renewed through this exercise of listening and compassionate action. But there is more; note the real enthusiasm with which the town's people go about helping Bianca evolve. They too are projecting their own desires on Bianca, and, in terms of concrete emotional interchanges, Bianca is becoming "real" to them too. Even adults need to play with dolls, it seems.

Lars's healing involves the recovery of the buried past. At one point he asked his brother "What did Dad do?" trying to fill in the gaps. Bianca and Lars visit the graves of Lars's parents, and Lars tells Gus that Bianca has been asking a lot about him and his past, and wants to know everything about him, so he wishes to take her to the wooded lake where he and his brother used to play as children. This trip enables Lars to have that long-needed conversation with his brother about their shared past. This area of wood and lake has a pastoral quality, which often evokes a sense of the lost time, a need to connect with its imagined innocence to improve the present. Lars shows Bianca their tree house, symbol of the brothers' happier time. There immediately follows a telling shot (Fig. 11.1): Lars has left Bianca on the ground and climbed up into the treehouse, and lying on his back, sings with some enthusiasm to himself the Nat King Cole song *L.O.V.E.*, which contains the pertinent lyrics "Love is all that I can give to you / Love is more than just a game for two / Two in love can make it / Take my heart and please don't break it / Love was made for me and you."

Note the image of Lars raised up above the world, singing with his eyes closed in his private reverie of love and wholeness. This scene underscores the protagonist's isolation, either here in happy fantasy or, as we shall see in *Ruby* as Calvin stays in his treehouse, in isolating resentment. He ends his singing abruptly, as if he was forgetful of Bianca, who, resting on the forest floor, looks particularly out of place, resembling a discarded doll. Lars's transition to a fuller engagement with the living will now pick up steam.

FIGURE 11.1 Lars in a tree house singing, Bianca on the ground.

Pygmalion's delusion was private. But beginning with Karin and Dagmar, and then extending to many community members, who treat her as human, the Lars-Bianca communication becomes dialectical; when Lars allows the community to craft/project a more complex life for Bianca, so Lars's life becomes more complex and human. Because they too claim to communicate with Bianca, they serve to give Bianca a personality independent of Lars's will, and as noted, they produce a different "Word of the Father." From Lars's perspective, Bianca starts acting independently. This community engagement is also enhanced by the common conceits that "love makes the world go around" and "all the world loves a lover," and that service to lovers brings benefits to all; in a sense it is Love, like the goddess of love, that enlivens the unliving doll. And because Lars's condition is so uncanny, and yet beautiful too, it brings out the most protective and loving qualities in people, which, exercised, can grow.

LARS BEGINS TO HEAL

Unused sides of Lars's personality blossom, a development unseen in the Pygmalion-Galatea relationship. Educational love should be dialectical; Plato in the *Symposium* 210a ff. suggested that the ability to love one person made one more able to love others. And soon, interesting and complicating undercurrents appear. Lars accepts an invitation to a party, having a pretty "hot" girlfriend to escort. We see Lars dancing alone, sobbing; later he tells Bianca he was crying because he is so happy; do those tears come from another place, where Lars feels the real vector of his loss? Two subsequent scenes suggest this possibility. In one, Lars reads a passage of *Don Quixote*, about the Knight's obsession with his beloved Dulcinea, who is Don Quixote's projected love object, as Bianca is Lars's fantasy, who has likewise tried to act the honorable gallant. The Knight also regrets that he had no hermit to confess to. We can imagine what Lars might need to confess to.

At the party Lars spied Margo enjoying herself, and later at work he found her happily carrying on with her new boyfriend. At times Lars stops and stares at her, imagining. Then, coming home one evening, expecting to play Scrabble with Bianca, he finds Bianca being primped by the ladies in preparation for a charity event. They have a fight, made possible because Lars has allowed the community to complicate his fantasy. Mrs. Gruner subsequently dresses Lars down, speaking her own Word about how he should respect Bianca's need to have a life of her own. The women drive off with Bianca; Lars goes outside and furiously chops wood in the chill darkness. Lars wallows deep in unhearing self-pity, declaring to the amazed, angry Karin that he does not know if Bianca will come back (as the child fears Mama will not come back), for people do not care. Here we see Lars's toxic fear of loss and also the narcissistic desire for total possession that forms the darker side of the Pygmalion myth. But that Lars allows a fight (and even surrenders) suggests his willingness to admit, at some level, a wider perspective.

When Margo introduces her boyfriend, Lars treats him rudely, and indulges in some borderline stalking. Later Lars confesses to Dagmar that he had asked Bianca to marry him (with all the forms of intercourse this implies), but she turned him down; of course, since *he* is Bianca's voice, this represents a discussion Lars is having with himself, about the need to move beyond Bianca. Later we observe Lars's car parked in some desolate spot, and Lars shouting to Bianca, "You can't talk to me that way." He even leaves his car, supposedly until she stops shouting at him. We wonder what Lars imagines Bianca saying.

Implicit in the Pygmalion narrative, the coming of age theme is palpable here as Lars explains to his brother that Bianca told him about societies that put young people through rituals, and if they survive, they know they are adults. Lars then asks a question whose answer he needs to know: when his older brother knew he was a man. Lars knows he needs to be recreated, to become "a real man" so he can have his "real girl." The brother's hesitant answer is that one becomes a man when one can do the right thing—for others, not just for oneself. Their father, although flawed, tried to do the right thing by not abandoning his children. Gus also needs to confront the past to heal; earlier he had told Karin that Lars's problems were worsened when he abandoned his brother, and he thought nothing of letting Lars live in the garage like the family dog. Now Gus can admit that he ran away from Lars, and did not try to do the right thing, and he now is sorry. And Lars says that was OK, the right speech act, so to speak, in that context.

Now, this emphasis on learning how to "be a man" can refer to acts of heroic daring, but *Lars* will also suggest that being a man requires the bravery to let a woman be herself. Many lovers (*Ruby*'s Calvin will be a prime example) prefer the beloved to remain dependent and unfree.[38] But now, instead of withdrawing or trying to reclaim total control of Bianca, Lars adapts to this apparent subjectivity in Bianca, at the same time expanding his ability to communicate with a truly real girl, a process that will involve a willed loss and the unmaking of his creation.

Pygmalion serves nobody but himself, but the true hero can heal others. As noted, Lars's office mates Kurt and Margo fight with toy figures as surrogates, often with Margo the aggressor. One day Margo finds her little teddy bear with a noose around his neck, a victim of Kurt's revenge, who declares the bear is dead. Lars overhears this and then sees Margo crying; she has broken up with her boyfriend. The teddy bear is clearly an object of comfort, a symbol of innocence, and this image of the hung innocent has powerful overtones. Lars comforts Margo by removing the noose and performing CPR (Fig. 11.2), infusing

---

38 Two famous Platonic myths highlight this problem. In the *Symposium* 193d–e a central point of Aristophanes' myth is that all lovers want to be is with each other, a real fusion of selves, while in the *Phaedrus* 238e–241d, Socrates explored the toxicity of an intense love relationship, suggesting how the lover wants to keep his beloved isolated and underdeveloped, fearing competition.

FIGURE 11.2 Lars performs CPR on Margo's teddy bear.

the little bear with the breath of life. The bear revives, part of a shared fantasy with the bear as the transition object that aids mutual communication.

Note Lars has entered into and enabled Margo's fantasy, her subjectivity, not his own. The rebirth of the toy bear foreshadows another rebirth. Margo suggests that Lars join her friends for bowling; when he announces that Bianca has a meeting, Margo is surprised when Lars then says that he will be free once he drops Bianca off. At the bowling alley Lars watches Margo dance around after a good shot. Gus's workmates arrive, and soon a vibrant game is in progress. Lars finally takes the plunge, and manages to score a strike. While leaving, Margo tells Lars she is glad he could bowl with her, but Lars responds that she should not get the wrong idea, that he would never cheat on Bianca. Of course, Lars protests too much. Outside the snow is falling; Margo notes how winter will not be over until Easter, the time of resurrection. And as evidence of the coming true thaw, Lars, once so afraid of contact, warmly clasps Margo's hand.

LARS AND THE DEATH OF BIANCA

Lars in its quite different conclusion addresses potential flaws in the canonical Pygmalion myth. The implied "problem with Pygmalion" is connected to the subthemes of isolation, narcissism, and implied incest, which in Ovid's version becomes explicit in the tragedy of Myrrha and Cinyras. Pygmalion imagined some sort of personality for the Galatea statue as he fantasized about it being alive. After all, one's fantasy of an ideal mate concerns both physical appearance and character. When Venus grants Pygmalion's prayer for a woman "like his statue," the resulting animated Galatea has his statue's physical appearance, and one supposed the personality Pygmalion imagined. There is no evidence that Pygmalion gains the ability to enter into a relationship with a woman possessing an independent subjectivity. Pygmalion and Lars create and animate their safe and personal fantasy-reflecting figure. But Lars, unlike Pygmalion, unlike Narcissus, will move beyond his reflection and kill (lovingly) that which he created.

Accordingly, Lars begins to express skepticism about Bianca's treatments. More tellingly, he informs Dagmar once more that Bianca will not marry him, and when Lars asks Bianca why, she sometimes cannot give a good reason, or *sometimes can say nothing at all.* The Bianca illusion is breaking down. At a subsequent church service the minister repeats the famous quote, "When I was a child I spoke as a child I understood as a child I thought as a child; but when I became a man I put away childish things" (1 Cor. 13:11). While Lars hears these words, he is looking at the very real Margo. It is time for him to put away his toys.

At the day's end Lars is seen mopping Bianca's brow, and he spends a restless night in the garage. The next morning he hysterically wakes up Gus and Karin; Bianca is unconscious! Bianca is rushed to the hospital, where Dr. Dagmar meets them. Lars asserts that Bianca is dying. Recall how fearfully Lars imagined Karin's possible death, touching the terrible consequences of his own mother's passing; but now it is Lars who has not only created life but also scripted death. As Dr. Dagmar notes, it is Lars who brought Bianca to life, and Lars is now letting her go, as young children let transitional objects go, just as his attraction to Margo is becoming evident, and he is realizing the limits of the artificial and is willing to accept the real, even though it contains the uncontrollable possibility of loss. The community, as before, rallies around Lars, with expressions of real grief themselves, joining in another essential form of communication.

Bianca is slipping fast, and, back from the hospital, Lars spends the night with her in the room of his dead mother, enacting the close bonds of life in the face of impending nonbeing. His romance with Bianca occurs mostly during dark wintertime, but now it is close to Easter and the icicles are visibly melting. After his night with Bianca, Lars goes outside amid the dripping icicles, and sees the massed display of flowers deposited for Bianca, along with many photographs of them. The three older women bring food, and come to sit with Lars, who connects the coming baby and the dying Bianca. One of the women is even knitting (as if one of the fates), and tells Lars "That is how life is—everything comes together."

At the end Lars, his brother, and an extremely pregnant wife take Bianca once more to that wooded and symbolic lake. Lars never had a chance to mourn his mother, and the blue blanket, which Lars once wore constantly, has been increasingly seen on Bianca.[39] At the lakeside, Lars tearfully kisses Bianca, the only kiss we ever see. Soon afterward the brother and wife discover Lars standing in the lake, lifting Bianca out of the water. Mythologically, bodies of water and lakes are points of transition, often between worlds. By lowering her

---

39 Jordan (2013).

into the lake, Lars both baptizes her and lets Bianca's magical being leave, as he also comes to peace with his mother's death[40] and, in a sense, is reborn himself.

At Bianca's well-attended funeral, where the pastor notes that they are not here to commemorate Bianca's death but her life, the life of a teacher who motivated the community to a great act of love and courage. Buried in the public cemetery, Bianca becomes an eternal part of the community; the importance of this status is made evident in the role of the public cemetery in that famous play about a small town and its own community across generations, Wilder's *Our Town* (1936), in whose last act Emily, a recently dead young mother, comes to realize the importance of every moment of life. Pygmalion's trauma-induced delusion was private and narrowly focused and, for all we know, perpetual. But Lars's fantasy was shared in a community of communications, first with his immediate family, and then with the whole town. They joined in the dialogue and delight in his delusion, to encourage him to speak the words that lead to wholeness and healing, and, in that generosity, are taught and healed themselves. As Dagmar noted, there can be good forms of madness.

During the graveside service Dagmar chats with Gus and closely surveys the proceedings; Margo stands beside Lars. Dr. Dagmar thoughtfully watches the couple; our shaman/Venus/Great Mother has done her work, and she quietly retires. Lars asks Margo to go for a walk. It is spring, and we suspect their communication is going to deepen. Margo is a real, even quirky, human being, and with her Lars should find one who will listen, and who has much to say. Lars now has a real chance at a real girl.

CONCLUSIONS: LESSONS FROM *LARS*

Lars has performed a heroic, if also a comic, role in a coming-of-age drama. He is the child of a shattered family, himself deeply wounded, sent into a kind of exile, into the dark wood of his decompensating mind symbolized by the garage apartment. He meets magic helpers who bring benefit and danger, and who have the power of listening as well as acting. Dr. Dagmar is a magic helper, a Venus/ Demeter/Mother Goddess, whose best help comes indirectly through her compassionate oracles. And the townspeople function as the supporting cast and extended family we all need to heal properly.

As noted above, it is useful to read different versions to understand the full potentials of a myth, and the varied human concerns it can engage. What words are not said, what issues not openly expressed, can be as important as what is present for our interpretation. Thinking about Ovid's Pygmalion in relation to *Lars*, we can now recognize the more limited scope of Ovid's presentation,

---

40 Interestingly, in the 2002 film *Simøne* the protagonist—after Simøne, a computer-generated movie star, has taken on a dominating life of her own—tries to "drown" her by infecting the program with a virus and tossing into the water a trunk that contains a cardboard image of Simøne and the now-corrupted computer files that generated her. See James (2011), 161–62.

which depicts how trauma can lead to exile and to a type of escape in a fantasy brought to life by the powers of desire and art, which is changed from fantasy to a kind of reality by a *dea ex machina*; but most of the problematics of this metamorphosis have been ignored by Ovid, and there is no evidence that anything but a baby has grown from that relationship.

Pygmalion achieves a new social status, but his psychological development is unknown. Save for the festival, the role of Pygmalion's community is absent. But *Lars* more deeply delves into the traumatic origins of the act of woman creation, and the suggestion of mental instability that blurs fantasy and reality, hinted at in the Pygmalion story, becomes explicit in *Lars*, as does the suggestion of a profitable artistic madness. *Lars* engages forcefully the narcissism that is central to the myth of the male creation of a perfect woman, the falling in love with oneself that is a form of spiritual incest and death; Lars's coming of age and implied heroic Quest is for the return to a type of sanity requiring a rejection of that narcissism and the bravery to engage the independent Other. All this requires assistance from a rather maternal community, which in turn is made more unified through their compassion. Lars, who speaks the "Word of the Father" to create Bianca, listens to, and then repeats, the Word spoken by the larger community whom he is willing to trust and be healed by. Thus we observe Lars growing and helping his townsfolk in ways that are absent from the Pygmalion story. This result also implies much about how we mutually construct and destroy each other through our interactions, and it presents a utopian vision of how that community might act through the cycles of life. In our next chapter we shall read *Ruby Sparks* in contrast to *Lars*, and thus explore its far less comforting vision.

Lars is a movie for this millennium in its juxtaposition of the old and new, of a consumerist technology that allows a customized Bianca to be bought combined with old issues of family trauma. Lars, Margo, and Kurt are presented as working adults and also children with their toys, in a way that feels modern. But the notion of the power of an engaged community, lost and idealized by moderns, is ancient. The brokenness and sensitivity of the man-child Lars likewise reflects a modern sensibility (note how many men-children there are in movies today[41]), even while his brother Gus reaches for ancient ideals of manhood. The image of the pregnant Karin and the dying Bianca, in the context of the revolving seasons, is also ancient. Many of our modern movies, in one way or the other, posit the need for a miracle to save us, and show protagonists who keep faith even in seemingly hopeless circumstances, which is the modern situation. There is a modern, pastoral sense of loss in *Lars*, reflected in the face of Dr. Dagmar. She is happy at the marvel of the healing she has seen, but senses it is beyond her.

41 See Nicholson (2015).

REFERENCES

Alegría, C. *Fugues*, tr. D. J. Flakoll. Curbstone, 1993.

Barolsky, P., and E. D'Ambra. "Pygmalion's Doll." *Arion*, vol. 17 no. 1, 2009, 1–24.

Blühm, A. *Pygmalion: Die Ikonographie Eines Künstlermythos zwischen 1500 und 1900*. European University Studies/ Publications Universitaires Européennes, 1988.

Dargis, M. "A Lonely Guy Plays House with a Mail-Order Sex Doll," http://www.nytimes.com/2007/10/12/movies/12lars.html, Oct. 12, 2007. Accessed July 22, 2016.

De Botton, A. "Why You Will Marry the Wrong Person," http://www.nytimes.com/2016/05/29/opinion/sunday/why-you-will-marry-the-wrong-person.html?action=click&contentCollection=N.Y.%20%2F%20Region&module=Trending&version=Full&region=Marginalia&pgtype=article&_r=0, May 28, 2007. Accessed May 30, 2016.

Ebert, R. "Lars and the Real Girl." *Chicago Sun-Times*, http://www.rogerebert.com/reviews/lars-and-the-real-girl-2007, Oct. 19, 2007. Accessed July 22, 2016.

Epstein, M. *The Trauma of Everyday Life*. Penguin, 2014.

Hersey, G. L. *Falling in Love with Statues*. University of Chicago Press, 2009.

Homer, S. *Jacques Lacan*. Routledge, 2005.

James, P. *Ovid's Myth of Pygmalion on Screen: In Pursuit of the Perfect Woman*. Bloomsbury, 2011.

Janan, M. "The Book of Good Love? Design vs. Desire in *Metamorphoses* 10." *Ramus*, vol. 17, 1988, 110–37.

Jordan, M. "A Psychoanalytic Look at *Lars and the Real Girl*," http://www.cgjung-page.org/learn/articles/film-reviews/917-a-psychoanalytic-look-at-qlars-and-the-real-girlq, 2013. Accessed July 22, 2016.

Karlinsky, H. "Review of *Lars and the Real Girl*," http://www.harrykarlinsky.ca/filmreviews/lars-and-the-real-girl-2007/, 2008. Accessed July 22, 2016.

Kris, E., and O. Kurz. *Legend, Myth, and Magic in the Image of the Artist: A Historical Experiment*, tr. A. Laing. Yale UP, 1979.

Law, H. H. "The Name Galatea in the Pygmalion Myth." *Classical Journal*, vol. 27 no. 5, 1932, 337–42.

Liveley, G. "Reading Resistance in Ovid's *Metamorphoses*." In P. Hardie, A. Barchiesi, and S. Hinds, ed., *Ovidian Transformations*. Cambridge UP, 1999, pp. 197–213.

Nicholson, A. "The Man-Child Movie Trend Must End," http://www.laweekly.com/film/the-man-child-movie-trend-must-end-5513746, Apr. 22, 2015. Accessed Aug. 24, 2016.

Ragland-Sullivan, E. "Lacan's Seminars on James Joyce: Writing as Symptom and 'Singular Solution'." In R. Feldstein and H. Sussman, ed., *Psychoanalysis and . . .* Routledge, 2016, pp. 67–88.

Reinhold, M. "The Naming of Pygmalion's Animated Statue." *Classical Journal*, vol. 66 no. 4, 1971, 316–19.

Remington, T. "Lars and the Real Girl: Lifelike Positive Transcendence." *SAGE Open*: 1–10. http://sgo.sagepub.com/content/early/2011/04/28/21582440114 08346, 2011. Accessed July 22, 2016.

Rosati, G. *Narciso e Pigmalione illusione e spettacolo nelle Metamorfosi di Ovidio.* Sansoni, 1983.

Salzman-Mitchell, P. *A Web of Fantasies: Gaze, Image and Gender in Ovid's Metamorphoses.* Ohio State UP, 2005.

———. "A Whole out of Pieces: Pygmalion's Ivory Statue in Ovid's *Metamorphoses*." *Arethusa*, vol. 41 no. 2, 2008, 291–311.

Scheff, T. "Social Treatment of Mental Illness." *Psychology Today* Online, https://www.psychologytoday.com/blog/lets-connect/200912/social-treatment-mental-illness, Dec. 3, 2009. Accessed July 22, 2016.

Scobie, A., and J. Taylor. "Perversions Ancient and Modern: Agalmatophilia, the Statue Syndrome." *Journal of the History of the Behavioral Sciences*, vol. 11 no. 1, 1975, 49–54.

Sharrock, A. "Womanufacture." *Journal of Roman Studies*, vol. 81, 1991, 36–49.

Sowa, C. A. *Traditional Themes and the Homeric Hymns.* Bolchazy-Carducci, 1984.

O' Sullivan, J. "Virtual Metamorphoses: Cosmetic and Cybernetic Revisions of Pygmalion's 'Living Doll'." *Arethusa*, vol. 41 no. 1, 2008, 133–56.

Tal, K. *Worlds of Hurt: Reading the Literatures of Trauma.* Cambridge UP, 1996.

Wheeler, S. *A Discourse of Wonders: Audience and Performance in Ovid's Metamorphoses.* University of Pennsylvania Press, 1999.

Winnicott, D. W. "Transitional Objects and Transitional Phenomena." In *Playing and Reality.* Tavistock Publications Ltd., 1971, pp. 1–35.

CHAPTER 12

RUBY SPARKS

Rereading Pygmalion and Narcissus

Have you ever found a red bra in your apartment and didn't know to whom it belonged? Has your dream girl/guy ever seemed to show up out of nowhere, barefoot and half clothed in your kitchen? Well, this happened to Calvin in the well-received 2012 independent film *Ruby Sparks*. The movie's screenplay was written by Zoe Kazan, and it was directed by Jonathan Dayton and Valerie Faris, famous for *Little Miss Sunshine*, a 2006 comedy-drama. Zoe Kazan, the daughter of well-known screenwriters and granddaughter of the famous director Elia Kazan, plays the role of Ruby. Paul Dano, who plays Calvin, was her partner in real life when the movie was made. This film opened to favorable reviews that stressed its clever screenplay and acting, how it offers a sleek and successful romantic comedy that deconstructs more conventional retellings of the Pygmalion myth, and its delving into the darker dimensions of male-female relations, being compared at times to the quirky *The Eternal Sunshine of the Spotless Mind* (2004). Some critics (e.g., Rex Reed) dismissed it as a breezy trifle.[1] Others were disturbed by misogynistic overtones, suggesting "Kazan winds up indulging in the very wish-fulfilment she initially sets out to deconstruct."[2]

Calvin is a high school dropout who wrote an "American classic" novel at nineteen and has been suffering writer's block ever since. He is now nearly thirty. His therapist recommends that he write one page about his unlikable dog Scotty. He subsequently dreams of a woman who is drawing a picture of the dog and begins to write about her, naming her Ruby Sparks, and making her a beautiful yet quirky and somewhat alternative girl, who gradually comes to life.

Is Calvin then a sort of magician, who manages to materialize his fantasy of the perfect woman and script every instant of his girlfriend's life? He is also like

---

1 http://observer.com/2012/07/ruby-sparks-rex-reed-paul-dano-zoe-kazan/. Accessed June 1, 2016.
2 Hornaday (2013).

PLOT SUMMARY

A young writer, Calvin, experiencing writer's block, dreams up a girl, writes about her, and in Pygmalion-like fashion falls in love with her. Ruby gradually comes alive. A passionate yet problematic relationship unfolds, where Calvin's male dominating and narcissistic tendencies become more and more perilous and toxic, until he decides to tell the truth and release her from his control by writing that she is now free. Months later, his novel about Ruby is published, and he happens to meet a Ruby lookalike in the park, foreshadowing a new relationship between the two.

Pygmalion, an artist able to construct the perfect girl, fall in love with her, and have her become real. Kazan even confesses that she was inspired by this myth and the sight of a discarded mannequin.[3] This chapter will look at the film and the myth from a gender perspective, focusing on three major aspects: the created beloved as fiction, the connections between Calvin and the mythical figures of Narcissus and Pygmalion, and the possibility of offering a feminist reading of the movie and myth in which, with the help of Kazan's millennial female take on the story, we can resist received male-biased interpretations of the tale.

THE COMING-OF-AGE AND HERO'S-JOURNEY PARADIGM

In *Lars and the Real Girl*, the overarching structure was the coming-of-age paradigm, perhaps better described here as "Hero grows through struggle to assume his proper adult status." In our last chapter we noted how Lars is a protagonist who faces obstacles and performs significant deeds on his life's "journey," conforming to a displaced form of the hero's journey. The same is true for Calvin. Like Lars, Calvin is in his late twenties (twenty-nine, more precisely), at the brink of another transitional moment in being about to reach thirty, an age when one stops being a "Young Adult" and is expected to assume greater responsibilities in life. The fact that he is constantly compared with Salinger, the author of what is considered one of the first American "Young Adult" novels, *The Catcher in the Rye* (1951), and the fact that he hasn't written anything of importance since he was nineteen, reveals him as someone stuck in his teens, at least in his feelings and attitudes, unlike his brother Harry (and Lars's brother Gus), who has gotten married, has settled down, and has a child and a nine-to-five job.

Narcissus (whose story, as we will see, is central for our interpretation) is at a transitional age, sixteen, in which *pueri* (young boys) in Ovid's *Metamorphoses* either make a successful passage to manhood or are doomed, as with Pentheus

---

3   Kazan herself (July 25, 2012, interview with Tasha Robinson, http://www.avclub.com/article/ iruby-sparksi-writer-star-zoe-kazan-on-love-relati-82855. Accessed July 14, 2016) points out that the inverse gender relation (woman creator of a perfect man) is not common, in part because women already have the biological capacity to create life and thus the fantasy is not so much part of the female psyche.

or Phaethon. Calvin lives, in many ways, like a young person, with no job, no schedule, no commitments. He even forgets his speaking engagements, does not dress appropriately for them, and doesn't check his telephone messages. At a speaking event, he is truly uncomfortable with the public's attention. This immaturity is evident during a therapy session, when he says he needs Bobby, a stuffed animal the doctor keeps for him—showing total regression in this conflicted young man. We even see him adopting a fetal position on the couch. We recall how Pygmalion is also somewhat childlike as he plays with the statue as if she were a doll,[4] and how Lars's companions Kurt and Margo also play with dolls. Even after Calvin finally accepts that Ruby is real, their dates seem a bit childish too: watching horror movies, going to game arcades, and dancing. The hero often must navigate a real or virtual underworld, where one of the threats is illusion, where the basic nature of the hero's very self is questioned. This psychological (and dangerous) journey is evident for Lars, but equally true for Calvin, especially since there are real (and unsolvable) questions about the real nature of Ruby and her relation to the mind of Calvin, who supposedly created her, but who loses control in the movie's dreadful climax.

WOMAN AS TEXT

Beyond the echoes of the Pygmalion narrative, *Ruby Sparks* also follows a narrative tradition in which characters in a story acquire independence despite the author's control and come to life or become aware that they are characters in fiction, as in the movie *The Truman Show* (1998) and the more recent film *Stranger Than Fiction* (2006).[5] This is another form of an intellectualized Pygmalion myth similar to what occurs in *Ruby*. The idea of a beloved who exists more as a text than as a living person has a strong presence in Latin literature, especially in Latin elegy, of which Ovid himself was a notable composer, with his *Amores* and *Ars Amatoria* in particular. This tradition certainly carries over into *Ruby Sparks*. The film's first image is the silhouette of a woman against the dazzling sun, a part of Calvin's dream, which is abruptly interrupted by the sound of an alarm clock. The girl asks for her "other shoe." This image makes us think of divine epiphanies (divine manifestations), and perhaps of the magical afternoon entrance of Ovid's mistress, Corinna, leading to exhilarating and exhausting sex (*Amores* 1.5). Like Calvin, Ovid is an author whose girlfriend and (problematic) love for her is probably largely a fictional creation.[6] And Ruby's epiphany is highlighted at the

---

4   See Barolsky and D'Ambra (2009), 19–20.

5   In literature we find good examples in the Spanish novel by Miguel de Unamuno, *Niebla* (1914), and the Italian play by Luigi Pirandello, *Six Characters in Search of an Author* (1921).

6   The modern understanding is that the elegiac mistresses of Ovid, Propertius, and Tibullus are fiction. For Corinna's fictionality and the elegiac mistress as a symbol for elegiac poetry, see also Veyne (1988), Wyke (1989, 2002), and Hallett (1984). Thus, in a rather Pygmalionic way, the poet is also in love with his own poetry.

FIGURE 12.1 "Ruby Sparks" DVD cover illustration.

film's end when Calvin, reading passages of his book for an audience, says "She came to me wholly herself. I was just lucky enough to be there to catch her." This ending also recalls the notion of writer as medium, the receptor of divine poetic inspiration: "words are not coming from you, but through you," as Calvin says.

Alison Sharrock in her "Womanufacture" notices that Pygmalion's ivory girl can be read as a metaphor for the elegiac *puella*, the love interest and mistress of the elegiac poet.[7] This connection between the statue and the textual girl that comes to life resonates well with the construction of Ruby. Note how the case cover for the movie's DVD shows the silhouette of Ruby literally coming out of the written words, out of typed letters (Fig. 12.1).

Interestingly, here the textual woman hints at the statue in her name: Ruby, precious stone (note that the clothes she often wears are indeed colors of the ruby, and so is her red hair), Tiffany (a middle name she disliked but that inevitably makes us think of the famous high-end jewelry stores), and Sparks, alluding to the dazzling quality of this stone. Pygmalion's maiden is made of ivory; various later traditions, including a series of famous paintings by Jean-Léon Gérôme, imagine her as made of marble, and thus this stone condition of the girl is transmitted in the classical tradition of the myth.[8]

---

7   Sharrock (1991b).

8   On the making of Pygmalion's statue out of ivory and its metapoetic resonances, see Salzman-Mitchell (2008). See also Hardie (2002), 206–26, for later representations. Some classical scholars even, and surprisingly, misread the material of the statue; see Solodow (1988), 2; and Anderson (1972), 498.

KEY TERMS

Resisting reading: a form of feminist reading that tries to find nonpatriarchal ways to interpret and deal with male-oriented texts

Narcissism: excessive self-absorption and love of oneself

Fetishism: sexual desire or pleasure through an object or body part

Pornography: Visual representations (through film or printed images or descriptions) of the naked body intended to arouse sexual desire

---

REFLECTIONS IN THE POOL: CALVIN'S NARCISSISM

The myth of Pygmalion has noticeable connections with the tale of Narcissus, whose best-known version is found in Book 3.339–510 of Ovid's *Metamorphoses*. Narcissus was a boy who rejected the amorous attentions of not only boys and girls but also the nymph Echo, who wasted away out of love for him: "Thus this nymph he had mocked, thus the other nymphs born in the waves and mountains, thus earlier he had mocked masculine unions. And so, a certain rejected lover, raising his hands to the heavens had said: 'So it is allowed that he himself might love, so he might not possess the beloved'" (Ovid, *Met.* 3.402–6).

Rhamnusia, or Nemesis, grants Echo's prayer. One day in the woods Narcissus saw his reflection in a pool and immediately fell in love with it. At first unaware that this was his own reflection, Narcissus finally realizes it is only an image of himself he loves. He despairs, beats his chest , and is finally turned into a yellow and white flower. Ovid himself alludes to Narcissus' reflection in the pool as a marble statue (419) and refers to his neck as ivory (*eburnea colla*, 420), and thus connects Narcissus with the artist himself.[9] Narcissus' beloved image of himself is only a hope, a shadow (*spem sine corpore amat, corpus putat esse quod umbra est*, "He loves hope without a body, what he thinks is a body is just a shadow," *Met.* 3.417; and *ista repercussae, quam cernis, imaginis umbra est*, "what you see is the shade of a reflected image," *Met.* 3.432), an *error* and a fleeting reflection (*credule, quid frustra simulacra fugacia captas?* "Credulous one, why do you, in vain, catch a fleeting reflection?" *Met.* 3.430), and a *mendacem . . . formam*, "a deceiving shape" (*Met.* 3.437).[10] In Pygmalion's and Calvin's case the illusion actually does become possible and real, and there is much of Narcissus in Pygmalion; this aspect of the myth is strongly explored in the film.

---

9   See Barolsky (1995), 255, for Narcissus as artist, "the first painter" (as Leon Battista Alberti mentions) more specifically.

10   For good discussions of Narcissus and Pygmalion, see also Rosati (1983); Salzman-Mitchell (2005), 95; and O'Sullivan (2008), 141–42. Hillis Miller (1990), 5, even relates Pygmalion's ivory maiden to Narcissus' image reflected in the pool; so when the statue wakes up and sees her creator, "it is as if Narcissus' reflection in the pool had come alive and could return his love."

Calvin writes not only about Ruby but also about himself in his novel-in-progress, accentuating his narcissistic tendencies. He tells his therapist: "The guy I'm writing . . ." "What's his name? " "Uh . . . Calvin. I'm gonna change it. Uh, anyway, there is a lot of me in him. . . . It's almost like I'm writing to spend time with her. . . . It's like I'm falling in love with her. . . . She's not real . . . she's some mother fucking product of my imagination!" Accepting Sharrock's suggestion that Pygmalion loves not exactly the love object but rather his own artistic capacity, we observe Calvin loving in part his own powers of creation.[11]

Before Ruby comes to life, after a rather depressing reception to celebrate the tenth anniversary of his first novel, pressured by editors, publishers, and public to produce something great again, Calvin goes home and is forced to sleep on the couch since Scotty has trashed his bed. Ruby appears again in a dream, that space of illusions and reflections, in her purple tights and white dress, and asks to draw his "cute" dog.

She says she is an artist: "I'm super good" (her many drawings will later cover the walls of Calvin's bedroom). This talent reminds us not only of Pygmalion, the extraordinary artist whose statue was superior to any woman born (*Met.* 10.247–49), but also of Zoe Kazan, the movie's screenwriter, who crafted this story from the treasury of her mind. In their dream conversation, Ruby does not know who Scott Fitzgerald is, suggesting her status as a "blank page," like the one in Calvin's typewriter, which Calvin will have the power to inscribe with his imagination. Dreams can function as divine omens. Calvin wakes up abruptly from the couch, inspired. He starts to write. He writes for days, in his study, surrounded by books, until Scotty brings him an unrecognized red shoe. After this period of intense artistic effort, the unreality of Ruby begins to turn real.

As noted, two recent modern American recreations of the Pygmalion myth, one set in the cold northern Midwest and the other in the sunny Southwest, require the intervention of a therapist, implying mental illness, as we saw explicitly in the case of Lars, but also exploration of hidden aspects of psychology. We presume that Calvin's need for Dr. Rosenthal is triggered by his frustration with his writer's block, his shame, his fear, and so forth. Calvin will be led by both the therapist and even more so by Ruby to confront his isolation and narcissism, which in turn may arise from earlier traumas. In *Lars*, Dr. Dagmar declared that "Bianca's in town for a reason." There may be a similar reason behind Calvin's creation of Ruby. But to get the process moving, Calvin's therapist suggested that he obtain Scotty, the dog, to help him connect with people. This hasn't quite worked out well so far; in many ways Scotty is also a projection of his owner. He is fearful, nervous, and not very friendly and pees like a girl (!), which of course makes Calvin feel "inadequate." Scotty reflects Calvin's

---

11 Sharrock (1991a), 169: "Like Ovid in *Amores* 1.2, Pygmalion is in love with love rather than with a love-object: he is in love with his own creative and erotic process."

own fears of failure, of rejection, of disappointing all the people who expect so much of him. Plus, Calvin has named him after F. Scott Fitzgerald, the famous American novelist, which even though meant as an honor is quite problematic because it may suggest that his owner is trapped in his world of fiction and literature; or as Ruby says, giving the dog this name makes him feel superior, or at least less insecure. As Ruby exclaims "Naming your dog after him . . . it is aggressive. Yeah—an aggressive gesture. . . . Kill your idols, man, I'm all for it."

The therapist subsequently assigned Calvin to write a page about some-one who sees Scotty "slobbery and scared" and likes him anyway. Accordingly, Ruby likes Scotty just the way he is as they meet in the park. But since Ruby is a creation of Calvin's imagination, doesn't this illustrate Calvin just liking himself? The three form a narcissistic triangle. The dog is a mirror of his owner, and the girl is a creation of the male artist. His brother Harry, having realized the written Ruby is real, even wonders: "You gonna marry her? Have kids with her? . . . Wouldn't that be like incest? Or mind-cest?" "I don't care. I love her," responds Calvin. Harry could have also added "narcissism," and we have noted how Pygmalion, who mates with his animated mind-child, also commits a type of incest. But at the same time, Calvin's Ruby externalizes the desire Lars, Bianca, and nearly all of us have: to be accepted as we are, with all our flaws. But the more different or exceptional we are, the harder that acceptance is to achieve, a problem several of our heroes have.

Michaela Janan, while discussing the connections between Narcissus and Oedipus (in terms of the dangers of knowing oneself), notes that "Theban king and Boetian boy share an excessive erotic attachment to their own flesh and blood; Oedipus' unwitting love for his mother, Jocasta, is paralleled and re-doubled in Narcissus' love for himself."[12] Gildenhard and Zissos also point out that "Oedipus and Narcissus unwittingly suffer from an active-passive schizo-phrenia that results from their envisioning the self as other."[13] One wonders if Calvin suffers from this same paradoxical desire. Harry's recognition that this is "mind-cest" implies that Calvin is in love with a part or his own self, a product of his "mind" representing his own reflection. This conundrum seems doomed to remain unresolved, since, in a significant ring composition, the movie's very final scene displays the trio again: Calvin with his dog in the park, where a Ruby lookalike is reading Calvin's novel about Ruby. And thus, like Narcissus eternally looking at himself in the waters of the Styx once in the Underworld (Ovid, *Met.* 3.502–3), Calvin perpetuates this cycle of never-ending specular love.

In *Metamorphoses* there are three levels of mirroring. First we have the over-arching narrator "Ovid," who tells the story of Orpheus, a famous bard, who in

---

12 Janan (2009), 159.
13 Gildenhard and Zissos (2000), 136. For the paradoxes in Narcissus and Oedipus, see that article as well.

his song narrates various stories of metamorphosis (just like Ovid in his epic), including that of the artist Pygmalion. And just like Calvin, Orpheus is also a "writer," a poet who creates fantasies with words.[14] The plot of the novel that Calvin ends up writing (*The Girlfriend*) seems to mirror the love story he is presently living. Thus, just as in Ovid, Calvin is trapped in a hall of textual mirrors, where he is at the same time author, artist, lover, and character, gazing on his beloved creation like Narcissus beside the pool, in love with his reflection.

Indeed, Calvin's narcissism is also hinted by the frequent appearance of pools. First, we see the older brother Harry reading the new manuscript by Calvin's swimming pool. These and other waters will soon become the space of fantasy, into which Ruby and Calvin, in a dream, will dive together. As in *Lars and the Real Girl*, we observe a pairing of down-to-earth (and married) older brother with disturbed (and more creative) younger brother whom he tries to help. When Harry thus tells Calvin that the type of girl he wrote is not real, Calvin replies that he's known women like Ruby. Harry responds: "Who, Lila? Not fucking Lila" and observes that the lover's honeymoon is quickly over and "women are different up close." He then asserts: "You haven't written a person. Okay? You've written a girl. . . . You don't know jack shit about women." Ruby is not a real person with faults, as all of us are, as is his own wife, but rather the male idea of a perfect "girl." Harry of course is the realist, holding down a "real job" with meetings and an office, in contrast to Calvin, who, freaked by Ruby's first manifestation, later calls his brother while hiding under his desk. Yet Calvin, as we later discover, is the serious one, refusing, for example, to join the fun when they are at his mother's house in Big Sur. Calvin's fantasy will soon have its beginning in his swimming (and reflecting) pool.

After Harry and Suzie leave, Calvin, back at the typewriter, produces an imagined scene of himself and Ruby eating burgers by his swimming pool. It is the space of dreams, illusions, and idealized reflections into which he has written himself. His comment to Ruby that he has nothing to regret, that "everything's been perfect so far," underscores his narcissistic tendencies and self-delusions. They soon find themselves in the water, engaged in a playfully romantic dance; Calvin tells her that she is the most beautiful girl he's seen. The dream-pool becomes the scene of Calvin's Narcissus-like projection. Yet just as Narcissus discovers his deception, in one of the movie's last scenes, after Ruby has left him, Calvin looks at his pool, now empty, from his den, bidding a kind of goodbye to his lost fantasy. The film's second pool is a communal space around which the family plays at their house in Big Sur, but Calvin remains aloft in the

---

14 As Wheeler (1999), 156, notes, Orpheus "caught in the loop of 'repetition compulsion' . . . attempts to master his loss of Eurydice by telling stories that repeat and vary the theme of bringing the dead back to life." On this, see also Salzman-Mitchell (2005), 77, who sees the Pygmalion tale as fulfilling Orpheus's dream to revive Eurydice.

tree house, reading. Ruby is in the pool but does not come to him, even when Calvin asks. The illusion of perfect satisfaction begins to shatter. Finally, a third swimming pool, located at his friend's book party, where Ruby strips to her undergarments to swim with another man, breaks the deception completely, like Narcissus realizing that the imagined perfection was unobtainable.

The merely written Ruby promises the ideal of the never-ending love, until the text merges with dream. Calvin, fallen asleep over the typewriter, is awakened suddenly by the telephone ringing. Reality calls again. Tellingly, Calvin works in a loft, which symbolically places him in a higher, superior space, as Narcissus and Pygmalion situated themselves above others, rejecting other real lovers and the world in general. Next morning, Ruby appears half-clothed in the kitchen, eating cereal from a red bowl. Of course, Calvin thinks he's gone insane or that it's all a dream ("It's not real. It's not real," he keeps repeating). Pygmalion could be read as delusional.

Besides the film's various pools, dreams are also prominent and act as reflecting spaces. It is in a dream that Ruby is first born, and just as with Narcissus' pool, dreams offer a universe of fantasy, unreality, where anything is possible, logical or not. Thus the story oscillates between the illusion and the real world, demarcated sharply by the various alarm clocks. And after waking up from his first dream, Calvin is faced with the mundane and unappealing reality of taking his dog out to go potty, a task almost as trite as the image of dry toast and dark coffee he has for breakfast.

Not only is Calvin looking at his own image ("this guy I write about") in the mirror of the text and has Scotty also as a sort of alter ego, but Ruby herself can be read as largely her author's reflection. She says that she doesn't drive (in Los Angeles!) and seems to lack a computer; Calvin writes on an old typewriter, and we do not see him using a computer till the film's end. She obviously doesn't work either, and she forgets to open mail and cash checks, like Calvin, who doesn't listen to his messages. Like Calvin, Ruby does not appear to have external commitments or schedules, and so she is not a real modern woman who, like others, struggles to work and love and negotiate with everyday life; she seems a more mythical being, a sort of ivory statue with no communal life beyond her creator's. Ruby's acceptance of Scotty "just the way he is" is a metonymy for Calvin's own self. Ruby is also a self-made artist, who, as she tells Calvin's mother, did not go to art school and thus did not have any formal education. Likewise, Calvin is a high school dropout, an autodidact who did not receive any schooling in writing and yet became successful. This suggests another species of isolation, that of the unschooled but successful artist who may believe he has nothing to learn from others. Ruby seems, like him, also to be an isolated artist, but one who is unsuccessful and thus nonthreatening to Calvin. And like Calvin, who has lost a parent, she is orphaned. Calvin, like Narcissus, seems to be gazing at a self-reflecting surface. But Ruby will later acquire a life beyond the confines of Calvin's reflection; thus the gender and power dynamics between them will become more challenging and then frightening.

Like other Pygmalion figures, the creator Calvin is a sort of father to Ruby; hence the relationship's slightly incestuous overtones ("incest? mind-cest?"). But, like a daughter who grows up, her image will eventually answer back. Yet the film's curious layers of mirrors go even further, since Zoe Kazan, who wrote the script to some extent mirroring the real-life love relationship she had with Paul Dano (Calvin), at least at the time of the film's production, though of course this is not *their* actual relationship. Thus as creator, Kazan turns the gender tables and artistically fashions a reflection of herself and Dano as characters who she, as scriptwriter, has power over.

THE ARTIST'S ISOLATION

Brenkman notices how Narcissus' pool in Ovid is strikingly isolated from the rest of nature: "that Narcissus would go to a place no one else had ever found neatly corresponds to his own characteristic isolation from the world of others."[15] Isolation indeed goes hand in hand with narcissism, and narcissistic characters tend to reject the world and dive deeply in the mirror of their own selves. What triggered Pygmalion's rejection of real women is the conduct of the Propoetides, who, because of their sexual excesses, were turned by Venus into the first prostitutes and then into stone.[16] *Sine coniuge caelebs / vivebat thalamique diu consorte carebat*, "Without a partner he [Pygmalion] was living as a celibate, and for a long while he was lacking a consort of the bed"; Ovid, *Met.* 10.245–46). Like Pygmalion, Calvin is a reclusive young man, perhaps depressed by his father's loss, an event mentioned several times, and has been celibate since Lila left him. The high (and now somewhat failed) expectations people have of him weigh heavy on him too, for Calvin, like some of our other heroes, has been a marvelous child (his friend Langdon Tharp even refers to him as "the boy wonder") who at nineteen wrote a world-famous novel but has done nothing since.

It is a common trope that truly gifted people feel usually alone and uncomprehended. So Calvin's response is to dive deeply into a fantasy. Even more apparent than in *Lars and the Real Girl* and Ovid's myth, the movie probes the struggles between the imaginary and real worlds. The viewer is asked, as in fairy tales or myths, to suspend disbelief and participate in this modern Pygmalion's fantasy, which will take some effort due to the logical impossibilities of the plot. Unlike Bianca, Ruby "is" real and everyone, not just her creator, can see her. Calvin might not be insane or suffering a delusion, as is Lars. But, just as Lars

---

15 Brenkman (1976), 305.
16 Feldherr (2010), 261, disputes that Pygmalion created his statue as a reaction to his dislike of the Propoetides: "Pygmalion never makes his miraculous sculpture as an ideal surrogate; he simply happens to make it while (*interea* 10.247) living as a bachelor."

must, Calvin must reconnect to and engage with the world. *Lars* suggests that its central character needs the help of family and the wider community, but these groups will perform a lesser, and more problematic role in Calvin's healing. But, as is also a modern trope, Calvin seeks out a therapist who will lead and advise him, as Dr. Dagmar does, through this transformation. In our discussion of *Lars*, we mentioned the status of the therapist as magic helper and shaman.

Harry understands what is happening and at the beginning of the movie encourages Calvin to go on dates: "Don't you wanna have sex, like, ever again in your life?" His brother is gradually becoming more and more reclusive, and thus an isolated girlfriend is the perfect match and self-reflection. As noted, Ruby, like Calvin, doesn't drive or own a computer. A car would allow Ruby the independence to go places, and a computer would, among other things, afford the possibility to communicate with others; in 2012, those who do not e-mail, tweet, use Facebook, etc., would be truly isolated beings! As with Lars's Bianca's, Ruby's parents are dead, which makes her both a woman in need of masculine protection and also one conveniently bereft of any family or community connections.

Further, while Calvin is locked in his own world, his brother Harry lives in reality. He understands the world is not perfect—there are lots of things he dislikes about his wife and having a child—but he has found some workable solutions, while Calvin excludes himself from anything potentially painful. Later Calvin explains that he has changed Ruby because he thought she was going to leave him. Now, who hasn't fantasized that he or she could "change" the beloved? And according to O'Sullivan, this is precisely what the whole myth of Pygmalion is about, "the lover's fetishistic efforts to obtain and subsequently contain the ideal woman."[17] The more mature Harry tells Calvin that his wife left once but came back; now he has to live, and struggle, with the constant fear that she will do so again. So though life is not perfect, "it is what it is," and this edginess about their relationship even makes Harry appreciate his Suzie more. Calvin will have to learn this lesson. As noted, Calvin has been alone since Lila left him, and has no friends either and ends up calling an old high school acquaintance when he needs to get out of the house, panicked at Ruby's mysterious presence. He travels with Ruby to Big Sur to see his rather overwhelming mother and her partner Mort, but Calvin becomes jealous that Ruby is spending so much time with other people. This trip is revealing in other ways. For a long time he avoided making this visit, in part because he is scared of, and does not want to consider, sharing Ruby with his family. Forced by Ruby, he agrees to go, but his tendencies to isolate himself from family and society are

---

17 O'Sullivan (2008), 134: "Here fetishism is taken to be a process by which a concurrently feared and desired object—in this case, a woman—is refashioned to conform to idealised notions of femininity in a bid to render her a compliant and familiar substitute for that unruly object and, in so doing, to tame her."

made evident. While everyone laughs, drinks, and smokes pot (also a communal activity), Calvin sits alone in a tree house, immersed in his own world of literature and texts, which reminds us a bit of Lars living alone in the converted garage house, separated from where his brother and sister-in-law live.

One wonders if Calvin's retreat to a tree house might arise from a need to distance himself from his mother; Oedipal issues may be suspected. Like Harry Potter and Percy Jackson, Calvin has a stepfather who, though not unkind, is a bit of a goof, something of a man-child himself; we see a parody of the Northern California new-wealthy-yet-aspiring-hippie generation here. With his biological father dead and a stepfather who does not offer overwhelming competition, the unconscious Oedipal desires in Calvin may emerge. The mother is still attractive and seems to possess some of the alternative and free-spirited nature that Ruby has. In fact, like Ruby she was also a painter in her youth. So perhaps Calvin created Ruby in the mirror image of his own mother and these reflections are rising uncomfortably close to the surface. Thus Calvin must hide aloft, way above the pool where everyone else is immersing themselves.

Mort, his mother's partner, who crafts wood as a hobby, gives Calvin a curious gift, a wooden chair. It is a cumbersome and rather odd object, but it is also a form of affection that Calvin has difficulties accepting, showing again his problems even engaging with his family, although since the gift comes from his mother's lover, there may be other complications. A sign of his reengagement appears toward the film's end, when Calvin, putting away the typewriter with which he created Ruby, gets a trendy Apple laptop, and, sitting in Mort's chair, writes his novel about his relationship with Ruby.[18]

NOT-SO-IDEAL WOMEN

As we remarked earlier in Ovid's myth Pygmalion rejects all real women. And so, the artist creates and lives in his own fantasy of what the ideal girl might be (*interea niveum mira feliciter arte / sculpsit ebur formamque dedit, qua femina nasci / nulla potest, operisque sui concepit amorem*, "In the meantime he auspiciously sculpted the snowy ivory with wondrous art, and gave it a form with which no woman can be born, and conceived a love for his own work"; *Met* 10.247–49). In a very male-oriented perception of what has happened, Pygmalion blames the Propoetides, while perhaps a feminist reading would see them as victims of Venus' cruelty,[19] although Ovid would have known that temple prostitution was considered an honorable service for the goddess Aphrodite/Astarte/Innana.[20] Furthermore, do we really know in what way the Propoetides supposedly rejected Aphrodite's

---

18 And as Paula James has suggested to us, one wonders if this chair—wooden, large, and oddly thronelike—may recall Pygmalion's original status as king.

19 Liveley (1999), 201–2.

20 For connections of the myth of Pygmalion with the cult of Venus, see O'Bryhim (1987), chap. 4, 118–59.

divinity? In fact, just as in the case of Hippolytus in Greek tragedy, it might actually mean that they rejected love and sex in general and thus were in fact exceedingly chaste, so the word *obscenae*, according to Anderson, is simply "looking back from their notorious period as prostitutes; before they blasphemed against Venus they were not *obscenae*."[21] So from the very onset of the myth, we have a misogynistic artist who sees women as basically harlots. Finally, Ovid tells us, the Propoetides were turned into stone.[22]

Calvin's celibacy, tied to his bitterness toward Lila (and perhaps to his low opinion of women in general) mirrors that of Orpheus, the composer of the story of Pygmalion, who rejects women after the trauma of losing Eurydice. Calvin, like Pygmalion, then creates his dream girl, as he recognizes, even when he is conscious of the problems of his new love. But before Ruby is manifested, Calvin seems to possess a generally negative impression of women, whom, as does Pygmalion, he sees as sexually mercenary, declaring: "Girls only want to sleep with me because they read my book in high school . . . they're not interested in me. They are interested in some idea of me." Yet, the emphasis on him as an "idea" accords with what he himself will do, falling in love with his own ideal made manifest in Ruby. At a party, Calvin makes similar comments to his ex-girlfriend Lila:

CALVIN: You think I was threatened by you?
LILA: No, Cal, why would you be? You're a genius.
. . .
LILA: You just had this image of who I was. And anything that I did that contradicted it, you just ignored. . . . All that I wanted was for you, I don't know, to care about me.
. . .
CALVIN: "You left weeks after my father died."
. . .
LILA: "The only person that you wanted to be in a relationship with was you. So I let you do that."

So Lila, in Calvin's twisted view of things, like the Propoetides, is hard-hearted as stone ("a heartless slut," as he describes to his therapist), only interested in his fame, but she also tells him things he does not want to hear, such as how he is self-centered and narcissistic, and how he projects his sense of being threatened into the behavior of others. The artist can reflect his desires upon his creation, and also his fears.

In contrast with the idealized Ruby, Mabel, a woman he briefly goes out with, is more palpably real, not particularly pretty, with little class or sense of

21 Anderson (1972), 495.
22 Feldherr (2010), 261, believes that "what Pygmalion turns away from are not real women but, as the order of the narrative hints, already stone representations of women." Yet we are not sure the text supports this.

Ruby Sparks (2012)	
Fox Searchlight (USA)	
Directors:	Jonathan Dayton and Valerie Faris
Writer:	Zoe Kazan
Cast:	Zoe Kazan (Ruby), Paul Dano (Calvin), Chris Messina (Harry), Annette Bening (Gertrude), Antonio Banderas (Mort), Aasif Mandvi (Cyrus Modi), Steve Coogan (Langdon Tharp), Elliot Gould (Dr. Rosenthal), Toni Trucks (Suzie), Deborah Ann Woll (Lila)

appropriateness, too sexually aggressive. She is a fan whom he meets at a book event, who immediately asks, "Do you want my number?" When they later meet for coffee, she even proposes that they go off and have sex in the middle of the day. Calvin is horrified. She is in many ways like the Propoetides, offering their bodies publicly. Calvin's name itself may hint at some sort of puritanism, e.g., John Calvin; and notice that his house is gleaming white,[23] perhaps a metaphor for his desire for purity. Just like Pygmalion, Calvin is disgusted by what he considers sexual excess and goes truly berserk when, at his friend's party, Ruby strips down and goes swimming in her underwear.

CALVIN: You were supposed to act like my girlfriend.
RUBY: I am sorry I wasn't acting like the Platonic idea of your girlfriend.
CALVIN: When you act a certain way you make people think you are a slut.
RUBY: I'm not your child. You don't get to decide what I do.
CALVIN: Wanna bet?

Note the threat implied, which leads to the movie's horrid climax, in which he forces her to recognize she is his creation and he has absolute power over her being. All this will be triggered by Calvin's feeling that Ruby is behaving like an overly sexual woman, attracting other men's attentions.

In *Ruby Sparks* his brother Harry represents the voice of the macho man interested in breasts, and sexualizing and reifying women. When Calvin first tells him of his dream of Ruby, he immediately asks, "What did she look like?" and finds it depressing that Calvin doesn't "even get laid in his dreams." Later Harry wonders if Calvin can physically alter his creation and give her bigger breasts, for example, as well as inquiring about her sexual preferences. Calvin seems initially respectful of Ruby's individuality ("I will never write about her again"), making a promise he will break. Thus when Ruby starts to refuse him sex and wants to get a job, do something, be her own person, he begins ever-more-unsuccessful attempts to "revise" her, until the movie's climax, where Calvin makes Ruby do denigrating things as if she were a mere puppet, as if he were punishing her for becoming one of the contemptible women he has met before.

In contrast to Calvin's negative view of women, his ideal girl fits into a more conventional mold. His perfect girlfriend is sexually faithful, although clearly

---

23 Contrast this relative sterility with the lush exuberance of his mother's place.

uninhibited, an artist but not successful enough to threaten Calvin. Note how Ruby is found very often preparing food in the kitchen; in her first entrance into the real world, we see her half-naked and cooking breakfast, a feast for the male gaze preparing a feast for the male stomach. Later Calvin says that she is "an amazing cook" and will be eager to learn to "bake a pie" from Calvin's mother. One further piece of evidence of the incestuous overtones is found when Calvin mentions that his mother, now an alternative and affluent middle-ager in the hills of Northern California, once used to wear polo shirts, cook dinner, and paint. And, as we noted above, at first Ruby seems to have no life or friends apart from Calvin. So this ideal Ruby is not, after all, too different from secluded Classical Greek and Roman women, and as chaste as Pygmalion's ivory maiden is meant to be.

RESISTING READINGS

But we need not accept Calvin's perspective. Contemporary critics suggest different ways of reading both the myth and the movies, asking questions such as: "What views of women does the film convey? How does it portray men's attitudes to women, and how does it explore questions of gender dynamics? What would be the role of a female viewer or a female-oriented reading of the story?" We note that, unlike other Pygmalion-themed movies, this is the creation of a woman, Zoe Kazan as scriptwriter and actress, which brings new, and perhaps positive, elements to this cinematic retelling.[24]

It is quite possible to resist the received patriarchal readings of Pygmalion's text, which focus, for example, on the artist's amazing capacity to create a perfect woman as wife, who will live for him in an idyllic happy ending, or the fact that the Propoetides are women of depraved morals. If we consider the movie and the creative process from Rich's perspective, Kazan as female creator of the tale "enters the old text with a new critical direction."[25] Amy Richlin posits three courses of action in respect to the treatment of male-biased texts, such as Ovid's Pygmalion narrative: "Throw them out, take them apart, find female-based ones instead."[26] Mary Devereaux, more specifically referring to this same problem in cinema, discusses various solutions to resist patriarchal perspectives by creating a countercinema, and "developing methods of dealing with existing texts," i.e., "re-reading . . . reading against the grain . . . revision,"[27]

---

24   Holden (2012): "Ms. Kazan's lovely, tart performance is the equal of Ellen Page's portrayal of the title character in 'Juno'. Both are impetuous screwball heroines who could have been created only by women." And he points out that if written by a man for a teenage audience, there would be a lot of misogynist sexual jokes, which are simply not there in *Ruby*.

25   Adapted from Rich (1972), 18. Liveley (1999) follows Culler (2008, using a 1982 edition), Fetterly (1978), and Rich (1972). See Rich (1972), 18, on reading "as a woman" and Culler (2008). Reading as a woman does not always mean that women do the reading, as indeed, women may have been conditioned to read as men. Culler (2008), 50–51. On this topic, see also Mills (1994), Introduction.

26   Richlin (1992), 161.

27   Devereaux (1990), 346.

which provide "an alternative to the passive readership which censorship assumes and in its paternalism, encourages."[28]

Various critical readers of Pygmalion's tale have searched for traces of female subjectivity despite the overarching male voice. Judith Fetterly's idea of the "resisting reader"[29] is helpful in guiding us to read texts "as a woman." Fetterly proposes a "re-vision," a "reading against the grain," and like Rich she considers this a method of "looking back, of seeing with fresh eyes, of entering an old text from a new critical direction."[30] Liveley tries to locate glimpses of female agency and subjectivity in the myth, suggesting, for example that the Propoetides may actually have resisted Venus by being chaste and living in celibacy. This approach would align our reading not with Ovid/Orpheus/Pygmalion, but rather with the women in the story. Liveley follows the same method when adopting the perspective of the ivory maiden who senses things (*sensit*) and can see the world with her own eyes, with the "potential for perceiving and interpreting the world as a living, viewing subject."[31] Traditional readings of the myth align with Ovid, Orpheus, and Pygmalion and accept the misogynist condemnation of the Propoetides (*offensus vitiis, quae plurima menti/ femineae natura dedit*, "offended by those many vices which nature gave to the female mind"; *Met.* 10.244–45) even before their transformation.

Amy Richlin in turn explores the image of the magician who appears to saw through a girl, to the awed admiration of the public. This matter of magic and the magician will be central in our understanding of the Pygmalion myth. In regard to texts that derive pleasure from violence, Richlin also notes that if pornography "is that which converts living beings into objects, such texts are certainly pornographic."[32] And thus the act of cutting up the lady is a pornographic form of body fragmentation as spectacle that produces pleasure, as do Ovid's many stories of rape. The question becomes, if one tries to "read as a woman," whether we can focus on the lady, rather than the magician as most ancient texts do. As we show below, the movie presents Ruby in this "cut-up" manner, as well as several scenes underscoring her status as a victim of a narcissistic magician.

RUBY WAKES UP

After an idyllic beginning of the relationship, which lasts for a while, Ruby begins to get bored and desires something new, like taking a class, getting a job, spending time outside the house. She starts to resist Calvin's sexual advances as well and goes as far as to suggest that she should spend one night a week at her

---

28 Devereaux (1990), 347.

29 Fetterly (1978).

30 Rich (1972), 18. For discussions of resisting reading and the gendered spectator more specifically applied to cinema, see Devereaux (1990).

31 Liveley (1999), 207 and passim for other examples of female agency in the story.

32 Richlin (1992), 158.

own apartment. Did Calvin actually know, or had he written, that she had her own apartment? This seems to take him by surprise and shows that Ruby is developing her own independence, forging her own life. Eburna—this is the name Sharrock gives to the ivory statue[33]—never acts this way. We have no idea where exactly this independence comes from, but it makes Calvin very uneasy; he wants her to stay home and satisfy him alone. Here we observe Kazan's feminist discourse foregrounding the manipulated and victimized nature of Eburna/Ruby. At the end Ruby is savagely made aware of her status as created and dependent on her creator, while her creator's truly toxic attitudes are evident. Here Kazan clearly deconstructs the usual manner in which this relationship is shown in movies, and this gives her refiguring of the ivory maiden a different nature from many traditional treatments.[34]

Is Kazan here deconstructing the myth, unmasking bit by bit its narrative of female oppression, even, to some extent, producing a more female-oriented version? We think she does a bit of all of this. Peter Brandshaw, in his 2012 *Guardian* review, takes this view: "Kazan prefers to emphasize the sadness, gender politics and downbeat reality of a relationship turning sour. A male writer might ask: what might it be like to create an ideal woman? This female writer asks: what is it like, having to be some man's idea of an ideal woman?"[35]

Clearly Kazan forces us to interpret the story from the victim's perspective. Asked about the film's feminist aspects, Kazan explained that she was interested in exploring the question of "being gazed at but never seen," where a woman appears not be understood properly but "in a way that wasn't unkind or alienating for men."[36] But do viewers really focalize with Ruby? We do perhaps sympathize with her incapacity to act independently and her status as victim of Calvin's whims and noxious insecurities. Calvin indeed "plays" with her as if she were truly a doll, for example making her speak French – indeed the educated language of proper young ladies in a traditional past – in order to gauge his controlling power.

Our film displays many allusions to magic. After meeting Ruby for the first time and not believing Calvin's story, Harry declares, "You are a writer, not Ricky Jay" (the famous stage magician). Calvin replies: "It's love. It's magic." At the movie's conclusion, reading from his newly published book, Calvin asserts, "One may read this and think it's magic . . . but falling in love is an act of magic. So is writing." Calvin is a type of magician, an illusionist who does not necessarily chop Ruby in two, but does separate and control her skills and abilities (and Ruby at some point teasingly says that Calvin is "such a control freak"). We

---

33 We use this name in this chapter to emphasize the statue's connotations as artistic creation (Eburna, from Latin *ebur*, "ivory," the material of the sculpture).

34 Although, as noted before, works such as W. S. Gilbert's *Pygmalion*, as well as Shaw's *Pygmalion*, allow the created to expose the flaws of the creator, and even to reject him.

35 Brandshaw (2012).

36 In Brady (2012).

can see a reification of the girl, as in pornography, which chops her into fragments. We are introduced to Ruby's presence in pieces. First Scotty brings him a shoe, only one, making the fragmentation quite apparent from the start. Then Calvin finds some female toiletries in the bathroom, and then some panties in a drawer. They are all red or purple. Before Ruby's first full manifestation, one night in the darkness Calvin opens the drawer and seems to fetishistically caress the red underwear, only an eroticized metonymy for her broken-up body. We finally see Ruby half-clothed (chopped in two in a way), with only a shirt on, barefoot in the kitchen. While the fragmentation of her body is not as obvious as in other movies like *Weird Science* or in the pieces of ivory that Pygmalion needs to make his statue, we are here seeing parts of Ruby scattered around the house, "in chunks" so to speak, all eroticized imaginings of her body.

The "makeover" is a pervasive element of Pygmalion-themed movies.[37] *Pretty Woman*, for example, is all about expensive dresses, and Julia Roberts' stunning beauty, and a body, which the camera focuses on. *She's All That* deals with the transformation of a girl from nerdy looking to hot babe, done by her "creator" of sorts, who, of course will fall in love with her.[38] The makeover per se in Ruby, if there is one at all, is subtler. There are no specific Cinderella-like transformations, but Ruby's colorful wardrobe is constantly highlighted, and it is hard to avoid gazing at her varied, bright red and purple clothes. Yet Kazan herself insists that one should not see Ruby as a "manic pixie dream girl" (a term coined by a blogger), as something "reductive, diminutive and . . . misogynist."[39] Kazan as female reader/writer exposes this manipulation of Ruby's body as a doll, a blatant sexual object, especially toward the end, which makes it impossible for the viewer to focalize entirely with the male creator, as do other films like *Pretty Woman*, which aim at the viewer's deception and continuation of the Pygmalionic illusion.

So even though Calvin initially seems a rather sensitive urbanite artist who has at least the intention to respect his woman (he tells Mabel, who says men never just want to talk, that he actually does and is not interested in only sex), we gradually discover his palpable disdain for women and a very low regard for their individuality. Kazan may not have explicitly wanted to be "unkind" to men, but the picture of Calvin is quite savage.

Paula James has noted that it is common for the created woman to raise complaints, even if only temporarily, in Pygmalion-themed films.[40] *Ruby Sparks* goes considerably further. Whereas in some ways the story is Calvin's first-person narrative, from a metanarrative perspective we can recognize Kazan as a Pygmalion, who, authoring the story, thus creates both Ruby and Calvin, mirroring herself

---

37 See James (2011), 34–36.
38 On *She's All That*, see James (2003).
39 http://www.vulture.com/2012/07/zoe-kazan-ruby-sparks-interview.html. Accessed June 1, 2016. See Greco (2012).
40 James (2011), 86–87.

and her experiences in the process. And thus Kazan makes Ruby question Calvin's seclusion when she complains that she is suffocated by the relationship:

RUBY: You don't have any friends.
CALVIN: I have you, I don't need anyone else.
RUBY: That's a lot of pressure.

Ruby clearly recognizes the narcissistic, rather incestuous aspects to the relationship when she argues that "there has to be space in the relationship. Otherwise, it's like we're the same person," and after their fight at the party she yells "I am not your child!" This is interesting because the parent- (or rather father-) child relationship is often a metaphor for "the relationship between the artist and his creation," as we mentioned before.[41] Ruby is beginning to wake up as woman and as an independent subjectivity, to resist the male-oriented versions of the myth, and even if she doesn't entirely manage to free herself, Kazan produces her resisting voice, as opposed to Pygmalion's voiceless Eburna. So, as Culler would put it, Ruby, Kazan, and we can read "as women" and present "a critique of the phallocentric assumptions that govern literary works," myths in our case.[42] We might see hints of female agency in the Ovidian text, but Ruby here gives our Eburna a full voice. The creation now rebels against her creator and voices a female-oriented reading of her situation.

Ruby, resisting isolation, expresses her will to visit Calvin's mother in Big Sur, and wins, despite his displeasure. She is able to point out his narcissism, and even asks for space in the relationship. And so, she goes off to art class one night a week; while Calvin waits at home, miserable, she has a fun time going to a bar with new friends. And appropriately, Calvin then cooks a meal for Ruby in a sloppy kitchen—we guess he doesn't cook that often—which she will never eat since she comes home late. While waiting, Calvin listens to "La donna è mobile" ("The Woman Is Fickle," the song at the beginning of Act III of Verdi's opera *Rigoletto*, 1851), which voices his view of women as untrustworthy and unstable. We note how Lars had a similar reaction when Bianca went out to a meeting; they supposedly had a date to play Scrabble. And it is, not surprisingly, after this night that Calvin decides to change Ruby, control her, with his writing power. "Ruby was miserable without Calvin," he writes, and immediately she phones saying that she wants to come home. But then Ruby gets too clingy, and Calvin cannot even read the paper. She cries because Calvin let go of her hand as they walked in the street. So Calvin, dissatisfied, changes her again: "Ruby was filled with the most effervescent joy." And so Ruby becomes constantly and impossibly euphoric. This foregrounds the inherent problems of falling in love with one's own creation and the need to interact with others in a "real" bond, as well as the impossibility of really knowing what we want. Accordingly, Calvin asks Harry, "How do I know it's real?" To which his brother

---

41 Sharrock (1991a), 176.
42 Culler (2008), 46.

wisely responds, "It's not." But even trying to return her to normal doesn't work, because she is still a fiction, a manufactured girl, and not a real person with her own thoughts. Thus, when Calvin writes "Ruby was just Ruby. Happy or sad, however she felt" Ruby becomes intolerably moody. Finally, her agency and subjectivity go too far for Calvin, and he begins to radically intervene.

Does the third of Richlin's possibilities apply here, and do we observe a female-oriented version of the myth? The movie's climax is deeply disturbing. As noted, when looking at the plot from the perspective of the hero's journey, this scene functions as the hero's death struggle, for it is a battle in which hidden power and evils latent in Calvin, that desire to be controlling at whatever the cost, now come out and viciously torment the woman he supposedly loves. It is a moment when overwhelming, and potentially ruinous, self-knowledge is gained. Will Calvin surrender to these forces? After their big fight in the party, Ruby is packing and ready to leave. Calvin declares she cannot do so because she is indeed not free, that, like a mechanic doll, he can control her every movement. He cruelly reveals that she is only a product of his own mind: "I'm not writing *about* you, I *wrote* you. I made you up . . . I can make you do anything . . . because you're not real." But at this point, she still has some autonomy and is able to retort, "You're sick. . . . If this is how you think about people . . . then you are in for a long, lonely fucked-up life. Do you hear me?" [Emphasis Ours] Then, to show his mastery, his misogyny, and his willingness to oppress her, through typing he makes her perform all sorts of degrading actions, such as jumping in a frenzy and screaming, "You're a genius. You're a genius" (Fig. 12.2), snapping her fingers uncontrollably, speaking French, barking like a dog, and even beginning a striptease. When he jams the typewriter keys, the exhausted Ruby collapses. Deeply shamed, he hangs his head. He tries to gently approach her, but she flees into the bedroom and locks herself inside. He finally "frees" her by writing: "As soon as Ruby left the house, the past released her. She was no longer Calvin's creation. She was free." Putting the manuscript right outside the locked door, he says: "Ruby, look at the last page. I love you." The following morning, Ruby and the note are gone, but she has left the manuscript and Calvin grieves for the loss of his fantasy.

FIGURE 12.2 What Calvin types, Ruby enacts.

This crisis is similar to and also different from the one we see in *Lars and the Real Girl.* There too we find a resisting Bianca, who shows her independence (getting jobs and going out without Lars, for example) and refuses to marry Lars, and who apparently even quarrels with him. Lars too has the power to regain control of the Bianca narrative, and he does so, but it is in a way we sympathize with, although it demonstrates his ultimate power. Enabled by Dagmar's diagnosis that Bianca is sick, Lars allows her to fade and die, at the same time demonstrating a deep tenderness to her. Of course, this is not a real human death, but rather the extinguishing of a beloved illusion that blocks his movement toward a "real girl." But Calvin instead must confront the real pathologies that lurk within.

The next scene shows Calvin playing golf with Harry, another traditional male-bonding activity. His brother asks what he has written lately. Calvin answers that he cannot write, but we soon see him sitting in the wooden chair with his new laptop trying to write the story. He now has something important to say, part of his self-transformation. Seven months pass by, and we find him in a bookstore reading from his new novel, *The Girlfriend.* Calvin is in a healthier, more productive place in life now—and perhaps we are to assume that he has turned thirty—and even shows some inclination to self-reflection as he goes back to the therapist.

HAPPY ENDING?

In large part the movie's reviews suggest that the romantic comedy appears to end well. Calvin is writing again and seems to have left his isolation behind, while Ruby has been liberated. Or has she really? The film's conclusion is quite troubling and puzzling. Calvin is walking the dog and telling him to go potty again. He sees a Ruby lookalike reading his novel in a park, a nice bit of ring composition that circles back to the film's beginning, perhaps ominously hinting at the perilous nature of this vicious cycle. Ruby asks what the name of his dog is, and after hearing the answer notices that it is also the name of the dog in the story she is reading. And yet she cannot connect this name to her own past. Despite her alleged freedom, her memories have been wiped out. She is now a blank page (let's note that a blank page on the typewriter is one of the first images in the film as well) in which a new relationship can be freshly inscribed.[43] Calvin again is not forthcoming and doesn't say who he is, but Ruby notices some familiarity: "Have we met before?" And he lies: "I don't know." She continues: "You seem really familiar. Maybe we knew each other in another life." And again he remains silent and only says, "I'm a writer." Ruby then recognizes him from the picture on the book jacket.

---

43 See Gubar (1981), 76–77, for the blank page as female that can be—almost sexually—marked by the male author. Writing is thus like an act of penetration; Gubar also notes that the acts of reading and writing have been understood in erotic terms.

RUBY: So that's why you look so familiar. . . . Can we start over?

CALVIN: Yes. May I sit down?

RUBY: Just don't tell me how it ends, OK?

CALVIN: Promise.

This clearly works as the "happy ending" for those who want to read the film as a typical rom-com. Apparently, there was a different ending planned initially but the producers suggested (demanded?) something else.[44] What would have happened if the film just ended with Ruby's liberation? With Calvin's acceptance that not all fantasies are possible? It would have probably been less marketable, but a much truer statement. Instead, the ending more or less fits the genre, but there are potentially tragic overtones visible. Calvin is hardly honest or sincere, a shaky start for a new relationship. There is a clear imbalance of power; Ruby doesn't know Calvin wrote her, and thus Calvin has the advantage of critical knowledge. Are we to assume that he will never tell her that he had once created her and set her free? Or if he does, aren't we back in the same unhealthy cycle of narcissism and male authority? What will happen then when he introduces this new Ruby to his brother and Suzie, or when he takes her back to Big Sur? Everyone who met her before will know who Ruby is, except for Ruby herself. Or will Calvin keep her imprisoned in the house in order to avoid this? One wonders: Since it is he is the one who set her free, isn't he the creator of that freedom and thus of this new Ruby as well? Perhaps the fact that she is written, set, and preserved as a character in the now-published novel means that indeed, he cannot change her; she is out of his hands.[45] Yet, this ending is impossible. It is not so easy to erase someone's past, and the community surrounding Calvin will of course know of Ruby's past existence.

The book this second version of Ruby reads functions like a mirror, where both Calvin and Ruby are reflected. With a new beginning for the couple looking very much like the earlier beginning of their previous relationship, with the dog, in the park (Fig. 12.3), are we to expect that things will be different this time? Yes, perhaps Calvin has lost the capacity to alter her with writing since he wrote that she is no longer his "creation"; she is, in a way, owned by the community of the book readers. We don't know, but the fact that he has knowledge of the past that she doesn't have is problematic. So this apparent uplifting ending may hide a much darker perpetuation of male fantasy and female oppression.[46]

---

44 Cf. http://collider.com/zoe-kazan-ruby-sparks-the-f-word-interview/. Accessed July 20, 2016.

45 We thank Monica Gale for this suggestion.

46 Note the comments of Lack (2012) on the movie's ending: "There, more than anywhere else, is where the film feels misogynistic to me. It doesn't quite vindicate Calvin's brutal actions, but it does absolve him without reason, and the closing beat shows that Ruby, even across multiple incarnations, will always be sucked back in to this awful man's orbit. The film presents the man as arbiter, pulling the strings and having his way at all times, and the women as puppet, subservient and helpless, without ever hammering home the destructive, disturbing nature of Calvin's actions."

FIGURE 12.3 Calvin and the new (?) Ruby.

The good thing, is that, unlike in Ovid's text, we have a woman writer to tell the story here, one who, if only momentarily, shows us how Eburna can wake up and resist the force of her creator.

RUBY SPARKS AS A MOVIE FOR OUR TIME

What makes *Ruby Sparks* a movie for the millennium? Even more than *Lars*, it presents a current "type," the man-child in need of maturation, which reflects the current, chaotic quest for social norms. The movie's scenes and settings situate it in a contemporary Southern California milieu. This movie is far more secular and worldly than *Lars*, which evokes dreams of the power of community and religion, and thus better reflects the increasingly desperate isolation closing in on us. We live in a world where we are in constant communication, through social media, text messaging, and e-mail, but we often do not communicate with each other and remain in a self-centered isolated world where indeed we seem to be in love with our own selves; think of people's self-construction and ex-hibition through Facebook. Indeed, Kazan noted the centrality of Los Angeles as the film's location, both a character and a setting for a film. Kazan sees Los Angeles as a place where one can easily feel alone and isolated, which is what Calvin is.[47] Compared to the therapist, family, and community found in *Lars*, their equivalents in *Ruby* are much less helpful. More modern, as compared to *Lars*, is the film's willingness to explore the toxic, exploitative dimensions of narcissism. Finally, the movie in a very fundamental way makes no real sense, and, even though it seems to have a "happy ending," a brief and logical consider-ation of the potential future of Calvin and his new-old Ruby conveys all manner of show-stopping obstacles. And this is what is depressingly modern about the movie. Zoe Kazan (who, considering her family background, must know a thing or two about the subjects she engages) can tellingly unmask illusions and gives the created female victim a dissenting voice, only to seemingly put her in another

---

47 Film Society of Lincoln Center (2012).

untenable situation at the end. In other words, the movie's ending suggests that the hidden moral of the story is that such love dreams are absurd, and that the artist's ability to produce such beautiful illusions serves like a drug to make us see the world, for a while, in Ruby-colored glasses.

REFERENCES

Anderson, W. *Ovid's Metamorphoses: Books 6–10*. University of Oklahoma Press, 1972.

Barolsky, P. "A Very Brief History of Art from Narcissus to Picasso." *Classical Journal*, vol. 90 no. 3, 1995, 255–59.

———, and E. D'Ambra. "Pygmalion's Doll." *Arion*, vol. 17 no. 1, 1995, 19–24.

Brady, T. 'Reality? Check!" http://www.irishtimes.com/culture/film/reality-check-1.551389, Oct. 12, 2012. Accessed Apr. 5, 2015.

Brandshaw, P. "Ruby Sparks. Review," http://www.theguardian.com/film/2012/oct/11/ruby-sparks-review, Oct. 11, 2012. Accessed Apr. 5, 2015.

Brenkman, J. "Narcissus in the Text." *Georgia Review*, vol. 30 no. 2, 1976, 293–327.

Culler, J. *On Deconstruction: Theory and Criticism after Structuralism*, 25th anniversary ed. Cornell UP, 2008.

Devereaux, M. "Oppressive Texts, Resisting Readers and the Gendered Spectator: The New Aesthetics." *Journal of Aesthetics and Art Criticism*, vol. 48 no. 4, 1990, 337–47.

Feldherr, A. *Playing Gods: Ovid's Metamorphoses and the Politics of Fiction*. Princeton UP, 2010.

Fetterly, J. *The Resisting Reader: A Feminist Approach to American Literature*. Indiana UP, 1978.

Film Society of Lincoln Center. "VIDEO: Q&A with Filmmakers and Stars of 'Ruby Sparks' | Filmlinc.com | Film Society of Lincoln Center." Filmlinc.com, Dec. 7, 2012. Accessed Jan. 6, 2013.

Gildenhard, I., and A. Zissos. "Ovid's Narcissus (*Met.* 3.339–510): Echoes of Oedipus." *American Journal of Philology*, vol. 121 no. 1, 2000, 129–47.

Greco, P. "Zoe Kazan on Writing *Ruby Sparks* and Why You Should Never Call Her a 'Manic Pixie Dream Girl'," http://www.vulture.com/2012/07/zoe-kazan-ruby-sparks-interview.html, 2012. Accessed Apr. 5, 2015.

Gubar, S. "'The Blank Page' and the Issues of Female Creativity." *Critical Inquiry*, vol. 8 no. 2, *Writing and Sexual Difference*, 1981, 243–63.

Hallett, J. P. "The Role of Women in Roman Elegy." In J. Peradotto and J. P. Sullivan, ed., *Women in the Ancient World: Counter-Cultural Feminism*. Women in the Ancient World: The Arethusa Papers. State University of New York Press, 1984, pp. 241–62.

Hardie, P. *Ovid's Poetics of Illusion*. Cambridge UP, 2002.

Hillis Miller, J. (1990). *Versions of Pygmalion*. Harvard UP, 1990.

Holden, S. "She's Everything He Wants, and Therein Lies the Problem." *New York Times* Movie Review, http://www.nytimes.com/2012/07/25/movies/ruby-sparks-starring-zoe-kazan-and-paul-dano.html?_r=0, 2012. Accessed July 17, 2015.

Hornaday, A. "Review of *Ruby Sparks*," http://www.washingtonpost.com/gog /movies/ruby-sparks,1226929.html. Accessed Oct. 15, 2016.

James, P. *Ovid's Myth of Pygmalion on Screen: In Pursuit of the Perfect Woman.* Bloomsbury, 2011.

———. "She's All That: Ovid's Ivory Statue and the Legacy of Pygmalion on Film." *Classical Bulletin*, vol. 79 no. 1, 2003, 63–91.

Janan, M. *Reflections in a Serpent's Eye: Thebes in Ovid's Metamorphoses.* Oxford UP, 2009.

Lack, J. R. "*Ruby Sparks* Review," http://wegotthiscovered.com/movies/ruby-sparks-review/, 2012. Accessed June 1, 2016.

Liveley, G. "Reading Resistance in Ovid's *Metamorphoses.*" In P. Hardie, A. Barchiesi, and S. Hinds, *Ovidian Transformations.* Cambridge UP, 1999, pp. 197–213.

Mills, S., ed. *Gendering the Reader.* Prentice Hall, 1994.

O'Bryhim, S. *The Amathusian Myths of Ovid Metamorphoses 10.* Dissertation. University of Texas, 1987.

O'Sullivan, J. "Virtual Metamorphoses: Cosmetic and Cybernetic Revisions of Pygmalion's 'Living Doll'." *Arethusa*, vol. 41 no. 1, 2008, 133–56.

Rich, A. "When We Dead Awaken: Writing as Re-vision." *College English*, vol. 34 no. 1, 1972, 18–30.

Richlin, A., ed. "Reading Ovid's Rapes." In *Pornography and Representation in Greece and Rome.* Oxford UP, 1992.

Rosati, G. *Narciso e Pigmalione: illusione e spettacolo nelle Metamorfosi di Ovidio.* Sansoni, 1983.

Salzman-Mitchell. *A Web of Fantasies: Gaze, Image and Gender in Ovid's Metamorphoses.* Ohio State UP, 2005.

———. "A Whole out of Pieces: Pygmalion's Ivory Statue in Ovid's *Metamorphoses.*" *Arethusa*, vol. 41 no. 2, 2008, 291–311.

Sharrock, A. "The Love of Creation." *Ramus*, vol. 20, 1991a, 169–82.

———. "Womanufacture." *Journal of Roman Studies*, vol. 81, 1991b, 36–49.

Solodow, J. *The World of Ovid's Metamorphoses.* University of North Carolina Press, 1988.

Veyne, P. *Roman Erotic Elegy: Love, Poetry and the West.* University of Chicago Press, 1988.

Wheeler, S. *A Discourse of Wonders: Audience and Performance in Ovid's Metamorphoses.* University of Pennsylvania Press, 1999.

Wyke, M. "Mistress and Metaphor in Augustan Elegy." *Helios*, vol. 16 no. 1, 1989, 25–47.

———. *The Roman Mistress: Ancient and Modern Representations.* Oxford UP, 2002.

DISCUSSION QUESTIONS FOR PART V

1. Starting probably with *Weird Science*, many movies like *Her* and *Ex Machina* have developed a technologized version of the Pygmalion myth, the ivory maiden turning into some sort of computer-generated ideal woman. What do we make of these modern versions of the story? What new dimensions do they add to Ovid's tale?

2. What other possible endings could *Ruby Sparks* have had, and how would it then engage with the Pygmalion myth and with perceptions of gender struggles and power?

3. Critics have connected the ivory maiden with the mythical Pandora. Can you see Ruby as Pandora? In what sense? What does it tell us about constructions of women, ancient and modern?

4. Pygmalion has often been discussed as a "viewer," and often as a male viewer who controls the gaze and has power over the female object of the gaze. Can we see this in *Ruby Sparks*? What role does the camera play in this?

5. How do we interpret the fact that Calvin and Harry often go to the gym in *Ruby Sparks*? Can we connect this to the myths of Pygmalion and Narcissus, or with issues of masculinity?

6. How does *Lars* (as well as *Ruby Sparks*) make you aware of how we do not see people as they are, but often see what we project upon them?

7. Imagine the new technology of twenty years from now, and how it may create an even more humanlike version of Bianca. How could the "problem with Pygmalion" become one of great social concern?

8. Reviewers have considered both *Ruby* and *Lars* as rather unrealistic. Which of these movies do you think is the more unrealistic, and why? Even though they are unrealistic, they do tell important general truths. Or do they?

9. Even though neither Lars nor Calvin is a hero in the sense that Perseus and Theseus are, they still go through a type of "hero's journey." How have these two movies and our chapters made you think differently about your own hero's journey?

10. Our chapters have pointed out two features present in these movies that are minimized or absent from Ovid's Pygmalion story: the role of trauma in causing the artist to create his Galatea, and the role of the community in helping the artist move beyond that trauma. How useful do you think these additions are? Do they provide valuable insights?

MYTHS AND MOVIES, MOVIES AND MYTHS

Everyone loves a good myth, and what better to bring those old stories to life than the magical new technologies of cinema that materialize those old worlds and gods for our eyes? Decades ago, the only way to "truly" study myth and Classics seemed to require philological and textually based analysis, accompanied by, of course the serious work of archaeologists and historians of the visual arts. And this is still perhaps the mode in many schools and universities around the world. Of course, as Classical scholars, we love line-by-line translation and a detailed commentary of texts. But, as the Classically inspired common saying goes, *tempora mutantur, nos et mutamur in illis.* "Times change, and we change in them." Philology has embraced new approaches and reached out to dialogue with other art forms and intellectual trends. Here is where our book inserts itself.

The new millennium, for all its downfalls and perils, has brought us to a world where the primacy of the visual is pervasive, and where the text has become to a certain extent secondary. Millennials are comfortable with images of all sorts; thus, as teachers and scholars, we recognize the power of moving pictures to communicate, reinterpret, recreate, and teach Classical myth. We want this book, which focuses on some major usages of myth in our millennial age, to help expand our understanding of myth to more teachers, more students, and more moviegoers, and to show that, in its own medium, movies are a good way to think about ancient stories (as well as being reflections of our own modern preoccupations). Thus, films like Miyazaki's Japanese mythological fantasy *Spirited Away* (2001) or *Pan's Labyrinth* (2006) can be valuable tools in courses where we learn about ancient myth, Hispanic culture, Asian studies, and gender-related issues. In the age of the World Wide Web, we appreciate how Classical myth is an ever-evolving, ever-transforming multiverse that never stops branching out, twining about and interpenetrating many other art forms and intellectual discussions. It is this conviction that not only inspired this book but also guides our teaching and research.

Although there is much fine scholarship on mythology and movies available (and to whose authors we are deeply indebted), we saw relatively little work that employs the formal and theoretical tools used in myth studies to explicate major mythological elements in narratives, rituals, and much else. Providing examples (although never comprehensive) of how to use these theories was a major goal of our book. We hope our examples are a spur for future research, which will enrich, contradict, and challenge our own interpretations. We also hope that, through providing new insights for teaching using movies—which, along with television and other video productions, are now the chief channel wherein people engage narrative and thus mythology—we can encourage the current generation to recognize themselves and their concerns in these myths-in-movies, as *we* once did in reading Vergil. Once those old stories spoke of the realities, ideologies, and political concerns of their times. They still do so today, and thus myths acquire a whole new meaning when set to speak about the modern issues of the last sixteen years. Of course, it is our very own interest that the Classics become ever more known, widely taught, and popular, an endeavor we greatly hope this book will foster.

APPENDIX

Further Readings on Classics in Film and Television

Aziza, C. *Guide de l'Antiquité imaginaire: Roman, cinéma, bande dessinée.* Les Belles Lettres, 2008.

Burgoyne, R. *The Film in World Culture.* Routledge, 2010.

Cyrino, M., ed. *Rome, Season Two: Trial and Triumph.* Edinburgh UP, 2015.

Cartledge, P., and F. Greenland. *Responses to Oliver Stone's* Alexander: *Film, History and Cultural Studies,* University of Wisconsin Press, 2010.

Day, K., ed. *Celluloid Classics: New Perspectives on Classical Antiquity in Modern Cinema.* Special issue of *Arethusa,* vol. 41 no. 1, 2008.

Drumond, H. *L'Antiquité au Cinéma. Vérités, légendes et manipulations.* Nouveau Monde Editions, 2009.

Ebert, J. D. *Celluloid Heroes and Mechanical Dragons: Film as the Mythology of Electronic Society.* Lisa Loucks Christenson, 2005.

Elley, D. *The Epic Film: Myth and History.* Routledge and Kegan Paul, 1984.

Fourcart, F. *Le péplum italien, grandeur et décadence d' une antiquité populaire.* Editions IMHO, 2012.

Joshel, S., M. Malamud, and D. McGuire, ed. *Imperial Projections: Ancient Rome in Modern Popular Culture.* Johns Hopkins UP, 2001.

Martin, M. *L'Antiquité au Cinéma.* Dreamland, 2002.

Meier, M., and S. Slanička. *Antike und Mittelalter im Film: Konstruktion—Dokumentation—Projektion.* Böhlau, 2007.

Michelakis, P., and M. Wyke, ed. *The Ancient World in Silent Cinema.,* Cambridge UP, 2013.

Morcillo, M., P. Hanesworth, and O. Lapeña Marchena, ed. *Imagining Ancient Cities in Film: From Babylon to Cinecittà.* Routledge, 2015.

Nisbet, G. *Ancient Greece in Film and Popular Culture.* Liverpool UP, 2006.

O'Brien, D. *Classical Masculinity and the Spectacular Body on Film.* Palgrave MacMillan, 2014.

Padilla, M. W. *Classical Myth in Four Films of Alfred Hitchcock.* Lexington Books, 2016.

Paul, J. "Cinematic Receptions of Antiquity: The Current State of Play." *Classical Receptions Journal,* vol. 2 no. 1, 2010, 136–55.

Perry, J. *Now Playing. Studying Classical Civilization through Film.* Oxford UP, 2014.

Pomeroy, A. *"Then it was destroyed by the Volcano": The Ancient World in Film and on Television.* Duckworth, 2008.

Prieto Arciniega, A. *La antigüedad a través del cine.* Universitat de Barcelona, 2014.

Renger, A.-B., and J. Solomon, ed. *Ancient Worlds in Film and Television.* Brill, 2013.

Rosen, G. *Now Playing. Studying Classical Mythology through Film.* 2nd edition. Oxford UP, 2016.

Rushing, R. *Descended from Hercules: Biopolitics and the Muscled Male Body on Screen.* Indiana UP, 2016.

Santas, C. *The Epic in Film: From Myth to Blockbuster.* Rowman & Littlefield, 2007.

Schulze-Gattermann, S. *Das Erbe des Odysseus: Antike Tragödie und Mainstream-Film.* Coppi-Verlag, 2000.

Smith, G. A. *Epic Films: Casts, Credits and Commentary on over 250 Historical Spectacle Movies.* McFarland, 1993.

Solomon, J. *Ben Hur: The Original Blockbuster.* Screening Antiquity Series. Edinburgh UP, 2016.

Voytilla, S., and C. Vogler. *Myth and the Movies: Discovering the Mythic Structure of 50 Unforgettable Films.* Michael Wiese, 1999.

Winkler, M., ed. *The Fall of the Roman Empire: Film and History*. Wiley-Blackwell, 2009a.

———, ed. *Gladiator: Film and History*. Wiley-Blackwell, 2004.

———. *The Roman Salute: Cinema, History, Ideology*. Ohio State UP, 2009b.

———. *Spartacus: Film and History*. Wiley-Blackwell, 2007a.

Wyke, M. *Projecting the Past: Ancient Rome, Cinema and History*. Routledge, 1997.

———. "Rome in the New Italy." In C. Edwards, *Roman Presences: Receptions of Rome in European Culture, 1789–1945*. Cambridge UP, 1999 (reprint 2007), pp. 188–204.

CREDITS

Figure 1.1 *Troy.* Directed by Wolfgang Peterson. 2004. Warner Brothers.

Figure 1.2 *Troy.* Directed by Wolfgang Peterson. 2004. Warner Brothers.

Figure 2.1 *O Brother, Where Art Thou?* Directed by Joel and Ethan Coen. 2001. Touchstone Pictures.

Figure 2.2 *O Brother, Where Art Thou?* Directed by Joel and Ethan Coen. 2001. Touchstone Pictures.

Figure 3.1 © Vanni Archive/Art Resource, NY

Figure 3.2 *Hercules.* Directed by Brett Ratner. 2014. Paramount Pictures.

Figure 3.3 *Hercules.* Directed by Brett Ratner. 2014. Paramount Pictures.

Figure 4.1 *Clash of the Titans.* Directed by Louis Leterrier. 2010. Warner Brothers.

Figure 4.2 *Wrath of the Titans.* Directed by Jonathan Liebesman. 2012. Warner Brothers.

Figure 4.3 *Wrath of the Titans.* Directed by Jonathan Liebesman. 2012. Warner Brothers.

Figure 5.1 *Immortals.* Directed by Tarsem Singh Dhandwar. 2011. Relativity Media.

Figure 5.2 *Immortals.* Directed by Tarsem Singh Dhandwar. 2011. Relativity Media.

Figure 6.1 *Pan's Labyrinth.* Directed by Guillermo del Toro. 2006. Estudios Picasso, Tequila Gang, Esperanto Filmoj.

Figure 6.2 *Pan's Labyrinth.* Directed by Guillermo del Toro. 2006. Estudios Picasso, Tequila Gang, Esperanto Filmoj.

Figure 6.3 *Pan's Labyrinth.* Directed by Guillermo del Toro. 2006. Estudios Picasso, Tequila Gang, Esperanto Filmoj.

Figure 6.4 *Pan's Labyrinth.* Directed by Guillermo del Toro. 2006. Estudios Picasso, Tequila Gang, Esperanto Filmoj.

Figure 7.1 *Such Is Life [Asi es la vida].* Directed by Arturo Ripstein. 2001. Wanda Visión S.A.

Figure 7.2 *Such Is Life [Asi es la vida].* Directed by Arturo Ripstein. 2001. Wanda Visión S.A.

Figure 8.1 *Harry Potter and the Chamber of Secrets.* Directed by Chris Columbus. 2002. 1492 Pictures. Warner Brothers.

Figure 8.2 *Harry Potter and the Chamber of Secrets.* Directed by Chris Columbus. 2002. 1492 Pictures. Warner Brothers.

Figure 9.1 Erich Lessing/Art Resource, NY

Figure 9.2 *The Hunger Games.* Directed by Gary Ross. 2012. Lionsgate.

Figure 9.3 Album/Art Resource, NY

Figure 10.1 *Percy Jackson & The Olympians: The Lightning Thief.* Directed by Chris Columbus. 2010. Fox 2000 Pictures.

Figure 10.2 Alan Lequire, Athena Parthenos. 1990. The Parthenon, Nashville, Tennessee. Photo by Gary Layda.

Figure 11.1 *Lars and the Real Girl.* Directed by Craig Gillespie. 2007. Metro-Goldwyn-Mayer.

Figure 11.2 *Lars and the Real Girl.* Directed by Craig Gillespie. 2007. Metro-Goldwyn-Mayer.

Figure 12.1 Bona Fide Productions/The Kobal Collection at Art Resource, NY

Figure 12.2 *Ruby Sparks.* Directed by Jonathan Dayton and Valerie Faris. 2012. Fox Searchlight Pictures.

Figure 12.3 *Ruby Sparks.* Directed by Jonathan Dayton and Valerie Faris. 2012. Fox Searchlight Pictures.

INDEX

V

Venus. *See* Aphrodite/Venus
Vergil, 8, 8n22, 12. *See also Aeneid*
Vietnam War, 279, 282n8, 300n79, 303
Virgin Huntress, 280, 285–90, 286f, 290
Virgin Mary, 171, 171n27
vision, darkness and, 268–71
Vogler, Christopher, 26, 114n52
Voldemort (fictional character)
    Harry Potter and, 22, 138, 259, 269n49, 272
    in *Harry Potter and the Chamber of Secrets*, 253–54,
       256–57, 259, 266, 268–73, 269n49
    immortality and, 137, 257, 257n9
    shrunken soul of, 208
    Tom Riddle becoming, 138, 148, 160, 256, 259,
       265, 270
Von Trier, Lars, 227, 240, 240n58, 242, 243n66

W

Wagner, Richard, 99n1
    on Achilles, 129
    Ring of the Nibelung cycle of, 6–7, 7f, 99, 129–30, 143
war story, 303
water
    as point of transition, 355–56
    women and, 263
The Wild One, 99
Winkler, Martin, 6–10, 40, 56
witch, Medea as, 221, 224, 227, 237–38, 241
withdrawal-devastation-return pattern, 52
women
    dangerous, 265
    in margins, 183–85
    misogyny, Hercules and, 106, 121, 121n64
    not-so-ideal, 372–75
    as reproductive bodies, 209n107
    scripts written by, 228, 246, 361, 375
    as text, 363–64, 364f
    transitions of, 301–2
    value of, 144
    water and, 263
Word of the Father, 340, 343–45, 348, 352, 357
wrath (*ira*), 231–32
Wrath of the Titans
    Agenor in, 131, 144, 145–52
    archetypes in, 131–35
    creation myth in, 130

Cyclops in, 146
family in, 19, 144, 152
fate in, 100
gender and, 21
goddesses missing in, 147n42, 153
gods falling in, 129–30, 133, 145, 151, 159, 161, 178
Hephaestus in, 146–48, 146n40
katabasis in, 15–16
labyrinth of Tartarus in, 147–49
Liebesman directing, 130
as millennial movie, 153
as peplum movie, 110
Perseus in, 4, 101, 121–22, 121n64, 129–30,
    137–38, 142–53, 174, 318, 329
plot summary of, 131
Poseidon and, 131, 144–45
ruling elite in, 45–46
as secondary epic, 12
surreal images in, 20
unintentional borrowing in, 6–7, 7f
Zeus in, 100, 143–47, 149–53, 149f
The Writer's Journey: Mythic Structure for Writers
    (Vogler), 26

Y

Yeats, William Butler, 39
"You Are My Sunshine," 73, 78, 80, 88

Z

Zeus
    in *Clash of the Titans*, 114–15, 131, 136–42, 151
    in Greek creation story, 23
    Hades and, 115, 142–43, 147, 150–51, 204
    Heracles/Hercules and, 103, 108, 116, 119, 134
    in *Immortals*, 100–101, 115, 158–60, 164, 167–69,
      172, 174–78
    Odysseus and, 67–68, 87, 89, 91
    in *Percy Jackson and the Olympians: The Lightning
      Thief*, 144, 315, 321, 329
    Perseus and, 132, 136–38, 140, 142–47, 149–53,
      149f, 168, 261, 272, 329
    Prometheus and, 133–35, 133n11, 284
    Theseus and, 139, 159–60, 167–69, 172, 172n28,
      174–78
    in Trojan War myth, 42–43, 53, 56
    in *Wrath of the Titans*, 100, 143–47, 149–53, 149f
    thunderbolt of, 18, 118, 146, 150, 308, 315